P9-CZV-542

BY DAVID MITCHELL

Utopia Avenue

Slade House

The Bone Clocks

The Thousand Autumns of Jacob de Zoet

Black Swan Green

Cloud Atlas

Number9Dream

Ghostwritten

The Reason I Jump
(TRANSLATOR, WITH KA YOSHIDA)

Fall Down 7 Times, Get Up 8
(TRANSLATOR, WITH KA YOSHIDA)

UTOPIA AVENUE

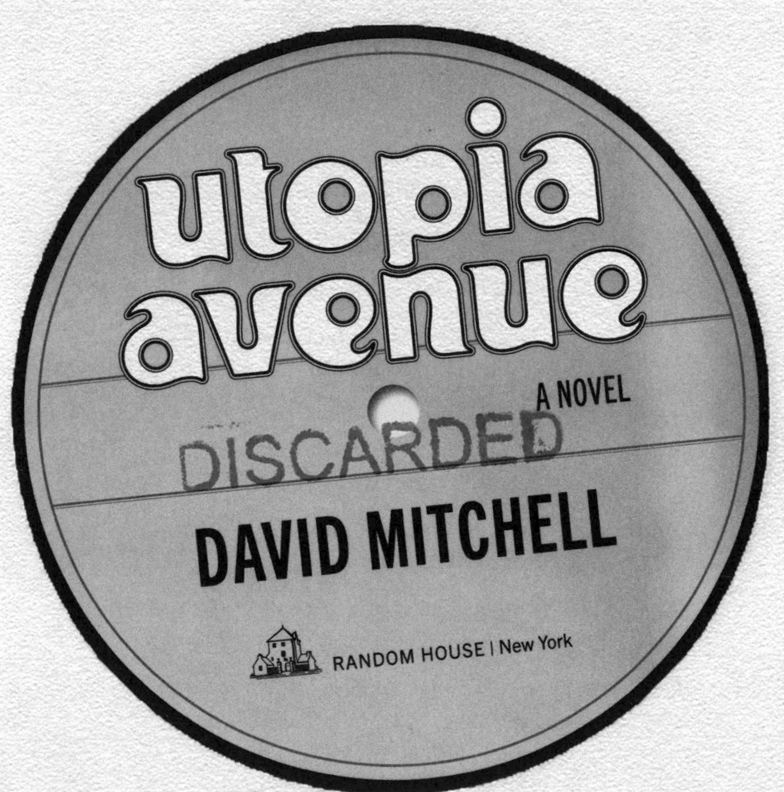
utopia
avenue
A NOVEL
DAVID MITCHELL
RANDOM HOUSE | New York

Utopia Avenue is a work of fiction. Names, characters, places, and incidents are the products of the author's imagination or are used fictitiously. Any resemblance to actual events, locales, or persons, living or dead, is entirely coincidental.

Published in the United States by Random House, an imprint and division of Penguin Random House LLC, New York.

RANDOM HOUSE and the HOUSE colophon are registered trademarks of Penguin Random House LLC.

Published in the United Kingdom by Sceptre, an imprint of Hodder & Stoughton, London.

LIBRARY OF CONGRESS CATALOGING-IN-PUBLICATION DATA

Names: Mitchell, David (David Stephen), author.
Title: Utopia Avenue: a novel / David Mitchell.
Description: First edition. | New York:
Random House, [2020]
Identifiers: LCCN 2020002646 (print) |
LCCN 2020002647 (ebook) |
ISBN 9780812997439 (hardcover) |
ISBN 9780812997446 (ebook)
Classification: LCC PR6063.I785 U86 2020 (print) |
LCC PR6063.I785 (ebook) | DDC 823/.914—dc23
LC record available at lccn.loc.gov/2020002646
LC ebook record available at lccn.loc.gov/2020002647

Printed in the United States of America on acid-free paper

randomhousebooks.com

2 4 6 8 9 7 5 3 1

FIRST U.S. EDITION

Book design by Simon M. Sullivan

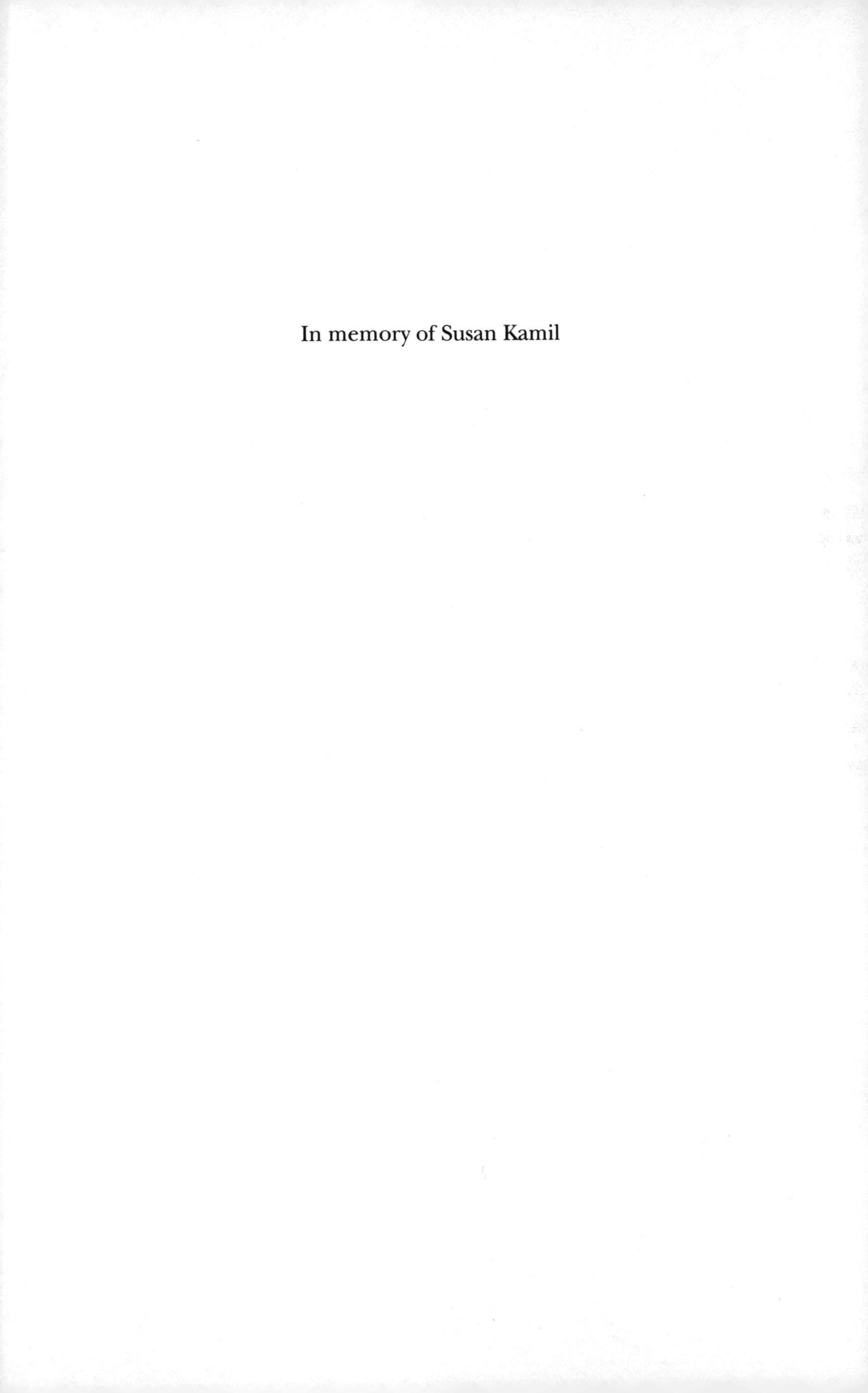

In memory of Susan Kamil

PARADISE IS THE ROAD TO PARADISE

SIDE ONE

1. ABANDON HOPE (Moss)
2. A RAFT AND A RIVER (Holloway)
3. DARKROOM (De Zoet)
4. SMITHEREENS (Moss)
5. MONA LISA SINGS THE BLUES (Holloway)

ABANDON HOPE

DEAN HURRIES PAST THE PHOENIX THEATRE, DODGES A blind man in dark glasses, steps onto Charing Cross Road to overtake a slow-moving woman and pram, leaps a grimy puddle, and swerves into Denmark Street where he skids on a sheet of black ice. His feet fly up. He's in the air long enough to see the gutter and sky swap places and to think, *This'll bloody hurt,* before the pavement slams his ribs, kneecap, and ankle. *It bloody hurts.* Nobody stops to help him up. *Bloody London.* A bewhiskered stockbroker type in a bowler hat smirks at the long-haired lout's misfortune and is gone. Dean gets to his feet, gingerly, ignoring the throbs of pain, praying that nothing's broken. Mr. Craxi doesn't do sick pay. His wrists and hands are working, at least. *The money.* He checks that his bankbook with its precious cargo of ten five-pound notes is safe in his coat pocket. *All's well.* He hobbles along. He recognizes Rick "One Take" Wakeman in the window of the Gioconda café across the street. Dean wishes he could join Rick for a cuppa, a smoke, and a chat about session work, but Friday morning is rent-paying morning, and Mrs. Nevitt is waiting in her parlor like a giant spider. Dean's cutting it fine this week, even by his standards. Ray's bank order only arrived yesterday, and the queue to cash it just now took forty minutes, so he pushes on, past Lynch & Lupton's Music Publishers, where Mr. Lynch told Dean all his songs were shit, except the few that were drivel. Past Alf Cummings Music Management, where Alf Cummings put his podgy hand on Dean's inner thigh and murmured, "We both know what I can do for you, you beautiful bastard;

the question is, What will you do for *me*?," and past Fungus Hut Studios, where Dean was due to record a demo with Battleship Potemkin before the band booted him out.

"HELP, please, I'm—" A red-faced man grabs Dean's collar and grunts, "I'm—" He doubles over in agony. "It's *killing* me . . ."

"All right mate, sit down on the step here. Where's it hurt?"

Spit dribbles from the man's twisted mouth. "Chest . . ."

" 'S okay, we'll, uh . . . get yer help." He looks around, but people rush by with collars up, caps down, and eyes averted.

The man whimpers and leans into Dean. "Aaa-*aaaggh.*"

"Mate, I think yer need an ambulance, so—"

"What seems to be the problem?" The new arrival is Dean's age, has short hair and a sensible duffel coat. He loosens the collapsed man's tie and peers into his eyes. "I say, my name's Hopkins. I'm a doctor. Nod if you understand me, sir."

The man grimaces, gasps, and manages to nod, once.

"Good." Hopkins turns to Dean. "Is the gentleman your father?"

"Nah, I never seen him till now. His chest hurts, he said."

"Chest, is it?" Hopkins removes a glove and presses his hand against a vein in the man's neck. "Highly arrhythmic. Sir? I believe you're having a heart attack."

The man's eyes widen; fresh pain scrunches them up.

"The café's got a phone," says Dean. "I'll call nine-nine-nine."

"It'll never arrive in time," says Hopkins. "The traffic's blue bloody murder on Charing Cross Road, do you happen to know Frith Street?"

"Yeah, I do—and there's a clinic, up by Soho Square."

"Exactly. Run there as fast as you can, tell them a chap's having a heart attack outside the tobacconist on Denmark Street and that Dr. Hopkins needs a stretcher team, *pronto.* Got all that?"

Hopkins, Denmark Street, stretcher. "Got it."

"Good man. I'll stay here to administer first aid. Now run like the bloody clappers. This poor devil's depending on you."

DEAN JOGS ACROSS Charing Cross Road, into Manette Street, past Foyles bookshop, and through the short alley under the Pillars of

Hercules pub. His body has forgotten the pain of his fall just now. He passes dustmen tipping bins into a rubbish van on Greek Street, pounds up the middle of the road to Soho Square, where he scares a pool of pigeons into flight, nearly loses his footing a second time as he turns the corner onto Frith Street, and bounds up the steps of the clinic and into a reception area where a porter is reading the *Daily Mirror.* DONALD CAMPBELL DEAD, declares the front page. Dean gasps out his message: "Dr. Hopkins sent me . . . a heart attack on Denmark Street . . . needs a stretcher team, on the double . . ."

The porter lowers the newspaper. Flakes of pastry cling to his mustache. He looks unconcerned.

"A man's dying," states Dean. "Didn't yer hear me?"

" 'Course I did. You're shouting in my face."

"Then send help! Yer a bloody hospital, aren't yer?"

The porter snorts inwards, deep and hard. "Withdraw a hefty sum of money from a bank prior to your encounter with this 'Dr. Hopkins,' did you?"

"Yeah. Fifty quid. So?"

The porter flicks crumbs off his lapel. "Still in possession of that money, are you, son?"

"It's here." Dean reaches into his coat for his bankbook. It's not there. *It must be.* He tries his other pockets. A trolley squeaks by. A kid's bawling his eyes out. "*Shit*—I must've dropped it on the way over . . ."

"Sorry, son. You've been hustled."

Dean remembers the man falling against his chest . . . "No. No. It was a real heart attack. He could hardly stand up." He checks his pockets again. The money's still missing.

"It's cold comfort," says the porter, "but you're our fifth since November. Word's got round. Every hospital and clinic in central London has stopped sending stretchers for anyone called Hopkins. It's a wild goose chase. There's never anyone there."

"But they . . ." Dean feels nauseous. "But they . . ."

"Are you about to say, 'They didn't look like pickpockets'?"

Dean was. "How could he've known I had money on me?"

"What'd you do if *you* were going fishing for a nice fat wallet?"

Dean thinks. *The bank.* "They watched me make the withdrawal. Then they followed me."

The porter takes a bite of sausage roll. "Hole in one, Sherlock."

"But . . . most o' that money was to pay for my bass, and—" Dean remembers Mrs. Nevitt. "Oh shit. The rest was my rent. How do I pay my rent?"

"You could file a report at the cop shop, but don't hold your breath. For the Old Bill, Soho's surrounded by signs saying, 'Abandon Hope, All Ye Who Enter Here.' "

"My landlady's a bloody Nazi. She'll turf me out."

The porter slurps his tea. "Tell her you lost it trying to be a Good Samaritan. Maybe she'll take pity on you. Who knows?"

MRS. NEVITT SITS by the tall window. The parlor smells of damp and bacon fat. The fireplace looks boarded up. The landlady's ledger is open on her writing bureau. Her knitting needles click and tap. A chandelier, forever unlit, hangs from the ceiling. The wallpaper's once-floral pattern has sunk into a jungle gloom. Photographs of Mrs. Nevitt's three dead husbands glower from their gilt frames. "Morning, Mrs. Nevitt."

"Barely, Mr. Moss."

"Yeah, well, uh . . ." Dean's throat is dry. "I've been robbed."

The knitting needles stop. "How very unfortunate."

"Not half. I got out my rent money, but two pickpockets did me over on Denmark Street. They must've seen me cash my bank order and followed me. Daylight robbery. Literally."

"My my my. What a turn-up."

She thinks I'm spinning her a yarn, thinks Dean.

"More's the pity," Mrs. Nevitt continues, "you didn't persevere at Bretton's, the Royal Printers. That was a proper position. In a respectable part of town. No 'muggings' in Mayfair."

Bretton's was indentured cocksuckery, thinks Dean. "Like I told yer, Mrs. Nevitt, Bretton's didn't work out."

"No concern of mine, I'm sure. My concern is rent. Am I to take it you want more time to pay?"

Dean relaxes, a little. "Honest, I'd be ever so grateful."

Her lips pinch tight and her nostrils flare. "Then this time, this time *only*, I'll extend the deadline for your rent payment—"

"*Thank* you, Mrs. Nevitt. I can't tell yer how—"

"—until two o'clock. Never let it be said I'm unreasonable."

Is the old cow putting me on? "Two o'clock . . . *today*?"

"Ample time for you to get to your bank and back, surely. Only this time don't flash the money as you leave."

Dean feels hot, cold, and sick. "My account's actually empty right now, but I get paid on Monday. I'll pay yer the lot then."

The landlady pulls a cord hanging from the ceiling. She takes a card from her writing bureau: BEDSIT TO LET—BLACKS & IRISH NEED NOT APPLY—ENQUIRE WITHIN.

"No, Mrs. Nevitt, don't do that. There's no need."

The landlady places the card in the window.

"Where am I s'posed to sleep tonight?"

"Anywhere you wish. But it won't be here."

First no money, now no room. "I'll be needing my deposit."

"Tenants who default on their rent forfeit their deposit. The rules are pinned up on every door. I don't owe you a farthing."

"That's my money, Mrs. Nevitt."

"Not according to the contract you signed."

"Yer'll get a new tenant by Tuesday or Wednesday. At the latest. Yer can't take my deposit. That's theft."

She resumes her knitting. "You know, I detected a whiff of the Cockney barrow-boy about you from the first. But I told myself, *No, give him a chance. Her Majesty's Printers see potential in the young man, after all.* So I gave you that chance. And what happened next? You abandoned Bretton's for a 'pop band.' You grew your hair like a girl's. You spent your money on guitars and Heaven knows what so you have nothing left for a rainy day. And now you accuse me of theft. Well, that'll teach me to second-guess myself. What's born in the gutter stays in the gutter. Ah, Mr. Harris . . ." Mrs. Nevitt's live-in ex-army goon appears at the parlor door. "This"—she glances at Dean—"*person* is leaving us. Immediately."

"Keys," Mr. Harris tells Dean. "Both of 'em."

"What about my gear? Stealing that too, are yer?"

"Take your 'gear' with you," says Mrs. Nevitt, "and good riddance. Anything still in your room at two o'clock will be in the Salvation Army store at three. Now go."

"God al-*bloody*-mighty," mutters Dean. "I hope yer die soon."

Mrs. Nevitt ignores him. Her needles click-clack. Mr. Harris grips the back of Dean's collar and hauls him up.

Dean can hardly breathe. "Yer choking me, yer scumbag!"

The onetime sergeant shoves Dean into the hall. "Up to your room, pack, and get out. Or I'll do more than choke you, you nancy-boy faggot layabout . . ."

AT LEAST I'VE still got my job. Dean tamps the coffee into the metal pod, clips it into the brew socket, and pulls down the handle. The Gaggia blasts steam. Dean's eight-hour shift has dragged. His body's bruised from the tumble he took in Denmark Street. It's a freezing night out, but the Etna coffee shop on the corner of D'Arblay and Brewer streets is warm, bright, and raucous. Students and teenagers from the suburbs are talking, flirting, arguing. Mods meet up here before hitting the music venues to take drugs and dance. Well-groomed older men eye up smooth-skinned youths in need of a sugar daddy. Less well-groomed older men stop in for a coffee before a visit to a dirty flick or a knocking shop. *Must be over a hundred people crammed in here,* thinks Dean, *and every man Jack of 'em has a bed to sleep in tonight.* Since he began his shift, Dean has been hoping that someone he knows who owes him a favor might drop by so he can cadge a sofa. His hope has grown feebler as the hours have passed, and now it's faded away. The Rolling Stones' "19th Nervous Breakdown" blasts out of the jukebox. Dean once worked out the song's chords with Kenny Yearwood, back in the simpler days of the Gravediggers. The Gaggia's nozzle dribbles coffee, filling the cup two-thirds full. Dean unclips the pod and empties the grounds into a tub. Mr. Craxi passes by with a tray of dirty plates. *Ask him to pay yer early,* Dean tells himself for the fiftieth time. *Yer've got no choice.* "Mr. Craxi, could I—"

Mr. Craxi turns around, oblivious to Dean: "Pru, wipe the farkin' counters at the front, they's disgr*azz*ful!" He barges by again, revealing a customer sitting at the counter, between the cold-milk dispenser and the coffee machine. Thirtyish, balding, bookish-looking, dressed in a houndstooth jacket and hip blue-glass rectangular glasses. *Could be a queer, but yer never know in Soho.*

The customer looks up from his magazine—*Record Weekly*—and meets Dean's gaze, unembarrassed. He frowns as if trying to place him. If they were in a pub, Dean would ask, *What d'yer think yer looking at?* Here, Dean looks away and rinses the pod under the cold tap, feeling the customer's eyes still on him. *Maybe he thinks I fancy him.*

Sharon arrives with a new order slip. "Two espressos and two Cokes for table nine."

"Two 'spressos, two Cokes, table nine, got it." Dean turns to the Gaggia and flips the switch, and milky foam settles on the cappuccino.

Sharon comes round to his side of the counter to refill a sugar pot. "I'm sorry you can't kip on my floor, honest I am."

" 'S all right." Dean sprinkles cocoa onto the cappuccino and puts it on the counter for Pru. "Bit of a nerve to ask yer, really."

"My landlady's half KGB, half Mother Superior. If I tried to smuggle you in, she'd ambush us and it'd be 'This is a respectable house not a bordello!' and she'd turf me out."

He fills the coffee pod for an espresso. "I get it. It's okay."

"You won't be sleeping under the arches, will you?"

"Nah, 'course not. I've mates I'll ring."

Sharon brightens. "In that case"—she hip-wiggles—"I'm glad you asked me first. If there's anything I *can* do for you, I'm here."

Dean's not attracted to this sweet but dumpy, dough-faced girl with raisin eyes too close together . . . *but all's fair in love and war.* "Could yer lend us a few bob till Monday? Just till I get paid?"

Sharon hesitates. "Make it worth my while, will you?"

Oh, yer flirty flirt. Dean does his half-grin. He yanks the cap off a Coke bottle. "Once I'm on my feet again, I'll pay yer a *ravishing* rate of interest."

She glows and Dean almost feels guilty at how easy it is. "I might have a few bob in my purse. Just remember me when you're a millionaire pop star."

"Table fifteen still waiting!" yells Mr. Craxi in his Sicilian Cockney accent. "Three hot chocolates! Marshmallows! Move it!"

"Three hot chocolates," Dean calls back. Sharon slips away with the sugar pot. Pru arrives to whisk the cappuccino away to table eight and Dean spikes the order slip. It's up to the two-thirds mark. Mr. Craxi should be in a good mood. *I'm bloody snookered if he isn't.* He starts on table nine's espressos. Donovan's "Sunshine Superman" takes over from the Stones. Steam hisses through the Gaggia. Dean wonders how much Sharon's "few bob" is likely to be. Not enough for a hotel, that's for sure. There's the YMCA on Tottenham Court Road, but he has no idea if they'll have a spare bed. It'll be ten thirty by the time he gets there. Once again, Dean combs through his list of Londoners who (a) might help him out and (b) have telephones. The tube closes around midnight, so if Dean shows up on a doorstep in Brixton or Hammersmith with his bass and rucksack and nobody's home, he'll be marooned. He even considers his old bandmates in Battleship Potemkin, but he suspects that bridge is well and truly burned.

Dean glances at the customer with the blue glasses. He's switched *Record Weekly* for a book, *Down and Out in Paris and London.* Dean wonders if he's a beatnik. A few guys at art college posed as beats. They smoked Gauloises, talked about existentialism, and walked around with French newspapers.

"Oy, Clapton." Pru has a gift for nicknames. "You waiting for them hot chocolates to make themselves, or what?"

"Clapton plays *lead,*" Dean explains for the hundredth time. "I'm a bloody *bassist.*" He spots Pru looking pleased with herself.

THE LITTLE COURTYARD behind the Etna's kitchen is a soot-encrusted well of fog with space for dustbins and not much else. Dean watches a rat climb up a drainpipe toward the square of underlit night-cloud. He draws a last lungful of smoke from his last

Dunhill. It's gone ten o'clock, and his and Sharon's shift is over. Sharon's gone off back to her digs, after lending Dean eight shillings. *That's a train ticket to Gravesend, if all else fails.* Through the kitchen door, Dean hears Mr. Craxi speaking Italian with the latest nephew to arrive from Sicily. He speaks next to no English, but you don't need any to serve up the bubbling vats of Bolognese sauce that, dolloped onto spaghetti, is the Etna's only dish.

Mr. Craxi appears. "So, you wanna'd a word, Moss."

Dean stubs out his cigarette on the brick-paved ground. His boss glares. *Damn.* Dean retrieves the stub. "Sorry."

"I don't got all night."

"Could yer pay me now, please?"

Mr. Craxi checks he heard correctly: "Pay you 'now'?"

"Yeah. My wages. Tonight. Now. Please."

Mr. Craxi looks incredulous. "I pay wages at Monday."

"Yeah, but like I said earlier, I got robbed."

Life and London have made Mr. Craxi suspicious. *Or maybe he was born that way.* "Is misfortunate. But always, I pay Monday."

"I wouldn't ask yer if I wasn't desperate. But I couldn't pay my rent, so my landlady booted me out. That's why I've got my rucksack and my bass in the staff cupboard."

"Ah. I think you going on holiday."

Dean does a phony smile, in case that was a joke. "If only. But, nah, I *really* need my wages. Like, for a room at the YMCA or something."

Mr. Craxi thinks. "You in the shit, Moss. But is your shit what you shitted. Always I pay wages at Monday."

"Could yer just lend me a couple o' quid? Please?"

"You have guitar. Go to pawnbrokers."

Blood from a stone, thinks Dean. "First off, I haven't paid the last installment, so the guitar's not mine to sell. That's what the money the robbers took was for."

"But you say it was for the rent money."

"Some of it was rent. Most of it was guitar. Second off, it's gone ten on a Friday night and the pawnbrokers'll be shut."

"I'm not your bank. I pay Monday. End of the story."

"How am I s'posed to *be* here on Monday if I've got double pneumonia after sleeping in Hyde Park all weekend?"

Mr. Craxi's cheek twitches. "You no here at Monday, is okay. I pay you fuck-all. A P45 only. Understand?"

"What's the *difference* between paying me now and paying me Monday? I'm not even bloody working this weekend!"

Mr. Craxi folds his arms. "Moss, you is sacked."

"Oh, for *fucksake*! Yer can't bloody do this to me."

A stubby finger jabs Dean's solar plexus. "Is easy. Is done. Go."

"No." *First my money, then my digs, now my job.* "No. No." Dean swats Craxi's finger away. "Yer owe me five days' pay."

"Prove it. Sue me. Get a lawyer."

Dean forgets he's five foot seven not six foot five and shouts in Craxi's face: "YER *OWE* ME FIVE DAYS' PAY, YER THIEVING BLOODY SHIT-WEASEL."

"Ah, *sì, sì,* I owe you. Here, I pay what I owe."

A powerful fist sinks into Dean's stomach. Dean folds over and lands on his back, gasping and shocked. *Second time today.* A dog is barking. Dean gets up, but Craxi is gone, and two Sicilian nephews appear at the kitchen door. One has Dean's Fender, the other holds his rucksack. They frogmarch Dean out through the coffee shop. The Kinks are singing "Sunny Afternoon" on the jukebox. Dean looks back once. Craxi glowers from the till with his arms folded.

Dean lifts an up-yours finger at his ex-employer.

Craxi makes a slashing gesture across his throat.

OUT ON D'ARBLAY Street with nowhere to go, Dean runs through the likely consequences of hurling half a brick through the window of the coffee shop. A police cell would solve his immediate housing dilemma, but a criminal record wouldn't help in the long run. He goes into the telephone box on the street corner. The inside is littered with Sellotaped-on pieces of paper with girls' names and phone numbers. He keeps his Fender close by, and his rucksack half propping open the door. Dean gets out a sixpence and leafs through his little black book. *He's moved to Bristol . . . I still owe him a fiver . . . he's gone . . .* Dean finds Rod Dempsey's number. He doesn't know Rod well, but he's a fellow Gravesender. He opened a shop in Camden selling leather jackets and biker accessories last month. Dean dials the number, but nobody answers.

Now what?

Dean leaves the phone box. Freezing fog blurs edges, smudges the faces of passersby, hazes neon signs—GIRLS! GIRLS! GIRLS!—and fills Dean's lungs. He's got fifteen shillings and threepence and two ways to spend it. He could walk down D'Arblay Street to Charing Cross Road, get a bus to London Bridge station and a train to Gravesend, wake up Ray, Shirl, and their son, confess that Ray's hard-earned fifty quid—which Shirl doesn't know about—was nicked within ten minutes of Dean cashing the bank order, and ask to sleep on the sofa. But he can't stay there forever.

And tomorrow? Move back into Nan Moss and Bill's? At the age of twenty-three. Later in the week, he'll take the Fender back to Selmer's Guitars and beg for a partial refund on what he's already paid. Minus wear and tear. Rest in peace, Dean Moss the professional musician. Harry Moffat'll find out, of course. *And laugh his tits off.*

Or . . . Dean looks down Brewer Street, to the clubs, lights, bustle, peep-shows, arcades, pubs . . . *I roll the dice one last time.* Goof might be at the Coach and Horses. Nick Woo's usually at the Mandrake club on Fridays. Al's at Bunjie's over on Litchfield Street. Maybe Al will let him sleep on his floor until Monday. Tomorrow he'll look for a new job at a coffee shop. Ideally, some distance from the Etna. *I can live off of bread 'n' Marmite till I'm paid again.*

But . . . what if Fortune favors the prudent? What if Dean rolls that dice one last time, spends his money on getting into a club, chatting up some posh girl with a flat of her own, who then clears off while Dean's in the bog? *Wouldn't be the first time.* Or what if a bouncer dumps him, pissed as a newt, onto an icy puke-spattered pavement at three in the morning with his train fare gone? The only way back to Gravesend then'll be shank's pony. Across D'Arblay Street a tramp sifts through an overflowing bin in the light of a launderette. *What if he once rolled the dice one last time, too?*

Dean says it aloud: "What if my songs are shit 'n' drivel?"

What if I'm just codding myself I'm a musician?

Dean has to decide. He takes out the sixpence again.

Heads, it's D'Arblay Street and Gravesend.

Tails, it's Brewer Street and Soho and music.

Dean flips the coin into the air . . .

"EXCUSE ME, DEAN Moss?" The coin falls into the gutter and out of sight. *My sixpence!* Dean turns round to see the possible queer beatnik from the counter at the Etna. He's wearing a fur hat, like a Russian spy, though his accent sounds American. "Jeez, sorry, I made you lose your coin . . ."

"Yeah, yer bloody did."

"Wait up, here it is, look . . ." The stranger bends down and retrieves Dean's sixpence from a crack. "There you go."

Dean pockets it. "So who are you, then?"

"My name's Levon Frankland. We met in August, backstage at the Brighton Odeon. The Future Stars Revue. I was managing the Great Apes. Or trying to. You were with Battleship Potemkin. You played 'Dirty River.' A great song."

Dean's wary of praise, especially from a possible queer. On the other hand, this particular possible queer is a music manager, and of late Dean has been starved of praise from anyone for anything. "I wrote 'Dirty River.' That's my song."

"So I gather. I also gather you and the Potemkins parted ways."

Dean's nose-tip is icy. "Got booted out. For 'revisionism.' "

Levon Frankland laughs straggly clouds of frozen breath. "Makes a change from 'artistic differences.' "

"They wrote a song 'bout Chairman Mao and I said it was a crock o' shit. The chorus went, *'Chairman Mao, Chairman Mao, your red flag's not a holy cow.'* Honest to God."

"You're better off without them." Frankland takes out a pack of Rothmans and offers Dean a smoke.

"I'm bloody skint without 'em." Numb-fingered, Dean takes a cigarette. "Bloody skint and neck-deep in the shit."

Frankland lights Dean's cigarette, then his own, with a fancy

Zippo. "I couldn't help but overhear . . ." He nods at the Etna. "So you've got nowhere to stay tonight?"

A platoon of mods marches by in their Friday night finery. On speed and off to the Marquee, Dean guesses. "Nope. Nowhere."

"I've got a proposal," decides Frankland.

Dean shivers. "Do yer? What kind o' proposal?"

"There's a band playing at the 2i's club tonight. I'd like your opinion as a musician on their potential. If you tag along, you can crash on my sofa. My flat's in Bayswater. It's not the Ritz, but it's warmer than under Waterloo Bridge."

"Aren't yer managing the Great Apes?"

"Not anymore. Artistic differences. I'm"—glass smashes nearby and demonic laughter rings out—"scouting for fresh talent."

Dean's tempted. It'll be warm and dry. Tomorrow he'll be able to cadge a bite of breakfast, get cleaned up, and work through his little black book. Frankland must have a telephone. *Problem is, what if this lifeline has a price tag attached?*

"If you'd feel vulnerable on my sofa"—Levon looks amused—"you can sleep in my bath. There's a lock on the door."

So he is a queer, Dean realizes, *and he knows I've guessed . . . but if he's not hung up about it, why should I be?* "Sofa's fine."

THE CELLAR OF the 2i's Coffee Bar at 59 Old Compton Street is as hot, dank, and dark as armpits. Two naked bulbs dangle above the low stage made of planks and milk-crates. The walls sweat and the ceiling drips. Yet only five years ago, 2i's was one of Soho's hippest showcases for new talent: Cliff Richard, Hank Marvin, Tommy Steele, and Adam Faith began their careers here. Tonight, the stage is occupied by Archie Kinnock's Blues Cadillac, featuring Archie Kinnock on vocals and rhythm guitar; Larry Ratner, bassist; a drummer in a vest whose kit is too big for the stage; and a tall, thin, wild-looking guitarist with pinkish skin, reddish hair, and narrow eyes. His purple jacket swirls and his hair dangles over his fretboard. The band is playing Archie Kinnock's old hit "Lonely as Hell." Within moments, Dean can see that not one but two of the Blues Cadillac's wheels are coming loose. Archie Kinnock is drunk, stoned, or both. He blues-moans into the mic—*"I'm looo-ooonely as hell, babe, looo-ooonely as hell"*—but he keeps fluffing his guitar part. Larry Ratner, meanwhile, is lagging behind the beat. His backing vocals—*"You're looo-ooonely as well, babe, you're looo-ooo-ooo-ooonely as well"*—are off-key, not in a good way. He barks at the drummer, "Too bleedin' slow!" in mid-song. The drummer scowls. The guitarist launches into a solo, sustaining a winding, buzzing note for three bars before checking in with the world-weary riff. Archie Kinnock resumes his rhythm part, sticking to the E-A-G underlay while the lead guitarist takes up the melody and, bewitchingly, inverts it. The second solo impresses Dean even more than the first. People crane their necks to watch the lead guitarist's fingers fly, pick, clamp, pull, slide, and hammer up and down the fretboard.

How's he even doing that?

MUDDY WATERS'S "I'M Your Hoochie Coochie Man" is followed by a lesser Archie Kinnock hit, "Magic Carpet Ride," which segues into Booker T. and the M.G.s' "Green Onions." The guitarist and the drummer play with accelerating verve while the two old hands, Kinnock and Ratner, drag the band down. The bandleader winds up the first set by saluting the double-figures audience as if he just blew the roof off the Albert Hall. "London, I'm Archie Kinnock and I'm *back*! We'll be out again soon for part two, okay?" The Blues Cadillac retire to the sunken bunker off to the side of the 2i's stage. Cream's "I Feel Free" wails from tinny speakers and half of the audience plod upstairs to buy Coke, orange juice, and coffee.

Frankland asks Dean, "Well?"

"Yer brought me here to see the guitarist, didn't yer?"

"Correct."

"He's pretty good."

Levon makes an is-that-all? face.

"He's bloody amazing. Who is he?"

"His name's Jasper de Zoet."

"Christ. Where I'm from yer'd get lynched for less."

"Dutch father, English mother. He's only been in England six weeks, so he's still finding his feet. Care for a splash of bourbon in that Coke?"

Dean holds out his bottle and receives a good glug. "Cheers. He's pissing his talent away on Archie Kinnock."

"He's like you in Battleship Potemkin."

"Who's the drummer? He's good too."

"Peter Griffin. 'Griff.' From Yorkshire. He salted his burns on the northern jazz circuit, playing in the Wally Whitby ensemble."

"Wally Whitby the jazz trumpet player?"

"The very same." Levon swigs from his hip flask.

"Does Jasper de Thingy write as well as play?" asks Dean.

"Apparently. But Archie won't let him play his own material."

Dean feels a throb of jealousy. "He's really got something."

Levon dabs his glazed brow with a spotted handkerchief. "Agreed. But he's also got a problem. He's too much his own man to slot into a preexisting act like Archie Kinnock's, but he's not a solo act either. He needs a handpicked gang of bandmates as gifted as he is, who'll spur him on and who'll be spurred on by him."

"Which band do yer have in mind?"

"It doesn't exist yet. But I believe I'm looking at its bassist."

Dean snorts a laugh. "Right."

"I'm serious. I'm curating a band. And I'm starting to think that you, Jasper, and Griff might just have that magic chemistry."

"Are yer taking the piss?"

"Do I look like I am?"

"No, but . . . what did they say?"

"I haven't approached them yet. You're the first piece in the puzzle, Dean. Very few bassists would be punctual enough for Griff *and* creative enough for Jasper."

Dean plays along. "And yer'll be the manager?"

"Obviously."

"But Jasper 'n' Griff are already in a band."

"Blues Cadillac is not a band. It's a dying dog. Putting it out of its misery would be an act of mercy."

A drop of sweat from the ceiling finds the back of Dean's neck. "Their manager'd beg to differ."

"Archie's *ex*-manager ran off with the piggy bank, so Larry Ratner's managing the band. Unfortunately, he's as good a manager as I am a pole-vaulter."

Dean swigs his bourbon and Coke. "So this is an offer?"

"A proposal."

"Shouldn't we have a tryout, at least, before we"—Dean stops himself saying *jump into bed together*—"decide anything?"

"Definitely. As Fate would have it, you have your bass here, and a fired-up audience. All I need from you is the nod."

What's he talking about? "This is Archie Kinnock's gig. He's got a bassist. We can't do an audition now."

Levon takes off his blue glasses and commences to clean the lenses. "But the answer to the question *Would you like a tryout with Jasper and Griff?* is *Yes,* yes?"

"Well, yeah, I s'pose, but—"

"I'll be back in a few minutes." Frankland puts his glasses back on. "I have an appointment. It shan't take long."

"An appointment? Now? Who with?"

"The Dark Arts."

WHILE HE'S WAITING for Levon Frankland to return, Dean stands in the corner guarding his bass and his rucksack. The Small Faces' "Sha-La-La-La-Lee" is playing. Dean's thinking the lyrics could be better, when a familiar voice says, "Mosser!" Dean stares back at his beaky-nosed, wide-eyed, goofy-grinning friend from art school, Kenny Yearwood. "Kenny!"

"So, yer still alive. Christ, yer hair's got longer."

"Yours is shorter."

"It's called 'getting a real job.' Can't say as I'm a fan. Was yer back at Christmas? Didn't see yer down the Captain Marlow."

"Yeah, but I had flu so I stayed at my nan's. Didn't call up any o' the old gang." *Couldn't face any of the old gang, more like.*

"Are yer still with Battleship Potemkin? I heard rumors about EMI signing yer or something."

"Nah, it all turned to shit. I left the band last October."

"Oh. Plenty more fish in the sea, right?"

"Let's hope so."

"So . . . who are yer playing with now?"

"Not . . . uh . . . well . . . kind of. We'll see."

Kenny waits for Dean to answer properly. "Are yer okay?"

Dean finds the truth is less exhausting than a lie. "It's been a bitch of a day, since yer ask. I got mugged this morning."

"Fucking hell, Mosser."

"Six bastards jumped me. I got in a couple o' decent punches but they took my rent money—all the money I had, in fact—so my landlady kicked me out. To cap it all, I got fired from the coffee shop I was working at. So yer find me neck-deep in shit, my friend."

"So where're yer staying now?"

"Someone's sofa till Monday."

"And after Monday?"

"Something'll turn up. Just don't tell anyone in Gravesend, all right? People gossip, then Nan Moss 'n' Bill 'n' my brother'll hear, and they'll fret 'n' stuff, so—"

"Yeah, sure, but look. Have a sub till yer back on yer feet." Kenny's wallet is out and he's slipped something into Dean's pocket. "That's five quid, not me going for a quick grope."

Dean's mortified. "Mate, I wasn't on the scav, I didn't—"

"I know. I know. But if the shoe was on the other foot, yer'd do the same for me, yeah?"

Dean considers giving the money back, for all of three seconds. Five pounds will feed him for a fortnight. "Jesus, Kenny, I don't know how to thank yer. I'll pay yer back."

"I know. Get yer record deal first."

"I won't forget. Honest to God. Cheers. I—"

Shrieks and shouts break out. A man's lunging through the crowd, knocking over punters left and right. Kenny dodges one way and Dean the other. It's Larry Ratner, the Blues Cadillac bassist, bolting for the stairs—chased by Archie Kinnock, who trips over Dean's Fender case, which has slid to the floor. Archie Kinnock lands awkwardly and thumps his head on the concrete ground. Ratner reaches the steep steps and bounds up them, two at a time, barging past startled patrons of 2i's. Archie Kinnock gets to his feet—his nose is half mashed—and bellows up the stairs, "I'm gonna rip your bleedin' heart out! Just like you ripped mine!" Then he staggers up the stairs after his bandmate and is gone, too.

Everyone looks at everyone else.

"What the hell was *that* about?" asks Kenny.

Dean edits and stores Archie's threat: *I'm gonna rip-rip-rip your heart out, just like you ripped mine.*

Levon Frankland appears. "Jeez, did you see that?"

"Couldn't miss it. Levon, this is Kenny, a friend from art college. We were in a band together in an earlier life."

"A pleasure, Kenny. Levon Frankland. I hope you both dodged hurricanes Kinnock and Ratner just now."

"Yeah," says Kenny, "by a few inches. What was that about?"

Frankland performs an exaggerated shrug. "All I know is gossip, rumor, and hearsay, and who listens to that?"

"Gossip, rumor, and hearsay about what?" insists Dean.

"Larry Ratner, Archie Kinnock's wife, a torrid affair, and financial irregularities."

Dean decodes this. "Larry was doing Archie Kinnock's wife?"

"An ounce of perception, a pound of obscure."

"And Archie Kinnock just found this out?" asks Kenny. "Just now? Halfway through a gig?"

Levon looks thoughtful and somber. "It might explain his homicidal rage, I suppose. What do you think?"

Before Dean can analyze the implications further, Oscar Morton—the Brylcreemed, owl-eyed manager of the 2i's club—steams by, heading to the sunken bunker.

"Would you mind keeping an eye on Dean's rucksack for a moment, Kenny?" asks Levon. "Dean and I may be needed."

"Uh . . . sure." Kenny looks as confused as Dean. The manager steers Dean by the elbow in the wake of Oscar Morton.

"Where're we going?" asks Dean.

"I hear knocking. Don't you?"

"Knocking? What's knocking?"

"Opportunity."

THE SUNKEN BUNKER smells of drains. Oscar Morton is interrogating the two remaining members of Blues Cadillac and doesn't notice Dean and Frankland slip in through the door. Jasper de Zoet is in a low-slung chair with his Stratocaster on his lap. Griff the drummer is pissed off. "Off the nearest cliff, I hope. I turned down two weeks at Blackpool Winter Gardens for this fookin' bollocks."

The 2i's manager tries Jasper de Zoet. "Will they be back?"

"I couldn't say." De Zoet sounds posh and indifferent.

"But what happened?" asks Morton.

"The phone went." Griff nods at the black telephone on the table. "Kinnock picked up. He just listened, frowning, for about a minute. His face turned to blue fookin' murder. He looked at Ratner. I thought, *Eh up, something's not right,* but Ratner didn't notice. He was restringing his bass. When whoever was calling finished, Kinnock hung up without saying a word and looked at Ratner, who finally noticed and told Kinnock he looked like he'd shat his pants. Kinnock asked Ratner, dead quiet, 'Are you shagging Joy? And have you bought a flat together with the band's money?' "

"Who's Joy?" asks Oscar Morton. "Archie's girlfriend?"

"Mrs. Joy Kinnock," answers Griff. "Archie's wife."

"Oh great," says Morton. "So what did Larry say?"

"Nothing," replies Griff. "So Kinnock said, 'It's true, then.' And Ratner came out with a load of garble about how they were waiting for the right time to tell him, and that the flat was an investment for the band, and how you can't choose who you fall in love with. Once he said the L-word, Kinnock turned full-on Incredible Hulk and . . . you saw him out there, right? If Ratner hadn't been sitting closest to the door and got away, he'd probably be dead."

Oscar Morton massages his temples. "Who called?"

"Not a clue," says Griff.

"Can you two play the second set?"

"Don't be fookin' daft," replies the drummer.

"Electric blues with no bass?" Jasper makes a dubious face. "It would sound one-dimensional. And who'd play harp?"

"Blind Willie Johnson just had a battered acoustic," says Oscar Morton. "No amps, no drums, no nothing."

"If you want me gone," says the drummer, "just pay up."

"I agreed to pay Archie for ninety minutes," says Oscar Morton. "You've done thirty. Until I get ninety, I owe you sod-all."

"Gentlemen." Levon speaks up. "I have a proposal."

Oscar Morton turns around. "Who are you?"

"Levon Frankland, Moonwhale Music. This is my client, the bassist Dean Moss, and we may just be your way out."

I am? thinks Dean. *We are?*

"The way out of what?" asks Morton.

"Of your dilemma," says Levon. "Outside are a hundred punters who'll soon start screaming for refunds. *Refunds,* Mr. Morton. Rents are up. Christmas bills are due. A hundred refunds is the last thing you need. But if you *refuse* . . ." Levon winces, ". . . half those kids are off their tits on speed. Things could get *very* nasty. Riotous, even. What will the City of Westminster magistrates make of that? You need to conjure up a new band. Without delay."

"Which *you* just happen to have," says Griff, "hidden cunningly up your large intestine?"

"Which *we* happen to have"—Levon indicates the players—"right here. Jasper de Zoet, guitar and vocals; Peter 'Griff' Griffin, drums; and introducing"—he slaps Dean's shoulder—"Dean Moss, bass prodigy, harp, vocals. Has Fender, will play."

The drummer looks at Dean askance. "You just happen to have a bass with you, just as our bassist runs out on us?"

"My bass 'n' all my worldly goods. I had to leave my bedsit in a hurry earlier."

Jasper has been strangely quiet throughout, but now he asks Dean, "How good are you, then?"

"Better than Larry Ratner," replies Dean.

"Dean's superb," says Levon. "I don't take on amateurs."

The drummer puffs on his cigarette. "Can you sing?"

"Better than Archie Kinnock," says Dean.

"So does a castrated donkey," says Griff.

"What songs do yer know?" asks Jasper.

"Uh . . . I could do 'House of the Rising Sun,' 'Johnny B. Goode,' 'Chain Gang.' Can yer two play those?"

"Blindfolded," says Griff, "with one hand up our jaxies."

"*I* run this venue," says Oscar Morton. "And if these three have never played together, how do I know they'll be any good?"

"You know they'll be good," says Levon, "because Jasper's virtuosic and Griff played in the Wally Whitby Five. Dean you'll have to take on trust."

Griff's growl sounds not displeased. Jasper isn't saying no. Dean is thinking, *I've got nothing to lose.* Oscar Morton looks sweaty and sick and needs one more push.

"I know showbiz is full of bullshit merchants," says Levon. "We've both met far too many. But I am not one."

The owner of 2i's releases a sigh. "Don't let me down."

"You won't regret it," promises Levon, "and for fifteen quid they're a steal." He tells the musicians: "Gentlemen, you get four pounds each. My commission is three. Agreed?"

"Hold your horses!" Oscar Morton is appalled. "Fifteen smackers? For three unknowns? You're putting me on!"

Levon stares back for a drawn-out moment. "Dean, I misread the situation. It looks as if Mr. Morton doesn't want a way out after all. Let's leave before the argy-bargy really kicks off."

"Wait wait wait!" Morton's bluff is called. "I didn't say I'd pay *nothing.* But I was only paying Archie Kinnock twelve."

Levon peers over his blue shades. "Ah, but we both know that Archie Kinnock's fee was eighteen pounds. Don't we?"

Oscar Morton hesitates for too long and is lost.

Griff darkens. "Eighteen? Archie told us it was twelve."

"Which is why you insist on paperwork," says Levon. "What's not written in ink on paper is, *de jure,* written in piss on snow."

A sweaty bouncer enters. "They're getting rowdy, boss."

Angry shouts find their way in: *"Where's the fackin' band?" "Eight bob for four songs?" "We've been had! We've been had! We've been had!" "Re-fund! Re-fund! Re-fund!"*

"What happens next, boss?" asks the bouncer.

"LADIES AND GENTLEMEN." Oscar Morton leans into the mic. "Due to"—a jag of feedback buys Dean extra seconds to check the leads—"unforeseen circumstances, Archie Kinnock's Blues Cadillac won't be joining us for Act Two . . ." The crowd jeers and boos. "But, *but,* we have a very special act lined up instead . . ."

Dean tunes up while testing the levels on Ratner's amp. Jasper tells him, "We'll go in A major. Griff, give us a driving canter, the way the Animals do it?" The drummer nods. Dean makes a ready-as-I'll-ever-be face. Levon stands with his arms folded, looking pleased. *It ain't yer who'll get torn to shreds by a mob of hopped-up Archie Kinnock fans if this goes tits up,* thinks Dean. Jasper tells Oscar Morton, "When you're ready."

"The 2i's is proud to present, for one night only . . . I give you . . ."

Only now does Dean realize they don't have a name.

Levon's face goes, *Okay, a name, think of a name!*

Jasper looks at Dean and mouths, *Any ideas?*

Dean's about to step in with—with what? The Pickpockets? The Evicted? The Penniless? The Anythings?

"I give you," bellows Oscar Morton, "the—Way—Out!"

A RAFT AND A RIVER

BY DAY THREE AFTER THE BUST-UP, ELF ADMITTED TO HERself that, this time, Bruce might not be coming back. The misery was incessant. Bruce's toothbrush, any song about a breakup, no matter how slushy, or even the sight of his jar of Vegemite in the pantry was enough to set her off sobbing. Not knowing his whereabouts was unbearable, but she was too afraid to phone their friends to ask if they'd seen him. If they hadn't, she'd have to explain why she was asking. If they had, she'd only humiliate herself and embarrass them by insisting on every last agonizing detail.

On Day Four, she went to pay her phone bill before she got disconnected. She stopped for a coffee at the Etna, where she bumped into Andy from Les Cousins. Before he even asked after Bruce, Elf blurted out that he was visiting relatives in Nottingham. Her lie appalled her. Pathetic, the speed at which she went from a modern girl who wasn't going to be treated like a doormat to a dumped dumpy ex-girlfriend. "Ex." She felt like Billie Holiday in "Don't Explain," minus the tragic glamour of heroin addiction . . .

All of which only partly explained why Elf slid her key into the lock of her own flat's door as quietly as a burglar. If, if, *if* Bruce had come home, she didn't want to startle him into taking flight. Stupid? Yes. Irrational? Yes. But broken hearts aren't clever or logical. Creaklessly, then, on a midweek afternoon in February, Elf let herself in, praying that Bruce would be home . . .

. . .

. . . AND THERE WAS Bruce's suitcase. His coat, his hat, and his scarf were draped over it. Elf heard him in the bedroom. She breathed properly for the first time in four days. She held his scarf to her face and inhaled its woolly damp Bruceness. Those Twiggy-thin fans who showed up to Fletcher & Holloway gigs, who gazed at Bruce, who glowered at Elf, they were wrong, wrong, wrong. Elf *wasn't* Bruce's stepping-stone. He loved her. Elf called, "I'm home, Kangaroo!" then waited for Bruce to reply, "Wombat!" and rush through to kiss her.

But when Bruce came through, his face was stony. LPs poked out of his rucksack. "Thought you were teaching this morning."

Elf didn't understand. "The class had flu . . . but hi."

"Thought I'd pick up the rest of my stuff."

Elf realized the suitcase by the door was not full of things Bruce was bringing back but removing. "You came when I was out."

"Thought it'd be better."

"Where have you been staying? I was worried sick."

"A friend." Flatly, like it was none of her business.

"Which friend?" Elf couldn't help it. If it was a male friend, Bruce the Australian should have said "a mate." "A girl?"

Bruce sighed like a patient grown-up. "Why do you do this?"

Elf folded her arms like a wronged woman. "Do what?"

"You're so possessive. That's why you pushed me away."

"Meaning, 'I'll do whatever I want and if you complain, you're a hysterical bitch'?"

Bruce shut his eyes as if at a throbbing headache.

"If you're dumping me, just tell me it's over."

"Suit yourself." Bruce looked at her. "It's—over."

"What about the duo?" Elf could hardly breathe. "Toby's about to offer us an album."

"No, he isn't." Bruce said it like she was a foreigner he had to speak loudly at. "The album isn't happening."

"You don't want to make an album?" Her voice was a husk.

"A&B Records don't want a Fletcher and Holloway album after

all. *'Shepherd's Crook,'* I quote, 'did not meet expectations.' No album. We're dropped. The duo's finished."

Below, a motorbike snarled through Livonia Street. Dispatch riders and petty criminals used it as a shortcut.

Two floors up, Elf wanted to dry-retch. "No."

"Call Toby if you think I'm lying."

"What about the gigs? Andy's given us the nine o'clock slot at Cousins next Sunday. There's the Cambridge Festival next month."

Bruce shrugged and jutted out his lips. "Cancel 'em, do 'em solo—do what you want." He put on his coat. "My scarf."

Elf's hand passed it to him. "If I need to contact—"

Bruce clunked the door shut behind him.

The flat was silent. Record label: *gone.* The duo: *gone.* Bruce: *gone.* Elf fled to her bed—*hers,* no longer *ours*—curled up under her blanket, and in that stuffy womb sobbed her heart out. All over again.

ON DAY NINE, February rain batters the Holloway family's mock-Tudor windows, erasing the muddy garden and Chislehurst Road. Lawrence, the besuited boyfriend of Elf's older sister, Imogen, is acting oddly. "So, um . . ." He half stands, sits down again, then leans forward. "So, um . . ." His fingers check his tie. "So, um, a . . . an . . . a, surprise announcement." Imogen gives him an encouraging smile, as if Lawrence is a nervous student in a Nativity play.

My God, thinks Elf. *They're getting engaged.*

One glance tells her that both her parents are in the know.

"Not that Mr. Holloway'll be surprised," says Lawrence.

"I'd say we're on 'Clive' terms now," says Elf's dad. "Eh?"

"Don't steal the lad's thunder, Clive," instructs Elf's mum.

"I'm not stealing anyone's thunder, Miranda."

"My God!" Bea, Elf's younger sister, acts concerned. "Lawrence is turning purple."

Lawrence is indeed blushing impressively. "I'm fine, I—"

"Shall I call nine-nine-nine?" Bea puts down her champagne glass. "Are you having an attack?"

"Bea," Elf's mum uses her warning voice, "enough."

"What if Lawrence combusts, Mummy? It'll take more than bicarb of soda to get Lawrence-stains out of the carpet."

Normally Elf would laugh at this, but since Bruce left, nothing's funny. Elf's dad takes charge. "Carry on, Lawrence, before you get cold feet about joining this madhouse."

"Lawrence is *not* getting cold feet," insists Elf's mum.

"Ah—uh—um . . . not at all, Mrs. Holloway."

"If Daddy's 'Clive,' " asks Bea, "shouldn't Lawrence call you 'Miranda,' Mummy? I'm only asking."

"Bea," groans their mum, "if you're bored, buzz off."

"And miss Lawrence's mystery news? It's not every day your sister gets engaged." Bea puts her hand to her mouth. "Oops. Sorry. *Was* that the mystery news? It's just a wild, wild guess."

A car backfires on Chislehurst Road. Lawrence puffs out his cheeks, relieved. "Yes. I asked Immy to marry me. Immy said . . ."

" 'Oh, go on then, if you insist,' " reports Imogen.

"Clive and I couldn't be more thrilled," says their mum.

"Unless England wins the Ashes," says Elf's dad, coaxing his pipe back to life. He gives Lawrence his corny wink.

"Congratulations," says Elf. "Both of you."

"Let's look at the ring, then, Sis," says Bea.

Imogen takes a box from her handbag. Everyone draws close. "Gadzooks," says Bea. "That didn't come from a cracker."

"It cost someone a fair whack," says Elf's dad. "My my."

"Actually, Mr. Hollo— Clive, my gran left it for me, for . . ." Lawrence watches Imogen slip it on, ". . . for my fiancée."

"Isn't that moving?" says Elf's mother. "Clive?"

"Yes, dear." Elf's dad gives Lawrence an arch look. "Two magic words you'll be saying often, from here on in."

Mum and Dad are a double act, Elf thinks, *like Bruce and me were.* Grief for "Bruce and Elf" squeezes her ribcage. *It hurts.*

"So," says Elf's mum. "Let's toast the happy couple, shall we?"

They all raise their glasses and chorus: "The happy couple!"

"Welcome to the Holloways," says Bea, in a Hammer horror voice. "You're one of us now . . . 'Lawrence Holloway.' "

"Thanks, Bea, but"—Lawrence gives his future sister-in-law an indulgent look—"it doesn't quite work like that."

"That's what the last two said," says Bea. "They're under the patio. Every year our patio is extended by one yard and Elf's murder ballad, 'The Lovers of Imogen Holloway,' gets a new verse. Odd."

Even their mum smiles at this, but Elf can't find it in herself to join in. "Let's lay the table."

Bea studies her not-quite-herself sister. "O-*kay*."

ELF HAS RECORDED a solo EP, *Oak, Ash and Thorn,* and a duo EP, *Shepherd's Crook,* with Bruce; her song "Any Way the Wind Blows" was recorded by American folk singer Wanda Virtue, who put it on a million-selling LP and released it as a Top Twenty single. With her royalty checks, Elf bought a flat in Soho, an investment that even her father begrudgingly approved. Elf can play a ninety-minute set of folk songs in front of three hundred strangers. She can handle drunken hecklers. She can vote, drive, drink, smoke, have sex, and has done all five. Yet bring her back to her family dining table, let her see Uncle Derek's watercolor of HMS *Trafalgar,* which she used to try to magic herself into like the children in *The Voyage of the Dawn Treader,* or the liveried stockade of *Encyclopedia Britannica* on the sideboard, and Elf's adult persona peels away, revealing the spotty, sulky, insecure teenager within. "That's plenty of beef for me, Dad."

"It's only two slices. You'll fade away to nothing."

"You do look pale, darling," observes Elf's mum. "I hope you're not going down with Bruce's mysterious . . . lurgy."

Elf extends her lie. "Laryngitis, the doctor said."

"Such a pity he missed Immy and Lawrence's big news." Elf is dubious. She suspects her mother of keeping a charge sheet of Bruce's crimes. These include living in sin with Elf, fueling Elf's delusions that music is a career, being a male with long hair, and being Australian. *She'll be happier about our bust-up than she is about Immy and Lawrence's engagement.*

Outside, rain bombards the crocuses to silky mush.

"Elf?" Imogen, and everyone else, is watching her.

"Crikey, sorry, I, uh . . ." Elf reaches for the mustard pot she doesn't want, ". . . Miles away. You were saying, Immy?"

"Lawrence and I are hoping that you and Bruce will play a few songs for us. At the wedding reception."

Tell them you've split up, thinks Elf. "We'd love to."

"Jolly good." Elf's mum surveys the plates around the table. "If everyone has Yorkshire pud, dig in."

Knives clink and the men make appreciative noises.

"The beef's out of this world, Mrs. Holloway," says Lawrence. "And the gravy's amazing."

"Miranda loves cooking with wine." Elf's dad cracks open the old gag. "She's even been known to put some in the food."

Lawrence smiles as if it's the first time he's heard it.

"Will you still teach," Bea asks Imogen, "after the wedding?"

"Not at Malvern. We're house-hunting in Edgbaston."

"Won't you miss it?" asks Elf.

"Life has chapters," says Imogen. "One ends, another begins."

Elf's mum dabs her mouth with her napkin. "It's for the best, darling. One can only juggle so much."

"Very sensible," agrees Elf's dad. "Being a housewife and mother is a full-time job. At the bank, we don't employ married women."

"*I* think"—Bea grinds the pepper mill—"that a policy designed to punish women for marrying should shrivel up and die."

Elf's dad rises to the bait. "Nobody's punishing anyone. It's simply a recognition of altered priorities."

Bea rises to the bait. "It still means women end up at the kitchen sink and the ironing board, as far as *I* can see."

Elf's dad rises to the bait. "You can't change biology."

"It's not about biology." Elf rises to the bait.

"Gosh." Her dad acts surprised. "What's it about, then?"

"Attitudes. Not so long ago, women couldn't vote or divorce or own property or go to university. Now we can. What changed? Not biology—*attitudes* changed. And attitudes changed the law."

"Ah, to be young"—their dad spears a carrot—"and be right about the ways of the world, by default."

"I UNDERSTAND YOU and Bruce are starting work on the new album next week, Elf?" says Lawrence, as Elf's mum serves up a ladle's worth of trifle from the Waterford crystal bowl.

"That was the plan, but there's been a—a mix-up at the studio. Unfortunately."

"So it's being postponed?" Bea's confused.

"Only for a week or two." Elf hates lying.

"What sort of 'mix-up at the studio'?" Elf's dad frowns.

"There was a double-booking," says Elf. "Apparently."

"Sounds *jolly* slapdash to me." Elf's mum passes the bowl of trifle to Elf's dad. "Can't you take your business elsewhere?"

Not only do I hate lying, thinks Elf, *I'm crap at it.* "I suppose so, but we like the engineer at Regent, we know the equipment."

"Olympic *did* do a lovely job with *Shepherd's Crook,*" says Imogen.

"A cracking job," echoes Lawrence, as if he knows the first thing about recording. Elf imagines the freshly engaged couple turning into Clive and Miranda Holloway in thirty years. One part of her recoils; another envies Imogen the clarity of her future life.

"If everyone has trifle," Elf's mum surveys the table, "dig in."

"How did you and Bruce meet, Elf?" asks Lawrence.

I'd rather scoop out my kidneys than answer this, thinks Elf, *but if I don't, they'll guess something's wrong, Mum'll winkle the whole sordid tale out of me.* "Backstage at a folk club in Islington. The Christmas before last. Australian folk music was a new thing, so everyone was curious to go and hear him. After the show I asked Bruce about his chord tuning and he asked about an Irish ballad I'd sung . . ." *and then we went back to his borrowed room by Camden Lock and by the New Year I loved him as hopelessly, as helplessly, as a girl in a folk song, and he loved me back as much. So I thought. But maybe he saw me as a way to leave sleeping on mates' sofas and pulling pints in Earl's Court behind. I'll never know. Nine days ago he discarded me like a crusty tissue . . .* Elf forces a smile. "Your and Immy's story at the Christian camp is much more romantic."

"But you're recording artists." Lawrence turns to Elf's mum. "What's it like to have a famous daughter, Miranda?"

Elf's mum finishes her wine. "I *do* worry where it'll all lead. Pop singers are here today, gone tomorrow. Especially the women."

"Cilla Black's doing all right," says Bea. "Dusty Springfield."

"Joan Baez in the States," adds Imogen. "Judy Collins."

"Let's not forget Wanda Virtue," says Bea.

"But what happens to them when all their starry-eyed fans move on to the next fad?" asks Elf's mum.

"Presumably they mend their ways," says Elf, "marry whoever's willing to overlook their shady past, and settle down to a life of ironing shirts and raising children."

Bea licks her spoon clean. "Bang, crash, wallop."

"Sensational trifle, Miranda," says Elf's dad, drolly.

Elf's mother sighs and looks out at the garden.

The rain whisks the water in the fishpond.

The gnome's nose drips, drips, drips, drips . . .

"I *wish* I could see a career in singing," says Elf's mum, "but I can't. All I see is Elf missing the bus on other careers."

I'm angry, thinks Elf, *because she articulates my fears.*

The clock out in the hall strikes two.

"Maybe Elf'll be a pioneer," suggests Imogen.

ELF PLAYS HER grandmother's piano while her family plus Lawrence sit and listen. She's wriggled out of singing by claiming to need to save her voice for later, but she can't wriggle out of playing without Imogen, Bea, and their mother suspecting something's wrong. The piano is an upright Broadwood with warm lower and bright upper tones. Elf mastered, first, "Twinkle, Twinkle, Little Star" at its keyboard, then scales, arpeggios, and a ladder of exercise books. The acoustic guitar may be the portable tool of the folk singer's trade, but Elf's first love—*before I liked boys, before I liked girls*—is the piano. Her grandmother died when Elf was only six, but she has a clear memory of the old woman telling her, "A piano is a raft and a river." Years later, on a February afternoon, on Day Nine of a broken, bloodied, and bruised heart, Elf finds herself improvising a melody around her grandmother's words: *A raft and a river, raft and a river, raft and a river.* It's the first musical idea she's had since Bruce left. She's grateful, too, for the minutes she spent without thinking about him . . . *Until now.* The song winds down, and Elf's family and brother-in-law-to-be give her a round of applause. The early daffodils in the vase on the mantelpiece have opened.

"That's lovely, dear," says Elf's mum.

"Ah, just mucking around, really."

"What's it called?" asks Imogen.

"It hasn't got a name."

Lawrence looks uncertain. "You just made that up?"

"There are tricks," says Elf. "To do with chords."

"That was brilliant. Could you play it in June?"

"If it turns into a song that's good for a wedding, then yes."

"Midsummer weddings are special," Elf's mum is telling Imogen. "Your father and I had a June wedding, didn't we, Clive?"

Elf's dad puffs his pipe. "And the sun's never stopped shining."

"June works for me, too," remarks Bea. "I'll be an ex-schoolgirl by then. Scary thought."

"Imogen said you're auditioning for RADA," says Lawrence.

"My first one's next month. If I pass that, I'll have the joy of a recall in May. Slap-bang during my exams."

"What are your chances?" asks Lawrence.

"A thousand applicants for fourteen places, give or take. Then again, what were Elf's chances of getting a record contract?"

Steam tumbles upward from the spout of a coffee pot.

"Just goes to show," says Imogen. "Aim for the sky."

The clock in the hallway gongs three times.

Elf finishes her coffee. "I'd better hit the road."

"Won't you cancel your Cousins spot tonight?" Bea asks. "With Bruce being too ill to sing, presumably?"

Elf has been clinging to the hope that by not canceling the gig Bruce might reappear and the last nine days be erased. Now the bill for her self-delusion is due. "I'll play a solo set."

"Surely Bruce won't let you go traipsing round Soho alone in the middle of the night?" asks her father.

"I've lived there a year without any trouble, Dad."

"Why don't I go along?" asks Bea. "As Elf's bodyguard."

"Not funny," says their mother, to Elf's relief. "Tomorrow's school. Having one daughter cavorting in Soho is bad enough."

"Why don't we go, darling?" Lawrence asks Imogen. "I've heard so much about the Cousins folk club."

"You have a long drive to Malvern tomorrow," says Elf. "Besides, a Cousins gig is like a home game. My friends'll be there."

THREE MONTHS AGO, Elf and Bruce dashed along the platform at Richmond station, her heart pumping, legs aching, breath rasping, beneath platform lamps haloed by mist. JESUS SAVES, promised a poster. The scent of chestnuts from an oil-drum roaster infused the twilight. A Salvation Army band was playing "While Shepherds Watched Their Flocks by Night." Bruce's stride was longer so he reached the last carriage well ahead of Elf and jumped aboard. "Stand clear of the doors," shouted the station master. "Stand clear—of—the doors!" Elf was sure she was doomed to miss the train, but Bruce grappled her aboard at the last possible moment and they tumbled onto a seat, joyful and gasping. "I thought," said Elf, "you'd left me behind."

"You're kidding." Bruce planted a kiss on her forehead. "Career suicide." Elf nestled her head under his chin, so her ear was over his heart. She breathed in the scent of his suede jacket and the ghost of his aftershave. He stroked her collarbone with his calloused fingertips. "Hello, girlfriend," he murmured, and Elf's nerves went *zzzzzzt. Take a photo of this,* a line came to Elf, *take a photo of this with your Polaroid eyes . . .* and she thought that even if she lived to be a hundred, she would never feel quite as glad to be alive as she was right then. Not quite.

. . .

THREE MONTHS LATER, Elf stands on the same platform at Richmond station that she and Bruce dashed along. There is no hurry tonight. There are delays on the District Line due to an "incident on the track" at Hammersmith: London Underground's favored euphemism for a suicide. Sunday evening pools in London's gardens, seeps through cracks and darkens streets. Nowhere is dry in West London tonight, and nothing is warm. The poster promising JESUS SAVES is peeling and scabby. She'll have less time than she planned to run through her old solo set list. The Cousins crowd will see an underrehearsed Elf Holloway play a duff set and conclude that when Bruce Fletcher left he took the magic with him. *They're bound to know by now—I'm the jilted Miss Havisham of the folk scene.* Elf looks into the dark window of a closed tearoom. Her reflection scowls back. She has never been the good-looking Holloway sister. Imogen's pretty in a wholesome, Christian way. Bea's status as the family beauty has gone unchallenged since infancy. Elf, relatives agree, takes after her father. *Meaning I bring to mind a pudgy middle-aged bank manager.* Not long ago in a club toilet Elf overheard a woman say, " '*Elf* Holloway'? '*Goblin* Holloway,' more like."

Elf's mum told her, "Make the most of your hair, darling—it's your best asset." It's blond and long. Bruce used to like burying his face in it. He complimented her body parts individually, but never her whole self. Or he'd say, "You look nice today," *as if there were days when I looked like a dog.* Elf always told herself that her talent as a folk singer would outweigh the fact that she doesn't look like Joan Baez or Wanda Virtue. Talent, she hoped, would bring forth the swan from the ugly duckling. Bruce's attentions made her believe that this was happening, but now he's gone . . . *I look at myself and I think,* "How forgettable." Her reflection asks, "What if you're just not as good as you think are?"

A one-clawed pigeon hops about on the track.

A fat rat a foot away pays it no attention.

There's a phone box up by the ticket barriers. Elf could call Andy at Les Cousins and plead laryngitis. It won't be hard to find a replacement for a Sunday-evening slot. Sandy Denny might be in, or Davy Graham, or Roy Harper. Several regulars have an album out—a whole LP, not just an EP. Elf could just go home to her flat, curl up under her blanket, and . . .

What? Sob yourself to sleep? Again? Do nothing until the last of the Wanda Virtue money is gone, then crawl back to Mum and Dad, penniless and careerless, contractless? If I don't show up at Les Cousins tonight, Bruce wins. The doubters will win. "Without Bruce propping her up, she's just an amateur who got lucky with one song—like, once." Mum will be proven right. "If you'd bothered to plan for your future like Immy, you'd have a Lawrence of your own by now, too."

Bugger that, thinks Elf.

LES COUSINS IS named after a French film, but everyone Elf knows pronounces it "Lez Cuzzins" or just "Cousins." Under its surreptitious sign, the narrow door is sandwiched between the Italian restaurant at 49 Greek Street and the wireless-repair shop next door. Elf descends the steep steps, glancing at the posters of Bert Jansch and John Renbourn, apostles of the folk revival. The fug of chatter, nicotine, and hash gets thicker. Waiting at the bottom is Nobby, an ex-fusilier who collects the entrance fee and assists the occasional drunk back upstairs. He greets Elf with an "Evenin', love. Parky out."

"Evening, Nobby." Elf resists an urge to blurt out, "Is Bruce here?" As long as she doesn't ask, it's possible he's shown up to apologize and resurrect the duo. Maybe he's onstage, setting up . . .

Andy sees her and waves from his corner bar where he serves Coke, tea, and coffee. No alcohol license means no closing time which means all-night shows. Every folk singer of note plays at Cousins, and Andy's wall of fame boasts Lonnie Donegan from the club's skiffle days, the Vipers, blues émigré Alexis Korner, Ewan MacColl and Peggy Seeger, Donovan pointing to the THIS MACHINE KILLS inscription on his guitar, Joan Baez and the dead-too-young Richard Fariña, Paul Simon, and Bob Dylan himself. Elf saw him four years ago play a new song called "Blowin' in the Wind" on this very stage, under the cartwheel and fishing nets, where a golden Australian named Bruce Fletcher is not waiting for her . . .

"Elf?" It's Sandy Denny, another habitué. "Are you holding up okay? I heard about Bruce. I'm so, so, so, *so* sorry."

Elf tries to act as if she's fine. "It's . . ."

"Old bollocks is what it is," declares Sandy Denny. "I saw him and his new squeeze in the café at the Victoria and Albert."

Elf can't breathe or speak. *I must.* "Oh, right." *So, it wasn't girls in general he wanted a break from—it was me.*

Sandy covers her mouth. "Oh, God . . . you *did* know?"

"Of course. Yeah. Yes. Of course."

"Thank Christ! I thought I'd put my foot in it. They were feeding each other cake and I thought it was you two, so over I went saying, 'Look at you two lovebirds!'—and then I twigged. *It's not Elf.* I just stood there like a lemon, not knowing what to say."

He took me to that café on our first date, Elf remembers.

"Bruce was Mr. Cool, of course. 'Hi, Sandy, this is Vanessa. She's a model at the Something Something Agency'—as if I'd know or give a shit. So I said, 'Hi,' and the model said, 'Enchanted,' like she'd just slipped out of some Noël Coward play."

Vanessa. There was a Vanessa at the party at Wotsit's house in Cromwell Road, in January. She was a model.

"Men," commiserates Sandy. "Sometimes I could just—" She flings her hand out and biffs a man walking by. "Oh, sorry, John."

John Martyn turns his wild-man's head and sees who it is. "Nae bother, Sandy. Breck a leg, Elf." He walks by.

"Beg pardon." Andy materializes. "Elf, I've heard the buzz. If you want to bow out, everyone will understand."

Elf looks over his shoulder at the exit, and sees further into her future if she leaves now. After staying with her parents for a few weeks, she'll work the summer at a typing pool, enroll at teacher-training college, get a job as a music teacher at a girls' school, marry a geography teacher, and look back at this moment, *this* one, when her future as a musician vanished. *Like a sandcastle in a wave.*

"Elf? What's the matter?" It's Sandy, looking worried.

"Are you going to vomit?" Andy's looking more worried.

ELF TIGHTENS THE D-string tuning peg. The faces are dark on darker with two dots of white where the eyes are. Cigarette tips glow moody umber. You don't need to smoke at Cousins: just breathe. Elf's nervous. It's been a while since she played solo. Even a duo is a gang. "For those of you here to see"—*say it*—"Fletcher and Holloway, apologies. Bruce isn't here . . ." her throat contracts, ". . . 'cause he dumped me for a flashier model. Literally, a model."

There's a collective gasp and several *huh*s and *what*s.

Elf nearly giggles. "The"—*say it aloud*—"the duo is over."

The till goes *chinggg*! People look at their neighbors in consternation. Not many knew, she guesses. *Well, they do now.*

Sandy Denny calls out: "It's his loss, Elf, not ours."

Before Elf starts crying, she jumps straight into "Oak, Ash and Thorn," her old show-opener and the first song she ever performed in front of strangers at the Kingston Folk Barge. Her voice is stiff and reedy and wavers on a couple of top Cs. Her slimmed-down, Bruce-less version isn't terrible, but it isn't great. Next, Elf strums the chords for "King of Trafalgar," her best song off the *Shepherd's Crook* EP . . . but she chickens out after the third bar of the intro. Without Bruce's guitar, it'll be anorexic. *What do I play instead?* The pause is growing. So she goes back to "King of Trafalgar," and fluffs the G minor to E7 on the bridge. Only the better guitarists notice, but the song feels skimpy. The applause is polite. Next she plays "Dink's Song" from the Lomax anthology. Bruce does a great banjo line over it, now missing; missing, too, are his upper octave "fare thee well"s. Better versions than Elf's can be heard at a dozen folk clubs up and down the country, right now. It occurs to Elf that she's still doing a Fletcher & Holloway set, but Fletcherlessly. *Now what? The new songs?* Of the four new songs intended for the *Fletcher & Holloway* LP, two are love songs for Bruce, the third is a blues-piano ode about Soho that doesn't have a name yet, and the fourth is a jealousy ballad, entitled "Never Enough." She doubts she'll be able to get through the Bruce songs without dissolving into a sobbing mess, so she plays "Wild Mountain Thyme." She forgets to change it to a female narrator, so she's locked into *"Will you go, lassie, go?"* not "Will you go, laddie, go?" At the line *"If you do not go with me, I'll surely find another,"* she thinks of Bruce and Vanessa undressing each other . . . *while I'm here singing stale old songs . . .*

Only now does Elf notice she's stopped playing.

There are coughs and shuffling in the audience.

They're wondering if I've forgotten the lines.

Others are wondering, *Is she cracking up?*

To which Elf would reply, *A good question.*

Elf realizes she's dropped her plectrum.

She's sweating through her makeup.

She thinks, *This is how a career dies . . .*

ABORT THE GIG. Leave with your dignity intact. What's left of it. As Elf lowers her guitar, a figure in the front row reaches forward. The spotlight's outer edge reveals a guy of about her age with feminine good looks: oval face, black hair down to his jaw, plush lips, clever eyes. He's holding Elf's lucky plectrum. Elf's fingers take it from his.

Elf was sure she was quitting. Now she's not.

To the left of the plectrum retriever sits a taller guy in a purple jacket. He addresses her semi-audibly, like a stage prompter: "If you do not go with me, I'll surely find another."

Elf addresses the audience. "I thought I'd revise this bit"—she starts to finger-pick—"to reflect the wreckage I call my love life . . ." She counts herself in and sings: *"Even if you go with me, I'll still sleep with another . . ."* she switches to an Australian accent *". . . 'cause my name is Brucie Fletcher, and I'll even do your mother . . ."*

Shrieks of glee slosh around the club. Elf finishes the song with no further revisions, and the applause is buoyant.

Oh, why not? She goes to the piano. "I'd like to road-test three new songs. They're not strictly folk, but . . ."

"Play 'em, Elf," calls John Martyn.

Elf grasps the hairiest nettle first and plays the intro to "Never Enough." During the middle eight she veers into "You Don't Know What Love Is." She saw Nina Simone do this at Ronnie Scott's—

splice a passage of one song into the middle of another. The two songs resonate. Elf returns to "Never Enough" and ends on a clanging unresolved F-sharp. Applause swells up and buoys her. Al Stewart's over to the side, clapping with delight. Elf returns to her guitar to play "Your Polaroid Eyes," and "I Watch You Sleep." Next, she sings a cappella a folk song she learned from Anne Briggs called "Willie o' Winsbury," cupping her hand to her ear à la Ewan MacColl. She sings the king's lines imperiously, his pregnant daughter's lines defiantly, and Willie's lines coolly. She's never sung it better. "Time for one more," she says, resuming her seat.

"Sing it, Elf," says Bert Jansch, "or Andy won't let you out."

If "Any Way the Wind Blows" is an albatross around Elf's neck, it's been a generous albatross. "So my last song is my big American hit." That D-string's loose again. "My big American hit for Wanda Virtue." The line earns its reliable laugh. Elf was singing this song years before she met Bruce, before he monkeyed about with the ending to make it segue into his Ned Kelly ballad. She shuts her eyes. *Strum down-up-down down-up.* A deep breath . . .

ONE ROUND OF applause, half a dozen hugs, many variations of *"You're better off without him,"* and several reviews of the new songs later, Elf gets to the stockroom that doubles as Andy's office. To her surprise, she finds four men squeezed into it, as well as Andy. Elf recognizes two: the good-looking plectrum retriever and his lankier neighbor who cued her "Wild Mountain Thyme" line. The third man has cloudy brown hair, a Regency mustache, lidded eyes that look like they're smirking, and a caddish air. The fourth, leaning against the filing cabinet, is a few years older. A big, bony face with receding hair, glasses with light-blue lenses, a halo of confidence, and a Prussian-blue suit with sunset-red buttons.

"The woman of the hour," declares Andy. "The new songs are corkers. Someone will record them, if A&B are too stupid to."

"Glad you approve," says Elf. "If you're all having a meeting, I'll come back."

"Less a meeting," says Andy, "more a plotters' huddle. Meet Levon Frankland. An old partner in crime."

The blue-glasses guy puts his hand on his heart. "Great show. Truly." He's American. "Those three new songs? Dynamite."

"Thanks." Elf wonders if he's gay. She turns to the darker shorter one. "And thank you for my plectrum."

"Any time. Dean Moss. Loved yer set. That pause, when yer made us think yer'd forgotten the words. Brilliant stagecraft."

Elf confesses: "It wasn't stagecraft."

Dean Moss just nods as if, after all, that makes sense.

Elf wonders if his face is familiar. "Have we met?"

"A year ago. Auditions for a talent show at Thames TV. I was in a band called Battleship Potemkin. You sang a folk song."

"That's it. We all lost to a child ventriloquist with a dodo thing," Elf recalls. "Sorry I didn't recognize you."

"*Pfff.* It was one o' them days yer want to forget. As well as that, I was working at the Etna coffee shop on D'Arblay Street till last month. Yer'd come in quite often, though I was stuck behind the machines, so yer prob'ly didn't notice me."

"I'm afraid I didn't. Why didn't you come out and tell me, 'Oy, I'm that guy from the Thames TV thing'?"

Dean looks at his hands. "Embarrassment, I s'pose."

Elf's not sure what to say. "That's very honest."

"I'm Griff," says the tousled, mustached one. "I play drums. I liked 'Polaroid Eyes' best. A cracker." He's an obvious northerner. "And this bleeder," Griff nods at the tall, skinny red-haired one, "is Jasper de Zoet. His real name, believe it or not."

Jasper shakes Elf's hand as if following instructions. "I've never met anyone called 'Elf' before." He sounds upper-class.

"It's the 'El' of 'Elizabeth' and the 'F' of 'Frances.' My sister Bea started it when she was little, and it's stuck."

"It's apt," says Jasper. "Your voice *is* elvish. I've played 'Oak, Ash and Thorn' over a hundred times. Your recording of 'King of Trafalgar' has remarkable"—he does a finger-twirl—"psycho-acoustics. Is that a word?"

"Possibly," says Elf, adding unguardedly, "If it is a word, it rhymes with 'Pooh sticks.' "

Jasper looks diagonally. "Or 'Why throw the Pooh sticks?' "

Ooo, thinks Elf. *Somebody else is a lyricist.*

Levon removes his glasses. "We have a proposal, Elf."

"Okay. Since you're a friend of Andy's, I'll listen to it."

"I'll make myself scarce." Andy hands her an envelope. "Here's your fee. It's the duo rate. You earned it." He exits.

"First, a little context." Levon Frankland shuts the door. "I'm a music manager. Raised in Toronto, but I went to New York to become a folk-singing colossus. My turtleneck sweaters were spot on, but everything else came up short, so I worked on Tin Pan Alley for a spell. First with a publisher, then with a booking agent who looked after British Invasion acts. I came to London four years ago to mind some American names on tour here and stayed on. I clocked up studio time gophering for Mickie Most, shifted into A&R for a year, and now it's management. An all-rounder, you could call me. Various people call me various things. I never take it personally. Cigarette?"

"Sure," says Elf.

Levon distributes his Rothmans. "Late last year, I had dinner with two gentlemen named Freddy Duke and Howie Stoker. Freddy's a tour agent based in Denmark Street. Old school, but open to new ideas. Howie's an American investor who recently acquired Van Dyke Talent, a middle-sized New York promotions agency. Freddy and Howie's big plan was—is—to merge the companies into a single-bodied two-headed transatlantic agency to be a gateway for British acts wanting to tour in the States, and vice versa. Foreign tours are a minefield without local knowledge. The music unions' regulations rob your will to live. So Freddy and Howie came to me with a fresh plan. How would I like to sign a small stable of talent, record demos, manage and get my acts signed and recorded, tour them via Duke-Stoker, and grow them into household names? I'd be operating from their offices in Denmark Street but with artistic autonomy. Duke-Stoker would pay seed money and my salary for a year, in return for a—relatively modest—cut of future profits. We'd shaken on it before the dessert trolley arrived. Lo, Moonwhale Music was born."

"New labels are springing up like mushrooms," says Elf.

"Most will last as long as mushrooms, too." Levon drags on his cigarette. "They sign the first gang of Paisley-suited likely lads they come across in Carnaby Street, blow their capital on studio fees, fail to get any radio play, and die of debt within twelve months. I want to curate a group by hand. No auditions. And we'll rehearse *before* we start gigging, so we're flawless from the get-go. Most revolutionary of all, I'm going to pay my artists a fair slice of the pie, not steal the pie and deny it ever existed."

"A novel approach," says Elf. "What kind of group?"

"You're looking at it," says Griff. "Dean on bass, Jasper on lead, yours truly on drums. Them two sing and write."

"What we're missing is a keyboard player," says Jasper.

So they're offering me a job, thinks Elf.

"A keyboard player who writes," says Levon. "Most bands can't crank out enough quality material to fill an album. But with Dean and Jasper and A. N. Other each bringing three or four songs along, we could put out an LP of original songs."

"So do yer know anyone who might fit the bill?" asks Dean.

"Someone with the right psycho-acoustics," says Levon. "Someone who can play organ licks and piano riffs."

"I feel like I'm being invited to run away with the circus," says Elf. "To be clear, you're *not* a folk group?"

"Correct," says Levon. "You'd be bringing the folk spirit to the picnic. Dean's got a bluesy sensibility, Griff's from jazz, and Jasper's . . ." They look at him.

"A bloody handy guitarist," says Dean. "I'm saying that despite the fact he's my landlord, not 'cause of it."

"Isn't a landlord someone you pay money *to,*" Griff ribs Dean, "and not just borrow money off?"

"Elf," says Levon. "I can *hear* how good you'd all sound. All I'm asking is that you jam with the boys. We have a rehearsal space at a bar in Ham Yard. Let's just . . . see."

"If yer don't like the circus," says Dean, "yer can leg it back and be home by teatime."

Elf drags on her cigarette. "Do you have a name?"

"We're thinking about 'The Way Out,' " says Levon.

"But it's not final," Dean assures her.

Good. "So if you're not a folk band, what kind are you?"

"Pavonine," says Jasper. "Magpie-minded. Subterranean."

"He ate a dictionary when he was little," explains Dean.

Elf tries again. "Okay—who do you want to sound like?"

The three musicians reply in unison, "Us."

DARKROOM

THE UFO CLUB VIBRATES AS PINK FLOYD SETS THE SHIP'S controls for the heart of the pulsing sun. Mecca's dancing, watching him. Her eyes are Berlin blue. Jellyfish of colored light breed and smear the dancers and Jasper's mind is set adrift. *Abracadabra, it's a boy, why not name him Jasper?* Why this name and not another? *A friend? The stone? A long-lost lover?* Only Jasper's mother knows, and she's asleep in a box on the seabed, off the coast of Egypt. *We come, we see, we hang around till Death snuffs out our candles . . .* Plenty more where we came from. A million per droplet of the stuff of life. Keeping track of each of us would drive God quite insane. Onstage Syd Barrett drags a comb along his Fender's slack-keyed strings. *A pterodactyl vents her grief.* Syd's no virtuoso, true, but stagecraft and Byronic looks make good the shortfall, amply. Meanwhile in the lighting rig, Hoppy throws a switch and Kurosawa's samurai circumambulate the walls. UFO's famous light show. Jasper's hand is drawing *8* and has been for a while: *8* is infinity, sat up. Words reach him, cracked and scratchy, like radio waves at dusk . . . *"If the doors of perception were cleansed every thing would appear to man as it is: Infinite. For man has closed himself up, till he sees all things thro' narrow chinks of his cavern."* Who said that? *I know it wasn't me.* Knock Knock? Or an ancestor? An azure jellyfish of light passes over Rick. Rick Wright plays keyboards—a Farfisa—in purple tie and yellow shirt. Pink Floyd signed with EMI last month. They spent this week at Abbey Road. Rick told Jasper earlier: "The engineer from Studio

B wandered in and said, 'The boys are on a break next door—fancy saying hi?' So in we went. John took the piss, George had a toothache, Ringo told a dirty joke." They listened to a song of Paul's called "Lovely Rita, Meter Maid." Mecca circles closer. Her syllables excite his ear: *"Ich bin bereit abzuheben."* Jasper's German's rusty, though Mecca's rubbing off the rust with every precious hour. "You feel you're lifting?" True enough, the Mandrax fuse is lit. The bouncers in the lobby here vend Londinium's purest gear, and here it comes and here it comes and *dot-dot-dot dash-dash-dash dot-dot-dot* . . .

. . . AND JASPER'S BODY'S where it was, dancing in the UFO club on Tottenham Court Road, but Jasper's mind is sling-shooting, first round irrigated Mars, then on and on and on and on to offspring-eating Saturn; then faster, Father, farther out, gaining on the speed of light where time and space solidify and here's that scratchy voice again: *"The glory of the Lord shone round about: and they were sore afraid. And the angel said unto them, Fear not: buckle up, enjoy the trip."* Bible black and starless, now. A comet's tail, a silver thread, unraveling and unspooling. Knock Knock. Who's there? *No, don't reply.* Let's think instead of saner things. Nick Mason's playing drums. Drums were here before we are. The rhythms of our mothers' hearts. Mecca leaves on Monday night. America will swallow her, like Jonah in the whale. We're pulsing now to Roger's bass, a Rickenbacker Fireglo. Roger Waters has a smile that is both cloak and dagger. Mecca's face becomes concave. It elongates, encircling him. *"My vegetable love should grow, vaster than empires and more slow."* Her face reflects his and his hers, and what reflection ever guessed that it is a reflection? Jasper asks, "Do you think reality is just a mirror for something else?"

Mecca's answer lags behind her waxy boyish lips: "*Ja, bestimmt.* This is why a photograph of something is more true than the thing." He puts her hand against his heart. Her face returns to normal. "Congratulations, I feel him kick. What day are you due?"

"Did I pass the interview?"

"Let's find a taxi."

. . .

A BLACK CAB is waiting outside the club. Mecca tells the driver, "Blacklands Terrace in Chelsea. Opposite John Sandoes Bookshop." Dark streets fly by. *Amsterdam wraps itself around itself: London unfolds, unfolds, unfolds.* She holds his hand, chastely. Only a few high windows are lit. Jasper still hears drumming. *A little Pink Floyd goes a long, long way.* The taxi stops. "Keep the change," says Mecca. A windy night, a pavement, a Yale lock, stairs, a kitchen, a low lamp. "I'll take a shower," says Mecca. Jasper sits at the table. She reappears, wearing a lot less than before. "That was an invitation." They shower together. Later, they're in a bed. Later, all is quiet. Later, a truck rumbles by, a street or two away. *Chelsea High Street?* Could be. Mecca's asleep. She has a big protruding birthmark on her back. Jasper thinks of Ayers Rock. The past and future seep into one another. He's on a lookout platform, with a view of a bay over roofs, gables, and warehouses. Cannon-fire. *This one must be a film.* Staccato thunder bludgeons his senses. The sky swings sideways. All the dogs are barking and the crows are crazed. A stout man, dressed for the Napoleonic era, leans on the railing, looking out to sea through a telescope. Jasper asks him if this is a dream or if the pill he took at the UFO wasn't just amphetamines.

The telescope man *clicks* his fingers. *Scrit-scrit.* Jasper's walking along a street. He comes to his aunt's boarding house in Lyme Regis. His wheelchair-bound uncle tells him, "You left us for a better life, remember? Piss off!"

Click. Scrit-scrit. Jasper passes Swaffham House at Bishop's Ely school. The principal stands in the doorway like a bouncer. "Move on, move on, nothing for you here."

Click. Scrit-scrit. The Duke of Argyll on Great Windmill Street. Jasper peers in through the engraved glass. Elf, Dean, Griff, himself, and Mecca are sitting at a table. "Half of my friends say 'The Way Out' sounds like a suicide textbook," explains Elf. "The other half say it's like a hippie going, 'Hey, way out, man!' If we were dreaming up a name now, from scratch, what would we choose?" They all look at Jasper's eye, including the other Jasper inside.

Click. Scrit-scrit. Dream-lit snow, or swirling blossom, or filigree moths obscure Jasper's vision. He's lost in a Soho even more labyrinthine than the real one. He looks for a sign. It emerges slowly, as obscurity sharpens into clarity. A street sign, in London street-sign font, reading UTOPIA AVENUE. *Click. Scrit-scrit . . .*

LETTERS SPELL P-E-N-T-A-X, inches from his face. *Click.* The camera is wound on—*scrit-scrit.* Mecca's wearing a cream Aran jumper that falls to her knees. She lines up another shot. *Click. Scrit-scrit.* Above her is a skylight of soiled sky. Crows tumble like socks in a drier. *What else?* A blanket. Crusty tissues. An electric fire. A rug. Jasper's clothes. Black-and-white photographs, dozens of them, pinned to the wall. Clouds in puddles, certain slants of light, commuters, tramps, dogs, graffiti, snow blowing in through broken windows, lovers in doorways, semi-legible gravestones, and whatever figments of London caught Mecca's eye and made her think, *I want to save you. Click. Scrit-scrit.*

She lowers her Pentax and sits cross-legged. "Morning."

"I see you start work early."

"Your eyes were . . ." she fails to find the right word ". . . moving like crazy under your eyelids. Were you dreaming?"

"Yes, I was."

"Maybe I'll arrange you as a series: *De Zoet, Asleep; De Zoet, Waking.* Or perhaps I call it *Paradise Lost.*" She pulls on navy stockings. "Breakfast is downstairs." She goes.

Jasper wonders if he and Mecca are still lovers, or if last night was their first and last time. He takes his time to dress, and spends a few minutes studying Mecca's photography.

SHE'S EATING A bowl of Weetabix in a staff kitchen and leafing through a fashion magazine. An electric kettle groans and wheezes. Jasper peers through the blinds onto a Chelsea backstreet. Gusts of wind herd dead leaves, shake a willow tree, and wrench a priest's umbrella inside out. Across the kitchen is a waist-high balcony. Jasper walks over and looks down at a large studio with an array of drapes, sets, lights, and tripods. A shot has been set up with hay bales and a couple of acoustic guitars as props. Jasper repeats what Dean said on entering the Chetwynd Mews flat: "Pretty cool digs."

Mecca asks, "What is 'digs'?"

"Accommodation. A flat, or a bedsit."

"Why 'digs'? Like, with a spade? Why?"

"I've no idea. I didn't design English."

Mecca makes a face that Jasper can't read. "Monday to Saturday, my boss Mike is here, with models, staff, and so on. I do donkey work—I help with shoots, much stuff. My 'digs' is free and Mike gives me film and the darkroom."

"Your photographs are special."

"Thank you. I'm still learning."

"There's a series of shots of a picket line."

"Dockworkers on strike in the East End."

"How did you persuade them to pose for you?"

"I just explain, 'Hi, I am a photographer from Germany, please can I shoot you?' A few say, 'Piss off.' One say, 'Take a picture of my willy, little Miss Hitler.' Most say, 'Okay.' To have your photo taken is to be told, 'You exist.' "

"It's as if they're there," Jasper speaks aloud, "staring at the viewer, working out if you're an enemy or not. Yet, really, they're just chemical reactions on paper. Photography's a strange illusion."

"On Thursday, at Heinz's digs, you played a Spanish song."

The kettle's rumbling now. " 'Asturias' by Isaac Albéniz."

"That. It gave me *Gänsehaut* . . . goosebumps, you say?"

"We do." The boiled kettle clicks off.

"Music is vibrations in the air, only. Why do these vibrations create physical responses? It's a mystery to me."

"*How* music works—the theory, the practice—is learnable." Jasper prizes the lid off the coffee. "*Why* it works, God only knows. Maybe not even God."

"So, photography is same. Art is paradox. It is no sense but it *is* sense. That coffee tastes of mouse shit. Tea is better."

Jasper makes a pot of tea and brings it to the table.

"Where are you going after here?" asks Mecca.

"I've got band rehearsal at two. Back in Soho."

"Are you good, your band?"

"I think we're getting there." Jasper blows on his tea. "We only started playing together last month, so we're still finding our sound. Levon wants us to perfect a ten-song set before we start gigging. He says he wants us springing fully formed from the brow of Zeus."

Mecca chews a spoonful of Weetabix.

"It's your last day in England, so maybe you have lots of goodbyes to make. But if you're free, tag along."

Mecca's half-smile must mean something. "Another date?"

Jasper worries he's got it wrong: "If it's not too forward."

" 'Forward'?" Possibly Mecca is amused. "We just had sex. It's a little late to be forward now."

"Sorry. I never know the rules. Especially with women."

"Is it only two days and three nights ago that we met?"

"Why?"

Mecca blows on her tea. "It feels much longer."

TWO DAYS AND three nights ago, Heinz Formaggio opened the door of a flat in an opulent crescent off Regent's Park. He wore a lounge suit, a tie embroidered with algebraic equations, and stern glasses. "De Zoet!" He gave his old school friend a hug that Jasper endured. "I *knew* it was you. Most callers do a long buzz—*bzzzzzzzzz*—but you did a *buzz-biddley-buzz-buzz, buzz-buzz*. My God, look at your hair! It's longer than my sister's."

"Your hairline's rising," said Jasper. "You're chubbier."

"Still a master of tact. You're right about my waistline, alas. Oxbridge fellows, I'm discovering, eat like kings." Party chatter and John Coltrane's "My Favorite Things" spilled into the corridor. Formaggio put his door on the latch and slipped out. "Before we go in, how are you?"

"I had a cold in November, a little psoriasis on my elbow."

"I'm asking about Knock Knock."

Jasper hesitated. He hadn't dared voice his suspicion to anyone in the band. "I think he's coming back."

Formaggio stared. "Why do you think so?"

"I hear him. Or I think I do."

"The knocking? Like before?"

"It's still faint, so I can't be sure. But . . . I think so."

"Have you been in touch with Dr. Galavazi?"

Jasper acted a headshake. "He's retired now."

Laughter rippled out of Formaggio's flat. "Do you have any of that medicine ready, in case you need it?"

"No." Jasper's gaze wandered down the curving corridor of the crescent building where Formaggio's uncle had his London pied-à-terre. There was an unpleasant number of big mirrors. "I'd need a referral to a psychiatrist. I'm worried about where a consultation may lead. If I get locked up here, I've got nobody to get me out."

"Dr. Galavazi could pull strings for you. Surely?"

Jasper was unconvinced. "I'll think about it."

"Do." His friend's frown unwrinkled. "Now, come in. Everyone's eager to meet a real live professional guitarist."

"I'm more semi-professional at present."

"Don't say that. I've been boasting about you. There's an itinerant German photographer here. She's a She, rather a striking She, at that. I'm reliably told she's a *Wunderkind.* I had the devil of a time working out who she reminds me of before it hit me—*you,* de Zoet. She's a female you. *And,* she happens to be unattached . . ."

Jasper wondered why Formaggio was telling him this.

HEINZ FORMAGGIO'S DINNER party was high-brow, academic, and free of drugs: the opposite of the musicians' gatherings that Jasper had been to since arriving in London last November. By midnight the caterers had gone and only five overnight guests remained. Jasper had intended to walk back to Chetwynd Mews, but the icy weather, the brandy, Miles Davis's *Kind of Blue,* gravity, and a sheepskin rug had changed his mind. He semi-snoozed as wine-oiled voices discussed the future. "I give late capitalism twenty more years," predicted the seismologist. "By the end of the century we'll have a Communist world government."

The philosopher issued a corvid rattle of Scouse laughter. "Bollocks! The Soviet Empire's morally bankrupt since we learned about the gulags. Socialism's a twitching corpse."

"Damn right," agreed the Kenyan. "Pinko-gray humanity will never share power with the rest of us. You all think, *What if they do to us what we've done to them?*"

"The Bomb lengthens the odds on *any* future," said the climatologist. "The future's an irradiated wasteland. Once a weapon's been invented, it gets used."

"The H-bomb may be different," answered Mecca the photographer. Jasper liked her brushes-on-cymbals voice. "If you use it, and if your enemy has it, your children die also."

"A right bundle of laughs, you lot," said the economist. "How about Martian colonies? TV-telephones? Jetpacks, silver clothes, robots who say 'Affirmative' instead of 'Yes'?"

The Kenyan snorted. "I'm betting on intelligent robots who see that *Homo sapiens* is breeding like rabbits and killing the planet, who do the sensible thing and use our weapons to wipe us out."

"What does the musician say?" asked the climatologist. "Whither the future?"

"It's unknowable." Jasper forced himself upright. "Fifty years ago, how many foresaw Hiroshima, Dresden, the Blitz, Stalingrad, Auschwitz? A big wall dividing Berlin in two? Television? Decolonization? China and America fighting a proxy war in Vietnam? Elvis Presley? The Stones? Stockhausen? Jodrell Bank? Plastics? Cures for polio, measles, syphilis? The Space Race? The present is a curtain. Most of us can't see behind it. Those who do see—via luck or prescience—change what is there by seeing. That's why it's unknowable. Fundamentally. Intrinsically. I like adverbs."

The song "Flamenco Sketches" finished. The LP clicked off. Silence was lush and lapping.

"A bit of a swizz, Jasper," said the philosopher. "We asked for a prediction and all you said was 'No idea' in an impressive way."

Jasper didn't have the mental wattage needed to refute philosophers. He picked up Formaggio's guitar. "May I?"

"You don't have to ask, maestro," said Formaggio.

Jasper played "Asturias" by Isaac Albéniz. Formaggio's guitar wasn't the best, but the half-dozen fell under the moon-swaying, sun-cracking, and blood-thumping spell, and when Jasper finished, nobody moved. "In fifty years," said Jasper, "or five hundred, or five thousand, music will still do to people what it does to us now. That's my prediction. It's late."

JASPER AWOKE ON Formaggio's uncle's sofa. He went to the kitchen, poured himself a mug of milk, lit a cigarette, sat by the rain-smeared window, and watched the dark naked trees lining the crescent. The lawns were dotted with crocuses. A milkman in a sou'wester swapped the empties for full bottles, doorstep by doorstep, putting jam jars over the foil tops to stop the birds getting to the milk. "You rise early," said Mecca. The thin pale young woman had her black velvet jacket on and looked ready to leave.

Jasper wasn't sure what to say. "Good morning."

"You play the guitar beautifully."

"I try."

"Where did you learn?"

"In a sequence of rooms over six or seven years."

Mecca's face became illegible.

"Was that a weird answer? Sorry."

"It's okay. Heinz said you are very *wörtlich*? Literalish?"

"Literal. I try not to be, but it's a hard thing to try not to be. Your voice is soothing. Like steel brushes on cymbals."

Mecca's face did what it had done a moment ago.

"That was weird too, wasn't it?"

"Steel brushes on cymbals. That's nice."

Ask her, thinks Jasper. "Do you know Pink Floyd?"

"Some of Mike's assistants talk about this band."

"They're playing at the UFO tomorrow night. I know Joe Boyd, who runs the club. If you'd like to go, he'll let us in."

Mecca's eyebrows went up. *Surprise.* "An official date?"

"Official, unofficial, date, no date. As you wish."

"A young lady in a foreign city must be careful."

"True. Why don't you interview me over dinner first? If I strike you as *too* weird, you can vanish while I'm in the gents. There'll be no hard feelings. I'm not sure if I can even do hard feelings."

Mecca hesitated. "Do you have a phone number?"

. . .

TWO DAYS, TWO nights, and a Sunday morning later, Ho Kwok's is steamy and loud with rapid-fire Chinese. A white porcelain cat with a swinging paw beckons good fortune in from Lisle Street. Jasper and Mecca are lucky to get a window seat.

"Chinatown's like Soho," says Jasper. "It's made by outsiders and the usual rules don't apply."

"An *Enklave*. Is the same in English?"

Jasper nods. A waitress brings jasmine tea and takes their order of wonton noodles, without comment. Outside, collars are up and hats are pulled down. Across the street, between a Chinese herbalist's and a dry cleaner, a man takes a battered guitar from a cardboard case into which he puts a few coins from his own pocket. He launches into a gravel-throated bash at the Rolling Stones' "Satisfaction." Before he reaches the second verse, three Chinese grandmothers appear. They wield brooms and tell him, "Go way, go way!" The busker protests—"It's a free bloomin' country!"—but the grandmothers sweep at his ankles. A few people stop and stare at the fun, and a skinny girl darts off with the coins in the busker's guitar case. The busker hares after the thief, trips over, lands in the gutter, and snaps his guitar's neck. He stares at his broken guitar in disbelief and looks around for somebody to complain to, or blame, or roar at. He finds himself alone. Gusts of March wind roll a can along the gutter, past his feet. The ex-busker hobbles back to his guitar case, loads up the broken instrument, and limps off toward Leicester Square.

"He can't get no satisfaction," says Mecca.

"He should have chosen his pitch more carefully. You can't just set up any old where and hope for the best."

"You do this busking a lot?"

"In Amsterdam, in Dam Square. London's riskier. As you saw. Or, people try to join in."

The waitress brings their order and four plastic chopsticks. Jasper holds his face over the hot pond of noodles, pork, half a soy-stained boiled egg, and Chinese cabbage. The steam softens his eyelids.

Click, scrit-scrit. Jasper looks sideways into the round eye of Mecca's Pentax and *click, scrit-scrit.* She replaces the lens cap.

"Are you never off duty?" asks Jasper.

"I want a souvenir. Before your band is famous."

"I want a souvenir of you. Would you lend me your camera?"

"Would you lend just anyone your guitar?"

"No. To you, I would."

Mecca passes him her Pentax. Jasper looks through the viewfinder at customers slurping noodles, nodding, joking, sitting in silence. The viewfinder frames Mechthild Rohmer, this unusual woman. She's staring back like a photographic subject.

"That's not the you I want to remember," remarks Jasper.

"What is the me you want to remember?"

"Imagine you've been away for two years in America. Imagine you're home at last. Imagine ringing the doorbell of your parents' house. They're not expecting you. This is a surprise. Imagine hearing their footsteps in the hall . . ." Mecca's face is changing, but it's still not quite right. "Imagine the sound of the bolt being slid. Imagine the looks on your parents' faces when they realize it's you."

Click, scrit-scrit.

ELF'S BOOGIE-WOOGIE ROLL, Griff's rimshots, and Dean's bass go from muffled to loud as Jasper opens the third-floor door marked CLUB ZED. The band is playing Dean's twelve-bar blues monster "Abandon Hope." Mecca hesitates. "You're sure they won't mind?"

"Why would they?"

"I'm an outsider."

Jasper takes her hand and leads her through the velvet curtain into a spacious room modeled on a Mitteleuropean salon. High armchairs sit around tables under dim chandeliers. Paintings and photographs of Polish military heroes watch from the wall. A Polish flag, riddled with bullet-holes from the Warsaw Uprising, is framed above the smoky-mirrored bar lined with a hundred vodkas. Many an anonymous Soho doorway, Jasper is learning, is a portal to another time and place. Club Zed is a jazzer's hangout as well as a Polish one, and it houses a fine Steinway grand and an eight-piece Ludwig drum kit on which Elf and Griff are playing while Dean wrings howls from his harmonica. The audience of two consists of Levon and Pavel, Club Zed's owner. They smoke cheroots. Dean notices Mecca and "Abandon Hope" clatters off the tracks. Elf and Griff look up and stop a few notes later.

"Sorry I'm late," says Jasper. "I was delayed."

"I bet you were." Griff's looking at Mecca.

"So this is *her*?" Dean asks Jasper.

"Yes, this is her," replies Mecca. "You are Dean, I guess."

Griff twirls his stick and does a *thump-thump*.

Introduce her, remembers Jasper. "So everyone, uh, this is Mecca. Levon, our manager, and Pavel, who lets us rehearse here."

Everyone says hello, except Pavel. He tilts his Leninesque head. "German, if I'm not mistaken."

"You are not. To do a wild guess"—she looks around—"you are from Poland."

"Kraków. Maybe you've heard of it."

"Why would I not know Polish geography?"

Pavel makes a *hmm* noise. "It's the history you people prefer to forget. The *Lebensraum* glory days."

"Many Germans do not say 'glory days.' "

"Really? The ones who commandeered my family home did. The ones who shot my father did."

Even Jasper senses Pavel's hostility.

Mecca speaks carefully. "My father was a history teacher in Prague. Before the Wehrmacht took him and sent him to Normandy. He did not wish to go, but if he refused, he would be shot. My mother escaped Prague ahead of the Russians to Nuremberg with me. So I know about history. *Lebensraum.* Genocides. War crimes. I know. But I was born in 1944. I gave no orders. I dropped no bombs. I am sorry your father died. I am sorry Poland suffered. I am sorry all Europe suffered. But if you blame me . . . for what I am—a German—why are you different from a Nazi who says, 'All Jewish are this' or 'All homosexuals are this' or 'All gypsies are this'? That is Nazi thinking. You think this way if you want but I will not. *That* way of thinking made the war. I say, 'Fuck all war.' Fuck old people who start them, who send young people to die in them. Fuck the hate that war makes. And fuck people who feed that hate, even twenty years after. The fucks is finished now."

Griff fires off a quick volley of drums and hi-hat.

"I will leave your bar, if you wish," says Mecca.

Don't go, thinks Jasper. Pavel stares at Mecca for a while. Everyone waits. "In Poland, we appreciate a good speech. And that was a good one. Would you care for a drink? On the house."

Mecca stares back. "In that case, I would like the very best Polish vodka, if you please."

"NO, NO, NO," Elf huffs. "G, A, D, E *minor.*"

"I bloody played E minor," protests Dean.

"No you bloody didn't," says Elf. "That was E. Here." She scribbles in her notebook, rips out the page and hands it to him. "Roll out the E minor at the end of the second and fourth lines, here, when I sing 'raft and river' and again on 'forgiven and forgiver.' Griff, could you play . . . featherier?"

" 'Featherier'?" Griff frowns. "Like Paul Motian?"

Elf frowns back. "Paul who?"

"Bill Evans's drummer. Shuffly, breathy, whispery."

"Try it. Jasper, could you shorten the solo by two bars?"

"Okay." Jasper notices Levon speaking in Mecca's ear.

"From the top, then," says Elf. "One and two and—"

"Sorry, folks, sorry." Levon stands. "Quick band meeting."

Griff plays a cymbal roll. Elf looks over. Dean lets his guitar hang. Jasper's wondering what this has to do with Mecca.

"We'll be needing band photos," says Levon, "for posters, for press, for—who knows?—album covers. By a happy fluke, a photographer has landed among us. The motion is, do we commission Mecca to shoot off a few rolls? Right now."

"Isn't Mecca off to the States tomorrow?" Elf asks.

"Yes. I shoot you now, develop the film tonight, and bring the best shots to Denmark Street tomorrow on my way to the airport."

"What about clothes and hair and stuff?" asks Griff.

"Mecca'll shoot while you're playing," says Levon. "*In situ.* Nothing cheesy. Think of those portraits on the Blue Note albums."

"You only said 'Blue Note' so I'd agree," grumbles Griff.

"You can see into my soul," agrees Levon.

"I vote yes," says Elf.

"I've seen Mecca's work," says Jasper. "I vote yes."

"No offense to Mecca," says Dean, "but shouldn't we hire a famous name? Terence Donovan. David Bailey. Mike Anglesey."

"Famous names," says Levon, "charge famous-name prices."

"Yer get what yer pay for in this world," says Dean.

"North of two hundred. Per shoot."

"I've always said," states Dean, "famous names're bloody ripoff merchants. *I* say we vote Mecca. Is it a full house, Griff?"

"Can you make me look like Max Roach?" the drummer asks the photographer.

Mecca considers. "If we apply much makeup, and print the negative, Max Roach's mother will mistake you for her son."

"Ooo, sharp as a blade and dry as the fookin' Sahara," says Griff. "The ayes have it."

THE DUKE OF Argyll on Brewer Street opens at six on Sundays. At a few minutes after six, the band plus Mecca shuffle into a nook by the window. The glass is frosted but for an engraved escutcheon through which Jasper can see passersby and the chemist opposite. It's a classy Victorian pub with brass fittings, upholstered chair backs, and NO SPITTING signs. Griff empties a paper bag of pork scratchings into a cleanish ashtray, and the band and Mecca clink their mismatched glasses. "Here's to Mecca's photos," says Dean, "being on our first LP cover." He downs half his pint of London Pride. "No harm being optimistic."

"Here's to 'A Raft and a River,' " says Griff. "Could be a single."

"Or a damn good B side." Dean wipes froth off his lip.

Elf raises her half-pint of shandy to Mecca. "Safe travels in the States. I'm jealous as heck. Think of me now and then, stuck here with this lot, while you travel around like a Jack Kerouac character."

Dean and Griff find this amusing, so Jasper acts a smile.

"You'll be touring America," predicts Mecca, "soon. You four have a special chemistry. It's *fühlbar*—what is *fühlbar*? I feel it."

" 'Palpable,' " suggests Elf.

A group files in wearing Carnaby Street fashion and longer hair than Jasper. Nobody gawps. In Soho it's the squares who are freaks.

"Guys," begins Elf. "I've been thinking."

"Uh-oh," interrupts Dean. "Sounds serious."

"I've tried to like the Way Out as a name. Truly. But I've failed. And half the people I've told it to keep saying 'the Far Out' by mistake. It's not sticking. Can we—please—think of a new name?"

"What," says Dean, "right now?"

"Soon it'll be too late to change," says Elf.

Jasper lights a Camel. Griff asks, "Crash us a fag."

" 'Crash us a fag' . . . " Dean misunderstands; or pretends to, for comic effect. Jasper isn't sure which. "Nah. A fag's a queer in the States. It'll give people the wrong idea. Keep looking."

"Write a joke book," says Griff. "Start with your sense of timing."

"I'm kind o' getting used to the Way Out," says Dean.

"Why settle for a name you've had to get used to?" asks Elf. "Why can't we have one that makes you think, *What a great name!* at first encounter? Mecca. 'The Way Out': Do you like it?"

"She'll agree with yer," says Dean. "She's a girl, too."

"I would agree with Elf also if I was a boy," says Mecca. " 'The Way Out' is flavorless. It is not even properly bad."

"Yeah, but yer German," says Dean. "No offense."

"To be German is not an offense to me."

"I *mean,* yer've got German ears. We're a British band."

"You do not wish to sell records in West Germany? We are sixty million. A big market for British music."

Dean exhales smoke ceilingwards. "Fair point that."

"To point out the obvious," says Griff, "most bands are 'the'—somethings. The Beatles. The Stones. The Who. The Hollies."

"Which is why," says Dean, "we shouldn't follow the herd."

" 'The Herd.' " Griff tries it for size. " 'Baa-Baa-Black Sheep'?"

Dean sips his London Pride. "My second choice for the Gravediggers was Lambs to the Slaughter."

"Great," says Elf. "We can come onstage in bloodied aprons and with a pig's head on a stick like *Lord of the Flies.*"

Jasper guesses this is sarcasm, but is less sure when Dean asks, "What did Lord of the Flies sing?"

Elf frowns, then asks, "Seriously?"

Dean asks, "Seriously what?"

"*Lord of the Flies* is a novel by William Golding."

"Is it? Frightfully sorry." Dean does a posh accent. "Not *all* of us read English at *university,* you know."

Jasper hopes this is banter and not a verbal knife fight.

"New American bands"—Griff muffles a burp—"have names that stick in the head. Big Brother and the Holding Company. Quicksilver Messenger Service. Country Joe and the Fish."

Elf spins a beer mat. "Nothing too wordy or gimmicky. Nothing too obviously desperate for attention."

Dean downs the rest of his pint. "So what *is* the perfect name, Elf? Fairy Circle? The Folk Tones? Illuminate us."

Griff munches a pork scratching. "The Illuminators."

"If I had a corker," says Elf, "I'd suggest it. But at the very least, something less random than the 2i's guy's misunderstanding? A name that sends a message about who we are as a band."

Dean shrugs. "So, who are we? As a band?"

"We're a work-in-progress," says Elf, "but looking at 'Abandon Hope' and 'A Raft and a River,' we're oxymoronic. Paradoxical."

Dean squints at her. "Yer what?"

"An oxymoron's a figure of speech made of contradictory terms. 'Deafening silence.' 'Folky R&B.' 'Cynical dreamers.' "

Dean assesses this. "Okay. Based on our catalogue of two songs. Yer turn, Jasper. It's Moss, one, Holloway, one, de Zoet, nil."

"I can't shit songs out on command," says Jasper.

"Maybe not the best metaphor," suggests Mecca.

Griff does his *gur-hur-hur.* "Ladies and gentlemen, please give a big hand to—the Song Shitters!"

Elf asks Jasper, "Do *you* think we need a new name?"

Jasper considers. "Yes."

"Any ideas up those embroidered sleeves?" asks Dean.

Jasper's distracted by an eye that appears in a clear swirl in the design on the frosted window. It's an inch from the pane. It's green. It meets Jasper's gaze, blinks, and its owner moves on.

"Sorry," says Dean. "Are we boring yer?"

I've been here before. "Wait . . ." *Dream-lit snow, or swirling blossom, or filigree moths . . . a street sign, on a wall . . .* Jasper closes his eyes. Words emerge from memory-hiss. "Utopia Avenue."

Dean makes a face. "Utopia Avenue?"

" 'Utopia' means 'no place.' An avenue *is* a place. So is music. When we're playing well, I'm here, but elsewhere, too. That's the paradox. Utopia is unattainable. Avenues are everywhere."

Dean, Griff, and Elf look at each other.

Mecca clinks her vodka glass against Jasper's Guinness.

Nobody says yes. Nobody says no.

"My darkroom is calling," announces Mecca. "I have a busy night." She tells Jasper, "You can be my assistant. If you want."

Dean and Griff clear their throats and exchange a look.

It means something but I don't know what.

Elf rolls her eyes. "Subtle as a brick, boys."

JASPER AND MECCA wait on the platform at Piccadilly Circus tube station. Groans, gusts, and echoes from the mouth of the Underworld resolve into half-melted voices. *Ignore them.* He lights a Marlboro each for Mecca and himself. The Piccadilly line is the deepest in central London, according to Dean, so its stations were used as bomb shelters during the Blitz. He imagines people huddled here, listening to explosions on the surface as powder trickled from the ceiling. Further up the platform, a cultured drunk is half singing Gilbert and Sullivan's "I Am the Very Model of a Modern Major-General" but he keeps forgetting the words and starts again.

"Can I ask a question that is not my business?" asks Mecca.

"Sure."

"Is Dean taking advantage of you?"

"He's not paying rent, it's true. But I'm not, either. I'm flat-sitting for my father. Dean's truly broke. Elf's flat only has one bedroom. Same story with Levon. Griff's living in a glorified garden shed of his uncle's. So Dean either stays in my spare room or he leaves London, and then we'd need a new bassist. I don't want a new bassist. Dean's good. So are his songs." The rails quiver. A train's approaching. "He spends most of his dole on groceries. He cooks. He cleans. If he takes advantage of me, and I take advantage of him, is it still taking advantage?"

"I guess not."

A sheet of newspaper spins along the track.

"He stops me staying too deep inside my head for too long."

Mecca drags on her cigarette. "He's very different from you."

"So's Elf. She keeps a little notebook to record her purchases in. So's Griff. The King of Chaos. We're all pretty different. If Levon hadn't assembled us, we wouldn't exist."

"Is this a strength or a weakness?"

"I'll let you know when I do."

The oncoming train blasts into the grimy light.

THE DARKROOM AT Mike Anglesey's studio is crimson black, save for a small rectangle of brightness under the projector. Fumes from chemicals stiffen the air. It's as quiet as a locked church.

Mecca murmurs, "One hundred seconds."

Jasper sets the timer and flips the switch.

Using a pair of tongs, Mecca dunks the print in the tray of developer fluid and tilts it to and fro to keep the liquid moving over the paper. "If I do this a million times, even, still it is magic."

As they watch, a ghost of Elf emerges on the paper, in a state of rapt concentration at Pavel's Steinway. Mecca has the same expression now. Jasper remarks, "It's like a lake giving up its dead."

"The past, giving up a moment." The timer buzzes. She lifts the print, lets it drip, and transfers it to the stop bath. "Thirty seconds."

Jasper sets the timer. Mecca has him tilt the tray of fixing fluid while she records timings and filter types. When the timer buzzes she flicks on the overhead bulb. Jasper's eyes hum in the yellow light. Mecca rinses the fluid from the print. "Photography needs lots of water, like all living things." She pegs the photo of Elf over the sink to drip dry, next to an Elf in full-throated song and an Elf tuning her guitar. Further along are a Griff in freak-out mode, a Griff with a cigarette dangling from his lips, and a Griff doing a drumstick spin. There's a shot of Dean's hands on the fretboard with an out-of-focus face above, one of him playing harmonica, and one of him smoking.

Is the past tense a trick of the mind?

Is sanity a matrix of these tricks?

Mecca turns to Jasper. "Your turn."

THEIR PULSES SLOW from demented to aquatic. Her coccyx presses into his appendix scar. He inhales her. She swirls into his lungs. His heart pumps her around his body. He covers their fused form with her blanket. Sweat puddles in a groove on her fuzzy neck. He laps it up. Ticklishly, she mumbles, *"Du bist ein Hund."*

He tells her, "Fox."

An angle-poise lamp slouches in the corner.

Later, she wriggles free of him, rolls over, slips on her nightgown, rolls back, and sinks into sleep.

01:11 A.M., says her clock. A classical LP is on her Dansette. Jasper clicks the PLAY toggle. An oboe has lost its way. Upon hearing a violin in the thorns, the oboe picks a path toward it, metamorphosing into what it seeks. *It's beautiful and perilous.* Sleep pulls Jasper down, hypnagogic fathoms down. *Nothing of her that doth fade, but doth suffer a sea-change into something rich and strange.* Far above, the hull of the steamer darkens the lilac sea. *Look.* A coffin sinks, trailing bubbles. Inside is Jasper's mother, Milly Wallace. From inside the coffin, Jasper hears a *knock . . . knock . . . knock . . .* Soft, yes, drowned, yes, persistent, yes, real? Yes.

Jasper wakes. 04:59 A.M. He listens to the knocks until they've gone. The whorls of Mecca's ear form a question mark.

. . .

UNDER THE STRIPLIGHT in the staff kitchen, Jasper studies the sleeve of *The Cloud Atlas Sextet.* Apart from the lines *Composed by Robert Frobisher* and *Overlapping solos for piano, clarinet, cello, flute, oboe and violin,* there are no words on the front. The back is even sparser: *Recorded in Leipzig by R. Heil, J. Klimek & T. Tykwer 1952,* and the label, Augustusplatz Recordings. Regarding the soloists, engineers, arrangers, and studio, there is nothing. Jasper wants to hear it again, but the record player is in Mecca's room and she's fast asleep. Using a biro and a notepad he finds in a drawer, Jasper draws a stave and hums his memory of the "Cloud Atlas" melody. It's in 4/4, simple enough, and starts on an F. *No, an E.* No. *An F.* The further along the melody he goes, the more it differs from Robert Frobisher's . . . *but I like it.* By the sixteenth bar, he realizes he's writing his first song since he arrived in London. He remembers seeing a guitar in the studio downstairs. It was on a hay bale, used as a prop. Jasper goes and finds it. It's so cheap it hasn't even got a maker's name, but it'll just about do.

After devising a chorus, Jasper starts looking for lyrics. Phrases of Mecca's from last night return. She was explaining the dangers of overexposure. "Without the dark there is no vision." What rhymes with vision? *Collision. Titian. Manumission.* It's a bold near-rhyme. *But how to contrive an uncontrived-looking link between slavery and photography?* Writing is a forest of faint paths, of dead ends, hidden pits, unresolved chords, words that won't rhyme. You can be lost in there for hours. Days, even.

Jasper plunges in.

"YOU'RE WEARING A tablecloth." Mecca yawns in the doorway. "You look like Grandmother in *Rotkäppchen.*"

The clock insists it's 08:07. "What? Who?"

"The wolf who ate Grandmother." Mecca's hair's a dark gold mess and she's wearing a blanket like a cloak. "The lost girl in the woods." The kitchen window is still dark, but Blacklands Terrace is waking up. A van with a phlegmy carburetor passes.

On the table is a pot of tea Jasper doesn't recall making, the core of an apple he doesn't recall eating, and a page of staves, notes, and lyrics he knows he wrote. "You're wearing a blanket."

Mecca pads over and looks at Jasper's notes. "A song?"

"A song."

"Is it good?"

Jasper looks at it again. "Could be."

Mecca notices the *Cloud Atlas* sleeve. "You like this LP?"

"Very much. I've never heard of Robert Frobisher."

"He is . . . *obskur.* 'Obscure.' The same word, yes?" Jasper nods. Mecca curls her legs up on the chair. "Robert Frobisher is not in *Enzyklopädie* so I asked a collector in Cecil Court. He was English. He studied with Vyvyan Ayrs in the 1930s. He died young, by suicide in . . . Edinburgh or Bruges? I forget. This record is his only work. A fire burned the warehouse, so it is very rare. The collector offered ten pounds for a good copy. True value is more, I think. Ten was his first offer."

"How much did you pay for it?"

"Zero." Mecca lights a cigarette. "At Christmas, Mike my boss had a party here, and the next morning, the record was left. By magic. To sell it does not feel right. So, if you like it, you keep it."

Say thank you. "Thank you."

"Now," says Mecca, "my final English bath."

"Do you need any help shampooing?"

An illegible look. "Finish your song."

"It's finished," says Jasper.

"Put me into a line, so when the radio plays it, I can boast to everyone, 'That part is me.' "

"You're already in it."

"May I hear the song?"

"Now?"

"Now."

"Okay."

Jasper plays the song from beginning to end.

Mecca nods, seriously. "Yes. You may shampoo me."

. . .

ON THE FIRST landing up the stairs from Denmark Street is a black-on-gold sign for THE DUKE-STOKER AGENCY. Jasper holds open the door and says, "Take a quick peek." Inside is reception, the receptionist's desk, a palm tree in a pot, framed photographs of Howie Stoker and Freddy Duke with Harry Belafonte, Bing Crosby, Vera Lynn, and others. Through a screen is a bustling office, two telephones ringing at different pitches, a typewriter's hammers slapping paper, and Freddy Duke, heard but not seen, barking into a telephone: "Sheffield is the twenty-*seventh* and Leeds on the twenty-*eighth—not* Leeds on the twenty-seventh and Sheffield on the twenty-eighth. Say it back!"

They climb the second flight of stairs to a logo of a whale silhouetted against the moon, stenciled onto a door: MOONWHALE MUSIC. The office is much quieter, much smaller and less populated than the busy agency below. Dust sheets cover the floors and Bethany Drew, hired by Levon to do everything at Moonwhale he doesn't, is on a pair of stepladders dabbing the coving with a paintbrush. Bethany is thirty, sometimes mistaken for Audrey Hepburn, unmarried, unflappable, and elegant even in the splashed dungarees she is wearing. "Jasper—and Miss Rohmer, I believe. Welcome to Moonwhale. I'm Bethany—office manager, dogsbody, and decorator."

"Jasper said you are very capable, Miss Drew."

"You can't believe that old flatterer. I'd shake your hand, but we can't have you flying to America with paint marks on you. I understand you're going straight to the airport from here?"

"Yes. My flight to Chicago is at six."

"And what's taking you to Chicago?"

"A patron is giving me a small show. Then I'll look for adventures and photograph what I find."

Jasper wonders why Bethany's looking at him. "It looks really professional," he says. "The paint job."

"So far, so good. Levon's expecting you . . ." Bethany nods toward Levon's office, partitioned by a pair of sliding doors. The doors are half open, revealing Levon pacing to and fro midcall, carrying a phone and trailing the cord. He mouths, "Two minutes."

Jasper and Mecca go to the bench along the front window. Mecca takes out her Pentax to compose a shot. Jasper sits down and shuts his eyes. He doesn't wish to eavesdrop on Levon's call, but ears don't have earlids. "Section two, clause three," says their manager. "It's there in black and white. Peter Griffin is engaged *as a session player,* not as an artist signed to Balls Entertainment for the rest of eternity. No 'release fee' is payable because there's nothing to release him from." Jasper guesses Levon's talking to his ex-bandleader Archie Kinnock's ex-manager. "I'm not off the boat yesterday, Ronnie. I'd say, 'Nice try,' but it's a moronic try."

Click, goes Mecca's camera. *Scrit-scrit.*

Tinny anger bleeds out of Levon's receiver.

Levon interrupts with a dry laugh. "You'll dangle me out of the window? Seriously?" Levon does not sound menaced. "Ronnie, has no old friend taken you aside and said, 'Ronnie, old son, you've gone the way of the dinosaur—get out of management, while you've still got a few quid in the bank'? Or is it too late? Are these rumors about your imminent bankruptcy true? Wouldn't it be awful if word got out that you're effectively trading while insolvent?"

A blast of abuse is ended by Levon hanging up. "What a freak show. Hi, Jasper, and welcome, Mecca, to my tiny empire."

"A beautifully decorated tiny empire," says Mecca.

"My, she's good," Bethany tells Jasper, to his confusion.

"Is that all you're taking to America?" Levon stares at Mecca's modest suitcase and middle-sized rucksack.

"It's all I own."

"Enviable," replies Levon.

Jasper asks, "Was that Ronnie Balls on the telephone?"

"It was," says Levon. "Archie Kinnock's ex-manager."

"Archie used to call him 'my ex-damager.' "

"He's claiming Griff's still under contract to Balls Management—but will let him go for a mere two thousand pounds."

"*How* much?"

"It's bullcrap and Ronnie Balls knows it."

"The glamorous world of showbiz, Mecca," says Bethany.

"It's very like the glamour of fashion photography."

"Speaking of photography," says Levon, "do I spy with my little eye something beginning with 'P' for 'portfolio'?"

Mecca holds it up. "They are ready for you to see."

"Come into my lair."

"HOLY CRAP." LEVON examines the photographs spread out on the pool table: four each of Jasper, Elf, Dean, and Griff; plus a few posed shots of the band, first in Club Zed, then a few outside shots during a lucky moment of sunshine in Ham Yard. "This one," he points to the picture of Elf at the piano, "it's more like Elf than Elf."

"I am glad the ten pounds is spent well," says Mecca.

Levon might be smiling. "Who said Germans aren't subtle?"

"A man who never went to Germany."

Levon takes out his cashbox and counts out ten pound notes, then adds an eleventh. "Your first dinner in Chicago."

"I'll toast you." Mecca slips the notes into a money belt. "Contact sheets and negatives are here, so you can print more."

"Perfect," says Levon. "We'll use them for press and for posters to flag up the band's first gigs. Next month."

Jasper realizes this is news. "You think we're ready to play?"

"We're going to book you a few student unions next month. It's only the foothills of Mount Stardom, but it's good to find your feet. My one concern is the lack of original songs."

"In fact," says Mecca, "he wrote one this morning."

Levon's head tilts back and his eyebrows go up.

"Just an idea I'm mucking around with," says Jasper.

"It's called 'Darkroom,'" says Mecca. "It will be a hit."

"I'm glad to hear that. Very glad indeed. Moving on to other news." Levon taps ash into the ashtray. "Elf called. Apparently you renamed the band in the Duke of Argyll yesterday."

"I made a suggestion," says Jasper. "Then we left."

"Elf told me that she, Dean, and Griff are all sold on Utopia Avenue. It's looking very like a fait accompli."

"I prefer Utopia Avenue to the Way Out." Bethany Drew glides in. "By a country mile." She surveys the photographs. "Goodness gracious. What fabulous images."

"These ones," says Mecca, "I am pleased by."

Levon's still on the band name. " 'Utopia Avenue' . . . I like it, but I'm worried. It sounds vaguely familiar. Where's it from?"

"It's a gift from a dream," says Jasper.

HALFWAY DOWN THE stairs to Denmark Street, Jasper and Mecca stand aside for a figure striding up, his trench coat flapping like a superhero's cape. He pauses his ascent. "Are you that guitarist?"

"I'm *a* guitarist," admits Jasper. "I don't know if I'm *that* one."

"Good line." The figure pushes back his fringe to reveal a thin white face, with one blue eye and one jet-black. "Jasper de Zoet. A damn good name. A 'J' and a 'Z.' Nice high Scrabble score. I saw you at 2i's in January. You magicked up a hell of a set."

Jasper mimes a shrug. "Who are you?"

"David Bowie, artiste-at-large." He shakes Jasper's hand and turns to Mecca. "Enchanted to meet you. You are?"

"Mecca Rohmer."

"Mecca? As in the place all roads lead to?"

"As in, the English cannot pronounce 'Mechthild.' "

"So you're a model, Mecca? Or an actress? Or goddess?"

"I take photographs."

"Photographs?" Bowie's fingers go to the gold buttons on his trench coat. They're the size of chocolate coins. "Of what?"

"I photograph what I wish to photograph," says Mecca, "for myself. I photograph what I am paid to photograph, for money."

"Art for art's sake and money for God's sake, eh? Your accent's a long way from home. *Deutschland?*"

Mecca makes a facial gesture that means, *Ja.*

"I dreamed of Berlin only the other night," says David Bowie. "The Berlin Wall was a mile high. Ground level was perpetual dusk, like René Magritte's *The Empire of Light.* KGB agents kept trying to inject my toes with heroin. What do you suppose it means?"

"Don't do heroin in Berlin," suggests Jasper.

"Dreams are basically garbage," suggests Mecca.

"Both of you could be right." David Bowie lights a Camel and nods up the stairs. "So, you're friends of Mr. Frankland?"

"Levon's our manager," replies Jasper. "I'm in a band with Dean and Griff from 2i's, and Elf Holloway on keyboards."

"I've seen Elf play at Cousins. You must be something. What name are you trading under?"

"Utopia Avenue." *That sounds good. That's us now.*

David Bowie nods. "Should do the trick."

"Are you thinking of working with Levon?" asks Jasper.

"No, this is just a courtesy call. I've signed my soul away elsewhere. I've a single out on Deram next month."

"Congratulations," Jasper remembers to say.

"Yeah." Smoke trickles from David Bowie's nostrils. " 'The Laughing Gnome.' Vaudeville psychedelia, you could call it."

"I have to get Mecca to Victoria Coach Station, so good luck with your gnome."

"As Our Savior said, 'It is easier for a camel to pass through the eye of a needle than it is to change music into money.' Be seeing you." He gives Mecca a salute and a heel-click—"*Bis demnächst,* Mechthild Rohmer." In a whirl of trench coat and hair, David Bowie resumes his climb to the top.

VICTORIA COACH STATION churns with engine noise, fumes, and nerves. Pigeons roost on struts and supports. Jasper tastes metal and diesel. People stand in queues looking tired and unlucky. LIVERPOOL. DOVER. BELFAST. EXETER. NEWCASTLE. SWANSEA. Jasper has visited none of them. *If Great Britain was a chessboard, I'd know less than a single square.*

"Hot dogs," calls a vendor from his trolley. "Hot dogs."

Mecca and Jasper find the Heathrow coach with only a minute to spare. As Mecca gives her rucksack to the driver to stow in the luggage hold, a large agile woman in a headscarf presses a wilting carnation into Jasper's hand and closes his fingers over it. "Only a shilling, love. Buy it for the young lady." She means Mecca.

Jasper gives the flower back, or tries to.

"Don't!" The woman looks shocked. "Or you may never see her again. Imagine how you'll feel if something happened . . ."

Mecca resolves Jasper's dilemma by taking the carnation herself, putting it in the woman's basket, and telling her, "Ugly."

The woman hisses at Mecca but moves on.

"Dean says I'm a nutter magnet," says Jasper. "He says I look both vulnerable and as if I have money in my wallet."

She frowns at him. For Jasper, frowns are even trickier to decipher than smiles. *Angry?* Then she cups his face and kisses his mouth. Jasper suspects this is their last kiss. *Press play and record.* "Don't change," she says. "Thanks for the last three days. I wish we had three months." Before he can answer, a large Indian family files onto the coach, forcing Jasper and Mecca apart. The grandmother is last, glaring at Jasper. A crackly Tannoy announces that the Heathrow coach is about to leave.

Jasper guesses he should say, "I'll write" or "When can I see you again?" but Mecca's future is not Jasper's to make claims on. She's not making claims on his. *Remember her now—face, hair, black velvet jacket, her moss-green trousers.* "Can I come with you?"

Mecca looks uncertain. "To Chicago?"

"The airport."

"Elf and Dean are expecting you at your flat."

"Elf usually guesses what's happened."

Mecca wears a new smile. "Sure."

ROADWORKS ON KENSINGTON Road make for slow progress. Jasper and Mecca watch shops, offices, queues at bus stops, double-deckers full of humans reading or sleeping or sitting with their eyes shut, rows of soot-blackened stuccoed houses, TV aerials sieving the dirty air for signals, cheap hotels and tenements with grubby windows, the mouths of tube stations swallowing people at the rate of hundreds per minute, railway bridges, the brown Thames, the upside-down table of Battersea Power Station, smoke gushing from its three working chimneys, muddy parks where daffodils wilt around statues of the forgotten, bomb sites where ragged children play among dirty pools and mounds of rubble, a bony horse hauling a rag-and-bone cart, a pub called the Silent Woman whose sign shows a woman with a missing head, a flower-seller in a wheelchair, billboards for Dunhill cigarettes, for Pontins Holiday Camps, for a British Leyland dealership, busy launderettes where patrons stare into the machines, Wimpy Bars, betting shops, sunless backyards where lines of damp washing stay damp, gasworks, allotments, fish-and-chip shops, locked churches in whose graveyards addicts sleep atop the dead. The coach ascends the Chiswick flyover and picks up speed. Roofs, chimneys, and gables slide by. Jasper considers how loneliness is the default state of the world. *Friends, family, love, or a band are the rare anomalies . . . You're born alone, you die alone, and for most of what lies between, you are alone.* He kisses the side of Mecca's head, hoping his kiss passes through her skull and lodges in a crevice in her brain. The sky glows gray. The miles pass. Mecca lifts the back of his hand to her lips and kisses it. That kiss could mean nothing. Or anything. Or something.

NEITHER JASPER NOR Mecca has been to an airport before. It feels futuristic. A man "checks in" Mecca's luggage, swaps her ticket for "a boarding card," and directs them to a door marked DEPARTURES. Most of the passengers are dressed as if they're going to a wedding or a job interview. They arrive at a doorway marked PASSENGERS ONLY BEYOND THIS POINT.

This is the end. They hug. *Ask if you can visit her in Chicago. Ask her to come back to London on her way home.* Her eyes drink him in. *Drink me up.* What to say? *Tell her you love her . . . but how would I know if I did? Dean says, "You just know" . . . but how do you know that you "just know"?* "I don't want you to go," says Jasper.

"Same here," says Mecca. "That's why I should."

"I don't understand."

"I know." She lifts his knuckle to her lips, then the queue shuffles her away. She looks back one last time, the way you're warned against by myths and fairy tales. She waves from the gateway and she's going, going . . . gone. *A person is a thing that leaves.* Jasper retraces his steps and joins another queue, for a coach back to Victoria. It's a cold March night. He feels what you feel when you've lost something, but before you've worked out what it is. *Not my wallet, not my keys* . . . In his jacket pocket he finds an envelope stamped "Mike Anglesey Studio." Opening it, he finds a photograph of the shot he took of Mecca in Ho Kwok's only yesterday, after Jasper asked her to imagine her homecoming in Berlin. *For once I don't have to guess what anybody's thinking. I know.* On the reverse side she has written a message.

Not bad for a beginner.
mit Liebe,
M.

SMITHEREENS

FOR A LOST TOURIST, THE DOOR OF 13A MASON'S YARD IN Mayfair would not merit a second glance. For Dean, it was a magic portal to the land where the in-crowd frolic, frequented by A&R men and producers; by columnists who can make or break you by tomorrow lunchtime; by masters of the realm and their daughters after a bit of exotic rock 'n' roll rough; by the designers of next year's fashions, the models who'll wear them, and the photographers who'll shoot them; and by musicians who no longer *dream* of success because they *have* it; by Beatles and Stones, Hollies and Kinks; by visiting Monkees, Byrds, and Turtles; by Gerry, with or without a Pacemaker; by Dean's future peers who'll tell him, "Send me a demo, I'll give it a play," or "Our support act just doesn't cut it—could Utopia Avenue step in?" Behind the door of 13A Mason's Yard is the Scotch of St. James club. Members only.

Dean told Jasper, "I'll do the talking."

He pressed the bell and an eye-level door slot snapped open. An all-seeing eye examined the pair. "And you gentlemen are?"

"Friends o' Brian's. Said he'd put us on the list."

The reply came, "Brian Jones or Brian Epstein?"

"Epstein."

"Then I'll just check my list . . . Ah, right, Brian is expecting . . . uh . . . Are you Neil and Ben, by any chance?"

Dean couldn't believe his luck. "That's us."

"Perfect. Let me double-check the surnames . . . so you'd be Mr. Neil Downe and your mate here's Mr. Ben Dover?"

"That's us all right," said Dean, then got the puns.

The All-Seeing Eye gleamed and the slot shut.

Dean pressed the doorbell again. The slot opened and the All-Seeing Eye peered out. "And you gentlemen are?"

"I was out of order just now. Sorry. But we *are* musicians. We're in Utopia Avenue. We're playing Brighton Poly tomorrow."

"Submit a membership application, plus fee, and management will consider the matter. Or get on *Top of the Pops* and the fee might be waived. Step aside, please."

A quiff, a nose, and a neck-ruff whooshed past Dean. The door of 13A half-opened and a burst of "How've yer been, Mr. Humperdinck?" escaped before the door closed again.

Dean jabbed the doorbell three times.

The slot snapped open. "And you gentlemen are?"

"Dean Moss. This is Jasper de Zoet. Remember our names. One o' these days we're coming in." He strode off across Mason's Yard.

Jasper trotted to keep up. "Maybe it's for the best. Our first gig's tomorrow. A hangover won't help."

"That smug shit was a shitting ponce."

"Was he? I thought he was quite polite."

Dean stopped. "Don't yer *ever* get pissed off?"

"I've tried, but I'm unconvincing."

"It's not a matter of 'convincing'! It's a bloody *emotion*!"

Jasper blinked. "Exactly."

THE TRAFFIC IS sluggish all the way from Waterloo to Croydon, so Dean doesn't have the chance to take the Beast above 30 mph. The gearstick is clunky as hell and the van keeps stalling at junctions. South of Croydon, they get stuck behind a slow convoy of caravans, so only now, beyond the yawn-and-you-miss-it town of Hooley, where the A23 crests the shoulder of the South Downs, is the road empty enough for Dean to put his foot down.

"It's not exactly built for speed," says Dean.

"She's a 'she' not an 'it,' " says Griff in the back. "And she's loaded up with four musicians and their gear."

When the speedo touches 45 mph, the Beast starts to shudder ominously.

"That doesn't sound good," says Elf.

Dean drops back down to forty and the shuddering subsides. "Griff, did yer actually test-drive this piece of crap?"

"Never look a gift horse in the mouth."

Dean had to borrow fifteen pounds from Moonwhale to pay his quarter share of this "gift." *More debt . . . I'm going to have to start serving coffees again, at this rate.* "Yer should *always* look a gift horse in its mouth. They're never gifts."

"We needed a van so I got us one," said Griff.

"Yeah—we needed a van. Not a twenty-five-year-old ex-hearse with holes in the floor yer can see the road through."

"Didn't see *you* putting in the legwork," says Griff.

"Well, I think the Beast has character," says Elf.

"As long as it gets us from A to B," says Jasper.

"Thanks for yer expert opinions," Dean retorts. "When the crankshaft shears off at two A.M. on the hard shoulder I'll let yer fix it with a bit o' 'character,' Elf. And when are *you,*" he asks Jasper, "getting your driving license so *you* can do that A-to-B bit?"

"I'm not sure I'd trust myself behind the wheel."

"How bloody convenient."

Jasper, predictably, says nothing. *Is he pissed off? Cowed? Or does he not give a toss?* Dean is still never sure what his flatmate-bandmate's thinking. Guessing gets tiring.

"There's a bloke in Wales," says Griff, "who'll sit your test for you. You pay twenty-five quid and a fortnight later your license arrives. Keith Moon got his that way."

The anecdote deserves a response, but Dean's heard it before. "Anyone got a ciggie?" Nobody replies. "Please."

Elf lights a Benson & Hedges and passes it to him.

"Ta. If this is the Beast's top speed"—Dean takes a drag—"we're in for some long bloody drives. Radio's knackered too."

"If someone gave you a million quid," says Griff, "you'd complain they didn't fookin' pack it right."

"Comrades," says Elf, schoolmarmishly, "tonight's our first gig. We'll make music history. Let love and peace reign."

The A23 curves out of the woods and climbs a hill.

Sussex unrolls all the way to the English Channel.

The golden afternoon is threaded by a silver river.

THE SKY TURNS dark. Dean sucks a toffee as the Beast passes through Pease Pottage, a village less quaint than its name. "If I had to choose *one* gig, it'd be Little Richard at the Folkestone Odeon. 'Bout ten years ago. Bill Shanks took us. Bill owns the record shop in Gravesend and sold me my first proper guitar. He drove my brother Ray 'n' me and a few of us down to Folkestone in his van. Little Richard . . . Jesus, he's a one-man power station. The screaming, the energy, the theatrics. The girls. I thought, *Well, now I know what I'm doing when I grow up.* Then, halfway through 'Tutti Frutti,' he was doing his thing, leaping on the piano, howling like a werewolf—when he stopped. Clutched his chest, went into a spasm . . . and hit the deck like a sack o' spanners."

The Beast passes a gypsy encampment in a lay-by.

"That was part of his act, right?" asks Elf.

"So we thought. *Little Richard's such a card,* we thought. *He's codding us,* we thought. But then the band noticed. They stopped playing. Then, dead silence. Little Richard lay there, twitching . . . and then stopped. Meanwhile a manager dashed up, tried to find a heartbeat, and shouted, 'Mr. Richard? Mr. Richard?' Yer could hear a pin drop. The manager stood up, dead pale 'n' sweaty, and asked if there was a doctor in the house. We all looked at each other thinking, *Bloody hell, Little Richard's dying on us . . .* A man called back, 'I'm a doctor, let me through, let me through.' He hurried up onto the stage, took Little Richard's pulse, uncorked a bottle, held it under his nose, and then this"—Dean overtakes a tractor pulling a load of horse manure—"ear-splitting *'Awop-bop-a-loo-bop a-lop-bam-boom!'* rang out. Little Richard sprang up—and the band came in bang on the chorus. The whole thing had been a put-on. Even the guys screamed! And it was on with the show."

Raindrops splatter on the windscreen.

The wiper *scree-scraws* ineffectually.

Dean drops down to 30 mph. "After the show, Shanks 'n' Ray and the others pissed off down the boozer. I was left to my own devices so I reckoned I'd go for Little Richard's autograph. Told the bouncer at the Odeon that I was Little Richard's nephew, and if he didn't let me in, he'd be in trouble. He told me to piss off. So I went round the back and joined the fans at the stage door. After a bit the manager showed up and said Little Richard'd gone already. They all believed him. The very same geezer who'd given it the whole is-there-a-doctor-in-the-house stunt. I played along but I sneaked back a minute later just as a window opened, three floors up. There he was. Little Richard, large as life. He took a few puffs of his joint, flicked away the butt, then shut the window. I did what any normal twelve-year-old Tarzan fan'd do. Climbed the drainpipes." The Beast approaches a bedraggled hitchhiker whose sign reads ANYWHERE. The ink is running. Dean asks, "Can we squeeze that poor bastard in?"

"Not unless he'll fit in the fookin' ashtray," says Griff.

"So you were climbing up the drainpipes," says Elf.

The Beast passes the hitchhiker. "Got to the third floor, where I shimmied up a diagonal pipe toward Little Richard's window . . . and the drainpipe came away from the wall. Fifty feet up! I lunged for the vertical section, grabbed it, and heard the pipe smash on the ground below. It looked like half a mile down. My only hope was to haul myself up to Little Richard's windowsill and go knock-knock-knock on the glass. It was that cloudy glass you can't see through. No one answered. I was clinging to the pipe like a koala but my hands were cramping up and my feet couldn't get any purchase. I knocked again. Nothing. Thought I was a goner—and if the window hadn't slid upward on my third knock, I would've been. It was Little Richard himself. Shiny quiff, pencil mustache, looking at this kid literally hanging on by his fingernails saying, 'Hello, Mr. Richard, can I have yer autograph please?' "

A bus flings a spume of spray onto the windscreen.

Dean's driving blind until the water's run off.

"You can't end on that cliffhanger," says Griff.

"First, he hauled me inside and gave me an earful 'bout how I'd just nearly killed myself but I was thinking, *This is amazing, I'm getting a bollocking off of Little Richard.* Then he asked who was in charge of me. I said my brother but he was in the pub. I told him my name and said I was going to be a star too. That softened him up a bit. 'Son,' he said, 'ain't *no* star ever went by the name of Moffat.' I said my mother's maiden name was Moss and he said, 'Dean Moss, that'll work,' and he wrote on a photo, *To Dean Moss, Climber to the Stars—from Little Richard.* Then one of his people escorted me out past the bouncer who hadn't let me in and my adventure was over. Ray 'n' the others thought I was making it all up till I showed them my photographic evidence."

A sign says it's twenty-seven miles to Brighton.

"Do you still have it?" asks Griff. "The photo?"

"Nah." *Do I tell them?* "My old man burned it."

Elf's horrified. "Why would your dad do such a thing?"

The middle classes have no bloody idea.

Dean's lip scar throbs. "Long story."

"NINA SIMONE AT Ronnie Scott's," says Elf. The Beast rattles through a village called Handcross. "I was seventeen. My parents would never have let me go into Soho alone, but Imogen and a boy from church chaperoned me into Satan's Lair. I'd been sneaking off to the Folk Barge at Richmond since I was fifteen but Nina Simone was in a higher league. Way higher. She floated across Ronnie Scott's like Cleopatra on her barge. A black orchid dress. Pearls the size of pebbles. She sat down and announced, 'I am Nina Simone,' as if daring you to contradict her. That was it. No 'Thank you for coming,' no 'I'm honored to be here.' It was our job to thank *her* for coming. *We* were honored to be there. A drummer, a bassist, and a saxophonist, that was it. She played a bluesy, folkie set. 'Cotton-eyed Joe,' 'Gin House Blues,' 'Twelfth of Never,' 'Black Is the Color of My True Love's Hair.' No banter. No jokes. No fake heart attack. Once, a couple were whispering too loud. She eyeballed the offenders and said, 'Pardon me, am I singing too loud for y'all?' The couple combusted on the spot."

A sign says Brighton is twenty miles away.

"In awe of her as I was, I never wanted to be Nina Simone," continues Elf. "I'm a white English folk singer. She's a black Juilliard-trained genius. She plays blues with her left hand and Bach with her right. I saw her do it. All I wanted was a few ounces of her self-assurance. I still do. Heckling Nina Simone would be like heckling a mountain. Unthinkable. Pointless. At the end she told the audience, 'I will sing *one* encore, and one only.' It was 'The Last Rose of Summer.' I was by the cloakroom with my sister when she left. One woman held up an album and a pen but Nina just said, 'I am here to S-I-N-G, not S-I-G-N.' A minder opened the door and off she departed to her secret London palace. I used to think you became a star by having hits. After that show, I started to think, *No—you are a star first, therefore you have the hits.*"

The Beast's wheel thumps into a pothole.

The vehicle jolts but carries on at 40 mph.

"Which is probably why I'm not a star."

"Until tonight," says Griff. "Until tonight."

A CHERRY-RED TRIUMPH Spitfire Mark II overtakes the Beast on a downhill stretch lined with orchards. *If Utopia Avenue ever makes real money,* thinks Dean, *I'm getting one o' them. I'll drive to Gravesend and slow down outside Harry Moffat's flat and I'll rev the engine once to say, "Screw" and again to say, "You" . . .*

The real Triumph Spitfire drives away, into the future.

The road is patchy with puddles mirroring the sky.

"What about your best show, then, Zooto?" asks Griff.

Jasper thinks. "Big Bill Broonzy once played 'Key to the Highway' just for me. Does that count?"

"Give over," says Griff. "He's been dead donkey's years."

"I was eleven. It was 1956. I was spending the summer in Domburg in the Netherlands. My Dutch grandfather was an old friend of the vicar in the town, and every year I'd stay with the vicar and his wife during the school holidays. That summer I made a model Spitfire out of balsa wood. It flew beautifully. It was the best I'd ever made. One evening, I launched it on my final throw and the breeze carried it over the high wall of the last garden in Domburg you'd want your prize glider to land in. The garden of Captain Verplancke. He had been in the wartime Resistance and had quite a reputation. The other boys told me I should go and get the vicar. Kids didn't just knock on Captain Verplancke's door at eight o'clock at night. But I thought, *The worst he'll do is just say no.* So in I went, up to the house and knocked. Nobody answered. I knocked again. Nothing. So I walked around the back and there, on Walcheren Island, a stone's throw from the North Sea, was a scene off a Mississippi whiskey label. Porch, lantern, rocking chair, and a big black man playing a guitar, hoarsely crooning in English and smoking a roll-up. I'd never spoken to a person who wasn't white before. I hadn't heard of blues guitar, let alone heard any. He may as well have been a Martian playing Martian music. Yet I was transfixed. What *was* it? How could music be so sad, so sparse, so dilatory, so jagged, so many things all at once? Pretty soon the guitarist noticed me, but he carried on playing. He played the whole of 'Key to the Highway.' At the end, he asked me in English, 'So, what's the verdict, Shorty?' I asked if I could ever learn to play like that. 'No,' he told me, 'because'—I'll always remember this—'you haven't lived my life and the blues is a language you can't lie in.' But if I wanted it enough, he said, then one day I'd learn to play like me. The vicar arrived at this point to apologize for my intrusion, and my audience with the mystery stranger was over. The next day, Captain Verplancke's housekeeper dropped by with the *Big Bill Broonzy and Washboard Sam* LP, signed with the words 'Play It Like You.' "

A sign says Brighton is only ten miles away.

"I hope nobody burned that LP," remarks Griff.

"I'll show it to you when you're next over," says Jasper.

"Did you get your model Spitfire back?" asks Elf.

There's a pause. "I don't remember."

. . .

THE BEAST PULLS into the Students' Union car park, where Levon is leaning against his 1960 Ford Zephyr. Dean steers the Beast into the adjacent space and kills the engine. There's no sign of Shanks's van. *We're still early.* The silence is sweet, as is the air as they climb out. Dean stretches. "Tomorrow Never Knows" escapes from a nearby window. The moon is a chipped cue ball. The Beast is attracting attention: one passing joker calls, "Oy, pal, where's Batman?"

Levon, too, assesses the band's new purchase with interest. "Well, it's definitely not a joyrider's magnet."

"She's a sturdy workhorse, is the Beast," states Griff. "And, thanks to my uncle, it's a fookin' bargain."

Levon scratches his ear. "How does she handle?"

"Like a tank," says Dean, " 'cept on corners, when she handles like a coffin. Won't go above fifty, either."

"We bought her for lugging gear," says Griff, "not for setting land-speed records. When did you get here, Levon?"

"Early enough to collect our check from the Students' Union. Once bitten by the we'll-post-it-on-Monday line, twice shy."

A gum-chewing girl passes Dean and eyes him up as if she's the guy and he's the girl. *Yes,* he thinks. *I'm in a band.*

"Well," says Levon, "this lot won't lug itself up the stairs."

"Give our roadies the evening off, did you?" asks Griff.

"If you get a gold disc," says Levon, "we'll talk roadies."

"If you get us signed," growls Griff, "we'll talk gold discs."

"Play a hundred scorching shows," replies Levon, "and recruit a legion of fans, you'll get signed. Until then, we all lug the gear. Three journeys'll do it. One of us stands guard. If you never trust anyone older than five and younger than a hundred not to steal your gear, you *might* just hang on to it. What is it, Jasper?"

"Us." Jasper's pointing at a noticeboard.

Dean's eyes skip over posters for ANTI-VIETNAM WAR SIT-IN; BAN THE BOMB, JOIN CND TODAY!, and WHY NOT TRY BELL-RINGING? before finding his own face in a 2x2 grid of the band's portraits, taken by Mecca. The reproductions have come out cleanly. UTOPIA

AVENUE is printed in a fairground font with an empty rectangle below for location, time, and price, if applicable.

"Welcome to the big time, boys and girl," says Griff.

"It came out pretty nicely," declares Elf.

"It looks like a Wanted poster," says Dean.

"Is that a good thing or a bad thing?" asks Jasper.

"It's the rock 'n' roll outlaw thing," says Elf.

"Less 'outlaw,' " Griff scrutinizes Elf's portrait, "more 'Employee of the Month.' No offense."

"None taken. Less 'outlaw' "—Elf studies Griff's portrait—"more 'Third in the King Charles Spaniel in a wig contest.' No offense."

THE VENUE IS a long thin hall, like a bowling alley, with a bar up near the door and a low stage at the far end. Windows run down one side with evening views of a treeless campus. To Dean, the whole place looks like it's made of Lego. The decorator was keen on glossy sewage brown. If full, the venue would hold three or four hundred. Tonight, Dean guesses, there are fifty. Ten more are gathered around the bar-football table. "I hope nobody gets hurt in the crush when we start."

"We're not on till nine," says Elf. "Plenty of time for a cast of thousands to walk on. Any sign of the Gravesend mob?"

"Obviously not." *Stupid question.*

"Excuse me for existing."

Two students approach from the bar. He has a musketeer's beard, a mauve satin shirt. She has a black bob, big mascaraed eyes, and a zigzag sleeveless one-piece that barely reaches her thighs. *I wouldn't say no,* thinks Dean, but she's staring at Elf as the musketeer speaks first. "I'm Gaz and my powers of deduction tell me you're Utopia Cul-de-Sac."

"Avenue." Dean rests his amp on the ground.

"Just my little jest," says Gaz. Dean thinks, *He's stoned.*

"I'm Levon, the manager. I've been dealing with Tiger."

"Ah, well, Tiger's otherwise engaged. He asked me to stand in and guide you to the stage. It's"—he points—"there."

"I'm Jude," says the girl. She's not stoned and speaks with a West Country twang. "Elf, I adore 'Oak, Ash and Thorn.' "

"Thanks," says Elf. "Though the music we're playing tonight'll be a little . . . wilder than my solo work."

"Wild's good. When Tiger told me you were in the band, I said, 'Elf Holloway? Book them now.' "

"She did." Gaz puts a proprietary hand on Jude's rear.

Dean thinks, *A pity.* "Better do the sound check."

"Just play loud," says Gaz. "It's not the Albert Hall."

"Could I ask . . ." Elf peers at the stage, ". . . where's the piano?"

Gaz's eyebrows fuse when he frowns. "Piano?"

"The piano Tiger promised to have ready onstage and tuned for the show tonight," says Levon. "Twice."

Gaz whistles softly. "Tiger promises a lot of things."

"We absolutely need a piano," says Elf.

"Bands bring their own instruments," adds Gaz.

"Not a piano they don't," says Griff. "Not unless they turn up in a fookin' removal van."

"I don't care if Tiger's otherwise engaged or not," says Levon. "He's paid to do the logistics. Just get him here."

"Tiger's undergone a metamorphosis," explains Gaz. "His Third Eye's opened. Here." Gaz touches his brow. "He set out last Tuesday and no one's seen him since. On the cosmic scale—"

"Look, Gaz," says Levon, "I don't give a shit about the cosmic scale. We're on the we-need-a-piano-now scale. Get us a piano."

"Man, your aggro is bumming me out. I'm not your skivvy. Wrong attitude. I'm doing Tiger a favor just by being here. I'm not the ents officer. Bugger this, man." He glances at Jude, who looks pained, and heads for the exit.

"Oy, Fuckface!" Dean steps after the departing stoner. "Don't—"

"Don't waste your energy." Levon grabs Dean's arm. "I'm afraid it happens with student unions from time to time."

"You booked us this gig. Why are we even bloody here?"

"Because student unions pay relatively well, relatively reliably, for relative nobodies. That's why we're here."

"But Elf needs a piano. How do we do our set?"

"I knew we should've loaded up the Hammond," says Griff.

"If yer *knew* that, Mr. All-Knowing Wise One," says Dean, "why didn't yer bloody say so when *I* said, 'Shall we load up the Hammond?' and everyone was all, 'No need, Levon's checked twice and there'll definitely be a piano'?"

Griff comes to within head-butting distance of Dean. "If anyone has the right to be pissed off, Mr. Arseypants, it's Elf. You're fine. You've got your bass."

"It's spilled milk," says Elf. "Next time, we'll load the Hammond. Levon, what do we do now? Cancel the gig and go?"

"Problem is, if the Students' Union cancel the check, I can't really get legal on them. If you can play for an hour, the money's ours. Forty quid. Divided by five."

Dean thinks about his debts and his bankbook.

"Let's think of it as a band practice," says Jasper. "It's not as if any press or reviewers are in the audience."

"But what do I play?" Elf scratches her neck. "If I had a guitar, I could at least do a couple of folk numbers."

A rowdy cheer explodes over at the bar-football.

"Sorry to butt in," it's Jude, who hasn't gone off with Gaz, "but I have a guitar you could borrow. If you like."

Elf double-checks this. "You brought a guitar here?"

Jude looks sheepish. "I was hoping you'd sign it."

THERE'S STILL NO sign of Ray, so Dean calls Shanks's flat from a phone booth in the lobby—Ray has no phone—to see if they even left. Nobody replies. *They're late, they hit traffic, they got a flat, they forgot . . . could be anything.* Back in the venue, night has blacked out the long glass wall. *This place must bleed heat.* A basic lighting rig hangs above the stage, but the lighting officer is on strike, so the bleak striplights stay on. "I've known morgues with better vibes than this," says Dean. Griff makes a few final adjustments to his kit. Off to one side, in a storeroom that smells of damp and bleach, Elf has finished tuning Jude's loaned acoustic guitar and is retouching her lipstick in a hand-mirror. "Any news of your brother?"

Dean shakes his head. "We may as well start."

"I don't think anyone else is going to show up," says Jude.

"The sooner we start," says Griff, "the sooner we'll get home."

"Break a leg," says Levon.

"Give me a list of legs to break and I'll work through it," mutters Dean. They walk up the three steps to the stage. Sixty or seventy people stand in a loose clump nearby. A few of them clap, led by Jude. Dean walks up to the mic. The room is 90 percent empty space. He's suddenly nervous. He hasn't performed live since the 2i's show, and that was all crowd-pleasing R&B standards. Tonight's set list is based on their own songs: Dean's "Abandon Hope" and his Potemkin-era "Dirty River"; Jasper's untested "Darkroom" and an instrumental, "Sky Blue Lamp"; Elf's "A Raft and a River," written for piano, performed without a piano, plus "Polaroid Eyes" and a few folkier numbers. "Okay," says Dean, "so we're—" The speakers howl feedback and the audience winces. *That's why yer do sound checks.* Dean fiddles with the mic and shifts it forward a foot. "We're Utopia Avenue. Our first song's 'Abandon Hope.' "

"We already have done, pal!" yells a wag at the bar.

Dean flicks an amiable V in the right direction, triggering a few gratifying *"Wooo!"*s. Dean makes eye contact with Jasper, Elf, and Griff. Griff takes a swig from his bottle of Gold Label. "When yer ready," says Dean. Griff flashes him the finger. "And a-one," says Dean, "and a-two, and a-one, two, three—"

GRIFF BURIES THE end of a lurching "Abandon Hope" under a rockfall of drums. *It's never sounded so shit at Pavel's,* thinks Dean. The half-arsed applause is more than they deserve. Dean goes over to Griff and says, "Yer played too fast."

"*You* played too fookin' slow."

Dean looks away in disgust. Elf's strumming was pointless and her harmonies were off. Jasper's solo failed to ignite. Instead of a three-minute firework display he offered a minute of squibs that went nowhere. Dean can't blame anyone but himself for fluffing the lyrics in the third verse, or for the croaked, wobbled, missed notes. Until this evening, he believed "Abandon Hope" was the best song he'd ever written. *Was I kidding myself?* He pulls Elf and Jasper into an emergency huddle, which Levon joins. "That was bollocks."

Levon starts: "Oh, I didn't think it was *all* that—"

"If we try 'Darkroom' without a piano," says Dean, "it'll die."

" 'House of the Rising Sun'?" suggests Jasper.

Dean's unimpressed. "Without an organ?"

"It's an old American folk song," Elf points out. "It predates the Animals by six decades, at least."

Dean wonders how long he'll be able to put up with her.

"Are we holding you lot up?" yells the wag at the bar.

"What do *you* want to play, then?" asks Elf.

Dean finds he doesn't know. " 'Rising Sun' it is, then."

"Once we win them over," says Jasper, "we'll do an original."

Dean goes over to Griff, who's opening another bottle of Gold Label. "Forget the set list, it's 'House o' the Rising Sun.' "

"Aye, sir, no, sir, three bags full, sir."

"Just bloody play it." Jasper steps up to the mic. "This next song's about a house of ill-repute in New Orleans, where—"

"There is . . . a house . . . in New Orleans . . . " begin the bar-football players, who haven't stopped playing since they arrived.

"Never heard this one before," calls out the bar wag.

UNTIL NOW, DEAN has thought of "The House of the Rising Sun" as an indestructible song, but Utopia Avenue are proving him wrong. Jasper's vocals sound constipated, posh, and twattish. Elf's harmony is a distraction in a song about male remorse. Dean walks too far from his amp and his piece-of-shit guitar lead unplugs itself from his piece-of-shit amp. The audience laughs as he scrambles back to plug it in again. Jasper doesn't cover for him and launches into the second verse without any bass to buoy it along. Griff plays ploddingly—*a deliberate fook you,* Dean suspects, *for daring to tell him he was playing too fast during "Abandon Hope."* Nobody in the audience is dancing. Or even swaying. They just stand there, their body language saying, *Well this is shit.* A group breaks off and leaves. Jasper's solo misfires again. *If he was this useless at 2i's,* thinks Dean, *I'd have never joined the band.* The swinging doors over by the bar keep swinging. *We're clearing the place out.* Dean joins the third verse, hoping Jasper will take the hint and drop away. He doesn't. He fingerpicks the last four bars minus drums and bass, like Eric Burdon's intro on the Animals' version, but it just highlights how inferior the whole performance has been. *Not an ounce o' showmanship,* thinks Dean. *Hopeless.*

On the final line, feedback jags out of the speakers. Not in a cool Jimi Hendrix way: in a bad village-fête-PA-system way. Someone shouts, "Heard better!" Dean can only agree. He looks at Levon, who stands with his arms folded, watching the dwindling audience.

They convene around the drum kit. "Pretty shit," says Griff.

" 'Pretty shit' 's too kind if yer ask me," says Dean.

"What's next?" asks Elf. " 'A Raft and a River' without a piano is going to sink without trace."

"What about an electric 'Any Way the Wind Blows'?" suggests Levon. "You've done it at Club Zed a few times."

"We were only pissing around," says Dean, who thinks Elf's signature song needs drums like an albatross needs propellers.

"We've nowt to lose at this point," says Griff.

"ANY WAY THE Wind Blows" is the least worst so far. Griff keeps the tempo slower than on Elf's recorded version, and Jasper ornaments each line. Dean finally clicks with Griff and they stay in lockstep. The mic barely picks up Elf's guitar, but only twenty people are left watching. Jude is still there, clasping her hands. She smiles at him, and Dean tries to smile back. The doors at the back swing open. Six or seven guys barge in and Dean thinks, *Trouble.* They're dressed more like mods than students. The barman folds his arms. A shout—"I *said,* FIVE *fucking* BEERS!"—is heard over the music, and the surviving audience turn around to look. The band plays on. Dean hopes someone is calling for the cavalry, and that Brighton Polytechnic's cavalry is more than a wheezing porter. Dean hears more shouts: "Yeah? If you won't serve us, I will!" There's an exodus from the bar area. Even the bar-football players stop and scuttle off.

The mods are helping themselves to beers. This should get the police involved, but Dean doubts they'll be here any time soon. The band reaches the end of the song, but only Jude and a couple of others applaud. The others melt away as the mods approach the stage, holding beers. Their leader has a bullish neck, rat's teeth, and a shark's eyes. He gestures at Elf. "When's she flashin' her udders?"

"This isn't that kind of show," says Elf.

"Customer's always right, honey pie," says Shark Eyes. "Boys?" He and his gang link arms and perform the cancan with the jerky malice of mods on speed. They advance to within a few yards of the stage, where the cancan stops as suddenly as it began.

"Play something, then," says a mod in a Union Jack jacket.

"None of your hippie bollocks," warns another.

Levon steps in front of the stage. "Lads, we play what we play. If you don't like the music, the door's back there."

Shark Eyes gurns mock astonishment. "A *Yank*? Fucksake. What are *you* doing here?"

"Canadian," says Levon, "and I manage this band, so—"

"If it looks like a faggot," Shark Eyes drops a glob of spit onto the floor, "dresses like a faggot, and squeals like a faggot . . ."

"You won't like our music," says Jasper. "You may as well leave."

"'*You may as well leave*'!" mimics Union Jack Jacket. "You *beastly* wuffians! Who are you? Little Lord Fauntleroy?"

"OY!" Griff stands up. "We're FOOKIN' *WORKING*."

With his vest and wild barbarian hair, Griff looks crazy enough to be a threat—but not to Shark Eyes, who starts laughing: "A Yank, a toff, a hippie moo, and a Yorkshire Yeti! It's like the first line of a fucking joke. What are you?" He's pointing at Dean. "The Pixie Bumboy?"

Off to one side, an arm swings and a projectile spins at Dean. He ducks, and Griff stumbles back clutching his head, falling over his drums. The cymbals clash like a punchline. Union Jack Jacket calls out, "One hundred and eightyyy!" like a darts scorer.

The mods hoot and laugh, but Griff doesn't get up. Levon and

Elf hurry over. Dean peers at the damage. Griff's face has a gruesome gash oozing blood. *The zigzag cap of the bottle,* thinks Dean, *or an edge on his drum kit . . .*

"Griff?" Levon's saying. There's blood on his shirt. "Griff!"

Griff mumbles, "Lemmegetmy'andsonth'fooker . . ."

Levon roars at the bar: "Barman! An ambulance! Now! An emergency! His eyeball's half out!" Dean doesn't think an eye *is* out . . . *but the mods don't know that.*

The barman shouts back, with a phone in his hand, "I called the porter! He's calling the cops and an ambulance!"

Dean shouts at the onlookers: "Remember their faces!" He points at the mods, whose smirks are fading. "The cops'll want witness statements. D'you *fuckers* know what that is?" He points at Griff. "That's five years' prison a head for GBH!"

A flash goes off. It's Jude, with a camera.

The flash goes off again. The mods take a step back, and another, and another, except for Shark Eyes, who marches at Jude, snarling, "Gimme that *fucking* camera!" Dean drops his Fender and jumps down from the stage. Now Shark Eyes is in a tug-of-war with Jude over her camera. He's roaring, "GIMME THAT, YOU BITCH!" It's a one-sided fight until Dean grabs a bottle of brown ale from a bystander and brings it down on Shark Eyes's head with all his might. Dean feels something crack. Shark Eyes lets the camera go and turns to look at his assailant, woozily. *Fuck,* thinks Dean. *Am I the one going to prison for five years?* To Dean's relief, Shark Eyes's gang hustle their leader from the scene of the crime.

DRIZZLE COATS THE Students' Union car park, and everyone in it, in a cool, wet layer. Most of the spectators have left. The mods have vanished into the night. "Your friend's injury looks worse than it probably is," says the ambulance man, discussing Griff. "But I'm guessing the duty nurse'll want to keep him in over the weekend. He'll be X-rayed, he'll need stitches, and there's a concussion risk with head injuries. On the whole, your friend's lucky he didn't lose an eye."

"I'll follow you to the hospital in my car," says Levon.

"I'm coming with you," states Elf.

"There's no need," says Levon.

Elf ignores him. "Dean can drive the Beast back, and . . ." Dean guesses she's stopped herself saying, "Jasper's not going to be much use to anyone." "I'm coming with you."

Dean asks the ambulance man, "Can we say goodbye to Griff?"

"Be quick, and don't expect sparkling conversation."

"He's the drummer," says Dean. He goes around the back and steps into the clean, cream-colored interior where Griff is sitting up on a trolley. Half his face is bandaged. He looks at Dean. "Oh, bugger. It's *you*. I've died and gone to Hell."

"On the bright side," says Dean, "if that scar turns out nice, yer'll get a lifetime of work in horror movies."

"How're you feeling?" Elf holds his hand. "Poor thing."

"Getting glassed is light entertainment up in Hull," says Griff. "Who's minding my drum kit? I don't trust them students."

"It's in the Beast," says Jasper. "We'll keep it at my flat."

"If yer snuff it," says Dean, "we'll flog it to yer replacement."

"Good luck finding a drummer who'll keep *you* on the beat."

" 'Scuse me?" There's a girl's voice behind them. Dean turns around to see Jude hesitating by the ambulance door. "Can I . . . ?"

"Come on up," says Levon.

"Sorry to barge in. I just . . . I feel awful, for you."

"Apologies *are* due from the Students' Union," says Elf, "but you've got nothing to be sorry for."

"Your music was fab." Jude tucks a fallen strand of her hair behind her ear. "Until you were so rudely interrupted."

"Wish I could agree," says Dean. "But thanks."

"Will you be back to finish the gig?" asks Jude.

The band look at each other. "Not unless we're paid blood money," says Dean. Levon *pfffs*. "We'll wait until Griff is back to full strength before planning our next move."

She glances at Dean. "So I guess it's bye, then . . ."

THE A23'S CAT'S eyes vanish beneath the Beast in sweeping curves. *Now you see 'em, now you don't.* The amps, drums, and guitars shift around in the back. *Four of us drove down,* thinks Dean, *and only two of us are going back.* Jasper has retreated into Jasper. Or maybe he's asleep. *What's the difference?* Dean wishes the Beast's radio worked. His mind is busy. *Thank God Ray didn't witness that shit-show.* Shanks, Ray, and Co. would have fought off the mods, but Utopia Avenue's disastrous debut would have had credible witnesses. *Sounding good in rehearsal doesn't count for shit if we can't do it onstage.* A band is only a band if it believes it is, and Dean isn't sure if he, Jasper, Elf, and Griff do. When push came to shove, they didn't click. He's got a working-class affinity with Griff, but Jasper's from a different planet. *The Planet of the Posh Weirdos.* Dean's lived with Jasper for eight weeks, but he still hardly knows him. Elf thinks Dean's an oik. *How could she not?* Her naughtiest swear word is "damn." Her parents will bail her out if her adventures in showbiz go wrong. She lives life with a safety net. *Even Griff's got a safety net.*

"Not me," mutters Dean.

"Did you say anything?" asks Jasper.

"No."

The Beast enters a tunnel of trunks and branches.

A dead pheasant is smeared into the road.

I need the others more than they need me, thinks Dean. Jasper could jump ship tomorrow. Any band in London would want him. *And then I can kiss my Mayfair flat goodbye.* Griff has the jazz circuit. Elf has a solo career to go back to. Levon has Moonwhale, an office in Denmark Street and, after tonight, Dean guesses, serious doubts about throwing good money after bad. *What have I got?* Utopia Avenue. Dean's future was supposed to take off tonight.

It blew up on the launch pad.

Smithereens.

MONA LISA SINGS THE BLUES

"WE DECIDED AN HOUR AGO," GROANS ELF. "THE THIRD TAKE'S best."

"Take six is more precise." Levon speaks on the control-room talkback. "Dean fluffed that descending scale."

"That adds to it," insists Elf. "It comes just as Jasper sings the word 'broken.' It's one of those happy accidents that—"

"Jasper's vocal's better overall on take six," says Levon. "And Griff played it more 'tick-tock-tick-tock,' too."

"If you want 'tick-tock-tick-tock,' " said Elf, "just get a giant hairy metronome in a vest to sit in the corner and record that."

"If the giant hairy metronome can get a word in." Griff lies on a saggy sofa, his angry new scar crossing his left temple. "Mosser's bass bled into my snare. Can we do a take seven with an absorber?"

"I left the absorber out on purpose," says Digger, Fungus Hut's in-house engineer. "Like the Stones. They let it bleed on purpose."

"So?" Dean is perched on an amp, picking his nose and not caring who sees. "We're not Stones clones."

"Taking a leaf from the Stones' book doesn't make you a clone, guys," says the tanned, tooth-whitened, *Playboy*-esque co-owner of Moonwhale, Howie Stoker. "Those boys are a gold mine."

"They're a gold mine 'cause they found their own voice, Howie," replies Dean, "and not by acting like bloody parrots."

"Nobody at Chess Records'd agree the Stones aren't parrots." Griff blows a smoke ring.

"None of this is the *point*!" Elf feels trapped in a circular nightmare. "Can we *please* just—"

"No, but, guys, here's an idea." Howie Stoker accentuates his speech with hand-chops. "Ditch that line, 'Down in the darkroom where a lie becomes the truth' and replace it with 'sha-la-la-la-la-dah sha-la-la-la-la-bah.' I had dinner with Phil Spector last week and he says sha-la-las are making a comeback."

"Definitely a thought, Howie," says Levon.

Shoot me first, thinks Elf. "Dean, it's your bass part. Take three or six. Choose one. Put us out of our misery."

"I've listened to them so much, my ears're on strike."

"That's why God invented producers," says Levon. "Digger, Howie, and I agree—take six is the one."

"We *were* agreed it was take three," Elf tries not to shout because then she'll be the hysterical female, "until *you*—"

"Take three led the field for a while," explains Levon, "but six rallied strongly and reached the finishing line first."

God give me strength. "A badly fitting metaphor is not a winning argument. Jasper. Three or six? It's your song."

Jasper peers out of the vocal booth. "Neither. I sound like Dylan with a cold. I'd like to do a croonier retake."

"Phil Spector has a saying," says Howie Stoker. " 'Don't let the good be the enemy of the best.' Is he right or is he right?"

"I'd say that's truly *sound* advice, Howie," says Levon.

You arse-licking pun-cracker, thinks Elf. "If we had all week I'd agree to try it five hundred ways. But we only have . . ." The clock shows 8:31 A.M. ". . . four hours and twenty-nine minutes to do two songs because we've spent *so much time on this one.*"

" 'Darkroom' 's the A side," says Levon. "This is the song that'll be coming out of a million radio sets. It has to be perfect."

"Shouldn't we hear how my and Dean's songs come out before deciding what's the A side?" asks Elf. "Otherwise—"

"No, but—" begins Dean, and a fuse blows in the brain of Elf, who slams her piano keyboard and tells the studio, "If anyone talks over me again I will ram my Farfisa up his arse."

The men look shocked, except for Jasper. Then they swap uh-oh-someone's-having-her-period looks.

"Miss Holloway?" Deirdre, Fungus Hut's receptionist, is at the door. "Your sister's in reception. She says she's expected."

Bea's been sent to save me from killing someone, thinks Elf. "Okay. Everyone. Do what you want with this damn song. I'm past caring. I'm going to the Gioconda. I'll be back at nine."

"Go ahead," replies their manager. "It'll do you good."

"I wasn't asking for permission, Levon." Elf gathers her coat and bag and exits without a backward glance.

OUT IN RECEPTION, fresh air wafts in from Denmark Street. Bea's looking at a wall of photographs of Fungus Hut's more famous clients. Elf admires her younger sister's new boyish haircut, her violet beret, her lilac jacket and knee-length boots. Nails and lips are a matching shade of plum. "Little sis. Look at *you*."

The sisters hug. "Did I go overboard? I was aiming at Mary Quant, but now I'm afraid I've gone Mary Mary Quite Contrary."

"If *I* was on the judging panel, I'd offer you a place based on your sartorial genius alone."

"You're biased." Bea points to a photograph of Paul McCartney. "If I stay here long enough, will Paul waft in on a wave of fabness?"

" 'Fraid not." Deirdre looks up from her desk. "That was March. Abbey Road was all booked up for the night. Just a one-off."

"Let's get breakfast," says Elf. "Better that I murder a bacon sandwich than a producer."

Howie appears from the studio door, hoicking up his trousers. "My my. And who's *this* delightful young lady?"

"My sister Bea," says Elf. "Bea, this is Mr. Stoker, who—"

"Gave birth to Moonwhale." Howie encases Bea's hand in both of his. "Though I keep my fingers in a number of pies."

Bea extracts her hand. "How jolly sticky for you."

Howie switches his smile to high beam. "And where are you in life's great adventure, Bea?"

"Finishing sixth form and aiming at drama school."

"Good. I've always said that beauty has a *duty* to be seen by the widest possible audience. You want to work in the movies?"

Deirdre slams her typewriter carriage back.

"That might be a possibility in the long run," says Bea.

"Funny you should say that," says Howie. "My old pal Benny Klopp—Benny's a big cheese at Universal Studios—tasked me to scout for English roses during my London sojourn. And you, Bea—I *can* call you Bea, right?—are one. You got a headshot on you?"

Bea frowns. "Do I have a what on me?"

"Headshot. A picture of your"—Howie draws a frame around Bea's breasts—"head. Benny's casting a film about Caligula. The emperor. You'd look a-*ma*-zing in a toga."

"I'm flattered," says Bea, "but I haven't even got into drama school yet. I have an A-level exam tomorrow."

"It's never too early to make connections in showbiz. Am I right, Elf?"

"As long as they're genuine. Sharks, shysters, and shite-hawks swim in these waters. Am I wrong, Howie?"

"Your sister," Howie tells Bea, "has an old head on her solid young shoulders. Do you know Martha's Vineyard?"

"No," says Bea. "Is it one of those pies you have a finger in?"

"Martha's Vineyard is a vacation resort in Massachusetts. I have a home there. Private beach, private quay, private yacht. Truman Capote's a neighbor. I have a fascinating idea. When Utopia Avenue flies over to conquer the US of A"—Howie presses his palms together like an Indian saying *Namaste*—"you come too, and stay at Martha's Vineyard as my houseguest. You'll meet Benny Klopp. Broadway movers and shakers. Phil Spector." Howie licks the corner of his mouth. "Your life will change, Bea. Trust me. Trust your gut. What's your gut telling you about me? Right now?"

"*GO CASTRATE YOURSELF with a rusty spoon, you crusty pervert* were the words that sprang to mind," Bea looks both ways as they cross Denmark Street, "but then I thought, *This is my sister's boss* . . . So I kept my mouth shut."

"Technically," says Elf, "he's Levon's boss, but it's true, he could still press the ejector button on us. So thanks."

A bicycle courier flashes by. Bea asks, "Dad's lawyer friend's still checking those contracts, right?"

"Yes. Hopefully he's up to the job. I could count the musicians who haven't been shafted on the fingers of no hands."

"Extra, extra!" hollers a raw-throated newspaper vendor in his tiny shack. *"Harold Wilson Found Dead in a Coffin with a Stake Through His Heart! Extra, extra!"*

Bea and Elf stop. They both look at the newspaper vendor who tells them, "I like to check if anyone's listening. Listening's a dying art. I mean, look at 'em all."

People hurry along Denmark Street in the May sunshine.

"Perhaps they hear you," suggests Elf, "but just think, *Ah well, that's another Soho eccentric.*"

"Nah," says the vendor. "Folks only hear what they expect to. Not one in a hundred has ears like you two."

THREE YOUNG MEN leaving the Gioconda café stand aside to let the sisters pass, *and to get a better look at Bea.* From their battered art folders and clothes, Elf guesses they are students at Saint Martin's College of Art, a minute away on Charing Cross Road. Bea breezes by as if the boys don't exist, and they file out of the café.

Elf asks, "What can I get you?"

"Just a coffee. Milk, no sugar."

"Not much of a breakfast," says Elf.

"I had half a grapefruit before I left."

"At the risk of sounding like Dad," says Elf, "is half a grapefruit enough for an audition? Let me get you a scone."

"No, really. I'm full of butterflies as it is."

"If you're sure." Elf orders a bacon sandwich plus two coffees from Mrs. Biggs, matriarch of the Gioconda, who relays the order through a hatch to a kitchen slave. The sisters take the window table. "What monologue did you settle on for the audition?"

"Joan of Arc from *Henry the Sixth, Part One.* And for my song, a pleasing ditty entitled 'Any Way the Wind Blows' by English songstress Elf Holloway. I didn't ask permission. Will she mind?"

"I'd say that Miss Holloway—whom I happen to know slightly—will be utterly delighted. Why that one?"

"It's beautiful unaccompanied, and because I happened to be upstairs while you wrote it—a story I *may* let slip to the panel, because I'm a shameless name-dropper. Where's the loo?"

"Down the steps, under the Mona Lisa picture. Be warned. It's a bit of a Journey to the Center of the Earth . . ."

THE KINKS' "WATERLOO Sunset" comes on the radio. Elf looks out at Denmark Street. Hundreds of people pass by. *Reality erases itself as it rerecords itself,* Elf thinks. *Time is the Great Forgetter.* She gets her notebook from her handbag and writes, *Memories are unreliable . . . Art is memory made public.* Time wins in the long run. Books turn to dust, negatives decay, records get worn out, civilizations burn. But as long as the art endures, a song or a view or a thought or a feeling someone once thought worth keeping is saved and stays shareable. Others can say, "I feel that too."

Across the road in a brick doorway, under a poster for Berkshire stockings, a couple are kissing. Elf's line of sight, the depth of the doorway, and the speed of the foot traffic are such that, chances are, the lovers are visible to Elf alone. They press their foreheads together and talk. *Arrangements, sweet nothings, promises, see-you-laters* . . . He's averagely good-looking but she's the first day of spring in a female body, Elf decides. Her poise, her clothes, her tomboyishness, her throat-length dark hair, and, most of all, that wild crooked smile.

You're ogling. Elf fumbles in her handbag for her packet of Camels, ferrets about for a lighter, and lights up. *I wasn't ogling, I was just looking.* Elf remembers the voice she heard on the 97 bus last January, shunting along Cromwell Road . . .

THE DOORBELL AT 101 Cromwell Road shrieked like a banshee. Music throbbed. "Sounds like the party's started," said Bruce. They had traveled back from Cambridge that day and Elf would have preferred to stay at her flat, but Wotsit was Bruce's oldest friend from Melbourne and he'd just arrived in London, so Bruce was going, and Elf was afraid that if she didn't go, he might not be back until the following morning, full of easy-to-believe lies about where he had spent the night. The door of 101 was opened by a gangly man in a peach Afghan coat, beads, and a straggly mustache. "Brucie Fletch! Get inside, it's freezing out!"

"Wotsit! How the bugger are you?"

"Alive. Well. Hydra was Paradise. You have to go."

"God, I'd love to. I'm stuck here for now, though."

"This," Wotsit turned to Elf, "must be . . . uh . . ."

Bruce stepped in. "The one, the only, Elf Holloway."

Elf shook his bony hand. "Bruce has told me a lot about you."

"Of all the gorgeous male Aussies in London," Wotsit had a toothy smile, "why pick this shameless larrikin, eh?"

"Sexual charisma," said Bruce. "Genius. My vast estate."

"That must be it," said Elf, who paid all the bills and expenses.

Wotsit ushered them down a hallway, past a mural of an elephant, a jade Buddha in a nook, and an Om prayer flag hanging in the stairwell. The *Freak Out!* album by the Mothers of Invention boomed through a marshy pong of dope, lentils, and incense. In the long lounge, thirty or forty people were chattering, drinking, smoking, dancing, laughing. "Hey, everyone," Wotsit announced, "this is Bruce and his good lady Elf." There was a small chorus of "Hi, Bruce!" and "Hi, Elf!" and someone gave Elf a beer. She had a few sips. A sleek woman in copper and gold with kohl-ringed eyes materialized. "Elf, I'm Vanessa. I a*dore* your records." Home Counties. "*Shepherd's Crook* overwhelms me. I do a bit of modeling, and I was at Mike Anglesey's studio in Chelsea for a Christmas knees-up, and at some point Mike put your EP on and told us all," Vanessa does a posh girl's Cockney imitation, " 'Get your shell-likes around this!' and . . . wow."

"Thanks, Vanessa," said Bruce. "We're proud of it."

Someone tapped Elf's shoulder. She turned to find Marc Bolan's big doggy eyes. "Where've you been hiding, Goldilocks?"

"Marc! Bruce and I have been—"

"I heard the *Shepherd's Crook* EP." Marc wore mascara, a leather jacket, and a knotted scarf. "Lots there to admire. The best songs reminded me of yours truly's new work, in fact. I've got these new songs that would fit *perfectly* on your label. It's an album's worth, really. Who should I speak to?"

"At Avebury? Toby Green. But it's only a small—"

"Toby Green. Got it. He'll *cream his pants* when he hears my idea: a song for each companion in *The Fellowship of the Ring*—with an interlude for Gollum and a climax for the One Ring itself."

Elf guessed she was supposed to be bowled over. She looked around for Bruce for clues but he had vanished. As had Vanessa.

"You *have* read *The Lord of the Rings*?" asked Marc Bolan.

"Bruce lent me the first volume, but if I'm honest—"

"I always tell girls: 'If you want to understand me, read *The Lord of the Rings* right now.' It's that simple."

Elf wished she had the nerve to say, "In that case, I'll avoid it like the plague." She said, "Good luck with the songs."

He kissed his forefinger and planted it between Elf's eyebrows. "I'll tell Toby Green you sent me."

Elf forced a smile but wanted to wash her face. "Bruce is around. He'll want to speak with you, too . . ."

BRUCE WAS NOWHERE. The bodies grew denser. The air grew smokier. The Butterfield Blues Band was on. Half an hour passed. Elf fended off a folk-bore, who took her to task for sullying the purity of the 1765 version of "Sir Patrick Spens" on her *Oak, Ash and Thorn* EP. Bruce reappeared. "Wombat, let me take you away from all this."

"Where were you? I just got cornered by—"

"The real party's up in Wotsit's room. C'mon." Bruce spoke low. "Everyone's waiting."

"Look, I'm not sure if I'm really in the mood for—"

"Trust me." Bruce gave her a conspiratorial wink. "The next few hours could change your life." He led her through bodies, up steps, up steeper steps, past snoggers, and up even steeper steps to a purple door. He knocked a pattern of knocks. A bolt was unbolted.

"Aha." The door was opened by Wotsit. "Sorry for the cloak and dagger"—he rebolted the door behind them—"but if word got out, the hoi-polloi would be kicking my door down." Wotsit's room was lit by a paper lamp on a tripod. Its beam revolved like a lighthouse's, traversing yellow walls, floorboards painted purple and yellow, and a boarded-up fireplace. Black tulips stood in a black vase. The window showed a South Kensington nocturne of chimney pots, TV aerials, and gutters. Six people sat or lay on beanbags, a low bed, and cushions. Vanessa from earlier said, "We thought we'd lost you. Do you know Syd?" Syd Barrett, the singer with Pink Floyd, was strumming a guitar and singing, *"Have you got it yet?"* over and over. He didn't appear to notice Elf. A man with an imperial beard, a rose-print shirt, and a shiny pate introduced himself. "Al Ginsberg. Great to meet you, Elf. Bill Graham's gonna *love* this." He held up Fletcher & Holloway's *Shepherd's Crook* EP.

"Allen Ginsberg the poet?" Elf checked with Bruce. "*The* Allen Ginsberg?" Bruce had a what-did-I-tell-you face.

"Don't believe *everything* you read about me," said Allen Ginsberg. "Just most of it. My friend Bill just happens to own the Fillmore Auditorium. You've heard of the Fillmore, right?"

"Of course. It's *the* venue in San Francisco, bar none."

"You'd fit *right* in there," said Ginsberg. "You're folkier than a lot of the acts, but you're not *just* folkie."

"We'd be over like a shot," said Bruce, "if Mr. Graham could sort the flights for us. Right, Elf?"

Elf was too stunned to do much but nod. "Definitely."

"I'm Aphra Booth." The woman in a denim suit was sitting against the far wall. "This reprobate"—she indicated the guy with a cloudy Afro who lay with his head in her lap and who raised a lazy hand—"is Mick Farren." Aphra Booth was another Australian. "I'm skeptical on the whole Doors of Perception thing, but in the spirit of scientific inquiry, I'd like to experience what I'm skeptical about."

This didn't make much sense to Elf, but Aphra Booth's demeanor prompted her to say, "Absolutely."

Syd Barrett detuned his guitar, still chanting *"Have you got it yet?"* in a quiet, demonic round.

"So, Elf." Wotsit indicated a shelf of drinks. "What's your rocket fuel? Brandy? A sugar cube?"

"Sorry to be square, but just a Coke, please."

"If you were square," said Wotsit, "you wouldn't be here."

"Bags Elf sits next to me." Vanessa patted a beanbag next to her. "Even if her talent makes me green with envy. Piano *and* guitar, you play? Isn't that just showing off?"

Elf sank into the beanbag, wondering if Vanessa was there with Syd or Allen Ginsberg. She was way above Wotsit's class. "I'm not that great on the guitar. Bruce calls me 'The Claw.' "

"Then *I* think Bruce is perfectly horrid."

Wotsit brought her Coke. "Enjoy the trip."

Elf guessed the phrase was an Australianism. "Thanks." She swigged a mouthful of dark sweetness.

"*You're* clearly not a virgin," observed Aphra Booth.

Elf guessed this was feminist forthrightness. "Um . . . neither are you, I guess."

Aphra looked confused. "Didn't you hear me earlier?"

"So, Elf." Bruce was doing his naughty-boy smile. "Me and Wotsit have given you an early birthday present."

"Oh?" Elf looked around. There was no sign of a gift.

"We all dropped acid ten minutes ago," said her boyfriend, "but it wouldn't be the same without you, so . . ."

Elf followed his gaze to her Coke, but dismissed the idea that Bruce would spike her drink with LSD as preposterous—until Wotsit giggled, snaggle-toothed.

"Sometimes you need a little push, Wombat," said Bruce.

Horrified, Elf put the bottle down. Shock trumped anger but anxiety trumped shock: Elf didn't want to start tripping in front of these strangers. She didn't want to start tripping at all. Bruce and a few of the Cousins crowd had dropped acid, but Elf was not attracted by the stories of archangels, or fingers turning into penises, or the death of the ego.

"Am I reading this right?" Aphra asked Bruce. "You put LSD in your girlfriend's drink without telling her?"

"Just relax into it," Bruce told Elf.

Elf stopped herself yelling, *"You stupid moron, how dare you?"* Allen Ginsberg was looking on, and to fail this acid test might be to kiss a gig goodbye at the mythical Fillmore. She looked at her bottle of Coke. She had only drunk about a quarter.

Bruce pouted on his beanbag. "It's your birthday present. You're not this square." He told Allen Ginsberg, "She's not."

"Have you got it yet?" sang Syd Barrett. *"Have you got it yet?"*

"No truly independent mind," said Allen Ginsberg, "is square. And if Elf isn't in the mood, a bad trip is far likelier."

Elf handed the Coke to Wotsit. "I'll hear about your adventures in the morning." Bruce looked sulky. Elf asked Aphra Booth. "Look after him, will you?"

"Certainly not. Do I *look* like his mother?"

ON CROMWELL ROAD, night had drawn a curtain of drizzle. A 97 bus groaned up to Elf's stop. Downstairs was packed, so she went upstairs and took the last free double seat near the front. She leaned her head against the glass and replayed the scene in Wotsit's room from various angles. Had she just turned down a lysergic acid golden ticket to San Francisco? Had she flunked a rite of passage? Was she a prisoner too afraid to escape from mind-prison? The bus stopped at the Natural History Museum. A tired-looking Caribbean woman appeared at the top of the stairs, making the quick-fire calculations women have to make when choosing a seat: *Where am I least likely to get hassled?* It must be doubly tricky if you're black *and* female, Elf figured, so she made a sisterly feel-free-to-sit-here nod at the seat next to her. The woman took the seat with a silent nod back. Within a minute she had fallen asleep. Elf studied her, sideways. She was Elf's age, give or take, with smoother skin, fuller lips, and thicker, curlier hair escaping from a headscarf. A silver cross rested on her clavicle behind the collar of a nurse's uniform . . .

"ELF HOLLOWAY IS a dyke," stated Imogen.

Elf sat very still. Imogen was in Malvern, a hundred and forty miles away, and not riding on the 97 bus in South Kensington.

"Dyke," repeated Imogen's voice. *"Dyke, dyke, dyke."*

Elf was either mad or hallucinating her voice.

"*You sleep with boys to hide what you are,*" said Imogen's voice. "*And you've fooled your friends, you've fooled our parents, you've fooled Bea, you've half fooled yourself—but you can't fool me. I'm your big sister. I know when you're lying. I always did. I know what you're thinking even as you think it. Bruce is camouflage. Isn't he, Your Dykeness?*"

Elf shut her eyes and told herself this was the acid-spiked Coca-Cola. Imogen wasn't here. She wasn't going mad. Truly mad people don't query their own sanity.

Rubbish, said Imogen's voice. *And I note you haven't denied that you're a dyke. Have you, Your Dykeness?*

Sitting meekly and pretending nothing was wrong and odd was, itself, wrong and odd, but Elf didn't know what else to do. A taxi would get her home more quickly, but if none appeared, she might start tripping by a wintry Hyde Park. She might imagine she's a fish out of water and jump into the Serpentine and drown.

"*Good riddance to bad rubbish. You're fat. Your songs are stupid. You look like a man in a wig. You're a failure. Your music is a joke. Bea only talks to you out of pity . . .*"

"GOLLY, YOU'RE RIGHT about the loos." Bea sits down, here and now, in the Gioconda Café, on a lovely day in April, a hundred nights after Elf huddled under her blanket in her flat waiting for the Imogen of the Mind to subside. "It really *is* a Journey to the Center of the Earth. I heard magma flows bubbling through the tiled floor." Bea sees the lovers in the doorway across Denmark Street, still snogging. "My, those two are going for it."

"I know. I don't know where to look."

"I do. He's a hunk. I like her miniskirt. Remember Mum's verdict on minis? 'If the goods aren't for sale . . .' "

" '. . . don't put 'em in the window.' "

The lovers pull away, their fingers intertwined until the last moment. They turn, take a few paces, turn again, and wave.

"It's like ballet," says Bea.

People sweep up and down Denmark Street. Elf twists a silver ring she bought from a market stall in King's Lynn on a sunny Sunday before a Fletcher & Holloway gig. Bruce didn't buy it for her—giving rings isn't his style—but it's proof that the Sunday was real, that there was a time when he loved her.

"So when's Bruce due back from France?" asks Bea.

YESTERDAY, ELF CAME home exhausted after eight hours of rehearsals. Waiting for her was a phone bill, an invitation for Fletcher & Holloway to play at a folk club last August in the Outer Hebrides, and a postcard of the Eiffel Tower. The mere sight of his handwriting tautened her innards:

Dear Wombat, I hope this
finds you tip-top. Paris is
amazing!!! Liberté, egalité,
fraternité and all that.
I have a weekly gig at Le
Gibus club – The flat I share
is above it. I busk on Les
Champs Élysées in my cork
on strings hat. The locals
are très amicables! Avec bises
Your humble Kangaroo, Bruce xxx

PARIS
613 - La Tour Eiffel illuminée
vue du Pont Alexandre III

Collectionnez les Cartes « IRIS »

Editions CHANTAL, 74, Rue des Archives, Paris

MEXICHROME

Elf Holloway
19c Livonia St.
London
Angleterre

Elf catalogued her thoughts. First, exasperation that the bastard had sent only one miserly card after a hundred days of nothing. Second, anger at its breezy tone—as if Bruce hadn't bruised her heart, sliced Fletcher & Holloway in half, and left her to sort out the mess. Third, a mortifying bliss at the "Dear," the "Wombat" and "Kangaroo," the *"avec bises"* . . . and dismay at the "flat upstairs I share." Share with whom? *"Très amicable"* French girls? Fourth, suspicion that the "Hope we're still friends" is a hedge-bet—as if Bruce is lining up a bed for when he gets back to London. Fifth, fresh anger at the way Bruce uses her. Sixth, a resolve to slam the door in his face if he shows up at Livonia Street. Seventh, a dread that she won't be able to. Eighth, disgust that one measly little postcard could still trigger a bout of Brucesickness. Elf ran a hot bath. She climbed in and read *The Golden Notebook* by Doris Lessing to take her mind off Bruce Fletcher, but in the event Bruce Fletcher took her mind off Doris Lessing. Elf kept imagining him and a French girl having baths together, him wearing nothing but his corks-on-strings hat . . .

"BRUCE IS STAYING in Paris a little longer," Elf tells Bea. A blind man walks by with his guide dog. "Australians like to see as much of Europe as they can when they're here." Elf turns to Bea, so she won't think Elf's avoiding eye contact.

"Happy Together" by the Turtles comes on the radio.

"So is Fletcher and Holloway on hiatus?" asks Bea.

The worst part is lying to Bea, thinks Elf. "Kind of."

"While you're recording with Utopia Avenue?"

Elf notices a cigarette lighter wedged between the ketchup and the HP Sauce bottles. On the side is enameled a red devil with a pitchfork, horns, and tail. She flicks the spark wheel and a flame appears. "I wonder if one of those dishy art students forgot it."

"What dishy art students?"

Elf snorts. "You'll have to do better than that at RADA."

Bea does Bea's impish smile. "If this was a story, one of them would come back in and say, 'Have you seen a lighter?' and you'd say, 'What, this lighter?' and he'd say, 'Thank God, my dying mother gave it to me on her deathbed' and your fates would be entwined forevermore."

Elf's smile is swallowed by a mighty yawn. "Sorry."

"You must be exhausted, poor thing. You were up at six?"

"Five. Graveyard-shift sessions are cheaper. Howie Stoker may be a millionaire playboy but he's not throwing money at Utopia Avenue willy-nilly."

"Are you making money, if it's not a rude question?"

"It's not. We're not. We've only done four gigs and our fee is minuscule. Minuscule gets divided five ways. I was earning more when I was headlining at folk festivals."

"So you're all paying to be in the band?"

"Kind of. I've still got a trickle of Wanda Virtue money coming in. Jasper's eking out an inheritance from his grandfather and stays at a flat his father owns in Mayfair. Dean's moved in with Jasper, so he's rent-free too. Griff's living in an uncle's back garden in Battersea. I should've invited you into Fungus Hut just now to introduce you, but I . . . was sick of the sight of them."

"Oh dear. What did they do?"

Elf hesitates. "Their default response to *any* of my ideas is to tell me why it's no good. An hour later, they'll arrive at the same idea—and truly not remember me saying it. Drives me *mental.*"

"Theater's the same. It's as if 'female director' is an oxymoron, like 'woman prime minister.' Are they always that bad?"

Elf makes a face. "Not always. Dean shoots his mouth off, but it comes from insecurity. I think. On charitable days."

"Is he good-looking?"

"Girls think so."

Bea makes a face.

"No no no. Never in a million years. Griff the drummer's a northern diamond in the rough. Anarchic, sweary, likes a drink. Great drummer. He's more at home in his skin than Dean. Jasper's . . . Mr. Enigma. Sometimes he's so spaced-out he's barely there. Other times he's so intensely there, he uses all the oxygen in the room.

Don't tell Mum and Dad, but he was in a psychiatric clinic in Holland for a while, and sometimes you think, *Yes, I believe it.* He reads a lot. Went to boarding school at Ely—there's real money on the Dutch side of his family. You should *hear* him play guitar, though. When he's on form, words fail me."

"Two coffees"—Mrs. Biggs arrives—"and a bacon butty." The sisters thank her and Elf takes a big bite. "Dear God, I needed that."

Bea asks, "So what does Utopia Avenue sound like?"

Elf chews. "A mix of Dean's R&B, Jasper's strange virtuosity, my folk roots, Griff's jazz . . . I only hope the world's ready for us."

"How have the gigs gone?"

"Our debut was abysmal. It ended with Griff getting hit by a bottle. He had to go to hospital. He's got a Frankenstein scar."

Bea covers her mouth. "Jesus Christ. You never said."

"We were this far"—Elf indicates half an inch—"from packing it in. Levon bullied us into going to our second gig, at the Goldhawk club. That went better. Until some Archie Kinnock fans showed up to hurl abuse at Griff and Jasper for 'stabbing Archie in the back.' We left round the back. Our third gig was at the White Horse in Tottenham, where ten people showed up. Ten. Then, joy of joys, some folkies arrived at the end to berate me for 'taking the thirty pieces of silver.' "

"That must have been horrible. What did you say?"

" 'What silver?' The landlord refused to pay. Levon preferred to stay on decent terms than get shirty, so my earnings for that night was half a shandy and a packet of nuts."

"I only wish you'd told me."

"You've got exams and auditions to worry about. I chose all this. Mum would call it making my bed and lying in it."

Bea lights a cigarette. "What about the fourth show?"

Elf chews a crispy bacon rind. "The Marquee."

"What? You played the Marquee? *The* Marquee? And you didn't invite me?"

Elf nods. "Don't hate me."

"Why didn't you say? I'd have rounded up half of Richmond!"

"I know. What if we were booed off?"

The crackle and sizzle of deep-frying escapes the kitchen.
Bea looks uncertain. "*Were* you booed off?"
Elf drops a sugar lump into her coffee and stirs . . .

THE MARQUEE ON Wardour Street was an underground tank of a venue, sloshing with a crowd of six or seven hundred. If someone had died, they would have stayed propped upright until after midnight. Elf was close to puking out of sheer fear. Utopia Avenue were second on a five-band bill entitled Anything Can Happen, arranged in order of fame, set-length, and fee. Below Utopia Avenue was a five-piece from Plymouth called Doomed to Obscurity. Above them were three major acts: Traffic, whose single "Paper Sun" was camped in the Top Five; Pink Floyd, London's underground band heading overground; and Cream, whose LP *Fresh Cream* was spinning on a million teenagers' turntables. A rumor was squirreling about that Jimi Hendrix was in the venue, or had been, or would be. Steve Winwood was in the office, just up those stairs, being interviewed by Amy Boxer for the *NME*. God knows what strings Levon had pulled to get Utopia Avenue on this bill, but Anything Can Happen was their biggest showcase so far. If they fluffed it, the gig could be their last showcase, too.

Elf had watched Doomed to Obscurity from the side, hoping they'd fulfill the promise of their name. None of the Pink Floyd, Traffic, or Cream fans called for an encore. "Shift over a mo, Elf." Levon and a Marquee dogsbody were staggering past with her Hammond. Elf fought an impulse to flee . . .

. . . AND SUDDENLY IT was time. Elf ordered her body onstage. Griff was setting up his kit. Dean and Jasper found the amp levels they'd marked at the sound check earlier. Elf's body didn't move. Her left hand was trembling, like her gran's who had died of Parkinson's. They had a thirty-minute slot. What if she pooched her chords on the "Darkroom" middle eighth? What if the crowd hated the electric "Any Way the Wind Blows"? What if the words flew out of her head on "A Raft and a River," like they had done at the White Horse?

"You'll be fine," said Sandy Denny.

"You're always here when I need you."

"Moroccan courage?" The singer offered her a lit joint.

"Yes." Elf inhaled, held down the peaty smoke, and let it all out again. The buzz was instant. "Thanks."

"A big crowd," said Sandy. "I'm mildly jealous."

"They're not here for us." Elf's fingertips buzzed.

"Oh, don't talk bollocks, nobody's—" Sandy flapped out a hand and splashed a passing roadie's beer. "Oops, sorry, mate. I've heard you rehearse. You've got something, you four. Just let it out. And if, *if,* the crowd are too stupid to appreciate it"—Sandy slapped the Marshall stack—"crank these monsters up. Atomize the bastards."

Dean appeared. "Hi, Sandy. Elf. Ready to go?"

Elf noticed her hand was steady again. "Do or die."

"Later, we shall imbibe spirits," promised Sandy.

Elf walked out and took her place at the keyboards. A chubby heckler leaning on the stage yelled out, "Strip joint's over the road, darlin'!" and his goons laughed. Liberated by the dope from a fear of consequences, Elf made a pistol with her fingers, aimed at the heckler's eyes, and—her face deadly serious—mimed shooting him, three times, complete with recoil at the elbow. The heckler's stupid grin faded. Elf blew away imaginary gun smoke, twirled her make-believe pistol around her trigger finger, slipped it into a make-believe holster, and leaned into her mic. The Marquee's impresario was supposed to introduce the band, but Elf waved him away. "We are Utopia Avenue," she told the Marquee, Soho, and all England, "and we intend to shoot you down." She glanced at Griff, who looked surprised, holding his sticks poised in his *Go* position; at Dean, whose approving nod told her, *Ready;* at Jasper, who was waiting for Elf's "A-one, a-two, and a—"

ELF DROPS A second sugar cube into her coffee. "It went pretty well. We started with 'Any Way the Wind Blows.' Then one of Dean's rockier numbers, 'Abandon Hope.' Then a new song of Jasper's, 'Darkroom.' Then my new one, 'A Raft and a River.' "

"Lucky Marquee. It's not fair. When can I hear it?"

"Soon, sis. Soon."

"Did you meet Steve Winwood?"

"Well . . . actually, after our encore he came up and said a few kind words about my Hammond playing."

"Oh, my God," says Bea. "What did you say?"

Elf inhales coffee steam. "I just squeaked, 'Thanks,' blurted out some stream-of-consciousness claptrap, and watched him go."

"Nice bum?"

"I honestly didn't notice." Sandie Shaw's "Puppet on a String" comes on the café's radio. "If I ever record anything this simpering, give me a stern talking-to about those thirty pieces of silver."

"She's getting more than thirty pieces, I bet. This song's everywhere." They listen to the chorus.

Suddenly Elf can't stand it anymore. "We've split up. Me and Bruce. The duo's finished. He's staying in Paris. He dumped me. In February. It's over." Elf's heart's pounding as if it's happening now. "Now you know." *I'm not going to cry. It's been three months.* She steels herself for Bea's shock and outrage.

Bea looks unfazed. "I guessed."

"How?"

"Every time his name came up, you'd change the subject."

"What about Mum and Dad and Immy?"

Bea examines her lilac fingernails. "If I've worked it out, Mum has. Dad's clueless. Immy? I'm *prrretty* sure she's not relying on Holloway and Fletcher for musical interludes at the wedding. Has she mentioned Bruce or your wedding booking lately?"

Actually, no. "Why didn't you say anything?"

"Tact." Bea drains her coffee cup. "Bruce was charming, but charm in a guy is a warning sign. Like black and yellow stripes in nature mean, *Watch out, there are stings near this honey.*"

Elf is trembling and isn't sure why. Her eyes meet the Mona Lisa's above Mrs. Biggs's till. The most famous half-smile tells Elf, *Suffering is the promise that life always keeps.*

"I really have to be off." Bea stands up and puts on her coat. "You go and record a masterpiece. Shall I tell Immy?"

"Please." It's the path of least resistance. "And Mum."

"I'll drop by your flat after the audition. If you want."

"Sure." Elf looks at the clock: 8:58. "Bea, tell me something. I've been to university. I've dropped out of university. I've survived the music scene for three years. You're still at school. How come you know so much while I know bugger-all? How does that work?"

"Basically," Bea hugs her sister goodbye, "I don't believe people." She lets her sister go. "Basically, you do."

PARADISE IS THE ROAD TO PARADISE

SIDE TWO

1. **WEDDING PRESENCE** (De Zoet)
2. **PURPLE FLAMES** (Moss)
3. **UNEXPECTEDLY** (Holloway)
4. **THE PRIZE** (De Zoet)

WEDDING PRESENCE

At the end of its eight-minute journey from the sun, light passes through the stained glass of St. Matthias Church in Richmond, London, and enters the dual darkrooms of Jasper's eyeballs. The rods and cones packing his retinas convert the light into electrical impulses that travel along optic nerves into his brain, which translates the varying wavelengths of light into "Virgin Mary blue," "blood of Christ red," "Gethsemane green," and interprets the images as twelve disciples, each occupying a segment of the cartwheel window. *Vision begins in the heart of the sun.* Jasper notes that Jesus's disciples were, essentially, hippies: long hair, gowns, stoner expressions, irregular employment, spiritual convictions, dubious sleeping arrangements, and a guru. The cartwheel begins to spin, so Jasper shuts his eyes and fights the slippage by naming the twelve, rummaging through boyhood scripture classes and church services: Matthew, Mark, Luke, John, a.k.a. the Fab Four; Thomas, Jasper's favorite, the one who demanded proof; Peter, who enjoyed the best solo career; Jude and Matthias, session players; and Judas Iscariot. *Our Heavenly Father's most sadistically deployed patsy.* Before Jasper can finish off the list, however, he hears a knock. Rhythmic, faint, a sonic room or two below the vicar's voice. Unmistakable.

Knock-knock, knock-knock, knock-knock.

He opens his eyes. The window has stopped spinning.

The knocking stops, too. *But I heard it. He's awake.*

Jasper was told this day would come. The agony of uncertainty is over, at least. *I was only ever on remission.* He glances at Griff, to his right, decked out in an improvised wedding suit. His hands are drumming, softly, on his thighs. To his left, Dean's trying to make one index finger turn clockwise and the other anticlockwise. *I like playing with these guys and I don't want it to end.*

Perhaps Queludrin could slow the onset.

Perhaps.

JASPER WAS FIFTEEN. Cherry trees around the cricket field blossomed wedding-dress white. Jasper lacked the body mass for rugby and the stamina for rowing, but he had the coordination, speed, and patience for the First XI cricket team. Jasper was fielding in the outfield as Bishop's Ely took on Peterborough Grammar. The grass was fresh-cut and the sun was raw. Ely Cathedral sat above the River Ouse like Noah's Ark. The captain, a boy named Whitehead, ran up to the wicket and delivered a yorker. The batsman smacked the ball in Jasper's direction. Shouts rang out. Jasper was already running to intercept the ball and scooped it up in mid-stride only a few feet shy of the boundary rope, preventing a four. His throw to Whitehead was accurate and earned a few seconds' worth of applause from the home supporters. Behind, or inside, or over the clapping, for the very first time Jasper heard the *knock-knock, knock-knock, knock-knock* that would change, redefine, and nearly end his life. It was like knuckles on a far-off door, down a corridor . . . Or a little hammer on the far side of a wall. Jasper looked around for its source. The spectators were all on the far side of the pitch. The nearest boy was a classmate, Bundy, about forty paces away. Jasper called out: "Bundy?"

Bundy's voice was nasal with hay fever. "What?"

"Do you hear that?"

"Hear what?"

"That knocking sound."

They listened to a Cambridgeshire morning's unscored music: a tractor in a nearby field; cars; crows. The cathedral bells began their count to twelve. Underneath, a *Knock-knock* . . . *Knock-knock* . . . *Knock-knock* . . .

"What knocking sound?" asked Bundy.

"That knock-knock . . . knock-knock . . ."

Bundy listened again. "If you lose your marbles and the men in white coats come to take you away, can I have your cricket bat?"

A fighter jet unzipped the horizon. Over the boundary rope, a chalk-blue butterfly grazed on the Queen Anne's lace. Jasper felt what you feel after someone leaves the room.

Whitehead was beginning his long run-up. The knocking had stopped. Or gone. Or maybe Jasper's hearing was especially acute and he had heard someone chopping wood. Or maybe he had only imagined it. Whitehead bowled. The wicket leaped from the ground. *"Hoooowwww-zzzzzzaaaaaaaattt!"*

"GIFTS CAN BE treasured for a lifetime or forgotten the next moment." The vicar of St. Matthias Church sounds, to Jasper, a lot like Prime Minister Harold Wilson. His voice is flat and buzzing, like a bee trapped in a tin. "Gifts can be sincere, or manipulative. Gifts may be material. Gifts may be invisible—a favor, a kind word, the end of a sulk. A sparrow on your bird table. A song on the radio. A second chance. Impartial advice. Acceptance. The gift of gratitude, which allows us to recognize gifts as gifts. Life is a continuum of giving and receiving. Air, sunlight, sleep, food, water, love. For Christians, the Bible is the gift of God's word, and buried within that vast gift, we find these treasured lines about gifts, given by Paul to a struggling church in Corinth: 'When I was a child, I spake as a child, I understood as a child, I thought as a child: but when I became a man, I put away childish things. For now we see through a glass, darkly; but then we'll see God face to face. Now I know in part; but then shall I know even as I am known. And now abideth faith, hope and love, these three; but the greatest of these is love.' "

Jasper, his ear pressed against a stone pillar, hears a heart.

The vicar continues: " 'The greatest of these is love.' When faith turns its back on you, the Apostle advises, just try to love. When hope is snuffed out, just try to love. I say to Lawrence and Imogen that on the days when marriage does *not* resemble a rose garden—and they, too, happen—just try to love. Just try. True love is the act of trying to love. Effortless love is as dubious as effortless gardening . . ."

Jasper looks at the flowers around the altar. *So this is a wedding.* He's never been to one before. He thinks of his mother, and wonders if she ever dreamed of having a wedding like this. Or if, when she discovered she was pregnant, that dream withered away. If you believe stories, romantic comedies, and magazines, a wedding day is the happiest day of a woman's life. A Mount Everest of joy. Everyone at St. Matthias Church looks quite serious. *In a church, in West London, on a ball of rock, hurtling through space at 67,000 miles per hour . . .*

"AHA, THE MYSTERIOUS missing diner." The man in the banquet hall at Epsom Country Club is too big for his chair. "Don Glossop, Dunlop Tires, an old pal of Lawrence's father." His handshake is a hand-clamp.

"Hello, Mr. Glossop. I remember you."

"Oh?" Don Glossop juts out his lower jaw. "From where?"

"I saw you in the church."

"Glad we got that cleared up." Don Glossop releases Jasper's hand. "This is Brenda, my better half. I'm told. By her."

Brenda Glossop has sculpted hair, prominent jewelry, and a sinister way of saying, "Enchanted."

"Tell me something," says Don Glossop, then sneezes like a donkey braying. "Why do so many young men nowadays *choose* to ponce around looking like girls? It's got so bad, I'm no longer sure which is which."

"Maybe you should look more closely," suggests Jasper.

Don Glossop frowns as if Jasper's answer didn't match his sentence. "But the hair! Why in God's name don't you get a haircut?"

Griff and Dean were with Jasper on the coach from St. Matthias Church. Jasper wishes he hadn't lost them.

Don Glossop peers into Jasper's face: "Cat got your tongue?"

Jasper rewinds. *Why in God's name don't you get a haircut?* "I like my hair long. It's that simple, really."

Don Glossop squints. "You look like a ruddy nancy-boy!"

"Only to you, Mr. Glossop, and—"

"Every—single—*person* in this banquet room'll take one look at you just now and think, *Nancy-boy!* I guarantee it."

Jasper avoids the onlooking faces. He sips water.

"I think you'll find that's *my* water," declares a voice.

Concentrate: "If every homosexual on Earth—if that's what you mean by 'nancy-boy'—had long hair, your statement might be logical. But long hair's only been fashionable for a few years. Surely, the homosexuals you've met were short-haired." Don Glossop looks blank so Jasper tries to help with examples. "In jail, or the Royal Navy, or public school, perhaps. One master at Ely was famous for interfering with boys, and he wore a wig like yours. Your logic is flawed. I suggest. Respectfully."

"What?" Don Glossop has turned pale maroon. *"What?"*

Perhaps he's hard of hearing. "I said, 'One master at Ely was famous for interfering with boys, and he wore a wig—' "

"My husband *means,*" Brenda Glossop says, "he has spent no time whatsoever consorting with 'types' like that."

"Then how could he be an expert on 'nancy-boys'?"

"It's common knowledge!" Don Glossop leans forward, dangling his tie in his food. "Nancy-boys have long hair!"

"Those awful Rolling Stones have long hair," says a woman with a frizzy halo of mauve hair. "And they're a disgrace."

"National Service would've sorted them out, but that's gone too now, of course." The new speaker wears a regimental tie and a medal. "Another nail in the coffin."

"My point exactly, Brigadier," says Don Glossop. "We didn't smack the Nazis for six just for a mob of guitar-twanging oiks to turn Great Britain into a land of yeah-yeahs and ooo-babys."

"That Keith Jagger's father worked in a factory," says Brenda Glossop. "Now he swans about in a Tudor mansion."

"And thanks to *The Evening News,*" says Frizzy Halo, "we now know exactly what goes on inside, don't we?"

"I hope Judge Block makes a proper example of 'em," says the brigadier. "No doubt *you* think they're the bee's knees."

Jasper remembers he's here. "I've never met them. Though I'd chance my arm and say their best music will outlive all of us."

"Their primitive mating calls aren't 'music,' " scoffs Don Glossop. " 'Strangers in the Night' by Frank Sinatra is music. 'Land of Hope and Glory' is music. This 'rock 'n' roll' is a poisonous racket."

"Yet to Sir Edward Elgar," says Jasper, " 'Strangers in the Night' might have been a poisonous racket. Generations pass. Aesthetics evolve. Why is this fact a threat?"

"Jasper." It's Elf's sister Bea, the one who's got into RADA. "Um, you're sitting at the wrong table."

"You can ruddy well say that again," says the brigadier.

"Oh." Jasper stands up and gives the guests at the wrong table a slight bow. *Be polite.* "Well, it was lovely to meet you all . . ."

AT THE CORRECT table, Jasper survives the prawn cocktail and the coq au vin, but by dessert he is drowning in dialogues. Levon is discussing changes to the tax system with an accountant from Dublin. Dean is discussing Eddie Cochran with Lawrence's best man. Griff is whispering into a giggling bridesmaid's hot-pink ear. *Look at them all.* Question; answer; witticism; fact; morsel of gossip; response. *How effortlessly they do it.* Jasper speaks fluent English and Dutch, good French, passable German and Latin, but the languages of face and tone are as impenetrable as Sanskrit. Jasper knows the tell-tale signs that he's failing to engage: the diagonal head-swivel; a gluey nod; narrowed eyes. He can disguise it as eccentricity, but after an hour, he crumples. Jasper doesn't know if his facial and tonal dyslexia is a cause or effect of his emotional dyslexia. He knows what grief, rage, jealousy, hatred, joy, and the normal spectrum of feelings are—but he experiences them only as mild changes of temperature. If Normals learn this about him, they mistrust him, so Jasper is condemned to act like a Normal and to fail. When he fails, Normals think he's shifty, or mocking them. Only four humans and one disembodied entity have ever accepted Jasper as he truly is. Of these, Trix is in Amsterdam, Dr. Galavazi is retired, and Grootvader Wim is dead. Formaggio is in nearby Oxford, but the Mongolian will never pass his way again.

Mecca, who might have been a fifth, is lost to America.

A person is a thing who leaves. Jasper estimates the time required by dessert, coffee, and further speeches. His watch says 10:10. That makes no sense. He holds it to his ear. *Time stopped.* Unable to concoct a plausible lie, Jasper slips away. He finds himself in a hallway lined with inoffensive English landscapes and carpeted with swarms of dots. A party of golfers spills through the front doors. They are talking at baffling speeds and volumes. A flight of stairs offers him a way out . . .

THE ROOFTOP TERRACE has a bench, flowers in pots, views over a golf course and the roofs and trees of Epsom. The afternoon is drowsy and pollinated. Jasper lights up a Marlboro and lies on the bench. Rudderless cloud-wrecks float, unmoored. *Breathe it in and breathe it out.* Jasper remembers summers in Domburg, at Rijksdorp Clinic, and in Amsterdam. *Time is what stops everything happening at once.* Jasper remembers last Thursday, looking out through the window of Levon's third-floor office. Garbage fumes ebbed in. On a flat roof a couple of streets away, three women sunbathed in bikinis. Possibly it was a knocking shop, Soho being Soho, and the women were between shifts. Two had black skin. One turned up a transistor radio and Jasper caught a faint whiff of Ringo Starr singing "With a Little Help from My Friends."

"Care to join us, Jasper?" It was Levon.

"I'm here." Jasper turned around.

"So what did they say?" asked Dean. "Have we got a deal?"

"Your second question first," said Levon. "No. We don't have a deal. All four labels turned us down."

For a moment nobody spoke.

"Hallelujah," said Dean. "Praise the Lord."

"You could've told us that on the phone," said Griff.

"What did they say?" asked Elf.

"Tony Reynolds at EMI liked the demos, but they already have one underground band in Pink Floyd."

"But me 'n' Elf sound nothing like Pink Floyd," objected Dean. "He did listen to all three demos? Not just 'Darkroom'?"

"Yes. I sat with him. But he wasn't budging."

"What about Vic Walsh at Phillips?" asked Elf.

"Vic liked the general sound but he kept asking, 'Who's the Jagger? Who's the Ray Davies? Who's the face?' "

"Who's the face of the fookin' Beatles?" asked Griff.

"My words exactly," said Levon. "Vic said, 'The Beatles are the exception that proves the rule,' and I said, 'No, the Beatles prove the rule that every great band is an exception.' He said, 'Utopia Avenue's not the Beatles.' I said, 'That's the whole point.' "

"What was Pye's fookin' excuse?" asked Griff.

"Mr. Elliot told me—I quote—boys won't 'get tribal' about the band because of Elf while girls won't 'cream their knickers' over Dean and Jasper because Elf's in the band."

"That's . . . absurd, insulting, and kind of incest-y, all at once," objected Elf. "What a limp reason for not signing us."

"Mr. Elliot hinted that if we ditched Elf and turned Utopia Avenue into Small Faces clones, he might be interested."

Elf did a *hfff* noise as if somebody had punched her.

"Obviously," said Levon, "I told him to take a hike."

"They take all of us or none of us," stated Griff.

Dean lit a cigarette. "What about Decca?"

"Derek Burke," Levon leaned back in his creaky chair, "saw you at the Marquee. He likes your energy, but isn't sure enough about the hybrid of styles to invest Decca's money."

"That's us snookered, then," said Griff. "The Big Four've given us the bum's rush. What now?"

"I won't deny it's a setback," said Levon, "but—"

"I'm skinter than I was in January," groaned Dean. "Half a year I've been living on solid air, and what've I got to show?"

"A great band," said Levon, "three great demos, a small but growing cohort of fans, five or six great songs. Momentum."

"If we're so fookin' great," growled Griff, "where's our record deal? Chas Chandler got Hendrix his in three weeks."

"And what about them?" Dean pointed at the posters of Dick Sposato and the Spencer Sisters. "They've got deals."

Levon folded his arms. "Hendrix is freak-out guitar R&B. Dick's an older crooner I've taken on as a favor for Freddy Duke. The Spencer Sisters sing arias for the masses and the *Songs on Sunday* audience. They're all easy to pitch. Utopia Avenue is not. You *are* unclassifiable: people *will* reject you, at first. If this upsets you—or if you think I'm not busting my ass—there's the door. You're free. Go. I'll have Bethany send the release documents."

Griff and Dean looked at each other and didn't move.

Jasper watched the clocks above Levon's head. One showed the time here, one the time in New York, one in Los Angeles.

"I was a bit out of order," admitted Dean.

Griff breathed in and out. "Aye. I might've been too."

"Half-assed apologies accepted," said Levon.

Elf tapped her cigarette. "What's our next move?"

FOUR MEN SIT around a low table: a shaven-headed abbot whose face is engraved on Jasper's memory; the abbot's acolyte; the magistrate of the city; and his trusted chamberlain. Dream-lit screens are adorned with chrysanthemums. The acolyte pours a glassy liquid from a gourd as red as blood into soot-black shallow cups. Birdsong is chromatic and glinting.

"Life and death are indivisible," declares the magistrate.

The four raise a cup to their host's strange toast.

The abbot drinks only when he sees the magistrate has drunk first. A few pleasantries are exchanged before Jasper realizes that a fifth guest—Death—is here too. Dabs of odorless poison were smeared inside the rough-hewn cups before the guests arrived. The poison dissolved in the rice wine and is now in the blood of hosts and guests alike. To ensure the abbot drank the poison, the magistrate and his secretary drank it too.

The abbot understands. This script is written. He reaches for his sword but his arm is stiff and wooden. All he can do is swing his fist at his cup. It skips across the empty floor. "The Creeds work, you human termite!" he tells the magistrate. "Oil of Souls works!" They speak of revenge, justice, buried women, and sacrificed babies until the chamberlain topples forward, quivering, scattering black and white pieces of the game of Go. He is followed by the acolyte. Spit and blood foam on their lips. A black butterfly lands on a white stone and unfolds its wings . . .

Knock-knock . . . Knock-knock . . . Knock-knock . . .

"Look at you, Sleeping Beauty."

JASPER OPENS HIS eyes and sees Bea, inches away, gazing down at him. She leans in and kisses his lips. Jasper lets her. Her fingers rest on his face. *It's nice.* Birdsong is chromatic and glinting. They've met twice: once when Elf brought her to see the band rehearse at Pavel Z's, and once at Les Cousins, where Utopia Avenue played a semi-acoustic set. Bea pulls her head back. "Don't tell Elf."

"As you wish," says Jasper.

"If you come across Sleeping Beauty, there's only one thing to do. But don't get any big ideas."

"I shan't. Princess Charming."

She sits on a bench opposite.

The roof garden. The country club. The wedding party. Jasper swivels himself upright. Rudderless cloud-wrecks float by, unmoored. *Breathe it in and breathe it out.* "Are the speeches over? How long was I asleep? We're supposed to be playing soon."

Bea counts off her replies: "Nearly. I didn't set a stopwatch. Yes, you are." She's wearing an ink-blue body-hugging dress. She possesses a sharp vivid beauty lacking in her sisters.

"You've changed your dress," says Jasper.

"Bridesmaids' dresses aren't my thing. Elf sent me to find you and give you a message." Below, a car door slams. Bea helps herself to Jasper's Marlboros and lighter.

Jasper waits patiently.

Bea breathes out smoke. "She says, 'Get your arse onstage in twenty minutes.' That was five minutes ago, so make it fifteen."

"Tell her, 'Thanks for the message: I'll be there.' "

Bea looks at him oddly.

Is she waiting for more? "Please."

"What's it like, being in a band with my sister?"

"Um . . . enjoyable?"

"How so?"

"She's talented. She's a good keys player. Her voice is ethereal and husky. Her songs are strong." An airplane scrapes by.

Bea slips off her shoes and sits cross-legged. Her toenails are sky-blue, like Trix's lamp.

Maybe I'm supposed to ask her a question. "How did you know where to look for me?"

"I just pretended I was you and thought," Bea mimics Jasper quite well, *"How do I get out of here?"*

"Was that difficult or easy?"

"I found you. Didn't I?"

A summer breeze sways lavender in pots.

Bea smokes and passes Jasper her cigarette. It's smudged pink with her lipstick. "Play 'Darkroom,'" she says. "I like 'Abandon Hope' and 'Raft and a River' too, but I think 'Darkroom''s your first hit. It's quite *Sergeant Pepper's*-y. Its colors. Its mood."

Jasper wonders what would happen if he touched her hand, but Trix told him to always let the lady lead. His throat is dry.

"You have heard *Sergeant Pepper's,* yes?"

THE CURTAIN BILLOWED out through Levon's half-open sash window. Jasper lay on the sofa and watched the others as they listened to side one. Elf sat cocooned in the velvet armchair, studying the lyrics. Dean was stretched out on the rug. Levon sat at the dining table, gazing at a bowl of apples. Griff was propped up against the wall, his hands and wrists twitching in sympathy with Ringo's. Nobody spoke. Jasper recognized the song that Rick Wright had told him about at the UFO Club.

After the carnivalesque "Being for the Benefit of Mr. Kite!" Levon flipped the record over. George Harrison's sitar cascaded around like a skittish comet . . . and metamorphosed into the clarinet of "When I'm Sixty-Four." Jasper noticed how two sounds make a third. The last track, "A Day in the Life," was a miniature of the whole album, like the way that the Book of Psalms is a miniature of the whole Bible. Lennon's "found" lyrics contrasted with McCartney's kitchen-sink lines. Together they glowed. The song's closer was an orchestral daymare finale spiraling upward to a final chord, slammed on dozens of pianos. The engineer raised the recording levels as the note fell away. Jasper thought of the end of a dream when the real world seeps in. It ended with backward laughing gibberish.

The stylus lifted off and the arm clunked home.

Pigeons cooed in the June trees of Queens Gardens.

"Shit the bed." Dean breathed a long and winding sigh.

"Wow," said Levon. "*Wow.* It's an inner travelogue."

"I always pegged Ringo as a jammy beggar," said Griff, "but . . . how'd he play them drum parts? I do not have a fookin' clue."

"The whole studio's a meta-instrument," said Elf. "It's as if they recorded it on a sixteen-track. But sixteen-tracks don't exist."

"The bass," said Dean, "is that crisp, it's like they recorded it last, as an overdub. Is that even possible?"

"Only if they recorded the other parts to a rhythm track playing inside their heads," speculated Elf. "Is *that* possible?"

"Good job they've stopped touring," said Dean. "They couldn't play that live in a month o' Sundays."

"Not touring," replied Griff, "freed 'em up to make this. They thought, *Fook it, we'll record what the hell we want.*"

"Only the Beatles can get away with not touring," Levon said. "Nobody else. Not even the Stones. Managerial footnote."

"Look at this sleeve." Elf held it up. "The colors, the collage, the way it opens up to reveal the lyrics. It's stunning."

"Our LP should look that classy," said Dean.

"That," Levon warned, "needs *real* love from the label."

"The lyrics in 'Darkroom' are pushing it," said Griff, "but 'Lucy in the Sky with Diamonds'? Surely that's LSD?"

"What 'bout that stuff 'bout 'I'd love to turn yer on' in that last one?" said Dean. "He's not talking about light switches."

"Have the Beatles just killed psychedelia?" asked Elf. "How could anyone possibly top that?"

"They've lit a fuse," said Levon. "'Darkroom' is perfect for the summer of *Sergeant Pepper's.* This settles it, for me. 'Darkroom' has to be the first Utopia Avenue single."

An ice-cream van was playing "Oranges and Lemons." The shimmering chords echoed off the stuccoed Georgian frontages of Queens Gardens. Jasper heard his name.

Everyone was looking at him. "What?"

"I asked," said Dean, "what yer thought o' the album."

"Why stick labels on the moon? It's Art."

TWO WEEKS LATER, Jasper sees a familiar face in the mirror above the adjacent washbasin. The reflected face belongs to Elf's dad. "Congratulations on the wedding, Mr. Holloway."

"Ah, Jasper. Enjoying yourself?"

Jasper stops himself saying *no* but *yes* would be a lie so he says, "The prawn cocktail was excellent."

For some reason Mr. Holloway finds this amusing. "These occasions are for, and by, the womenfolk. I never said that."

Jasper notes that now he shares secrets with Elf's sister and Elf's father. "Thanks for having your lawyer look at our contracts."

"Time will attest to Mr. Frankland's financial probity, but my lawyer assures me you didn't sign your soul away this time around."

Jasper attempts a witticism. "They come in handy, I'm told."

Mr. Holloway's reflection frowns. "I beg your pardon?"

It fell flat. "Um . . . in folklore and religion, the soul is a useful thing to hang on to. That's all."

The roller-towel rattles. "Ah." The older man's voice changes timbre. "Elf tells me you went to Bishop's Ely. The top brass at my bank includes a few Old Elysians."

"I was only at Ely until I was sixteen. Then I moved to the Netherlands. My father's Dutch, you see."

"How does he feel about you forfeiting the advantages of a top education on a 'pop group'?"

Jasper watches Elf's father dry his hands, finger by finger. "My father leaves me to my own devices."

"I've heard the Dutch are a permissive bunch."

" 'Indifferent' might be truer than 'permissive.' "

Mr. Holloway pulls down the towel for the next user. "This much I do know. Any candidate for a job at *my* bank who played in a 'band' would be rejected. Whatever school he went to."

"So you disapprove of Utopia Avenue?"

"I'm Elf's father. The band harms her prospects—and what about the occupational hazards? What if that bottle at Brighton had hit Elf? Scars may suit a chap, but they disfigure a girl."

"The worst clubs have cages to protect the performers."

"Was that meant to reassure me?"

"Well"—*a trick question?*—"yes."

Mr. Holloway's stab of a laugh echoes off the walls. "To top it all, this so-called 'underground culture' is awash with drugs."

"Drugs are everywhere. Statistically, a fifth of the wedding guests are taking Valium. Then we have tobacco, alcohol—"

"Are you being willfully dim with me?"

"I don't know how to be willfully dim, Mr. Holloway."

The bank manager frowns as if a column of figures won't add up. "*Illegal* drugs. Drugs that—that 'hook' you and . . . make you jump off buildings, and so forth."

"Do you mean LSD, specifically?"

"According to *The Times,* there's an epidemic."

"That's a lurid word. People choose to use recreational drugs. Some of your employees may even use them."

"I assure you they do *not*!" His voice goes up.

"How do you know?" Jasper's stays low.

"Because none of them are 'junkies'!"

"You enjoy a glass of wine, but you're not an alcoholic. The same is true with drugs. It's the *pattern* of consumption that does the damage. Heroin's an exception, however. Heroin's awful."

A toilet cistern goes *drip, drip, drip.* Mr. Holloway clasps his head. *Exasperation?* "I've heard your song 'Darkroom.' The lyrics are . . . Well, are you admitting that the song is drawn from . . ."

Jasper knows not to guess the ends of other people's sentences.

". . . personal experiences of . . . drug-taking?"

"'Darkroom' was inspired by a young German photographer I met. She had a darkroom. Psychotropic drugs and I wouldn't mix well. I've a condition that LSD might well inflame. Amphetamines aren't *as* dangerous, but I'd drop notes, fluff lyrics, and so forth if I took them. I'm afraid I'm really rather straight."

Mr. Holloway narrows his eyes, glances around the gents, and looks back. "And, um . . . Elf?" He's sweating.

"Elf's the same."

"Ah." Mr. Holloway nods. "You are a strange fish, young man. But I'm glad we had this talk."

"If I am a strange fish, I am an honest strange fish."

The door bangs open and Griff wafts in, backward. His hair is askew, his scar is livid, and his tie is tied around his head. "King Griff'll be back," he tells at least two laughing women, "once he's sunk the *Bismarck*." The door swings shut. "Eh up, Zooto. Dean thought you'd flown off with Puff the Magic Dragon."

Mr. Holloway gapes at Griff. *Dismay?*

Mr. Holloway looks back at Jasper. *Anger?*

Mr. Holloway storms out. *Who knows?*

"What's up with him?" asks Griff. "It's a wedding, not a funeral."

UTOPIA AVENUE START their slot with "Any Way the Wind Blows." Elf sings and plays her acoustic guitar; Griff limits himself to brush-work, except for the point in the song when he got hit with the bottle at Brighton Poly—when he thumps on his bass drum, spins a stick in the air, and catches it like a bandleader. The second song is Elf's new song-in-progress, "Mona Lisa Sings the Blues." She plays it on the piano. Dean complements her bass keys while Jasper noodles a solo in the middle. The women listen closely to the lyrics, which are changing with every rehearsal. Griff takes up his sticks for a beefy "I Put a Spell on You" with Dean on vocals and Elf vamping on piano. Some of the younger guests begin dancing so the band stretch it out. Jasper plays a saxophonic solo on his Stratocaster. Looking up, he sees the bride and groom dancing. *If I was better at envy, I'd envy those two; they have their families and they have each other.* Bea is dancing, too, with a tall dark handsome student, though she looks at Jasper, who hands the solo to Dean, who plays a slapping bass run. Clive and Miranda Holloway stay seated. Jasper wishes he could read Elf's father's expression. He's placed his hand on his wife's, so maybe he's calm again. *Music connects.* The Glossops are sitting in their chairs with their arms folded, stiff and visibly disgusted even to Jasper. *Music can't connect everyone . . .*

Yet Jasper notices Don Glossop's foot tapping and, almost imperceptibly, his wife's head nodding in time to the rhythm.

Or maybe it can.

THE SOUND OF knocking Jasper heard on the cricket field during the match against Peterborough Grammar didn't reoccur that day, or the next, or the next. Jasper persuaded himself it hadn't occurred at all. Late one afternoon, the master of Swaffham House sent Jasper to the cathedral with a satchel full of sheet music for the chorister. An east wind was rising. It tore the last of the blossoms from the cherry trees and shoved Jasper along the Gallery, one of Ely's medieval streets. Up ahead, he heard a door being slammed open and shut and open and shut and open, and as he passed an archway, a wooden gate, torn loose from its hinges, bowled past him with demonic force, missing his sixteen-year-old head by no more than twelve inches, and smashed into kindling against a wall across the road. It could have snapped Jasper's neck, cracked his ribs, or staved in his skull. Shaken by the near miss, Jasper nevertheless hurried onward to the cathedral, through the great door, and into the cavernous gloom. Candles flickered. The organist wove chords. A few tourists were shuffling around, but Jasper did not pause to observe the masterpiece of medieval architecture. It was a bad evening to be out on. He walked around the cloisters to the chapter house, where the chorister had his office. He approached the door and was about to knock, when—

Knock-knock . . .

Jasper hadn't knocked, but he had heard the sound.

He looked around for an explanation.

There was no explanation. Cautiously, Jasper raised his knuckles to knock again—

Knock-knock . . .

He hadn't touched the door.

Was someone knocking on the *inside* of the door?

Why? A prank? Was this funny?

How were they timing it? There was no spyhole.

A third time Jasper readied his fist to knock.

Knock-knock . . .

Someone must be in the chorister's room.

Jasper tried the door. Stiffly, it opened.

The chorister was behind his desk, across the room, reading *The Times.* "Ah, de Zoet. You know, a chap of your manners really should know better than to enter a room without knocking . . ."

PURPLE FLAMES

DEAN STEERS THE BEAST OFF THE A2 AT THE WROTHAM ROAD roundabout. *It's a miracle we got this far.* They'd had a flat tire at Blackheath. Dean and Griff changed it while Jasper sat by the roadside. *How come the rich own the world when they're so bloody useless?* The Beast's engine is snarling. *If the carburetor's buggered, that's another fifteen quid gone, easy, on top of the fiver for a new tire.* Despite two or three gigs a week, Dean still owes Moonwhale and Selmer's Guitars an impossible number of pounds. *I had more spare cash when I worked for Mr. Craxi . . . We need a record deal, we need a hit, we need to raise our gig fee.* Past the twenty-four-hour Watling Street café, favored by long-distance truckers on the London-Dover-Continent run; past the old army barracks, mothballed for a future war; past a maze of council houses that was all fields when Dean was a boy; and over the lip of Windmill Hill, where gravity takes over and pulls the Beast down into Gravesend's spillage of roofs; its cheek-by-jowl streets, alleyways, bomb sites, building sites, cranes, the railway to Ramsgate and Margate, steeples, gasworks, the new hospital sticking up like a box, blocks of flats, and the sewage-brown Thames, where barges dock at Imperial Paper, at Smollet Engineering, at the Blue Circle Cement works and, over on the Essex side, the Tilbury power stations. Smoke from the factory chimneys hangs over this hot, still, late July afternoon.

"Welcome to Paradise," pronounces Dean.

"If you think this looks grim," says Griff, "just try Hull in the middle o' January."

"Paradise is the road to Paradise," says Jasper.

Whatever the bollocks that *means,* thinks Dean.

"It all looks very . . . authentic," says Elf.

Is she taking the piss? "Meaning?" asks Dean.

"Nothing," says Elf. "It was a pleasantry."

"Sorry it's not all lovely like Richmond."

"No, *I'm* sorry I'm such a clueless little rich girl, so out of touch with reality. I'll watch *Coronation Street* to make amends."

Dean presses the clutch and lets the Beast coast downhill. "I thought yer were taking the piss."

"Why would I?"

"It's hard to tell with yer . . ."

" 'Clueless little rich girls'?"

Dean says nothing for a bit. "I'm on edge. Sorry."

Elf huffs. "Yeah. Well. Playing for the home crowd's a big deal." The slope steepens and the Beast gains momentum. *Truth is,* thinks Dean, *I'm worried Jasper and Elf'll take one look at Nan and Bill and Ray and think,* Who are these troglodytes? *I'm worried Nan and Bill and Ray'll take one look at Jasper and Elf and think,* Christ, who are these la-di-dahs? *I'm worried we'll get booed offstage at the Captain Marlow. I'm worried we'll be a laughingstock. And most of all, the closer I get to Harry Moffat, the colder and sicker I feel . . .*

"WHAT THE BLUE bloody *fuck* are yer playing at?" Dean's dad glared down at him. The Queen Street market was in full swing and Dean's skiffle band, formed that very week, were playing "Not Fade Away." Bill and Nan Moss had organized a whip-round and bought Dean a real live Czechoslovakian Futurama for his fourteenth birthday. It stayed in tune for a whole song. Dean had already collected a few coppers in the tobacco tin. Kenny Yearwood and Stewart Kidd were singing and playing a washboard but it was Dean's band, Dean who had learned the chords, Dean who had claimed the pitch, Dean who had stopped Kenny and Stewart chickening out. Girls were watching. A few looked impressed. For the first time in months he felt more joyful than flat, sick, and gray. Until his dad arrived. "I *said,* what the blue bloody fuck are yer playing at?"

"We're only busking, Dad," Dean managed to reply.

" 'Busking'? You're *begging.*"

"No, Mr. Moffat," Kenny Yearwood began, "it's not like—"

Dean's dad pointed a single finger. "Fuck off. Both of yer."

Kenny and Stewart Kidd gave Dean a pitying glance, and went.

"What would yer mother say? Eh?"

Dean swallowed hard. "But Mum plays the piano. She—"

"At home! In private! Not where the whole world can see! Pick that up." Dean's dad scowled at the tin of coins and led him across the street to the collection box for a guide-dog charity outside Mr. Dendy's newsagents. It was colored and shaped like a black Labrador. "All of it. Every farthing." Dean had no choice. Every coin went through the slot on the dog's head. "Pull a stunt like this again, that guitar's a goner. I don't care *who* bought it yer. Am I clear?"

Dean hated his dad, hated himself for not standing up to him, and hated his dad for making him hate himself.

"AM I *CLEAR*?"

Vodka fumes and tobacco. That Harry Moffat smell.

Passersby slowed down to rubberneck.

Dean wished he could kill his dad right then.

Dean knew his Futurama was vulnerable.

Dean addressed the hollow dog: "Yes."

ELF VAMPS A piano solo in "Moon River" on Nan Moss's piano. Dean breathes in the smell of bacon fat, old carpet, old person, cat litter. Nan's entire ground floor, Dean guesses, would fit into Jasper's lounge at Chetwynd Mews. Jasper looks as relaxed as Jasper ever does, and the four generations of assembled Mosses and Moffats are more curious about than disapproving of Dean's exotic bandmates. *So far.* Griff, who grew up in a two-up-two-down, would feel at home here, but he's taken the Beast down to the Captain Marlow to set up and meet a friend from his Archie Kinnock days. White-haired and crinkled, Nan Moss hums, sways, and half sings along to "Moon River." Bill, Nan's common-law husband and no mean piano player himself, nods at Elf's style. Loud Aunt Marge and quiet Aunt Dot look on benignly. Their sister, Dean's mum, watches from her photo frame. Next along is Dean's brother, Ray, Ray's pregnant wife, Shirl, and their two-year-old, Wayne, enacting motorway crashes with his Dinky cars. Jasper sits in the corner of Nan's parlor beneath a chevron of porcelain ducks. Dean studies his flatmate. They've shared boxes of cigarettes, boxes of Durex, boxes of eggs, tubes of toothpaste, books, pints of milk, guitar strings, bottles of shampoo, colds, and Chinese takeaways . . . Sometimes he's childishly unguarded; other times, he's like an alien passing himself off as an earthling. He mentioned a breakdown he had at school, and a spell in a clinic in Holland. Dean didn't probe. It felt wrong. He isn't even sure if Jasper's detachment from the real world is a cause or a scar of those days.

Elf ends "Moon River" with a spangly glissando.

The small audience pays her in warm applause.

Wayne smashes a car into a truck and says, "Ka*booom!*"

"Oh," says Nan Moss, "that was lovely, weren't it, Bill?"

"Bloomin' lovely. How long've yer been playing, Elf?"

"Since I was five. My grandmother taught me."

"Start 'em young," says Nan Moss. " 'Moon River' was our Vi's favorite. Dean's mum. She and Marge and Dot all played piano, but it was Vi who took to it."

"If you shut your eyes just now," says Aunt Marge, "it might've been Vi playing. That fiddly bit in the middle, 'specially."

"In another life," says Aunt Dot, "Vi could've been something, I reckon. Musically, I mean."

"Dean inherited her gift all right," says Aunt Marge.

"Mustn't let this steak-and-kidney pud get cold, eh?" says Bill. Aunts Dot and Marge set about dishing up the food.

"Can the audience hear a piano," Ray asks Elf, "with thousands o' girls screaming and throwing their knickers at God's Gift there?" He nods at Dean.

"The knicker-throwing hasn't started yet," says Elf. "Once he's been on *Top of the Pops,* maybe. Acoustics depend on the venue, mics, amps. We have a Farfisa keyboard in the van. I have a Hammond as well, but it weighs a ton. They both pack quite a wallop."

"Don't it take a lot o' nerve"—Shirl's putting on Wayne's bib—"getting up onstage in front of a crowd of strangers?"

"I suppose," says Elf. "But either you get used to stage fright, or you stop. Nan, that's oodles."

"An army marches on its stomach," says the matriarch. "Right. If we're all served . . ." Everyone clasps their hands. Nan says grace: "For what we are about to receive, may the Lord make us truly grateful. Amen." Everyone joins in the "Amen" and eats. Dean thinks how food, like music, brings people together.

"This pie is perfection," states Jasper, as if assessing a solo.

"Serves up a juicy compliment, this one," says Aunt Marge.

"Actually," states Dean. "He doesn't. He says it as he sees it."

"My nose is a mouth." Wayne shoves a carrot up a nostril.

"Wayne, that's revolting," says Shirl. "Take it out."

"But yer said I can't pick my nose at the table."

"Ray, tell him."

"Do as yer mother says." Ray manages not to laugh.

Wayne sticks his little finger up his nostril. "It's up further." Now it's less funny. "It's stuck!" He sneezes the carrot out at high velocity onto Dean's plate. Even Shirl sees the funny side.

"So, who'll dish the dirt on the teenage Dean?" asks Elf.

"Oh, Lordy," says Bill. "How many hours do we have?"

"Yer'd need days," says Ray, "just to scrape the surface."

"Lies, lies, lies," says Dean. "More lies."

"Ah, but who's the rock 'n' roll rebel now, eh?" Ray forks a lump of kidney. "And who's the responsible husband?"

Only 'cause yer shot yer tapioca up Shirl's muff when her eggs were ripe. Dean picks up Wayne's spoon from the floor.

"It wasn't easy for Dean," says Nan Moss, "after his mum passed away. Wasn't easy for anyone. His father had a . . ."

"A bit of a rough patch," offers Bill, catching Dean's eye.

"Exactly." Nan continues: "Ray left to do his apprenticeship at Dagenham, and Dean moved back in with his dad, at the old house on Peacock Street, but that didn't work out. So Dean moved in with me and Bill here, for three years or so, while he was at Ebbsfleet College of Art. We were *that* proud."

"But instead o' becoming the next Picasso," says Ray, "he turned into the guitar genius we know 'n' love."

"*He's* the guitar genius." Dean jerks his thumb at Jasper. "Yer were there at the Marquee, Ray."

"If I can play," says Jasper, "it's because I practiced in lieu of living. It's not a method I recommend."

"To achieve anything in this world," says Bill, "yer've got to put the work in. Talent's not enough. Yer need discipline too."

"Dean did some smashing art," says Aunt Marge. "That's his, above the radio." Everyone looks at Dean's print of the jetty at Whitstable. "His heart was always in the music, mind. He'd be up in his room, doing his tunes until he got them note-perfect."

"Like now." Jasper spears a runner bean. "Lesser bassists go *oompa-oompa,* like a tuba player. Dean does these fluid runs"—he puts down his fork to mime it—"*bam-bam-bi-dambi-dambi, bam-bam-bi-dambi-dam.* He plays bass like a rhythm guitar. It's great." Jasper eats the bean.

Dean's a little embarrassed by this factual praise.

"See that shield?" Nan points to a trophy and recites the inscription: " 'Best Band, Gravesend 1964—The Gravediggers.' That was Dean's group. We'll dig out the photo albums later."

"Ooo, the photo albums." Elf rubs her hands.

A motorbike thunders by, rattling teacups on the dresser. "That's that Jack Costello," grumbles Aunt Marge. "Puts his boy Vinny in the sidecar, treats the town like his private racetrack."

"Yer won't mind my asking, Jasper," says Aunt Marge, "but are you posh? Yer dead well-spoken. Like a BBC announcer."

"I was raised by my aunt in Lyme Regis until I was six. She kept a boarding house and money was always tight. But then I went to a boarding school in Ely, which is very posh indeed. Unfortunately, a toff's accent is no guarantee of a toff's bank balance."

"How could yer aunt afford a posh school?" asks Bill.

"My father's family—the de Zoets—stepped in. They're Dutch."

Aunt Marge adjusts her dentures. "And they're wealthy, are they, Jasper, if yer don't mind my asking?"

"Can we spare the poor lad the third degree?" asks Dean.

"Oh, he doesn't mind, do yer, Jasper?" says Aunt Marge.

Jasper appears not to. "I'd describe the de Zoets of Zeeland as rich, rather than wealthy."

"Aren't rich and wealthy the same thing?" asks Shirl.

"The rich know how much money they have. The wealthy have so much, they're never wholly sure."

"Where was yer mother in all of this?" asks Aunt Marge.

"My mother died when I was born."

The women tut sympathetically. "Poor love," says Aunt Marge. "At least Ray and Dean knew their mum. Having no memories of her at all, that must be tough. Yer should've warned us, Dean."

"I warned yer not to give him the third degree."

Nan's cuckoo clock cuckoos seven times.

"It can't be seven o'clock already," says Elf.

"Funny stuff, is time," observes Aunt Dot.

DEAN WAS FIFTEEN. Cancer and morphine had half erased his mother. He dreaded the visits to her ward and he knew that dreading them made him the worst son in England. Death turned every other topic into a futile evasion, yet how can people who aren't dying discuss death with people who are? It was a Sunday morning. Ray was in Dagenham. Dean's dad was doing overtime at the cement depot. Nan Moss and the aunts were at church. Dean never saw the point of church. "God works in mysterious ways" seemed no different from "Heads I win, tails you lose." If prayer worked, Dean's mum wouldn't be dying. Dean had come to the hospital with his Futurama. His mother was asleep when he arrived, so Dean practiced quietly. He worked through a tricky picked arrangement of "The Tennessee Waltz." When he got to the end, a fragile voice said, "That's nice, love."

Dean looked up. "I've been practicing."

A ghost of a smile. "Good lad."

"Sorry if I woke yer."

"There's no nicer way to be woken."

"Do yer want to hear another one?"

" 'Play it again, Sam.' "

So Dean stuck with "The Tennessee Waltz." The son focused on the fretboard, and missed the exact moment his mother slipped away . . .

JASPER PLAYS A pyrotechnic solo at the end of "Smithereens." Elf lays down glowing slabs of Hammond chords. Griff is drumming thunder and lightning. Dean's fingers, not Dean, are playing his bass runs, letting Dean look out over two hundred heads in the annex of the Captain Marlow. He glimpses friends who want to see him succeed; one-time rivals who hope he crashes and burns; older men who see in the band something they once had, or once could have had; young men out on the piss and the pull; girls with Camparis and Babychams and cigarettes; and Dean thinks, *Gravesend, yer punched my face, yer kicked my balls, yer told me I was useless, a joke, a tosser, a fairy, but LISTEN to Utopia bloody Avenue. We're getting bloody good and behind that scowl, that sneer, yer know it.* There'll be a few of Harry Moffat's cronies out there. *You tell him we set this place on fire.* Jasper reaches the end of round one. Dean looks over and, as he expected, Jasper keeps his eyes on his Strat's fretboard to signal that he wants another round. Most people have never heard a wah-wah pedal played live, and Jasper's mastery of the gadget is stupendous. *I'll take credit for the song, mind, thank yer very much.* A couple of practices ago, Elf suggested changing the lyrics from "All dreams end as smithereens" to "Smithereens are seeds of dreams." Dean tried it, and the song's gone from being a downer to an upper. Jasper suggested Elf sing harmony on that one "seeds of dreams" line: and everyone in the room, Pavel Z included, groaned with pleasure. Toward the end of his time in Battleship Potemkin, Dean gave up sharing his songs; that band always made the songs worse. Utopia Avenue is the opposite. The band is a song-refining machine.

Jasper's coming down from his solo; Dean looks at Griff who nods; four bars to go . . . three bars to go . . . two . . . one . . . and an *Okay* look from Elf . . . and Jasper pauses—they all count off a shared clock—*one, two, three, four*—and smash the ending into drummed, pounded, plucked, twanged molecules . . .

. . .

APPLAUSE IS THE *purest drug,* thinks Dean. He wipes his face on a cloth beer mat and slurps his pint of Smithwick's. "Cheers, everyone." The applause goes on and on. There's less velveteen on view than you get at a London gig, more plain shirts, denim, and flat caps. The Captain Marlow is a both-fish-and-fowl pub. It's just a few doors down from the Gravesend Working Men's Club and the first good pub the men from Blue Circle Cement reach with their pay packets. A hipper crowd—by Gravesend standards—is lured in with pinball, a jukebox, and a live act twice a month. Off to one side, Levon is standing with a man Dean doesn't know. *If he's a boyfriend, they'd better be bloody careful.* The applause is subsiding, and Dean leans into the mic. "Thanks for coming out, and thanks to Dave and Sylv for having us." He peers at the bar at the back where Dave Sykes, the teddy-bear-faced landlord, waves back. "I'm Dean Moss, I'm Gravesend born 'n' bred, so if I still owe anyone a fiver from when I skipped town, I'll pay yer back after the show"—Dean tightens his G-peg—"if yer lend me a tenner first."

Griff fires off a comedy *Psssh . . . ta-boom!*

"So here's the band: on keyboards, Miss Elf Holloway!"

Elf plays the intro to Beethoven's Fifth on the Hammond. A genius calls out, "Yer can play with my organ anytime, darlin'!"

"Sorry"—Elf uses her stock reply—"but I don't play on toy instruments." Griff does another *Psssh . . . ta-boom!*

"On drums," says Dean, "from the People's Republic of Yorkshire: Peter 'Griff' Griffin—or, for short, Griff!"

Applause. Griff performs a drum explosion; stands and bows.

"On guitar," says Dean, "Mr.—Jasper—de *Zoet*!" Jasper wah-wahs the final line of "God Save the Queen." Applause.

Someone calls out, "Jasper the fuckin' Fairy, more like!"

Jasper steps forward, shields his eyes, and scans the crowd for the heckler. "Who's talking to me?"

"Over 'ere!" The heckler waves. "Get a fackin' haircut!"

Shit, thinks Dean, *here comes Brighton Poly part two.*

Jasper peers closer. "What? And look like *you*?" He said the first thing that came into his head, but even the heckler's laughing.

Dean hurries things along while the going's still good. "This next one's by Jasper. It's called 'Wedding Presence,' and a-*one* and a-*two* and a-one two *three*—"

NEXT UP IS Dean's old song "Seemed Like a Good Idea at the Time," a gutsy, rootsy "Mona Lisa Sings the Blues," Booker T.'s "Green Onions," "Darkroom," a ten-minute "Abandon Hope"—by the end the whole room is yelling out, *"I'll rip-rip-rip your heart out, just like you ripped mine"* as if they've known it for years—"A Raft and a River," an Animals-esque "House of the Rising Sun," a beefed-up "Any Way the Wind Blows," and the Beatles' "Day Tripper" sung by Elf with all the "she's" turned into "he's." For a second encore they play the Gravediggers' best song, "Six Feet Under," penned by Dean when he was seventeen. Dean's two fears—that the trippiness of Jasper's songs would be lost on the brown ale crowd, or that Gravesend wouldn't let Elf play without bombarding her with smutty heckles—don't come to pass, and when Dave Sykes switches on the houselights Dean is sweaty, his voice is croaky, and his fingertips are raw, but he's high on the gig. Dean, Jasper, Elf, Levon, and Griff make an impromptu rugby scrum by the drum kit.

"Lads, we fookin' *stormed* it!" states Griff.

"You can say that again," says Elf.

"Lads, we fookin' stormed it," repeats Griff.

"That is *such* a corny gag," says Elf.

"Sensational," says Levon. "Something'll happen soon. You can't play *that* well and word not get out."

I bloody well hope so, thinks Dean.

"Your turn, Jasper," says Elf.

Everyone looks at Jasper. "To do what?"

"Say how you fookin' *feel,* you nonce," says Griff.

Jasper considers. "I feel . . . we're getting better?"

THEIR CIRCLE OF five is entered and dispersed by the world. "Yer'll be paying me back that fiver any day soon," says Kenny Yearwood.

Dean says, "Believe me, I cannot wait."

"If Mum could've seen yer," says Ray, "she'd be so proud."

"She did see it, love," says Aunt Marge, pinching Dean's cheek.

More encounters with old classmates, teachers, and people from Dean's old life continue until, after a couple of pints, a girl comes up. "You won't remember me," she begins, "but—"

"Jude. Brighton Poly. Yer lent Elf a guitar. How are yer?"

She's pleased. "You need a record deal. Right now."

"I've written to Santa," says Dean. "Fingers crossed."

"It's only July. But have you been naughty or nice?"

Flirty flirty. "How's Gaz? Was that his name?"

"I do not know and I do not care to know."

Praise be the Lord. "I'm dead sorry to hear that."

"Yeah, I bet you are."

Dean inhales her perfume. "What're yer doing here?"

"My brother likes his music, and he said a band called Utopia Avenue was playing. My ears pricked up, and hey presto."

"I'm amazed yer bothered after the last time."

"I wouldn't have missed it for the world."

Shanks pops up behind her, signaling that they need to go.

Dean signals for two more minutes. "Me and Jasper are staying over at a friend's here in town. D'yer want to . . . ?"

My my, say Jude's lifted eyebrows. "One step at a time, Speedy Gonzales. My brother's driving me back to Brighton. I've got a job at a cosmetics wholesalers. But . . ." she waves a folded-up square of paper, ". . . if you're free—as in *not seeing anyone else*—here's my work number. You'll have to pretend to be a customer or my boss'll get suspicious. Plus, that's written on *Mission: Impossible* paper that'll turn to dust in forty-eight hours." She reaches inside Dean's jacket and slips the paper in. She gives him a peck on the cheek. "Call me. Or repent at your leisure. Seriously—the band's great. You're going to be famous."

SHANKS PUTS THE nozzle to his mouth and smoke curls down the hookah's neck—*bubble, bubble, toil and trouble*—and into his well-tanned lungs . . . and out, in clouds of cauliflower.

"Are these things legal?" Kenny asks.

Shanks mimes the scales of justice. "The apparatus, yes. The herbal cocktail in the vase might excite the fuzz. I pay insurance." A long and living hush unfurls. Jim Morrison sings about The End. "Oy, Deano—are we doing okay?"

"Very," says Dean. He takes the nozzle's nipple, squeezes it between his lips, thinks of Jude, and . . . *Suck it up, bubbly-bubble, here it comes, now hold it in* . . . And lets it out again. "It's . . . like . . ." *Words are failing me tonight.* "Breastfeeding plus levitation."

Brother Ray rocks with laughter. Not a sound comes out.

"You 'n' Jasper," Kenny says, "are like a married couple."

Jasper's face reminds Dean of Stan Laurel's as he thinks this through. "Let's not go there." He sucks upon the nozzle. The hookah's nothing new to him. Jasper lived in Amsterdam.

Dean asks, "Would they dig us over in Amsterdam?"

Jasper's words reverberate a bit ahead of time. "First we need a record deal. Otherwise, it's amateur hour."

Our end-o'-the-rainbow record deal. Dean feels lost in space and needs to take his bearings. Shanks's flat above his shop, the fabled Magic Bus. The wee small hours. Who's who? Yours truly; Shanks the Shanks; his lady friend called Piper; brother Ray; Kenny Yearwood; Jasper and a girl who just appeared, post-gig, with clear designs on Herr de Zoet. She says her name is Ivy. The six of them are motionless. A Rembrandt. *See? I know art.* Painted by the candle's brush upon the living dark . . .

. . . TILL SHANKS DISPELS the Rembrandt spell with a flutter-by of words. "You four were something else tonight. Out of this freaking world! One o' these days soon, I'll be shooting off my mouth, 'Oh, yeah, yeah, me 'n' Dean Moss go back—we saw Little Richard—I taught him his first chords . . .' Those songs! 'Darkroom,' 'Smithereens,' 'Mona Lisa' . . . each one could be a hit. Don't you reckon, Piper?"

"FM radio in Seattle would eat you with a spoon."

"I hope it happens soon. I ain't got a pot to piss in."

Jasper isn't listening. His ear is being whispered in by Ivy, Ivy, Ivy. He looks at Shanks, who reads his mind. "Spare room's down the landing, kids. It's only got a single bed. Daresay that'll do you." Ivy leaves, the way cats do, dissolving into shadow. Dean makes sure Jude's number's safe. *It's still here in my jacket.*

Brother Ray warns Jasper, "Mate, I'm impressed. My cock's as stoned as I am." Jasper shrugs.

"A word o' warning," pipes up Kenny, "a scientific fact. Gravesend girls are eggs on legs—all you do is sneeze on one and suddenly they're three months late, the family's banging down yer door, all calling you the daddy. Ray here knows of what I speak."

Ray mimes the hangman's noose. Ray takes the holy nozzle . . . and expels a genie, limb by smoking limb. "Make sure yer wear a thingie. Yer came prepared, I hope?"

Jasper does a Scout's salute and follows after Ivy.

"What 'bout you?" Ray's asking him. "Getting any oats?"

Piper floats away. "Think I'll retire discreetly, boys, to spare my virgin blushes—see you in the morning."

Stoned Dean takes another toke—*Suck it in, bubbly-bubbly, hold it and release*—and hopes the topic's gone away.

"What 'bout you?" Ray's asking him. "Getting any oats?"

Anything for a quiet life. "Not much. There was a girl from St. John's Wood at Elf's sister's wedding. We had a weekend at her place. That's all for June."

"Yer jammy git," says Kenny. "All Tracy ever says is, 'No engagement ring, no sex—what bit don't yer understand?' I should just drop her now, but her dad's my boss. Utter bloody nightmare."

It's Ray's turn: "Some days are good. I like being a dad. Mostly when Wayne's unconscious. But Shirl's a moody cow, as often as not. I had more crumpet when I was single. Every day she's turning more into her mother. Marriage is a prison, funded by the prisoners. What d'yer reckon, Shanks? Yer've been through the grinder twice."

Shanks puts the Doors back into their sleeve and puts on the Velvet Underground. "Marriage is an anchor, lads. Stops you drifting onto rocks, but stops you voyaging as well."

The first track on side one, "Sunday Morning," pulls Dean up inside it. Nico's half a note off-key but sounds the better for it.

Ray sits up and asks, "Who's Elf seeing, then?" Dean's too relaxed to answer. Ray gently kicks Dean's foot. "Who's Elf seeing?"

Dean lifts his head. "Some projectionist, in Leicester Square."

Kenny asks, "Have you or Griff or Jasper ever had a nibble?"

"Elf? *Jesus,* Kenny, *no.* It'd be like shagging yer sister."

Now Kenny sits up. "Yer *what*? *You*'ve been shagging Jackie?"

THE HOOKAH'S SPELL is fading. Dean lies where he lies on Shanks's Turkish carpet. He remembers his father telling him, "Yer've stayed at yer nan's for long enough. High time yer came back home." He told Nan Moss, "Thanks for all yer've done, but Dean belongs with me. Vi'd agree, God bless her soul." Who could object to that? He moved back in on New Year's Day. His mum had died in September. As winter turned to spring, his list of jobs grew longer. Cooking, shopping, cleaning, laundry, ironing, polishing the shoes. Everything his mum once did. "The world don't owe yer a living," his father said, "any more'n I do." Harry Moffat had always liked his drink, but Dean was shocked to see him drink a bottle of Morning Star a day—a cheap and nasty vodka. He functioned fine. No one guessed. Not the neighbors, no one at work. His dad was still a charming rogue once he left the house. At Peacock Road, "bad" slid into "worse." He made rules. Impossible rules. Rules that always shifted. If Dean stayed out, he was dossing around. If Dean stayed in, he was sat on his arse. If Dean didn't speak, he was a stroppy shit. If Dean spoke, he was lippy. "Hit me, then, if yer fancy a pop. Go on. Let's see what happens." Dean never dared. Father press-ganged son into his noble-widower act. Dean had to stow the empty bottles in a different bin each day. Answering the phone was Dean's job too. If his dad was blotto, he'd say, "He's just popped out." Dean did what was necessary, exactly like his mother. He lied to Ray. "Yeah, can't complain, how's Dagenham?" What was Ray supposed to do? Give up his apprenticeship? Try to reason with the man? If reason worked on alcoholics, there'd be no alcoholics. But when Dean started art school, something had to give . . .

. . .

BONFIRE NIGHT. DEAN was sixteen. He came back from a firework party at Ebbsfleet and found his father frowning over the *Mirror* on the kitchen table. The day's bottle of Morning Star was empty.

Dean just said, "Evening."

"Give the boy a prize."

Dean drew the kitchen curtains, noticing a small bonfire in the garden incinerator where they burned rubbish, leaves, and weeds, usually on a Saturday. That day was a Friday. "Had a bonfire, I see."

"Some old shite needed burning."

"I'll say g'night, then."

Dean's father turned the page.

Dean went upstairs to his room—and noticed the sickening absences, one by one, like punches to his gut. His Futurama guitar. His Dansette. His *Teach Yourself Guitar* books. His signed photo of Little Richard. Dean heard the bonfire crackle.

He rushed downstairs, past the man who'd done this, and out into the frosty air to see what could be salvaged . . .

The bonfire was burning nicely. Only the Futurama's fretboard remained, its varnish bubbling. Purple flames licked its neck. The Dansette was a spindle and blackened Bakelite. The books were sheets of ash. The signed photograph of Little Richard was gone. Dean's dad had added lumps of coal and a few firelighters. The purple flames toasted Dean's face. The smoke was oily and toxic.

Dean went back inside. "Why?" His voice shook.

"Why what?" Dean's father still didn't look up.

"What was the point o' that?"

"Till now yer've been a work-shy long-haired pansy with a guitar. Now yer just a work-shy long-haired pansy. That's"—Dean's dad looked up—"a step in the right direction."

Dean got his rucksack and packed his nine albums, twenty singles, a packet of guitar strings, his birthday cards from Mum, his best clothes, mock crocs, photo album, and his notebook of songs. He said goodbye to his old room for the last time and went downstairs. Before he could undo the chain, a force hurled him down the hall. Dean's ear smacked into a doorframe. Footsteps approached on the lino. Dean slid himself vertical. "What? Yer going to keep me locked up here?"

"No son of mine's a guitar-twanging fairy faggot."

Dean looked into the hard eyes and hated them. Was his dad in there? Was the vodka talking? "Yer dead right, Harry Moffat."

"Yer *what*?"

"I'm not yer son. Yer not my father. I'm off. Now."

"Piss and wind. It's high time yer stopped fannying about with art 'n' music 'n' this shit and got yerself a *real* job. Like Ray. I warned yer, but now I've—I've—I've *taken action.* Yer'll thank me for it."

"I'm thanking yer now. Yer've opened my eyes, Harry Moffat."

"Say that again—once again—and by fuck you'll regret it."

"Which bit, Harry Moffat? The I'm-not-yer-son bit, or—"

Dean's jaw cracked, his skull smacked the wall; his body thudded; and he came to on the lino. He tasted blood. Pain in his skull and jaw tapped in time with his pulse. He looked up.

Harry Moffat looked down. "See what yer made me do?"

Dean got up. He checked his mouth in the mirror. A cut lip, blood, a mashed gum. "Is that what yer used to tell Mum? When yer hit her? '*See what yer made me do*'?"

Harry Moffat's sneer was gone.

"No secrets in Gravesend. The whole town knows. '*There goes Harry Moffat, beat his wife like a carpet, she got cancer and she died.*' Never to yer face. But they know."

Dean undid the chain and stepped into the November night.

"I'm *done* with yer!" shouted Harry Moffat. "Yer hear me?"

Dean kept walking. Curtains were twitching.

Peacock Street smelt of frost and fireworks.

SEVEN YEARS AND a quarter of a mile away, Dean wakes to the sound of rain and Kenny snoring on the sofa. Someone has put a cushion under Dean's head. Ray's in the armchair, asleep. The hookah is surrounded by glasses, bottles, ashtrays, peanut shells, cards. Dean pads into the kitchen for a mug of water. Gravesend water tastes less soapy than London water. He sits at the table and munches a Jacob's cracker. From its high shelf, a spider-plant has unfurled tendrils over a tapestry of a god with an elephant's head and a photo of Shanks and Piper somewhere foreign and sunny. The furthest Dean's ever been from Gravesend was a Battleship Potemkin gig in Wolverhampton. His share of the cut was less than a pound. He would have earned more busking at Hyde Park Corner. *Is Utopia Avenue a cul-de-sac? We were good last night, but that was a home match . . . What if nobody wants us?* Roofs step down from Queen Street to the river. Tugs pull a freighter out of Tilbury Docks. As the freighter's middle section clears the hospital, its name is revealed to Dean a letter at a time—STAR OF RIGA. Shanks's Gibson acoustic sits on the chair opposite. Dean tunes it and, accompanied only by the hiss of rain and his own thoughts, he lets his fingers strum and pick . . .

"One o' yours?" Ray stands in the doorway of Shanks's kitchen.

Dean looks up. "Hmm?"

"That tune."

"Just something I'm messing about with."

Ray drinks a mug of water. "Aunt Marge was right, Mum'd be *that* proud. It'd be ' 'Course, *Dean always was the artistic one.*' "

"It's you she'd be proud of. ' 'Course, *Ray always was the one who applied himself.*' She'd spoil Wayne rotten, too."

Ray sits down. "Are you 'n' Dad going to bury the hatchet?"

Dean plays a discordant twang. "He's the original hatcheter." A droplet of rain runs down the window. "Bill's been more of a dad to me. You, too. And Shanks."

"I'm not trying to excuse him, but he's lost everything."

"We've been here before, Ray. '*It's the vodka's fault,*' '*His dad slapped his mum 'n' him about too,*' '*He went through hell watching Mum die,*' '*Refusing to call him "Dad" is a childish grudge that's eating me up.*' Miss anything?"

"No. But if he could unburn yer guitar, he would."

"Told yer that himself, did he?"

Ray makes a face. "He's not a man to discuss his feelings."

"Stop. This isn't a grudge. It's consequences. If yer want him in yer life, great. Bully for you. That's yer choice. I don't want him in mine. That's *my* choice. End o' story. Just . . . stop."

"Men his age can and do drop dead. 'Specially if their liver's fucked. The dead can't sign peace treaties. And he's still yer dad."

The dead can't sign peace treaties, thinks Dean. *Good line.* "Genetically, legally, yeah, he's my father. In every other sense, he's not. I've a brother, a nephew, Nan, Bill, two aunts, but not a dad."

Ray heaves out a long sigh. Drains gurgle.

Shanks's phone in the hallway starts ringing.

Dean doesn't answer: Shanks is a man with fingers in many pies and any pie might be calling. Their host's bedroom door opens, and his footsteps thud up the hallway. "Yeah?" A long pause. "Yeah, he is . . . Yeah . . . Who shall I say is calling?" Shanks appears in the doorway. "Dean, son. It's yer manager."

"LEVON? HOW DID you know I was here?"

"The Dark Arts. Is Jasper there?"

"Sort of. He's with a girl."

"I need both of you at Denmark Street."

"But it's Sunday morning."

"I know. Griff and Elf are on their way."

This sounds like urgent bad news. "What's happened?"

"Victor French happened."

"Who's Victor French?"

"The A&R scout for Ilex Records. He was at the Captain Marlow last night. He wants to sign Utopia Avenue."

He wants to sign Utopia Avenue. Six little words.

I have a future after all. Shanks's hallway is listening.

"Hello?" Levon sounds worried. "Still there?"

"I am," says Dean. "I heard. That's . . . Bloody hell."

"Don't buy your Triumph Spitfire yet. Victor's putting in an offer for three singles, then an album, if—*if*—interest builds. Ilex isn't one of the Big Four, but it's a solid offer. Being a middle-sized fish in a small pond could work better for the band than being a tadpole in a lake. Victor wanted to sign you last night, but I pushed for more money and told him EMI were sniffing. He called his boss in Hamburg this morning for approval—and it's a yes."

"Yer never told us last night's gig was an audition."

"No good manager would. Get dressed, get Jasper, get on the next train to Charing Cross, get to Moonwhale. We've got details to discuss ahead of a meeting at Ilex tomorrow."

"Okay, see yer. Uh, thanks."

"Any time. Oh—and, Dean?"

"Yeah?"

"Congratulations. You've earned this."

Dean hangs up. The phone pings.

We've got a bloody record deal.

"Mate?" His big brother appears from the kitchen, looking concerned. "Yer okay? Yer look like someone's died."

THE PLATFORM ROOF drips. The mouth of the tunnel drips. Signage, cables, and signals drip. Pigeons huddle on the dripping girders of the dripping footbridge. The platform is an archipelago of damp patches between puddles. Dean's right foot's wet. He has to take his boots back to the cobbler. *No,* Dean realizes. *No, I don't. I'll walk into Anello and Davide in Covent Garden and I'll say, "Hi, I'm Dean Moss, I'm in Utopia Avenue, we just signed with Ilex Records, so kindly show me the best bloody boots yer've got."* Dean snorts a laugh.

"What's funny?" asks Jasper.

"My mind keeps wandering off, and I sort o' forget, and I think, *Why am I feeling so fantastic?* Then I remember—*Oh, yeah, that's it, we've got a record deal!*—and it all goes *boom!* again."

"It is good news," agrees Jasper.

"West Ham winning three–nil away at Arsenal is 'good news.' Getting a contract is . . . *orgasmic* news. And *you* get it on top of a real orgasm. Yer should be in a state o' rapture."

"I guess so." He opens his packet of Marlboros. "Two left."

They light up. "I'm half-afraid," says Dean, "I'll wake up on Shanks's floor and this'll all be a hookah dream."

Jasper holds out his hand. Raindrops splash on his palm. "That's not dream-rain. It's too wet."

"Expert in these matters, are yer?"

"Unfortunately, yes."

Dean looks up the London-bound railway tracks. He thinks of his younger selves, gazing up the same tracks toward a formless future. He'd like to send a telegram back in time: *You'll be ripped off, mugged, and shat on, but Utopia Avenue's waiting for yer. Hang on in there.* The tracks quiver. "Here comes the train."

DEAN AND JASPER have their own window seats. Dean looks out onto the far platform, into the waiting room for eastbound trains, and sees Harry Moffat sitting by the window. He's reading a paper. Before Dean can hide, Harry Moffat looks up and stares straight back. Not maliciously, not accusingly, not mockingly, not despairingly, not imploringly. It's a simple "Yes, I see you"—like a telephonist putting through a call. Harry Moffat can't have planned this encounter. Dean didn't know he was going to be on this train until ten minutes ago. Why is Harry Moffat traveling to Margate on a rainy Sunday morning in July? A holiday? Harry Moffat doesn't do holidays. Harry Moffat returns to his paper . . . and at this angle, Dean can no longer swear it's him. They are, after all, two rainy windowpanes and twenty rainy yards apart. There's an undeniable resemblance—the glasses, the posture, the thick dark hair, but . . . *it might not be.* The London-bound train tenses, takes the strain, and heaves away. The man does not look up again.

"What is it?" asks Jasper.

Gravesend station slides into the past.

"Someone I thought I knew."

UNEXPECTEDLY

LEVON'S PARKED CAR WAS HOT AND AIRLESS. ELF YAWNED and checked her makeup in her hand-mirror. *It's running.* "Is it Thursday?"

A concrete mixer rumbled by, churning fumes and dust.

"Friday." Dean lay in the backseat, his notebook open on his chest. "Oxford tonight. Southend tomorrow. Don't look now. It's Lovely Rita, Meter Maid." A traffic warden walked past, examining the meter. Dean called, "Lovely day." She did not reply.

Elf yawned again. "Last time Bruce and I did a gig at Oxford, a student accused us of looting songs from the proletariat. Bruce told him he grew up having to walk through snake-infested bush to an outdoors dunny every time he needed to take a shit, so Oxford Varsity Boy could kiss his arse."

"Huh." Dean was only half listening.

Elf wondered what Bruce was doing at that very second. *Who cares? I've got Angus.* "So. Oxford tonight. Southend tomorrow."

"Southend tomorrow."

"Ever played there?"

Dean wrote something in his notebook. "Once. With Battleship Potemkin. At the Studio at Westcliff. Lots of mods. They hated us, so here's hoping they don't recognize me."

Elf switched on the car radio: "Even the Bad Times Are Good" by the Tremeloes was playing. "Why's this at number fifteen when 'Darkroom' is nowhere? It's rubbish."

"Airplay, airplay, airplay. The piano part's pretty good."

"Where's *our* airplay? 'Darkroom' 's piano part is incredible."

"If you do say so yourself."

"I do."

"It's a chicken 'n' egg thing. If we don't climb up the charts, we don't get airplay. If you don't get airplay, no chart entry."

"What do other bands do?"

Dean rested his notebook on his chest. "Sleep with DJs. Have a record label rich enough to pay the stations. Write a song so irresistible that it practically plays itself."

Elf turned the radio dial, finding the final bars of the summer's biggest hit. The DJ rounded it off: "Scott McKenzie, still going to San Francisco, and still wearing flowers in his hair. You're tuned to *The Bat Segundo Show* on Radio Bluebeard one-nine-eight long wave, brought to you by Denta-dazzle gum, now in triple mint *and* fruity toot. Time for one more summer sizzler. Stevie Wonder's 'I Was Made to Love Her.' Weren't we all, Mr. Wonder?"

Elf switched the radio off and sighed.

"What's wrong with Stevie Wonder?" asked Dean.

"Every time it's not us I feel sick."

Dean screwed the cup-lid off his Thermos and poured himself a cupful of cold water. "Thirsty?"

"Parched. Which side have you drunk from?"

"No idea." Dean handed it through the gap between the seats. "What's a spot of oral herpes between bandmates?"

"When did you become an expert on oral herpes?"

"No comment."

Elf drank. A guy and a girl rode past on a scooter. "How did Jasper and Griff wriggle out of these courtesy calls again?"

Dean sighed through his nose. "Griff, by being so rude Levon doesn't dare send him. Jasper, by sounding like he's on drugs."

"So you and I are being punished for being polite and sane."

"Me, I'd rather be doing this with you than stuck in the belly of the Beast with Griff, lugging the gear round."

A lunchtime lollipop lady took up position on the pelican crossing and directed a crocodile of infants across the road.

The nib of Dean's pen scratched his notebook.

Elf asked, "Still doing those lyrics?"
"When you're not asking me stuff."
"Can I take a look? I'm *booo*ooo*ooo*oored . . ."
Dean surrendered and handed her the notebook.

Fireworks split the sky at night
A hundred rockets screamed and fell.
You swung the axe with all your might
at my guitar and gave it hell.

My record player was next to catch
it. Little Richard had to pay.
You poured on paraffin, one match
lit—awop-bop-a-loola-awop-bam-bay.

Elf smiled at that and Dean asked, "What? What?"
"Good line. '*Awop-bop-a-loola.*' "
Dean looked relieved. "What d'yer think 'bout—"
"Ssh. Let me finish."

Hope that bonfire in the garden
still burns purple in your eyes,
still turns my future into carbon,
still smolders, your November prize.

"Don't dream bigger than I do."
"You are what I say you are."
"You'll do what I tell you to." Go
tell your friend, the morning star.

"An X-ray of the soul," said Elf. "Is it about your dad?"
"Uh, not exactl—uh . . . kind o' . . . Yeah."
"Do you have a title yet?"
"I was thinking about 'Still Burning.' "
Not great, thought Elf, scanning the lines.
"Don't yer like it? Have yer got a better one?"

Elf scanned the lines. "What about 'Purple Flames'?"

Dean thought. An articulated lorry rumbled by. "Maybe."

"You've deployed trochaic tetrameter, I see."

"I've got some ointment for that, but you can't have sex for a week after the symptoms have cleared up."

Elf tapped the page. "*Dum*-dah *dum*-dah *dum*-dah *dum*-dah. '*Hope* that *bon*fire *in* the *gar*den.' A '*dum*-dah' is a trochee. The word '*tro*chee' is also a trochee, which proves Greeks were show-offs. The word iamb—a 'dah-*dum*'—is also an iamb. Your lines are four trochees long—fiddly bits aside—so it's a trochaic tetrameter."

"So that's what yer learn in posh schools." Dean put a fruit pastille in his mouth and offered her the tube.

Elf took one. Lemon. "At the *poshest* posh schools—like Jasper's—you study meter in Latin and Greek. Not just English."

"At the *shittest* shit schools—like mine—yer study smoking, skiving, dodging shit, and petty theft."

"Crucial skills for the Great British workplace." Elf reread the lyrics. Lemony saliva floods her mouth. "No chorus, no bridge?"

"Not sure if it needs one. If an X-ray of the soul has a catchy chorus, is it still an X-ray of the soul?"

" 'Tell your friend, the morning star.' It's lonely."

"Morning Star vodka was Harry Moffat's main food source."

Dean tended to veer away from discussion of fathers, but Elf sensed that a locked door was ajar. "If he ever got in touch—if, say, we end up recording that song . . . what *would* you do?"

Dean didn't reply for a while. "I've spotted him in Gravesend, now 'n' then. Sat in a barber's. At the market. Waiting for a train. But I just blank him out. S'prisingly easy. Since that"—he nodded at his notebook—"Bonfire Night, we never spoke again. Not once."

"How about when Ray and Shirl got married?"

"Ray fixed it so Harry Moffat was at the register office, and I was at the reception. Never the twain. Happy days."

Elf looked at the lyrics again. "These lyrics aren't an olive branch, but they are a message. *You exist, and I still think about you.* If he was totally dead to you, why write it?"

Dean tapped cigarette ash out of the window.

He's gone moody. "Sorry if I overstepped the mark."

"No, no. I was just envying how, if yer want to say something, yer just say it. Is that education? Or is it being a girl?"

"It's easy being the Enlightened One about other people's families." Elf fanned herself. "So why a song about your dad now?"

Dean frowned. "Something just says, 'My turn,' and it won't leave yer alone till yer do it. Isn't that how it is for you?"

I thought I knew Dean pretty well by now, but I was wrong. "Ye-es. He must be complex. Harry Moffat, I mean."

" 'Complex' is one word. If yer just met him one time, yer'd think, *Life 'n' soul o' the party.* If yer knew him better, yer'd think, *Nice enough fella, but something's a bit off.* If yer were family, yer'd know why he's got no friends. He doesn't drink to get drunk. He drinks to act normal. And his idea o' normal got really bloody nasty."

A dustcart drove by. Bare-chested binmen clung to the side, one with an Action Man's physique, one with a darts player's.

Elf asked, "Why didn't your mum leave?"

Dean frowned. "Shame. A mother who walks out on her husband's a failure. That's what a lot o' people think. I s'pose she was worried 'bout what'd happen to me 'n' Ray, too. She was afraid it'd be hand-me-downs 'n' bread 'n' marge and never going on holiday. When it comes to divorces, it's the breadwinner who has the money for a proper lawyer. There's always a sort o' twisted hope, too. Hope that last time *was* the last time. That he's mellowing out."

"That's twisted logic more than twisted hope," said Elf.

"Agreed." Dean dropped his cigarette stub out of the window. "The best-selling type."

"Your father still lives in the house you grew up in?"

"Till about a year ago, when he was in a car smash. He got away with scratches but the Mini he hit was a write-off. The driver's in a wheelchair and his ten-year-old daughter lost an eye."

"God, Dean," said Elf. "That's awful."

"Yep. It was an accident waiting to happen, mind. 'Cause he was drunk, the insurance company wouldn't pay the compo, so he had to sell the house. He's in a council flat. The cement works'd sacked him. So he had to sign on. Ironic, that. That was why he was so dead set against me being a musician—he was sure I'd just end up on the dole. His drinking buddies stopped standing him rounds. He got barred from pubs. By that point I was thinking, *Okay, if it wasn't Harry Moffat I'd feel a bit o' pity* . . . But it *is* Harry Moffat. I just thought, *Yer've made yer bed, now lie in it.*"

"Has he tried to get help?"

"Ray told me he's going to Alcoholics Anonymous. Who knows how that'll work out? What's Harry Moffat without his Morning Star?"

Levon returned, climbed in, and wiped his face on a spotted handkerchief. "Holy crap. When I was chart-hyping for Buster Godwin, chocolates and flattery got the job done. Now they want your first-born child." Levon took an envelope from the glove compartment and put in five one-pound notes. "A naked bribe."

"Can't *I* have that?" asked Dean. "Or can't we just buy a million copies of our single in shops?"

"The brutal truth is, the world doesn't give a shit about 'Darkroom' and we have a fortnight to make it care. So whatever it takes to flog this single, we do. Which means me bribing an asshole in a Slough record shop so he'll report inflated sales figures. It also means you"—Levon looked at Elf—"coming in with me to schmooze the creep. And you"—Levon turned to Dean—"wooing the shop girls with wilting roses. Ready? Once more unto the breach . . ."

"PETER POPE." THE trout-lipped manager of Allegro Records stroked Elf's hand. "At your service." Engelbert Humperdinck sang "There Goes My Everything" on the stereo. "Welcome to my 'HQ.' "

Elf retrieved her hand. "It looks super, Mr. Pope."

"We boast branches in Maidenhead and Staines, too. On Saturdays, trade is humming. Is that not so, girls?"

"Absolutely, Mr. Pope," intoned the two shop assistants. Both were young women Elf's age, but leggier and twiggier.

"Mmmmmm," purred Peter Pope. "We have six listening booths. Six. Our competitor by the railway station only has three."

"Allegro is the only reputable retailer in the Slough area," declared Levon. "Care for a smoke, Mr. Pope?"

Mr. Pope pocketed the whole packet. "We cater to all palates, from Ellington to Elvis to Elgar. Is that not so, girls?"

The two assistants said, "Absolutely, Mr. Pope."

"Meet Pale Becky and Dark Becky," said Peter Pope. "Girls. Miss Elf Holloway is a true English nightingale."

"Nice to meet you," said Elf.

Pale Becky's smile said, *We'll decide that.*

Dark Becky's smile said, *Yes, you're in a band, yes, you have a single out, but who's here begging for favors?*

"Here's a little something"—Dean gave the Rebeccas a bouquet each—"from Utopia Avenue."

"Fancy that," said Dark Becky. "Twelve red roses."

"What *will* we tell our boyfriends?" fretted Pale Becky.

"That they're the luckiest fellas in Slough, Maidenhead, and Staines," replied Dean. Elf could have puked, but the Two Beckies looked at each other like reluctantly impressed judges.

"The stocktaking won't do itself, girls," said Peter Pope.

"No, Mr. Pope." They retreated to the stockroom.

The manager turned to Levon. "So, Mr. Franklin. My little *dolce per niente?*" Levon handed him the envelope of money. It vanished into Peter Pope's jacket. "I own your EP *Oak, Ash and Thorn,* Miss Holloway. It and you are exquisite."

Elf tried to look pleased. "Thank you, Mr. Pope."

"There's a piano in my office." The manager's eyes swiveled to a door. "Once upon a time, Allegro sold musical instruments."

"Is that so?" asked Elf. "Why did you stop?"

"My brother stole that side of the business." Peter Pope sucked in his cheeks. "No. Your ears do not deceive you."

"That doesn't sound very fraternal," said Levon.

"I never waste a thought on that backstabbing thief or his pigpen of a shop by the station. Success is the sweetest revenge. But since both you and a piano are to hand, Miss Holloway, would it be horribly greedy of me to request a tune? All for myself, I mean?"

Levon said, "We're on a tight schedule, I'm afraid—"

"A sweetener," Pope patted his jacket pocket, "*adds* to the sales figure for the chart compilers at *Melody Maker.* A private audience with Miss Elf Holloway playing 'Any Way the Wind Blows' will *multiply* those figures by a factor of . . . ten."

Elf could smell Peter Pope's body odor.

Levon's face told Elf, *It's your decision.*

Here was a chance to nudge "Darkroom" up the charts to where a DJ might sit up and take notice. "Just one song, then."

"We'll be listening at the keyhole," half joked Dean.

"You could," Peter Pope pinched his lips into a triumphant pucker, "if there was a keyhole. Mmm*mmm*."

Elf told herself not to worry. It was just one song.

THE BACK OFFICE of Allegro Records was beige, tidy, and had a view of dustbins. Filing cabinets lined the walls. A black upright piano stood across from the desk. On the piano sat a framed photograph of a stern woman in buttoned-up clothes. Peter Pope closed the office door and lowered his voice. "Miss Holloway, I must warn you. Your manager, I think he's a . . . you know . . . one of . . ."

Elf had no intention of discussing Levon's homosexuality. "His private business is his private business, Mr. Pope, and—"

He exhaled egg fumes. " 'Business' is the whole point! It's all *his sort* care about. You have read *The Merchant of Venice*?"

Elf was baffled. Peter Pope's blackheads were like sweaty braille bumps. *"The Merchant of Venice?"*

"If your manager is one of *them*"—he stabs his sausage finger at the door—"I very much fear for your career."

Elf didn't understand. Until she suddenly did. "Hang on—are you asking me if Levon's Jewish?"

Peter Pope's nostrils flared. "Of course. Is he?"

Elf's first instinct was to say, "No, he's not Jewish at all!" but then she stumbled; to deny Peter Pope's accusation would be to validate the gravity of the charge—and what was wrong with being Jewish in the first place?

By now Peter Pope was smiling at his powers of deduction. "They hide. I seek. I find. Mmm*mmm*. It's the noses."

"What? Would you be happier if they all embroidered a Star of David on their smocks?"

"Oh, you *hip young things* gobble up their propaganda like Jelly Tots. Wake up! CND? Run by Jews. BBC? Ditto. LSD? Invented by Jews. Bob Dylan? A Jew. Brian Epstein? A Jew. Elvis Presley? A Jew. Your counterculture is a Zionist smokescreen."

"Do you seriously believe this?" asked Elf.

"Who do you think ushered Adolf Hitler into power? The Rothschilds. They *knew* the way to the State of Israel was through the concentration camps. All down history, they've been pulling the levers. I described it for *The Times* but my exposé was censored."

"Maybe *The Times* needed proof," suggested Elf.

"Amateurs might leave 'proof' lying round, but the Zionists don't. That's why we can be sure they're running things."

"So your only proof is your lack of proof?" asked Elf.

"Don't be ridiculous. Forty days *exactly* after sending my exposé to *The Times,* I was invited to join the Slough Masonic Lodge. Oh, I sent the trouser-tuggers packing. Peter Pope is not for sale." He lit one of Levon's cigarettes and took a few puffs.

The sooner I play it, the sooner I'm out of here. Elf sat at the piano and played a quick D scale to wake her fingers . . .

. . . IN THE FINAL verse, scissors snipped close to her ear. Elf yanked her head away from the blades. Peter Pope peered at a long lock of Elf's hair, pinched between his forefinger and thumb. He looked sexually aroused. Elf jumped off the piano stool, banging her knee. She was shaking. "Why—why did you cut my hair off?"

"A chap's entitled to a souvenir." Peter Pope twirled the scissors around his finger. He brushed his cheek with the lock of her hair, savoring Elf's disgust and liking it. "Your hair's like Mother's."

Elf hurried over to the door. Nightmarishly, the knob wouldn't work. She turned it the other way, not daring to look back, and was out, into a record shop on a Friday afternoon in Slough.

Lulu was singing "Let's Pretend" on the shop stereo.

Levon was flicking through the jazz albums.

Dean was chatting up Pale Becky, by the look of it.

The shop bell dinged as a customer entered.

Levon looked up. "That didn't take long. All well?"

Elf was about to say, *"No, that pervert just snipped off a strand of my hair!"* But what could Levon do? Tell Peter Pope to give the lock of hair back? She didn't want it back. If she reported the manager to the police, the desk sergeant would laugh. What law had the shop manager broken? If the slimy creep told *Melody Maker* that "Darkroom" had sold eight hundred copies across his three stores instead of eighty, who's to say that wouldn't nudge it into the Top Fifty?

"I'll treasure the memory of my private audience." Peter Pope appeared. There was no sign of Elf's hair. "Till the day I die."

Elf didn't trust herself to answer.

"So," said Levon, "Mr. Pope, we can rely on your support?"

"My word is my bond." Peter Pope smiled at Elf, opened and closed his fist, like a toddler waving goodbye. "Don't be a stranger, Nightingale." His trout's lips blew her a kiss.

THE TROUT ON Elf's plate gazes up. Lunchtime chatter fills the Seven Dials restaurant. Elf's mother, Imogen, and Bea are looking her way. *They asked you something.* "Sorry, what was that? I was distracted by my trout. It reminded me of a manager. In Slough."

"He must have made quite an impression," says Elf's mum.

"Mmm*mmm.*" Elf sinks her fork through the trout's eye.

Bea recites the John Betjeman poem: "*Come, friendly bombs, and fall on Slough! It isn't fit for humans now. There isn't grass to graze a cow. Swarm over, Death.* Then, of course, bombs really *did* fall. Betjeman must have felt absolutely dreadful."

"I went to Slough for a teaching seminar once." Imogen dabs her mouth with her napkin. "There are worse places."

Bea spears a gherkin. "I can see the roadside signs: '*Welcome to Slough: There Are Worse Places*—Imogen Holloway.' "

"Imogen Sinclair now," their mother reminds her.

"Still can't quite get my head round that," says Bea. "Mum, there's *un petit goutte* left in here. Go on." She tips the remnants into her mother's champagne glass. "You're only fifty once."

"Bless you, dear," says her mother. "Though 'a drop' is feminine, '*une petite goutte.*' You can run into trouble if you guess your genders wrongly."

"In French grammar as well as certain Soho clubs," says Bea. Her mother and sisters give her a look. "So I'm told. By Elf."

"Funny." Elf dismembers the trout with her fork. "Levon said to send you all his best wishes, before I forget."

Elf's mum is pleased. "Send mine back. He was quite the gentleman at Immy's wedding. *Ever* so well-presented, and so well-spoken. I imagine he'd be a very fair-minded boss."

"We're lucky," says Elf. "Most managers in show business are just one step up from the Kray Twins."

"Bea's flying the nest, come September," Imogen reminds their mother. "Have you thought of going back to work?"

"Oh, I'm hardly kicking my heels, what with the Rotary Club, the Women's Institute, the garden . . . not to mention your father."

Bea slices her quiche. "Do you miss teaching, Immy?"

Imogen hesitates. "I've hesitated too long, haven't I?"

"Marriage takes acclimatization, darling," says their mother. "For you and Lawrence. But don't worry. You'll get there."

Imogen squishes peas onto her fork. "It's what we sign up for, isn't it? House and home and all that."

"In the meantime," says Bea, "we can live a vicarious rock 'n' roll life via our jive chart-topping sister."

Elf harrumphs. "Not even 'chart-scraping.' "

"It's still early days," says Imogen.

Elf loads a forkful of fish onto a buttery potato. "Early days is all most bands get. Pop's not as cottage-industry as folk. Overheads are bigger. Studio fees. Marketing. Forty-nine out of fifty acts fail before they get a sniff of fame and fortune."

"You'll be the one in fifty," says Imogen. "My friends are still talking about the songs you did at the wedding."

"I loved that 'Mona Lisa' one," says their mum. "Goosebumps. Why didn't you release that as a single, darling?"

Good question. "Because there are two other songwriters in Utopia Avenue, and we all want a crack of the whip."

"How did you decide on the first single?" asks Bea.

. . .

THREE MONTHS AGO, the day after the Gravesend gig, Elf's first thought was, *It's got to be "Mona Lisa."* The problem was, Dean nominated "Abandon Hope" and Jasper voted for "Darkroom."

"Pretend I'm Victor French," Levon suggested. "Pitch me why *your* song should be the one."

" 'Abandon Hope' 's got a great riff," said Dean. "It gives us all a chance to shine. Plus, I need the money more than Elf 'n' Jasper."

Elf didn't smile. "If we release 'Abandon Hope,' we'll get pigeonholed as a blues band. It's very bloke-y."

"And 'Mona Lisa' 's very girlie," objected Dean.

"You're guys," said Elf, "so guys'll listen to us anyway. If we release 'Mona Lisa,' we'll get girls buying our records, too."

It was Jasper's turn. " 'Darkroom' has a psychedelic vibe. It's our song for the British Summer of Love."

The clocks above Levon's desk ticked. "All three could be hits," said their manager. "It's a lucky problem. Griff?"

"I don't know," said Griff. "But you've got to sort this fairly. By the end of Archie Kinnock's first band, all Ratner and Kinnock and the others did was squabble over fookin' royalties."

"So what do yer suggest?" asked Dean. "Pool all the songwriting money from the singles, and divvy it up equal?"

"Or credit all songs to the three of us?" suggests Jasper. "Lennon-McCartney. Jagger-Richards."

"I did that with Bruce for the Fletcher and Holloway EP," said Elf. "It made more problems than it solved. If the EP had sold, the problems would've grown even nastier."

"We could leave it all up to Ilex," suggested Levon. "Tell them, 'You decide and leave us out of it.' "

"No thanks," said Dean. "Our music, our decision."

"We should roll a dice, then," announced Jasper.

"You . . . *look* like you're being serious," guessed Levon.

"I am. Whoever rolls the highest has the first single. The second highest roll decides the second single. The third, the third."

"That's bloody nuts," said Dean. "Even for you."

"One dice. No blame. No bitching. Why's that nuts?"

Elf looked at Dean, who looked at Levon, who looked at Elf.

Jasper placed a red dice with white spots on the coffee table.

"You ain't half a weird fooker sometimes, Zooto," said Griff.

"Is that a good thing or a bad thing?" asked Jasper.

Griff shrugged, smiled, and frowned, all at once.

Dean picked up the dice. "Are we actually doing this?"

"It's bizarre," said Levon, "but I admit, it's . . . fair."

"It beats having a blazing, inconclusive row," agreed Elf.

"Bigger things've turned on the toss of a coin," noted Griff.

"The answer's yes, then," concluded Dean. "We're doing it."

After a pause, the three songwriters nodded.

Levon held up his palms in resignation. "Fine. But don't let Ilex know. Or anyone in the press. It's . . . eccentric. Who throws first?"

"I do," said Jasper. "Clockwise from the dice-owner."

"Right," said Dean, "as if there's a rulebook."

"There is," replied Jasper. "Rule one: If there's a draw, *only* the draw-ers throw again. Rule two: If the dice leaves the table, the thrower re-throws. Rule three: You shake the dice in your cupped hands for five seconds then you *throw* the dice—you can't 'place' it. Rule four: The result is final. No whinging. No best-ofs."

"Blimey," said Dean. "All right. You go first. Dice-owner."

Jasper shook the dice vigorously in his cupped hands; then dropped the dice. It landed on 3.

"Could be worse." Dean scooped up the dice. "Could be better." He kissed his cupped hands, shook the dice, and let it fall. It clattered, skidded, and landed on 2. "Shit."

Without fuss or ritual, Elf shook the dice, and threw it. It dropped onto the glass and landed on 6 . . .

. . . but skidded off the edge and onto the floor.

"Throw again!" said Dean. "Second rule. Throw again."

"I'm not deaf, Dean." Elf re-threw. She got a 1.

"WE ROLLED A dice," admits Elf in the Seven Dials restaurant.

"A dice?" checks their mother. "A dice?"

"It seemed better than a shouting match."

Bea munches celery. "Does the record company know?"

"They don't need to. As it happens, Victor the A&R man wanted 'Darkroom.' He may be regretting it now. It's done nothing."

"Nobody can accuse *you* of slacking, darling." Her mum sounds indignant. "You're all working like Trojans."

"We are." Elf finishes her champagne. It's now fizzless. "And we have nothing to show for it."

"Not true." Imogen reopens this week's *Melody Maker* and reads out the review: "*Take a prime cut of Pink Floyd, add a dash of Cream, a pinch of Dusty Springfield, marinate overnight and whaddaya get? 'Darkroom,' a smashing debut served up by newcomers Utopia Avenue. Could be destined for great things.*"

"A nice thirty-word write-up is better than a nasty one." Elf squishes her thumb onto breadcrumbs. "But without airplay we're just four keen beans paying to be in a band."

"Don't get cold feet now," says Bea.

"I like recording, when the guys aren't being"—*dicks*—"idiots. I love playing live. We're upping each other's games as songwriters. But the sharks, creeps, setbacks, the miles and miles in the van, the feeling that nobody's listening . . . it wears you down. I can't say you didn't warn me, Mum."

"Big of you to say so, darling."

"I'll say this too. Having two worried parents is a gift Dean and Jasper don't have. Gosh, I'm blethering. It's the champagne."

"If you can blame the champagne," says Elf's mum, "so can I. When you told us you wanted to swap university for folk-singing, your father and I had our doubts."

"*Uuuuuu*nderstatement," sing-songs Bea.

"We were afraid you'd be taken advantage of. That you'd—"

"End up penniless and up the duff," stage-whispers Bea.

"Thank you, Bea. But look what you've done, Elf. A song on an American LP that went gold. Two EPs. Six hundred people paying to see you at Basingstoke town hall. You're doing what you want to. Despite all the obstacles. That's why I—we—and Dad too, even if he doesn't say so, are *jolly* proud of you."

"It won't get any better than this." Bea holds up her glass. The four of them clink over the table. "To 'Darkroom.' "

They drink. Elf records the memory.

Imogen clears her throat. "Speaking of being up the duff . . ."

Elf, Bea, and their mother turn to look at her.

Their mouths are already starting to droop.

"I meant to wait until the coffee," says Imogen, "but the champagne's gone to my head as well . . ."

I'M GOING TO be an aunt. Denmark Street is hot as engines and smells of tar. Pigeons row, not flap, through the humid air. Still half aglow from the champagne and buzzing from the coffee, Elf crosses Charing Cross Road. The doors of Foyles bookshop are open to ventilate the shady interior, and Elf feels the pull of its shelved labyrinth . . . *But I need more unread books piling up like I need a bout of thrush.* She walks through the ten-yard tunnel at the end of Manette Street under the Pillars of Hercules pub. A midday rent-boy says, "Love the hat, sweetheart." Elf nods graciously. Greek Street smells of drains. Sleeves and skirts are short. Elf passes two Caribbean-looking women chatting in rapid-fire patois. One is burping a baby girl, who vomits milky gloop down her mum.

I'm going to be an aunt. Elf hurries down to Bateman Street and round the corner to the continental newsagent. She runs her thumb up the rack of *Le Monde, Die Welt, Corriere della Sera, De Volkskrant.* She and Bruce used to dream about Paris. He's there now . . . *while I'm working my arse off to flog a single nobody wants.* A dustbin buzzes with flies. A rat noses about. Jefferson Airplane's "White Rabbit" escapes through the open door of Andromeda Records. Elf resists the temptation to go in and see how many copies of "Darkroom" . . . then succumbs and doubles back. On the New Releases shelf she counts fourteen singles; earlier there were sixteen. Two copies sold in two hours. If that happened at, say, five hundred record shops nationwide, that's one thousand copies since eleven A.M. . . . or four thousand during an eight-hour day . . . *times six days, that's twenty-four thousand singles . . . But who am I kidding?* This is Soho, where Utopia Avenue is known. How many "Darkroom"s are the likes of Peter Pope likely to sell? Elf leaves the shop, worried.

Never mind. I'm going to be an aunt. In the window of Primo's, a boy feeds his girlfriend ice cream from a knickerbocker glory. He pulls out his licked-clean spoon. He looks plain. She's gorgeous, like a she-wolf. *I wish I was him.* She squashes the thought and crosses Dean Street into Meard Street. It narrows into an alley as dim as dusk where a prostitute pulls a john through a side door, her finger hooked through his belt. The alley ejects Elf onto the sunny side of Wardour Street. Cherries on a greengrocer's stall gleam. Elf joins the queue. A few yards away there is a telephone box. A pane of glass is missing, and Elf hears the yelling woman inside: "This ain't no divine conception, Gary! It's yours! You PROMISED! Gary? GARY!" The woman falls silent. Elf thinks, *A classic folk-song narrative.* The woman stumbles out of the phone box. Her mascara's running. She's pregnant. She plunges into the market crowd, sobbing. The receiver rotates on its cable like a body on its rope.

I'm going to be an aunt. Elf asks for a quarter-pound of cherries. The man weighs them, hands her the brown paper bag, and pockets her coins. "You're looking pale today, pet. Burn the candle at both ends, and soon you've got no candle." Elf commits the line to memory and walks up Peter Street, squishing a cherry in her mouth. Summer oozes through the torn, sun-warmed skin. She spits out the pip. It plops down a drain.

A funeral cortège is blocking Broadwick Street. Elf steps into the launderette to let the group pass. Chain-smoking Mrs. Hughes, her hair in curlers, appears with a basket of laundry. "Nelly Macroom passed away last week. Her family's got the chipper on Warwick Street." Mrs. Hughes taps ash onto the floor. "She went to get her usual at Brenda's salon last week. Her snooze in the perming helmet turned out to be eternal. Lucky so-and-so."

"Why lucky?" asks Elf.

"Her last-ever hairdo was on the house."

The hearse draws level. Elf glimpses the coffin between the bodies of the living.

"At your age," says Mrs. Hughes, "you think getting old and dying's what other people do. At my age, you think, *Where did it all go?*

If you want to do something, do it. 'Cause your turn to be in that box, it's coming. No doctor, no diet, no nothing'll keep it away. It'll be here. Quick as"—she snaps her fingers and Elf blinks—"*that.*"

LIVONIA STREET IS a cobbled cul-de-sac with an alley that cuts through to Portland Mews, used only by Soho locals or lost tourists. Elf slips her key into the door marked *9*, between a secretive locksmith on one side and a seamstress's shop, run by several Russian sisters, on the other. Elf's flat is upstairs from Mr. Watney, a widower who lives on the first floor with his corgis, minds his own business, and is nearly deaf, a useful quality in a pianist's neighbor. In the dingy hallway Elf finds three letters and a bill on the doormat, all for Mr. Watney. She props them on the shelf by his door and climbs two flights of scuffed steps to her own front door. Inside, Angus's shoes are placed side by side and Fats Domino is singing "Blueberry Hill" on the radio. Angus calls from the bathroom, "Miss Holloway, I presume?"

Elf slips off her shoes. "Mr. Kirk, I trust."

"Be warned, if you're in company," Angus has a full-tilt Highlands accent, "I'm in the nip."

"At ease, soldier, I'm alone." She hangs her handbag and hat on the coat stand and goes through to the steamy bathroom.

Angus is in the bath, reading *Oz*. His groin is hidden by a raft of bubble-bath foam. "Your modesty preserver is the same shape as Antarctica." Elf takes the chair. "You're boiled pink."

"How was lunch?"

"I'm going to be an aunt. Imogen's three months gone."

"Brilliant news. Right?"

"Definitely."

"You can show the wee sprog how to roll joints. Then when Imogen finds out, it'll be 'But, Mam, Aunty Elf said I could!' "

Elf flexes her toes. They're tired from her heels. "What's showing at the Palace tonight?"

"*In the Heat of the Night* on screen one. I'm doing *Bonnie and Clyde* on screen two. I could smuggle you in, if you fancy it."

"It's Basingstoke tonight."

"Just tell 'em you'd rather be with your Highland hunk."

"It won't wash, alas. Six hundred tickets sold so far."

Angus makes an impressed noise. "When are you leaving?"

"Five. The Beast's at Jasper's. Are you starting at six?"

"Aye, but I need to go by my bedsit, drop off my crusty cacks, and pick up some fresh ones, so I should leave here by four."

Elf looks at her watch. "It's almost two thirty now, so . . . we have ninety minutes to ourselves, Mr. Kirk."

"We could play three games of Scrabble."

"We could boil twenty eggs, one after the other."

"Or listen to *Sergeant Pepper's*. Twice."

Elf perches on the bathtub, tilts Angus's head back, and kisses him. She thinks of the she-wolf in the window of Primo's. She opens her eyes to see if Angus is watching her. Bruce always does. *Did.* Angus never has. It makes her feel in charge.

"Deep beneath the frozen wastes of Antarctica," intones Angus, "an ancient menace awakes . . ."

ANGUS DOZES OFF. Elf wonders what it's like to be the guy. Her pillow squishes Angus's face out of shape. Every lover is a lesson and Angus's lesson is that kindness is sexy. The Beach Boys are singing "Don't Talk (Put Your Head on My Shoulder)" on Radio Bluebeard. It's a much weirder song than it admits to being, Elf thinks. The wild swans in the mobile over her bed rotate on their endless flight through time. Bea made it for her as a housewarming present. Angus makes a growling noise in his sleep. The gawky, deep-eye-socketed Scot has grown on her. They met in May, he slept over a few nights in June, and now he's here more nights than not. She introduced him to the band last week. Dean liked him and Jasper liked him, as much as Jasper likes anyone. Griff was a bit off with him. Elf likes the novelty of not going out with a musician. Angus thinks music is magic, which makes Elf a magician. She doesn't love Angus with that punch-drunk love she loved Bruce with, but liking him is enough. Angus is also proof that she likes men, and that the voice on the number 97 bus was a malicious lie, not a suppressed truth.

Right?

Obviously.

Elf lights a cigarette and shoots out smoke at the swans. *Thank God for the Pill, and for the female GPs who'll prescribe it.* The Beach Boys finish their harmonies, and the next song is so familiar it takes Elf a few free-falling seconds to identify it and a few more seconds to believe it . . .

"Darkroom"—her chords, her Farfisa—is coming from her Hacker radio. In comes Dean's bass; in comes Griff's snare drum; and here's Jasper's Lennon-esque phrasing: "*You took me to your darkroom and you slipped inside my mind . . .*"

Elf's heart wallops. *IT'S US!*

"*. . . where negatives turn positive, where IOUs are signed . . .*" Pirate radio audience sizes are anybody's guess, but surely tens of thousands are hearing Utopia Avenue right now. Fifty thousand? A hundred thousand? *What if they hate it? What if they see I'm bluffing it? What if they love it? What if they rush out and buy it?* She wants to hide. She wants to savor this once-in-a-lifetime first. She wants to tell everyone she knows. "Angus!"

"Wassityeahwha?"

"Listen! The radio!"

Angus listens. "That's you."

Elf can only nod. They listen to the whole song. Bat Segundo only speaks after Elf's closing refrain. "That slice of pop perfection was 'Darkroom,' a brand-new song by Utopia Avenue. They're English, they're happening, and they're this week's Tip-for-the-Top brought to you in proud association with Rocket Cola, the with-it pop drink for the with-it crowd—and if that didn't give you goosebumps, please see your doctor because you may well be dead. Before Utopia Avenue was the Beach Boys, 'Don't Talk (Put Your Head on My Shoulder),' and coming up before we go to the news, we—"

Angus turns off the radio. "You'll be on *Top of the Pops.*"

"Only if they send a limo to pick me up," says Elf. Angus isn't smiling, so Elf adds, "I'm joking."

"I'm not," replies Angus. "This is the start."

Don't even dream it, Elf warns herself.

. . .

DEAN PICKS UP: "We were just on Bat Segundo."

"I know. I know! Did Jasper hear it too?"

"Dunno. He's out. Griff's not here yet. Should I name my first child 'Bat' or 'Segundo'?"

"Dean Bat Bluebeard Segundo Moss."

"This is liftoff, Elf. I bloody feel it."

"So do I. So do I."

Dean laughs. "I . . . God . . . The radio! *Us.* The Beach Boys!"

"I'll call Moonwhale. See you later."

"See yer."

BETHANY PICKS UP: "Good afternoon—Moonwhale Management?"

"Bethany—'Darkroom' was on Bat Segundo."

Bethany's tone turns to giddy delight. "Did you catch it?"

Elf laughs. "I caught it."

"I'll put you through to Levon."

Levon is pleased in his urbane Canadian way. "Congratulations. It's the start of the start. You're off the blocks."

"Did you know?"

"For once, no. Funnily enough, though, Victor French called earlier to say John Peel's playing 'Darkroom' on *The Perfumed Garden* tomorrow, but Bat beat him to the draw. It's only two plays, but one's enough to trigger a chain reaction. The Home Office—"

Angus is waving from Elf's front door. Elf blows him a kiss. Angus pretends to be shot through the heart and staggers off.

"—is closing down the pirate radio ships any day now, so no more Radio Bluebeard or Radio London. But I'm reliably informed John Peel and Bat Segundo are in talks with the BBC to work on Radio One. They're pals, and a nice lunch with both of them would be a smart investment, if you're free next week."

"You bet."

"I'll set something up. And . . . sorry, Elf, Bethany's saying Ilex is on the other line."

"Go."

"I'll see you at De Zoet Towers later."

. . .

ELF GOES TO the kitchen window to watch Angus exiting her building into Livonia Street below. He disappears into Berwick Street without a backward glance. She goes to the bathroom and asks her reflection if she just dreamed that Utopia Avenue was on the radio.

"It happened," her reflection tells her.

"Will you still be my face if I'm famous?"

"Kiss me," replies her reflection.

So Elf does, on the lips.

Jasper's right . . . mirrors really are strange.

Her reflection laughs, and Elf goes to straighten up her bed, but Angus has already done it. She goes back to the kitchen and pours herself a glass of milk, just as the key turns in the door. She wonders what Angus forgot. His coat?

"Hiya, Wombat!"

The floor sways like the deck of a ship.

"Hey," says Bruce, "you're spilling that milk!"

So I am. She puts down the bottle.

He says, "Take two. 'Hiya, Wombat!' "

Everything is still and very quiet.

"Wh-what-wh—why? How—"

"Overnight ferry." He dumps his rucksack by the coat stand. "Haven't eaten since Calais—so there's *very* little I wouldn't do for a cheese 'n' ham sarnie. So how in hell have you been?" He runs his hands back through his lush golden hair. He's deeply tanned and a little older. "God, I missed you."

Elf takes a few steps back, into the kitchen cupboard. "Hang on—wait—I . . ."

Bruce looks confused, then not. "Ah . . . You didn't get my postcard, I guess?"

"No."

"All praise Royal Mail. Or maybe the French *facteur* cocked up." Bruce walks over to the kitchen sink, slaps water over his face, pours himself a mug of water, and drinks. He eyes her up. "New hair, right?

Lost a few pounds, too." He drapes himself along the sofa, showing midriff. "Cheese and pickle'll do fine, if you've got no ham."

Elf feels as if she's in the wrong play. "You dumped me. You pissed off to Paris. You *do* remember that?"

Bruce winces. " 'Dumped'? We needed oxygen. We're artists."

"No. You don't," she steels her voice, "dump me, break my heart, then turn up and act like the last six months never happened."

His jokey pout says, *Am I in the doghouse?*

"I'm serious."

His jokey pout fades. "I thought you'd be pleased. I came straight here from Charing Cross. I . . ."

"Maybe Vanessa will be pleased. I've got *very* mixed feelings."

Bruce scrunches up his face as if he can't quite place the name . . . "Oh, *her*? Oh, Wombat. Jealousy doesn't suit you."

So she dumped him. "Try Wotsit."

"Wotsit's back in Greece. People move on."

"What if I've moved on too?"

Bruce pretends she didn't just say that. "Hey, I heard about Utopia Avenue. Review in *Melody Maker.* Nice one. May I?" He takes one of her Camels from the little table and lights up.

Elf fights an impulse to knock it from his hand.

"A long way from Islington Folk Den, eh? I'm proud of you."

Elf notices she has no desire to tell him about "Darkroom" on *The Bat Segundo Show.* "Look, I've got a gig tonight, so—"

"Cool. I'll come along and guard your handbag with my life. I could even play, if you're a guitarist short. Where's the gig?"

"Basingstoke, but—"

"One of those nowhere places?"

Elf sighs. *I have to say it.* "You walked out, Bruce. It's over. We're over. And I'd like my key back."

Bruce lifts his eyebrows, like a teacher waiting for the truth to emerge. "And are we 'seeing' anyone else?"

"Give me my key. Please." Elf hates that "please."

But Bruce's cockiness ebbs away. The fridge shudders into silence. "What's good for the gander's good for the goose, I s'pose."

He puts the key on the arm of the sofa. "Sorry. About February. About everything. The more of a dingo's arse I am, the more I bluster. I know I can't wave a magic wand, fix the damage . . ." His voice wobbles. "Or bring back Fletcher and Holloway."

Elf's throat contracts. "True."

"Thinking that you still hate me, that's . . . the worst. Before I throw myself off Waterloo Bridge"—he makes a brave face—"could I . . . could we . . . part as mates?"

Careful. Elf folds her arms. "Your apology's a few months late, but okay. We're parting as mates. Goodbye."

Bruce shuts his eyes. To Elf's surprise, they start to stream. "God, I hate my guts sometimes."

"I can understand why," says Elf. "Sometimes."

He dabs his eyes on his granddad shirt. "Shit, I'm sorry, Elf. But . . . I'm in a bit of trouble."

Drugs? Syphilis? Crime? "Tell me."

"The arse fell out of France. The cops beat me up for busking on the Champs-Élysées. They nicked my guitar. My flatmate did a runner with my savings, clothes, everything. I'm broke. I've got two francs, seven centimes, eight shillings, and a threepenny bit. I—I—I came via Toby Green's office." Bruce is red and sweaty. "He was out, but his secretary checked our *Shepherd's Crook* royalties."

"It's not a lot."

"It won't buy a cup of pigeon food. I know I'm a king of the shits for asking *you,* of all people, but . . . I honestly, *honestly,* don't have anyone else to turn to. So I'm . . ." he takes a deep breath to compose himself, ". . . I'm begging. Please. If there's any way you can help . . . any way at all . . . please . . . help."

THE PRIZE

"A VERY VERY *VERY* GOOD EVENING, LADIES AND GENTLEMEN, and welcome one and *all* to this week's *Top of the Pops.* I hope you're feeling fit and well, and if you're not feeling fit and well, I hope this next half hour cheers you up." The golden mop-topped Jimmy Savile smiles for the TV camera. "So, how's about we start off with a nice, brisk number from one of the best new bands of the summer—and, gentlemen, do not adjust your TV set when you cop a load of the *scrrr*umdiddley*ump*tious keyboard player! With no further ado—in at number nineteen with their debut song 'Darkroom'—the one, the only, the weird, the wonderful . . . Utopia Avenue!"

Electric APPLAUSE signs light up; a cheer goes up; Jasper glances offstage at Levon, Bea, Dean's girlfriend Jude, and Victor French from Ilex. *Here we go.* The intro comes over the PA and the thirty or forty hip young things selected for the dance floor sway to Elf's chords, which she now pretends to play on her unplugged-in Farfisa. Bea and Jude spent three days on Elf's outfit: an American Indian squaw look with a tasseled suede, embroidered headband and glass beads. Dean is in a dusty-pink frock coat he bought at the Marshmallow Cricket Bat. He does an Elvis lip-curl for the camera. Griff, drumming on a kit with sound-deadening rubber mats and a special plastic cymbal that goes *Tssh!,* sports a jazzer's loose shirt and a psychedelic waistcoat. *Vocals.* Jasper leans into the mic and lip-syncs his vocal track. A second camera moves closer to Elf. A producer told them that Elf's the first woman ever to "play" an instrument on *Top of the Pops.* Jasper moves in to the mic:

You took me to your darkroom
where secrets get undressed.
Jerusalem is east of there,
and Mecca's to the west . . .

Dean joins Elf at her mic for the second chorus. He points into the camera's lens and out of millions of TV sets across Great Britain. After the bridge a third camera moves in to catch Griff's drumburst before Jasper's solo. He plays it on his unplugged-in Strat as he would onstage, complete with bent notes and shading. Back to Elf and Dean for the last chorus, cut off midway by a big cheer from the audience. APPLAUSE! Their three minutes are up.

An assistant hustles the band offstage as Jimmy Savile, nestling in a bevy of miniskirted women, introduces the next band on the adjacent stage. "How's about that, then, ladies and gentlemen? 'Darkroom' by Utopia Avenue and isn't it a cracker? Now then now then now then. Three clues about our next guests. Clue one: they're all quite *small.* Clue two: they have *faces.* Clue three: they're *itchy* and live in a *park.* Who can they be? Why, it's the Small Faces and their latest dotty ditty—'Itchycoo Park'!"

FROM THE WINGS, Jasper and Griff watch Diana Ross and the Supremes mime "Reflections." Jasper sees the whites of Diana Ross's eyes. Elf joins him and Griff. Diana Ross, Mary Wilson, and Cindy Birdsong make every other act look amateurish. *Us included.* Their poise, dark skin, and silver gowns are perfect for black-and-white screens. Jasper—and most of Great Britain, he guesses—is entranced by their minimal choreography, how they embody the song, serve it, mean it. No other song on the show—"Itchycoo Park," Traffic's "Hole in My Shoe," the Move's "Flowers in the Rain," and the Flowerpot Men's "Let's Go to San Francisco"—struck Jasper as believed in by anyone, from writer to punter.

When "Reflections" ends, Diana Ross responds to the loud applause with a modest wave and a smile before she and the Supremes are ushered past. As she passes Jasper, he inhales a few of the molecules left in her wake.

"Think we'll get there someday?" Elf asks, in a low voice.

"Where?" asks Jasper.

"America."

Jasper considers the question.

"If Herman's fookin' Hermits can," growls Griff, "*we* will."

WHILE ENGELBERT HUMPERDINCK ends the show with "The Last Waltz," the backstage party at the BBC Lime Grove Studios—"Slime Grove" to its friends—kicks off the London scene's Thursday-to-Sunday weekend. Musicians, managers, groupies, wives, columnists, and hangers-on are circulating, plotting, flirting, bitching, and backstabbing. Levon, Jasper, and Howie Stoker are in the corner with Victor French and Andrew Loog Oldham. Elf and Bruce—his hand on her hip—are with Bea, Jude, and Dean in a huddle with half of Traffic.

The reappearance of Elf's ex-boyfriend, and Elf's abrupt ejection of Angus, triggered a big argument at Pavel Z's when Elf brought Bruce to meet the band. As far as Jasper could tell, Dean was angry with Elf for taking Bruce back because Dean thought Bruce had treated Elf badly in the past, and might treat her badly again. At that point, Bruce left, telling Elf he'd get dinner ready for when she came home. Elf got angry with Dean because she thought her choice of boyfriend was none of Dean's business, especially when Dean was two-timing Jude with the Patisserie Valerie waitress from Scunthorpe. That made Dean even angrier, which made Elf even more scornful. Griff began a few drumming exercises, which made both Dean and Elf angry with him. Griff played louder. Jasper was by then totally lost. Why, he wondered, do Normals get so worked up about who's having sex with whom? Surely people who want to sleep with each other will do so, until one or both no longer want it. Then it ends. Like the end of the mating season in the animal kingdom. *If everyone just accepted that, there would be no more heartache.*

Maybe Dean is accepting it now. Griff is on a sofa with giggling girls and a saucer-eyed Keith Moon miming a story involving lots of bouncing. Jasper checks his facts: *I'm in a band; we got signed; I wrote a song; it's at number nineteen; we just mimed it on* Top of the Pops. *Millions saw it.*

Yes, these facts appear to be reliable.

Jasper thinks of "Darkroom" as a cloud of dandelion seeds, floating across the airwaves, taking root in minds from the Shetlands to the Scillies. They fly through time, too. Perhaps "Darkroom" will land in the minds of people not yet born, or whose parents are not yet born. *Who knows?* Jasper bumps into a helmet of gold hair, a lime shirt, and a magenta tie. He apologizes to Brian Jones of the Rolling Stones.

Brian Jones says, "No bones broken." He puts a cigarette into his mouth and asks, "Got a light?"

Jasper obliges. "Congratulations on 'We Love You.' "

"Oh, you like that one, do you?"

"It's a relentless knock-out."

Brian Jones holds in smoke, then sighs it out. "I play Mellotron on it. Mellotrons are bitches. It's the delay. Ought I to know you?"

"I'm Jasper. I play guitar in Utopia Avenue."

"Nice for a holiday. Wouldn't want to live there."

Jasper wonders if that was a joke. "Why are you the only Rolling Stone here?"

Brian Jones frowns. "Between us . . . I don't quite know."

"Why not?"

"Things get lodged in my head, sometimes."

"What kind of things?"

"Well, the notion that we were doing 'We Love You' on *Top of the Pops* tonight. So I dropped everything and had Tom drive me in . . . only to find a lot of baffled BBC chaps who assured me that no, in fact the Stones *aren't* performing on the show and never were."

"So . . . someone made a hoax call, are you saying?"

"No. It's more like a message in my head."

Jasper thinks of Knock Knock. "A message?"

Brian Jones slouches against the wall. "Or the *memory* of a message. But when you try to find out where it came from, there's nothing. Like . . . graffiti that vanishes the moment it's read."

"Are you high?" asks Jasper.

"I wish."

"Are you ever visited by incorporeal beings?"

Brian Jones moves the curtain of gold hair from his bloodshot eyes and looks at Jasper properly. "Speak to me."

DURING JASPER'S TEN years at Bishop's Ely, he made no enemies worthy of the title and only one friend. Heinz Formaggio was his roommate and the son of Swiss scientists. Three weeks after the first *knock-knock* on the cricket pitch, when the number of "incidents" had reached double figures, Jasper told his roommate what he was hearing. They were under an oak tree during a free period. Formaggio leaned against the tree while Jasper spoke for half an hour. He didn't reply for a while. Bees perused the clover. Lines of birdsong got tangled up. A train crossed the fen, heading north.

"Have you told anyone else?" Formaggio finally said.

"It's not the sort of thing I want to advertise."

"Damn right."

A burly groundsman pushed a lawnmower.

Jasper asked, "Do you have any theories?"

Formaggio knitted his fingers. "I have four. Theory A posits that the *knock-knock*s are a fabrication to seek attention."

"They're not."

"You are morbidly honest, de Zoet. Theory A is dismissed."

"Good."

"Theory B posits that the sound is made by a supernatural entity. We might christen him, her, or it 'Knock Knock.' "

"It's a he. 'Supernatural entity' isn't very scientific."

"Ghosts, demons, angels are *anti*-scientific, and yet, in a straw poll, I'd wager more people believe in these things than believe in the General Theory of Relativity. Why 'he'?"

"I don't know how I know. He's a he. I'm no fan of Theory B. Being a majority is no guarantee of being right."

Formaggio nodded. "Also, ghosts manifest. Angels intervene. Demons terrorize. They don't just make knocking noises. This smacks of a third-rate séance. Let's reject Theory B for now."

Through the open windows of the music room, across the lawn, wafted the sound of thirty boys singing *"Summer is a-cumin in . . ."*

"You'll like Theory C the least. It posits that Knock Knock is a psychosis, with no external reality. In a nutshell: you're nuts."

Boys spilled out of the Old Palace down the slope.

"But I hear Knock Knock as clearly as I hear you."

"Did Joan of Arc really hear the voice of God?"

A cloud shifted and the oak tree cast a dappled net. "So the more real Knock Knock feels, the crazier I am?"

Formaggio took off his glasses to clean the lenses. "Yes."

"Before that cricket match, I was the only one living in my head. Now there are two. Even when Knock Knock isn't knocking, I know he's there. I know that sounds crazy. I can't prove I'm not, I suppose. But can you prove I am?"

Through the window of the music room came the music master's voice: *"No no no—that will not do!"*

"So what's Theory D?" asked Jasper.

"It's Theory X. Theory X concedes that Knock Knock is neither a lie nor a ghost nor a psychotic episode but an unknown, X."

"Isn't Theory X just a fancy way of saying, 'I'm clueless'?"

"Literally so: we have no clues. Theory X is about gathering them. Have you tried to engage with Knock Knock?"

"Every day at prayers, I sort of 'broadcast' a message: *Speak to me* or *Who are you?* or *What do you want?*"

"No reply so far?"

"No reply so far."

Formaggio blew a ladybird off his thumb. "We need to think scientifically. Not like a boy who's afraid he's insane or haunted."

"How do we think scientifically?"

"Record the durations, times, and patterns of the knocks. Analyze the data. Are the 'visitations' random? Are there patterns? Observe. Is Knock Knock tied to Ely, or will he travel to Zeeland in July?"

Bells rang, doves cooed, a mower mowed. "Could Knock Knock be some kind of messenger? If so, what's the message?"

"A '*KNOCK-KNOCK-KNOCK*' IN your head isn't much of a message." Brian Jones cuts in before Jasper gets to what happened next. "Is that a birthmark? Or a Hindu spot?" The Rolling Stone is peering between Jasper's eyebrows with drug-constricted pupils. He taps the place. "Here. It's closing. It's shy. Ought I to know you?"

"I'm Jasper. I play guitar in Utopia Avenue."

"In Gloucestershire, 'jaspers' are wasps." Brian Jones asks someone over Jasper's shoulder. "I say, Steve. Do you East End herberts call wasps 'jaspers'?"

"We don't call the little bastards nothing. We just splat 'em." Steve Marriott of the Small Faces hands Jasper a brown ale. "Welcome to the big time. And for His Satanic Majesty"—Steve Marriott presses a small Ogden's snuffbox into Brian Jones's palm—"Happy birthday."

"Is it today?" Brian Jones blinks at the box. "Snuff?"

Steve Marriott squeezes a nostril flat and mimes a snort.

"*Oh.* In that case, I'm off to powder my nose . . ."

Jasper takes a swig from the brown ale.

"You just broke the first rule," says Steve Marriott. "Never accept a drink from a stranger. Could be spiked."

"You're not a stranger," says Jasper. "You're Steve Marriott."

The singer smiles as if Jasper has made a joke. "That chick in your band. Is she a gimmick, or does she really play?"

"Elf's no gimmick. She plays. She sings. She writes."

Steve Marriott juts out his jaw. "It's novel, I'll give you that."

"There's Grace Slick. Jefferson Airplane."

"She sings, she's sexy as hell, but she don't play."

"Rosetta Tharpe."

"Rosetta Tharpe *has* a band. She's not *in* one."

"The Carter Family."

"They're a real family first who became a band second."

"Now then, *now* then." A hand grips Jasper's shoulder, a nasal

Yorkshire voice fills his ear. "There's enough star wattage in this room to light up Essex, but I came straight to *you,* good Sir Jasper, to congratulate you on popping your *Top of the Pops* cherry." Jimmy Savile puffs a fat cigar. "How was it for you?"

"It all went by in a bit of a blur," admits Jasper.

"That's what the ladies tell young Stephen here." Jimmy Savile leers at Steve Marriott. "Who is arisen from the dead."

"Hadn't noticed I'd died, Jimmy," says Steve Marriott.

"The artist's always the last to know. Jasper: Is Captain Didgeridoo over there knobbing your lusty, busty organ player?"

"If you mean Elf and Bruce, they share a flat, yes."

"She's a bit old for you, Jimmy, surely," says the singer. "I mean, she's over sixteen. Legal, like."

"Ooofff!" Jimmy Savile's chin juts out. "Marriott's right hook strikes again! Is that what you're aiming at when your Adventures in Stardom sputter out? Boxing? I can't see it myself. Not with that physique. You're not called the 'Small' Faces for nothing. How does it feel, Young Steven? Getting utterly, royally fleeced out of every last penny by Don Arden? Not even owning the clothes you stand up in? Don't you just want to shrivel up and die? I know I would."

Even Jasper can identify the hatred in Steve Marriott's face.

"So sorry if I touched a raw nerve," says Jimmy Savile. "Shall I lend you the bus fare home?"

CHIN-*CHINGGGGGG!* HOWIE STOKER, freshly returned from Saint-Tropez, sporting a turquoise blazer, taps a wine glass with a spoon in the private function room in Durrants Hotel. His week in Saint-Tropez has deepened his tan. *If he was a roast chicken,* thinks Jasper, *he was in the oven twenty minutes too long. Chinggggggggg!* Howie's gaze circumambulates the private room. Guests include Freddy Duke of the Duke-Stoker Agency, underneath Moonwhale; Levon, in a raspberry-and-vanilla-striped suit; Bethany, with her hair up, black pearls, and a black dress; Elf still in her *Top of the Pops* warrior squaw getup; Bruce Fletcher in rusty flannel and shark's tooth necklace; Bea Holloway, dressed like an acting student at RADA; a pale art student called Trevor Pink who's come with Bea and has pink paint on his hands, *so he's easy to remember;* Dean in his Union Jack jacket; Dean's girlfriend Jude, who's fractionally taller than Dean; Griff; Humpty-faced A&R man Victor French; and whippet-faced publicist Nigel Horner. *Too many eyes.* Social gatherings are archery ranges and memory tests.

Chinggggggggggggg! A hush descends.

"Friends," Howie Stoker begins, "Moonwhalers and well-wishers. I'd like to say just a few words. So I shall! When I told my buddies back in New York I was venturing into the music biz in London, a typical reaction was, 'Howie, are you nuts? A Wall Street maestro you may be, but you're a showbiz novice and those limeys'll milk you dry!' My enemies just laughed, fit to bust, at the prospect of Howie Stoker losing his goddamn shirt. Well. Those sons of bitches sure as hell aren't laughing now! Not now that my *very first signing's very first single is in the UK Top Thirty!*"

Cheers and applause bubble up and spill over.

"We're here today because of five *truly* talented individuals," says Howie Stoker. "Let's name 'em and shame 'em, one by one."

Five? wonders Jasper. *He must be including Levon.*

"First: our gorgeously proportioned, lyre-strumming, ivory-tinkling Queen of Folk. The one, the only, Miss Elf Holloway!"

Applause. Aristocrats look down from paintings spaced around the room. Elf's smile strikes Jasper as complicated.

Howie Stoker turns to Dean. "Plenty of folks say that a bassist is a failed lead guitarist. I say, 'Horse pucky!' Round of applause!"

People applaud. Dean lifts his glass jauntily.

Howie Stoker pushes on. "Drummers are unjustly the butt of too many jokes. Jokes like . . ." Howie unfolds a sheet of paper and puts on his glasses ". . . *'What's the difference between a drummer and a savings bond?'* Anyone? *'One will mature and make money.'"* A few polite smiles. Griff nods, like he's heard it all before. " *'What has three legs and an asshole?'* No? *'A drum-stool!'* One more? Here we go: *'What do you call a beautiful woman on the arm of a drummer?'"*

Griff makes a megaphone of his hands: "A tattoo."

"You're treading on my lines, Griff! Next up—the man who penned Utopia Avenue's first hit, first of many, I have no doubt.

Our King of the Stratocaster, Jasper de Zoet!" He mispronounces Jasper's name and raises his glass. Jasper avoids all the eyes by focusing very hard on the flake of pastry on Howie Stoker's lapel.

Chinggggggggggg. "I'm not a man to blow my own trumpet," says Howie Stoker, brushing his lapel, "so I won't bang on about my instrumental role—pun intended, you betcha—in creating Utopia Avenue. So I'll let the results speak for themselves and say a few words about my guide and my mentor—my own 'gut instinct.' Expertise is cheap. Expertise you can learn, hire, or poach. But guts? You've got it or you ain't. Am I right, Victor?"

The A&R man raises his glass at Howie. "Too true, Howie."

"You see? And when I first met Levon at Bertolucci's on Seventh Avenue, where Rob Redford, Dick Burton, and Humph Bogart often eat, my gut said, *Howie, this is your man.* Same story when I heard the tapes of the band's Marquee show. My gut literally sat up and told me, *This is your band.* When I met Victor at the Dorchester—why stay anywhere else when *en frolique* in London, right?—my gut said, *This is the label.* Bang bang bang! Over *sixteen thousand sales* and one stellar performance on *the* English TV showcase prove that my gut was on the money again."

"Guts," Griff says in Jasper's ear, "are full o' fookin' shit."

"Do you know the best part?" Howie Stoker's grin sweeps the room. "This is just the beginning. Victor, I think the hour is nigh for your surprise announcement, *s'il vous plaît.*"

"Thanks for that inspirational speech, Howie," Victor French says. "I do indeed bear glad tidings. I just got off the blower with Toto Schiffer in Hamburg. Ilex's head honcho. He's given us the green light to record *not only* a follow-up single to 'Darkroom' but also . . . an LP."

Bea, Jude, and Elf let out a spontaneous "Wooh-wooh!"

"Back o' the fookin' net!" says Griff.

Dean tilts his chair. "Thought yer'd never ask."

"You'll need to get cracking," Victor French tells the band. "We want the LP in the shops well before Christmas."

"No problem," promises Levon. "The band has a stack of gig-polished songs ready for vinyl."

"Ideally, we'll release a second single a week before the album," says Nigel Horner. "Maximum noise is the name of the game."

"I'll review the gig book first thing," says Levon. "Ditch a few of the smaller-fry bookings to make room for studio sessions."

"Any chance of a real studio this time?" asks Dean.

"Fungus Hut did a good enough job on 'Darkroom,' " says Victor French. "Competitive prices, too."

Levon straightens his tie. "I know the band will repay Mr. Schiffer's faith with one of the albums of the year."

"You're being very quiet, Jasper," comments Howie.

Jasper isn't sure if this is a criticism or an invitation to speak. He sips at his wine glass and finds it empty.

"We'll need a couple of new songs out of you," says Nigel Horner. "Something as catchy as 'Darkroom.' Please."

"I'll do my best." Jasper wants all the eyes off him. He has to concentrate on what he's afraid he can hear.

"Me 'n' Elf write songs too, yer know," says Dean.

Here it is . . . a steady knuckle-on-wood. *Knock . . . knock . . . knock . . .* quieter than Dean's protestations, but louder than it was the other day. Nobody else hears it. This message has only one addressee.

JASPER FOLLOWED FORMAGGIO's advice and kept a notebook entitled "K^2" for the twelve months between April 1962 and April 1963. In it, he recorded the times, durations, and contexts of Knock Knock's "episodes," written in Dutch. Jasper adopted musical notation to describe the varying styles of knocking: *f* for *forte, ff, fff, cres.* for *crescendo, bruscamente, rubato,* etc. The data established several facts. Knock Knock's visits tended to cluster close to noon and midnight. Visits were as likely to occur when Jasper was alone as they were when in company, in the shower, studying, in choir, or in the refectory. As the year progressed, the frequency increased from two, three, or four visits a week to two, three, or four a day. Knock Knock accompanied Jasper to his summer lodgings at Domburg in Zeeland. The knockings lengthened from the triad of *knock-knocks* heard on the cricket pitch to complex strings of knocks that lasted up to a minute. They also grew louder or nearer. Jasper sensed an intelligence behind the knocks. Sometimes the quality of the knocking sounded desperate, or angry, or grim. Attempts to communicate with Knock Knock—tap once for yes, twice for no—came to nothing. Despite this increased activity, as the months passed, Jasper grew accustomed to him. As aural hallucinations went, a knocking sound was relatively innocuous. It wasn't a voice claiming to be God, or the devil telling him to kill himself, or even the hanged Jacobite reputed to haunt the stairwell of Swaffham House. Compared to Jasper's classmates who endured epilepsy, the aftereffects of polio, blindness in one eye, or even a severe stammer, Knock Knock was an easy cross to bear. The loyal Formaggio told nobody, and maintained his curiosity about his roommate's oddity, but days might pass without the boys mentioning it. Days that Jasper would soon look back upon as the closing of a golden age.

"THOSE LYRICS," VICTOR French tells Jasper, "in the last verse of 'Darkroom': '*We hid under trees from the rain and the dice; but under the trees the rain rains twice.*' I don't know what it means, but I know what it means." A hotel waiter is pouring coffee into china cups from a narrow-spouted silver jug. Port is distributed on silver trays. "Where do words like that come from?"

Jasper wishes he could celebrate *Top of the Pops* by smoking a joint on a rowing boat on the Serpentine, away from Victor French and Howie Stoker and anyone who requires him to act. "It's hard to talk about writing. I get my words from the same place where you get yours: the language that calls itself 'English.' What catches your eye, or ear, are the combinations I put those words into. Ideas float in, like seeds, from the world, from art, from dreams. Or they just occur to me. I don't know how or why. Then I'll have a line, which I try to massage so it scans into the rhythm of the whole. I have to consider rhyme, too. Am I choosing an easily rhymeable last word? Is it too easy to rhyme? Cliché that way lies. Never rhyme 'fire' with 'desire.' Or 'hold me tight' with 'tonight.' If it's too artful, it sounds contrived. 'Pepsi-Cola' and 'Angola.' "

"Fascinating." Victor French glances at his watch.

Bruce swaps his empty port glass for a full one. "Elf looked incredible on the TV monitors earlier. The camera adored her."

"We all scrubbed up nicely," says Elf.

"I'm waiting for *Vogue* to call about a cover issue," says Griff. "I may get a matching scar on the other side of my face."

"Any woman on *Top of the Pops* gets a lot of camera time," says Elf. "We're an exotic species on the show."

"It's your folk background," says Bruce. "Folk's all about rapport and authenticity. That's what the camera picked up on."

Dean exhales a blade of smoke. "Yer reckon folk music's got a monopoly on authenticity, do yer, Bruce?"

"If you screw up in a folk club, there's nowhere to hide. There's no hordes of screaming girlies to cover you. You're naked."

"Sounds like I've been visiting the wrong clubs," quips Howie.

"So the question is," says Bruce, "which of Elf's songs is going to be the follow-up single?"

"Let's discuss this another time," says Elf.

"We settled this in June, Bruce," Dean looks for an ashtray and uses a saucer, "while yer were dipping in and out and in and out of Gay Paris. Jasper gets the debut, I get the follow-up, and Elf gets the third single. That's also why Elf got the B side on 'Darkroom.' Which she's paid the same royalties for as Jasper's A side, by the by."

"It might be wiser," says Victor French, "to see what comes out of the first few sessions at Fungus Hut before deciding."

"Victor's right," says Bruce. "He's seen a hundred one-hit wonders die early because they cocked up the second single. The follow-up *must* display the band's range of flavors."

Dean's turning pink. "We're not a bloody ice-cream parlor."

"Mate," says Bruce, "this is the autumn of the Summer of Love. When I hear 'Abandon Hope' I hear doom and gloom. To adapt Howie's pithy phrase, it's Not Very Now. Elf's new song, though—'Unexpectedly'—it's *so* now, it's next year. Right, Howie?"

Jasper doesn't think that Howie has heard "Unexpectedly," but Moonwhale's chief investor purses his lips and nods. "Surely there's no harm in seeing what comes out of the sessions."

"I appreciate everyone's interest," says Elf, "but—"

"If the second hit's an Elf Holloway song," says Bruce, "our fans will dig that Utopia Avenue is yin and yang. They'll think, *There's nothing this band can't do.* Girls will dig the band. 'Abandon Hope' 's a fab little tune, Dean, don't get me wrong, but if it follows on from 'Darkroom,' Utopia Avenue'll get put into a pigeonhole labeled 'Cream Clones.' Then when Elf sings lead on the *third* single, all your blues fans'll think, *What's this girl doing in my band?* Imagine a new Rolling Stones single, sung by some chick. Di-*saster.* We have to establish that Elf's a core singer *now.*"

Dean addresses the room. "Ain't no one going to say it?"

"Say what?" Bruce's smile is illegible to Jasper.

"Sleeping with Elf doesn't earn yer voting rights."

A few gasps, a few mumbles; everyone looks at Elf.

"Guys," says Levon, "let's just mellow out a little . . ."

"How Elf amuses herself in her spare time's her business," says Dean. "What *is* my business is the band. Long 'n' short of it is, Bruce, yer've got no bloody vote in Utopia Avenue. None."

Elf sighs. "Can we all stop this? We should be celebrating."

"I don't *want* a vote, Dean." Bruce speaks like a patient teacher. "Yes, I'm Elf's feller, yes, I'm a lucky man, no, I'm not in the band. But if I see you cruising straight at an enormous iceberg, I'm not going to shut up. I'm going to yell, *'Watch out for that bloody enormous iceberg!'* And if 'Abandon Hope' is your next single, I'm afraid that's an iceberg."

"Remind me," says Dean. "How many Top Twenty hits've *you* had lately, Mr. McCartney? I've gone 'n' forgotten."

Bruce smiles, confusing Jasper. "You don't have to be a Beatle to have valid views about the music business. Dean."

"Acting like yer the King of Showbiz when yer've got fuck-all on yer CV'll make yer look a twat. Twat."

BRAKES SCREECH ON the cobbles of Mason's Yard. The stars are out. A few doors away, the Indica Gallery is having a late private view. Jasper hears laughter. "Here we go again," says Dean. The two Utopians stand before the door of 13A. Four months have passed since they tried to blag their way in using Brian Epstein's name. The

Beatles' manager took his own life only a fortnight ago. It was global news for a day or two. "Yer new pal promised he'd put our names down, yeah?"

"Yes," replied Jasper. "Though it was just after he'd had a bump of cocaine in the BBC toilets, so . . . no guarantees."

"Nothing ventured, nothing gained." Dean presses the golden doorbell. It rings. The window slot snaps open and the all-seeing eye appears. "Good evening, gentlemen."

"Hi," says Dean. "Um, so we're, um, uh, actually—"

"Mr. Moss, Mr. de Zoet," says the eye. "How are you?"

Dean looks at Jasper, then back to the eye. "Fine. You?"

"Congratulations on *Top of the Pops,*" says the all-seeing eye. "The first of many appearances, I'm sure."

"Cheers," says Dean. "I didn't expect, uh . . ."

The eye-slot snaps shut and 13A opens, revealing a bald man with a wrestler's build dressed like a stagecoach driver. Music and chatter spill out. "Welcome to the Scotch of St. James. I'm Clive. The management instructed me to offer you membership. The office'll send the paperwork along to Moonwhale in the morning, but for tonight, please step inside . . ."

HIGH WALLS, BEAUTIFUL people, next year's fashion, eyes that don't miss a trick, a corridor that ends in a salon. Smoke is thick, lamplight is foaming, mirrors might be doorways or might be mirrors. Jasper avoids these as best he can. Diamonds dangle, laughter boomerangs, champagne is golden, walls are tartan, bottles line shelves, rumors are spreading, faces are famous but at odd angles, talent is hungry, talent is assessed, lips are glossy, teeth are shown, perfume is French, yobs are northern, debutantes loll and flirt with the rough and the smooth, age woos youth, youth weighs up the pros and cons, senses commingle. Booths line walls. A real stagecoach sits in a corner. Music throbs up from the cellar. "Stick with me, darlin'!" exclaims a man's voice, "and you'll *fart through silk.*" Jasper feels as if he's wandered into a zoo without cages.

Dean mutters in Jasper's ear, "*Look!* Michael Caine. George Best. No, *don't look.*"

Jasper looks. The famous actor's laughing at something a swarthy, bearded, shorter man's saying. "Who's George Best?"

"Yer seriously don't know who George Best is?"

"I seriously don't know who George Best is."

"One o' the best three footballers on the planet."

"Right. I'll get the drinks. What'll you have?"

Dean makes a face. "What d'yer drink in a place like this?"

"My grandfather always used to say, 'If in doubt, ask for a whisky on ice.' "

"Perfect. Cheers. I'll pop to the bogs. Be right back."

Jasper edges a path to the bar, where three voices are bellowing to penetrate the dim din. "Yes, Eppy made the Beatles a fortune," says Voice One, "but he *gave* the merchandising away. Eppy was just a furniture salesman who got very, *very* lucky."

"How come the boys stuck with him?" asks Voice Two.

"Aha," says Voice Three. "*My* driver heard it from Ringo's driver that they'd agreed to give him the heave-ho when they got back from their weekend with the Maharishi in Wales."

"But Eppy got wind of the dastardly plot," says Voice One. "See? His 'accidental overdose' starts to look less accidental."

"Stuff and nonsense," says Voice Two. "He swilled down too many pills, that's all. Eppy always was more ham than bacon . . ."

"STAND AND DELIVER." Sporting a Mexican hat, Brian Jones is ensconced in a booth with two women. "Your whisky or your life. Glad you got here." There's no sign of Dean, so Jasper hands Brian Jones his glass of Kilmagoon. *I can always get another when Dean shows up.* "Meet Miss Cressy"—Brian Jones indicates a willowy girl with dark ringlets—"and Miss Cressy's bosom friend . . ."

"Nicole." She flutters her fingers. "Hi." A Mary Quant bob half hides her eyes. "Do I know you? It's the hair."

"Jasper was on *Top of the Pops* this very eve," says Brian Jones.

"I knew it!" Nicole awards herself a round of applause. "Character *is* hair. Like Brian's magic golden mop."

"The source of my sun-god virility," agrees Brian Jones.

"If we shaved it off," adds Miss Cressy, "nobody would know him from a bleached Mr. Potato Head."

"You're a Leo," Cressy tells Jasper.

"Pisces," replies Jasper.

"That's exactly the source of your pain. You're a spiritual Leo trapped in a material Pisces."

Jasper guesses he's being flirted with, but Cressy looks young enough to have school in the morning. "I don't complain."

"That's the Leo talking," says Nicole. "Most men are frightful whingers. They should try having hair plucked from their privates. Oops." She puts her finger to her lips. "That just slipped out. I'm a *teensy* bit squiffy. I blame wicked Mr. Jones."

Brian Jones clinks his glass with Jasper's. "The health of the salmon." He puffs on Nicole's cigarette. Apollo is flaking.

"You were going to tell me more about the messages you get in your head," Jasper says. "Then Steve Marriott came up."

Brian Jones's eyes dart around Jasper's face. "Was that only this evening? It feels like much longer ago."

"I'll cast a spell of protection," says Nicole. "I did a witchcraft course. My teacher was Morgan le Fay in a former life."

"Miss Cressy," says Brian Jones, "fingers off my nipples, please. There's a time and a place."

"Which is *not* what he said in the loos at the Flamingo club," Cressy tells Jasper. "Oops. It slipped out."

"Ladies," says Brian Jones, "my friend and I need a little privacy. Amuse yourselves for a few minutes."

"Spoilsports," pouts Nicole. The women vacate the booth.

Brian Jones leans in. The brim of his hat touches Jasper's head. "Me, Keith, and Mick were living in a shithole in Chelsea. They started then. It comes and goes. Sometimes they're friendly. They'll say, '*Damn good job, Brian.*' Other times they'll tell me what a piece of shit I am. Others it sends me off on wild goose chases. Like tonight. '*Lime Grove Studios! Go go go go go!*' Do you think it's just my unconscious? Perhaps I've done too much acid. Do I sound like a crank?"

"I don't judge anyone. I was in an asylum for two years."

Brian Jones is hard to decipher. "I ought to know you."

Nearby, a tray of glasses is dropped. A cheer explodes.

Hurry. "Has your voice ever struck you as evil?"

Brian Jones drinks whisky. "Why do you ask?"

JASPER LAY IN Matron's room at Bishop's Ely. A headache had turned cyclonic. Matron had given him an aspirin, then had to run an errand. Thunder ricocheted across the Fens. The May afternoon was dark as an eclipse. There was a *knock-knock* at the door. Jasper waited for whoever it was to come in, or go.

There was a *knock-knock* at the door.

Jasper called, "Matron's not here."

There was a *knock-knock* at the door.

Jasper called, "Come in, then."

There was a *knock-knock* at the door.

Jasper guessed it was a timid first-year. He swung off the bed, his brain banging his skull's interior, and walked over to the door.

Nobody was in the corridor outside.

Jasper guessed it was a prank and shut the door.

Immediately there was a *knock-knock* at the door.

Jasper flung open the door.

Nobody was in the corridor. Nobody.

Jasper's eardrums popped. He shivered.

Knock Knock? thought-spoke Jasper. *Is that you?*

Nobody replied. Jasper closed the door.

There was a *knock-knock* at the door.

The knocking could only be in Jasper's head.

The first bullets of rain smashed on the window.

Like knuckles on wood came a *knock-knock.*

Jasper felt Knock Knock watching him with the intensity of a marksman, or a psychologist, or a bird of prey. Rain smattered Ely's old stones, old slates, the river, its tarmac and the roofs of cars. A cacophony broke over Jasper—*knock*knock*knock*-KNOCK-*KNOCK*-KNOCK-*knocketty*-knock. He stumbled back to bed and pulled the blanket over his head. Jasper recited, "I'm not insane, I'm not insane, I'm not insane . . ." guessing this was exactly what the insane do as they vanish down the helter-skelter.

Abruptly, the knocking stopped.

Jasper waited for it to begin again.

He emerged from his blanket.

The rain had stopped. Water dripped.

There was a *knock-knock* at the door.

Jasper's only recourse was to refuse to answer.

After another *knock-knock,* the door opened, and a nervous first-year in a uniform two sizes too big stepped in. "Hello. Is Matron here? Mr. Kingsley says I look like death warmed up."

THAT NIGHT, JASPER had a dream of cinematic clarity. Snow was falling onto a mountain temple of high walls, curved roofs, and pine trees. The dream was set in Japan. Women swept wooden walkways with rustic brooms. Several were pregnant. A curving tunnel lit by dream-light led into a domed chamber. It housed an erect-backed, kneeling goddess, three or four times the size of a human woman, sculpted from a block of night sky. Her cupped hands made a hollow the size of a cradle. Her eyes gazed into the hollow. Her predatory mouth opened wide. *If the shrine of Shiranui is a question,* spoke a thought, *here is the answer.* Swaying flames were moonflower blue and silent. Realizing he had been lured to that place to be sacrificed, Jasper fled back down the curving tunnel to the temple. Wooden screens slid shut behind him. *Knock, knock, knock, knock.* He reached his room at Swaffham House in this world, bolted the door, and hid in his bed. But still he heard it. *Knock-knock, knock-knock . . .* Knock Knock was knocking a hole in the wall between the snowy temple in Japan and his room in Ely, and this mustn't, *mustn't* happen . . . but it already had . . .

"SHIT," SAYS BRIAN Jones. "Sounds like a bad trip." The smoke in the Scotch of St. James turns the lights brown. Jasper keeps drinking his whisky but his glass never empties. The Stone asks, "Were you all acid-heads at this school of yours?"

"The only acid we knew were acid drops, the boiled sweets; hydrochloric acid; and battery acid. This was still 1962."

"Was 'Heinz Formaggio' a real name?" asks Brian Jones. " 'Heinz' as in Baked Beans? 'Formaggio' as in 'cheese' in Italian?"

"Yes. He's German-Italian-Swiss. *Outside* a bad trip, have you ever experienced anything like Knock Knock?"

Brian Jones squints. "My messages are nasty sometimes, but your Knock Knock sounds—"

"IT'S A NIGHTMARE, de Zoet!" A familiar voice reached him across a vast divide. "You're having a nightmare. Jasper! Wake up."

Jasper sat bolt upright, staring at a face he knew, but not yet sure if it was Now, Then, or Will Be.

It was Formaggio. Confusingly, they were in their dorm. Jasper had thought he was in Matron's room. The knocking had ceased.

"You were talking in a foreign language," said Formaggio. "Not Dutch. This was *really* foreign. Chinese or something."

The alarm clock said a quarter past one.

"What happened?" asked Formaggio.

There was a *knock-knock* at the door.

Jasper looked at Formaggio, hoping he had heard it.

There was a *knock-knock* at the door.

"Did you hear that?" Jasper was trembling.

"Hear what? You've got me worried."

FORMAGGIO WAS GRIM. "So it's worse now than it's ever been before?"

"Like my skull's a wall and this is a hammer."

"Have you kept data?"

"Formaggio, keeping my sanity's the best I can manage."

"And there's been no dialogue?"

"None. He just knocks. Without letup."

"Is he knocking now?"

"Yes."

"That must be terrifying."

"Now I know what that word means."

"Can I try something?"

"Anything."

Formaggio looked into Jasper's eyes as if peering into a cave entrance. "Knock Knock. We want to ask some questions. Knock once for no and twice for yes. Please. Understand?"

The knocking stopped. The silence of Swaffham House was blissful. "He's gone quiet," said Jasper. "I think he—"

Knock-knock, came the answer, loud and clear.

Jasper was astonished. "Two knocks. Did you hear it?"

"No, but . . ." Formaggio thought. "If he hears me, he's wired into your auditory nervous system. Knock Knock? Can we call you that?"

Knock-knock, came the reply. "Yes," said Jasper. "Two knocks. Does this make me more crazy or less crazy?"

"Knock Knock: Do you know what Morse code is?"

A pause was followed by a single knock. "No," said Jasper.

"Pity." Formaggio leaned forward on his bed. "Knock Knock, do you exist independently of de Zoet?"

Knock-knock. "Yes," confirmed Jasper.

"Knock Knock. Do you think of yourself as a demon?"

A pause. *Knock.* "No," said Jasper.

"Did you once have a body, like me and de Zoet?"

Knock-knock. "A strong yes," said Jasper.

"Knock Knock. Do you know the name of the country we're in?"

Knock-knock. "Yes," said Jasper.

"Is it France?"

Knock. "No," said Jasper.

"Is it England?"

Knock-knock. "Yes," reported Jasper.

"So you know the year is 1962, Knock Knock?"

Knock-knock. "Another yes."

"Knock Knock, how many years have you been resident in de Zoet? Can you knock once for each year?"

Slowly, as if to ensure Jasper wouldn't lose count, Knock Knock knocked sixteen times. "Sixteen."

"Sixteen? All of de Zoet's life, then?"

Knock-knock. "Yes."

"Are you older than de Zoet?"

A firm *knock-knock.* "Yes."

"How old are you?" asked Formaggio.

Ten knocks were followed by a pause. Jasper said, "Ten," and the knocks continued to twenty. "Twenty." The knocks went up to thirty. "Thirty." Jasper continued in this way, up to a hundred. Two hundred. A couple of minutes passed before the knocks finally stopped and Jasper reported, "Six hundred and ninety-three."

Swaffham House was utterly silent.

"Let's try this." Formaggio went to his desk and drew a grid with letters on a sheet of writing paper. He brought it to Jasper's bed and laid it on the blanket:

	1	2	3	4	5
1 –	a	b	c	d	e
2 –	f	g	h	i	j
3 –	k	l	m	n	o
4 –	p	q	r	s	t
5 –	u	v	w	x	y
6 –	z				

"These numbers are x-y coordinates," Formaggio explained in his Knock Knock voice. "You spell out words, letter by letter. Columns first, then rows. So if you want to spell the word 'sun,' you'd knock four times"—Formaggio indicated the fourth column across—"pause, then four times again"—he counted down the rows—"to get the *s,* once across and five times to get the *u,* four then three times for the *n.* Understand?"

A crisp *knock-knock.* "He understands," said Jasper.

"Great. So, Knock Knock: What do you want?"

Knock Knock knocked twice and waited for Jasper to say, "Two"; then three times. *L.* Formaggio wrote the letter on a jotter. Next came four and two knocks for *i;* and after two minutes, l–i–f–e–a–n–d–l–i–b–e–r–t–y

had appeared. Jasper hadn't considered that the squatter in his skull might also be a prisoner. Formaggio asked, "How can we give you life and liberty?"

Knock Knock got to work again.

d–e–z–o–e–t–m–u–s–t

Knock Knock stopped there, or appeared to.

Old pipes in the walls juddered and groaned.

" 'De Zoet must' what?" asked Formaggio.

The knocks began again, and spelled:

d–i–e

Formaggio and Jasper looked at each other.

Every hair on Jasper's arms was standing up.

"Why?" asked Formaggio. "What's de Zoet done to you?"

Knock Knock's reply came rapidly and sharply:

t–r–e–s–p–a–s–s

"But you're the one in *his* head," said Formaggio.

Blow by blow, the answering knocks spelled out:

i–n–t–h–e–b–l–o–o–d

Jasper stared at the letters.

"It's like a cryptic crossword," said Formaggio.

A crossword for you, thought Jasper, *but a death warrant for me.* "Formaggio, I can't do this anymore."

"But this is the most incredible thing I've ever—"

"Stop. Please. Stop this. Now."

STUFF OF LIFE

SIDE ONE

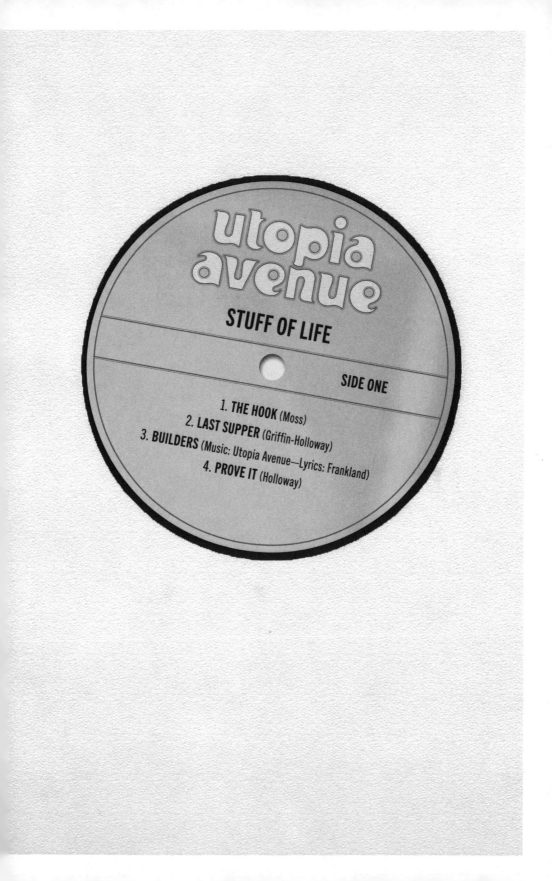

1. **THE HOOK** (Moss)
2. **LAST SUPPER** (Griffin-Holloway)
3. **BUILDERS** (Music: Utopia Avenue—Lyrics: Frankland)
4. **PROVE IT** (Holloway)

THE HOOK

"PICK A NICE FAT BASTARD." DEAN'S DAD TOOK A MAGGOT from the jar and held it up to the hook. "Squeeze him *very* gentle-like. Below the head. Yer don't want to kill him, yer just want his mouth to open . . . Open wide, that's it . . . See? Feed him onto the hook . . . Like feeding a thread through a needle." Dean watched up close, fascinated and disgusted. "Twist the hook out of his arse, just so the point shows. See? That way he can't slide off, but he'll still twitch a bit and the fish won't rumble he's a maggot on a hook. He'll just think, *Oh, dinner, yum,* bite 'n' swallow . . . and then the hook's lodged in him good 'n' proper-like. Then guess who's dinner after all?" His dad smiled. It was a rare sight. Dean smiled too. "Check yer weight 'n' float're tied proper one last time—they cost a few bob—and then yer ready to cast." His dad stood up, reaching halfway to the sky. "Stand back, we don't want *you* getting snagged on the hook and flying into the river. Yer mum'd never let me hear the end of it." Dean trotted back down the jetty, almost to the shore. His dad held the rod back over his shoulder and cast. Weight, float, maggot on a hook flew over the glossy Thames, and landed with a plop and a splash many yards out.

Dean trotted back. "It went *miles*!"

His father sat down with his feet dangling over the edge. "Hold it. Good steady grip. Both hands." Dean obeyed while his dad swigged from the bottle in a brown paper bag. The river slid by. The river slid by. The river slid by. Dean wished it could be like this all the time. Father and son did not speak for a while.

"The mystery o' fishing's this," said Dean's dad, "what's the hook, who's got the rod, what's the maggot, what's the fish?"

"Why's that a mystery, Dad?"

"Yer'll understand when yer older."

"But ain't it obvious what's what?"

"It changes, son. In a heartbeat."

THE TIP OF Amy Boxer's fang indents her lip. "When I chat with John or Paul, or the lads in the Hollies, I'm speaking with guys who met at school. They're as close as brothers. They plodded around the talent shows, they survived the variety circuits, they slaved in dives like the Cavern. Compared to them, don't you feel . . . a little"—the *Melody Maker* reporter has to raise her voice over the noise of hammering—"manufactured?"

Levon's office in Moonwhale is not, today, an oasis of calm. A toilet cistern burst in the Duke-Stoker office downstairs. Tradesmen are repairing the damage noisily.

"Does our music sound manufactured?" asks Jasper.

"Are you saying we're the fookin' Monkees?" asks Griff.

"Not the Monkees' biggest fans, then?" asks Amy Boxer.

Levon intervenes. "We wish Davy, Michael, Peter, and, uh . . ."

"Scrotum-chops," grunts Griff, from his hangover-recovery position on the sofa, with a black cowboy hat over his face.

"Micky Dolenz," says Elf. "Don't be mean."

"We wish the Monkees all the very best," says Levon.

Amy Boxer's fishnet tights make a nylon scratching noise when she crosses her legs. Dean tries to focus on her hands. Ruby fingernails and three or four rings on both hands. Her biro leaves a trail of longhand. Her tendons flex in her forearm. Her accent is Essex. "*The—very—best* . . . Got it. So that night at Les Cousins, Elf, when a suave Canadian, a corblimey Cockney, a starving Viking, and a wildman drummer invited you to join their merry band, what passed through your mind?"

"Hang on," interrupts Dean: " 'A corblimey Cockney'?"

Levon's hand gesture says, *Let this one pass, let it pass.*

"Readers love a good creation myth. *We formed after getting locked in a barn* or *We were adrift in a lifeboat and nearly had to eat each other* is so much meatier than *Our manager assembled us like an Airfix kit.* Our female readers are also curious, Elf, about being the only girl in a band of guys."

In Bethany's office, three typewriters clatter and ping; space has been made for two sister-secretaries from Duke-Stoker.

Elf biffs the question back. "How is it for you at *Melody Maker*? Pop journalism isn't known for respecting women."

"God, Elf, don't get me started. Sweary, preening, horny boys who rewrite the rulebook as it suits them. Sound familiar?"

Elf nods wearily. "If a man makes a mistake, it's a mistake. If a woman makes one, it's 'Told you so!' Does *that* sound familiar?"

Levon looks neutral. Jasper's staring into space. Griff stays under his hat. "Who here treats yer like that?" asks Dean.

"In the studio, anyone with testicles treats me like that."

"I bloody don't."

"Watch. Watch how everyone reacts to one of *my* ideas, compared to an idea from a guy. Watch and learn."

Dean lights a Dunhill. *Either someone's on her period or Bruce is putting ideas into her head.*

"Let's focus on the forming of the band," suggests Levon.

"So why *did* you join this band of brothers?" Amy Boxer's pen is busy. She's looking pleased with herself.

Elf sips her coffee. "The morning after we met at Les Cousins, we went to Club Zed up on Ham Yard, just to jam for a while. The musical chemistry was good, for four strangers." She gestures at the sleeve of *Paradise Is the Road to Paradise,* propped up on the glass table. "It's only improved since."

"Nice . . ." Amy Boxer's pen scratches. The sound of sawing starts up. "You and your boyfriend, Bruce Fletcher, put out an EP last year. *Shepherd's Crook.* Which I enjoyed, by the way. I'm curious, is Bruce jealous of your success in Utopia Avenue?"

"You're allowed to say, 'No comment,'" says Levon.

"Bruce is happy for me and the band . . ." replies Elf.

Only 'cause there's more cash to sponge, thinks Dean.

". . . and he's put together a demo of his own songs. Our success has got his creative juices flowing."

Bruce Fletcher doesn't "flow," thinks Dean. *He dribbles.*

Amy Boxer looks a little dubious. "Any luck so far?"

"There's some early interest. Duke-Stoker have been plugging it in the States, and Dean Martin's people have been in touch. Gladys Knight too. Shandy Fontayne."

"Shandy Fontayne?" The reporter looks at Levon, reluctantly impressed. "When Bruce's first song goes gold, maybe I'll interview him. But Elf, don't you miss your artistic independence, now you have to haggle over musical decisions with these three?"

"Yer such a bloody shit-stirrer," mutters Dean.

The reporter is amused. "Just doing my job."

Elf hesitates. "Obviously, a band's a democracy." Elf taps ash from her Camel. "You get your own way sometimes, but if you want your own way every time, you have to not be in a band anymore."

Amy Boxer transcribes the quote. "You're sitting quietly at the back, Jasper. First, that surname, 'de Zoet.' Am I saying it right?"

"No. 'Zoet' rhymes with 'loot,' not with 'poet.' "

"Noted. Is it true you're from aristocratic stock?"

"Once upon a time, my father was sixtieth in line to the Dutch throne, but recent babies expelled him from the top hundred."

This is news to the others. "Yer never told me," says Dean.

"The subject never came up," says Jasper.

"Why the fook *would* it?" asks Griff.

Jasper shrugs. "Does it matter?"

Dean nearly tells Amy Boxer, "That's Jasper in a nutshell," but she's asking, "Do you think of yourself as British or Dutch?"

"I don't think about it at all, unless people ask."

"And when people ask, how do you respond?"

"By saying, 'I feel both.' Usually, they reply, 'You can't be both.' I say, 'I feel both.' And the conversation grinds to a halt."

She taps her teeth with her biro. "What does Bishop's Ely school think of an alumnus on *Top of the Pops*?"

"No idea," says Jasper. "TV sets are banned there."

"Several musicians I've interviewed in the last month used the word 'genius' to describe your guitar work. How do you plead?"

"People should listen to Jimi Hendrix and Eric Clapton before lobbing language like that at me."

"How gratifying was it when 'Darkroom' hit the Top Twenty?"

It peaked at number sixteen, thinks Dean, *then sank like a bloody stone, despite* Top of the Pops.

"Dean and Elf write too," Levon reminds the reporter. "That's why *Paradise* is so varied and devoid of padding."

"I'm curious," says Amy Boxer. "The first time you played the LP to your record company, how did they react?"

GÜNTHER MARX SAT in his office, framed by a view of Tower Bridge, and uttered not one syllable. Squally rain tumbled up the Thames. Victor French sat beneath a canvas of red and yellow dots. Publicist Nigel Horner sat by a state-of-the-art Grundig turntable. *Paradise Is the Road to Paradise* pumped through four Bose speakers. Günther's gnarly index finger might have tapped during "Smithereens." He tilted his head during Elf's piano solo in "Mona Lisa Sings the Blues." He made a turn-it-over gesture to Nigel Horner at the end of side one. Jasper's "Wedding Presence" and Elf's ballad "Unexpectedly" came and went without prompting a flicker. Dean found himself sweating during "Purple Flames." Elf did a Procol Harum–esque organ solo, which Dean loved and had got Digger to splice onto an earlier take. It ruled the song out as a single, which cut Dean's field of contenders for the glory and publishing money down to "Abandon Hope" and "Smithereens." Halfway through Jasper's song "The Prize," Günther's head began, very slightly, to bob in time. Dean felt sick. "The Prize" finished. The stylus lifted. The Grundig clicked off.

Neither Victor French nor Nigel Horner was going to commit to an opinion before their overlord had spoken. Which he did not do before Dean ran out of patience. "Do yer like it or not, Günther? Or are we s'posed to guess?"

Nigel Horner and Victor French winced.

Günther made a steeple of his hands. " 'Darkroom' did well. Most bands would follow the proven formula. Correct?"

"Very often," said Victor French, "in general, yes."

"Yet the only song on the LP that sounds like 'Darkroom' "— Günther leaned back—"is 'Darkroom.' This album sounds as if three separate bands recorded it. Not one."

"Is that a good thing or a bad thing?" asked Dean.

Günther removed a wooden box from his desk. He opened it. Dean noticed Victor French swap a look with Nigel Horner. Günther took a cheroot from the box and scalped it with a tiny guillotine. Dean crossed his legs. Günther announced: "*Paradise Is the Road to Paradise* will be in the shops and the album chart Top Forty by Christmas. Well done."

A wash of relief passed through Dean's body.

"I have no doubt it'll perform *very* well," said Levon.

Günther is scalping cheroots. "We'll throw everything we have at *Paradise* and a new single. Radio, gigs, magazine interviews, everything. Let us now smoke a cheroot." He handed one to everyone. "It's a little custom. It goes back to my U-boat days."

"Does it say 'Cuban' on that box?" asked Elf.

"They fell off a boat," said Günther.

"ILEX ADORED THE album," Levon tells Amy Boxer. "Every time a song finished, Günther the managing director said, '*That*'s the masterpiece.' When the next song came on, he did the same. At the end, he said, 'It's a whole album of goddamn masterpieces.' " Levon speaks so persuasively, Dean almost remembers it happening.

"Isn't Ilex a brave choice? They've got a strong classical catalogue but you're their first pop signing, pretty much."

"EMI and Decca made overtures," replies Levon, "but we thought, *No.* The future belongs to swifter, hungrier labels."

Amy's pressed-together lips reply, *If you say so.* "Let me turn to you now, Griff. What's your story?"

The drummer lifts his cowboy hat and opens one eye. "Five pints at Ronnie Scott's, a chaser or two, then things get hazy."

"I've already noted you're the band joker. But seriously."

Griff growls, swivels upright, and slurps coffee. "The Drummer's Tale. I was a sickly boy and I spent a lot of time in Hull Royal Infirmary. There was a children's band, and I took to the drums. When I got out of hospital, I got roped into a brass band as the drummer-boy. Later, Wally Whitby took me under his wing."

"My dad likes Wally Whitby. 'Yes Sir, That's My Baby.' "

"Wally took me around the northern circuit. Pontin's holiday camp at Southport. Butlin's in Skegness. I liked the life. The ladies liked me better with my drums. Wally's an old pal of Alexis Korner, so when I came to London to seek my fortune, Alexis got me work in blues and jazz clubs. That led to Archie Kinnock's Blues Juggernaut. Several misadventures later, Archie gave Jasper a tryout for his new band, the Blues Cadillac. That didn't last . . ."

"The 2i's bar incident is becoming the stuff of legend," says Amy. "Do the ladies still like you with your drums?"

"Ask Dean about the ladies, Miss Cheeky." Griff lies down again. " 'The Goat of Gravesend,' they call him. Fookin' shameless."

"They'll be calling him 'The Songsmith of Gravesend,' " says Levon. "Thanks to 'Abandon Hope.' Out today. Which Dean wrote."

"Mmm . . ." Amy Boxer finishes transcribing Griff's story before looking at Dean. She has a *screw-you*-ness that Jude lacks. Jude is nice, sweet, and loyal, and if Dean had never left Gravesend and wanted a nice girl to settle down with, a Jude would've been perfect. *But fame changes the rules.* Melody Maker *reporters understand that, but hairdressers from Brighton don't.* "So," says the reporter. " 'Abandon Hope.' It's a brave choice for a second single."

"Why would that be, Miss Boxer?"

A sharp little smile. " 'Amy' is fine. I'm not my mother. It's a straight R&B number. No psychedelic jiggery-pokery."

"Nothing straight about its hook. Once its hook's in yer, there's no swimming off. One in the verse, one in the chorus."

"And a song's only as good as its hook, do you think?"

By way of answer, Dean *da-dah*s the hook of the Kinks' "You Really Got Me" until Griff names the track. Then Griff *da-dah*s a different song, adding air drums. After a few seconds, Jasper says, " 'Taxman,' off *Revolver.*" Jasper thinks, then sings the tune of his chosen hook for three lines before Elf lays the "Hound Dog" lyrics over the fourth. "Though the way you sang it," Elf adds, "it sounded more like the theme to *Born Free.*"

"Looks as if you play that game often," notes Amy.

"Thanks to 'Darkroom,' " Elf replies, "we're doing more longer journeys in the Beast. Our van. The Hook Game is a staple."

"Dean's well known for his hooking talents," Griff tells Amy. " 'Specially in the men's bogs in Soho Square."

"Griff is, of course, joking," says Levon.

Amy jots something down. "What I meant about 'Abandon Hope' being brave was: Don't you think fans of 'Darkroom' will hear 'Abandon Hope' and feel flummoxed?"

"On *Sergeant Pepper's,* that Indian track of Harrison's sits cheek-by-jowl with 'When I'm Sixty Four.' Sitar to oboe, like . . ." He snaps his fingers. "Does that flummox yer? Or do yer think, *Bloody Nora, that's clever*?"

Amy Boxer looks unconvinced. "Neither of those songs is a single. Did Ilex choose 'Abandon Hope,' or was it a band decision?"

"We chose it." Dean looks at the others. Jasper is off in Jasperland. Elf studies her nails. Griff is under his hat. *Thanks a bloody bunch,* thinks Dean.

A little silver dagger hangs in the hollow of Amy Boxer's throat. "Did Ilex agree? Or did you have to twist their arm?"

"CONCERNING THE NEXT single," declared Günther Marx at Ilex HQ, "I am in two minds." His office was infused with cheroot smoke. "Either 'Mona Lisa Sings the Blues' or 'The Prize.' Opinions?"

"The band," said Levon, "nominate 'Abandon Hope.' "

"The first song on the first side," said Dean.

Günther wrinkled his nose. "It is too nihilist."

Dean didn't know the word. "It's just nihilist enough."

"It's a strong opener for an album," said Victor French, "but that doesn't necessarily make it the best single."

"The question, Dean"—Nigel Horner wrinkled his whippet face—

"is why would today's teenagers go nuts for a song about getting mugged and evicted and none of it mattering because the Russians'll nuke us anyway?"

"They *do* go nuts for it," said Dean. "At our gigs."

" 'Mona Lisa' will put Elf in the spotlight," said Victor French. "I see girls buying it in big numbers. They'll identify with a woman battling the odds in a hostile world."

"I agree with Victor," smarmed Nigel Horner, "about 'Abandon Hope' *and* I'd vote for 'The Prize' as the next single. Any kid dreaming of stardom'll dig it—and if there's one type of song DJs love to play, it's the type that praises DJs."

Dean looked at Levon. Levon looked like a man working out if he wanted a shit or not. Dean wanted to shout, *'We agreed this! The bloody dice!'* "No. We've chosen 'Abandon Hope.' It's gritty, it's got the end-o'-the-world stuff in the air right now. And if we do another Jasper song, people'll think we're a poor man's Pink Floyd."

"The reality is this." Günther stubbed out his cheroot. "Ilex spent thirteen thousand pounds on *Paradise Is the Road to Paradise.* Therefore, Ilex chooses the singles."

Dean stubbed out his cheroot. "No."

Günther, Nigel Horner, and Victor French looked at Dean first like men checking they'd heard right, then like men realizing they had. Günther spoke quietly: "What do you mean, 'No'?"

"The band chooses the single."

Levon jumped into action. "Moonwhale and the band are grateful for the investment, Günther, of course—"

"Quiet." Günther made a *Halt* sign. "Elf. Do you not wish to prove the band is not men with a novelty keyboardist in a frock?"

"Divide 'n' rule, Günther?" Dean sniffed. "Subtle."

Elf looked out of the window. "I agree to wait my turn."

"*Thank* you," said Dean. "So you see—"

Günther wasn't going to be distracted. "What is this 'agree'? This 'turn'? Do I detect"—he drew an oval in the air—"a plot?"

"The band is keen to . . ." Levon chose his words, ". . . nip jealousies in the bud by treating its songwriters equitably."

Günther studied the words. "So . . . you conspired—between yourselves—to release first a de Zoet song, *then* a Moss song, *then* a Holloway song. Is this the . . ." he searched for the word, ". . . gist?"

"It's a gentleman's agreement," said Dean.

"And my opinion is"—Günther *pfff*ed—"immaterial? And, Elf, why do you come *after* the boys? Is this the modern feminism?"

"Elf's not last because she's female," said Jasper. "She's last because she only rolled a one."

Dean cursed the educated idiot's honesty.

Günther flinched. Nigel Horner and Victor French looked askance. "What are you talking about?"

"When she rolled the dice," explained Jasper. "I got a three, Dean a two, and Elf a one. That's why her single is third."

Günther released a *"Hah?"* "If you believe I decide a major commercial decision on a *dice,* you're living in the Cloud Cuckoo Land. No. In a padded cell in the Cloud Cuckoo Land. Listen—"

"*You fookin'* listen!" Griff leaned forward. "It's *us* lugging our arses up the M2 night after freezing fookin' night while you're tucked up in bed. *Us.* It's *us* dodging bottles, or not"—he touched his scar—"flung by mods on hoppers. *Us.* So if you want your thirteen thousand quid back, we choose the fookin' single. Not you. *Us.* And 'Abandon Hope' 's the next single."

Thank you, thought Dean. *At bloody last.*

"So your threat," summarized Günther, "is this. 'Do what we say, or we sabotage our own careers'?"

"Nobody's threatening anyone," said Levon, "but I'd ask you just to give us this one. It's how the band want it."

"I sign the checks and *we*"—he indicates Victor and Nigel Horner—"choose the singles. That is how *I* want it."

"Fook this." Griff stubbed his cheroot out on the sofa's arm, dropped it on the carpet, got up, and left the office.

"He's bluffing," stated Nigel Horner. "He'll be back."

"Don't be daft," said Elf. "He's from Yorkshire."

"Drummers are two a penny," stated Victor French. "If he just quit, which he appears to have done, we'll simply hire a new one."

"No, yer bloody won't." Dean stood, defiantly. Elf stood, resolutely. Jasper stood. Levon stood, mumbling, "Oh, great."

"What?" Günther Marx's voice soared. "A walkout? A strike? Not so clever. Simply, I'll fire all of you."

"And kiss yer thirteen grand goodbye?" asks Dean. "How'll that look when yer speak to Toto Schiffer at Berlin HQ?"

Günther's face changed. *"Blackmail?"*

"I'VE NEVER KNOWN a label so eager to accommodate its artists as Ilex," Levon tells Amy Boxer. "Günther Marx is a visionary. He's a member of the Utopia Avenue family. Quote me on that."

"My my," says Amy. "That's a glowing review. Back to you, Dean. You're not related to royalty as well, are you?"

"I'm the Duke of Edinburgh's love child. *Shh.*"

"The band have deep respect for the Royal Family," said Levon.

Amy sipped her coffee and shot a *He is a worrier, isn't he?* look at Dean. "Your titles are nihilistic. 'Smithereens,' 'Abandon Hope,' 'Purple Flames.' Are you the Angry Young Man of Pop?"

That word again. "How d'yer mean, 'nihilistic'?"

"Bleak. Fierce. A belief that life is meaningless."

"Oh. Right. Yeah, well, if something pisses me off, I might write a song about it. That don't mean I think life's meaningless."

"What kind of thing pisses you off?"

Dean lights a Dunhill and takes a drag. The hammering downstairs starts up. "What pisses me off? Music critics who play God. People who use fancy words to lord it over yer. Men who hit women. Bent coppers. Old men who think 'I fought the war for you lot' ends any argument. The nobs who killed pirate radio. Anyone who shits on someone's dream. Pies that've got more air than filling, The Establishment, for skimming off the cream. The rest of us, for letting the bastards get away with it."

"Well, I did ask," says Amy. "Isn't Jasper 'Establishment'?"

Dean's housemate looks his way. "No. Jasper's cool."

"And I'm as common as muck," says Griff, "so when Dean needs to talk ferrets, outdoor bogs, or socialism, I'm right here."

Amy Boxer's silver dagger glints. "If you all hit the big time and are buying mansions in Surrey as a tax write-off, will you still be 'common as muck'? You've had a nibble of stardom. Haven't things started to change already?"

"STONE—THE—SODDING—*CROWS*, DEANO!" Stewart Kidd stood in the hallway, gawping at Jasper's flat. "Talk 'bout landing on yer feet." Kenny Yearwood was speechless. Rod Dempsey's eyes darted from item to item, fitting to fitting. Dean guessed he was totting up the value. "Yer not going to do the place over, are yer, Rod?"

Rod just cackled as his eyes kept scanning.

"This really is yer digs?" checked Stew.

"This is my digs," replied Dean.

"It's like out o' *Playboy,*" said Stew. "Yer've got the telly. Yer've got the stereo. Got a helicopter pad on the roof, have yer?"

"Jasper's dad bought the place as an investment. Jasper's the caretaker, and I'm Jasper's caretaker, I s'pose."

"So where's Jas-*pah* now?" Kenny did a posh accent.

"Oxford. He's back tomorrow. And just so's yer know, he'd never take the piss out o' *your* accent."

"Punch his bloody lights out if he tried," said Kenny.

Stew was still gazing at the flat. "Yer've been living here since January and yer only inviting us for a gander *now*?"

"Ain't Dean's fault," stated Rod Dempsey. "It's a brutal game, showbiz. Bet he hardly has time to take a crap."

"Yer not wrong," said Dean. "Shoes off, Stew. House rules."

Stew went *Huh?* but Rod Dempsey was already unstrapping his biker boots. "This flooring's worth more than yer aunt Nelly's house and everything in it."

"Including yer aunt Nelly," added Kenny. "Who charged top dollar in her day. Worth every penny, mind. Like yer mum."

"Hilarious." Stew unlaced his shoes. "Can I take a wazz, or would it stain the gold toilet bowl?"

"Down the passageway, second on the left."

Stewart followed the directions while Kenny went to inspect the record collection.

"I'm glad for yer, Dean." Rod Dempsey had a checkered reputation in Gravesend. At sixteen, he was sent to Borstal for torching his truancy officer's car; at eighteen, he joined a biker gang; at twenty, he fell through a skylight during a burglary and lost an eye. He left prison homeless, jobless, and penniless, but Bill Shanks loaned him enough to open a market stall dealing in biker gear. Now he had a shop in Camden Town.

"You too," Dean told him.

"We use the gifts we're given. Speaking of which." From his jacket he took a tin of Nipits licorice pellets and gave it to Dean.

Inside was a lump of hash as big as his thumb.

Dean held it up. "Standing by for takeoff . . ."

ARE YOU EXPERIENCED boomed out of Jasper's speakers. Dean stretched out on the fleecy rug, sinking into Noel Redding's bass on "The Wind Cries Mary." The darkness was colored by a glow-in-the-dark Dutch gnome called Mr. Kabouter. Kenny passed him the joint. "Spill the beans, Rock Star."

Dean toked. He floated and sank. "What beans?"

Stew knew what he meant. "How many girls've had the Dean Moss Experience in yer shag-pad?"

"I don't notch 'em on my bedpost."

"Are yer in double figures?" probed Kenny. "Are yer still knobbing that hairdresser from Brighton?"

Dean passed the joint to Rod. "This is God's own dope."

"Helmand Chestnut, brought from Afghanistan in the panels of a VW van. Seeing as we've got history, I can get it you at cost."

It dawned on Dean that Rod Dempsey wasn't dealing only in biker accessories. "I'll bear that in mind."

"The hairdresser," Kenny reminded him. "Yer stalling."

Dean's conscience gave him a slap. "I see Jude on 'n' off."

"Yer *bastard,*" groaned Kenny. "Why did I give up the music? I soddin' hate my job. The gaffer's a ponce. Shop steward's a berk."

"But yer've got a girlfriend," pointed out Stew.

"She's all nag, no shag." The dope made Kenny confessional. "I tell her, 'Let's just do it.' She gets weepy, and goes all, 'Are yer playing me for a fool, Kenny?' If I was Dean, if *I* was on *Top o' the* shittin' *Pops,* I'd give her the heave-ho, swan around Soho 'n' drop acid 'n' sleep with models 'n' hippie chicks and *do* something with my life. I'm dying in Gravesend."

"Follow in Dean's footsteps, then," said Rod. "Like they say with the football pools, 'If you are not in, you cannot win.' "

Kenny toked. "For two pins, I'd move up tomorrow."

Dean considered giving an honest account of how the modest advance from Ilex hadn't paid off his debts to Moonwhale, Selmer's Guitars, and his brother; how his slice of the "Darkroom" money won't add up to three wage-slips from a union job like Kenny's . . . but their envy tasted too good. "It ain't all cakes 'n' ale."

"Says he with a flat in Mayfair . . ." Stew took the joint. "With his mug on the telly and a bird he 'sees on and off.' "

"All shag, no nag," remarked Kenny.

"Got any famous mates yet?" asked Stew.

For a few seconds Dean considered saying no. The bass on "3rd Stone from the Sun" giddy-upped. "Does Brian Jones count?"

"*The* Brian Jones?" Stew gaped. "From the Rolling Stones?"

"Of course he bloody counts," said Kenny. "Brian Jones!"

Dean buzzed with the dope. "We bump into each other on the scene. We talk guitars, venues, labels. Just between us, he's a bit slow to buy his rounds." Dean's half-fib grows into a lie. "Unlike Hendrix. Jimi'd give you the shirt off his back."

"Yer know Hendrix?" asked Kenny. "I don't bloody believe it!"

But they did believe it, and Dean's escape from Gravesend never felt so secure or so triumphant. He passed the joint to Rod, whose one eye housed a tiny, reflected, grinning, glow-in-the-dark Mr. Kabouter, in on the secret.

LATER THAT EVENING, Dean and Kenny were waiting at the bar of the Bag o' Nails. Rod and Stew had gone to find a table. Dean slipped five one-pound notes into his friend's pocket. "That's that fiver yer lent me last year. The 2i's bar. Not a quick grope in yer trousers."

"Cheers, Dean. Thought yer'd forgotten."

"Never. Yer saved my arse. Thanks."

"Yer've come a long way since then."

"S'pose so."

"Seriously, I want a bite o' this," said Kenny. "London. Could I doss on yer sofa for a bit?"

Dean pictured Kenny trading on the scene as Dean Moss's best mate, and didn't relish the idea. "What'd yer do here?"

"What you've done. Get a guitar, write a few songs, put a band together. I wasn't the *worst* guitarist in the Gravediggers, was I?"

"Mate, it's a cutthroat game."

"It's working out sweet enough for you."

"Yeah, but I've practiced guitar for . . . *years.*"

"Or I could dust off my art diploma, get a job at *Oz* or the *International Times.* Or sell antiques up the Portobello. Or set myself up as a photographer. All I need's a base. So . . . yer sofa?"

He's got no idea, thinks Dean. "Thing is, it ain't my sofa. It's Jasper's dad's, and he could turf us out at any time. If yer serious, yer'll need somewhere more stable. It's Rod yer want to speak to."

Before Kenny cottoned on that he was being given the brush-off, Dean caught the barman's eye. "Four pints o' Smithwick's!"

THE LAST BAND on at the Bag o' Nails was a five-piece from Ipswich called Andronicus. They weren't great, but they kept up a driving, danceable beat and Dean, in his Napoleon coat from I Was Lord Kitchener's Valet, invented a new dance called the Flamingo. He couldn't afford the coat, but he figured he'd soon be able to. Dean felt overwhelmed by love. Love for his brothers and sister in music, Jasper, Elf, and Griff. Love for Levon, whose name had "love" hiding inside it. Love for his mum, who'd slipped away with the wonderful, the marvelous, the beautiful "Tennessee Waltz." Dean wiped his eyes. Love for Little Richard, for saving that snotty Tarzan boy at the Folkestone Odeon. Love for Nan Moss and Bill. He swore he'd buy them a bungalow in Broadstairs, maybe, with his first royalty check from "Abandon Hope," or the second check, or the third.

Love for Ray, his nephew Wayne, and, okay, pregnant Shirl his sister-in-law. Harry Moffat could wait for his handout in Hell—even Rod's happy pills had limits. But Dean felt love for the pirate-eyed Rod, who supplied these magic pills at cost. Love for Andronicus and every other musical mediocrity whose murk let Utopia Avenue shine all the brighter. Love for Jude, fast asleep in Brighton. Dean had been ordinary too, not so long ago. Love for Stew and his old friend Kenny—even if he didn't want to babysit him. Love rotated its beam like a lighthouse on a rock. When Andronicus finished, Dean went to the bar and told the barman, "Drinks for my friends!"

The barman asked, "Who're your friends?"

Dean looked at the faces. "All of 'em!"

The barman looked dubious. "*All* of them?"

"Everyone! The lot! Put 'em on my tab."

"Who are you again?" replied the barman.

"Dean Moss. My band's Utopia Avenue. We were on *Top of the Pops* last month. And I would like a tab."

The barman did not say, 'Sorry, Mr. Moss, I didn't recognize you.' The barman said, "Can't open a tab without the boss's say-so."

The magic blue pill did not rescue him, and, dimly, Dean realized that twenty onlookers would tell twenty others who would tell twenty others that a tosser called Dean Moss had made an utter prat of himself in the Bag o' Nails.

"It's okay, Dermott." Rod Dempsey appeared at Dean's shoulder. "I'll guarantee the tab. Standard ceiling."

The barman's face changed instantly. "Ah, well, in *that* case . . ." he looked back to Dean, ". . . Mr. Moss has a tab."

Dean burned with gratitude. "Rod, I . . ."

Rod made an it's-nothing gesture.

Dean jumped onto a table. "Bag o' Nails! Whatever yer having, ask at the bar to put it on Dean Moss's tab. *Dean Moss.* My band's Utopia Avenue. Our album's *Paradise Is the Road*—" A surge to the bar nudged Dean off his stool, and he half fell to the sticky floor. Hands lifted him up, laughing, and a string of brand-new lifelong friends toasted him with the Singapore Slings, Manhattans, triple

Scotches, Babychams, and pints of stout that Dean, Dean's talent, and Dean's generosity had paid for. His friends loved "Darkroom," and Dean promised them "Abandon Hope" would blow their minds.

The night became aquatic. Girls asked, "So you really *are* a pop star!" Dean said, "It's a dirty job but someone's got to do it," or "I am now, but I started off as a boy with a crazy dream." Girls asked if he knew any Stones or Beatles. Girls listened to his true lies with wide eyes. Girls shepherded Dean to the dance floor. One slid her hands around the back of his neck. He must have asked her name because she put her lips to his ear, like a fish nibbling the maggot on a hook. "Izzy Penhaligon."

"WOULD I STILL be working class," Dean repeats the question, "if I had a mansion in Surrey, a Triumph Spitfire, 'n' all that shit?"

Amy Boxer—*Amy*—nods as if she knows the answer.

A one-legged pigeon lands on the ledge of Levon's window.

Who cares? "Ask me when it happens."

" 'When it happens'?" asks Amy. "Not 'if'?"

"Yeah. 'When.' " *Cheeky cow.*

Scratch, scratch, scratch, goes Amy's pen.

"Are yer going to make me out to be an idiot?"

Amy looks up, doesn't say no and doesn't say yes.

"Amy's okay," Levon tells Dean. "We go back a ways."

Dean scratches an itch at the base of his spine. "That thing she wrote about John's Children made 'em look like pillocks."

"They didn't need my help," says Amy, "to look like pillocks."

"John's Children?" Elf knows them. "The ones who tried to upstage the Who by getting the crowd to wreck the venue?"

"The Who could shit a turd each into a bucket," grunts Griff, "and that bucket'd *still* be a better band than John's Children."

"Ooh, can I quote you on that?" asks Amy.

"Utopia Avenue," said Levon, "wish John's Children—"

"Aye, quote me on it," says Griff.

Amy's biro scratches her notepad. "One last question for all of you, if I may. When I listened to *Paradise Is the Road to Paradise,* I kept wondering about politics. We live in revolutionary times. The Cold War. The end of empires. The erosion of authority. Attitudes to sex and drugs. Should music mirror change? Should music try to trigger change? Can it? Does yours?"

"It's easier when they ask about pets and favorite food," mutters Griff, still under his cowboy hat.

" 'Abandon Hope' ends with the atom bomb," says Elf.

" 'Mona Lisa' has feminism at its core," remarks Jasper. "Its 'sister song,' so to speak, is Nina Simone's 'Four Women.' "

"Even 'Darkroom' has a with-it free-love friskiness," suggests Dean. "It's not 'xactly 'I Want to Hold Your Hand.' "

"You each nominated someone else's song," says Amy.

"That's us," growls Griff. "One big happy family."

"Yet 'A Raft and a River' is an ode to music," Amy continues. " 'The Prize' is about the swings and roundabouts of success. 'Purple Flames,' one of my songs of the year by the way"—she looks at Dean, who throbs with pleasure before reminding himself that critics are the enemy—"is acutely, nakedly personal. These aren't political."

"Where does it say a band can't be both?" asks Elf.

"Now 'n' then yer get a song that's both great music and makes a statement," says Dean. " 'For What It's Worth.' 'Mississippi Goddamn.' 'A Change Is Gonna Come.' But a whole album o' stuff busting its guts to be Political with a capital *P*? That's not pretty. I should know. I was in Battleship Potemkin."

"The Beatles, the Stones, the Who, the Kinks," says Griff. "They're not trying to change the world. They don't buy their mansions by writing anthems about CND or making a socialist paradise. They're just out to make fookin' good music."

"The best pop songs are art," says Jasper. "Making art is already a political act. The artist rejects the dominant version of the world. The artist proposes a new version. A *sub*version. It's there in the etymology. Tyrants are right to fear art."

"And music scares 'em shitless," says Dean. "It's the hooks. Once music's in yer, it's in for good. The best music's a kind o' thinking.

Or a kind o' *re*thinking. It doesn't follow orders." *Bloody hell,* thinks Dean. *I sound intelligent.*

EARLY ON SUNDAY morning after the Bag o' Nails, Dean stood outside Izzy Penhaligon's house feeling stupid. London's edges and signs were blurred by a cold fog that Dean's Napoleon coat did little to keep out. Nobody was around. The night had been a disappointment. Izzy Penhaligon kept flinching, and her parting words were, "I think you'd better leave now." They hadn't exchanged phone numbers. He set off down Gordon Street, discovering only when he reached Euston Road that he had walked north instead of south. He waited at a bus stop for a number 18. He wondered where Kenny and Stew had ended up last night. He'd said his friends could kip at Chetwynd Mews, a promise he conveniently forgot when Izzy Penhaligon said, "Come back to mine." He thought of how Harry Moffat had needed vodka to feel normal, and wondered if he himself needed sex to feel normal, or loved, or successful, or real. The idea was unpleasantly plausible. The number 18 bus continued not to show up, so Dean set off down Euston Road on foot. A number 18 overtook Dean thirty seconds later. Its conductor watched Dean's attempts to flag it down as the bus was swallowed by fog.

Dean turned into Gower Street. As he pounded along the pavement, a guitar line marched along with him. He adjusted it, distorted and spiky and metallic, two bars long. The first half of the phrase asked a question that the second half answered. A perfect hook. He skirted Bedford Square. Dead leaves clung to trees. Morwell Street, where he used to live, opened on his left. Dean entered its narrow gullet. Visibility was down to ten paces or so. He passed Mrs. Nevitt's house. He thought of the five pounds she had stolen from him. Her sign, BEDSIT TO LET—BLACKS & IRISH NEED NOT APPLY—ENQUIRE WITHIN, sat on her windowsill. In the gutter, he noticed a loose cobble and decided it had been put there for a reason. Checking nobody was emerging from the fog in either direction, Dean hurled the cobble through the window. It entered with little fuss—just a brief, musical shattering of glass. He jogged away, exhilarated. Nobody called out, nobody saw him—a secret he would take to his urn.

Oxford Street was populated only by a few refugees from Saturday night. In Soho Square a wiry black dog was dogging a chubby pale bitch. Sex is the puppet-master, he thought, and scribbled the five words on an old bus ticket with a biro. Elf says, "If you don't write it down, it didn't happen." Rhymes cropped up: *disaster, sticking-plaster, faster and faster.* He passed the clinic where "Hopkins" had sent him running for a stretcher all those months ago. London is a game. It makes its rules up as it goes along. One of Mr. Craxi's nephews was mopping the floor of the Etna café. Dean considered dropping by Elf's flat in Livonia Street with croissants from the French bakery, but remembered Bruce would be there. If Dean could click his fingers and erase Bruce Fletcher's existence, no questions asked, no murder investigation, he wouldn't hesitate. In fact, he clicked his fingers now, just on the off chance it would work. He'd be seeing Elf at Pavel Z's for rehearsal. They were playing in Brixton that night. Not too far to drive. He emerged from Soho onto Regent Street, a curved fog-canal, and crossed into Mayfair. He decided to ring Jude after he'd had a bath. He decided to treat her better. Even Griff was calling him a tart. Dean should send her some flowers. Girls like flowers. He might turn his hook into a song for Jude, he thought, or write a song *around* her, like "Darkroom" was around Mecca. At the Polish grocer's on Brook Street, Dean bought a box of eggs, a loaf of bread, a *Daily Mirror,* and a packet of Dunhills. "Foggy day," said the man.

"Foggy day," Dean agreed. He walked into Chetwynd Mews and climbed the five or six steps to his front door. He was safely home. Luck had been on Dean's side. He fished out his key . . .

INSIDE, A GIRL's boots were placed neatly in the porch. Jasper appeared to have returned from Oxford early and with company.

Dean called, "Jasper?"

No reply. Probably they were in bed. The air was peaty with dope-smoke. Mr. Kabouter was still on. Dean crossed the lounge to let in some air and light and yelped at the sight of Jude watching him from the armchair. The eggs hit the floor. "*Shit,* Jude! Yer gave me a heart attack!"

Jude said nothing.

The shoes in the porch were hers. "I just popped out to buy some aspirin. A while ago. Everywhere I tried was out. Traipsed halfway across the city. Just for aspirin! Unbelievable. Fancy some eggs?" He opened the box. Three were smashed. "Pre-scrambled eggs. Or d'yer fancy an omelette?"

Jude stared at him.

"So, is, uh . . . Jasper at home?"

"He arrived the same time I did." Her voice was off-key. "He let me in. He's gone out again. I didn't ask where."

"Right. Well. Nice to see yer."

"I called you last night to see if your flu was better, but nobody replied. So I thought I'd come up, to take care of you. I took the early train to Victoria. Nobody answered the door."

"Yer must've *just* missed me," said Dean, "before I left."

"You're a crap liar, Dean."

Dean acted baffled. "Why would I lie to yer?"

"Don't. Please."

"Don't what?"

"Don't treat me like the mug I am."

Dean wished he was safe in the future where this scene was a past mistake and he no longer felt like King Shit.

Jude rubbed her eye. "Everyone said you'll think the rules don't apply to you. I defended you. I said you had your feet on the ground." She stood up, went to the door, and put on her coat and boots. "I'd like to say, 'I wish you the best,' but I don't want my last words to you to be a lie. So . . . I hope you'll find a better version of yourself than the one you are now. For your sake."

Dean felt scuzzier than a bag of pond weed.

Jude closed the door behind her.

"DEAN?"

Amy's looking at him. So is everyone else in Levon's office. Bethany's phone rings next door: "Good afternoon, Moonwhale?" The international clocks chop up minutes. "Sorry. What was the question?"

"I was just saying," says Amy, "if you *want* to dish me up any final tales of rock 'n' roll depravity, I won't turn them away."

"Oh. Yeah. Sorry. No. In bed by ten o'clock with a mug o' cocoa and *Golfing Weekly,* that's me."

"I can picture it." Amy packs her handbag and stands up. "Well, I think I have everything, so . . . I'll leave you to it."

Levon stands and slides the doors open. "When is the piece likely to run, would you say?"

"Next week's issue."

"And a review of the album?" asks Levon.

"That, I've already written."

Dean scrutinizes her face for clues.

The tip of Amy's fang indents her lip. "Relax. Why bother writing eight hundred words on a band if I've trashed their album?"

Dean shakes Amy's hand. She looks him straight in the eye.

DEAN STARED AT the chair Jude had sat in. It still held the faint ghost of her body heat. Lust had caused all this trouble. Hunting girls *was* a kind of addiction. Sex with these strangers brought him no pleasure. Dean swore to start treating women the way he treated Elf—like people, basically. Dean heard the telephone ring. He turned off the water and went to answer it. "Hello?"

"Morning, yer dirty stop-out."

"Rod. Sorry I . . . sort o' disappeared on yer last night."

"No explanation necessary, Romeo. Seal the deal?"

"A gentleman never tells."

"Yer naughty rock god. Bit of yer magic dust fell on Kenny."

"Yeah?"

"Oh yes. Last seen heading off for Hammersmith with a witchy maiden. Do the boy good. He's got cum backed up to his sinuses. Stew slept on my sofa in Camden. He's just left."

"All's well that ends well, I s'pose."

" 'Xactly. So, after such a brilliant night, it feels rude to talk 'bout money, but will yer be settling up by cash or check?"

Time brakes sharply, like a train. "For the pills?"

"Nah. Yer bar tab at the Bag o' Nails."

Dean remembered. "Yeah. 'Course. And it came to . . ."

"Ninety-six quid plus a bit o' change."

Time came off the rails like a train crash.

Dean didn't have a spare ninety-six pounds.

Dean didn't have a spare fiver.

"Dean?"

"Uh . . . yeah."

"Oh, good. Thought I'd lost yer. After yer went, I closed yer tab. The Bag o' Nails isn't the cheapest bar in London. Yer made a generous gesture, but people take the piss. I hope that was okay?"

"Yeah. Thanks."

"Is this line all right? Yer sound only half there."

As Dean was trying to work out how you tell a friend that you can't pay them back an unexpectedly enormous drinks bill, his mind was hijacked by a memory of a hook sliding into a maggot's mouth: *Twist the hook out of his arse,* said Harry Moffat, *just so the point shows. See?*

POST-INTERVIEW, ELF AND Jasper are clearing up the coffee cups while Bethany runs through the calls Levon missed. Griff is motionless beneath his cowboy hat. Dean sees a woman's glove on the arm of the sofa. "Look, Amy left a glove."

"Fancy that." Elf gives Dean a loaded look.

"I'll see if I can catch her."

"She'll be streets away by now," says Jasper.

"Or," Elf says airily, "a lot nearer."

"When is a glove a lobster pot?" asks Griff.

Dean hurries out of Levon's office, out through Moonwhale's door, and down to the landing of the Duke-Stoker Agency, where Amy is smoking a cigarette.

Dean dangles the glove. "Lost: one suede glove."

"Fancy that." She takes it. He pinches it more tightly. Her face says, *You're cute, but not that cute.* He lets it go.

"Do I get a reward?" He takes out his packet of Dunhills.

"You get to give me your telephone number."

Yer cheeky, beautiful, slinky, curvy bitch.

"If I give yer my number, how do I even know yer'll call?"

"You don't." Amy holds up her lighter.

Denmark Street washes and ebbs up the stairs.

Dean holds his cigarette in her flame.

LAST SUPPER

UPSTAIRS AT THE DUKE OF ARGYLL, GRIFF BEGAN A HEAD-count while waiting for his next Guinness to appear. Under a halo of Christmas lights, Bethany, her theater-director boyfriend, and Petula Clark were numbers 1, 2, and 3; the well-groomed quartet of Levon, a biochemist called Benjamin, Pavel Z, and the Move's manager were 17, 18, 19, and 20; Jasper, Heinz Formaggio, and the scientist from Kenya were 36, 37, and 38; DJs John Peel and Bat Segundo were 44 and 45; and Elf and Bruce, sharing a moment in a nook, were 59 and 60. Bruce was pressing his forehead against Elf's and talking and she was smiling the smile only lovers smile. Griff feared for Elf. A crash was coming. He extracted a Benzedrine from a pillbox in his jacket pocket, faced the window, and popped the bringer of peace and joy to all men. Below in Brewer Street, workers hurried home, collars up and hats down. Across the street, above a greengrocer's, a boy of ten or so watched Griff through a window. Griff held up a hand in greeting. The boy sank away into gloom.

"Suffering is the one promise life always keeps."

Griff turned to find two young women sporting blood-red lips, lethal-looking hatpins, fishnet gloves, fur stoles, and artful cleavage. He wasn't sure which of them spoke. "Aye."

"We've never officially met," said one.

"But we've watched you play," said the other. "Often."

"We're your biggest fans," they said together.

Griff was both spooked and wanted to laugh.

"I'm Venus," said one. "As in the goddess."

"I'm Mary," said the other. "As in the virgin."

"Here's yer Guinness, Wild Man o' Rock." Dean handed him a pint. "It's the Battle o' Waterloo in the bar. Who do we have here?" He gave Griff a sly-old-dog look; Griff fired back a never-met-'em-before look. "This is Venus and Mary," he replied. "In person."

"Hello, Dean." Venus and Mary spoke in perfect stereo.

Dean looked from one to the other. "Wow."

"We've seen you eleven times now," said Mary.

"We've played *Paradise Is the Road to Paradise* over two hundred times," said Venus. "We're on our third copy."

"We've memorized the lyrics. We collect your press clippings. Even from the *Hull Gazette.* We know your birthdays."

"Know the colors of our front doors too, do yer?" joked Dean.

"Your and Jasper's door is bright red," said Venus. "Elf's door down on Livonia Street is bare metal, but the internal one to her apartment is black. Yours used to be creosoted wood." Venus looked at Griff. "But now it's mushy-pea green."

Before Griff could work out what to think about this, Amy arrived holding a huge martini. "It's bedlam down there." She saw the two groupies and read the situation. "My God, I *love* your look. The lacework on those corsets . . ."

"We ransacked our dead grannies' wardrobes," said Mary.

"We thought, *Why leave it to the moths?*" said Venus.

"Why indeed?" said Amy. "Are you sisters?"

"Sisters on Utopia Avenue," explained Venus. "We enjoyed your feature, Amy. You're *Melody Maker*'s best writer."

"By a mile," said Mary. "You never suck up to bands, but you never shit on them. We think you're good for Dean."

Amy glanced at Dean and sipped her drink. "I'm glad you deem me to be worthy of him."

"He's glowing," said Venus. "More than he did when he was going out with that hairdresser. Just don't break his heart."

"Or we'll eviscerate you," they intoned together.

Amy could only smile. "I have been warned."

Mary touched Griff's pint. "May I wet my whistle, Griff?"

Griff found himself handing her his stout. She drained off a quarter and passed it to Venus, who drank a similar quantity.

"Guinness tastes to thirsty people . . ." began Mary.

". . . how blood tastes to vampires," said Venus. "It's the iron." She handed Griff back his half-empty glass.

Levon, standing on a chair, was hailing the room through a hand megaphone, "Okay, folks, okay, folks, a few words, *IF YOU PLEASE* . . ." The racket subsided. "Thank you, one and all, for being here, at the end of a hectic day, a hectic week, a hectic year. We have a lot to celebrate today. Not only the release of Utopia Avenue's brand-new single, Dean's song 'Abandon Hope' . . ."

A cheer went up and Dean raised a hand.

". . . but also *Paradise Is the Road to Paradise.*" Levon held up the LP to louder cheers. "Only eleven weeks ago, it was a gleam in the band's eye. Only seven weeks ago, Elf, Jasper, Dean, and Griff finished recording the last song at Fungus Hut. To my mind, the results speak for themselves."

A ragged shout of approval; much applause.

"A few reviewers pissed on our strawberries . . ." Levon dampened down cries of "Death to Felix Finch!" and "Eunuchs in a harem!" ". . . but, on the whole, the album earned the reception we'd hoped for. The British music press has no wiser critic than Miss Amy Boxer of *Melody Maker*—who happens to be with us tonight."

Cheers broke out. Amy waved. Dean clapped hard.

"If Amy doesn't object," Levon continued, "I'll read from her review for *Paradise.*" The reporter made a be-my-guest gesture, while Levon unrolled a copy of *Melody Maker,* put on his glasses, and turned to the right page: "Here we go: *Question: What do you get if you cross an Angry Young Bassist, a folk-scene doyenne, a Stratocaster demigod and a jazz drummer? Answer: Utopia Avenue, a band like no other. Their debut LP,* Paradise Is the Road to Paradise, *is one of the Must Own albums of 1967. The range and quality of the songwriting is formidable. Bassist Dean Moss serves up 'Abandon Hope,' a slice of mean streets R&B. 'Smithereens' is a lonesome howl for broken dreams. 'Purple Flames' is a seven-minute epic of riffs, power, soul-searching and maturity.*"

Cries of "Hear, hear" and "Well said, Amy" break out.

Levon sipped his rum. *"Elf Holloway's ethereal, gutsy voice is well known to her legions of fans. Revelatory on* Paradise, *however, are her chops as a keyboard player. Listen to her scorching Hammond solo on 'Purple Flames,' or the prismatic playing on 'Darkroom.' Miss Holloway's new songs are also top notch. 'A Raft and a River' is an electric-folk ode to music, while 'Unexpectedly' is a torch song whose torch flares up again."*

"White hot, baby!" Bruce held his arms aloft like a champion, then kissed Elf. Griff looked at Dean. They rolled their eyes.

" 'Mona Lisa Sings the Blues' is the mightiest of the three. No wittier exposé of the roles a woman has to navigate in a Man's, Man's, Man's World has ever been etched into vinyl. A future single, surely?" Levon looked up. "I think we would all agree, yes?"

More applause. Venus and Mary applauded in rhythmic unison, Griff noticed, like a single pair of hands.

"Which brings us," Levon continued, *"to Jasper de Zoet. Comparisons with Messrs. Clapton and Hendrix are, for once, merited. De Zoet plays acoustic passages, feedback squalls, space-blues with startling alacrity. He wrote Utopia Avenue's breakout hit, 'Darkroom,' the strangest love song ever to grace* Top of the Pops. *'Wedding Presence' is a dreamy waltz to dance among the chandeliers. De Zoet's third offering is 'The Prize,' about a journey to the brink of stardom. It echoes Dylan's 'Desolation Row' but, like the LP it concludes, it is its own glorious beast."* Applause.

Griff fished out a Marlboro, put it into his mouth, and patted his pockets to locate a lighter; Mary was ready with a match. Venus blew it out. Their eyes were four full moons.

"Home lap," said Levon. *"To overlook Griff Griffin's role in Utopia Avenue would be criminal. Griffin chugs like Charlie Watts, explodes like Keith Moon, swings like Ginger Baker."* Venus and Mary gently squeezed Griff's right and left biceps. It was both spooky and arousing. *"The Moss-Griffin rhythm section is the invisible force that unifies this remarkably diverse album.* Paradise Is the Road to Paradise . . ." Levon swept his gaze around the upstairs room ". . . *has the makings of a classic.* Amy, I could not have declared my love for Utopia Avenue so skillfully myself."

More applause. It was all getting too lovey-dovey for Griff. He put down his glass on the mantelpiece.

"Where're yer off to?" asked Dean.

"Busting for a wazz."

GRAFFITI WAS WRITTEN on the calamine-pink wall at eye level above the urinal. Maybe it was witless smut, or maybe it was witty smut, but Griff couldn't muster the energy to turn the letters into words, so he let the hieroglyphics be. The plughole gurgled. He sucked the last life out of his Marlboro and dropped the stub into the small yellowish pond. It hissed. The door banged open and Friday night pub noise swilled in. A moment later Dean was unzipping his fly at the adjacent urinal, singing the theme tune to *Born Free.* "So," said Dean. "Venus 'n' Mary."

"What about them?"

"It's pur-*retty* clear they want to fondle yer tom-toms."

"Groupies are groupies."

"Yer point being?"

"They want a pop star. They don't want me."

"So? Yer still get to do the ravishing. Or ravishing*s*."

Griff thought of Elf and Bruce.

"Just plunge in," said Dean. "What're yer 'fraid of?"

"Pubic lice and five varieties of the clap, for starters."

"Yer know what we say about female hygiene in Gravesend."

"Why do I suspect," said Griff, "that the next words out of your mouth'll put me off my food till next fookin' Easter?"

Dean acted wounded. "Wholesome advice for my comrade-in-arms is all I'm offering yer: *If it smells like chicken, keep on lickin'. If it smells like trout, get the fuck out.*"

Griff tried not to smile. "You are foul."

"It's a gift." Dean zipped his zipper. "Seriously, threesomes don't come along that often, and yer mojo needs a workout. That's why yer've been all pale 'n' quiet 'n' . . . hungry-looking."

TWO WEEKS LATER, standing with his tray of fish and chips and bottle of Coke, Griff looks around the Blue Boar motorway services restaurant. Two tribes occupy the place during the graveyard shift. The truckers have short hair, plaid shirts, bad backs, and swelling bellies. They pore over the *Mirror,* the *Sporting Post,* or road atlases and discuss routes, miles per gallon, speed traps, and dangerous bends. The showbiz tribe are musicians and performers, plus managers, roadies, and entourage, if applicable. Male hair tends to be shoulder-length, and costumes this year are paisley, velveteen, and ruffled. They gossip about labels, signings, venues, musical instruments, and which promoter went mysteriously bust before receipts from the last tour were paid. Of Griff's brother, Steve, there is no sign. Griff isn't worried. It's an icy night and traffic is slower than usual. The Beatles' table is free, so Griff heads over with his tray to claim it. Everybody on the British touring circuit refuels at the twenty-four-hour Blue Boar, located in Watford Gap, a notional border—not near Watford, despite the name—between the north and the south of England. When Jimi Hendrix first came to London, he heard the Blue Boar mentioned so often that he assumed it was a hip club in Knightsbridge or Soho.

Griff sits in Ringo's seat because it has a sight line on the Beast, parked close to the restaurant. He isn't assuming a brother performer would be so low as to smash a window and make off with an amp, but he can't assume they won't. He tucks in. After the drive to Birmingham, playing support for the Move at the Carlton Ballroom, and the drive back here, he's famished. The fish isn't fresh by Hull standards, but he's too hungry to care. He sprinkles vinegar from the sticky bottle and bites into the slab of cod. Jasper sits down with a plate of eggs, beans, grilled tomatoes, and toast. "Nice and warm in here. Is this the Beatles' table?"

"Aye. That's George's seat you're sitting in."

Jasper cuts a precise square of toast and loads it with a cargo of baked beans. "Are you sitting in Ringo's?"

"You're a mind reader, Zooto."

Jasper chews slowly. " 'The Hook' sounded good."

"It's Dean's best song. Don't tell him I said that."

Dean rolls up next with his bacon butty and a hill of chips and takes McCartney's seat. "Seen who's over in the corner?"

Griff follows Dean's nod. "Herman's fookin' Hermits. Purveyor of poppy jingles so sugary your teeth'll fall out."

"Those poppy jingles took them on a twenty-date tour o' the States," says Dean. "Think we could play support for them?"

Elf takes John Lennon's seat. She has a pie. "I spy with my little eye something beginning with HH."

"I was just saying," says Dean, "wouldn't it be great if we were their support act in America?"

Elf tucks a paper napkin into her blouse. "I'd rather we got there under our own steam than hanging on Herman's coattails."

"It takes a *hell* of a lot o' steam to cross the Atlantic," says Dean. He forks a chip, glumly. *Meaning,* Griff translates, *more than a number sixteen hit and a flop that peaked at number seventy-five.* Levon told the band that their second single has dropped out of the Top 100 after the Birmingham show, and Dean was unusually quiet on the long drive over.

"We're not bland enough to be a support act," says Jasper. "The headliners want you to make them look better."

"Same story tonight," says Elf. "The Move's manager was all 'Have a great show' when we started, but after 'The Prize' he was telling Levon, 'Get 'em off, they're only the sodding warm-up act.' "

"Archie Kinnock once took the Yardbirds along for a twelve-night tour of the north," says Griff. "Know how long it lasted? Three dates. They stole the fookin' show every night. Archie couldn't stand it. Eric Clapton wrote 'Green-Eyed Monster Blues' about it."

"I thought that was about a woman," says Jasper.

Griff squishes mushy peas onto a big chip. "Now you know. Eh, wasn't it classic when Elf said 'If you hold your ticket over a naked flame, you'll see the words *Our LP is out now*'—and that one wazzock actually did it and set his fookin' ticket on fire!"

"I stole that from Peggy Seeger." Elf squirts ketchup onto her chips. "So 'The Hook' went down a storm again tonight, Dean."

Dean scowls at his bacon sandwich. "Unlike 'Abandon Hope,' which went down like a lead balloon. Ilex didn't push it. That's the problem. They should've put adverts in *NME* and *Melody Maker.*"

Griff looks at Elf. Elf looks back. "Lots of great songs don't sell shit, Mr. Sulkypants. Lots of shit songs sell like hotcakes. Look at Herman's Termites. Ilex won't drop us yet."

"Griff's right, Dean," says Elf. "It's not the end of the—"

"It's a bloody disaster." Dean shoves his plate away.

"Oh f' fooksake!" Griff loses patience. "A famine in China, an earthquake in the Philippines, Hull City losing to Leeds: *that's* a fookin' disaster. Fookin' get over it or go and get a job in a café."

Dean huffs and puffs. "Next time I try to push for something, if there *is* a next time, Ilex'll be all 'Don't think so: what 'bout the time yer thought "Abandon Hope" was a Top Ten hit?' "

The Blue Boar plays a syrupy Muzak "Silent Night."

"If we'd released 'Mona Lisa,' " says Dean, "we'd have a song in the Top Ten over Christmas."

"There's no way of knowing that," insists Elf.

"That's what Amy reckons. It's what you reckon too."

"Self-pity *really* doesn't suit you, Dean."

"Hey." Jasper dangles his watch. "It's officially Christmas Eve."

"Kiss and make up," says Griff, "or you'll be on the naughty list."

"I'm not kissing *that*," snorts Elf. "I'd rather kiss . . ."

"Peter Pope?" suggests Dean.

Elf's anger wilts, a little. "Mmm."

"Sorry," says Dean.

"Blame the dice," says Elf.

"Here's to never abandoning hope." Jasper raises his glass of Tizer. He betrays an occasional fondness for puns.

"Here's to Utopia Avenue," says Dean. "Now in all good record shops, between T for Shirley Temple and V for Gene Vincent."

Griff lights a cigarette. "Nine songs we got down, in two weeks. Most LPs have shit in to pad out the sandwich. Not ours."

"All we need," says Dean, "is for a million people to agree and . . ." He's distracted by someone over Griff's shoulder. *"Marcus?"*

Griff turns around to find a guy wearing a pink caftan, turquoise glasses, a black cape, and a runic headband.

"Dean! Fancy meeting you here."

"That's the Blue Boar for yer. Elf, Griff, Jasper: this is Marcus Daly. Guitarist of the Battleship Potemkin."

"The same Marcus," asks Jasper innocently, "who sacked Dean for saying the Chairman Mao song was sonic gonorrhea?"

Marcus looks shifty. "Water under the bridge. Dean ought to thank me, by rights. *Top of the Pops?* An LP? I mean . . . *shit.*"

Dean smothers a burp. "What's with the new wizardy look? Can't imagine that going down too well on the picket lines."

Marcus scratches his neck. "Chris is an accountant, Paul went to India after a girl, so me and Tom formed Battleship Aquarius."

Dean stares. "What happened to using the capitalist pop song to turn the proletariat on to Marxism?"

"One night at a gig in Dartford a fight broke out during 'Workers United.' It turned into a brawl. We had to leave the stage. I mean, chairs were flying. Teeth were flying. The pigs were called. Eight people were arrested, another dozen got taken to hospital. When we went back for our gear, it had all been nicked. There was nothing for it but to drive back. But we couldn't because our van was gone, too. That's when I realized: the real revolution that people are crying out for isn't political, it's spiritual."

"So you boot Dean out for not kowtowing to your red flag," says Griff, "then you scrawl cosmic runes all over that same flag?"

"Everything happens for a reason," says Marcus. "At Dartford, the cosmos spoke to me. I wrote a bunch of songs around mystic themes, updated our image"—he holds up his cape—"and, lo and behold, our gig fee's fifty pounds a shot."

Dean's eyes go wide. "Fif-*ty* or fif-*teen*?"

"Fif-*ty*—five-oh. We've got a manager now. He's in talks with Decca. It's all about energy flow. Potemkin was blocked. Aquarius flows. Come see us at Middle Earth in the New Year. Our music says it all better than I can. Got to rush, but Merry Christmas and all that. Nice meeting you all . . . Ta-ta." Marcus Daly is gone.

"You look in shock," Griff tells Dean.

"He used to insist we call him 'comrade.' "

"The decade is going insane," says Elf.

"Is that a good thing or a bad thing?" asks Jasper.

"EVENING, ALL." STEVE arrives less than a minute later. He's wearing an oxblood leather jacket, a thick sweater, and a pleased smile. "Elf, Jasper, Dean, good to see you again and uh . . ." He frowns at

Griff. "What's-his-name, the drummer guy? I always forget that one."

"My first name's 'You May Be Older Than Me,'" replies Griff. "My surname's 'But I'll Still Kick Your Arse You Cheeky Git.'"

Steve smiles and sits down. "Sorry I'm late. There was a crash near Luton." His smile fades. "Traffic was down to a single lane."

"It was slow going from Birmingham, too," says Elf.

"Like an ice rink in parts," says Dean. "Freezing fog."

"We just finished our grub," says Griff. "Are you hungry?"

"I had a pasty before I left. We ought to be off soon. Any tea left in that pot, mind? I could do with a whistle-wetter."

"I'll get yer a cup," says Dean.

"How was the Birmingham show, then?" asks Steve.

"Not too shabby." Griff looks at Jasper and Elf.

Elf nods back. "We've got some new songs since you saw us at Derby. Griff here played like a demon. As usual."

"You're exactly like him." Jasper looks from Steve to Griff and back. "And exactly different."

"I got the looks and brains," says Steve. "Obviously."

"And all the bullshit, too," adds Griff. "Obviously. You picked up the car without any trouble?"

"Aye. Uncle Phil's pal lives out Wembley way, so it's the right side of the city. A Jag. Three years old, only twenty thou on the clock. Suspension like driving on air. Worth the trip down."

"It's worked out well for getting you home on Christmas, too," remarks Elf. "I feel like a gangster, handing over a witness."

"If he wasn't coming back to Hull for Christmas," says Steve, "Mum was going to have him kidnapped and brought back in the boot of a car. This way, he gets to drive."

Dean returns with a cup. "Here you go, milord."

"Thanks, pal. I'm ready for this." Steve pours himself a cup, slurps, and tilts his head back. "Ah . . . that's better. Before I forget, I've got a job for you all." Steve takes out three copies of *Paradise Is the Road to Paradise* and a black marker. "Would you all mind signing these?"

"The thrill hasn't worn off yet." Dean takes the marker. "Who're they for?"

"One's for Wally Whitby, one's for our Mum and Dad, and one's for me. When you're bigger than the Beatles I'll flog it and retire from my career in the motor trade."

"Wally *does* know it's not trad jazz, right?" checks Griff.

" 'Course he does. He saw you do 'Darkroom' on *Top of the Pops.* He were down Price's Records the very next morning, telling everyone how he discovered you when you were twelve. He still brings your press clippings to Mum."

Dean passes the records and the marker to Griff.

"You must be right pleased with that cover," says Steve.

They all gaze at the photograph of the Gioconda café, with Elf, Jasper, Dean, and Griff in the window seats. By using a long exposure, the photographer added the blurry ghost-trails of passersby, a dog, and a cyclist. A street sign reading UTOPIA AVENUE was fixed to the wall on the top left; on the bottom right, a newspaper board reads PARADISE IS THE ROAD TO PARADISE.

"I bloody love it," replies Dean.

"It took a while to get right," replies Jasper.

"We blew Ilex's art budget twice over," says Elf.

Griff signs his name over a pale window.

"An LP's like a baby," says Elf. "Us four made it . . ."

". . . not sure where you're going with this," says Dean.

Elf goes *ugh.* "You know what I mean. You want what you've made to have the right face. The artwork's the face."

THE FRIGID AIR penetrates Griff's coat and fillets his flesh from his bones. "It's fookin' Siberia out here!" Each word is a puff of white vapor. The party reaches the Beast. "Right, then," Griff tells his bandmates. "See you on the thirtieth."

"Me 'n' Jasper'll cook something at De Zoet Towers," Dean tells him. "Our last supper of 'sixty-seven can't be the Blue Boar."

"Right you are," says Griff. "I'll bring the stomach pump."

"Don't open your prezzie till Christmas Day," says Elf, "or it'll vanish in a puff of regret. Have a lovely time with your family."

"Aye, you too."

Jasper shakes his hand. It's formal and oddly intimate.

"Merry Christmas, yer northern wazzock," Dean tells him.

"Peace on Earth, you great southern ponce," replies Griff.

Utopia Avenue minus Griff climb into the Beast. Elf sits at the wheel and coaxes it into life on the third try, with the choke out. She wipes condensation from the windscreen and gives Griff one last fluttery wave before driving away onto the slip-road.

Steve leads him over to a moonlit S-type Jaguar.

"Look—at—*you*." Griff strokes the bonnet.

"Want to drive?"

THE M1 HURTLES out of the northern dark, bringing a sign reading HULL 102 and motorway lamps on tall poles. A truck's rear lights stay at a constant hundred yards. The Jaguar is warmer, comfier, and quieter than the Beast. It handles like a dream. *Safer, too,* thinks Griff. "If the album sells, would you look out for a better van for us? A Bedford, maybe."

" 'Course," says Steve. "You'll be needing a roadie."

"At some point. Why? Fancy the job yourself?"

"Debs would not be impressed. All them groupies."

Griff thinks of Venus and Mary and wonders. "The musician's life isn't what it's cracked up to be from the outside."

"Stardom's getting stressful, is it?" asks Steve.

"One song in the Top Twenty isn't 'stardom.' "

"Do you get recognized much?"

"Can't say I do. We've only been on the telly the once. Dean's the pretty one, Jasper's Mr. Guitar God, and Elf's the golden lass in a gang of likely lads. People forget the drummer. Suits me to a T."

A Triumph Spitfire overtakes them in the fast lane.

"Too fast, you daft twat," Steve tells the driver.

"How's Debs?" Griff asks. "Still at the hairdressers?"

"Debs. Aye. She's a bit . . . it's not easy, all her friends are having babies, or second babies, or third, and Debs is pleased for them, of course, but every time, every christening, she's like, 'When's our turn?' Every month, it's like, 'Maybe this time.' But every time, it's like, 'Nope.' It hits Debs really hard." Steve lights a cigarette. He's never discussed the topic as directly as this.

Griff sees it isn't easy. "Must be tough, like."

"There comes a time when you think, *Maybe it's not going to happen for us.* So . . . well, this is our big news, really, Pete. We've got a meeting with the adoption people, in the New Year. To explore what's involved, like."

Griff glances sideways. "Big step, Steve."

"Big step." Steve pulls out a fancy ashtray from the dashboard and taps his cigarette. "Feels right. There's nothing wrong in hoping for the best, but . . . after five years, you start thinking, *Hang on—I'm a fookin' ostrich, here. It's time we face the facts and try something else.*"

"Does Mum know?"

"Aye, it were Mum who gave Debs that little nudge. We've been thinking about it, but the first step's hard, like."

Griff overtakes a slow Morris Minor. "I can imagine."

A motorway bridge passes overhead at 50 mph.

"I also imagine you and Debs being brilliant parents."

"Fingers crossed, eh."

"I'll teach your kids to drum."

A SIGN READING HULL 75 glows, grows, and is gone.

"I always liked that 'Hull' is such a short word," says Griff.

"Makes sense."

"It's got the same number of letters as 'home.' And starts with an *h*."

"So does 'hell,' mind."

"Aye."

"There's lots of *B*s down south. Brighton, Bristol, Bournemouth, Bedford. They're bastards. They all merge into one big 'Birmstolmouthford.' "

"Do the others know?"

"Elf's guessed, but she's too classy to ask. When I'm driving, she reads the signs out, like she's talking to herself. Dean hasn't twigged. I doubt he's heard of dyslexia. Jasper . . . who knows?"

"Is Jasper a bit . . ." Steve searches for a word. "Touched?"

"He's a strange 'un. When Archie Kinnock got him in for the

Blues Cadillac, I thought, *He's up his own arse.* When I got to know him better, I thought, *Maybe all toffs are like that.* But Jasper's no toff. His dad's a millionaire, but Jasper's eking out a small dollop of money his granddad left him. He needs Utopia Avenue to work too, or he's fooked. These days my take on Jasper is, he's just a bit mental—but who isn't, to some degree, so live and let live, right? It's Dean who gets my goat the most. A human fookin' yoyo! Half the time he thinks he's God's gift: the other half, he's a bag of nerves that he's *not* God's gift. Sure, his mum died when he was a boy and his dad slapped him about, but fook it. We've all got a sob story, but we don't all act like bolshy pricks."

"Is he as bad as Archie Kinnock?" asks Steve.

"Oh, compared to Kinnock, Dean's a walk in the park."

A sharp moon rises over a pale hill.

Steve turns up the heater. "What about Elf?"

ON THE LAST morning of the *Paradise* sessions, back in November, Jasper and Dean were twenty minutes late. Griff had been listening to Dave Brubeck's "Take Five," so he tried keeping a 5/4 time signature, just to warm up for the session. Elf joined in on Dave Brubeck's piano part. Griff asked himself, *How many women in the world could do that?* Elf stopped the improv, asked Digger to set up the drum mics, and asked Griff to lay down a 5/4 drum track. He kept the five-legged shuffle going for five whole minutes until Elf—now in full producer mode—waved him to a stop. She instructed Digger to replay the drum track through Griff's headphones, and asked Griff to improvise cymbals, hi-hat, gong, and tubular bells over it—anything he wanted—within the 5/4 frame. Elf held her earphones over one ear to catch both the drum track and Griff's overlay. "Don't overthink it, Griff. Just play what's in your head."

Griff started with a tom-tom and came in with a minute's solo in the style of Cozy Cole. Then he grabbed his sticks and played a solo, heavy on backbeats and rimshots, with a snare interlude. Elf watched his hands with a faraway smile on her face. Griff showed off an Art Blakey press-roll; a skipping run of ostinato; an Elvin Jones rolling triplet pulse; some swing-era cymbal-playing; and a glorious free-form crescendo as Elf's hand slowly rose . . . and . . . fell. Griff stopped his overlay. The original drum track ran for five bars.

Thump! two three four *five*

Thump! two three four *five*

Thump! two three four *five*

Thump! two three four *five*

Thump! two three four *five*—and . . .

Stop.

Elf just shook her head. "Fabulous."

Digger's voice came through on speaker. "Got it."

Griff took off his earphones. "So what's it for? Is it a song you're working on? Or . . ."

"I'd call it a song *we're* working on. If I do anything with it, you're getting a writing credit."

Griff imagined their names in brackets on the record label—(*Holloway-Griffin*). The studio door burst open. Dean and Jasper burst in. "Our train got stuck in the tunnel for a quarter of an hour up by Tottenham Court Road. Some poor sod threw himself on the line. What've yer been up to? Twiddling yer thumbs?"

"THEY BROKE THE mold when they made Elf," says Griff. "I weren't sure about her at first. I couldn't see her surviving the slog of clubs. I thought Dean, Jasper, and me were fine as a trio. But Levon insisted we ask her for a tryout, and . . . yeah, he was right. I was wrong. She drives. She carries the gear. She's bulletproof against hecklers. Onstage, she's two musicians for the price of one: a fookin' great keys player—and that voice. It's instantly her."

"That 'Mona Lisa' gets under your skin. It makes Debs cry."

"Elf's problem's her taste in men," says Griff. "Fookin' chronic. She's back with this Australian singer . . ."

"Love's blind," says Steve, "and is no fan of eye doctors. So . . . do you see you and her as an item?"

"Me and Elf?" Griff splutters a laugh. "No. No no no."

"What's so funny? She's got the right curves and bits."

He imagines Elf's response. "Maybe if we weren't in the same band . . . but sex can't compete with music."

"If you say so. So *are* you getting any?" asks Steve.

"Any what?"

"Oh, butter wouldn't melt in his mouth."

Griff thinks of Mary and Venus. They moved into his new flat the night of the *Paradise* party at the Duke of Argyll. They have a key and come and go as they wish, but most nights, the three of them share a bed. They cook and clean. They smoke dope together. They tell him next to nothing about themselves, and Griff has stopped probing. *If I find out too much,* Griff half fears, *they'll vanish in a puff of reality.* They don't make the usual demands. They don't want gifts. They don't want access to parties. They are absolutely in control. And Griff is fine with his abdication of control. He doubts their affair—*if that's the right word*—can last. Maybe that's why he hasn't told anyone about them, not even Dean, who met them briefly. Mary and Venus are one of the strangest paragraphs in his life. "No," Griff lies to his brother. "I'm still on the prowl . . ."

HULL 40, SAYS a road sign. The Jaguar's needle touches 40 mph. *Even I can do the maths.* It's 2:15 A.M. now, so they'll get to Albert Avenue in forty minutes, give or take.

"Will Dad still be up, do you reckon?" asks Griff.

"He'll be on the sofa," predicts Steve. "He'll say 'By heck, look what the cat dragged in.' And he'll look at your mustache and say, 'Something's stuck to your lip, son. Is it a squashed mouse?' "

"Good old Dad. Always standing by with a big shiny needle, in case we get too puffed up."

"Don't go thinking he's not proud as punch. This is the man who once bragged to his passengers how his son was Yorkshire's youngest-ever professional drummer. And now you've been on the BBC, there's no stopping him. He's even dug out that biscuit-tin drum kit me and him put together for you."

Griff glances sideways. "You're joking."

"He'd kept it in his shed." Steve is strobed by the orange gleam of a motorway light. His brother laughs. "He even—" Steve's face changes to wide-eyed horror. Griff looks ahead and sees the truck ahead jack-knifing and tipping over. A second, oncoming truck is ripping up the center barrier. Its undercarriage fills the Jaguar's windscreen. Griff's hauling at the wheel like a sailor in a storm. Tires shriek. The steering locks. *We'll need a miracle to—*

"WE'RE ALL RIGHT." Steve's voice, from light years and inches away. A croak. Something's pressing into Griff. He's squashed. *That truck hit us. It was bad. I'm alive. So's Steve. Where there's life . . .* Griff opens one eye. The other eye is gone. *I can still play the drums with one eye. One leg, one arm, that would be harder. One eye, I can do.* Orange light seeps into the wrecked car. Steve's bent like an Action Man with its limbs twisted the wrong way. The floor's the roof. *We flipped over.* Griff tries to move his right arm. Nothing happens. *Not fookin' good.* Griff tries moving his legs. Nothing. He's not in pain. A mercy. An ominous mercy. *If your spine's snapped you won't feel pain.* A noise comes from Steve's mouth. Not words. A bubbling gurgling. Griff says, "It's okay, we'll be okay," but what comes out is, "Shkay, ee'll eeshkay." Like Griff's granddad after his stroke. *Or like I'm bladdered.* Blood dribbles from Steve's mouth. It drips up his face, the wrong way. Black as oil in orange light. Pooling in his eye sockets. Dripping off his eyebrows. He splutters feebly. Griff says, "Steve, stay with us." It comes out as "Shtee, shaywhus . . ." A tide comes rushing in.

THUMP-THUMP, THUMP-THUMP, THUMP-THUMP, thump-thump, thump-thump. A tide goes out. Griff reenters his body. *My pulse.* A jagged groan. He's cold. That's good. People freezing to death feel warm. Steve's next to him. Steve's very still. Maybe he's saving his strength. *I'd like stars. There should be stars.* There's Steve, the roof, a thousand bits of glass scattered on the floor. Which was the roof. There are the pedals. A, B, C. Accelerator, brake, clutch. Close enough to touch. *If only my arms worked.* Glinting amber from the M1 lights. Voices. A long way off. Or tiny, tinny, and close. Coming through the speaker, late at night, under the blanket, in his and Steve's old room at Albert Avenue. "Love Me Tender." Dean strums it sometimes when he does his Elvis impression. Elf looks across the Beatles table at the Blue Boar. Jasper glances up at the end of "Purple Flames," ready to kill the song stone dead on the same beat. "Cyril! Over here! Bring the cutting gear!" Why? *The accident.* What accident? *This accident.* Griff tries to call out, to tell them Steve needs help first. His voice isn't working. It just isn't. *Where there's life there's hope.* But that ain't necessarily so. There's a song. About things you're liable to read in the Bible. Griff's mum sang it as she hung out the washing. *Stars.* A spring day. Griff was the boy at the window. *Stars.*

Waiting for his life to start.

BUILDERS

RAIN DRUMMED ON THE UMBRELLAS AND ON THE COFFIN LID. Rain whisked the water in the rectangular hole: seven feet long, three feet wide, and, famously, six feet deep. Levon pitied the gravediggers who had shifted these one hundred and twenty-six cubic feet of cold wet earth. Somebody sobbed. When the chapel bell fell silent, the vicar—who had a bad cold—began: "In the sweat of thy face shalt thou eat bread, till thou return unto the ground; for out of it wast thou taken: for dust thou art, and unto dust shalt thou return . . ." Yobbish crows in the yews half smothered the Book of Genesis. The vicar's voice began to crack and fade, like a dying amp. "Tragedy . . . Only the Almighty understands . . . Gave so much, had so much yet to give." A percussive *boom boom boom,* deep as a bass drum, struck the outer edge of Levon's hearing. *The North Sea, perhaps.* His feet were wet. His socks sponged up water from the sodden turf. As the vicar wound up his brief address, a line to sign the book of condolence formed. Levon thought they should have done this during the service in the chapel, out of the rain. Sixty or seventy people filed past Mr. and Mrs. Griffin and their eldest daughter and son, both in their thirties. Gloves on gloves. Levon shook their hands in turn. The family resemblance was immediate. "I'm sorry," he told Griff's dad, the bus driver. Such inadequate words, Levon thought, but then what words would begin to dent this grief? Mr. Griffin looked back like a man who could not understand how this day could be happening. "I'm sorry," he told Griff's mum, from whom Griff got his chin. Her eyes were sunken and red.

Her lips twitched as if to say 'Thank you,' but no sound escaped. Levon doubted she knew who he was. At the end of the line, a sexton offered a trowel for anyone who wanted to tip some earth onto the coffin in the grave. About half did. Elf, ahead of Levon, shook her head and swallowed a sob. Dean put his arm around her and escorted her off. Jasper took the trowel, looking around him like an observant anthropologist in the field. The hollow rattle of wet earth on wood was, to Levon's ear, the saddest sound he had ever heard.

BACK AT THE Hull Royal Infirmary, bandaged, plastered, and trussed, Griff listened to Levon's account of Steve's funeral. He avoided eye contact. Levon tried not to stare at Griff's shaven skull; they had removed his hair to fit the metal plate. Levon stuck to the facts. The facts were starkly eloquent. Somebody down the corridor was coughing his guts out—an incessant, barely human, smoker's cough. It was Griff lying in the bed, but Griff wasn't Griff anymore. This Griff looked like he'd never smiled in his life, and never would smile again. Frank Sinatra crooned "Have Yourself a Merry Little Christmas" on the hospital radio, even though Christmas had come and gone. "More grapes?" asked Elf.

"No, ta."

"A ciggie?"

"Don't mind."

"Got yer a fresh box o' Dunhills." Dean put a cigarette to Griff's lips and lit it.

Griff held the smoke in his lungs for a while. "I don't know if I'm coming back." His voice was a shadow of its old self. "I can't think about drumming. Or gigs. Or chart positions. Steve's dead."

"We understand," said Levon.

"No you don't." Griff rubbed his red eyes. "You think I'm only saying this because Steve's dead. But I don't know if I want it anymore. It's so fookin' hard. Night after night after night after night."

"This isn't like you, mate," said Dean.

"That's the point. I'm not the me I was. My brother's dead. I was driving."

"Nobody's saying this was your fault," said Elf.

"Not the cops," agreed Dean, "not Steve's wife. Nobody."

"Fault," sighed Griff. "Fault, fault, fault. I shut my eyes, and I'm back there. On the motorway. I know what's coming. I can't change the ending. It's always the same. The truck. Me, Steve, there. Upside down like a fookin' bat. I can't fookin' sleep."

"Have you told the doctor?" asked Elf.

"*More* pills? I'm a walking Boots the Chemist. Well. Moot fookin' point. I'm a lying-down Boots the Chemist."

"Your dad said the doctor said—"

"That could've been my funeral. If I hadn't put my seatbelt on. If the truck'd hit us differently. If the car had flipped over another way. The whole fookin' universe, a gazillion little ifs. If, if, if. So fookin' easily, *I* could be dead in that box . . ."

The man in the next bed along snored.

It would have been funny, in other circumstances.

"But you aren't dead in that box," said Jasper.

"And Steve is. That's what's killing me, Zooto."

IT WAS STILL raining when the train back left Hull, early the next morning. Roofs, an estuary, a fleet of trawlers, a hard town, a football stadium, and bands of rain rolled into the past. Nobody had the heart for small talk, and there was only one subject that wasn't small talk: What now for Utopia Avenue? Elf got out *The Bell Jar* by Sylvia Plath. Jasper had *The Magic Mountain* by Thomas Mann. Dean was reading the *Daily Mirror.* Thinking about other things was not a luxury available to a manager. Levon had canceled the New Year's gig at the Hammersmith Odeon and all bookings for the next month, adding up to four hundred pounds in fees no longer coming in to Moonwhale. Bills were due. Moonwhale's landlord, the Inland Revenue, and the telephone company did not care about Steven Griffin's tragic death. Levon still had to pay Bethany. Fungus Hut. Fire insurance. *Paradise Is the Road to Paradise* had crawled up to number fifty-eight on the album chart, but "Abandon Hope" had flopped. Ilex were "disappointed." Victor French had told Levon that the third single would need to "perform substantially better" than "Darkroom." Victor had not needed to add, "Or we'll be dropping the band." Levon thought of Don Arden's aphorism about having to woo a record label three times: first, when they sign the act; second, when you need their money to promote the band; third, to get them to stick with the act after a song flops. Levon thought of Mussolini's son-in-law's aphorism: *Victory has a thousand fathers, but failure is an orphan.* Gazing out at the bleak landscape, Levon felt orphanlike. Many people's view of a band manager was formed by the acerbic, exploitative bully in *A Hard Day's Night.* The reality was much harder. Depending on the band, Levon had been a gopher, moneylender, drug-supplier, fall-guy, shrink, pimp, ego-stroker, babysitter, punching bag, and diplomat, as the situation demanded. If your act got rich, you might make money. If your act stayed poor, you got poorer. Utopia Avenue was Levon's last, best shot. Levon liked them as people. Most of the time. He loved their music. But he was exhausted. London was grinding him down. The weather was gray. The gay scene was infested with blackmailers, the vice squad, and chancers. He missed having someone to love. A manager's life was gruelingly thankless. Could they not say, "Thank you, Levon, for believing in us and busting your ass for us morning noon and night?" Just once? When things went right for a band, it was down to their God-given genius. When things went wrong, blame the manager.

Fact one: the band needed a new single out in the New Year—"Mona Lisa Sings the Blues"—and they needed to promote the hell out of it from Land's End to John o' Groats. And in Europe.

Fact two: this wouldn't happen without a drummer.

DEAN REACHED THE back page of the *Daily Mirror.* Levon had a clear view of the front, promoting the "I'm Backing Britain" campaign to save British industry by getting workers to put in an unpaid half-hour every day. Pye Records was bringing out a campaign single by TV face Bruce Forsyth, and DJ Jimmy Savile was working for nine whole days as a volunteer porter in Leeds General Infirmary. JIMMY'S DOING HIS BIT—ARE YOU?! read the caption. For Levon, the whole campaign belonged in the hinterlands of Bad, Stupid, and Naïve. The train rocked Dean, Jasper, and Elf to sleep.

A headache was hatching in Levon's brainstem, but he had to think. That was his job. Griff said he wasn't sure if he'd be back. Was this grief talking? Or was it act one of a breakdown? Or a genuine wish to leave the grueling life of a musician? Should Moonwhale seek to terminate Griff's contract? What about future percentages? Howie Stoker and Freddy Duke wanted a return on their investment. All Levon had to show them was a modest hit and an LP that had sold poorly. What if "Darkroom" had been a fluke? What if "Abandon Hope" was the real indicator of Great Britain's appetite for the band he had handcrafted? What if the real action wasn't in London anymore? What if the epicenter had shifted to San Francisco?

The band drove Levon crazy. Dean's demands for money they hadn't earned yet. Elf's insecurities. Jasper's day-to-day uselessness. Now Griff was wavering. Levon lit a cigarette. He looked out of the window. Still northern, still rainy, still drab.

He remembered arriving in New York, still deluded enough to believe that he was going to be, simultaneously, a Greenwich Village Baudelaire-in-exile, a beatnik folk singer, and author of the Great Canadian Novel. Ten years on, the only part that smacked of any truth was "exile." Propelled by an impulse he hadn't felt in years, Levon turned to the last page of his accounts book.

LEVON'S WATCH INSISTED that ninety minutes had passed. From the five pages of scribblings and crossings-out, four simple verses emerged. He made a neat copy on a fresh page.

Love found me when I was young.
A tent, a lake, a shooting star.
I built Utopia in my head, where
We could be the way we are.

They beat me up, they kicked me out,
They fed me to their godly flames.
"Pervert," "monster," "deviant"
Were just some of the nicer names.

Conform, conform, or be cast out.
The dogma is intense.
To build your own Utopia is
A criminal offense.

What is plotted will unravel.
What is built slip out of joint.
Good intentions get forgotten.
Makes you wonder, what's the point?

Levon knew it wasn't Robert Lowell or Wallace Stevens, but it had passed the time. Self-pity can lift one's mood. The landscape now was as flat as a prairie but wet, crisscrossed with wide ditches and drainage channels. A cathedral floated into view. Levon wondered which one it was. Lincoln? Peterborough?

"Ely." Jasper yawned. "Where I went to school."

"So that's Ely. Fond memories?"

"Memories," replied Jasper.

Levon closed his notebook.

"You wrote a poem."

If Elf or Dean had asked, Levon might have lied. "Yes."

"Please can I read it?"

Levon was curious about Jasper's curiosity. He acted on instinct, said, "It's just verses," and handed over the notebook.

Jasper's eyes flickered down the lines.

Then he read it a second time.

The train jolted out its own rhythm.

Jasper handed it back. "It works."

THE TRAIN STOPPED at a country station, but as it screeched away, it jolted to a halt. The light in the compartment went out. The driver informed the passengers of a "mechanical situation." Levon wiped an eye-slit on the fogged-up window and read the station name: GREAT CHESTERFORD.

"A notorious spot for breakdowns," said Jasper.

Half an hour later, the driver announced that "A mechanic had been dispatched to investigate the mechanical situation."

"Love the tautology," said Elf.

"Bloody British Rail," groaned Dean.

A hailstorm swept over the Fens. The stuffy compartment got stuffier. Three babies bawled at once. Sneezers seeded the air with germs. Levon had aspirins, but when he poured tea into the cup-lid of his Thermos to wash the tablets down, he found it laced with tiny shards of glass from the interior of the flask. Levon pooled saliva in his dehydrated mouth to swallow the chunky pills. They lodged in his esophagus. He sucked a Polo mint and finally got the pills down. He blurted out the truth: "We need a hit single. Urgently."

"We'd all like one o' them," said Dean.

"No. We *need* a hit single. Or it's over."

"What d'yer mean, 'it's over'?"

"Our deal with Ilex."

Elf looked uneasy. "They're dropping us?"

"Says bloody who?" asked Dean.

"Says Günther Marx. And commercial logic."

"But you saw Griff," said Elf. "Mentally, physically, spiritually, he's not ready to come back."

"That is true, Elf. And so is this: if we don't put out a hit single and promote the shit out of it, there'll be no band to come back to."

"Griff'll be on his feet again soon." Dean sounded scornful. "And if Ilex don't want us, screw 'em. We'll switch to a label that does."

"Name one." Levon's headache was getting worse. "The last single flopped. *Paradise* is not selling well."

"So are yer saying we get a new drummer?" asked Dean. "Screw that too. If Ringo Starr got hit by a bloody great truck—"

"The Beatles have millions in the bank and a back catalogue that shits out money every hour. Utopia Avenue have fuck-all in the bank, Dean, and we have no back catalogue."

"Hang on, Levon," said Elf. "Hang on. Are you saying you want to sack Griff because his brother just died in a horrific car crash and he's too full of grief to play? Seriously?"

"I am laying out the facts. Because somebody has to. Or there is no band. Of course we give Griff time. Of course. But you heard Griff. You saw him. It is entirely possible he won't be back."

"Drummers like Griff don't grow on trees," said Elf.

"You think I don't know that?" asked Levon. "I chose him! But a drummer who can't drum isn't a drummer. Jasper. Speak."

Jasper drew a spiral on the steamy glass. "Eight days."

"Speak English, not Cryptic Crossword. Please. I have a headache as big as East Anglia."

"My Dutch grandfather used to say, 'If you don't know what to do, do nothing for eight days.' "

Dean asked, "Why eight?"

"Less than eight is haste. More than eight is procrastination. Eight days is long enough for the world to shuffle the deck and deal you another hand."

Without warning, the train shuddered into motion.

The passengers raised a weary ironic cheer.

THE APPLAUSE FOR "Waltz for Debby" dies down. "Thanks," says Bill Evans. "Thanks a lot. So, uh, this next one I wrote after my father's passing. It's called 'Turn Out the Stars' and . . . uh, yeah . . ." The taciturn American balances his cigarette on the ashtray and leans in low over the keyboard. He half shuts his eyes. His hands take over.

Levon recalls Elf playing her freshly composed "Mona Lisa Sings the Blues" on this very Steinway in a well of sunshine half a year ago. He thinks of Griff in his hospital bed. *All that work, those meetings, phone calls, letters, the favors I cashed in, the crap I took from Howie Stoker, from Victor French, from everyone—all to get* Paradise *recorded and released, all turning to shit . . .*

Shut up and listen. The greatest jazz pianist in the world is playing ten yards away. Pavel appears and places a glass of vodka on the little table. He gives Levon's knee a consoling pat in a way no straight man would and withdraws, exposing Levon to a neighboring patron's stare. The man saw. Levon's unease and involuntary guilt is calmed by the man's sympathetic expression and cocked eyebrow.

Levon knows that roundish, storied face. Late fifties, a gray quiff, almost cherubic, had things gone differently . . .

Francis Bacon. Archly, the painter nods. Levon looks to his left and right—*me?* Francis Bacon's lips twist into a pert smile.

BILL EVANS'S UNFOLDING rendition of "Never Let Me Go" washes Levon in memories—intimate, painful, vivid. What was; what never was; what should have been; and what is, right now, on the first weekend of the New Year. The extended Frankland clan and favored members of his father's congregation will be gathering in the family home in Kleinburg, outside Toronto, to welcome in 1968. The Christmas tree will still be up. Levon hasn't been a welcome guest for ten years. He was not invited to his sisters' weddings. *I'm used to this . . . I got over it a long time ago.* Christmas and New Year's are hard, though.

"I'm Francis. Might I intrude?" Francis Bacon is leaning in. "You see, my friend Humph lured me along, describing Mr. Evans in rapturous terms—but frankly, I'm what's called 'lost at sea.' " The artist speaks queer English with a terse Irish underlay. "I saw how transported you were, so I've plucked up my courage to ask you for a pointer or two."

Is Francis Bacon hitting on me? wonders Levon. "I'm hardly a jazz buff, but . . . sure, I'll answer the best I can."

"You're buff enough for me. So, would 'Why doesn't he just play the damn tune the way it goes?' be a silly question?"

"Only if 'Why doesn't Van Gogh just paint the damn sunflowers the way they look?' is a silly question."

Francis Bacon performs a chortle, then looks mock-coy. "You must think me an awful old dunderhead."

"No. People who don't ask are dunderheads. To pianists like Bill Evans, what matters is less the melody itself and more what the melody *evokes.* Like Debussy. When Debussy's Preludes appeared, he had their titles—*"Des pas sur la neige," "La cathédrale engloutie,"* so on—printed at the end of the score, so the music could speak for itself, free of textual interference. For Mr. Evans there, a hummable tune is interference. The tune's the vehicle, not the destination." A few people move away, giving a view of the square-jawed, heroin-gaunt pianist. "I don't know if you're more at sea than you were before I started talking."

"You're saying he's an impressionist?"

Have I strayed into a French novel, wonders Levon, *where characters talk about art for page after page?* "Correct."

"Yes, that helps." He eyes Levon up. "Are you a Soho habitué? Or am I succumbing to wishful thinking?"

"We've not met. My name's Levon."

"My. I've never met a Levon in the flesh. Your accent's a long way from home. Canadian?"

"That's impressive. Most people guess American."

"You have a cultured, civilized air."

"You flatterer, Mr. Bacon. I'm a bit of a gypsy, really. I left Toronto at nineteen. For various reasons, I've never made it back."

"I'm from darkest Wicklow and I have no intention of making it back." Francis Bacon makes a shuddery face. "Your glass is empty." He looks around like a spy in a melodrama before producing a hip-flask. "Care for a little bone-warmer? Fear not, you shan't wake up naked in my garret. Unless you absolutely insist."

Only in Soho. "Why not?" Levon remembers topping up Dean's Coke with whisky in the 2i's basement. That, too, was a seduction of sorts. "I must be honest—I won't be the best of company tonight."

Francis Bacon pours. "And why would that be?"

"A business matter. I won't bore you. I'm only here because Pavel, the owner, bullied me into coming out."

"Here's to friends who know when to bully us"—the artist clinks his glass on Levon's—"and to a speedy resolution."

"Here's hoping."

"Ah, Humph." The painter addresses a man in his forties wearing a cable sweater. "Pull up a pew, as they say. Humph, meet my newest friend, Levon. We haven't reached the surname stage yet."

"Levon Frankland." Levon holds out his hand.

Humph has a kind face and firm handshake. "Humphrey Lyttelton. So you're a fan of Bill's?"

"Yes. Even more after tonight. Humphrey Lyttelton the jazz trumpeter, by any chance?"

"I have been known to torment unfortunates with that instrument, yes. Levon Frankland the manager, by any chance?"

Levon's surprised. "That's right."

"Then I know about your drummer. I'm a friend of Wally Whitby's, your boy's old mentor. How's he holding up?"

Where do I begin? "His brother's dead. He was driving. He blames himself. The whole thing's hit him very hard."

"Once I knew a stable-boy," says Francis Bacon. "He used to say, 'Grief is the bill of love, fallen due.' I can't recall his face or even name, but I remember that line. Isn't it odd, what sticks?"

THE WALLS OF the Colony Room Club are slime green. Thirty or forty faces, drink-flushed, drink-ravaged, and purgatorial, hover in the narrow enclosed space. A pianist is playing "Whisper Not" on an upright piano in the corner. Christmas decorations and stories crisscross the bar. A Scottish voice crows: "So the judge looked down at me from on high and asked, 'Didn't you think it peculiar that all the men were dancing together?' I told His Honor, 'Milord, I'm Inverness born and bred. How would I know what you southerners get up to of a Saturday night?' " Ornate lamps are reflected in the liver-spotted mirror. Unusual bottles and watchful eyes gleam; gossip bubbles and froths; the fallen and fading stare from framed photographs; aspidistras stand in bronze pots; and Muriel Belcher, steely empress of the Colony, is perched on a stool at the end of her bar, sipping a pink gin and stroking a white poodle. "Utopia Avenue?" She owns a sixty-a-day rasp of a voice. "Sounds like a field of four-bedroom houses at the edge of Milton Keynes."

"I'd be a shit of a lot richer if it was." Levon drains his glass of something thick and Turkish. He's uncertain what liqueur he's drinking because the fiery liquid stripped away his taste buds.

"*I* thought management was a one-way street to fame, fortune, and free shank 'n' loin," says George the Cockney. "Francis's manager's coining it and all *she* does is throw a party now 'n' then."

"Thou shalt not badmouth Valerie from the Gallery," says Francis. "It's biting the hand that feeds the hand that feeds you."

"I was under the impression"—Lucian the artist has a fox's eyes—"that screwing your artists is a perk of the job."

" 'Screw' as in 'screw' or 'screw' as in 'screw'?" asks Gerald with the windswept white eyebrows.

"Neither," replies Levon. "The boys are straight and I don't have what it takes to cheat them."

"Levon's father is a reverend." Francis rolls the *R*s.

"*Someone*'s going straight to Hell, then," says Muriel.

"Exactly what he told me the last time we met," Levon hears himself saying, and blames the Turkish liqueur. "Verbatim."

"*My* father's last words to me," says Gerald, "were, and I quote, 'If you set foot on this estate again I'll string you up and flog you until you're crow meat'—unquote."

"By 'I don't have what it takes to cheat them,' " Lucian the artist asks Levon, "do you mean, 'I don't know how to cheat them'? Or do you mean, 'I'm too honest to cheat them'?"

"The latter," replies Levon. "I wanted to see them as a long-term investment." *Or as a sort of family, now I think of it.*

"So 'ow *would* a manager rip off a band," says George the Cockney, "if yer *weren't* so full o' bloody scruples, like?"

Levon's glass is mysteriously full again. "Some managers cook the books and pocket the difference between declared and actual earnings. There're crooked contracts, where you get your client to sign away copyrights for a bowl of soup or a shitty percentage. From then on, the goose is laying its golden eggs for you. There're complex tax scams. Charity gigs that aren't really for charity. Lots of ways."

"Why don't yer clients cotton on 'n' stomp yer skull in with a length o' lead piping, say?" asks George the Cockney.

"Often, the talent doesn't *want* to believe it, because that would prove they're gullible morons. They prefer to look away. I know one manager who gets the talent so hooked on drugs, they're too fried to ask about the money."

"But wouldn't that strategy kill his clients?" asks Gerald.

"Exactly. The dead do not sue for fraud. I know another who got his band to sign a blank page over which he typed a power of attorney. He cleaned them out. When they finally scratched together the money to sue him, he produced a second affidavit they had all signed, forfeiting their right to sue him, in *any* circumstances—including the forging of affidavits."

"A twisted sort of genius," announces Muriel the owner. "So why, exactly, do you believe honesty pays?"

"A small slice of a big pie is more pie than a stolen half of a small pie," replies Levon. "Is what I thought."

"Fraud is tawdry," says Jerome, a regular. "*I* pass state secrets to my handler at the Soviet Embassy. That's treason. A proper crime." The others roll their eyes. "One can be hanged for it, you know."

"What do you think, Francis?" asks a random voice.

"What *I* think is, we ought to mark our first colonization of nineteen sixty-eight in style—Ida?" The barman looks around. "Champagne all round! Unleash the Krug!"

The bar cheers. Momentarily, Levon panics—he only has a couple of quid—but Francis tosses a bundle of banknotes to Muriel. A few flutter to the floor. "Will this do the trick, Mother?"

Muriel does the maths at a glance. "I'd say so."

"Donate any surplus to the Soho Home for Geriatric Poofs. Jerome's going to need a roof over his head."

Jerome pretends to find this droll as he retrieves the fallen notes. Levon notices him stuffing a few into his pocket. Champagne is uncorked and glasses are filled. The piano falls quiet. "Queens, queers, stiffs, straights, squares, givers, parasites, mediocrities, fellow artists, hypocrites, crooks, honest souls, old friends"—Francis catches Levon's eye—"dark handsome strangers, and Muriel, who maintains this enchanted outpost of Utopia. For a brief spell, we share a stage. Others are coming to kick us off. But while you're here, write yourself a good part. Act it well." He looks around the bar. "Act it well. There's nothing else to say because there's nothing more to say. Wisdom is platitudes gussied up."

Someone at the back calls out, "Happy New Year to you too, you miserable fuck!" and Francis bows. Levon knocks back his glass of champagne. *It tastes of liquid starlight . . .*

LEVON DRINKS A galaxy. The pianist is playing "I've Got You Under My Skin." Lucian buys him a pisco sour with Angostura bitters. *Does he want to get me drunk too?* Levon's confused. *He's a straight observer, slumming it with the queers . . .* Francis has a word in Levon's ear: "My gallerist's brother-in-law has opened a music club, tucked away behind Regent Street. They're having dinner at Harkaway's. Would you care to tag along, as my guest? It might be a frightful bore, but I can promise the freshest seafood in London." Levon can't recall his answer, but now he's walking up Bateman Street with Francis the artist and Jerome the fantasist. An icy wind gropes Levon's tenderer spots. It sobers him up a little. Francis stops at the corner of Bateman and Dean streets. "Do you know, I'm in the mood for a flutter? Let's go to Penrose's."

SERVED IN A pea-green porcelain boat, the mussel shells are blue-black on the outside and flint gray inside. Harkaway's restaurant is housed on the ground floor of the Kingly Street Hotel. Candles are beeswax, linen is starched, cutlery is heavy. It's far above Levon's budget, but he's enjoying not worrying about the band for the first time since the grim news about Griff's accident reached him on Christmas morning. Jerome is bragging about his victory at roulette in the casino. Levon's memories of Penrose's are splintered and distant, a losing streak at blackjack viewed through the wrong end of a kaleidoscope. Francis, Jerome, and Levon have joined a larger party of gilded people. Levon features in the story as a minor character—"Our poor Canadian cousin" who "got well and truly Waterloo'd" at blackjack. Jerome is trying to needle him, but the needles aren't sharp enough to irritate. Besides, his memories of Penrose's feel as unreliable as Jerome's. Levon half recalls running into Samuel Beckett at the casino bar; and yet there were no witnesses, and such a random encounter sounds far-fetched, even to Levon. His neighbor at the table is an alleged duchess—of Rothermere, or possibly Windermere, or maybe even Van der Meer—and—

unless Levon dreamed this part—is George Orwell's widow. "These oysters are or*gas*mic. Have one."

Levon slurps at the shell she brings to his lips. He washes it down with Château Latour. Francis ordered six bottles. Even the French sommelier was mildly impressed by the bill-trebling order.

"I've never met a music mogul before," the duchess says.

If I was Dean, I'd be all over her like a rash. "I've never met a widow of George Orwell before," says Levon.

"What do I need to know about you?" asks the duchess.

That I prefer men, thinks Levon. "I'm not a true mogul."

"But you *do* choose the stars of tomorrow, as it were?"

"Only in the sense that punters in a betting shop 'choose' the winner of the two-fifteen at Aintree. I only have one major act signed. Well, 'major' in a 'still minor' way. Well, 'potentially major.' So you see. No mogul."

"If you have designs on Levon's lolly," Jerome tells the duchess, "think again. Has anyone here even heard of Utopia Street?"

"Avenue." Levon twigs too late that Jerome got it wrong on purpose. *Fuckface.*

"I'll wager more people know Levon's pop group than ever heard of *you,* Jerome Blissett, master spy, professorial parasite, and part-time paint tormentor."

Jerome smiles at Francis's little witticism. Francis does not. Levon knows the man is butchered on the inside.

The duchess whispers to Levon, "You cut your lip. Oyster shell. That must have been me."

"It's nothing." Levon dabs his lip with his napkin and is unduly entranced by the way the linen drinks up his blood. *Osmosis.*

"How are your new paintings coming along for the new exhibition, Francis?" asks a Dickensian caricature.

"Modern slavery. Valerie from the Gallery wants another six by the end of . . . some month. I don't recall. It's soon."

George Orwell's widow asks, "Are you satisfied with what you have so far?"

"No artist is ever satisfied with his work," replies Francis. "Except Henry Moore."

Jerome swallows an oyster. "I met Salvador and Gala Dalí in Paris last month. He's putting together a new show, too."

"Fancy. The Great Masturbator is doing art, now?"

"I saw the Jackson Pollock retrospective at the New York Met," says the Duchess of Somewhere. "Do you rate him?"

"I rate him most highly," says Francis. "As a lacemaker."

It's Battle Royale, thinks Levon. *He's assassinating rivals, one put-down at a time.* A sole meunière appears with a pillow of string beans. It smells of butter, pepper, and the sea.

SEVERAL GLASSES OF Château Latour later, the door of the gents at Harkaway's veers this way and that. Levon commands it to stay still. Sulkily, it obeys. Levon's deflating his bladder at the urinal. *Urinal.* The capital U: *U* for *U-bend.* A familiar figure shambles across the periphery of his vision. A cubicle door is bolted. The tiles in front of Levon are off-white and ink-blue. He thinks of the Delftware on his mother's dresser at the reverend's rectory in Kleinburg, Toronto. *Of the band plus me,* thinks Levon, *only Griff and Elf have sane relationships with their fathers.* A few seconds pass. A few more seconds pass. A few more seconds pass. Levon buttons his fly and goes to wash his hands. "Look at *you,* swanning around casinos and nightspots with a famous sugar daddy." It's Jerome, his face in the mirror. "Just remember this: I've known him for years. I'm an artist. You're a bean counter. You're a tick. Piss off or I'll contact my KGB handler and have you vanished. The police would never even find your body."

The scarier Jerome tries to be, the more pitiful he becomes.

Jerome misreads Levon's silence as proof of successful intimidation. "Your plan'll never work."

Levon is curious. "Plan?"

"You're hardly the first, darling. Swap your arse-crack for a few Francis Bacon originals, flog 'em for a life of Riley."

Levon dries his hands, bins the towel, and turns around to face his adversary. "First, my arse-crack is not for sale, and—"

"Oh, you think the cock-struck dotard's invited you along for the quality of your conversation?"

"Second, why would he give art to a stranger? He's no fool. And third—"

"George milked him for thousands, and now George's family's blackmailing the idiot."

"You really should've listened to my 'third.' "

"I am agog."

A toilet flushes. An artist emerges from the cubicle.

"Francis!" half shrieks Jerome. "We were . . ."

"Tell your comrades in Moscow," says Francis, " 'Let me in, it's all over, nobody in London will even spit on me now.' "

Jerome forces his mouth to smile. "You and I are too grown-up to bicker over a silly misunderstanding."

"If you're still here when I finish washing my hands," Francis goes to the basin, "I'll have the manager send you the bill."

A CAVE-BLACK PASSAGEWAY off Dufours Place swallows them. A twist and a turn later, Levon and Francis emerge in a tiny courtyard with grated windows and ruckled paving. A neon sign stamps two words on the bricked-in dark: LAZARUS DIVES.

A statement, a promise, or a warning?

The door opens at Francis's approach and closes behind them. Inside is dim and reddish. A voice says, "Welcome back, sir." Francis mumbles something. "Of course, sir, if you vouch for him," and then, "Extremely generous of you, sir." Steps lead down to an arched cellar vibrant with Jimmy Smith's molten Hammond and Stanley Turrentine's volcanic sax. Levon can't determine the size of the club, if that's the right word. Discreet booths with tables and benches are arranged around a dance floor of flagstones. It may have been a crypt, once upon a time. Most of Lazarus Dives's clientele is male, though a few women are dancing amid the queerness as if none of this is a big deal. Men flirt at the bar, hold hands, touch. Several eye up Levon. Which is flattering, because Levon's still dressed for a Bill Evans gig, not for a Soho club where men meet men. *No, idiot, it's because you're with Francis fricking Bacon.* The last face is dangerously handsome. Thick black curly hair, darkish skin, chest visible to his solar plexus, like a satyr from Greek mythology. Levon thinks, *I'm going to know you very well,* then dismisses the idea. "It's Bloody Mary o'clock."

"A Bloody Mary would be perfect. How did you know?"

"A proper night out is both bomb making *and* bomb disposal. Two Bloody Marys, if you'd be so kind . . ." A giant barman nods. A hairless mod and a bearded hippie are locked in a yearning kiss.

"I've never heard of this place," says Levon.

"All tastes are catered for." The artist's face is inches away.

Levon stares back at a man twice his age.

Francis plants a strange, slow, pouted kiss on Levon's lips. Their eyes stay open. Lust is absent. *It's a ritual.* Francis pulls back and massages the muscles and fascia of Levon's face: not gently, not painfully. "Our persecutors maintain that"—Francis sighs the word, regretfully—" 'homosexuals' violate Nature's law. A decrepit falsehood. Nature's law is oblivion. Youth and vigor are fleeting aberrations. This truth is the canvas on which I paint."

A boy with a face like a girl or a girl with a face like a boy slides open a Swan Vesta matchbox. Inside are two white pills. Francis puts one in his mouth and swallows it. Levon looks at the other. Asking "What is it?" is not an option. *Acid, aspirin, vitamin C, a placebo, cyanide . . . it could be anything.*

Levon swallows it. Francis tells him, "Good boy."

A BASSIST, A drummer, and a keyboardist set up an oscillating drone, heavy with reverb. The drone seduces even non-dancers like Levon into dancing. A man in a nightshirt and facepaint is spinning plates on poles. He's up to thirteen. *One for each guest at the Last Supper,* thinks the reverend's son. *It's like the UFO Club was before the tourists flooded it.* A skinny man in sunglasses joins the band and lays tenor sax lines over the drone. They stab, slalom, wheel, and ululate. *Less commercial than Stockhausen, but they're perfect for Lazarus.* The Satyr, incredibly, is orbiting Levon, or vice versa. *He could have any guy in the place.* His lips are full and serious. His eyes inspire vertigo. *I could fall inside them and never reach the end.* His skin is bathed in dark red light and beaded with sweat. The pill is sharpening Levon's senses like speed and giving him a Mandrax glow. *No hallucinations,* he thinks gratefully, *unless this place is one, or this evening, or the whole of my life.* The Satyr leads Levon off the dance floor. His palms are scaly with calluses; clearly the Satyr works with his hands. They pass through another door, into a small room furnished for assignations with a single bed, clean sheets, a chair, some cords. It's as warm as a body. A red lamp glows like embers. The nameless band's bass throbs. The Satyr pours Levon a glass of water from a jug. It's cool and fresh. The Satyr drinks from the same glass. He holds an apple to Levon's lips. It's tart and lemony. The Satyr bites the same apple.

THEY TALK, A little, in the naked darkness. Both are cautious about giving details away. *Up those magic stairs awaits a harsh reality and we can't be too careful.* The Satyr is a native Dubliner called Colm. He calls himself "Black Irish"—a descendant of Spanish sailors from the shipwrecked Armada fleet, "though that's a yarn used to cover a multitude of sins." Levon says he's in music publishing. Colm says, "I'm a sparky"—adding, "electrician" when he sees Levon doesn't know the word. Colm asks if it's true "yer old tubby uncle feller" is one of the greatest painters of the century. Levon says, "*The* greatest, to my mind." Colm asks if Levon's "with him." Levon says no, he's just along for the ride. Levon takes a biro from his jacket and writes his number on Colm's left palm. "You can wash me away or you can call me." There's a tattoo of a cross over Colm's heart. Very gently, Levon sucks it. Afterward, Colm asks Levon if Levon's his real name; Levon says yes, it is—what about Colm? He says yes, it is. When Levon wakes, the Satyr is gone. Methodically, Levon checks that his wallet, watch, and pen are still in his jacket and trousers. Everything is in its right place.

PICTURES OF THE Nativity, in crayon. Snowmen. Eyes on upside-down chins. Fairy cakes. Jokes about Newfies and Nova Scotians. Goals in junior ice hockey. Book reports. A cake rack. Prayers to God to make him normal. Crusty tissues. A bonfire of love poems to Wes Banister. Shoveled paths through snow. Camping trips with the Baptist Boys Adventurers. Fumbles with Kenton Lester in a tent in the Adirondack Park. *That Game,* Kenton called it. *"Wanna play That Game?"* Kenton's face twisted with pleasure. Shooting stars. Later, furious denials. Outrage! Promises to himself to be more careful. Promises, when Kenton's family moved to Vancouver. Sticky fantasies. Essays. Exams. His bed in a room at the University of Toronto. Friends. Talk of Freud, Marx, Northrop Frye. Trips to see foreign films. Roll-ups. Poetry. Visits to folk clubs. "That Game" with a married judge, on the sixteenth floor of the Inn on the Park, one Saturday. Another Saturday. Another. Scandal. His father, shouting. His mother, sobbing. A meeting about an electrotherapy clinic. A decision. A six-hour bus journey to New York. Decorations for his tiny room in Brooklyn. Poetry. A job in the post room of a Wall Street brokerage. Enough money to buy a guitar. Songs. Trips to Greenwich Village. Advice from Dave Van Ronk: "Kid, we're all put on this earth for a reason, but molesting that guitar, it ain't yours." Sex with boys of a dozen races, creeds, and sizes. *Yes, sizes.* A job at a record shop on 29th and 3rd. A desk with the Mayhew-Reeves agency. The Beatles at Shea Stadium. *Their manager, Brian Epstein, he's one of us . . .* A poky office at the Broadway West Agency. A passport application. London! Trips with artists to Paris, to Madrid, to Bonn. Repair jobs on fragile egos. Letters to his mother and his sisters. His third, fourth, fifth Christmas out of Canada. A letter from his elder sister: *"Dearest Lev, this is ridiculous, you're my brother . . ."* Photographs. A partial, secret family reunion at Niagara Falls. An office at Pye. A stint at managing the Great Apes. A top-floor flat in Queens Gardens. Cordial relations with A&R men. A handshake with Howie Stoker and Freddy Duke. A call to Bethany Drew. Plans. A trip to see Jasper de Zoet play in Archie Kinnock's group. A trip to 2i's with Dean Moss. Utopia Avenue, or three-quarters of. Elf Holloway. Takeoff! Small tours. A deal with Victor French at Ilex. "Darkroom." The album. More dates for the new year. A trip to Hull. Cancellations. Apologies.

What we make, we are.

Levon is waking up . . .

. . .

CHILLY LIGHT SEEPS in. Levon is lying on a battered sofa in a messy sitting room. Books. Bottles. Bowls. *Objets.* A mirror, cracked into a jagged flower of shards. He has no idea where he is. He remembers Colm—but remembers Colm had left. Levon sits up. *Delicately.* Sash windows, overlooking a London mews, much like Jasper's but with higher sides. A soggy winter sky, like sodden toilet paper. Levon is fully clothed. He needs a bath. His keys and wallet are on the corner of the coffee table. The smell of cigarettes and beef drippings. The door opens and Francis Bacon peers in wearing a smoking jacket over pajamas. He has a black eye and his lip is cut. "Ah, you're alive. That simplifies matters."

"What happened to you?"

"Nothing happened to me."

"But your face! Somebody beat the crap—"

With casual finality: "You're mistaken."

Levon remembers Lazarus Dives: *All tastes catered for.*

"Hair of the dog." Francis hands him a tomato juice.

Levon sniffs it. "A Bloody Mary?"

"Don't argue with Nurse."

Levon sips the red gloop and feels better. "It's good."

"I've given a little thought to your predicament."

"My predicament?"

"Your drummer, the band, doubt, failure, et cetera."

"I told you all that?"

"In the taxi, you spilled your guts, so to speak."

Now he mentions it, thinks Levon, *I think I did . . .*

Francis Bacon lights a cigarette and tops up his Bloody Mary with a generous glug of vodka. "Levon, I don't know you from Adam. We may meet again, or we may not. London's a metropolis and a village. You're not an artist per se, but you enable the artists who make the art. What you are is an enabler. An assembler. A builder. This is a calling. You don't get the glory. You don't get remembered. But you don't get devoured. And you do get the money. If that's not good enough, go and play golf." A mouse watches from behind a jar of turpentine on a shelf by Francis's shoulder. "If this drummer boy of yours emerges from his Nighttime of the Soul, good. If he doesn't, get another. In any event, stop feeling so fucking sorry for yourself, and get back to work." The artist downs his Bloody Mary. "Now, I'm going up to my studio to follow my own advice. When you leave, pull the front door shut. It needs a good, hard *slam.*"

IF JANUARY WAS a place, it would be Kensington Gardens this morning. The trees are bare and dark. The flowerbeds are flowerless. It may be Sunday, but there's no sun to be seen or felt. The sky is somehow not quite there. Gulls, geese, and ducks on the Round Pond honk and bellow. It's cold. Nobody lingers for long. Nobody lingers at all. Levon's glad of the scarf he stole from Francis Bacon's coat stand. He'll return it if his conscience insists, but he doubts it will. The shops around Paddington are mostly shut. Few cars are about. No kids are playing in Queens Gardens. He climbs up to his flat, starts a bath running, cleans his teeth, makes a pot of tea, and brings it into the bathroom on a tray. He retrieves his notebook from its drawer, sinks into the hot soapy water, and reads the four verses he wrote on the train from Hull. *I need a final verse.* Levon knows it's on its way. A new verse, to flip the whole poem on its head. He wonders if Colm has scrubbed his biroed number off his palm, or if the telephone might ring today.

Maybe in the next few minutes.

Maybe in the next few seconds.

PROVE IT

A GLOW IN THE STAGE LIGHTS OF MCGOO'S, EIGHT WOMEN rest their pints of bitter on the stage. Four are in tears. Two are mouthing the words, prayerfully. *Gotcha!* thinks Elf. Until two Thursdays ago, Utopia Avenue was thought of as a male acid-flecked R&B band with a novelty girl. Elf suspected that most of the women at their gigs were girlfriends in tow. Since she mimed singing "Mona Lisa Sings the Blues" for the ten million viewers of *The London Palladium Show,* however, things have changed. McGoo's is a Jack-the-laddish venue in Edinburgh—Steve Marriott and the Small Faces are here next weekend—but nearly half of the house tonight is female. As Elf hits the high E of the final chorus and Jasper, Dean, and Griff fall quiet, her vocal is accompanied by, surely, a two-hundred-strong female choir blasting at top volume. *I couldn't sing off-key if I tried,* she thinks, and doubles the usual length of her final "Bluuu*uuu*-uuu*uuues* . . ." *Screw it,* she thinks, *I'll go another four bars* . . . Dean gives her a my-my-my smile. Jasper extends his falling note, and Griff sits out the extra beats before playing the cymbal crescendo. The band is only two songs into a twelve-song set and he's on industrial painkillers but he's doing well. The sound of his gong is buried under cheers, stomps, and applause. "Thank you," says Elf into the mic, looking at the eight women up front. One, the Queen of the Picts with wild black hair and arms like cables, makes a megaphone of her hands: *"We came althaway fro' Glasgee f' thassong, Elf, an' ye fookin' nailed it!"*

Elf mouths, "Thank you," at her and leans into her mic. "Thanks, everyone. I wish we'd come here months ago."

More applause, and blurred shouts, calls, and whistles.

"Holy God, I've missed this," continues Elf. "There were times in the last couple of months when the future didn't look so great . . ."

The Pictish Queen calls out, "We know what ye've been through right enough, Elf!"

". . . but Edinburgh and Glasgow, you've brought us back and—" People shout, *"Perth!"* and *"Dundee!"* and *"Aberdeen!"* and *"Tober-fookin'-mory!"* and Elf laughs. "Okay, okay—Scotland, you've blown away the darkness. So, our next song is . . ." Elf looks for her set list. "My set list just combusted. Dean? What's next?"

Dean calls over, "How 'bout yer new one?"

Elf hesitates. She's pretty sure "Smithereens" was the third song, and Dean isn't one to give up the spotlight. " 'Prove It'?"

Dean speaks into his mic. "Scotland, help us out. Elf's written a new song and it's bloody great. D'yer want to hear it or what?"

McGoo's roars with approval. Griff plays a drumroll. Dean cups his hand to his ear. "Didn't quite catch that, Scotland. Was it Some Old Bollocks yer want next? Or was it Elf's new one?"

The roar articulates itself: "ELF'S NEW ONE!"

Dean looks at Elf with a seems-pretty-clear face.

"Okay. Okay. You've done it now." Elf flexes her fingers and starts her piano intro. Hush falls. She stops. "It's called 'Prove It' and it's kind of, sort of, semi-, quasi-autobiographical . . . so, it's about wounds that are still raw, so if I rush offstage halfway through, leaving a vapor trail of misery and tears, you'll know why." She resumes her intro. The triad-based short piece was in her notebook for years, waiting for a home. Now it has one. Once its sixteen smoky bars are played out, Elf looks at Dean, who checks with Jasper, who glances at Griff, who counts off, "One, two, *one-two one-two*—" *Boom! Chacka-boom! Chacka-chacka-chacka-chacka-boom!* In comes Dean's bass march and Elf's doomy piano riff, and by the fifth bar, the audience are clapping out the rhythm already. Elf leans into her mic:

"They're jealous of me!" he left with a shout.
She was his fool so she followed him out.
He was the Romeo, she his subplot.
A dignified scene I'm afraid it was not.
"I'll prove it," she cried, "my love for you —
I'll prove it, I'll prove it, I'll prove it."

THE CLOCK IN Fungus Hut said 7:05 and Elf had to think: 7:05 P.M., or 7:05 A.M.? The evening, she decided. The band had started the November sessions for their first album with the low-hanging fruit of the older songs, but these kept evolving in the studio. By Friday of the first week—day five of ten—they were still on song three, Elf's "A Raft and a River," and badly behind their schedule of a song per day. Elf wanted jazzier drums and worked with Griff on a rippling, choppy arrangement with wire-brushes. By the tenth take, she was happy. The RECORDING sign went off and Bruce slipped in, winking at Elf and taking a stool in the corner of the control room. Digger pressed playback. The tapes revolved.

The song began. Elf kept glancing at Bruce.

Bruce just sat and listened with his eyes shut.

Elf loved the take, and wanted Bruce to love it too.

"It's a beautiful thing," said Levon.

"Done 'n' dusted," said Dean.

"Nice work," said Griff.

"Agreed," said Jasper.

Bruce appeared still to be making up his mind.

"Great." Elf told herself that just because she and Bruce loved each other didn't mean he had to love everything she recorded.

"I'll mark this tape as the master, then," said Digger. "You've got till a quarter to eight before I kick you out."

"Who's in after us?" asked Dean.

"Some kid of Joe Boyd's. His name didn't stick. Nick Duck, Nick Lake, or something. I need to clean some of your shit up."

"Time for a run-through of 'Wedding Presence'?" suggested Levon. "It'll save time tomorrow morning."

Elf couldn't stop herself. "Did you like it, Bruce?"

She sensed Dean, Levon, and Griff swapping looks.

Bruce breathed in. Bruce breathed out. "Honestly?"

Elf's heart shriveled. "Of course."

"Well. If you want a folk-jazz curio, mission accomplished. I *know,* I'm not *in* the band"—Bruce glanced at Dean—"but in my *asked-for* opinion, the song's suffocating. What's wrong with playing the beat on the first and third?"

"I asked Griff to 'drum the river,' " said Elf.

Bruce paused. "Right."

"If *my* girlfriend'd put together a song like 'Raft and a River,' " stated Griff, "I'd be less of a cold fookin' fish about it."

Bruce sniffed. "Elf and I believe honesty matters."

"Oh, aye? 'Honest,' like when you fooked off to Paris?"

Elf felt scorching up her neck, face, and ears.

Bruce did his easy smile. "It's a good song, but it's buried under too much smart-arsery on top. Word to the wise. If you want to know how to record Elf, play *Shepherd's Crook.*"

"We *could* try another take," began Elf, "with a more basic—"

"*No,* Elf," said Dean. "It's great as it is."

"I wouldn't touch it," said Jasper.

"No *fookin'* way," said Griff.

"If a basic drum pattern's beneath you, Griff," said Bruce, "I'll play it, and you can—"

"Lay one fookin' finger on my kit and I'll ram—"

"Stop it," groaned Elf. "Just stop it. Stop it."

"If your corner needs defending, Elf," Bruce told his girlfriend, "it's my duty to do that."

"Yer Knight in Shining Armor act'd be more convincing, Sir Bruce," said Dean, "if yer weren't such a bloody leech."

Bruce laughed. "*I'm* a leech? And you're living rent-free in a luxury flat in a Mayfair mews *how,* again?"

Dean stood up. "Yer want to take this outside?"

"Guys, let's just cool it," intervened Levon.

"I *am* cool." Bruce put on his jacket. "No, I don't want 'to take this outside,' Dean. Not because I'm *afraid* of you. I'm just not fifteen years old anymore. Elf, love, I'll see you later."

Bruce left without another word.

"Dean!" Elf is quivering with anger. "What if I insulted Amy in front of you? Or discussed Jude, or all your Away Dates, just to rub her nose in it? Griff, how *dare* you bring up Paris? Bruce was only trying to *help*—and you tore strips off him? What is it with you two? Un-be-fucking-lievable!"

Dean and Griff looked at each other, unimpressed.

Elf grabbed her bag and walked out.

THREE MONTHS LATER, onstage at McGoo's, Elf goes operatic on the last "Prove it!" of the first verse, and hyperenunciates the *t* of "it." Jasper bends the G down, like a motorbike roaring off a quarry's edge. He glances up at Elf, who nods at Griff tapping on his hi-hat: *five, six, seven, eight* . . . Next verse. Elf glances at the Pictish Queen and the Seven Sisters. They're all staring up at her, wide-eyed, hooked, smoking, nodding in time. Word has reached Scotland about who and what inspired the song, Elf guesses . . . *if "inspired" is the right word.* Even Felix Finch wrote about the rumors surrounding Shandy Fontayne's Top Five hit in his *Daily Post* column last week. Levon was pleased the band had won its first inches in a real newspaper, without him lifting a finger. *Unless it was Levon who told Finch,* it only now occurs to Elf, who dismisses the idea. Whatever the source, the column inches doubled the following day with an angry denial from Shandy Fontayne's office and a letter to Moonwhale promising legal ruination if the "public slander" against Bruce Fletcher is traced back to Elf Holloway. No doubt there's more to come. *Melody Maker* and *New Musical Express* are stirring the pot. When next week's editions hit the newsstands, the story looks set to boil over. If asked by anyone, Elf's supposed to say, "Our legal counsel has advised me not to comment"—but Ted Silver, Moonwhale's lawyer, didn't say she couldn't sing about it. Elf plays the glissando into the second verse and sings with sharpened edges:

He'd write a hit that'd prove 'em all wrong
And he'd run at the front of the pack. But
He hunted a hit and no hit came near.
He stared at the page but the page stared back.
"I'll prove it," he swore, "I've the Midas touch —
I'll prove it, I'll prove it, I'll prove it."

AFTER RUNNING OUT of Fungus Hut, Elf caught up with Bruce outside the Gioconda café. They went in and sat at the back and ordered two bacon sandwiches. Traffic's "Hole in My Shoe" played on the radio. "Dean and Griff were prize shits to you just now. Yet you're so calm. You're . . . just great."

Bruce stirred sugar into his coffee. "As the Good Lord said, 'Let he who has never been a prize shit cast the first stone.' And"—he made a guilty face—"they had a point. About Paris. To my shame."

Elf kissed her forefinger, reached across the table and planted it between his eyebrows. "Ancient history."

Bruce smiled an I-don't-deserve-you smile. "Fact is, I think Fletcher and Holloway make Utopia Avenue a bit insecure. 'Darkroom' was a minor hit—but what would it be without Elf Holloway's keys and harmonies? A third-rate 'See Emily Play.' What've they ever done to compare to *Shepherd's Crook*? Griff played drums on two lesser Archie Kinnock LPs. Dean's got Battleship Potemkin on his CV, who only ever recorded a couple of demos, and Jasper's got 'Darkroom.' As for Levon—sure, he's a decent manager, but being Mickie Most's gopher for a few months doesn't mean you know your way around a control desk. I just wish they were man enough to say, 'Bruce knows stuff we don't. Let's learn from him.' But that's guys for you. Competitive idiots."

Elf wished her family could meet this new improved Bruce. No invitations to Chislehurst Road had been issued. Bea had been over a few times after drama school, which Bruce was grateful for. He said he was willing to wait and prove by his actions that he'd done a lot of growing up in the last twelve months.

Mrs. Biggs arrived with their bacon sandwiches. Bruce sank his teeth in and ketchup oozed out. "God, I need this."

Elf dabbed ketchup off Bruce's chin with a napkin . . . and an abdominal twinge told her that her period was on its way. She wasn't late, but she felt relief. Then, she wondered if, just *if,* she and Bruce ever had a kid, what a half-Fletcher-half-Holloway co-creation would look like.

"I finished off 'Whirlpool in My Heart,' " said Bruce. "It's sounding pretty sweet, if I do say so myself."

"What did you decide about the chorus?"

"Like you said, it sounded better slower. Thanks."

"You're *so* welcome. You're making a real go of this."

"You're the inspiration, Wombat. You, 'Any Way the Wind Blows,' and Messrs. Moss, Griffin, and de Zoet. I'm not your bandmates' favorite person, but I dig how they've shaken the Soho music tree to see what falls out. Your best teachers aren't always your friends. Sometimes your best teachers are your mistakes."

"Write that line down," Elf insisted, "or it didn't happen."

Bruce obeyed, using a biro and paper napkin.

"Wouldn't it be easier," asked Elf, "to get a band together?"

Bruce clicked his tongue and shook his head. "We've been through this, darling. If I was away as often as you four, we'd drift apart. I'm not losing you twice. No. And think about the big-name solo artists who can't, or don't, write their own songs. Elvis. Sinatra. Tom Jones. Cilla. Really, there's loads. Cliff Richard. I can do this. I live with a piano. I've got contacts. Freddy Duke. Howie Stoker. Lionel Bart. Look how good 'Any Way the Wind Blows' has been for you. Three or four of those out in the world and I could plan for our future a little. So. Songwriter-for-hire. That's the ladder to the stars I'm on, and that's the one I'm sticking to."

Elf leaned across the table and kissed her boyfriend.

Bruce licked his finger. "I don't deserve you, Wombat."

"I'll help any way I can. What's mine's yours, Kangaroo."

JASPER SLOTS A solo into "Prove It" unlike anything he's tried in rehearsal. It's glorious. *I don't know how he does it.* She glances at Dean, whose face tells her, *I don't know either.* Jasper eschews guitar-theatrics, but the music finds a way onto his face. There's muted bliss at a sweet chord, muffled surprise when an improvisation swings up to a new place, or a half-hidden ferocity when his Stratocaster howls. *Only when he's playing,* realizes Elf, *is his face legible.* Jasper's solo ends on a blistering Iron Man yowl, and his glance her way means, *Your turn.* Elf takes up the piano figure and expands it into a boogie-woogie solo. *I love my job,* thinks Elf. If there is a deeper fulfillment than watching strangers connect with a song she's written, she has never found it. Musically, "Prove It" is closer to Chicago blues than to the folk music Elf played from the Richmond Folk Barge to the Les Cousins chapters of her life. *Maybe a brass section, if we ever put this on record.* Yet, to Elf's mind, folk is more an attitude than a genre and its tropes. If a song acknowledges the lives of the lowly, of servants, the poor, the shafted, immigrants and women, then in spirit Elf calls it folk music. It's political. It says, *We matter, and here's a song about us to prove it.* She ends the solo on D2, the second D from the bottom, her favorite note on the keyboard. She looks down at the Pictish Queen and her sisters and thinks of barmaids in Toulouse-Lautrec paintings. *They're worn, tired, ill-used, and dream-lit, yearning for a better life . . . but unbreakable, too.* The boys play quietly now, to usher in the "sleep verse." Elf sings hard against the mic so she can soften her voice.

As Soho dreamed deep she played her piano,
The chords came first, the lyrics by stealth.
He lay in her bed and he liked what he heard —
"What's hers is mine—she said it herself—so
I'll take it, adapt it, and smarten it up,
And improve it, improve it, improve it."

THE MORNING AFTER returning from Steve's funeral in Hull, Elf woke in the predawn murk. The city played its backing track while Bruce snored softly. Elf heard a waltz. It came from her piano, in its nook off her kitchen. She wasn't afraid. Nothing threatening could play music so soulful, so divine. She saw the pianist's hands. The right hand played overlapping minims: C to C an octave below; F to F, the same; B flat to B flat; E to E. The left hand played jazzlike sixths; blue jazz, not red jazz. It ended. Elf wanted to hear it again. The pianist obliged. This time Elf paid attention to the right-hand thirds: E and G; D and F; C and E; then a yo-yo back up to A and G, where the hand opened wider; a thumb on F and pinkie on B flat . . .

Elf put on her dressing-gown, went to her piano, got a sheet of manuscript paper, wrote out the C, F, B flat, and E sequence, then let the topography of the waltz rise up again . . . There. The first half was very close to how the dream-pianist had performed it. The third quarter needed more guesswork. Elf played a few chords as quietly as she could. By the final quarter, the milk float had jingle-jangled up Livonia Street. Elf had to compose the final bars herself, using the musical logic of the first half. Then it was done. Three pages of music. Elf played the piece through, knowing it was finished.

"Morning, Wombat." Bruce appeared. "That's pretty."

"Sorry I woke you. A song arrived in my sleep."

Bruce shuffled over, yawned, and peered at the manuscript. "Has it got a name?"

It had, Elf discovered. " 'Waltz for Griff.' "

Bruce made a face. "Guess *I'll* have to get myself into a near-fatal accident on the M1, too. 'Ballad of Bruce,' you can call mine."

A FORTNIGHT AFTER the funeral, Levon drove the band back up to Hull to see Griff. The visit was not a success. They passed the Blue Boar but none of them had the heart to suggest a stop. Griff was out of hospital and living at his parents' house. His dad, a bus driver, was out at work, covering a colleague's illness. Griff's mum was shriveled by grief and anxious about Griff's state. He never left the house, barely left his room, and didn't want to speak with anyone. She served them cakes and tea in the front parlor. Elf helped her arrange the flowers. Griff came downstairs. His bruising was much better, the plaster was off, and his hair was starting to grow, but his humor and curiosity were gone. His answers were curt.

"Any thoughts about coming back at some point?" asked Levon.

Griff just looked away, lit a cigarette, and shrugged.

"It's a bloody long drive for a shrug," said Dean.

"Didn't fookin' ask you to come," replied Griff.

"We don't want to rush you," said Levon, "but—"

"Why are you fookin' here, then?"

"McGoo's in Glasgow offered us the third Saturday next month," Levon explained. "Four weeks from now. Good money. Great exposure. If we do it, I *think* I can persuade Ilex to rush out 'Mona Lisa' as a single. But we'd need to tour the living bejesus out of it in March. I know you're in mourning. It's not fair to ask you. But we've got to know. Are you on board or not?"

Griff shut his eyes and sank back into the armchair.

A motorbike drove by. Elf remembered Dean's Nan's house in Gravesend. That was a happier place in happier times.

"Can we do anything that'd help you back?" asked Levon.

Griff made no reply.

Elf heard a train in the distance.

"What would Steve want you to do?" asked Jasper.

Elf flinched at the rawness of the question.

Griff stared at Jasper, murderously.

Jasper looked back as if they were discussing the weather.

A minute may have passed.

"Fook off," said Griff, and left the room.

They drove back to London in near silence. Elf thought how quickly the Wheel of Fortune spins. The future of Utopia Avenue was suddenly up in the air. Yet a week before Bruce had sold an option on his song "Whirlwind in Your Heart" to Andy Williams's company for $800. It was only an option, but the money was real.

It was late when Elf finally got home. Bruce poured her a glass of wine, massaged her feet, and listened to her sad account of the sad day. Elf had a bath and they went to bed.

DEAN'S BASS HANGS loose while he plays his harmonica thirstily, texturing the notes by flapping his palm over the vents. The sound loops-the-loop in the low cavern of McGoo's, a winged solo with teeth, and Elf vamps the bass line on the piano. Griff keeps time with rim-shots and Jasper plays his Stratocaster like a rhythm guitar. The crowd's gripped. *It's the best feeling—you write a song—you work on it—you polish it—you tweak it—you play it—you watch hundreds, thousands, more thousands inhabit it . . . Holy cow, I love what I do.* There'll be adjustments, but Elf knows that "Prove It" will make the next LP. *If Ilex want a next LP.* Elf doesn't want to jinx the future by assuming there is one, though this show is giving her hope that Utopia Avenue is properly back—and, somehow, better than before. Word will get back to Victor French. Having Griff back behind the drum kit gives her hope, too. She looks at the drummer. He's still not playing Dean's heavier numbers with quite the thump he used to, but he's doing well . . .

LEVON TRIED TO speak to Griff in the first week of February. Griff refused to come to the phone. Levon sent a telegram asking him to put a call through to Moonwhale. Griff did not reply. Levon drove back to Hull—again—with Elf. When they arrived, Griff's mum was in floods of tears. Griff had slipped out of the house two days previously, leaving only a note in his dyslexic handwriting that might have read, *Gone away for a bit don't worry, Pete*—but it was hard to be sure. None of his friends or family in Hull knew where he was—in fact, they had hoped he'd gone back to London. Levon left a letter with his dad to give Griff if he came back. It gave Griff a deadline of Friday to tell them if he wanted to carry on in the band or not. If they didn't hear from him, they would assume it was a no and audition for a replacement. Elf and Levon began the long drive back to London for the second time in ten days.

At lunchtime on Thursday, Elf's telephone rang as she staggered into her flat with her and Bruce's laundry. "Hello?"

Pips peeped, a coin clunked, and a Yorkshireman said, "Eh up."

"Griff?"

"Elf."

"Are you leaving the band?"

"Don't be soft. Why? Do you want me out?"

"Don't *you* be soft. None of us does. But you vanished."

"And now I've unvanished."

"Have you told Levon and the others?"

A pause. "Could you tell 'em?"

"Uh—sure. I'll try. Levon's been out of town and Jasper and Dean might have left. It's great news. But . . ."

"But what?"

"We thought we'd lost you. Why did you change your mind?"

A pause. Elf hears the noise of a pub.

"I . . . worked out what Steve'd want me to do."

Elf waited for Griff to tell her, but he didn't. "Okay."

"Are you rehearsing at Pavel's today?"

"Yes." Elf looked at the clock.

"See you there, then. Usual one o'clock kickoff?"

"Whoa, wait—are you here in London?"

"Aye. The Duke of Argyll."

"Round the corner?"

"Money's going." The pips peeped.

DEAN'S HARMONICA FRAYS at the end of the solo, McGoo's roars, and Dean takes up his bass again, pleased as hell with himself because there are few prizes as hard-won and golden as the approval of six hundred Scots, especially if you're English. He checks with Elf—who nods, *Ready*—and Dean's bass line comes in over her left hand, freeing her up for the next verse. In folk music, there is an element of acting in character: Elf, after a lengthy solo, would need to summon up the song's character again and switch from soloist to wronged ex-virgin, highwayman, whaler—and the audience would be required to play along with the artifice. If "Prove It" is working, it's because Elf is singing as herself and from her exposed heart. This is why it's painful and this is why it's powerful. She looks at the Pictish Queen and tells her true story of love, betrayal, and loss:

One Wednesday morning she ironed his shirts,
When she heard her own song on the radio.
"How dare you?" she cried; "Calm down," he said,
"I taught you all that you know—and
Prove that it's yours, if you can, go ahead —
Just prove it—in court—just prove it."

. . .

"SO YER BACK," Dean said to Griff at Pavel Z's. Elf hadn't been able to reach him or Jasper that lunchtime and could only leave a message for Levon with Bethany at Moonwhale. Now all three arrived at Pavel's bar at once.

Pavel Z was drying glasses with a cloth.

Griff was adjusting his drum stool. "Aye."

Levon shot Elf a glance: *Did you know?*

Her look told him, *Yes, but just go with the flow.*

Griff tightened a wingnut.

Elf played a few Bill Evans chords on the Steinway.

"Are you fit enough to travel?" asked Levon.

Griff played a quick cascade around his kit, thwacking the cymbal last of all. "I'd say I am. Are you?"

Dean and Levon turned to Jasper.

The heroes of Poland watched from the wall.

Light fell in a bright curtain through the skylight.

Griff took out a cigarette and looked for matches.

Jasper walked over and flicked open his Zippo.

"Obliged." Griff leaned forward, Dunhill in his mouth.

"Any time." Jasper put his lighter away and unclipped his guitar case. "So we've all been working on this new thing of Elf's . . ."

A BLUR OF days passed. Elf was doing some ironing to Radio 1. The Hollies' "Jennifer Eccles" was playing. The song was less trippy than the band's last single, "King Midas in Reverse." Elf wondered if psychedelia had been a flash in the pan, like Dean had always claimed. Tony Blackburn introduced the next song: "Coming up now is the wonderful Shandy Fontayne, a Texan singer who scored a string of hits three or four years ago. I hope you love her lovely new release, 'Waltz for My Guy,' as much as I do, because I think it'll be one of *the* hits of sixty-eight . . ."

The intro sounded familiar. Elf couldn't put her finger on why. The C, F, B flat, and E sequence gave the song a jazz feel, but a brass section pulled it in a bluesier direction. Shandy Fontayne came in with the vocal melody. Elf found herself predicting its every turn. At the chorus, the sickening truth smacked her in the face: "Waltz for My Guy" was "Waltz for Griff," with a brassy production and lyrics. The tune and chords weren't merely similar: they were exactly the same. This was theft. She smelt singed cotton. Her new Liberty blouse was burning . . .

BRUCE'S KEY TURNED in the lock. "God, those lads *still* can't play 'Greensleeves' without murdering it . . . What's up?"

"You stole my song and sold it to Shandy Fontayne."

Bruce did an I'm-so-innocent-I-can't-possibly-have-heard-what-I-thought-you-just-said face. "What?"

"You sold my song to Shandy Fontayne. Or Duke-Stoker did. Or someone did. Tony Blackburn played it on Radio One."

"Stole it?" Bruce looked bemused. "Listen to yourself. Why would I need to steal a song from anyone? Freddy Duke says I can write. Lionel Bart says I can write. Lots of Howie's clients say I can write. Are they all wrong? Is that what you're saying?"

"I'm saying"—Elf felt starved of oxygen—"that 'Waltz for My Guy' is 'Waltz for *Griff,*' with lyrics and a cheesy chorus."

"I've got to tell you, Elf, you're sounding weird—"

"Don't, don't, don't. Don't make this about me. Don't."

Bruce stood there. Out in Livonia Street a dog was barking. "Look. We live, breathe, eat, sleep together. Maybe—*maybe*—I *imbibed* a musical phrase or two. Why get hysterical?"

"*Imbibed?* It's the same song!"

"But 'Waltz for My Guy' has a chorus. A brass section. Lyrics. *My* lyrics. How *can* it be 'the same song'? Anyway, you've had a million ideas from me."

"Name me five. Three. No, name me one."

"The lyrics for 'Unexpectedly.' "

"Are you serious? I asked for your opinion on a few *lines.* That's *not* the same as me taking one of your songs and *you* only finding out when you hear it on the radio."

Bruce shook his head, as if stupefied by the illogic of the female brain. "Why can't you be *pleased*? When 'Darkroom' hit the Top

Twenty, nobody was happier than me. If 'My Guy' does *half* as well as Shandy Fontayne's people reckon, I—*we*—will be in clover."

It was like arguing with a tennis-ball launcher: *pop, pop, pop*—always a comeback. "Did you think I wouldn't notice? Did you think the record would flop? Or did you just not care?"

Bruce sighed. "Why must you always do this?"

Elf was supposed to say, *Do what?* So she didn't.

Bruce told her anyway. "You always cast yourself as the injured party. I stole *nothing*. 'My Guy' is a Bruce Fletcher song."

Elf was pushed past the point of no return. "Then Bruce Fletcher is a liar and a thief."

The hurt-boyfriend mask evaporated off Bruce's face. "Yeah?" Even his voice had changed. "Prove it."

JASPER SITS ON the edge of McGoo's drum-riser and strums his Strat. Dean's nod means, *I'll bow out after one more round.* Elf hits diminished and augmented chords in rapid progression. Tony Blackburn was right about "Waltz for My Guy": after only two weeks it's at number eleven in the US charts and number three in the UK, behind only Petula Clark and the Monkees. Last week Shandy Fontayne flew over for *Top of the Pops* at Lime Grove. Bruce was in Shandy's entourage in the company of "ravishing model Vanessa Foxton," according to Felix Finch's column. According to Dean, who heard it from Rod Stewart, who knows these things, Bruce has been "twanging her G-string" since he got back from Paris.

Bruce wears Italian suits now. His credit is excellent. The royalties will soon be thundering in. Elf will receive not one penny, cent, pfennig, yen, or lira. Ted Silver, the lawyer for Duke-Stoker Agency and Moonwhale Management, concluded that while the musical similarities between "Waltz for Griff" and "Waltz for My Guy" were strong, a defending lawyer would argue that Elf could not prove that she had composed "Waltz for Griff," could not prove that Bruce had heard it, and could not prove that Bruce had plagiarized the song. Elf could well be liable for Bruce's legal fees as well as her own. If she went to the papers with the story, Bruce could countersue for defamation, leaving Elf vulnerable to the loss of two fortunes, not just one. "What should I do, then?" she asked. Ted Silver suggested needles and a voodoo doll.

Griff, Dean, and Jasper stop playing, leaving Elf to carry "Prove It" home on her piano. McGoo's hushes so as not to miss a word. The spotlight shines on the piano. Two little dots are reflected in the Pictish Queen's eyes. Her skin turns gold. So do Elf's hands . . .

A thief needs a fool to ply his trade,
A gullible fool who'll trust anyone;
A lover needs a cure for a serious illness.
A singer needs a lawyer and a gun.
"I'll prove crime pays," said Romeo, "I will,
I'll prove it, I'll prove it." He's proving it still.

STUFF OF LIFE

1. **NIGHTWATCHMAN** (De Zoet)
2. **ROLL AWAY THE STONE** (Moss)
3. **EVEN THE BLUEBELLS** (Holloway)
4. **SOUND MIND** (De Zoet)
5. **LOOK WHO IT ISN'T** (Moss)

NIGHTWATCHMAN

ENGINES CHURN BELOW THE WATERLINE, THE GRUBBY SEA foams up, and the *Arnhem* pulls away from the concrete Harwich quay. Jasper feels the deck begin to lift, fall, and tilt with the swell of the open sea.

"Amsterdam," says Griff. "Here we come."

"Legal dope," says Dean. "Here we come."

"Tolerated, not legal," Levon corrects him. "Be discreet. Please. Trouble with the cops could impinge on future tours."

The *Arnhem* blasts out three honks on its mighty horn.

"Is it true," says Griff, "that in the red-light district, the hookers stand in glass cubicles that you see into from the street?"

"It's true," says Jasper.

"Oh, goody gumdrops," says Elf. "Dirty mags without the mag."

Jasper's pretty sure she's being sarcastic.

"If *you* go," Elf tells Dean, "don't tell me. I don't want to have to lie to Amy. Actually, I *won't* lie to Amy."

"Pure as the driven snow, me." Dean clutches his heart.

"This is the boat you took every summer?" Levon asks Jasper.

"Every summer. A driver would pick me up at Ely, drive me to Harwich, and put me aboard. My grandfather was at the other side to take me to Domburg."

"And Domburg's where the de Zoets live?" asks Elf.

"The de Zoets live in Middelburg, the capital of Zeeland. I used to board with a vicar at Domburg, on the coast."

"Why couldn't yer just stay with yer family?" asks Dean.

"Family politics," replies Jasper.

"Didn't you mind being sent off across the North Sea, all on your own, to stay with strangers?" says Elf.

Jasper thought of himself, standing at this railing, buffeted by the same North Sea wind, watching everything he'd ever known flatten into a knobbly smear on the horizon. "Saying no wasn't an option. I had nowhere else to go. I like ships. I was born on one."

"The ruling classes, eh?" says Dean.

Salty air fills their lungs. Runaway shadows cross the crumpled sea. Gulls hover alongside the *Arnhem.* "It was an adventure," says Jasper. "I felt like a boy in a story."

TRESPASS IN THE blood. Jasper awoke seven years ago, the morning after he and Formaggio had communicated with Knock Knock. He felt a sick dread in his guts and a sharp-knuckled *knock-knock-knock-knock-knock-knock* at the top of his skull like an angry downstairs neighbor hitting his ceiling with a broom handle. It stopped and started several times a minute, water-torture style, as if bent on destroying Jasper's sanity. He had no appetite and skipped breakfast. The first period was history but Knock Knock buried Mr. Humphries's discourse on the Hundred Years' War so Jasper asked to be excused on the grounds of a migraine. He went to Matron via his room, picking up the "alphabet matrix" Formaggio had made the night before. Matron gave him an aspirin—which had no effect on the knocking—and sat knitting for a while. When she left the room, Jasper asked his tormentor aloud what his price of peace was. The answer was a barrage of *KNOCK-KNOCK-KNOCK*s. Jasper understood that no further correspondence was to be entered into.

Formaggio came to see him before lunch. "Christ, you look terrible. Is it still . . ." He rapped his knuckles together three times.

Jasper nodded. Marshaling sentences was like trying to perform mental arithmetic while someone shouted random numbers into his face. "Telegraph my grandfather. If I get sectioned in an English hospital, I've got no guardian here to get me out."

Formaggio nodded and went away. More hours limped on under heavy showers of hard knocks. They were getting louder. Jasper felt hairline splits crisscross his mind. The headmaster arrived with Dr. Bell from the town surgery to give Jasper a proper examination: Formaggio's telegram had reached Grootvader Wim. Knock Knock fired off a cannonade of blows that brought tears to Jasper's eyes. After testing Jasper's pulse, reflexes, blood pressure, vision, and hearing, Dr. Bell ventured a diagnosis of "extreme nervous migraine" and prescribed sleeping pills and a mild opiate solution. Formaggio returned after supper, but speaking was now nearly impossible. "I don't know if it's demonic possession or madness or a brain tumor," said Jasper, "but this is killing me."

Formaggio asked Matron and the headmaster if Jasper could sleep in their dorm where Formaggio would be on hand if his friend's condition worsened. The headmaster agreed, and Jasper took two sleeping pills before he lay down on his own bed. In lieu of counting sheep, he listed the ways a schoolboy in Swaffham House could kill himself: a noose made of his school tie; drowning in the River Ouse; slicing his veins with his Swiss Army knife; resting his head on the King's Lynn–London railway line . . .

. . . Knock Knock jolted Jasper back to consciousness. His alarm clock said two. Formaggio was asleep. Jasper's own body felt unfamiliar, as if his mind had been transplanted as he slept. The knocking was relentless, merciless . . . Some impulse prompted Jasper to get out of bed and check his reflection in the mirror in his wardrobe. A stranger's eyes regarded him. The stranger within knocked his knuckles against the inside of the mirror and, for a split second of pain, revealed his true form: a man, older, shorter than Jasper, with East Asian eyes, in ceremonial robes. His head was shaven.

He was gone.

Of its own volition, Jasper's knuckle struck the mirror again and the figure reappeared, possessed Jasper's fist, and *KNOCK-KNOCK-knockknockknockknockknockknockknockknockknockknockknockknockknock-knockknockknockknockknockknockknockknockknockknockknockknock-*

knockknockknockknockknockknockknockknockknockknockknockknock-knockknockknockknockknockknockknockknockknockknockknockknock-knockknockknockknockknockknockknockknockknockknockknockknock-knockknockknockknockknockknockknockknockknockknockknockknock-knockknockknockknockknockknockknockknockknockknockknockknock-knockknockknockknockknockknockknockknockknockknockknockknock-knockknockknockknockknockknockknockknockknockknockknockknockknock-knockknockknockknockknockknockknockknockknockknockKNOCK-KNOCK-KNOCK-KNOCK-KNOCK-KNOCK-KNOCK "De Zoet! De Zoet! De Zoet!"

Formaggio had hauled Jasper away from the mirror and was pinning him down on his bed. His knuckles were cut and bloody. "You were sleepwalking! You were dreaming!"

"No I wasn't," said Jasper.

UTOPIA AVENUE WALK down the gangplank at Hook of Holland. A chopped rainbow rises over the warehouses and wharves. Levon carries a suitcase in each hand. Jasper and Dean carry their guitars. Amps, keyboards, and drums will be provided at the TV studio and at the Paradiso, so Griff and Elf carry only their overnight bags. They enter the new customs area at Hook of Holland port. Jasper is reassured by the design of the place, by the fonts on the signs, by the sound of Dutch and the facial habits of the speakers. He reaches the front of the queue and hands over his Dutch passport. The heavyset officer studies Jasper's photograph, then frowns at Jasper's long hair. "But it says *here* you're male." He speaks with a Flemish accent.

A joke. The hair. "Yes, I get that quite a lot."

The officer nods at Jasper's guitar case. "Machine gun?"

Another joke? Jasper shows the man his Stratocaster.

The officer makes an unreadable face and looks behind Jasper to Elf, Griff, Dean, and Levon. "Is that your band?"

"Yes. The older one's our manager."

"Huh. Are you lot famous?"

"Not very. We might be soon."

"What do you call yourselves?"

"Utopia Avenue."

The officer double-checks Jasper's name. "Are you related to the de Zoets of Middelburg? The shipping family?"

Experience has taught Jasper to be evasive. "Only distantly."

THE CHANGING ROOM at AVRO TV boasts four chairs facing four mirrors lit by four naked lightbulbs, a coat stand, two squashed cockroaches on a floor of broken tiles, and a view of dustbins. "We've hit the big time now, baby," mumbles Dean.

"At least it doesn't smell of piss and beer," says Elf.

"Relax here for twenty minutes," says the assistant.

Jasper looks away from the mirrors. *I doubt that.*

"Here, you do preparation," says the assistant. "Two minutes before your slot, I will deliver you to the studio stage. You will perform the songs 'The Darkroom' and 'Mona Lisa Sings the Blues.' After, Henk will conduct a short interview. Is there anything that you need in addition?"

"A ball of opium as big as my head," says Dean. "Please."

"This you may buy in the city. After the show."

Applause washes down the corridor outside as Shocking Blue, a four-piece psychedelic band from The Hague, start the show.

"I will be back." The assistant shuts the door behind him.

"Bloody Nora." Dean turns to Jasper. "There's no holding you wild Bohemian swinging Dutch freaks back, is there?"

Irony, sarcasm, or sincere? Jasper does an all-purpose shrug.

"I'd like a quick word with the Hollies' manager." Levon puts on his blue glasses. "Don't do anything I wouldn't."

"That gives us plenty of scope," says Elf, as tradition dictates.

Jasper slips his jacket over a hanger, hooks the hanger over the mirror, sits down, and gets out his Rothmans.

"But why *do* mirrors give you the creeps?" asks Griff. "Granted, aye, you're no oil painting, but you're not *that* revolting."

"They just creep me out." Jasper avoids the specifics.

"Oooh, hark at Captain Mysterious," says Griff.

"Phobias are irrational," says Elf. "That's the point."

"The things I'm afraid of are all pretty sensible," says Dean. "Beeswarms. Atomic war. Surviving an atomic war."

"The plague," says Griff. "Elevator shafts. Elf?"

Elf thinks. "Forgetting lines onstage. Fluffing songs."

"If that happens," says Dean, "just sing in fake Hungarian and when people say, 'What's that?' say, 'It's avant-garde.' "

"Avant-garde a clue," says Griff. "I left my sunglasses in the makeup room. I'll be right back." He stands up to go.

"*That* old trick," says Dean. "Yer just after Miss Makeup Artist's number, yer old dog. I'll come along. Want to cop yer face when she turns yer down."

"I'd like to see Shocking Blue," says Elf. "Coming, Jasper?"

Peace, quiet, and a cigarette are inviting. "I'll stay here."

THERE'S A *KNOCK-KNOCK-KNOCK* on the changing-room door.

It's okay, Jasper assures himself. "Hello?"

A face with a square jaw, a restless stare, and brown hair. "Jasper de Zoet, I presume." The visitor has a deep American voice.

Jasper knows him. He's formerly of the Byrds. "Gene Clark."

"Hi. Mind if I disturb you?"

"You're welcome. Just mind the roaches."

Gene Clark peers down to examine the squashed bugs. "There but for the grace of God." Jasper's unsure what a normal response might be so he shrugs and hopes for the best. The visitor is dressed in a fuchsia shirt, loose mauve string tie, green trousers, and gleaming Anello and Davide boots. He pulls a chair out. "Just wanted to say, I *really* dig your LP. Your guitar playing's out of this world. Did you teach yourself?"

"I had a Brazilian teacher for a while. Mostly I taught myself. In a long continuum of rooms."

The singer looks as if Jasper's answer was strange. "You taught yourself good. When I heard 'Darkroom,' I thought, *How in hell did Pink Floyd get Eric Clapton to play with 'em?* It's great."

That's a compliment, Jasper realizes. *Give one back.* "Thank you. The album you made with the Gosdin Brothers is a banquet. 'Echoes' is remarkable. That uphill F major seventh is ingenious."

"So that's an F major seventh?" Gene Clark taps ash. "I call it 'F demented.' I liked how the album turned out. Too bad it sold shit.

It came out the same time as my old band released their *Younger Than Yesterday* LP and it vanished down a hole . . ."

Jasper guesses that it's his turn to speak. "Are you touring?"

"Just a few dates, here in Holland and Belgium. They dig me here. Enough for a promoter to fly me over, anyway."

"I thought you quit the Byrds because of a fear of flying?"

Gene Clark stubs out his cigarette. "I quit the Byrds 'cause I was *tired* of flying. Tired of that life, of the screams, of the faces, of the fame. So I quit. Fame molds itself onto your face. Then it molds your face. Fame brings you immunity from the usual rules. That's why the law doesn't like us. If a freak with a guitar doesn't have to abide by the rules of the great and the good, why should anyone? Problem is, if fame *is* a drug, it's hard to kick."

"But you did kick it, Mr. Clark," says Jasper. "You walked away from the American Beatles."

Gene Clark examines the callus on his hand. "I did. And guess what? Now it's gone, I want it back. How do I earn a living without fame? Playing coffee houses for beer money won't cut it. I miss being someone. When I had fame, fame was killing me. Now it's gone, anonymity is killing me."

Shocking Blue's "Lucy Brown Is Back in Town" wafts down the corridor. The saxophone solo's great. The song itself is not.

"We'll give you a home in Utopia Avenue," says Jasper.

Gene Clark flashes his smile as if Jasper was joking. "Am I life's greatest fool? Is all pop just a fad? Do we all get replaced by some new Johnny Thunder and the Thunderclaps after X many years? Or could we still be in this game when we're sixty-four? Who can tell?"

"Time," says Jasper.

THE LAST CHORDS of the recorded "Mona Lisa Sings the Blues" die away and the assistant producer holds up a Dutch sign saying APPLAUS. The audience obliges. Jasper recognizes Sam Verwey, his old busking partner and classmate at the art college. Verwey gives him a double thumbs-up. The band is ushered over to a sofa alongside Henk Teuling. The presenter of *Fenklup* is a walrus of a man dressed like a civil servant. Addressing the camera, he speaks scholarly Dutch as if to atone for the show's hippie visuals. "The British band Utopia Avenue, playing 'The Darkroom' and 'Mona Lisa Sings the Blues.' Their guitarist Jasper de Zoet is 'half Dutch'—and a scion of the famous de Zoet shipping family. Am I correct?"

"Mostly," replies Jasper. "Shall we speak in English?"

"Naturally." Henk Teuling gives a magnanimous smile and indicates Elf. "Why don't you introduce this lovely lady first?"

"This is Elf," says Jasper, "who wrote 'Mona Lisa.' "

Elf gives a cool wave at the camera and makes a valiant stab at *"Goodag, Nederlands."*

Members of the audience shout, "We love you, Elf!"

"So I must ask," says the host, "why are you in a band with three guys? This is very unconventional. Did you apply to join the band? Or did the band invite you?"

"We . . . sort of auditioned each other," says Elf.

"People suggest you were hired as a gimmick."

Elf's face becomes more complicated. "I'm hardly likely to say yes to that, am I? I mean—were you hired as a gimmick?"

"But an elf is a little magic person with pointy ears. Yet you are not little, not magic, and do not have pointy ears."

"It's a family nickname. My birth certificate names are 'Elizabeth Frances.' 'El' plus 'F' makes 'Elf.' "

Henk Teuling takes this in. "I see. Do you dig Amsterdam?"

"I love it. It's so . . . improbable. Yet here it is."

"Precisely so." Henk Teuling turns to Griff. "You are . . ."

Griff's brow furrows. "I'm a fookin' what?"

"You are the drummer of Utopia Avenue."

Griff looks over at the drum kit, astonished. "Holy shit. You're right. I *am* the drummer . . ."

"And tonight you make your international debut at the Paradiso, here in Amsterdam. What does this show mean to you?"

"It means I get to be interviewed by Henk Teuling."

Henk Teuling nods as if considering a line of Immanuel Kant and turns to Dean. "You are Dean Moss. A bass guitarist. You wrote a song we did not hear just now entitled 'Abandon Hope.' It was released as a second single. It was a flop. Why?"

"One o' them mysteries," says Dean. "Like, who hired yer?"

Henk Teuling smiles illegibly. "The British sense of humor. I am an eminent music critic in the Netherlands, and well qualified to present this program. Which brings us to Utopia Avenue's LP, *Paradise Is the Road to Paradise.*" He shows the camera a copy of their album. "Some people say this LP is schizophrenic. How do you respond? Anyone?"

"How can an LP be schizophrenic?" asks Dean. "That's like saying, 'Your helicopter is manic depressive.' "

"Yet, in fact, on this album we hear acid rock, folk with acid effects, R&B, folk interludes, passages of jazz. So 'schizophrenic' is, in fact, an apt adjective for such inconsistency of style."

"Wouldn't the adjective 'eclectic' be more apt?" asks Elf.

"But into which *category* of music," Henk Teuling asks the three males, "can Utopia Avenue be located? Our viewers at home will be worrying about this question. The *category.*"

"Locate it in an eclectic category," states Dean.

Jasper's attention wanders off and finds Sam Verwey, who mimes hanging himself with a noose. *A joke.* Jasper mimes a smile. He finds he's looking for Trix.

"You have a view on this issue, Jasper?" asks the eminent critic.

"You're like a zoologist asking a platypus, 'Are you a duck-like otter? Or an otter-like duck? Or an oviparous mammal?' The platypus doesn't care. The platypus is digging, swimming, hunting, eating, mating, sleeping. Like the platypus, I don't care. We make music we like. We hope others like it too. That's it."

The producer is making a time's-up gesture. Henk Teuling addresses the camera. "We will finish here. Some people will find the music by these four platypuses unfocused, confusing, and too loud. Some people *may* enjoy it. I will prejudice no one. Next up, making their third appearance on *Fenklup* with their newest hit, 'Jennifer Eccles,' I am proud to present a genuine British pop sensation—the Hollies!"

THE BLACK SINGEL Canal reflects the streetlamps spaced along its curving banks. Pale globes fragment, resolve, fragment, resolve. Jasper crosses the narrow bridge and enters Roomolenstraat, exactly the kind of street that foreigners picture when they think of Amsterdam: brick-paved, with lampposts, tall narrow houses with tall narrow windows, steep gables, and flower boxes. Halfway along its modest length, he finds the number he is searching for and a name-plaque atop the brass doorbell: GALAVAZI. Once Jasper's thumb is on the doorbell, however, his resolve fragments. He's no master of social etiquette, but he's pretty sure that normal people telephone before turning up on a doorstep after five years. *More than that, if you push this bell, Knock Knock's return is official.* Jasper senses the present bifurcate, right now. *Or I could walk away and hope for the best.*

A builder's van rumbles up Roomolenstraat. Jasper has to stand on the doorstep to let the van pass. The van slows down, and both the driver and the passenger—*a son?*—give Jasper a lidded stare, as if memorizing his face for a police artist. *I could have been you,* Jasper thinks, looking at the son, *easily—it's all Y-junctions, from Alpha to Omega . . .* His thumb is still on the doorbell. Just a *little* more pressure, and one future comes into being at the expense of another. *No.* The door opens anyway. Dr. Ignaz Galavazi addresses Jasper in his Frisian-flavored Dutch. "Ah, excellent timing, Jasper. In you come now, out of the cold. Dinner's ready."

DR. GALAVAZI'S HIGGLEDY-PIGGLEDY kitchen is spotless and daffodil yellow. "My wife's in Maastricht, visiting her family." The doctor ladles stew into Jasper's bowl. He's older, his throat is saggier, but his white hair still looks blown backward as if he's facing a gale. "She'll be sorry she missed you."

"Pass on my compliments," Jasper remembers to say.

The herby steam feels good on his cold skin.

"I shall. How are you finding London?"

"Labyrinthine."

"We both find much to admire in your gramophone record. Naturally, 'modern music' to me means Poulenc or Britten, but if culture doesn't evolve, it dies. I sent a copy to Claudette Dubois, too. She's teaching in Lyon now. She's 'happy as Larry'—as the English say—about you and Utopia Avenue."

"Pass on my compliments. Please."

"I shall. Little did I know that when I let her test her newfangled ideas at Rijksdorp, we were hatching 'the Dutch Jimi Hendrix.' That's what *De Telegraaf*'s calling you, and even I have heard of him. *Bon appétit.*"

Jasper's taste buds investigate. *Calf's tongue, rosemary, cloves . . .* "Were you expecting guests today, Doctor?"

The doctor breaks open a crusty roll. "Why do you ask?"

"The soup. You made enough to feed a rugby team."

Dr. Galavazi's lips twist. "It's a fiddly old Jewish recipe of my mother's. Collecting the ingredients is quite a quest, so I make a lot to justify the trouble. We have a refrigerator now. It'll keep for a week. Also, I had a hunch—and hopes—that a former patient might drop by." He has a certain look. *Amusement?*

Jasper hunts for clues: *a former patient . . .* "Me?"

The doctor sips his beer with pleasure. "Who else?"

"You must have many former patients."

"Not many whose name is printed in giant letters outside the Paradiso. Not many perform on *Fenklup,* either."

"At Rijksdorp, you used to say that television turns the human brain to cottage cheese."

"For you, I made an exception. I imposed upon a neighbor. The program was idiotic, but you all played superbly, I thought. Identical to the gramophone."

Jasper bites a soft butterbean. "On TV, we mime."

"Is that so? My, my. More's the pity Henk Teuling didn't mime his interview. Have another bowl. It's good to see you eat."

THE PSYCHIATRIST SERVES green tea and lights his pipe in his book-lined study. These two aromas remind Jasper of Rijksdorp. Dr. Galavazi's voice lulls. "Is this purely a social call, Jasper, or am I correct in thinking there's a professional aspect to it, as well?"

"How retired are you, Doctor?"

"Us old shrinks never retire. We just vanish in a puff of theory." He sips his tea. "Seeing you on my doorstep earlier, I guessed you were here to talk business." The doctor sips his tea. "Was I wrong?"

Outside a cyclist in a hurry rings a frantic bell.

Say it. "I think I can hear him again."

The doctor makes his thinking-growl. "Knock Knock? The Mongolian? Another?"

"You still remember my case."

The doctor's pipe smoke smells of chicory, peat, and pepper. "Disclosure: your case was good to my career. After *Psychiatry Forum* published my JZ paper, colleagues from Vancouver to Brasília, New York to Johannesburg contacted me with reports of the very same phenomenon: of patients with diagnoses of schizophrenia who reported visits by an entity who ameliorates the psychosis. Only last May we held a conference in Boston on 'Autonomous Healer Personae'—AHPs. If my zeal seems vampiric, I apologize—but, yes, I remember the facts of your case very well."

"If psychiatrists weren't a *little* vampiric, psychiatry wouldn't exist and I'd probably be dead."

The doctor doesn't deny this. "I'll help in any way I can."

Things cost money. "Thank you, but my grandfather is dead, and I'm not exactly on a steady wage, so—"

"There will be no fees. All I ask is that I can publish my findings."

"It's a deal." Jasper guesses that a handshake is appropriate.

Dr. Galavazi smiles as he shakes Jasper's hand, then reaches for his notepad. "So. How much time do we have now?"

"Our sound check at the Paradiso is at eight."

The doctor's clock says six fifty-five. "Just the basic facts for now, then. Why do you think Knock Knock is coming back?"

"I've heard him over the last few months. He's still distant and it's still faint, but he's awake. I *think* I first heard him at a nightclub in London, about a year ago."

Deep growl. "Were you on drugs at the nightclub?"

"An amphetamine. I saw him in a dream, too."

"The monk in the mirror?"

"Yes."

Another growl. "Perhaps it would be strange if you *didn't* dream about such a traumatic figure in your life."

"If . . . an invisible man moved into this house, Doctor, you couldn't see him, but you'd sense him. I sense Knock Knock, here . . ." Jasper touches his temple. "It's like it was at Ely, at Rijksdorp too, before the Mongolian. The Mongolian said I'd have five years. My five years are up."

Dr. Galavazi's biro is busy. Jasper thinks of Amy Boxer, who has been sleeping over in Dean's room at Chetwynd Mews a lot since November. "Have you ever taken any hallucinogenic drugs?"

"No. I've heeded your warning."

"Have you taken Queludrin or any antipsychotic drug?"

"No. I don't have any. I haven't approached a doctor. The British lock more people up than is generally known."

Dr. Galavazi puffs his pipe. "What happened in this dream about Knock Knock?"

"It was like a film I was watching. A historical film, set a few centuries ago. I saw Knock Knock—a monk or abbot—being poisoned by some kind of governor . . ." Jasper gets his journal out of his satchel. "It's on the first page. I've written down other dreams I thought were significant too. They're dated."

The psychiatrist takes the journal. Jasper guesses he looks pleased. "May I borrow this, and transcribe anything of interest?"

"Yes."

He opens the first page. "An excellent habit."

"My friend Formaggio says, 'What isn't carefully recorded is gossip and guesswork.' "

"He's right. Are you still in touch?"

"Yes. He's studying the brain at Oxford."

"Remember me to him. He's a smart boy. I take it you've heard nothing from the Mongolian since Knock Knock's—what shall we call it?—'reawakening.' "

"Correct. The Mongolian is long gone."

"At Rijksdorp, you told me he was just passing through, like a 'barefoot doctor.' "

"That's correct."

"And you still believe now . . . that he was real?"

The clock's pendulum thinly sliced half a minute.

"Yes," said Jasper. "I do. Unfortunately."

"Why 'unfortunately'?"

"If your theory is correct, and the Mongolian was a mental sheriff I created to lock up my psychosis, there's hope I could do it again. But if *I'm* right, and the Mongolian was real and came to Rijksdorp by fluke, my prognosis is not good."

Outside a woman shouts, *"Watch where you're going!"*

"You must feel like a nightwatchman, Jasper, who knows only that danger is coming, not when or from which direction."

"That's not a bad simile."

"Why, thank you." Dr. Galavazi sips his green tea. "I'd like to read this"—he holds up the notebook—"review the facts, and conduct a fuller interview than we have time for this evening. For now, I'll give you a prescription for Queludrin. Take it to a chemist before you return to England so that if a full relapse does occur you'll have a little breathing space."

Say "Thank you." "Thank you."

The psychiatrist thinks. "One thing more. In Boston, I met a psychologist based at Columbia University in New York. He's an odd fellow, with unorthodox methods, to say the least. But I've come to respect him greatly. He's curious about AHPs in general—and the patient JZ in particular. May I share tonight's conversation with him?"

"Yes. What's his name?"

"Dr. Yu Leon Marinus. He's Chinese. To look at. But that's not the whole story. Most people just call him Marinus for short."

THE LONG SOLO in "Purple Flames" grows ever longer as Jasper finds a secret passage deep inside. The high roof, vaulted murk, arches, and windows evoke the Paradiso's origins as a Nonconformist house of worship. *Worship still happens here,* thinks Jasper. *Not of us four, but worship of music itself. Music frees the soul from the cage of the body. Music transforms the Many to a One.* The Marshall stacks vibrate his skeleton. *We touch something divine.* His Stratocaster speaks of ecstasy and despair. *We're not gods, but we are channels for something that is godlike.* Jasper could die here and now and not feel short-changed by life. He looks at Dean, who knows that the end is nigh. Jasper closes with a flashy bend of the top two strings and Dean rips into the final verse like a blowtorch. His vocals are twice as powerful as they were a year ago, in part thanks to Jack Bruce from Cream, who appeared backstage after their McGoo's gig in Edinburgh and gave him some pointers about singing while playing bass. He has also taken some formal singing lessons and now has an extra half-octave at either end of his comfort zone. Elf is in no mood to be upstaged, and slams into a particularly pyrotechnic Hammond solo. Jasper wonders if Guus de Zoet or his half-brothers are out there in the Paradiso. *Unlikely.* Wouldn't they have got in touch? *Who knows? If normal people are difficult to read, the de Zoets are cryptic crosswords . . .*

BACKSTAGE, JASPER LOSES the others in a merry-go-round of faces who appear to know him. Sam Verwey is one of the few he can name. "So, de Zoet. You left Amsterdam a nobody and come back a fully fledged pop star. My pupils think you're God. When I tell them we used to busk together in Dam Square, they think I'm bullshitting them, so I'm taking this picture of us . . . Smile!" A flash explodes in Jasper's eyes and brain.

"A triumph!" roars Big Smiler. "A coronation! An apotheosis!"

"Need any gear?" asks a pinstriped Mr. Toad. " 'Shrooms, dope, Bennies, bombers? You name it, I got it."

Big Smiler becomes Loud Laugher. "Why the hell have you stayed away for so long, eh? Amsterdam *needs* you . . ."

"They'll be shitting cold puke now at De Zoet HQ," remarks the Queen, who can't possibly be on the balcony, smoking a doobie.

"Thijs Ogtrot from *Hitweek,*" says an undertaker's face. "Is it true you spent two years at Rijksdorp asylum?"

From the balcony Jasper spots the Paradiso's manager talking with Levon and Elf in the bar below. *How do I get to them?*

"So the question is, Jasper," says Backslapper, "can your current management take you up to the next level?"

Jasper finds the wrong stairs. "His only friend was his guitar," a teacher at the Conservatory explains. "His graduation piece was called 'Who Shall I Say Is Calling?' It *dripped* sound . . ."

"Coke, weed, Dexy, Purple Hearts," murmurs Mr. Toad, by Jasper's ear. "Satisfaction guaranteed. Ever tried acid?"

"Or will they be puking cold shit?" asks Queen Juliana. "The skeleton in the family cupboard—on *Fenklup*! Priceless!"

"You and I made love on Monday." A woman's painted her face like a Rorschach inkblot test. "Astrally. Yes. It was me."

Jasper's in the gents, washing his hands. He tells Miss Rorschach, "Perhaps it was Eric Clapton."

"Now you're famous," begins Big Smiler, down in the bar, "all sorts of leeches'll come crawling out of the woodwork . . ."

"Thijs Ogtrot from *Hitweek*," says an undertaker's face. "You wrote 'Darkroom' in the same acid session where John Lennon wrote 'Lucy in the Sky with Diamonds.' True or false?"

". . . and they'll want favors or money," adds Big Smiler. "You'll need to get better at saying *'Rot op!'*"

"The question is," says Backslapper, "how long can a solo genius like Jasper de Zoet prosper in the confines of a band?"

"*Who* did you score off?" Mr. Toad's face is knitted up. *Anger.* "Not a podgy little Belgian fuck with a quiff like Tintin?"

The Lecturer offers him a joint. "So, the dean wants you to give a lecture for Founders' Day . . ."

"Bloody Nora." Dean staggers up. "In the bogs just now was these two *blokes* snoggin' 'n' gropin' each other! *Uuuuuugh* . . ."

". . . about anything you like," says the Lecturer. " 'Art, Love, and Death,' 'Dispatches from Soho,' 'Counterculture' . . . Do say yes."

"Thijs Ogtrot from *Hitweek*," says an undertaker's face. "Your father wants you cut out of your grandfather's will. True or false?"

"So all I need is five hundred guilders up front to pay for the studio," says Big Smiler. "Cash is best."

Jasper sees the Rorschach woman with her hand inside Griff's shirt. "On Monday we made love astrally, but tonight . . ." she whispers in Griff's ear, and burrows her hand downwards.

"Take your producer's fee from future sales," says Big Smiler. "Big bucks, guaranteed. What have you got to lose?"

THE MARCH NIGHT is coal gray, indigo, and starlit. The air is crisp and cool along Prinsengracht. Spring's nearly here. A bicycle bell rings. Jasper steps out of the way: the cyclist leaves a low *"Taak"* as he passes. A song from long ago and a delicious whiff of *bitternbollen* fried meatballs leak from an amber-lit bar. Jasper pauses at the corner of Amstelveld and holds up his thumb to test the half-moon's blade. *It's comfortable being an Amsterdammer again.* The English distrust duality. They equate it with potential treachery. In the Netherlands, having a German, French, Belgian, or Danish parent is no big deal. The city's bells begin their midnight round. Iron boom by bronze chime, stroke by stroke, the proud houses and the churches fade away. The conservatory and the poky room above the bakery in Raamstraat, where Jasper lodged for three years, vanish. Going, going, gone are the squalid brothels, shipping offices, and scruffy cafés; the venerable hotels, fussy restaurants, and concert halls; the Paradiso, the Rijksmuseum, and the ARPO studios; Dam Square, the shuttered-up souvenir shops, and the Anne Frank House; maternity wards and cemeteries; Vondelpark, its lake and chestnuts, lindens and birches, not yet in leaf; the city's sleepers and the city's insomniacs; even the bells in their towers that weave this impossible vanishing act melt out of reality until all that remains of Amsterdam's ancient future is a brackish marsh, swept by gales, home only to eels and gulls, hut-dwellers with leaky boats and hungry dogs . . .

GRAFGRAVERSGRACHT IS AN oddity among Amsterdam's waterways for being a cul-de-sac canal. Tourists blunder in only by accident in search of a shortcut to the zoo. Born-and-bred Amsterdammers have told Jasper to his face that no such canal exists—that its very name, "Gravediggers Canal," is proof of a prank.

Yet here it is, complete with street sign, legible in the light of a half-moon. Its respectable residents are asleep, but at the far end, in the triangular attic window of 81 Grafgraversgracht, is a dab of sky blue. Jasper walks the length of the short canal to the door below the lamplit window. He presses the top bell to the rhythm of a Dutch nursery rhyme: *"Boer wat zeg je van mijn kippen . . ."* a pause, "*. . . Boer wat zeg je van mijn haan?"* Jasper waits.

Maybe she's asleep and forgot to switch the lamp off.

Jasper waits. *I'll count to ten, then slip away . . .*

Four floors above, the window opens. A key chimes on the cobbles. Jasper picks it up. It's attached to a Superman key ring. Quiet as a burglar, he lets himself in and climbs up to the fourth story, past bicycles, cooking-gas cylinders, and a roll of old carpet. At his approach, the door at the very top opens . . .

THE ONE-BAR ELECTRIC fire is lava red. It bleeds into the light of the sky-blue lamp to make a purple glow. Helen Merrill's muslin-and-silk voice is singing "You'd Be So Nice to Come Home To" on the record player. Trix stands in a furry bathrobe embroidered with *Il Duca Hotel, Milano.* Thirty, slender, a dash of Javanese, steamy from the bath, hair up. "Good heavens. It's Mr. Platypus."

"Can I come in?"

Trix lifts her eyebrows. "Lovely to see you too."

I should have said hello. "Sorry. Hello. It's lovely to see you."

Trix stands aside and shuts the door behind him. "I was about to go to bed and cry myself to sleep. I thought your groupies must be feasting on the bones of my poor red fox."

Jasper hangs his coat on the antlers. "Irony."

"My, my, haven't we gotten clever in London?"

Jasper slips off his boots. "Sarcasm?"

"Don't get too good at normality."

"There's not much danger of that."

Trix prepares two glasses of rum and ice.

The clock on the shelf says it's five o'clock.

Jasper's watch says it's three minutes to midnight.

"It wound down months ago," says Trix. "Time's noisy."

They each take one end of the sofa, drawing their feet up, and sit facing each other. "*Proost,* Mr. Platypus."

"Proost." They drink. Rum burns Jasper's esophagus.

"How was the Paradiso?"

"The show went well, but the party afterward was too much. I slipped away when nobody was looking."

"Your album's selling like fresh herrings. The de Zoets of Middelburg are having an emergency board meeting about you now. Your father will be there, addressing his shareholders: 'The family skeleton in the cupboard is playing guitar on *Fenklup*! What is our official policy on this?' Your bassist is dishy."

"Dean's smaller in real life than he is on television."

"The four of you look very close."

"If you're in a band with someone, you get to know them well."

"Like family?"

"I'm not an expert on the subject but maybe, yes. I live with Dean. He looks out for me, I suppose. He makes sure I don't forget things. Griff is fearless. He doesn't worry. He's good at living. Elf is like a sister. I imagine. She's good at understanding what people mean. Like you. All three of them—and Levon, our manager—know about my emotional dyslexia, I think. We don't discuss it. They just cover for me, when I need it."

"How very English of them." Trix lights a Turkish cigarette. "What's it like? Stardom?"

"People kept asking me that at the Paradiso, and when I said, 'I'm not really a star,' they became . . . hard to read."

Trix considers this. "They may think you're holding out on them because you think them unworthy of illumination."

"The reality isn't at all like the fantasy."

"When did that ever matter?"

Jasper finishes his rum and peers through the base of the glass at the candle flames, the sloping walls, draped fabrics, the electric fire, the incense-breathing Indian goddess. "I've missed your anthropology classes, Trix."

"You're the one who crossed the English Channel to find his fortune and left me tearing my hair out with misery."

Did I? Was she? No—she's smiling. "Irony."

She biffs his calf with her foot. "Give the boy a prize."

· · ·

THE HALF-MOON SHINES in through Trix's window onto her homemade four-poster bed. *A celestial body never dies,* Jasper tells the moon, *but you never get to curl up with another body, either.* "It's lucky you played at the Paradiso this side of April," says Trix. "I'm moving to Luxembourg. For good."

"Why?"

"To marry a Luxembourger. You're my last fling."

You say, "Congratulations." "Congratulations."

"On my marriage? Or about you being my last fling?"

"I meant"—*was she joking?*—"your marriage."

"Well, it's about time. I'm not getting any younger."

"That's true."

Trix's torso twitches. She's smiling.

"What? Was that funny? Why?"

Trix twirls Jasper's hair around her finger. "No jealousy, no 'How could you, how dare you?' You're nearly an ideal man."

"Not many women agree."

Trix makes a noise that may mean skepticism. "You didn't teach yourself that trick with your tongue, did you?"

Jasper thinks of Mecca and her room above the photographer's studio. *It's still yesterday in America.* "What'll happen to the shop when you've gone?"

"I've sold it to Niek and Harm. They'll still get obscure LPs from Brazil and poor conservatory students will still get a discount."

"Amsterdam won't be the same without you."

"Bless you, but Amsterdam won't notice a damn thing. The city's changed since we stayed up late redesigning the future and crashing the royal wedding." Trix traces her forefinger along Jasper's clavicle. "Remember the free white bicycles? Nobody repairs them now. People think, *Why can't somebody else do it?* Or they paint them black and lock 'em up. Provo is winding down. New revolutionaries have grabbed the megaphones. Humorless ones. The ones who quote Che Guevara like he's a close personal friend. 'It is better to die on your feet than live on your knees.' They'll say, 'You can't make an omelette without breaking eggs,' as if a demonstrator's spine, or a policeman's skull, or an elderly widow's window is only an egg. Time for us Utopianists to clear the stage for the Molotov-cocktail brigade. I want no part of it."

"Who is the future Monsieur Trix van Laak?"

"A horse breeder. He's a little older, and not exactly Adonis, but he's rich enough to be my last best suitor, smart enough to value a clever wife, and worldly enough to let my past stay in the past." Trix taps the tip of Jasper's nose. "His mother disapproves. She called me a social climber. I called her an Alpinist with oxygen tanks. I'll win her around."

An ember eats an incense stick. Sandalwood.

"You'll ride horses every day," says Jasper.

"I'll ride horses every day," agrees Trix.

DR. BELL OF Ely wasn't sure about Jasper going on a twelve-hour sea crossing in the grip of a nervous breakdown with only Formaggio to mind him, but the headmaster was adamant. He had been an army cadet when *he* was sixteen, and a blast of sea air might be the very medicine young de Zoet needed. Jasper was too battered by Knock Knock's campaign against his sanity to express an opinion. Telegrams had been sent to Jasper's grandfather, who would be waiting at Hook of Holland. Later, Jasper worked out that his school's concern was to ensure that he lost his marbles as far away from Swaffham House as possible, ideally in another country. There was a car to Harwich. Dr. Bell had entrusted Formaggio with a few pills to give to Jasper if his condition deteriorated. Before the car was halfway to Harwich, Jasper's condition deteriorated. The *knock-knock-knock-knocks* were merging into one solid impact. The pills softened it, a little, but didn't stop the assault. Jasper and Formaggio boarded the *Arnhem*. It was a choppy crossing. The boys sat in the second-class lounge, Formaggio only leaving him to throw his latest sick-bag over the side. Some soldiers bound for West Germany laughed at the vomiting Formaggio and pasty-looking Jasper in their poncy uniforms before, eventually, taking pity on them.

"Have a mouthful o' this, you poor bastard." An army flask. Tea and gin, to settle their stomachs. The *Arnhem* docked under a late sky. The squaddies bade them good luck and were swallowed by the world. Grootvader Wim waited in his Jaguar, where the new immigration building stands. He spoke English to Formaggio. "I shan't forget your kindness. Jasper, I'm taking you directly to a clinic near Wassenaar. All will be well. All will be well. You're in the Netherlands now . . ."

JASPER WALKS BACK down the stairs from Trix's room to Grafgraversgracht. By the tenth or twelfth flight of steps, he works out that his body is in Trix's bed, far above, yet the steps carry on until the dreamer arrives at an earthen passageway. An old woman is expecting him. She places a finger on her lips—*Hush!*—and points to a spyhole in the wall. Jasper looks through. Beyond is an ossuary, or a prison cell, or both. Knock Knock, dressed in his ceremonial robe, sits on a whale's jawbone holding a knife in one hand and a shinbone in the other. The bone is inscribed with notches. *Like Robinson Crusoe,* thinks Jasper, *keeping track of days on his island.* Knock Knock's gaze meets Jasper's. A mechanism is triggered. The two swap places. Jasper is now a prisoner in the deepest under-cellar of Knock Knock's mind, with no hope of rescue or escape. He cannot even die his way out. The eye at the spyhole—Knock Knock's eye—vanishes. Jasper is left alone for eternity to draw the blade across the notched shinbone, like a violin bow . . .

. . . and a metallic shriek fills Jasper's head. He wakes in Trix's bed to the sound of a tram's steel wheels. His heart thuds. He's flooded with relief that he's not in that doorless ossuary anymore. Once the tram has passed, the only sounds are Trix's breathing, the sigh of rain on Amsterdam's roofs and canals, the distant boiler of 81 Grafgraversgracht, and night ebbing away. It's hard to know one from the other.

We trust our lovers not to harm us.

The bells of Osterkerke skim out five plangent chimes. Jasper borrows Trix's brown furry bathrobe and pads to the bathroom. Ointments, jars of creams, and bottles of gloop. Avoiding the mirror, Jasper splashes water onto his face. He feels something he would call "change-ache" but he doesn't know if it's a real emotion or not. He goes to Trix's kitchenette and eats an orange. He boils the kettle on the hob but takes it off the heat before the whistle wakes the lady of the house. He takes his mug of tea to Trix's table. A silver horse with opal eyes watches him. Lines are buried in the last few hours. Carefully Jasper proceeds to excavate.

A song, a crowd, a coronation,
a merry-go-round, a deal—
a city so improbable,
it's not exactly real.

Doctor, liar, teacher, leech;
pusher, mystic, hack—they
crashed the gates of paradise.
I snuck out through the back.

Gravedigger's night, a sky-blue light,
a chime, the key that turned your lock.
Stairs, the dark, a magic lamp,
A fox who didn't have to knock.

A cigarette from Istanbul,
A glass of fire and ice—
A clock that wound down months ago.
A clock we wound up, twice.

A silver horse with opal eyes,
incense from Hindustan—
I, who rarely understand,
You, who often can.

You slept on like a tiny bird,
a bell, all's well, a far-off call—

I slept like a fugitive,
if I slept at all.

A curse, a demon, maybe worse,
a knife, a bone, a notch—
I am the lone nightwatchman.
This is my night watch.

ROLL AWAY THE STONE

SIX POLICEMEN ENTER THE CHECK-IN HALL AT ROME AIRPORT, followed by a chief who removes his sunglasses and scans the crowd. Dean imagines a gunfight between the cops and the businessmen at the Aeroflot counter, who turn out to be KGB. Screams, havoc, blood. Dean dodges the bullets to rescue that hot *signorina* in the pink jacket. The KGB guys are shot. The King of Italy pins a medal onto Dean. The *signorina* in pink takes Dean to meet her father, whose castle sits atop a hundred acres of vineyard. "I 'ave no sons of my own," he hugs the brave Son of Albion, "until today . . ."

Back in reality, the chief is joined by a photographer.

He looks familiar. *He is.* He did a shoot of the band at their hotel. He spots Dean, Griff, Jasper, and Levon, and points. The chief strides over, his men following in V-formation. *He doesn't look like he's after an autograph.* "Uh . . ." says Dean. "Levon?"

Levon's speaking with the clerk. "One moment, Dean."

"I'm afraid we don't have that long."

The chief is here. "You is the *gruppo* Utopia Avenue?"

"How can we help you, officer?" asks Levon.

"I am Captain Ferlinghetti, Guardia di Finanza. This." He taps the leather bag Levon has strapped to his chest. "What is in?"

"Documents. Valuables."

He makes a beckoning gesture. "Show." Levon obeys. Captain Ferlinghetti removes the envelope. "What is?"

"Two thousand dollars. The band's earnings from the four gigs. *Legal* earnings, Captain. Our promoter, Enzo Endrizzi—"

"*No,* is not legal." The captain stuffs the money into his pocket. "All. You come. Now. There are questions."

Levon is too stunned to move. They all are. *"What?"*

"Make *concerti* in Italia, profit in Italia, taxation in Italia."

"But our paperwork's in order. Look." Levon unfolds a receipt in Italian. "This is from our promoter. It's officially—"

Captain Ferlinghetti declares: "*No.* Not *valido.*"

Levon changes timbre. "Is this a shakedown?"

"We make arrest here? For me is same." The officer addresses the clerk at the Alitalia desk in rapid-fire Italian. Dean catches the word *"passaporti."*

Nervously, the clerk holds out their passports—which Dean snatches and puts into his jacket pocket.

Captain Ferlinghetti thrusts his face into Dean's. "GIVE."

I know a bent copper when I see one. "Our flight leaves in half an hour. We're going to be on it. With our bloody money. So—"

Pain splits Dean from his groin. The departure hall spins. Dean's cheek smacks the floor. A supernova detonates, inches from his face: a flashbulb. Levon remonstrates. Dean's vision recovers. The photographer is closing in for a floor-level shot. Dean swivels and launches a horse-kick. His heel crunches plastic and lens against jawbone. A scream. Boots pound Dean. He curls into a fetal position, protecting his hands and balls. *"Bastard! Bastard!"* yells Captain Ferlinghetti; or, *"Basta! Basta!"* The kicking stops. Dean's wrists are yanked behind his back and cuffed. The passports are removed from his jacket. He is hauled onto his feet. Griff is objecting, swearily. Orders are dispensed in Italian. The party is marched off. "There'll be legal consequences," Levon was saying, "I promise you."

"*Conseguenze* is only beginning now." Captain Ferlinghetti puts his sunglasses on. "*I* promise *you.*"

"WHAT A WHIRLWIND," Elf said to Dean. "Amsterdam in March, six nights supporting the Hollies . . . now Italy. By airplane."

Dean peered out. Their plane had reached the top of the runway.

"Well, 'Purple Flames' is number nine there. Did I mention that? Can't quite recall."

"Not for ten minutes, at least," says Elf.

"Levon should've held out for first-class tickets."

"Right, and I should've insisted on Gregory Peck meeting me at the airport to drive me around like Audrey Hepburn."

Dean checked on Jasper in the aisle seat. He was sickly pale, hiding behind sunglasses and chewing gum. "Cheer up, matey. If we drop like a rock we can do bugger-all about it, so why worry?"

Jasper's fingers gripped the armrest.

The stewardess spoke over the intercom: "Please check that your seatbelts are securely fastened . . ." Mighty engines revved. The airplane vibrated.

Elf peered past Jasper and Griff to ask Levon, "Is this normal?"

"Totally. The pilot's got one foot on the gas and one on the brake, so when he releases the brake, the plane is hot off the—"

The passengers were pressed back as the Comet 4 lurched forward. A *"woooooo"* filled the cabin and Dean found Elf's fingers digging into his wrist . . . Everything juddered, rain beads on the window became rain streaks, the floor tilted upward, the horizon tilted down, the airplane lifted, Elf muttered, "Oh my God oh my God oh my God . . ." Below, depots, a multistory car park, trees, a reservoir, the M4 and trunk roads dropped . . . A soggy life-size model of England; the snaking Thames, Richmond Park, the ark-like glasshouse in Kew Gardens . . . then the window went misty; the fuselage shook as if gripped and shaken by a giant hand. Elf asked, "Is that normal?"

"Just a little turbulence," said Levon. "It's fine."

Dean tapped Elf's hand. "Elf . . . my wrist?"

"Oh, God, sorry. It looks like a dog bit you. Oh . . . Jesus, look—at—*that*!" They saw clouds *from above*. Sunlit, snow-white, and mauve; whipped, rumpled, and steel-brushed . . .

"Ray ain't never going to believe this," said Dean.

"How would you capture that," asked Elf, "musically?"

"Jasper," said Dean, "yer've got to see this. Really."

Jasper, if he heard Dean, ignored him. So Dean and Elf watched the clouds. "That's the most beautiful thing I've ever, *ever* seen," said Elf.

"Me, too." A slight tickling sensation alerted Dean to a strand of Elf's hair caught on his stubble. He gently untangled it. "I'll return this to its rightful owner."

TWO COPS FROM the snatch squad sit with the band in the back of the police van. It's similar to a Black Maria on the inside, Dean notes. Benches run along the walls and light comes only through a thick grille along the top of the driver's compartment. Dean's midriff, arse, and groin are already throbbing with future bruises. His hands are still cuffed. The guards light up. They have handguns. "Hey, pal," Dean asks. "*Amico.* Cigarette, *per favore?*"

The guard's amused headshake means, "*'Amico'? Really?*"

"That money in your bag," Griff asks Levon. "It *is* legit?"

"Entirely," says Levon. "But it's not in my bag anymore."

"Wasn't carrying it all in cash a bit risky?" asks Griff.

"If you think carrying cash is risky," Levon retorts, "try accepting a check from a foreign promoter you've never worked with. Watch it get magically canceled by the time you're home."

"That copper knew yer had it," says Dean, "and which bag yer were carrying it in, too. Bloody fishy, if yer ask me."

Levon sighs. "Yup. Only Enzo knew I had it."

Griff asks, "Why would our own promoter rat us off?"

"Enzo keeps the net profit on five sold-out theater shows. The captain gets a juicy slice. Everything's hunky-dory. Fuck it. I should've brought Bethany with us to spirit the money home separately. Getting fleeced in showbiz is the price of admission, but I thought I'd paid my dues. Now, if Enzo swoops in to straighten this out, I'll owe him an apology. But if he stays AWOL, we'll know."

Nobody speaks for a minute or so. "Thank God Elf took the early flight," says Dean. "Thank God for that."

"You're not wrong," says Griff.

The police van thumps over a pothole.

"Money's only money," says Jasper. "We'll make more."

"Could Ted Silver get the two thousand back?" asks Griff.

"This is Italy," states Levon. "Our case might get to court by nineteen seventy-five, if we're lucky. Seriously. No, the best scenario is a swift deportation."

"What's the worst scenario?" asks Dean.

"Let's not think about it, but unless someone from your embassy is telling you it's safe, sign *nothing*. Remember. The Italians invented police corruption."

THE FOUR STEP out of the van, blinking and dazzled, in the walled yard of a police station. It's an ugly one-story building with a flat roof. Dean stumbles. Griff steadies him. Beyond the barbed-wire-topped wall they see a motorway bridge, a factory chimney, and a housing block. A guard shoos them inside. Every last person in the waiting area, from ten-year-olds to priests to pregnant women to the desk sergeant is puffing on a cigarette. Conversation ceases and heads turn to look at the exotic foreigners. The party is led through a blast-proof door into a processing room. Captain Ferlinghetti awaits. "*Allora,* you like my hotel?"

"It's a shithole," says Dean, fake-amiably. "D'yer know that word? 'Shithole'? Full of shits. Like you lot."

"Cool it, Dean," mutters Levon. "Just cool it."

"You all is held for violations of currency, and *you*"—he smirks at Dean—"for assaulting police officers."

"Piss off. *You* assaulted *me.*"

"Who believe a criminal, thief, liar? Empty pockets here." He indicates four shallow wooden boxes on the counter.

"You've already stolen two thousand dollars off us," says Griff. "How do we know we'll ever see our stuff again?"

"No. *You* steal from the people of Italy."

"Captain Ferlinghetti," says Levon, "please call Enzo Endrizzi. He'll explain the misunderstanding."

Ferlinghetti displays a weakness for gloating. "Who is 'Enzo Endrizzi'?" His grin says, *I'm lying and I don't give a shit that you know I'm lying*—which means, Dean guesses, that their promoter set them up. Levon, Griff, and Jasper, meanwhile, have emptied their pockets as instructed. Dean asks, "How'm I s'posed to empty my bloody pockets with my hands tied, Captain Genius?"

"Is true. So, I empty the pockets." The captain comes around to Dean's side of the counter via a liftable flap.

"Yer could just take the cuffs off," points out Dean.

Ferlinghetti turns Dean's jacket pocket out over the tray. A few coins rattle out—and a misshapen lump wrapped in tinfoil.

What the bloody hell's that? "That ain't mine."

"Is from your pocket. I see it fall. My sergeant see, also."

The desk sergeant juts out his lower lip. *"Sì."*

Ferlinghetti unwraps the tinfoil. Inside it is a lump of hash. The chief's eyes widen like a bad actor's. "Cannabis? I hope is not."

Now Dean's worried. "Yer put it there yerself!"

Ferlinghetti sniffs the lump. "Smell like cannabis." He scrapes it with his thumbnail and dabs his tongue. "Taste like cannabis." He shakes his head. "Is cannabis. Is bad. *Very* bad."

"We demand a lawyer," states Levon, "and consular access to the British and Canadian embassies. Immediately."

Ferlinghetti scoffs, "*Pfff.* Is Italia. Is Sunday."

"Telephones, lawyers, ambassadors. We know our rights."

The captain leans over the counter. "Here is not London, is Roma. *I* decide 'rights.' *I* say"—he flicks Levon's nose—*"no."*

Levon jerks his head back at the oddness of the attack. The deputy starts to prod Dean down a corridor.

"Oy!" Dean realizes that there may be worse things in store than indignity. "Where're yer taking me?"

"Private suite," the captain tells him, "in the Hotel Shithole."

"Sign nothing, Dean," Levon yells after him. *"Nothing."*

THE ITALIAN PROMOTER was not waiting for the band at Arrivals, so Levon went off to find a telephone kiosk to call the Endrizzi office. Dean's first impression of Italians was that they smiled more often and more brightly than the British. Their hair was better, their clothes more stylish, and they spoke with hands, arms, and eyes as well as words. He watched two big macho guys greet each other with a peck-kiss, peck-kiss on either cheek. "On the bright side," Griff muttered, in a voice too low for Elf to hear, "if Italian men *are* mostly gay, it leaves the field wide open, like."

Dean's pores inhaled the warm air. "I love it here."

"We haven't even left the airport yet," said Elf.

"The one, the *only*—Utopia Avenue!" A man approached with open arms, with a silver tooth, a cream shirt, and a booming voice that needed turning down from ten to three or four. "I am"—he put his hand over his heart—"Enzo Endrizzi, your promoter, admirer, friend. And you"—he chose Jasper first—"are Jasper de Zoet, *il maestro.*"

"Mr. Endrizzi." He offered a hand.

The promoter clasped it in both of his. "Enzo, always." He turns to Dean. "Dean Moss, *il cronometro.*"

Il what? "Cheers for bringing us over, Enzo."

"Is your fans who bring! They write, they *telefono* me, they *crazy* for 'Purples Flames'! You write this song, Dean, yes?"

Dean swells a little. "As it happens, yeah, that's one o' mine."

"A song *stu-pen-doso.* We make gigs, do *interviste,* and next week we go up, up, up to number *one* in Italia. And *you,* Elf 'Olloway, *la sirenessa.*" He raised Elf's hand to his lips.

"Nice to meet you, Mr. Endrizzi. Enzo."

"You break ten thousand hearts this week, in Torino, Napoli, Milano, Roma." He turned to Griff. "So you are . . . not Levon? No no. You is 'Greef Greefin' because you do a lot of 'grief' for me, is right?" Enzo made a pistol of his hands and cackled. " 'Stand and deliver! Your money and your life!,' eh?"

"Levon will be back any minute," said Elf. "He went to phone you. There was a little confusion over the arrival time."

Enzo sighed. "For Anglo-Saxons, time is a master. For Mediterraneans, time is a servant."

ENZO'S FIAT MINIBUS thumped along the Italian highway at twice the top speed of the Beast. Driving was a big silent bruiser whom Enzo introduced as "Santino, my right-hand man *and* left-hand man." The highway cut through hills of beige and heat-proof green. Suburbs emerged from bomb-site rubble. Cranes reached halfway to heaven. Tall dark trees corkscrewed upward. Traffic swerved, lawlessly. People honked horns instead of signaling, and traffic lights appeared to be ornamental. Jasper retained his sickly pallor from the flight. "Were you born in Rome, Enzo?" Elf asked.

"Cut my arm, the Tiber River flows out."

"Where d'yer learn yer English?" asked Dean.

"From GIs, from Tommies, in Rome, in the war."

"Weren't kids evacuated to the countryside?" asked Elf.

"No place is safe. All Italia a battlefield. *Certo,* Roma was magnet of bombs, but so is other cities, and if you at wrong time, wrong place, *boom!* In July in 1943, *biiiiiig* raid destroyed San Lorenzo. Royal Air Force. Three thousand dead. My parents also."

"That's horrible," said Elf.

"Is twenty-four years ago. Many water under bridge."

"London had the shit bombed out of it too," said Dean.

Enzo flashed his silver tooth. "By Italian Air Force?"

"Mussolini was on Hitler's side, right?"

"*Certo*—Mussolini's men killed my uncles and cousins, who was partisans in the north. A movie, a story, is simple: good *contro* bad. Reality is"—his fingers waggled and interwove—"*così.*"

Dean wondered if European history might be more complicated than in the war films he'd seen growing up.

"Disaster is the mother of opportunity," said Enzo. "GIs arrive, they give Marvel comics, I learn English, they had dollars, I get things they need, I take commission, I eat that night. Black-market people, they help me, I help them. Is Italian way. To be young was protection. If military police catch a man, they shoot. If they catch a boy, usually no. Was my university of the life. I learned to *'uss-ssel.*"

"What was that, Enzo?" asked Griff.

Dean worked it out. "'Hustle'?"

"Exactly. *'Uss-ssel.* Is a skill I use still, as promoter."

The Fiat was cut off by a school bus. Santino beeped his horn, leaned out his window, and yelled, never mind that at the speed they were traveling his words couldn't possibly reach the offending driver. Kids leaned out of the bus windows and made a stabbing hand gesture at Santino, with the index and little fingers pointing straight, like a pair of horns. "What's that about?" asked Dean.

"Is *cornuto.* Horns of man of wife who go with other man."

"A cuckold," said Elf. "Folk songs are full of them."

A farmhouse flew by. A shallow-angled roof, narrow windows, biscuit-colored stone walls. Sloping fields were cultivated with rows of what looked to Dean like Kentish hops.

"Is a vineyard," said Enzo. "Grapes, for the wine."

Dean wondered who he'd be if he'd been born in that house and not in Peacock Road, Gravesend. He wondered if identity is drawn not in indelible ink, but by a light 5H pencil.

THE GRIDDED HIGH window is no more than a foot wide and six inches in height. *A head might fit through but never the body.* A blade of dusty sunlight falls on the rusty bed frame and crusty mattress. A shit-spattered porcelain hole in the corner exhales evil vapors. The floor is clammy concrete. The graffitied walls are blotched with mold. The steel door has an eye-slot and a floor-level hatch. Nowhere to sit but the mattress. *Now what?* He hears the muffled din of the motorway, scraps of distant Italian, and the *drip, drip, drip* of a cistern.

Hopefully Ferlinghetti only wants to scare us into forgetting the two thousand dollars.

Dean has no idea about drugs penalties in Italy. The Rolling Stones had their drugs charges overturned recently. *But they're the Stones, and that was England.*

Minutes creep by. Dean's indignation is cooling. The beating he took is starting to hurt. He wonders how Elf's doing, and how Imogen's holding up. The death of an infant puts his predicament in perspective. Levon, Jasper, and Griff know he's here. He wasn't abducted without witnesses. He's British. *Italy's not Russia or China or Africa, where they could take me round the back and put a bullet in my head.* Dean's trial—*if it comes to that*—would be a drawn-out, costly headache. Why bother when they can just deport him? Last, Dean is not a nobody. He's a somebody with a song in the Italian Top Five. Last night Utopia Avenue filled a two-thousand seater in Rome . . .

"TWO THOUSAND PEOPLE!" Griff half shouted into Dean's ear over the din in the wings of the Mercurio Theatre. "From Archie Kinnock to *this* in fourteen months! Am I fookin' dreaming?" Sweat-drenched, Dean squeezed Griff's shoulder as he drank. Dean was hoarse, wrecked, jubilant, and temporarily indestructible. This last round of roars and whistles was for the band, but also for Dean's new song, "The Hook," a work in progress. The Mercurio Theatre liked it just as much as "Darkroom" and "Mona Lisa." The applause settled into a marching giant's *clap, clap, clap, clap, clap, clap, clap, clap, clap* . . .

Levon appeared. "A third encore? They want it."

Elf glugged from her water flask. "I'm game."

"I never turn down two thousand Romans," said Griff.

"Seems rude to say no," agreed Dean. "Jasper?"

"Sure."

Enzo appeared, smiling like a promoter on the last night of an amply profitable tour. "Friends, you is all *fan*taaaaaa*stici*!"

"So's this crowd," said Dean. "They're mental."

"In England, you . . ." Enzo mimed zipping his lips. "In Italia . . ." he posed operatically, ". . . we show! This noise is noise of love."

"We're singing in a foreign language too," said Elf, wonderingly. "Imagine a British audience going this crazy"—she gestures out through the wings—"for an Italian act."

"They study the lyrics," explained Enzo, "they *feel* the music. Your songs, Elf, they say, 'Life is sad, is joy, is emotions.' Is universal. Jasper, your songs say, 'Life is strange, is wonderland, a dream.' Who does not feel so, sometimes? Dean, your songs say, 'Life is a battle, is hard, but you is not alone.' You, Greef, you is a drummer *intuitivo*. Also, your Italian promoter is a genius."

A somber man spoke into Enzo's ear. Enzo translated, "He ask, 'Please play a song before they break his theater.' "

"We've done the whole album," said Griff.

"And all our stash of covers," said Dean.

"Jasper's new one," said Elf. "All those in favor?"

The band plus Levon said, "Aye."

"I'll introduce it," said Dean. "Enzo—how do yer say 'We love you too' in Italian?" He had Enzo repeat the phrase until he had it by heart. They filed back onto the stage to be greeted by a Godzilla-size roar. Jasper strapped on his guitar. Griff took his place. Elf sat at the piano. Dean leaned into his mic: *"Grazie, Roma—anche noi vi amiamo . . ."*

A woman shrieked, *"Dean, I want you, baby!"* or possibly, *"Dean, I want your baby!"*

"Grazie tutti," said Dean. "One more song?"

Rome howled, *"Sììììììì!"* and *"Yeeeeeesss!"*

Dean cupped his hand to his ear. *"Che cosa?"*

The answer was louder than a Comet 4 taking off.

This is a drug, Dean realized, *and I am an addict.* He looked at Elf. Her look back said, *You charmer.* "Okay, Roma. You win. This next song really is our very last song tonight . . ."

A giant groan of disappointment fell to Earth.

"But, I promise, we'll come back to Italy very soon."

The groan pulled out of its dive into a cheer.

"This is by Jasper. It's called 'Nightwatchman.' "

CHAMPAGNE CORKS POPPED. The perfume of lilies was giddying. Very good friends of Enzo flowed in. Half the city appeared to be a very good friend of Enzo. One of them met Dean in the bathroom and gave him a long line of superb cocaine. A galaxy exploded in Dean's brain. The champagne turned into purple wine. The changing room became a VIP enclosure in the kind of nightclub Dean once fantasized about, with huge chandeliers, women dripping diamonds, fresh from a scene in a James Bond film. Men chortled over cigars and talked in huddles. An Italian guy from a fresco was whispering into Elf's ear. She was smiling. Dean posted her a look that said, *Someone's on the pull, I see.* Elf's look back said, *What can I say?* Enzo's very good friend with the cocaine took Dean to another bathroom for another bump. A jazz trio was playing "I Got It Bad and That Ain't Good" when Enzo and Levon appeared. They both wore grave expressions. They crouched by Elf and spoke. Elf's face changed. Her hands covered her mouth. Levon looked sick and haggard. The handsome suitor vanished.

Dean guessed someone had died. He went over. "What?"

Elf opened her mouth but couldn't yet say it.

"Elf's nephew," said Levon. "Imogen's baby, Mark. A cot death. He died sometime yesterday night."

The club frolicked on as if none of this had happened.

"Oh, Jesus," said Dean. "Twenty-four hours ago?"

"My assistant she tell me only now," insisted Enzo Endrizzi. "The *telefono* between England and Italy, not is good . . ."

Elf was shaking and breathing heavily. "I have to go home."

"We're leaving tomorrow afternoon," Levon reminded her.

"The first flight in the morning," Elf told Dean.

Levon looked at Enzo, who nodded. "Is possible. My very good friend, he's the brother of a boss of Alitalia . . ."

Elf was looking about her, unable to process anything.

"Let's get yer back to the hotel," Dean told Elf. "Yer've got to pack 'n' everything. I'll sleep on yer sofa, too . . ."

EVENING ENTERS THE cell. The slatted rectangle of sky turns orange, then plague-brown. Dean's body is aching and sore from his beating. A sickly lamp, bolted to the wall above the door, flickers on. *Eight o'clock? Nine o'clock?* They took Dean's watch.

Looks like I'm in for the night, thinks the prisoner.

Dean wonders if the others are in solitary, too. The flight the band were due to have boarded will have landed at Heathrow.

Elf will be at Imogen's house in Birmingham.

I'm in trouble, thinks Dean, *but Imogen must be in hell* . . .

Neither Elf nor Dean slept much last night. Elf talked about her three visits to see her tiny nephew, and how Mark gurgled at his aunt on her last visit. She wept. Dean offered to leave, worried that she might prefer to be alone. She asked him to stay. They dozed for an hour or so. Then the taxi arrived.

She'll think they're back in London now.

Nobody will have noticed his and Jasper's absence yet. Griff's flatmate won't be raising any alarms. It'll take Bethany a while to smell a rat tomorrow, but with luck she'll call Enzo Endrizzi by mid-afternoon. Then the cavalry should be mobilized. *I hope.* The floor-level hatch slides open. A tray appears. Dean kneels down by the hatch and fires questions out: "Oy! Where are my friends? Where's my lawyer? How long—"

The hatch snaps shut. Footsteps recede.

Two slices of white bread spread with margarine, a plastic cup of tepid water. The bread tastes of paper. The water tastes of crayons. *So much for great Italian food.*

Time passes. The hatch slides open. *"Vassoio,"* says a man.

Dean crouches down by the hatch. "Lawyer."

The voice repeats itself: *"Vas-soi-o."*

"Ferlinghetti. *Fer-lin-ghetti.*"

The hatch snaps shut. Keys jingle. A heavy lock in the door grinds. A big cop with a big nose, big mustache, and big gut steps inside. He holds up the tray, points at it, and tells Dean, *"Vas-soi-o."*

"*Vassoio.* Tray. Got it. Lawyer? Ferlinghetti? Embassy?"

The big cop's nasal snort means, *Dream on.*

"Grazie mille, Roma." Dean quotes the line Enzo taught him at the Mercurio Theatre. *"Anche noi vi amiamo."*

The cop hands Dean a skimpy roll of skimpy toilet paper and a blanket and slams the door shut. Dean lies down, hungry for an apple, his guitar, a newspaper, or even a book. Thoughts whisper: *What if Günther Marx and Ilex throw yer to the wolves? What if Ferlinghetti decides to send yer down just for a laugh?*

The light above the door clicks off. The cell is dark.

A little light enters under the door. That's it.

Why were you such a jealous hypocrite with Amy?

DEAN WISHES THAT he hadn't flown off the handle when he saw Marcus Daly of Battleship Aquarius drooling over Amy at the 100 Club in Oxford Street two weeks ago. He wishes he hadn't told Amy to cut the night short, prompting her to reply, "Go if you want, but I'm staying," and forcing him to leave or to stay and look like a toothless fool. He wishes that when Amy got back—to her own flat—he hadn't actually said, "What time do yer call this?" As if he was her father, not a lover. Dean wishes, too, he hadn't started interrogating her like Inspector Moss of Scotland Yard. He wishes he hadn't called her a "Leech with a Typewriter." He wishes he hadn't called her a paranoid bitch when she told him she knew about the Dutch girl in Amsterdam. *How did she know?* Dean wishes he hadn't flung a marble ashtray into her glass-fronted cabinet, like Harry Moffat on a three-day bender. He wishes he had been man enough to apologize the next day instead of hiding at Chetwynd Mews and letting Amy leave his stuff in a box at Moonwhale. When he went in for a band meeting the day after, Bethany had a look in her eyes and the look said, *Coward.* Dean could not disagree. It was no way to say goodbye.

HE WAKES IN the Hotel Shithole. He's itchy. He inspects his torso. It's speckled with insect bites. Several are smeared with blood where he scratched them in his sleep. *What wouldn't I do for a cigarette?* He gets up and pees in the shithole. His pee smells like chicken soup. He's thirsty. He's hungry. In the last twenty-four hours he's eaten . . . *fuck-all, is what.* He knocks on the door. It hurts his knuckles. "Hello?" Nobody comes. "HELLO?"

Nobody comes. *Don't give up.*

He knocks out the bass line for "Abandon Hope" . . .

Footsteps clomp. The eye-hatch snaps open. Dean thinks of the Scotch of St. James. *"Stai morendo?"*

Meaning? Dean asks for *"Aqua, per favore."*

A blast of pissed-off Italian. The hatch snaps shut.

Time drags. The food-hatch snaps open. Breakfast is almost the same as dinner. The bread is staler. There's coffee served in an aluminum mug but the foam on the surface looks worryingly like phlegm. He thinks about trying to scoop it off to get at the coffee below, then pictures Ferlinghetti's satisfaction so he leaves the coffee on the tray untouched. He thinks how the middle classes—the Clive and Miranda Holloways of the world—go from cradle to grave believing that every police officer is a devoted servant of the law. A chant rises up from Dean's recent memory.

Fuck the pigs!
Fuck the pigs!
Fuck the pigs!

RINGRINGRING!

RingRingRing!

RingRingRing!

The doorbell at Chetwynd Mews woke Dean up. His head pounded. The day before, the band had played a festival in a field near Milton Keynes. Elf had gone on to Birmingham to visit Imogen, Lawrence, and her baby nephew, Mark. Dean, Griff, and Jasper had brought the Beast back to London, popped a pill, and gone to the Ad Lib club. Jasper had left with an Olympic show-jumper from Dulwich and Griff with an Avon Lady, leaving Dean to woo a laughing-eyed half-Cypriot—until Rod Stewart waltzed up and stole her away. The pool of Ad Lib's 2 A.M. leftovers was by then a puddle. He walked back to the flat with a strong suspicion that the Swinging Sixties weren't all the papers cracked them up to be, even for a musician who had been on TV not once but twice . . .

RingRingRing! "Oy! Deano! I can see yer boots!"

Kenny Yearwood. Guilt propelled Dean to the front door. His hometown friend was living in a Hammersmith commune with a lentil-eating, tarot-reading girl called Floss. Dean had visited his art college buddy and Gravediggers bandmate exactly once. Kenny had played him a few forgettable self-penned songs, suggesting Dean "add a few finishing touches" and record them with Utopia Avenue under a Yearwood–Moss credit. Dean had laughed at the joke until he realized Kenny was serious. They hadn't met since. Kenny left messages a couple of times, but Dean assured himself he was too busy to call back. Then Griff had his car crash and Kenny slipped off Dean's "to-do" list.

"Open up," called Kenny through the letter box, "or I'll huff 'n' I'll puff 'n' I'll *blow*—" Dean opened up, and was shocked by Kenny's wholesale transformation from Gravesend ex-mod to West London hippie: caftan, headband, poncho. "Yer can run but yer can't hide."

"Morning, Kenny. Floss, how's tricks?"

"It's the afternoon, yer dope," said Kenny.

"The afternoon of the big demo," said Floss.

"Yer what? What big demo?"

"The biggest demo of the decade," said Floss, "against American genocide in Vietnam. We're gathering in Trafalgar Square and marching to the U.S. Embassy. You *are* coming?"

If the United States government was hell-bent on turning a luckless country in Asia into an inferno of death and forcing American teenagers to go and fight and die there, Dean doubted that walking down Oxford Street blowing whistles would change its mind. Before Dean could say so, a young woman floated up the steps to Jasper's front door, opening a packet of Marlboros. "Hi, Dean, I'm Lara. Can we talk as we walk? Mustn't miss Vanessa Redgrave."

Lara looked superimposed onto the gray March afternoon. She wore a man's black parka, open at the front, jeans, boots. Her black hair was streaked with red and she looked capable of anything.

Unspent lust woke Dean up. "I'll grab my coat."

SPEECHES ECHOED OFF the National Gallery. *"The American war machine won't stop until every man, woman, child, tree, ox, dog, cat is killed . . ."* Trafalgar Square was jammed with hippies, students, trade unionists, CND supporters, Trotskyites, and concerned citizens of all stripes and none. *"The economic crisis facing Great Britain and America has its roots in this suicidal war in Vietnam . . ."* Hundreds more watched from the edges while the police guarded the Whitehall and Pall Mall exits leading to Downing Street and Buckingham Palace. *"We have traveled from West Germany for a new society, a better future, where imperialism, where war, where capitalism belong only in the dustbin of history . . ."* The crowd generated a dim roar by its mere existence. Kenny put the number at ten thousand, Floss at twenty thousand, and Lara thought it closer to thirty. Whatever its size, the crowd was a power grid. Dean felt his own nervous system connect to it. Scores of Vietcong flags were clustered around the foot of Nelson's Column. Placards passed like pages: HELL NO WE WON'T GO!; VICTORY TO THE VIETCONG!; WE ARE THE PEOPLE OUR

PARENTS WARNED US ABOUT. Dean wondered how any of this would stop B-52s bombing Vietnamese villages.

After the speeches, the mass of people began to drain up Charing Cross Road. Kenny, Floss, Lara, and Dean followed the flow. Past the Phoenix Theatre, past Denmark Street, past Selmer's Guitars, where Dean's debt was paid off, finally. Past the doorway that led into the defunct UFO Club. At Tottenham Court Road, the crowd flowed left along Oxford Street. A young squaddie, acne on his face, emerged from the tube station. Peace demonstrators yelled abuse: *"How many kids did* you *kill, Soldier Boy?"* before a paternal copper pushed him back down into the tube. *"Long—live—Ho Chi Minh! Long—live—Ho Chi Minh!"* Oxford Street itself was shuttered, as if in preparation for invasion. Dean thought he glimpsed Mick Jagger, but wasn't sure. Floss and Kenny told him they had heard John Lennon and his new girlfriend, Yoko Ono, were marching with the crowd. Whatever the truth, Dean felt the power. He and it were one. The road was theirs. The city was theirs.

"Do you feel it too?" asked Lara.

"Yeah," said Dean. "Yeah, I do."

"Do you know the name of this feeling?"

"What?"

"Revolution."

He looked at her, sideways.

Lara looked back. "We're marching with the suffragettes, the Durruti Column, the Communards, the Chartists, the Roundheads, the Levellers, Wat Tyler . . ."

Dean didn't admit he hadn't heard of these bands.

". . . with everyone who stuck two fingers up to the bloodsucking Establishment of their age and said: 'FUCK YOU.' Causes change, but power is in flux and its ownership is temporary."

"What's yer surname, Lara?" asked Dean.

"Why do you ask?"

"One day yer going to be famous."

Lara lit a Marlboro. "Lara Veroner Gubitosi."

"Wow. That's . . . long."

"Most names on Earth are longer than 'Dean Moss.' "

"S'pose so. Are yer Italian, then?"

"I'm from many places."

They turned into North Audley Street, where the march was funneled south: *"Hands—off—Vietnam! Hands—off—Vietnam!"* Faces watched from Mayfair townhouses. Two blocks south lay Grosvenor Square. Cordons of police and a defensive line of Black Marias walled off the American Embassy: a squat, modernist five-floor bunker, topped by an eagle.

"Didn't the SS have an eagle too?" asked Floss.

The crush from behind grew as demonstrators ahead filled the road around the square. The big area of grass and trees in the center of Grosvenor Square was walled off by police, who had badly underestimated the size of the crowd they needed to contain. Exits from the square were blocked, so the thousands of marchers at the front had nowhere to go. The crush grew denser until the barriers around the park in the square gave way, in several places at once. A body fell on top of Dean and a heel pressed his knee into the soft turf. A roar rose up, like at the start of a football game or a battle. If the day had been a summery pop single, it was now flipped over onto its darker, rockier B side . . .

DEAN WAS LIFTED up by Lara Veroner Gubitosi, who murmured in his ear, "Let the love-in begin," and was lost in bodies. Whistles blasted. Smoke stained the air. Kenny and Floss were nowhere to be seen. The sun had dimmed to half-light. *"Fuck the pigs! Fuck the pigs! Fuck the pigs!"* Officers manning the lines around the square retreated back to the police phalanx in front of the embassy. Who was on whose side? What were the sides? Projectiles rained. A tinkle of glass—a ragged cheer—*"We got a window!"* Another cheer. *"Another one!"* Screams. *"Ho! Ho! Ho Chi Minh! Ho! Ho! Ho Chi Minh!"* An earthquake? In London? Horses charging, a dozen or more, straight at Dean. Mounted officers swung truncheons like Victorian cavalry swinging cutlasses. People ran under the trees, where the branches were too low for the mounted police. Dean fled into the path of another horse and into the path of another and into the path of another, and tripped, saving his skull from a skull-crushing truncheon by a whisker. A hoof slammed the turf inches away from his head. Dean scrambled to his feet, finding a rag of hairy scalp stuck to his hand. A man with an LBJ mask hurled a smoke bomb at the police. Dean ran in the other direction but no longer knew which direction that was. The battle line kept looping in on itself. Louder, louder: *"Ho! Ho! Ho Chi Minh! Ho! Ho! Ho Chi Minh!"* A gang of coppers caught a man and pounded, pounded, pounded him with truncheons and boots. "That enough love an' peace for yer?" They dragged him off by his hair. *"Out of the way!"* A copper was being stretchered past, his face like a butcher's tray. Dean wanted out of Grosvenor Square. The band was due to fly to Italy in forty-eight hours. Getting arrested would be bad: a trampled hand, disastrous. But where was the exit? Police blocked the Brook Street exit with a wall of Black Marias into which they were slinging protesters indiscriminately. *"Fuck the pigs! Fuck the pigs! Fuck the pigs!"* A black horse pranced Dean's way. A hand grabbed Dean's scruff and pulled him onto a doorstep. "Mick Jagger?"

Dean's rescuer shook his head. "Nah, I'm an impersonator. Go thataway, this ain't no place for a street-fighting man." He pointed to the mouth of Carlos Place, where the police were letting people out of the square.

Dean made no eye contact as he passed through the uniformed filter. He remembered the end of the nursery rhyme: *Here comes the chopper to chop off your head.* He walked down Adam's Row. Through an archway, he saw a gang of three kicking a hippie on the ground. They had shaved heads, like monks, and one had a Stars-and-Stripes flag T-shirt. What tribe were these? Not mods, not rockers, not Teds. They worked methodically. Their victim had curled into a shuddering ball. One of the shaved-heads noticed Dean watching. "Yeah? Want a taster too, do yer, yer cunt?"

Dean ran through his options. He walked away . . .

. . . *LIKE A COWARD.* Dean revisits the scene on a bedbug-infested mattress in a police cell in a suburb of Rome. Kenny, he found out the next day, had been arrested and had had his nose broken. *And now it's my turn to spend a night in a cell.* If Harry Moffat could see Dean now, banged up in prison, he'd laugh his tits off. *"I fuckin' told yer so!"* Or maybe not. He'd had a letter from Ray the day before they left for Italy. A contact at Alcoholics Anonymous had got Harry Moffat a job working nights as a security guard. One slip off the wagon, though, and he's out. *But for now, he's a nightwatchman. Like Jasper's song. Ray says he's changed a lot. Maybe Ray's right. Maybe I've been carrying a hatchet so long I don't even notice it.*

A mosquito flies into Dean's field of vision.

It settles on the wall by his head.

Dean splats it and inspects the wreckage.

Have yer forgotten how the old bastard used to belt Mum? If that's not worth a lifelong hatchet, what is?

Lunch arrives. It's a mug of instant soup. Dean can't identify the flavor. He can only hope it hasn't been gobbed into. There's an apple and three biscuits with the word TARALLUCCI baked into them. The biscuits are bland, but the sugar's welcome. Footsteps approach and a key turns. It's Big Cop making a beckoning gesture. *"Vieni."*

Dean's hopes surge: "Are you letting me go?"

"Hai uno visitatore."

THE WINDOWLESS INTERROGATION room is lit by a striplight speckled with flies, living and dead. Dean sits at the table, alone. He hears a typist on the other side of the door. Two men are laughing. Minutes limp by. The men are still laughing. The door opens.

"Mr. Moss." An Englishman in a pale suit, riffling through papers. He looks over his gold-rimmed glasses. "Morton Symonds. Consular Affairs at Her Majesty's Embassy."

Ex-military, thinks Dean. "Good afternoon, Mr. Symonds."

"Not for you, it isn't." He sits ramrod straight. He places an Italian newspaper in front of Dean and points to a photograph. "This is not the publicity your Mr. Frankland was hoping for."

The photograph shows Dean Moss being frog-marched out of the airport with his hands cuffed. "Is this a national paper?"

"It certainly is."

Then if I know my Mr. Frankland, thinks Dean, *he'll be over the bloody moon.* "At least they printed my best side."

A pause. "Do you think this is all a lark?"

"Dunno 'bout 'lark.' The way I've been treated's a farce. What's the story with the others?"

Morton Symonds performs a small *huh.* "Mr. de Zoet and Mr. Griffin have been released without charge. They're staying at a *pensione* near the airport. Mr. Frankland is being questioned about tax obligations and monetary control violations."

"Which means what?"

A sigh. "You can't just take five thousand dollars out of the country. There are laws against it."

"It wasn't five. It was two. And why not? We earned it."

"Immaterial. And, for you, the least of your problems. You're being charged with common assault"—Morton Symonds checks a file—"assaulting a police officer, resisting arrest, and, most gravely, drug trafficking." He looks up. "Still a lark, is it?"

"It's bullshit is what it is. They punched *me.* See?" Dean stood, undid his shirt, and showed his bruises. "I might've kicked a reporter 'cause he shot off a flash in my face but the dope—was—*planted.*"

"The authorities beg to differ." The consul scans the newspaper article. "I quote, 'Captain Ferlinghetti of the Polizia Fiscale told reporters, "Our handling of these hooligans sends a message to foreign celebrities: if you flout Italian laws, you will regret it." ' " Symonds looks up. "You're facing jail, Mr. Moss."

"But I didn't do what they said I did."

"It's your word against that of an Italian police captain. You're facing a minimum sentence of three years, if found guilty."

It won't come to that. It won't come to that. "Do I get a lawyer? Or is it trial by witchcraft?"

"The state will engage a lawyer. Of sorts. But Italian justice is more glacial than British. You'll be held for at least twelve months."

Dean pictures his cell. "Bail?"

"No chance. The judge will assume you're a flight risk."

"So why're yer here, Mr. Symonds? To gloat at an oik with girl's hair? Or d'yer help people who didn't go to Oxbridge too?"

Symonds is mildly amused. "I'll submit a standard plea for clemency, citing your youth and inexperience."

"When'll I hear if the plea's worked or not? Today?"

"Monday's a slow day in Italy. Wednesday, with luck."

"Are there any fast days in Italy?"

"No. The upcoming election doesn't help."

"How long can they hold me before charging me?"

"Seventy-two hours, unless a magistrate grants an extension. Which is amply possible in a case like yours."

"Can I see my friends?"

"I'll ask, but the captain will tell me that he can't have you orchestrating your stories."

"The only story is, 'A bent little Mussolini planted drugs on an innocent Brit.' Can I have a toothbrush—or access to my suitcase, for clean clothes? My cell's a bloody khazi."

"It was never going to be the Hilton, Mr. Moss."

Twat. "I'm not asking for the Hilton. I'm asking for a mattress that isn't crawling with bedbugs. Look at these bite marks."

Symonds looks. "I'll mention your mattress."

"Yer wouldn't have a packet o' fags on yer, would yer?"

"It's against the rules, Mr. Moss."

HOURS DIE SLOWLY back in Dean's cell. He imagines Ferlinghetti imagining him starting to crack. The prisoner's only countermove is not to crack. He imagines his Fender around his neck and works through the bass parts on *Paradise Is the Road to Paradise,* song by song. He plays "Blues Run the Game" on an imaginary acoustic. He imagines the flat in Chetwynd Mews and surveys it, room by room, searching for details he didn't know he'd stored away: smells; the feel of the boards through his socks; the spider plant; the tobacco tin he keeps his weed in; the pirate on that tin; the resistance of the lid as you open it. He imagines having to do this for three years. He senses a crack. *Stop it.* A jug of water is put through the hatch, with a sliver of soap and a used toothbrush. He drinks half of the water, then uses the remainder to give himself a stand-up wash over the shithole. He gives the toothbrush a miss. Through the gridded window, his second evening of captivity fades. The lamp flickers on. Dean hears another mosquito; sees it; tracks it; kills it. *Sorry, mate, but it's you or me.* Dean does a hundred sit-ups. His underpants stick to his skin. The light clicks off. *What if I don't get out? What if I don't see Elf 'n' Ray 'n' Jasper 'n' Griff 'n' Nan Moss 'n' Bill again?*

Dean lies down on the bed. It squeaks.

But I will see them again. Griff won't see his brother again. Imogen won't see her son again. Elf won't see her nephew again. Those candles're snuffed out. Mine are still burning . . .

IN A HEART of the eternal labyrinth known as Rome, Dean came across a hidden square. A rust-speckled blue sign read PIAZZA DELLA NESPOLA. Old men played chess in the shade of a tree. Women talked. Boys bragged, laughed, and kicked a ball about. Girls watched. A dog had three legs. The piazza was warm in a way Gravesend is never warm. Its flagstones and cobbles gave up the stored heat of midday. Dean heard a clarinet, but he couldn't work out through which window, over which balcony, the melody was calling. He wished he could notate it, like Jasper or Elf. Dean knew it would be gone, later. He knew he should get back to the hotel, over the river, over the bridge, but some spell made him linger. On the offal-pink wall, on crumbling plaster, on terra-cotta bricks, graffiti read, CHIEDIAMO L'IMPOSSIBILE and LUCREZIA TI AMERÒ PER SEMPRE and OPPRESSIONE = TERRORISMO. Starlings streamed through gaps of sky. A tall, narrow gateway drew Dean up a half-dozen steps and into a church. Gold glittered on darkness. Incense hung in the air. People came in, lit candles, knelt, prayed, and left like customers in a post office. Dean didn't believe, but here it didn't matter. He lit a candle for the dead: for Mum, for Steven Griffin, and for Elf's baby nephew, Mark. He lit another for the living: for Ray, Shirl, and Wayne; for Nan Moss and Bill; for Elf, Jasper, Levon, and Griff. A small choir sang. Pure vocal stacks rose all the way to the distant roof. Dean had to leave, but a part of him never would. In memory and in dream, he'd revisit this lacuna in time and in space. The place was a part of him now. Every lifetime, every spin of the wheel, holds a few such lacunae. A jetty by an estuary, a single bed under a skylight, a bandstand in a twilit park, a hidden church in a hidden square. The candles at the altar did not burn out.

DAY THREE BEGINS. Tuesday. *Elf and Bethany must know by now.* Bedbugs have snacked on Dean again. He wonders if Symonds mentioned the mattress to Ferlinghetti. *What wouldn't I give for one cigarette?* Rod Dempsey told Dean that a British prison is like a rough hostel. There are tribes and gangs, but if you keep your head down, you get through it. Would an Italian prison be as survivable? He doesn't speak the language. When he's out, what then? Johnny Cash managed a career after prison, but Dean's no Johnny Cash. Jasper and Elf couldn't be expected to sit around twiddling their thumbs until 1971. Footsteps approach. The hatch in the door slides open. A breakfast tray is pushed through.

"My friends? My lawyer? Ferlinghetti?"

Everything on the tray is the same as yesterday.

"New cell?" Dean asks through the hatch. "New mattress? Ambassador? Cigarette? Acknowledge my sodding existence?"

The hatch snaps shut. Dean eats the bread. He scoops off the froth and chances the coffee. He thinks of Nan Moss's apple pie and battered cod and chips. He puts the *vassoio* by the hatch. "Don't make an enemy o' the screws," Rod Dempsey told him. "The fuckers've got the power o' life 'n' death over yer . . ."

Dean wonders if Symonds has lodged that appeal for clemency yet. He wonders if Elf or Bethany believes he was stupid enough to take drugs through an airport. He wonders how things are at Elf's sister's. Footsteps approach. Dean's pretty sure it's Big Cop. The hatch snaps open. The tray is exchanged for a half-roll of toilet paper. The hatch snaps shut. There's more paper on the roll than yesterday. *Does this mean I'm not going anywhere?*

Dean thinks about the thing called "freedom."

All his life he'd had it but didn't even notice it.

Time passes. Time passes. Time passes.

Footsteps approach. The hatch in the door snaps open.

A tray is pushed through. Bread, a banana, and water.

Lunch. The banana's old and foamy. Dean doesn't mind.

Symonds said he has to be charged within seventy-two hours.

Ferlinghetti made it clear whose word is the real law.

Dean leaves the tray by the hatch.

Yes, sir, no, sir, three bags full, sir . . .

Good prisoners might get an extra banana.

I thought I knew boredom: I never had a bloody clue.

Small wonder half the prison population's on drugs.

It's not to get high: it's to kill time before time kills you.

Armed columns of days, weeks, months, and years march toward Dean out of the future. A first hearing. Transfer to a real prison. *I'll look back at this boredom when I'm banged up with a psycho cellmate with sexual frustration and pubic lice and I'll think,* "Christ, those were the days . . ."

Dean sets himself the task of doing a hundred sit-ups.

As if that'll keep yer safe in a real prison wing.

His underwear feels disgusting. A bag of clean washing is waiting for him at the launderette near Chetwynd Mews. It'll be clean and smelling of soap powder. It may as well be on the moon.

GRIDDED MOONLIGHT LIES on the concrete floor. The whole of Day Three passed with no word from anyone. Dean should be at Fungus Hut this week, recording a demo for "Nightwatchman." Or "The Hook." Dean's stomach growls. Supper was a jug of water, a stale roll, an inch of salami, a cup of cold rice pudding. A conversation would be nice. No wonder people lose their sanity in prison. People say, "Where there's life there's hope," but every saying has a B side and this one's is "Hope stops you adapting to a new reality." Dean is an inmate. Inmates can't be pop stars. He wonders if his arrest is in *Melody Maker.* He expects Amy's line will be "Let's hope the Italians throw away the key." Fleet Street will agree, if anyone notices that Utopia Avenue's lesser songwriter has been detained in Italy. *"Bravo, Italy! Lock the bleeder up!"* The public won't believe the cannabis was planted. The public believe what the papers tell them. Nan Moss and the aunts might not, but Harry Moffat will. *He'll want to believe it . . .*

What if Harry Moffat dies while I'm in prison?

Alcoholics aren't known for long lives.

Dean tells his cell, "Harry Moffat's dead to me already."

If that's true, why do you think 'bout him so much?

Once upon a time in Gravesend, a gang of kids threw Dean's schoolbag down the railway embankment and Dean came home in tears. His dad put him in his car and they drove around Gravesend until Dean identified the bullies. "Wait here, son." Harry Moffat got out and went over. Dean couldn't hear what his dad said, but he watched the kids' faces. They went from cockiness to ashen dread. Harry Moffat returned to the car and said, "I doubt they'll be bothering you again, son."

It was simpler when Harry Moffat was a monster.

The moonlight's gone. The cell is darker.

Maybe the night sky has clouded over.

Maybe the moon has shifted its position.

THE SOUND OF rain. Day Four. Tuesday. *No.* Wednesday. Wednesday? *Something has to happen today.* Why?

Why must something happen today?

The toilet smells worse. Dean folds his prison blanket and scrubs his teeth with the prison toothbrush. *Now what?*

What wouldn't I give for one cigarette?

Or a notebook and pen. He'd like to work on a song, but if he thinks of brilliant lyrics and forgets them, it'll torment him.

Then I'll just have to remember them. Dean starts off with the old blues trope: *Woke up in the Hotel Shithole.* That's no good. The BBC will ban it and kill the single. What about—

There's a jangle of keys in the lock of the door.

Here is Big Cop, making a bored come-with-me gesture.

. . .

LEVON STANDS UP as Dean enters the interview room. He's freshly shaved in a clean shirt. *A good sign.* Big Cop locks them in. "Bloody hell," says Dean, "I could hug yer."

Levon opens his arms. "I promise not to lose control."

Dean hasn't smiled in three days. "I am one stinky bastard. Yer might pass out if I come closer. What's happening? Where're the others? Are yer in the clear?"

"I am. Jasper and Griff are well—just worried about you."

"Elf?"

"She's been in touch with Bethany. It's awful, of course. One thing at a time. Are you holding up okay?"

"Depends on what happens next. That guy Symonds was talking 'bout a three-year sentence."

"Bullshit. Günther's lawyers have taken to the air. Even prior to the fake drugs bust, your arrest was riddled with errors. Time's short, Dean, so let me get to the point. Very soon Mr. Symonds and El Capitano will walk in with a confession-cum-apology. '*Sorry for punching the nice policeman. I didn't know cannabis was illegal. Let me go and I'll mend my ways.*' Sign it and you'll be free to go . . ."

Relief floods through Dean. *I'm going home.*

"And yet I'm asking you to refuse to sign it."

"Yer kidding." *Oh no he isn't.* "Why?"

"On Sunday I placed a call to the Canadian consul and had *him* place a few calls to London. On Monday, Bethany got busy and contacted a few allies, including a certain Miss Amy Boxer."

Dean winced. "Amy? 'Ally'?"

"When she stopped laughing, she wrote a three-hundred-word piece about Utopia Avenue's mistreatment by the dastardly dagos—and sent it to a pal at the *Evening Standard* who ran it in Monday's edition."

Dean's confused. "Amy did that for me?"

"Amy did it for Amy, but she did it, and that's the main thing. After the *Standard* hit the stands, the *Mirror* came calling."

"The *Record Mirror*?"

"The *Daily Mirror.* National circulation, five million. By midmorning tea break yesterday, all five million readers knew that Dean Moss, working-class hero of British pop, was facing thirty years in a foreign jail for a crime he did not commit."

"*Thirty?* Symonds told me to expect three."

Levon shrugs. "Is it my fault if they don't check their facts? Better yet: a two-page exclusive in the *Standard* with Dean Moss's fiancée, pop journo Amy Boxer: 'Star's Sweetheart Says "God Help My Dean in Third-World Hell-Hole."' It's a publicist's wet dream."

"Her last words to me were, 'I'm dialing nine-nine-nine.'"

"Only in reality: not in print, where it matters. Amy had the shoot done at that Catholic church off Soho Square while she was praying for you."

"Amy's as religious as Chairman Mao."

"I know she's talented, but *that* was genius. Bat Segundo dedicated his show to you and played 'Purple Flames,' 'Mona Lisa,' and 'Darkroom' back to back. The *Financial Times* cited your case in a piece on British citizens in corrupt foreign jurisprudences. Then—I've saved the best until last—we have the vigil."

"What vigil?" says Dean. "In fact, what *is* a vigil?"

"A dawn-to-dusk gathering of two hundred fans outside the Italian Embassy. 'Free Dean Moss' placards. A fan in a flat opposite is playing *Paradise* nonstop through the window. Harold Pinter's said he'll pitch up tomorrow. Brian Jones, if he can get out of bed. Elf's going to make a speech, despite the awfulness at Imogen's. Even the weather's on our side. It's embarrassing the shit out of the Italians."

Dean tries to grasp all this. "Why don't the fuzz move in?"

"A municipal peculiarity. The Mayfair cul-de-sac through which the embassy is accessed isn't a public thoroughfare, so the landlord has to serve an eviction notice. It'll take weeks. So the police can guard the building, but they can't disperse the vigil."

Dean begins to grasp it. "And in the meantime, we're getting coverage, glorious coverage."

"Bethany's been fielding press calls every hour. Including American stringers. Orders are flying in. Vinyl is flying out. Günther called. He says hi. Ilex is printing thirty thousand *Paradises*.

And"—Levon places his fingertips together—"if you're still behind bars tonight, the *London Post* is flying Felix Finch out first thing tomorrow. He'll interview us, then join us on your grand homecoming. You should be out on Friday."

"And will the *Post* be paying us for this interview?"

"Initially they offered us two, but I played them off against the *News of the World* and we agreed on four."

"Four hundred pounds for one interview? Bloody hell."

Levon smiles sweetly. "Bless his heart. Four *thousand.*"

Dean stares. "Yer never joke about business."

"I do not. I propose this. Half the four thousand pounds goes to you. You're the one doing bird. The remaining two thousand pounds replaces the tour fees that Ferlinghetti took, so you'll get twenty percent of that, too. Acceptable?"

Two thousand quid for six days picking my arse in a police cell? That's more than Ray earns in a year. "Shit, yeah."

Symonds and Ferlinghetti make their entrance.

"Mr. Symonds and Captain Ferlinghetti," says Dean.

They sit down. Symonds speaks. "I trust Mr. Frankland has explained how lucky you are, being allowed to scuttle out of this with a rap on the knuckles?"

Ferlinghetti puts a pen and a typewritten page in front of Dean. The paragraphs are in English and Italian. Dean scans it, finding the words *confess, wrongdoing, unprovoked, possession of cannabis, apologize,* and *treated with dignity.*

Dean rips the confession down the middle.

Ferlinghetti's jaw drops like a cartoon villain's.

Symonds takes a carefully controlled breath.

Levon's face is telling him, *That's my boy.*

"You no *want* go home?" demands Ferlinghetti.

"Of *course* I do," Dean addresses Symonds, "but I never hit a copper, and that cannabis was planted. P'rhaps yer'll believe me now. If I *was* guilty, yer'd not see me for dust. Would yer?"

Symonds looks troubled. "The Italian state is handing you a pardon. I must advise you to take it." Ferlinghetti unlooses a string of pungent-sounding Italian at the consular official. Symonds sits calmly until the captain is finished. "He's saying that there's no guarantee this pardon will be repeated."

"We're at cross-purposes here," replies Dean. "I've been beaten black 'n' blue by Italian police. I've had drugs planted on me by this"—Dean points without looking him in the eye—"*Ferlinghetti.* I don't want a pardon, Mr. Symonds. I want a bloody apology. In writing. And till I get one"—Dean stands and presses his wrists together—"it's the Hotel Shithole for me."

Ferlinghetti looks angry but also, Dean thinks, anxious.

Symonds addresses Levon. "If this is about publicity, be warned. It's high-stakes poker and your boy's liberty's at stake."

"One moment." Levon is scribbling rapidly in his reporter's notebook. "The columnist Felix Finch at the *Post* asked me to keep track of proceedings, ahead of his arrival tomorrow . . . So. Where were we? 'Poker.' 'Publicity.' No no no. Let me assure you, this is Dean's decision. *I* suggested he do the wretched deal. But as you see, Dean's a man of moral fiber."

"Yer a decent bloke, Mr. Symonds," says Dean. "We got off on the wrong foot. Sorry 'bout that. I was scared. But look me in the eye. If yer were me—innocent—would yer sign that confession?"

Her Majesty's Consular Representative sniffs, looks away, looks back, twitches his nose, and takes a deep breath . . .

ALBERT MURRAY, MEMBER of Parliament for Gravesend, meets flight BA546 on the tarmac at Heathrow Airport along with the *Post* photographer. The evening sky has the drama and colors of an exploding battleship. Dean, Levon, Griff, and Jasper—still jittery from the flight—are ushered aside for brief introductions and handshakes, not before fifty or sixty or seventy girls on the viewing platform atop the terminal building spot the party and shriek *"Deeeeeeaaan!"* A sign is draped over the safety rail: DEAN WELCOME HOME. Dean waves. The Monkees and the Beatles get many hundreds, *but they started off with tens, once, surely.* He can't help but notice the signs read DEAN, not JASPER or GRIFF. *"Deeeeeeaaan!"*

Levon steers Dean back to the parliamentarian. "The band's truly touched you found the time, Mr. Murray. And arranged such glorious weather for Dean's homecoming."

"Nothing's too good for a Gravesend hero. We were proud of his music before, but now we're proud of his backbone."

Felix Finch inserts himself. "Felix Finch, sir—of *A Finch About Town*. Would you elaborate on Dean's backbone?"

"With pleasure. The Italian Gestapo did their damnedest to get Dean to kowtow. But did he? Did he *heck*. I read your column from time to time, Mr. Finch, so I know we'd disagree on a lot, politically. But can we not agree, me as a socialist and you as a dyed-in-the-wool Tory, that in that godforsaken dungeon in Rome, what Dean Moss showed was true British bulldog spirit? Can we not agree?"

"We most certainly can, Mr. Murray." Finch's pencil captures every word. "Superbly put, sir. Superb."

"Rightio," says Albert Murray. "Time for a few pictures."

The columnist, the politician, the manager, and Utopia Avenue stand as the photographers' flashbulbs pop and dazzle.

AN AIRPORT OFFICIAL escorts the band through a VIP entrance. The immigration man tells Dean he doesn't need to see *his* passport—but could he write "To Becky, with love" and sign his daughter's autograph book? Dean obliges. Steps lead to a corridor, to more steps and a side room next to a busy-sounding conference room. Waiting there are Elf, Bethany, Ray, Ted Silver, and Günther Marx and Victor French from Ilex. First, Dean hugs Elf. She looks hollowed, like Griff in the days after Steve's death. He murmurs, "Hey. Thanks for coming."

"Welcome back, jailbird. You've lost weight."

"Trust you lot to go skiving off in Italy," says Bethany.

"Nan Moss 'n' Bill 'n' the aunts send their love," says Ray. "They was planning a prison bust. Seriously."

"Enzo Endrizzi's made himself the most famous crook in Europe," says Ted Silver. "Professional suicide."

"Did you write a prison ballad?" asks Victor French.

"We could rush it out before the next album," says Günther.

Dean examines the sentence. "The *next* album?"

The German is almost smiling. "Pending negotiations."

I didn't think today could get any better. Dean looks at Levon who tells him, "Günther wanted to give you the good news."

"Let's get incarcerated more often," says Griff.

"Next time," says Dean, "*you* get banged up. *Greef.*"

Griff cackles. Jasper looks as pleased as Jasper ever looks. Elf looks complicated. Victor French is peering through the slats of a blind. "You should see this." Utopia Avenue and their manager look into the function room. There must be thirty reporters and photographers waiting for the press conference. Up front is a TV camera with THAMES WEEKEND TELEVISION on the side.

"That," says Levon, "is the next chapter."

EVEN THE BLUEBELLS

THE TAXI DRIVES OFF. ELF STARES AT IMOGEN AND LAWrence's house. Her suitcase stays by her feet. Honeysuckle blooms around the porch. Her father's Rover stands in the drive, behind Lawrence's Morris. The other car must belong to Lawrence's parents. The day had been a sleep-deprived blur, of saying goodbye to Dean and the others in Rome; a drive to the airport; the flight; navigating Heathrow; a coach to Birmingham; a taxi, all the time thinking, *Faster, faster* . . . yet now that she's here, Elf's courage has deserted her. *What can I say to Immy? What can I possibly do?* The late April afternoon is cruelly perfect. A thrush sings, very near. A word, "threnody," arrives in Elf's head. If she once knew what it meant, she doesn't now. *You'll never feel ready for this, so just begin.* She picks up her suitcase and walks to the front door. The upstairs bedroom curtains are drawn, so Elf taps on the front window quietly, in case Imogen is sleeping. The net curtains part and Elf's mother looks out, inches away. Normally her eyes would have lit up. Today isn't "Normally."

LAWRENCE, HIS PARENTS, Bea, and their parents greet her in the living room. Everyone is whispering. Imogen is upstairs, "resting." Her husband is miserable, broken, and looks five years older than he did a fortnight ago, when Elf was last here. She tells him she's sorry, appalled by the inadequacy of the phrase. Lawrence nods. Elf's father and Mr. Sinclair exude uncertainty about what to exude.

Her mum, Mrs. Sinclair, and Bea are red-eyed and weepy. Bea takes Elf to the kitchen. "Mark had started sleeping through the night. Immy gave him his last feed at midnight on Friday and put him down for the night. She and Lawrence fell asleep. Immy woke at six thirty. She thought, *Great, Mark's slept through,* and went to see him." Bea shuts her eyes and tears well up. She breathes in, breathes out, breathes in, breathes out. Elf holds her. "So, yeah. Mark was where she left him. But . . . not alive."

The electric kettle boils and clicks off.

"Lawrence called the ambulance, but . . . Mark was gone. They sedated Immy. Lawrence called his mum and dad first, who called ours. They got here yesterday. I came up this morning. Dad called the hospital where Mark"—Bea swallows noisily—"was taken. The coroner said he may have had a cardiac defect but until the autopsy—tomorrow or Tuesday, depending on . . . uh . . ." Bea's focus lapses ". . . how many people died in Birmingham over the weekend. Sorry. I couldn't think of a nicer way to say it. I didn't sleep."

"Me neither. Don't worry."

Bea grabs a tissue. "We're getting through boxes and boxes. I shouldn't bother with makeup for a while."

Elf asks, "Have you seen Immy?"

"Only for a few minutes this morning. She's an awful mess. She was asleep for much of yesterday. Being awake is torture. She's taking Valium. She saw Mum for a few minutes. Lawrence is in and out of her room. Just keeping an eye on her. I called Moonwhale yesterday at, uh . . . I don't know, two-ish. Bethany put a call through to your Italian promoter's office and called *me* back to say she'd left the message with his secretary in Rome . . . What is it, Elf?"

Elf realizes that Enzo Endrizzi knew about Mark before they performed at the Mercurio Theatre but had said nothing. *So the show would go ahead.* "I didn't know until . . . midnight."

"Well, it wouldn't have made any difference. I'll make that cuppa. There's ginger nuts somewhere . . ."

Footsteps come down the stairs. It's Lawrence. "Elf? She'd like to see you. Just you, for now."

Elf feels trepidation and guilt that she and not Bea or the two mothers-on-tenterhooks are being summoned. "Now?"

Lawrence nods. "Yes, if that's, uh . . ."

"Of course," says Elf. "Of course. Of course."

"I'll put a cup of tea on a tray for her, too," says Bea.

"It'll be a comfort to speak to her sister," says Mrs. Sinclair.

ELF CLIMBS THE carpeted stairs to the landing. The letters M, A, R, and K are on the nursery door. *The only pain worse than seeing the letters,* Elf guesses, *would be taking them down.* She takes a quick look inside. The same two blue and two pink walls. The mobile of little ducks, the simple cross on the wall, the pile of nappies on the changing table. Talcum powder still scents the air. The teddy Elf had bought and named John Wesley Harding still sits on the chest of drawers.

Mark is dead. Him, and all Mark's future selves—a toddler mastering verticality, a boy bunking off school, a youth fixing his hair for his first date, a man leaving his hometown, a husband, a father, some old bloke watching the TV and declaring, "The entire world has lost its mind!" None would now exist.

She puts down the tray. She composes herself.

Elf crosses the landing to the bedroom. "Immy?"

"ELF?" GRIEF-SCOOPED, WRUNG-OUT Imogen is propped up in bed. She's wearing a nightie under a dressing gown. Her hair is disheveled. It's the first time in years Elf has seen Imogen without a dab of makeup. "You're here."

"I'm here. Bea made us tea."

"Mm."

Elf brings the tray to the nightstand. She notices an ashtray and a packet of Benson & Hedges. Imogen quit smoking three years ago. "I'm taking Valium," says Imogen. Her voice is dulled and plodding. "Is it like marijuana?"

"I wouldn't know, Ims. I've never taken Valium."

"Did you really fly back from Italy today?"

"Of course I did."

"You must be tired." She indicates the upright armchair in the window bay. Their mother had nursed Imogen, Elf, and Bea on it and, for eight weeks, Imogen had breastfed Mark.

Sunlight passes through daisies on the curtain.

Elf remembers to breathe. "I have no idea what to say."

"I've had, 'I'm so sorry.' I've had, 'It's just awful.' I've had, 'It's like a bad dream.' Mostly, people just cry. Dad cried. It was so weird that for a few seconds I didn't think about Mark. People are . . . are . . . Oh, sorry. I can't finish my sentences very well."

"Valium and grief will do that, I suppose."

Imogen lights a cigarette and slumps into her pillow. "I've started smoking again."

"I'm on no high horse. I'm on twenty a day."

"You can cry yourself dry, Elf. Did you know that?"

"I did not." Elf opens the window to let a little air in.

"It's like when you vomit and vomit until there's nothing left, but you still vomit, and it's only air. Like that, but with my tear glands. Like that song, 'Cry Me a River.' Who sings that?"

"Julie London."

"Julie London. I'm learning all sorts of things. Mark was wrapped in his Winnie-the-Pooh blanket, and when it was time for the ambulance man to take him, my arms, my body, wouldn't let go. My arms just gripped. As if *that* was any use. At that stage. Where was I when his heart was stopping? Here. Sleeping."

Elf tries to hide her eyes. "Don't think that way."

"How, Elf? Can *you* control what you think?"

"Not very well. Distraction helps, a little."

"My breasts get sore. They're still making milk. They haven't cottoned on. I have to express it by hand, the doctor said, or I'll get mastitis. If you ever want to write the saddest song in the world, you can use that."

Elf feels her tears starting. She helps herself to a Benson & Hedges. "I'll never ever write a song like that."

Imogen looks at Elf across a void. "Do I sound mad?"

The blossom outside the window in the late sunshine is heartbreakingly beautiful. "I'm not a psychologist," says Elf, "but I'm pretty sure that people who are mad don't ask, 'Am I going mad?' I think they just . . . *are.*"

Imogen's shallow breaths grow further apart. She murmurs, "You always know the right thing to say, Elf."

Elf watches her sister fall asleep. "If only."

THE CRICKETER'S ARMS Hotel by the Sparkbrook roundabout is adorned with cricketing memorabilia, photographs, and signed cricket bats mounted in small glass-fronted boxes. Bea, Elf, and their father are staying at the hotel and eating dinner in its restaurant. Elf gives a potted version of the band's Italian tour, and her dad musters an account of the Richmond Rotary Club's gala. Bea talks about her upcoming role as Abigail Williams, villainess of *The Crucible.* Arthur Miller the playwright is due to give a couple of classes at RADA next week. *Small talk,* thinks Elf, *is Polyfilla you fill cracks with so you don't have to watch them widening.* The food arrives. Shepherd's pie and peas for their dad, salad and an omelette for Bea, and a bowl of minestrone soup for Elf. The soup contains bits of everything else on the menu.

"It's awful to see her like that," says Bea.

"It's awful to be so helpless," says Elf.

"She's not on her own," says their dad. Outside, across the car park, traffic goes round and round the roundabout. "It won't hurt this much forever. One day your sister will be back again. Our job is to help her get from here to there. What is it, my darlings?"

The sight of Bea crying has set Elf off.

"So much for my wise words of solace," says their dad.

THE THREE HOLLOWAYS have the residents lounge to themselves. Bea and Elf forget to pretend they don't smoke, and their dad forgets to voice his disapproval. The news on TV shows French police storming the Latin Quarter in Paris to take down protesters' barricades. Teargas was fired, stones hurled, hundreds of injuries sustained, hundreds of arrests made. "Is that how you build a better world?" asks Elf's dad. "Pelting the police with stones?"

In Bonn, a vast crowd of students marched on the German parliament to protest against new emergency laws. "If I had my way," says Elf's dad, "I'd give 'em a country of their own. Belgium, for example. I'd tell 'em, 'It's all yours. You sort out food for millions, organize sewage, banking, law and order, schools. You keep them safe in their beds at night. All the boring, nitty-gritty stuff. Hearing aids. Nails. Potatoes.' Then come back in twelve months and see what kind of a dog's dinner they've made of it . . ."

In Vietnam, an American base called Khâm Duc has been overrun by the North Vietnamese. Nine U.S. military planes were shot down, and hundreds of soldiers and civilians killed. "The entire world," declares Elf's dad, "has lost its mind."

Bea and Elf exchange a look. Their father rarely watches the news without uttering the phrase at least once.

"I'm off to bed," says Elf. "It's been a long day."

MONDAY IS CLOUDY. Elf telephones Moonwhale from the hotel to ask Levon to cancel the band's gigs later in the week. She's never canceled a ticketed gig in her life. Moonwhale's line is engaged. Their dad drives Elf and Bea around the cricket ground to Imogen's house. Elf's mum lets them in.

"How was the night?" whispers their dad.

"Pretty rotten," replies their mum.

"Can we see her?" asks Bea. "Is she up?"

"Later, love. She's asleep now. Lawrence and his father have gone to the hospital to meet the coroner."

"Right, then," says Elf's dad. "That lawn needs a mow." Bea and Elf peg out some washing and walk to the shops for groceries and cigarettes. In the newsagent's, Shandy Fontayne comes on the radio singing "Waltz for My Guy." Bea's watching her. Elf says, "If I don't laugh, I'll cry." Elf buys Imogen a packet of Benson & Hedges and the week's *Melody Maker.* Back at the house, Imogen is downstairs, staring at a jigsaw of a tulip field and a windmill their mother is working on. Elf wishes she could say, "You're looking better," but it would be an obvious lie.

Elf tries calling Moonwhale again, but the line is still engaged.

She tries Jasper's flat, but nobody replies. She wonders if anything's wrong, then tells herself not to be paranoid.

Elf and Bea are preparing a salad when the Sinclairs arrive back. They enter through the back door. "Well," reports Lawrence's dad, "the coroner's put 'Accidental Infant Death' on the certificate. Which says everything and nothing."

There's a raw sob. Imogen's hands are covering her mouth.

"Oh, *pet.*" Mr. Sinclair is horrified. "I didn't see you, I . . ."

Imogen turns to run upstairs but her mum's blocking the way, so she spins back and lurches through the kitchen into the garden.

"I thought she'd be upstairs," says Lawrence's dad.

"It's the message, Ron," Elf's mum assures him, "not the messenger. I'll go and be with her."

Elf makes a vinaigrette while Bea chops cucumber. The sound of the lawnmower stops. Elf's mum comes in, looking shaky. Elf's dad's with her. "Immy wants to be alone," she explains.

"I'm so sorry," repeats Mr. Sinclair. "I'm so sorry."

"Don't be, Ron," says Elf's dad. "She had to hear somehow, and now it's over and done with, she can . . . process the news. It's for the best." He goes to call his office from the phone in the hall.

Bea switches on Radio 3 for sonic cover. It's twiddly Mozart.

Imogen returns from the garden, red-eyed and distraught.

It's a play, thinks Elf. *Exits and entrances, nonstop.*

"There's salad, pet," says Mrs. Sinclair.

"I'm not hungry." Imogen goes upstairs. Lawrence follows. Elf remembers the engagement lunch at Chislehurst Road in February last year. *If we could read the script of the future, we'd never turn the page.* Elf's mum announces, "I think I'll pop out to the shops. A bit of fresh air will do me good."

Bea and Elf clear up the dishes. A few minutes later, they hear Imogen, sobbing.

"It's a tough time," says Mr. Sinclair.

"The toughest," agrees Elf's dad.

A news bulletin comes on Radio 3. Riots and arrests in Paris have continued all morning. "*We* didn't have a university education given to us on a plate," says Elf's dad, "did we, Ron?"

"That's the problem, Clive. It *is* given them on a plate, so they don't value it. They smash it up like spoiled toddlers. It's all these lefty yobboes. At British Leyland, management can't show their faces without eggs and abuse. Where's it all going to end?"

"The entire world," says Elf's dad, "has lost its mind."

"Was there any of this in Italy last week, Elf?" asks Mr. Sinclair.

Elf explains that the tour was a week-long treadmill of van travel, setting up, performing, and grabbing what sleep you could before the next day's drive. "Martians could have invaded and we wouldn't have noticed."

After coffee, Bea announces that she'll return to the hotel. "I'm surplus to requirements here. I've got to write an essay on Brecht." The good-natured exchange between Elf's and Lawrence's fathers over who'll run Bea back to the Cricketer's Arms is settled by Bea, who puts her coat on and says, "I'm walking."

A little later, Lawrence comes downstairs, whispering, "She's taken a pill, she's sleeping now." He goes out too.

"You can't beat a bit of fresh air," says Elf's dad.

"Quite right," agrees Mr. Sinclair. "Quite right . . ."

Elf tries calling Moonwhale a third time. The line's still engaged. She tries the Duke-Stoker Agency. She can't get through. She tries Jasper's flat. Nobody replies. She asks her dad if today's a bank holiday. "Definitely not, pet," says her dad. "Why?"

It feels as if Utopia Avenue has ceased to exist. "Nothing."

CUT GRASS SCENTS the tepid air. Elf borrows secateurs and gloves from the shed and gets to work on the brambles and weeds at the far end of the garden. Fronds of willow sway. Bluebells uncoil from Midland clay. A song thrush is warbling nearby. *Yesterday's?* It's still invisible. Elf thinks about her flat, empty for a week, and hopes all is well. The door is sturdy and the windows inaccessible, but Soho is Soho. The bottle of milk in the fridge will have curdled by now.

"You missed a bit," says Imogen's voice.

Elf looks up. Her sister is wearing a duffel coat over her dressing gown and Wellington boots. The glimmer of humor in her remark is absent from her face. "I'm leaving the nettles. They're good for butterflies. New fashion trend or what?"

Imogen sits on the low wall dividing the upper lawn from the sunken, boggier end. "I was a bit wobbly, earlier."

"Be as wobbly as you damn well want."

Imogen looks at the house. She snaps a twig.

"Shall I ask everyone to give you space?" asks Elf.

A noisy motorbike churns up the midday suburban drowse.

"No. Stay. Please. I'm afraid of the silent house."

The motorbike drives off. Its racket fades to nothing.

"Each time I wake," says Imogen, "just for a moment, I've forgotten. The misery's there, pressing in, but I've forgotten why it's there. So for that moment, he's back. Alive. In his cot. He was starting to recognize us. He'd *just* started smiling. You saw. Then . . ." Imogen shuts her eyes, ". . . I remember, and . . . it's Saturday morning, all over again."

"Fucking hell, Ims," says Elf. "It must be torture."

"Yes. Yet when the torture ends . . . when I stop feeling this . . . he really will be gone. That torture's all I've got of him. Torture and breast milk."

A bee heavily laden with pollen draws ovals in the air.

I have no idea what to say, thinks Elf. *None.*

Imogen looks at the pile of weeds Elf has pulled up.

"Sorry if I uprooted any botanical marvels," says Elf.

"Lawrence and I were thinking of putting in a gazebo down here. Maybe now we'll just leave it to the bluebells."

"Can't argue with bluebells. They even smell blue."

"I brought Mark out here, when they were blooming properly. Three or four times. That was all. Those were the only times he . . . felt the Great Outdoors on his face." Imogen looks away, then at her hands. Her nails are a mess. "You assume you have forever. We had seven weeks. Forty-nine days. Even the bluebells lasted longer."

A snail is crawling up the brickwork. Gluey life.

"It was a tricky birth," says Elf. "You had to recover."

"It wasn't just a torn perineum. There was uterine damage, and . . . it turns out, I—I . . . can't get pregnant again."

Elf is very still. The day carries on. "That's definite?"

"The gynecologist says it's 'extremely unlikely.' I asked, 'How extremely?' He said, 'Mrs. Sinclair, "extremely unlikely" is the gynecological term for "will not happen." ' "

"Does Lawrence know?"

"No. I was waiting for the right moment. Then . . . Saturday—" Imogen tries to reel in the right verb but fails. "So I've just told you, instead of my husband. I'll never be a mother again. And Lawrence won't be a father. Biologically. Unless he thinks, *I didn't sign up for this, and* . . . Oh, I go round and round and round."

An unseen kid is kicking a ball against a wall.

Thump-pow, goes the ball, *thump-pow, thump-pow.*

"It's your body," says Elf. "Your news. Your timing."

Thump-pow, goes the ball, *thump-pow, thump-pow.*

"If that's feminism," says Imogen, "sign me up."

Thump-pow, goes the ball, *thump-pow* . . .

"It's not feminism. It's just . . . true."

Thump-pow, thump-pow . . .

ELF SITS AT the piano in the deserted function room at the Cricketer's Arms and practices arpeggios. She's been thinking of Imogen all evening. Her mind needs to do something else for a little while. Outside, it's raining. The TV newsreader in the residents lounge is just audible, but his words are not. Elf senses a melody is waiting. *Sometimes it finds you, like "Waltz for Griff," but sometimes you track it by the lie of the land, by clues, by scent, almost* . . . Elf draws a stave as a statement of intent. She settles on E flat minor—*such a cool scale*—with her right hand and plays harmonies and disharmonies with her left to see what sparks fly off. *Art is unbiddable; all you can do is signal your readiness.* Wrong turns, eliminated, reveal the right path. *Like love.* Elf sips her shandy. Her dad appears. "I'm off to bed. See you later, Beethoven."

Elf glances up, "Okay, dad. *Sleep tight* . . ."

". . . *don't let the bedbugs bite.* Night, love."

Elf carries on, linking rightness with the next rightness along. *Art is sideways. Art is diagonal.* She tries flipping it, playing bass arpeggios with a treble overlay. *Art is tricks of the light.* Elf transcribes notes on her hand-drawn stave, bar by bar, asking and answering musical questions every four bars. She tries 8/8 time but settles on 12/8: twelve quaver beats per bar. She happens upon a middle section—*a glade in a forest, full of bluebells*—that she half identifies as, and half creates from, "The Lord Is My Shepherd," played upside down. She reprises the opening theme at the end. *It's changed by the middle, like innocence changed by experience.* She plays with rubato, legato, and dynamics. She runs through the whole thing. It works. *A few rough edges, sure, but . . .* Nothing strained. Nothing naff. Nothing staid. No words. No title. No hurry. Not yet. She murmurs, "Bloody hell, you're good."

" 'Scuse me," says a man.

Elf looks up.

It's a barman. "I'm closing up for the night."

"God, sorry. What's the time?"

"Quarter past midnight."

IN THE MORNING, when Elf and Bea arrive in the restaurant of the Cricketer's Arms for breakfast, Elf's dad's expression tells her something's happened. She thinks, *Imogen*—but she's wrong. Clive Holloway slides his *Telegraph* across the table, pointing at an article. Elf and Bea read:

UTOPIA AVENUE IN DIRE STRAITS

Pop group Utopia Avenue, best known for Top 20 hits "Darkroom" and "Prove It," were detained on Sunday afternoon by Italian authorities at Rome Airport as they attempted to leave the country. Band manager Levon Frankland is in custody for alleged fiscal evasion and guitarist Dean Moss was arrested after drugs were found on his person. The British Embassy in Rome confirmed that both men have sought consular assistance but declined to comment further. Band lawyer, Ted Sil-

> ver, issued a statement: "Dean Moss and Levon Frankland are innocent of these defamatory, trumped-up charges, and we look forward to clearing their names at the earliest possible opportunity."

"Fff"—Elf turns a Griff-esque profanity into—"*ffflaming* heck."

"That's a turnup," says Bea.

"That could've been *you.*" Her dad speaks quietly, so other guests tucking into their breakfasts don't hear.

"No wonder my calls were unanswered," says Elf.

"You'll be leaving the band, I trust?" says her dad.

"Let's get the facts first, Dad."

"This is the *Telegraph,* Elf. These *are* the facts."

"What about 'innocent until proven guilty'?" asks Bea.

Cutlery clinks. "The National Westminster Bank," their dad lowers his voice further, "can't have managers whose families are mixed up with the wrong sort. Drugs? Fiscal evasion?"

"Only idiots carry drugs through airports, Dad," replies Elf. "Especially if you're a guy with a guitar and long hair."

"Then maybe Dean *is* an idiot." Her dad taps the paper.

He is in some ways, but not this one. "The British police plant drugs on people. Why wouldn't Italian police do the same?"

"The British police force is the envy of the world."

Elf feels her temper heat up. "How do you know that? Have you been around the world, asking everyone?"

"If it was Elf's name in that article," says Bea, "as it would be, if she had gone to the airport with the others, whose word would you trust? Hers? Or what the Italian police say?"

Clive Holloway peers at his daughters over his glasses. "I'd believe Elf—because she's been raised properly. More's the pity we can't say as much for everyone." He folds up the newspaper as the waitress approaches. "Full English, please. Crispy bacon."

BETHANY PICKS UP on the second ring and Elf pushes the sixpence into the slot. "Bethany, it's Elf."

"Elf! Thank heaven. Do you know the news?"

"Only what the *Telegraph* wrote."

"There's lots more. Where are you calling from?"

"A kiosk. A hotel in Birmingham."

"Give me the number. I'll call you back . . ."

Moments later, the phone rings and Elf picks up. "All ears."

"First, the good news. Jasper and Griff are in the clear. They're holed up at a hotel near the airport. The bad news. Levon and Dean are still in custody. Günther at Ilex has engaged the best Italian lawyers that deutschmarks can buy, however, and promises to call as soon as there's news."

"Where's Enzo Endrizzi in all this?"

"Mysteriously AWOL, which smacks of a stitch-up. Press interest is off the scale. Amy Boxer, of all people, has been leading the charge via the *Evening Standard*."

"I dread to ask, but whose side are they all on?"

"Ours. The *Telegraph* was a little sniffy, but it's 'Get Your Dago Hands Off Our Boy' from the *Mirror,* 'Bent I-Ties Stitch Up British Star!' from the *Post.* Ted Silver's friend at the Foreign Office thinks the authorities in Rome want to be seen to be cracking down on 'foreign influences.' They didn't anticipate this brouhaha. Friends and fans of the band are staging a vigil outside the Italian Embassy in Mayfair. It's a diplomat's nightmare."

Elf feels gears turn and levers shift. "What do I do?"

"Keep your head down. I'm drafting a press release. I'll say you're safely in England and you're overwhelmed by the support for Utopia Avenue at this dark hour, et cetera—but if the story keeps growing, hacks might come sniffing."

"Oh God. The last thing we need is reporters at the door."

"Exactly. How is Imogen?"

Elf doesn't know where to begin . . .

HOT TEARS WELL from Imogen's sore eyes. Elf hands her a tissue. "He must've known. He must've wanted his mum. He must've been afraid, he must . . ." Imogen shakes and curls up like a child fitting into a hiding place. "Last night I heard him crying. My milk started up and I woke in the dark and was halfway to the door when I remembered, and my nightshirt was damp so it was out with that bloody breast pump and then when it's done I have to wash the milk down the sink, and—" Imogen fights for breath, as if her grief has turned to asthma. Elf clasps Imogen's hands. "Breathe, sis, breathe. Breathe . . ." Radio 3 is turned on in the kitchen downstairs.

The curtains are drawn against the sunshine.

AFTER LUNCH, WHICH Imogen doesn't join, Elf returns to the end of the garden to carry on with the weeding. She and time forget about each other.

"You've missed a bit," says a voice.

It's Lawrence, holding a tray with a teapot.

"That's what Immy said yesterday."

"Is it? Well, um . . . Mum's made gingerbread."

"Great. Thanks. I'll just . . ." She rips out a cable of bramble, takes off her gloves, and joins Lawrence on the wall. "Is she still asleep?"

"Yeah. Her safe haven. As long as she doesn't dream."

Elf dunks her gingerbread man, head first. "Mmm. It's good."

"So, the crematorium called. Mark's service is tomorrow. Four o'clock. There was a cancellation, apparently."

"Who cancels at a crematorium?"

"I . . . uh, didn't think to ask."

"Ignore me, I'm just being an insensitive idiot."

"Your dad told me about Dean and Levon," says Lawrence. "Stuck in Italy. You must be worried."

Elf is worried, but Mark's death leaves space for nothing else. "They have lawyers. You're family. My place is here."

Lawrence lights a cigarette. "I never knew how death messes with language. *Are* Immy and I still a 'family,' now Mark's gone? Or . . . are we demoted back to a 'couple'? Until . . . I don't know."

Elf remembers what Imogen told her yesterday. It's an uncomfortably heavy secret to have to keep. She sips her tea.

"If I say, 'Mark *is* my son,' " Lawrence continues, "it looks like I'm denying that Mark's gone. Like I'm crazy . . ."

The unseen kid is kicking a ball against a wall again. Elf guesses this is his or her regular practice time.

". . . but if I say, 'Mark *was* my son,' it's . . ." Lawrence steadies himself. "It's unbearable. It's too . . ." He almost laughs at how he's almost weeping. "Sad. God. Someone needs to invent a verb tense that you only use for the . . . for people who have . . . gone."

Willow fronds swish and flick around them. *Like horses' tails.* "Use 'is,' " says Elf. She thinks of Jasper's strange detachment. Sometimes it's a superpower. "If other people think I'm crazy, let them."

Thump-pow, thump-pow, thump-pow . . .

WEDNESDAY MORNING IS bright. The windows in the dining room of the Cricketer's Arms are open. Warm air seeps in. Elf, Bea, and their father wear black. This morning he has bought the *Post.* He shows the girls Felix Finch's column:

VIGIL ON UTOPIA AVENUE

Two hundred fans of British popsters Utopia Avenue held a vigil outside the Italian Embassy in Three Kings Yard, Mayfair, yesterday in protest at the detention of the band's guitarist Dean Moss and manager Levon Frankland in Rome. Italian authorities accuse the pair of possessing drugs and fiscal impropriety, but "Not so!" say band and fans alike, who presented a petition demanding Dean and Levon's release to an Italian consular official. Songs by the detained musician were sung, with more enthusiasm than technique. Rolling Stone Brian Jones joined the vigil and told Your Humble Finch, "I've been at the receiving end of some pretty rough justice myself, and I'm in no doubt that the Italians are playing the same dirty game. If they have real evidence that Dean and Levon have committed crimes, let them press charges. If they don't, they should let Dean and Levon go—with an apology for wasting everyone's time."

Mr. Jones's sentiments were echoed by Rod Dempsey, a close friend of Dean Moss, who sported a Union Jack jacket. "It's a scandal that toffs at the Foreign Office won't pull their fingers out to clear the name of a British artist of Dean's cali-

> ber. Would they be so blasé if he had gone to Eton?" When I asked Mr. Dempsey if he intended to return tomorrow, he avowed that he would return for as long as it took.
>
> Whether or not Utopia Avenue's music is one's cup of tea, Your Humble Finch feels a grudging respect for the gathering in Three Kings Yard. They prove that British youth can make its opinion known without resorting to the disgraceful scenes erupting all over Europe. If the vigil stays within the four-square posts of the law, I concur with the placard waved by one demonstrator with a shock of pink hair: PAWS OFF DEAN MOSS!

"A Rolling Stone is not my idea of a knight in shining armor," says Elf's dad. "Felix Finch, however, could make a big difference."

"It's a miracle the fuzz haven't put the boot in," says Bea.

" 'Fuzz'?" Their dad acts the horrified father. "The 'boot'?"

"I'm surprised the friendly bobbies"—Bea acts coy—"haven't dispersed the protesters. Have you met this Rod Dempsey, Elf?"

"Only in passing." Elf keeps to herself that Dempsey is Dean's drug dealer, and that he once made an artful pass at her.

"Will you be attending this 'vigil'?" asks Elf's dad. "Because I'd be much happier if you stayed well away."

"Today I'm only thinking about Mark."

EDGBASTON CREMATORIUM IS a pebble-dash shoebox-shaped building, with a mock-Greek portico bolted onto the front and a tall chimney at the rear. Spruces fail to conceal an industrial estate, the motorway flyover, and six identical tower blocks. To Elf, these Homes in the Sky look like vertical prisons. Waiting in the reception area is Imogen's friend Bernie Dee, whom Elf remembers from her sister's wedding. She enfolds Imogen in a hug. "Oh, my dear. My poor, poor dear." The silver cross around her neck could belong to a vampire hunter.

Two doorways are labeled "Memorial Room A" and "Memorial Room B." Slot-in letters on the A door read KIBBERWHITE 3:30 P.M. B reads SINCLAIR 4 P.M. A full-throated rendition of "When the

Saints Go Marching In" booms out of A. After it ends, the doors fly open and at least a hundred people spill out into the afternoon. Most look and sound Caribbean. Tropical colors are mixed with black. "Bessie always loved a damn good singalong," says a lady. Her friend replies, "She joined in at the end, I swear. I knew it was Bessie by how off-key it was . . ."

After the Kibberwhite party has gone, the waiting room feels bleaker than before. Bernie Dee, Elf's mum, and Mrs. Sinclair make small talk. Imogen and Lawrence sit in silence.

A few minutes before four o'clock, the funeral director ushers the nine mourners into a room with space for thirty or forty. The lighting is harsh and the floor is scuffed wood. The walls are tobacco-stained white. A piano sits in the corner. Mark's small coffin rests on a conveyor belt. *Like a parcel in a lost and found office.* A nearly new blue rabbit sits on the coffin. Elf's mum holds Imogen's arm and guides her to the front. Elf wishes the sight didn't make her think of Imogen's wedding day. The roses are white.

BERNIE DEE'S ADDRESS is well crafted and well meant but is, ultimately, based on the "God works in mysterious ways" message. *Not that I know how to attach meaning to Mark's death.* "As we bid goodbye," concludes Bernie Dee, "to the body that housed Mark's soul for so brief a time, we'll listen to a favorite hymn of Imogen's." She looks at the funeral director. He lowers a needle onto crackly vinyl and a choir begin, "O God, Our Help in Ages Past."

Imogen's voice is shaky but loud. "No."

Everybody, funeral director included, looks at her.

"No. Stop playing that. Please."

The funeral director lifts the needle.

Bernie is worried. "Is there a mistake, Immy?"

"I—I asked for it, but . . . it's the wrong choice." Imogen swallows. "Mark should've had a lifetime of music. Nursery rhymes, pop songs, dances, and all sorts of music. I don't want him to, to leave us . . . to . . . a hymn you play at funerals."

"We didn't bring any other records," says her mum.

"Elf." Imogen turns to her sister. "Play something."

Elf's nervous. "I haven't prepared anything, Ims."

"Please. Anything. Something for Mark." She's fighting back tears. "Please."

"Of course, Ims. Of course I will." Elf walks over to the piano. The funeral director lifts the lid for her. She sits on the stool. *But what?* "A Raft and a River"? She could make a decent stab at the *Moonlight Sonata* from memory, but any mistakes would stand out a mile. *Scarlatti's too lively.* Then Elf remembers the composition she wrote at the Cricketer's Arms last night. She's carrying it in her handbag, in case a set of lyrics occurs to her. Elf puts the exercise book on the music holder and plays the still untitled sixty-six bars from beginning to end. Playing it more slowly makes it change color. It lasts perhaps five minutes. As Elf plays, Imogen recovers her composure. She goes over to Mark's coffin and kisses the lid. Lawrence does the same. They hold each other and cry. The two bereaved grandmothers join them, with Bea.

Elf's composition comes to an end.

Its ghost fills the silence that follows.

Imogen tells the funeral director, "It's time."

Elf walks over and takes the blue bunny.

Everyone's fingertips rest on the white coffin.

The funeral manager presses a discreet switch.

The conveyor belt clunks into life.

The smooth lid slides from under their fingers.

Mark's coffin passes through a curtain.

Beyond, a mechanical screen is lowered.

Even the bluebells lasted longer.

ON THURSDAY MORNING, Elf meets Bethany in the spiral rush of Piccadilly Circus tube station. Londoners pour from the diagonal tunnels each minute, each with tragedies, histories, comedies, and romances. Shoeshiners work hard and quickly. Newspaper sellers work through their queues at high speed. Bethany is wearing a stylish blue hat, silk scarf, and Jackie Onassis sunglasses.

"I almost didn't recognize you," says Elf.

"That's the idea. A reporter was lurking outside Moonwhale. He tried to shake down the bicycle courier for gossip. How's Imogen?"

"She's at Richmond with my parents." Elf looks for words. "Grief is a boxer, my sister's a punchbag, and all we can do is watch."

"Then watch," says Bethany, "stitch up her cuts and help her get to her feet again when she's flat out."

Elf nods. There's nothing else to say. "So. What's happening with Levon and Dean?"

"They're all over the press like a rash. This, from the *Post* . . ." Bethany has an article pasted into a notebook. Under a picture of Dean onstage at McGoo's:

'NOT WITHOUT MY HONOUR!'

The saga of heart-throb Dean Moss, arrested in Rome on Sunday on a dubious drugs charge, took an EXTRAORDINARY new twist yesterday when the Utopia Avenue guitarist refused to buy his repatriation by signing a confession of guilt. Mr. Moss, who penned the Top 20 hits "Darkroom" and "Prove It," insists that the contraband was PLANTED by the arresting detective. Charges of fiscal impropriety against band manager Levon Frankland have already been DROPPED. In a statement issued via his lawyer, Mr. Moss explained his courageous decision: "I'd do almost anything for this ordeal to be over and see my friends, my family and my country—but signing a false confession for a crime I didn't commit is beyond the pale."

"I can hear 'Land of Hope and Glory,' " says Elf.

"Levon and Freddy Duke can hear cash registers in record shops across the land. Oh, and Ted Silver told me to tell you BBC Radio have a reporter in Three Kings Yard. There'll be others."

"Don't tell me I'll be on the lunchtime news."

"Lunchtime *and* dinnertime."

Elf thinks of her father eating his sandwich in his office at work. *What if I say the wrong thing?*

"I'm giving Amy Boxer the lead interview, if that's okay."

"Fine by me." Elf thinks of Dean in his cell in Italy. His fate may depend on her getting this right. "I feel out of my depth, Bethany."

"You had two thousand Italians eating out of the palm of your hand last Saturday, I've been told."

"Yes, but that was a performance."

"So is this. That's why we're meeting early. Let's find a quiet spot, sit down with a coffee, and work out a few lines . . ."

ELF ENTERS THREE Kings Yard under its archway, flanked by A&R man Victor French and Moonwhale's lawyer Ted Silver. The courtyard is packed. A cheer goes up and stays up. Elf suppresses an urge to bolt. *Dean needs this.* Dozens of people call out her name. In seconds, it becomes a chant: *"Elf! Elf! ELF! Elf! Elf! ELF! Elf! Elf! ELF!"* Young people. A few older faces. The sharply dressed. Unshaven hippies. *"Elf! Elf! ELF! Elf! Elf! ELF!"* A smattering of mods. A trio of jugglers. A Westler's hot dog vendor. A hurdy-gurdy man. *Harold Pinter? "Elf! Elf! ELF! Elf! Elf! ELF!"* "Smithereens" is playing from an upstairs window. Reporters block Elf's path: "Arthur Hotchkiss of *The Guardian,*" says a newshound in a houndstooth jacket. "What are your hopes and fears for the counterculture?" *"Elf! Elf! ELF! Elf! Elf! ELF!"* He's jostled out of the picture by a hairless bulldog: "Frank Hirth, *Morning Star*—what is Utopia Avenue's view on the struggle of the proletariat?" *"Elf! Elf! ELF! Elf! Elf! ELF!"* A Jack-the-lad slips in: "Willy Davies, *News of the World.* What's yer vital statistics, Elf, and who's the hunkiest man in pop?" *"Elf! Elf! ELF! Elf! Elf! ELF!"* Elf swerves away, and an American voice says: "Don't forget to breathe." She's young, Spanish-looking, and beautiful. *"Elf! Elf! ELF! Elf! Elf! ELF!"* The woman cups her mouth to Elf's ear. "I'm Luisa Rey, *Spyglass* magazine, but that doesn't matter—good luck and don't forget to breathe."

Elf breathes. "Okay."

Ted Silver escorts her through the crush to a crate under a lamppost. Victor French puts a mic in her hand. *What if I forget my speech?* Bethany clasps her shoulder: "You memorize entire folk songs word-perfectly, remember. You can do this." Elf nods and climbs onto the crate. The *"Elf! Elf! ELF! Elf! Elf! ELF!"* becomes another cheer, louder and longer than the first. A needle is lifted off "Smithereens." Hundreds of faces look back. Dozens of cameras click. People watch from the surrounding windows. She quietens the roar with a hand gesture.

Breathe. "Morning, all." Elf's voice issues from an amp lashed to the lamppost. Her words echo off the walls of Three Kings Yard. "I'm Elf Holloway from Utopia Avenue and I'm here—"

A woman shouts, *"We know 'oo you are, Elf darlin'!"*

"Oh, hi, Mum, thanks for showing up." Elf's quip gets a warm laugh. "Seriously, everyone. Thanks for your support. I'm here because my friend Dean is rotting in jail in Rome . . ."

A braying chorus of *"Boooooo!"* and *"Shame!"*

". . . where he has been beaten and denied access to a lawyer. The Italian police called him a drug smuggler." *Short sentences,* Bethany advised. *Hemingway not Proust.* "That—is—a—lie. Dean was given a choice. Confess to that lie and walk free—or refuse to sign the confession and return to his cell. He refused."

A medium-size roar and nodding, approving heads.

"Some call Dean Moss a publicity seeker. Some say Dean goaded the Italian police into arresting him, for the publicity. That—is—nonsense. *Who,* of sound mind, would risk getting banged up in a foreign prison for years for a few column inches?"

A man is aiming a mic at her, adjusting levels on a box.

"Some call Dean Moss a yob and a thug. That—is—a—lie. Dean hates violence. Let's follow his example—please. For Dean, be friendly to the embassy staff. This isn't their doing. Likewise, give the police guards an easy day's work. They're Londoners too."

Don't forget to breathe. "That's what Dean Moss isn't. Here's what Dean Moss is. He's a working-class boy. He knows what it's like to not have enough. Dean is no saint, but he'd give you the shirt off his back if you needed it more than him. He's decent. He's kind. He's a writer of songs that show life in its pain and its glory. Songs that tell us we're not alone. Dean is my friend. So please. Can we bring our friend home?" A mighty roar fills the courtyard.

"Can we bring him home?"

The crowd replies with a bigger roar.

Third time is the charm: "Can—we—bring—him—home?"

The roar is mighty. Elf steps off the crate. The crowd surges forward. Cameras click and flash in her face. Ted Silver, Victor French, and Bethany and a few big guys Bethany has dragooned form a phalanx to get Elf out of Three Kings Yard and into the taxi. It moves off. Elf's heart is beating like crazy. "How did I do?"

SOUND MIND

ANTHONY HERSHEY'S HOUSE IS A BIG EDWARDIAN RESIDENCE on Pembridge Place. The wall is high and topped with spikes. Two bouncers at the wrought-iron gates check off partygoers' names on a list before letting them in. Jasper sees the top of a striped marquee in the back garden. "Someone's not short of a few bob," says Griff. "House like that in a posh street like this . . . what d'you reckon, Deano? Hundred grand?"

"Easy. Cop a load o' them cars. An Ace Cobra. Austin-Healey . . . a Jensen Interceptor. D'yer think they're all his?"

"Wipe the drool off your chin," Elf tells him. "When the new album sells a million, you'll be able to buy your very own."

"On our royalties? I'll be lucky if I can stretch to a rusty Mini. D'yer reckon there'll be film stars 'n' that at this party?"

"Stands to reason," says Elf. "He *is* a director. How officially single are you, again? I lose track, rather."

Dean acts being shot in the heart. *Comedy,* thinks Jasper. "The only film of his I saw was that *Gethsemane,*" says Dean. "All that stuff about Jesus 'n' drug addicts 'n' whatnot. Over my head."

"The film club at Amsterdam conservatory put on an Anthony Hershey retrospective," says Jasper. "His best work is phenomenal." Jasper checks the time: 5:07. "Levon's late."

"Maybe he's stuck in a *Colm*-plicated situation," says Griff. Elf winces. Dean half smiles and growls. Jasper's not sure what's going on but is saved by a taxi pulling up. It's Levon. He pays and jumps out. "Wow, you're all here on time."

"What d'yer take us for?" huffs Dean. "A bunch o' knob-head rock stars who think the world's at our beck 'n' call?"

Irony? Jasper doesn't find out because the others take full note of Levon's sharp new suit with turquoise trimmings.

Griff wolf-whistles softly.

Elf says, "Someone's been shopping."

Dean feels the lapel. "Savile Row?"

"You have to look the part to cut the deals, my friends. How's 'Roll Away the Stone' shaping up?"

"We're up to take twenty," says Jasper.

Levon makes a face Jasper can't read. *Disappointment?* "Soon is good, folks. Victor's serious about it being a single."

"Tell him he'll hear it when its melodic genius is at peak perfection," states Dean. "It'll be worth it."

Levon lights a cigarette. "*Please* don't blow the album budget on one tune. Your credit with Ilex is better now *Paradise* is in the Top Thirty, but it's no bottomless overdraft."

"Looks like the bagpipes and Bulgarian choir are out, Dean," says Elf. "So why are we here?" She nods at the Hershey house. "Bethany didn't have any details. We're thinking 'soundtrack.' "

"Or," says Dean, "did Mr. Hershey see my rugged good looks in the papers last month and think, *There's my leading man*?"

"Aye, that'll be it," says Griff. "He's making *The Ugly Wanker from the Black Lagoon,* and thought, *He won't need makeup.*"

"*Ooh,* yer bitch," says Dean. "Or does Hershey want the band in a film, like the Italian guy who put the Yardbirds in *Blow-up*?"

"Michelangelo Antonioni," says Levon. "Elf's barking up the right tree—soundtrack. Think of today as a pre-interview for a job yet to be defined. Enjoy yourselves. But not *too* much."

"Why're yer looking at me when yer say that?" asks Dean.

"You're paranoid. Let's step into the lion's den, shall we?" Levon looks both ways and crosses the road.

ON JASPER'S SECOND day at Rijksdorp Sanatorium, Dr. Galavazi issued a diagnosis of severe aural schizophrenia and searched for a drug to alleviate the symptoms. Queludrin, a German antipsychotic, emerged as the most effective treatment. The sense of Knock Knock's tenancy remained, but the "interior hammering" ceased. It felt to Jasper that his mental intruder had been confined to an attic. The sixteen-year-old was now free to take stock of his new surroundings. The psychiatric facility was hidden in a forested area between the town of Wassenaar and dunes fringing the North Sea. A single-story clinic connected two large 1920s houses, which served as Rijksdorp's male and female wings and housed a total population of only thirty. A high wall surrounded the site and the gate was guarded. Residents' private rooms could not be locked, though NIET STOREN signs were generally respected. Jasper's top-floor room was furnished with a bed, a desk, a chair, a cupboard, shelves, and a washbasin. The mirror was removed at his insistence. The barred window looked onto canopies of trees.

Jasper's nickname was De Jeugd, the Youth. He was Rijksdorp's youngest resident. The Trappists were a group of manic-depressives who spoke only in occasional short sentences. The Dramatists passed their days with gossip, intrigues, and internecine struggles. The Conspirators fomented delusional theories about the Elders of Zion, Communist bees, and a secret Nazi base in Antarctica. Jasper remained Non-aligned during his residency. Sexual liaisons in the clinic were forbidden in theory and difficult in practice, though not unknown. Two men on Jasper's floor had sex now and then, but ten years in an English boarding school had accustomed him to furtive gay sex. His own libido was, perhaps conveniently, dimmed by Queludrin.

Days at Rijksdorp began with a seven A.M. gong, followed by an eight A.M. gong to announce breakfast. Jasper sat at a Non-aligned table and spoke little while he ate his rolls and cheese and drank his coffee. Residents then reported to the pharmacy for their medication in alphabetical order. Jasper's *Z* ensured last place. Mornings consisted of treatments appropriate to individual diagnoses: psychotherapy, behavioral therapy, or just "community work" for those willing and able to perform light chores in the kitchen or garden.

Afternoons were the patients' own. Jigsaw puzzles were popular, as were a table-tennis table and bar-football. Some patients memorized poems, songs, or "turns" for the Dramatists' hotly debated Saturday revue. Grootvader Wim and Dr. Galavazi were initially keen for Jasper to continue with the Bishop's Ely curriculum, but when he opened the textbooks, he knew that he and school had parted ways forever. An ex–classics teacher from Apeldoorn nicknamed the Professor enlisted Jasper as a chess opponent. He played slow, fierce games. A nun from Venlo ran a Scrabble league. She invented new words and rules to ensure victory, and cast religious curses if challenged.

Weeks became months. In August Jasper agreed to Dr. Galavazi's proposal that he venture outside the Rijksdorp grounds. Within a few yards, he felt his pulse elevate and gravity strengthen. His vision swam. He hurried back through the gate, convinced that it wasn't only Queludrin but also Rijksdorp's walls that kept Knock Knock at bay. He admitted that this was irrational, but so was an Oriental monk who appeared only in mirrors and sought to drive Jasper insane. Dr. Galavazi, fearful that his young patient was too dependent on Queludrin, reduced his 10 mg dose to 5 mg. After a day, Jasper felt Knock Knock stir. After two, he felt a *thud-thud, thud-thud, thud-thud* on the wall of his skull. After three, he saw Knock Knock's dim reflection in a soup spoon. On the fourth day, Jasper's dosage was returned to 10 mg.

All through the autumn, Grootvader Wim visited. If "enjoyed" was the wrong word for these visits, Jasper valued the fact that one person, at least, came to see him. Three- or four-word sentences were Jasper's upper limit, but Wim de Zoet had volunteered in the Great War and was used to men suffering from shellshock. He spoke for both of them, reporting on de Zoet family affairs, news, Domburg, books, and chapters of his own life. Jasper's father, Guus, visited once. It did not go well. Guus de Zoet, unlike Wim, couldn't hide his distress at Jasper's fragility, or his nervy disgust at the more visibly mentally ill patients. Guus's wife and Jasper's half-siblings did not visit. Jasper did not mind. The fewer the pitying witnesses to his collapse, the better. Jasper's only other connection with the world was Heinz Formaggio, who wrote every week from Ely, Geneva, or wherever he happened to be. Some weeks he sent only a scribbled postcard; others it was a ten-page epic. Jasper tried to reply, staring at "Dear Formaggio" for half a day, lost in the infinity of possible first lines until he gave up. The lack of a reply never discouraged Jasper's former roommate.

IN NOVEMBER, A protégé of Dr. Galavazi's from the University of Leuven named Claudette Dubois took up an eight-week work placement at Rijksdorp. Her thesis proposed that music might have positive effects on some psychiatric patients, and she was keen to test a few of these ideas. "Come in," she told Jasper, as he entered the consulting room. "You're my very first guinea pig." Various wind, string, and percussion instruments were arranged on a table. With a smile like a misbehaving child, Miss Dubois asked him to choose one. He picked the guitar, a Spanish-built Ramirez. He liked its feel on his thigh. He strummed, and had a sense that his future had just changed. His fingers remembered G, D, A, and F from a couple of guitar lessons he had had after his encounter with Big Bill Broonzy in Domburg. Jasper told Miss Dubois about the encounter. He had not spoken so many sentences for months. He asked to borrow the guitar for the day. She lent him the instrument and a manual by Bert Weedon called *Play in a Day*.

Jasper didn't realize the title wasn't a literal command, and was angry with himself for having mastered only two-thirds of Bert Weedon's methodology by the next session. Each of his fingertips required a sticking plaster. Miss Dubois was impressed, but made the ongoing loan of the Ramirez conditional upon Jasper performing at the Saturday revue. Jasper had no choice. When he played, he forgot he was a scared dropout wasting away in a psychiatric facility in the Netherlands. When he played, he was a servant and a lord of Music. On Saturday, he played a simplified "Greensleeves." In future years, Jasper would experience the live adoration of thousands, yet no applause would ever quite equal what he earned that

Saturday from a motley group of schizophrenics, depressives, fantasists, doctors, nurses, kitchen staff, and cleaners. He thought, *I want to get better.*

WHEN MISS DUBOIS returned to Leuven she entrusted her Ramirez to Jasper, saying she expected further progress by the spring. Shortly before Christmas, Jasper played his grandfather "Yes Sir, That's My Baby" and Duane Eddy's "Forty Miles of Bad Road." Grootvader Wim had missed a couple of visits due to illness and was joyful and shocked at Jasper's rapid progress. He engaged a Brazilian guitarist married to a Dutchwoman in Den Haag to give Jasper weekly lessons at Rijksdorp. Jasper's "turns" at the Saturday revue grew in complexity and length. He slipped in a few of his own compositions, describing them, if asked, as "a traditional Argentinian folk song." For Christmas, Jasper received a Philips record player—with earphones—from "The De Zoet Family," which meant Grootvader Wim. Miss Dubois gave him Abel Carlevaro's recordings of Bach and Manuel Ponce. His Brazilian teacher gave him Andrés Segovia's *Master of the Spanish Guitar* and Odetta's *Odetta Sings Ballads and Blues.* Jasper spent the whole day transcribing Odetta songs, note by chord by line. He didn't consider himself a singer—but he needed to hum the vocal line, so why not sing the words? Jasper performed Odetta's "Santy Anno" at the first Saturday revue of 1963 and took an encore. He could have taken two, but his Brazilian teacher warned Jasper that a musician should leave an audience wanting a little more.

That winter was severe. Canals froze across the Netherlands but the Elfstedentocht race across Friesland was aborted as all but sixty-nine of ten thousand skaters succumbed to hypothermia and frostbite. Jasper worked on mastering guitar exercises by Francisco Tárrega, Jasper's father visited Rijksdorp before his annual departure for South Africa. Jasper played "I've Got It Bad (and That Ain't Good)" and Tárrega's "Étude in C." This time, his father left Rijksdorp later than planned. The following week, the nun from Venlo died in her sleep. Jasper composed "Requiem for the Scrabble

Cheat" in her honor. Some residents were moved to tears. Jasper enjoyed the power his music gave him over their emotions.

Spring brought tulips and a reversal. One April morning Jasper thought he could hear a far-off *knock, knock, knock* . . . By evening he was sure. Dr. Galavazi speculated that Jasper was acquiring an immunity to Queludrin. He tried alternative psychotropics but the knocking grew nearer and louder until the doctor agreed to increase Jasper's Queludrin dosage to 15 mg. Formaggio sent him the complete set of Harry Smith's *Anthology of American Folk Music*. Jasper felt an affinity for the blues tunes. With his Brazilian teacher, he mastered Tárrega's "Recuerdos de la Alhambra." It was so beautiful that Jasper could hardly breathe. Buds unfolded. Insects spilled. Woodpeckers hammered. Birdsong drenched the woods around Rijksdorp. Jasper broke down into violent sobs, but couldn't say why. A trip was organized to nearby tulip fields. Jasper got on the bus, but before they were out of Rijksdorp Wood, he found himself struggling to breathe. The bus had to take him back. Jasper's first anniversary as a patient came and went. Would there be a second, a third, a tenth?

The knocking started again. Dr. Galavazi increased the Queludrin dosage to twenty milligrams. "That's the last time," he told Jasper. "It's killing your kidneys." Jasper felt like a cat on its ninth life.

One August day, Grootvader Wim appeared with Heinz Formaggio, who was six inches taller, bulkier, and sported a half-beard and a gabardine suit. He was to sail from Rotterdam to New York the following day. An institute in Cambridge, Massachusetts, had awarded him a scholarship. The friends sat beneath the almond tree. Jasper played "Recuerdos de la Alhambra." Formaggio spoke about their Ely classmates, theater, sailing in Greece, and a new science called cybernetics. Jasper's news was confined to the routines of a psychiatric hospital. He longed to be free of his battle with a demon or, if Dr. Galavazi was correct, a psychosis posing as a demon. Later, as Grootvader Wim's car carried Formaggio off to his brilliant future, Jasper understood that death is a door; and asked himself, *What does one do with a door?*

. . .

THE DOOR OPENS onto a hallway swirling with laughter, anecdotes, and the *Getz/Gilberto* LP turned up loud. Lilies and orchids burst from Grecian urns. A staircase curves toward a modernist chandelier. A man in his forties floats over, radiating a host's bonhomie. "Dean I know from last month's papers. Elf's the girl. Jasper, the hair. Which leaves Griff—and Levon. Who else could you be? Welcome to my Midsummer Ball."

"The honor's ours, Mr. Hershey," says Levon.

"It's Tony," insists the director. "No standing on ceremony here. My wife said you were in a recording studio when she called. Tell me I'm not your man from Porlock. I'd never forgive myself."

"You averted a murder," says Griff. "Things were turning ugly about a keyboard solo."

"Is this the hallway and staircase where you shot the party scene in *Cat's Cradle*?" asks Jasper.

"Well spotted! I'd *utterly* blown the budget, so this was one less set to build. I say, Tiff? Tiff!" He beckons to a woman with a golden bouffant, a dress of swirling blues and pinks, flared pantaloons, and bare arms. "Look who's arrived!"

"Utopia Avenue." She walks over, smiling. "And Mr. Frankland, I assume." Jasper guesses she's fifteen years younger than her husband. "Delighted you could make it—at such short notice."

"We wouldn't have missed it for the world," says Elf. "Your home's breathtaking, Tiffany."

"Tony's accountant told us to turn the *Battleship Hill* money into bricks and mortar or hand it over to the Inland Revenue. It's perfect for parties but, golly, it's a nightmare to keep on top of."

"Tiffany introduced me to your *Paradise* LP," says the director. "This was before that awful Italian business. It's a sublime record."

A compliment, thinks Jasper. "Thanks." *Be agreeable.* "We think so too." Everyone looks at him. *I said something off-key.*

"What's remarkable," says Tiffany Hershey, "is that my favorite song changes every time we play it."

"So what song's yer favorite right now?" asks Dean.

"Where do I begin? 'Unexpectedly' pulls my heartstrings. 'Darkroom' sends shivers down my spine, but if you tied me up and *forced* me to choose . . ." she looks at Dean, ". . . 'Purple Flames.' "

Dean says nothing. Jasper guesses he's pleased.

"If it's not too cheeky, Tiffany," Elf brings out an autograph book from her handbag, "would you mind ever so?"

"How awfully sweet," says Tiffany, taking the pen. "It's been simply ages since I signed anything. Except checks."

"My mum took my sisters and me to see *Thistledown* at the Richmond Odeon. Afterward my sister Bea announced, 'I'm going to be an actress.' Now she's in her first year at RADA."

"Oh, my golly!" says Tiffany Hershey. "What a story!"

"See, Tiff?" says Hershey. "Your fans haven't gone anywhere."

Tiffany Hershey writes: *"To Bea Holloway, my sister in drama, Tiffany Seabrook."* "*Thank* you," says Elf. "She'll have this framed."

"What's your new film about, Tony?" asks Jasper.

"It's what Hollywood calls 'a road movie.' A London pop star is told he has only a month to live and hitches to the Isle of Skye to address unfinished business. He's accompanied by the ghost of his dead sister, Piper. Adventures and epiphanies along the way guaranteed. Emotional climax. Twist in the tail. The End—until the Oscars flood in."

"Who's playing the star," asks Levon, "if it's not an impertinent question?"

"It's a moot and pressing question. Should I go for an Albert Finney or a Patrick McGoohan? Or for a bona fide singer who's actually, you know, lived through it?"

"Cast the Real McCoy," says Dean. "Every time. I'll do it. I've got bags o' free time over the next few months, right, Levon?"

He looks and sounds as if he means it, but Jasper guesses from everyone else's smile that he was joking, and that it's not a serious offer. Jasper acts a smile. "Do you have a title?"

"*The Narrow Road to the Deep North,*" says Tiffany.

"That's jolly evocative," says Elf. "I love it."

"The title's from Bashō," says Jasper. "The Japanese poet."

"*Someone's* an omnivorous reader," says Tiffany.

"I had lots of time to read when I was young."

"Before you joined the Old Farts' Club, you mean?" The director says it half smiling, but Jasper doesn't get the joke.

"Tiffany will be making her acting comeback as Piper." Hershey sips his Pimm's. "After four years away."

"Five," says Tiffany Hershey. "Six, by the time it's out. Your song, Jasper, 'The Prize' "—Tiffany turns to Jasper—"reminds me of 'Tomorrow Never Knows.' How conscious was that?"

"Not very," says Jasper. A pause. *Do they want more?*

"John's here, you know," says Anthony Hershey.

"No fookin' way!" says Griff. "Lennon? Here? At this party?"

"In the living room, I believe," said the host. "By the punchbowl. Tiffany, would you make the introductions? I was on a quest to find some green olives for Roger Moore . . ."

"THREE FACTS." THE man by the punchbowl is not John Lennon, but an older man with bad teeth, a shark's-tooth necklace, and evangelical eyes. Tiffany and the others move off, but Jasper likes facts. "Fact one: UFOs from other stars visited Earth during the Neolithic era. Fact two: ley lines were their navigation aids. Fact three: where ley lines converge, we have a landing site. Stonehenge was the Heathrow Airport of pre-Roman England."

"A real archeologist might point out," says an Australian woman, "that a fact is only a fact if it's derived from proof."

"How lucky we are," says the ufologist, "that the anarchists can spare Aphra Booth for the day. The Ivory Tower Brigade did indeed bleat at my book and I gave them the response I now offer Miss Booth. 'My book contains six hundred pages of proof: piss off and *read* the damn thing!' " He pauses to enjoy the laughter. "Did they take my advice? Of course not. Academics are thought-policed from cradle to grave. During my lost years at Oxford, I attended their conferences. I had but one question: How did human societies as far-flung as the Nile Valley, China, the Americas, Athens, Atlantis, India, et al., invent metallurgy, agriculture, law, and mathematics within decades of one another? Their answer?" The ufologist mimed someone with Parkinson's looking up a word. " 'Oh, let me check my textbook . . .' " He mimes turning a page. " 'Ah, yes, here it is . . .

Coincidence!' Coincidence. The last refuge of the bankrupt intellectual."

"If the skies over Stonehenge once swarmed with little green men," asks Aphra the Australian, "where are they now?"

"They fled in disgust." The ufologist's smirk fades. "The Visitors gave us the wisdom of the stars. We used it for warfare, slavery, religion, and trousers for women. And yet, and yet. Our myths, legends, and literature are *replete* with entities from other planes of being. Angels and spirits, Bodhisattvas and fairies. Voices in the head. My hypothesis unifies these phenomena: *These beings are extraterrestrial in origin.* For millennia they've visited us, to see if *Homo sapiens* is ready for the Final Revelation. The answer has always been 'Not yet.' But that 'Not yet' is turning into 'Very soon.' UFO sightings are multiplying. Psychedelics are guiding us to higher states. Soon, extraterrestrials will initiate a sea change. Or, as I call it in my book, a 'star change.' "

A thoughtful silence settles. Someone says, "Far out."

The expression is new to Jasper. He guesses it means "Wow."

"If you were a sci-fi writer," Aphra Booth taps her cigarette, "I'd think, *Well, it's clichéd drivel, but his fans'll go, 'Far out.'* Or, if you'd fabricated a cult, I'd think, *Scientologists, Hare Krishna, and the Vatican peddle* their *hogwash, you may as well peddle yours.* But what sticks in my craw is how you tosh up your drivel in the lexicon of science. You piss in the well of knowledge."

"We should thank Miss Booth," says the ufologist, "for revealing how academia thinks. *If I don't believe it, it's not knowledge.*"

Aphra Booth exhales smoke. "Fifty years from now, you'll look back at this horseshit and cringe with embarrassment."

"*You'll* look back in fifty years, and think, *Why was my thinking so shackled and anal?*"

"Shackled *and* anal?" Aphra Booth stubs out her cigarette. "My God, how we give ourselves away . . ." She walks off, stepping aside for Elf, who is with an exotic-looking young woman in black velvet with silver designs.

"Jasper, there's someone I'd like you to meet. This is Luisa."

"Hello, Luisa," says Jasper.

"I love your music." Luisa sounds American. "I adore Elf's songs, I hasten to add"—the women exchange a bright look—"but I played 'Wedding Presence' so often, I wore out the track. It's numinous, if I can use that word."

Numin, thinks Jasper, *from "divine will."* "Thank you. Are those comets embroidered on your jacket?"

"Uh, yeah. Stylized ones."

"Luisa did them herself," says Elf. "I got an *E* for Needlework and the remark, 'Could try harder.' Scarred for life."

"Are you a ufologist?" Jasper asks the American. "Or a fashion designer?"

Luisa finds the questions amusing. "Neither. I'm a journalism student, here on a Fulbright scholarship. Lucky me, right?"

"I doubt luck has anything to do with it," objects Elf.

"Aw, shucks. I was in Three Kings Yard when Elf had her Martin Luther King moment."

"God, that all went by in a blur," says Elf. "I don't recall what I said, but I sure as heck know it wasn't 'I have a dream . . .' "

"Too modest, Elf. I covered the story for *Spyglass* magazine, and I quoted you, and hey presto—my first byline in an international publication. So. I owe you."

"Ah, stuff and nonsense." Elf's smiling in a way Jasper hasn't seen since before the death of her nephew.

"Do you guys have any plans to tour in the States?" asks Luisa. "They'd eat you with a spoon in New York, in LA."

"Is that a good thing or a bad thing?" asks Jasper.

"Oh, it's good," says Luisa. "Definitely good."

"Our label's mooting a short U.S. tour," says Elf, "now *Paradise* is selling in reasonable numbers. Who knows?"

HALFWAY DOWN THE curving stairwell, Jasper hears a voice. "Hello, Mr. Famous." Its owner has one blue eye and one black eye. He's dressed in a black suit with silver buttons and white piping. "We met on the stairs last time, too," says David Bowie. "I was on my way up, then. Now I'm going down. Is that a metaphor?"

Jasper shrugs. "If you want it to be."

David Bowie looks behind Jasper. "So . . . is Mecca here?"

"Her last letter was from San Francisco."

"Where else? Ninety-nine people, you forget instantly. Mecca's one in a hundred. Five hundred. She shines."

"I agree."

"Jealousy is not a demon that tortures you."

"Women go with who they want to go with."

"Precisely! Most men are 'Me Tarzan, you Jane.' I'm jealous of your sales, though. If it's not a cheeky question," David Bowie leans in, "did Levon cook the whole Italian affair up?"

By chance, Levon is in Jasper's line of sight, topping up Peter Sellers's wine glass at the foot of the stairs. "Not unless he's ten times craftier than we know."

"Mine's ten times crappier than I thought. My singles got no airplay. My label didn't promote the album. It flopped, too."

"I bought it, David. I found a lot to admire."

"*Ugh.* A glass of whisky and a revolver would be kinder."

"Sorry if I've offended you."

"No. Excuse my thin skin." David Bowie runs his hand through his ginger hair. "I've been the Next Big Thing since I left school, but I'm *still* broke. Hobnobbing with stars at Anthony Hershey's Midsummer Ball is nice, but tomorrow I'll be Xeroxing reports in a shitty office. What if my only talent is kidding people I have talent?"

Two women in thigh-length boots pad by.

"Overnight success," says Jasper, "takes a few years."

David Bowie swirls the ice in his glass. "Even yours?"

"Three years of busking in Dam Square. After"—*can I trust him?*—"a long spell in psychiatric care."

David Bowie meets Jasper's gaze. "I didn't know."

"A discreet clinic in Holland. I don't advertise it."

David Bowie hesitates. "My half-brother Terry's in and out of Cane Hill Hospital, near my parents' house."

Jasper shakes his head, like a Normal might. *Or should I nod?*

"I was with him, actually, when his first episode happened. We were walking down Shaftesbury Avenue, and he started screaming about the tarmac cracking and magma oozing up. For a few seconds

I thought he was joking. I was like, 'Okay, Terry, it's gone far enough.' But he meant it. These two coppers thought he was high so they wrestled him to the ground—into the magma that was now burning Terry's flesh. Fucking terrifying stuff, psychosis."

Jasper remembers Knock Knock in mirrors. "It is."

David Bowie crunches an ice cube. "I worry it's ticking away in me, too. Like a time bomb. These things run in the family."

I know it's ticking in me. "I've got two half-brothers. So far, they're fine. The de Zoet side of the family blame it on my mother."

"How did you get it under control?"

"Psychiatry. Music helps. A . . ." *What to call the Mongolian?* ". . . a kind of mentor." Jasper drinks his punch and lays out his theory. "A brain constructs a model of reality. If that model isn't too different from most people's model, you're labeled sane. If the model *is* different, you're labeled a genius, a misfit, a visionary, or a nutcase. In extreme cases, you're labeled a schizophrenic and locked up. I'd be dead without Rijksdorp sanatorium."

"Madness is a label you can't peel off, though."

"You write about it, David. Or atypical states of mind. Perhaps your phobia will make you famous."

David Bowie's nervy smile comes and goes. "Got a ciggie? Lennon cadged my last one. Like the Scouse millionaire he is."

Jasper gets out his packet of Camels. "Is he still here?"

"Yes, I think so. He was in the cinema."

"What cinema?"

"Anthony Hershey has a cinema in the basement. How the other half live, eh? Down that corridor, past that big Ming vase thing"—he points—"there's a door. You can't miss it."

THE STEEP STAIRS descend at right angles. Posters of films line the glossed walls. *Les Yeux sans visage. Rashōmon. Das Testament des Dr. Mabuse.* The stairs continue for longer than is likely. They end in a small lobby that smells of bitter almonds. A woman, absorbed in her needlepoint, occupies an armchair. Her head is hairless. "Excuse me, is this the cinema?"

The woman looks up. Her eyes are voids. "Popcorn?"

Jasper sees no sign of popcorn. "No, thank you."

"Why do you play these games with me?"

"I don't understand."

"That's what you always say." She pulls a cord. Curtains part to reveal a slab of darkness. "Enter, then."

Jasper obeys. He cannot see his own hand. Another curtain touches his face. He steps into a tiny auditorium of six rows of six seats. Each one is occupied except for an aisle seat on the front row. Through the cigarette smoke, a title is projected onto a screen: *PanOpticon.* Jasper's shadow hunches low as he makes his way to the free seat. If John Lennon is here, Jasper fails to recognize him. The film begins.

IN A BLACK-AND-WHITE city of winter, an omnibus shoulders its way through a crowd. A careworn middle-aged passenger looks out at busy snow, newspaper vendors, policemen beating a black-marketeer, hollow faces in empty shops, and a burned skeletal bridge. Jasper guesses the film was shot behind the Iron Curtain. Getting off the bus, the man asks the driver for directions. By dint of reply, the driver nods at the enormous wall obscuring the sky. The protagonist walks along its foot, looking for the door. Craters, broken things, wild dogs. Circular ruins where a hairy lunatic talks to a fire. Finally the man finds a wooden door. He stoops and knocks. *Knock-knock.* No reply. *Knock-knock.* A tin can is hanging from a piece of string vanishing into the masonry and the man speaks into it. "Is anybody there?" The subtitles are English, the language is all hisses, slushes, and cracks. Hungarian? Serbian? Polish? "I'm Dr. Polonski. Warden Bentham is expecting me." He puts the can to his ear and hears what sounds to Jasper like drowning sailors. *Knock-knock-knock.* The prison door opens. A hood of tiredness gathers around Jasper's head. He submits . . .

. . . AND WAKES IN a tiny cinema, lit by the mercury sheen of the vacant screen. Jasper looks around. Everybody's gone. The film's over. "Sorry for your loss," says a cultured voice next to him.

Jasper swivels and sees a face from an album cover: Syd Barrett. Pink Floyd's ex-singer is printed in black and white on the glowing dark. "How was the film? I nodded off."

Syd Barrett runs a Rizla along his tongue. "People who never set foot beyond the Land of the Sane just don't understand."

"Understand?"

Syd Barrett taps the long joint on its filter. "How indescribably sad it is, here on the outside. Got a light?" Jasper finds Grootvader Wim's lighter and holds up the flame. The big spliff in his lips, Syd leans in. He fills himself with smoke and offers the spliff to Jasper. The hit is instant. It is not just cannabis. Syd's words arrive late and fragmented, as if bounced off the moon. "We think we are a One, but you and I know an 'I' is a 'Many.' There's Nice Guy Me. Psychopath Me. Wife-beater Me. Narcissist Me. Saint Me. I'm-all-right-Jack Me. Suicidal Me. The Me Who Dares Not Speak My Name. Dark Globe Me. I is an Empire of 'I's."

Jasper thinks of Knock Knock. He wonders if a whole minute ever passes when he hasn't thought of Knock Knock. *Only inside music.* He asks, "Who is the emperor, Syd?"

Syd Barrett stares back through black holes, opens his mouth, and puts out the joint on his tongue. It hisses.

ANOTHER FILM BEGINS. The screen glows blue. Stippled sea, glazed sky, a bandage-colored coastline. Onscreen, a White Star liner fills the shot. Its horn blasts three times. A caption reads OFF THE COAST OF EGYPT, NOVEMBER 1945.

Cut to—deck of the SS Salisbury. The captain squints at the prayer book: *"Lord God, by the power of your Word you stilled the chaos of the primeval seas . . ."* The man is a northerner not given to theatrics. He recites the prayer as if reading nautical protocol: *"You made the raging waters of the Flood subside, and you calmed the storm on the Sea of Galilee."*

Cut to reveal—the deck. Passengers and crew stand around the coffin. A haggard nurse holds a three-day-old baby. The baby is crying. The captain pushes on. *"O Lord, as we commit the earthly remains of Milly Wallace to the deep, grant her peace . . ."*

Cut to—Two English ladies look down on the service from the railing of the first-class deck. "A tragedy," remarks the first lady.

"My maid heard from Mrs. Davington's girl that *she*"—the woman points a gloved finger at the coffin—"was no 'Mrs.' Wallace at all, but an unmarried 'Miss.' "

"Servants are such incorrigible gossips."

"As if they've nothing better to do. Apparently, *Miss* Wallace was originally a nurse who went out to Bombay on 'the fishing fleet,' if I may use the vulgar term. One of those young women who go to India with the purpose of netting themselves a better catch than they might at home. Miss Wallace, it seems, overestimated her talent as an angler. *She* got 'hooked' by a Dutchman, who," she whispers, *"already has a wife and family in Johannesburg . . ."*

The first lady's eyes open wide. "Is *that so*? Was he brought to any kind of justice? Couldn't the governor intervene?"

"Once the U-boat menace was over, the scoundrel hightailed it to South Africa. Miss Wallace was left alone, in *that* state, in Bombay, with nothing but a third-class passage. What with the delays at Bombay and Aden, however, and nature taking its course earlier than expected . . ."

"While it takes two to tango," the first lady fans herself, "one would need a heart of stone not to feel for the poor woman."

Zoom in on . . . the coffin, and Jasper at three days old.

Second lady voiceover: "Look at the sorry mite. Motherless, illegitimate. Hardly the best start in life, is it?"

Four sailors in uniform carry the coffin to the edge of the railing. A fifth plays "The Last Post."

Cut to—underwater. The hull of the *Salisbury* floats above. The sun is an orb of dazzle. A coffin plunges through the roof of the surface. Fish dart away. Milly Wallace's coffin sinks . . . sinks . . . sinks and settles on the ruckled seabed. The *Salisbury*'s propellers churn and rumble. The vessel moves off, leaving strains of Saint-Saëns's "Aquarium" in its wake. Fish inspect this latest offering.

For the first time he can remember, Jasper's eyes swell with tears. It is an alien, astonishing sensation. *So this is how it feels.*

Might Milly Wallace have a message? The coffin grows until its lid fills the screen. Jasper presses his ear against the wood . . .

Knock —

Knock knock *knock —*

KNOCK! KNOCK! KNOCK!

KNOCK! KNOCK! KNOCK!

Jasper's up and running for the exit . . .

PEOPLE FILL THE corridor, talking, flirting, drinking, smoking, arguing. Jasper's gasping for breath. His heart's thumping. The knocking didn't follow Jasper up the steep Escher-like stairs, but the sense of a death sentence did. *Knock Knock's excavating himself and there's nothing I can do about it.* Brian Jones appears in a cape, beads, and gold. "I've a bone to pick with you." His breath is yeasty and ill. "The lyrics in 'The Prize.' I recognize a few lines. From that night in the Scotch."

Jasper hauls his thoughts from Knock Knock to the ailing Stone. "It's true. Some of them are yours. Thank you."

"The magic word." Brian Jones makes the sign of the cross. "I absolve you. See? I come up with *tons* of ideas for Mick and Keith but all I get from them is sarcasm. *I* ought to write songs, you know. Even Wyman's got one on *Satanic Travesties.* That settles it. I begin. Tomorrow. Got any drugs?"

"Lord de Zoet of Mayfair and King Brian of Cotchford Farm." Rod Dempsey, Dean's drug dealer, sidles up. "Did I hear my favorite three words in the English language, or did my ears deceive me? 'Got any drugs,' was it?"

"Rescue me, Sir Rodney of Gravesend," says Brian Jones. "I daren't leave the house with so much as an aspirin nowadays."

"For you, my friend," Rod Dempsey slips a packet into Brian Jones's waistcoat pocket, "the doctor is always in." He turns to Jasper. "Prellies, Mandy, Miss Mary J. Acid as pure as driven snow."

"Another time, maybe."

"Easy come easy go, that's me. Brian, I'll drop by yer crib next week to settle yer tab. It's mounting up. Neither a borrower nor a lender be." Rod Dempsey winks and exits between bodies.

Dean arrives through the same gap. "Jasper. Mr. Jones."

"Fellow jailbird." Brian Jones grips Dean's shoulders. "I've had the most mind-blowing wheeze. Let's you and me make a prison film! Mick's doing one. Some gangster bollocks. Him and Anita get naked in a bath and Keith's as jealous as hell. That's what I call justice . . . Anyway, we'll get Hershey to direct ours. We'll call it *The Unbreakables*. What do you say?"

" 'How much dough?' and 'Where do I sign?' "

" 'A ton of' and 'In blood on the dotted line.' "

"Then I'm in, Brian. One o' them Oscar statues'd look just the ticket on my nan's piano."

"Perfect. I'll speak with . . . with my people. I'm off to the little boys' room to open my present from Dempsey. See you later."

They watch him go. "As if he could put together a cheese sandwich," says Dean. "Let alone a film. Where've yer been hiding for the last three hours, flatmate? I thought you'd buggered off early."

"I fell asleep in the cinema."

Dean gives him an odd look. "Yer've been to the cinema?"

"There's one in the cellar. Syd Barrett was there. I think."

"Syd's here? There's too many famous people at this party. It's bloody ridiculous. Just bumped into Hendrix coming out o' the bog."

"Is John Lennon still around?"

"Thataway." Dean points down a crowded passageway of bookshelves. "With his Oriental lady, talking to someone who looks *very* like Judy Garland. Haven't seen hide nor hair of Elf for a while. Levon's mingling. Colm's around somewhere. See yer at the flat if I don't see yer later, or see yer at Fungus Hut tomorrow if I don't see yer at the flat . . ."

"Sure."

Jasper doesn't get far before his path is blocked by Amy Boxer, Dean's ex-girlfriend and the *Daily Mail*'s newest ace reporter. "I would say, 'Fancy meeting you here!' but, really, who *isn't* here?" Amy Boxer taps ash into a crystal bowl of potpourri. "Tony and Tiffany have played it *very* clever. I presume they've given you the whole 'We're making a rock 'n' roll movie but should we cast actors, singers, or both' shtick?"

" 'Shtick'?" Jasper doesn't know the word.

"Jasper, sweetie, the Hersheys have lured London's starriest to their Midsummer Ball, ensuring it's both the event of the season *and* a mammoth pre-audition for a film that may"—Amy Boxer presses in close to let Princess Margaret and Lord Snowdon pass by—"or may not get made."

"I had no idea," says Jasper.

"Which is why," Amy tugs Jasper's tie like a bell-rope, "*ding-dong ding-dong,* you're adorable. You know, you still owe me for getting you all out of jail in Italy. What are your plans for paying me back? *Ding-dong ding-dong?*"

THE TWILIT SKY is slate and mother-of-pearl. The floodlit swimming pool is afternoon blue. The marquee on the back lawn pulses with inner light, and a trumpet plus jazz piano trio plays "Summertime." Jasper drifts over to Griff, who's surrounded by a huddle of models, actresses, intelligentsia, and who-knows-who. "I couldn't sleep. There was screaming from the next cell—all night long. It was in Italian, so I didn't know exactly what were going down until the morning after. There, on my breakfast tray . . ." Griff drops his voice to a hush, "plopped in my baked beans, was a *human thumb.*"

Squeals of disgust. A voice asks in Jasper's ear, "Now, is that for real? Or is the cat's imagination getting the better of him?"

Jasper turns to find curious eyes, framed by an Afro and a snakeskin top hat with a bright blue feather. *I know you . . .*

"Chuffin' heck!" Griff looks over. "It's Jimi Hendrix!"

"That's your solo album, Jimi," says Keith Moon. "Right there: *Chuffing Heck, It's Jimi Hendrix!* I'm calling mine *Man on the Moon.* Or does that sound too much like a gay porno mag?"

"Utopia Avenue, I dig you cats." Jimi Hendrix shakes hands with Griff and Jasper. "Your album's out there."

Return a compliment, thinks Jasper. "*Axis* is seminal."

"I can't listen to it, man," says Jimi Hendrix. "The sound quality's a fuckup. I left the original master in a cab—"

"Or *Man* in *the Moon?*" wonders the Who's drummer. "Or is that even smuttier? Once you start, you can't stop . . ."

"So we used a crumpled copy of Noel's. Chas had to iron out the tape. Literally. With an iron. Where do you cats record?"

"Fungus Hut," says Jasper, "on Denmark Street."

"I know it. The Experience made our very first demo there."

"Or do I go with my first choice," says Keith Moon, "*Howling at the Moon*? I'll be on the cover—a hairy werewolf—howling . . ."

"What's your setup on 'Smithereens'?" Jimi is asking Jasper. "I can't work out if it's a fuzz pedal."

"I plugged my guitar into an old Silvertone of Digger's. The cone in the speaker was ripped. That gives it the torn sound."

"Uh-huh. And is it a Strat or Gibson on that now?"

"I only own a Strat. A sailor in Rotterdam"—a body cannonballs into the pool—"sold it to me. A 1959 Fiesta Red. The tone's not as seismic as yours—no fuzz pedal, no spiral coil—but it's versatile. It's good and growly for Dean's new prison song."

"Yeah, I read 'bout your Roman holiday. Jail's heavy shit."

"You were lucky Fleet Street rallied to your cause," says Brian Jones. "They're baying for my blood. For one bag of weed—planted by Detective Pilcher. The bastard even gave me the choice: 'Do you want to be done for weed or for coke?' "

"The Establishment is scared shitless that your defiance is contagious," says a heavyset man with stern glasses. Jasper knows he is a famous playwright but the name eludes him. "If *you* get a happy ending for flicking the *V*s, why should any pleb tolerate the factory floor? That way revolution lies."

"Bang bang, you're dead." A very small boy in a cowboy hat, dressing gown, and slippers shoots the playwright with a toy gun.

"Who isn't, in the long run?" asks the playwright. *"They give birth astride of a grave, the light gleams an instant, then it's night once more."*

The boy scans the circle of giants for his next victim. He chooses Jimi Hendrix. "Bang bang, *you're* dead too."

"Hey, Shorty. There are days when I see the appeal."

The boy twirls his gun and slots it into his holster as Tiffany Hershey arrives. "Crispin! Who told you you could come down?"

Crispin replies, "Bad Boy Frank," as if the matter is settled.

"My son has a coterie of imaginary friends," explains Tiffany. "Frank takes the rap for Crispin's misdemeanors."

The playwright swaps his empty wine glass for a full one from a passing tray. "A healthy imagination is a gift for life."

"Crispin's imagination is beyond 'healthy,' " says Tiffany.

"Yer a *mum*?" exclaims Dean. Jasper hadn't noticed him arrive. "Seriously? I had no—"

Crispin fires his gun at Dean. "Bang bang, you're dead."

Tiffany Hershey tells Dean, "I'm a mum twice over. Hence my screen hiatus. Righto, Crispin, let's get you back up to Aggy before this turns into A Midsummer Eve's Massacre."

The small boy hasn't finished. He aims his gun at Jasper and squeezes the trigger, slowly. Jasper looks down the barrel, eye to eye with the man Crispin will be. "Whenever you're ready . . ."

The small boy sighs like a world-weary adult. "Not you." He swivels the gun toward Brian Jones—"Bang bang, *you're* dead"—and Keith Moon, "Bang bang, you too."

Keith Moon hams it up. "It's all going dark, dear boy."

"Go to the light, Keith," Brian says, in a ghostly voice. "Go toward the light . . ."

"Don't encourage him," says Tiffany, but Keith Moon groans hammily, grips Brian Jones's elbow, and together they totter backward over the edge of the swimming pool . . . They slap into the water, drenching bystanders. Shrieks and laughter fill the terrace.

A SAXOPHONIST CARVES out a muscular "How Deep Is the Ocean?" Jasper is crawling along a pale shaft about four feet wide and three feet high. The ground is soft. *Turf.* Jasper's shuffling on his hands and knees. The walls of the shaft are linen. He touches the roof. *Wood.* His knuckles rap *knock-knock.* A mistake. *Knock-knock.* It's undeniable. *Soon, soon, soon.* All Jasper can do is keep the Queludrin to hand and keep shuffling onwards. *Look . . . shoes.* Side by side. Men's shoes. Women's shoes. Slipped-off shoes. Open sandals with painted toenails. *I'm underneath the tables in the marquee.* He remembers realizing this before. He remembers realizing he remembered realizing this before. Jasper wonders how long this chain goes back. His hand encounters a puffy thing. A bread roll. He squeezes it into a doughy globe. It squelches. *Knock-knock.* Jasper reaches the far corner. He turns right. *No choice.* This is not the first circumnavigation of the Undertable. *I've lost my watch. Time doesn't care.* Along the shaft, at the next corner, a head appears. Another undertable shuffler. Twenty feet away, fifteen, ten, five . . . The two inspect one another.

"You're you, aren't you?" asks Jasper.

"I think so," says John Lennon.

"I've been looking for you since I got here."

"Congratulations. I'm looking for . . ." He needs a prompt.

"Looking for what, John?"

"Something I lost," says the Beatle.

"What have you lost, John?"

"My fuckin' mind, pal."

LOOK WHO IT ISN'T

THE SPANKING NEW CHERRY-RED TRIUMPH SPITFIRE MARK III handled the sharp bends around Marble Arch as if it was steered directly by Dean's mind. A purring 1296cc engine, walnut dashboard, oxblood leather seats, top speed 95 mph, "But she'll kiss the hundred," said the sales manager, "if you're heading downhill and feeling naughty." Zipping along Bayswater Road with the roof down, under sunshine and leaf-shadow, Dean passed a Mini, a cement truck, a bus packed to the gills, and a cab carrying a man in a bowler hat and stopped on a sixpence at the traffic lights by the Hyde Park Embassy Hotel. Men pretended not to stare, envying Dean his car and the mysterious woman in Philippe Chevallier sunglasses and a snow-white headscarf at his side. Dean, for sure, would envy Dean something rotten if he wasn't already him. An album at number seventeen in the charts. Brian Jones's and Jimi Hendrix's numbers in his little black book—and £4,451 still in his bank account even *after* paying for his new car. A car that would have cost three or four years of pay packets if he'd got a job in a factory like Ray. Like Harry Moffat told him to. He rested his hand on the gearstick, inches away from Tiffany Hershey's caramel thigh. His gearstick vibrated.

"No buyer's remorse, then?" asked the actress.

" 'Bout *this*? Yer codding me."

Casually, she patted his hand. "It's a work of art."

Was that a pat or a touch? "Thanks for coming along, Tiff. Did yer see that sales-twat's face when he realized who yer were?" Dean did his posh voice. " 'Oh, you're a friend of the Hersheys? I'll fetch Mr. Gascoigne.' "

"Tony's sorry he couldn't join us. When the Americans come to town, he drops everything."

Dean wasn't sorry about anything. The lights turned green, he pressed the accelerator, and the Spitfire slid forward. Turbulence played with loose strands of Tiffany's hair. The lights were red again at Kensington Palace Gardens. Her suede glove rested on Dean's hand. "Would it be *awful* of me to ask for a lap of Knightsbridge, Buck Palace, and Pall Mall? I haven't felt this free for . . . years."

"I'm due at Fungus Hut at twelve, but I'm yours till then."

"You *are* a darling. Take the next left."

"There's gates and a copper. Can yer drive down here?"

"With Tiffany Seabrook in an open-top Triumph, yes."

Dean turned left and slowed to a halt at the gates.

"What an *utterly* beautiful morning!" Tiffany removed her sunglasses and beamed. "We're having luncheon with the Yukawas at the Embassy of Japan. May we pass?"

The policeman looked at Tiffany, the car, and Dean, in that order. "Right yer are, miss. Enjoy yer lunch, sir."

"Useful skill, acting," remarked Dean, as they moved off.

"Everyone acts. The trick is to do it well and reap rewards."

The Spitfire hummed down a tree-lined avenue of embassies. Most of the flags were unfamiliar to Dean. Old empires were coming unstitched and new nations cropping up every year. Not long ago, Dean was facing three years in a Roman prison: now he was flying down Embassy Row in a Triumph Spitfire, and coppers were calling him "sir." Dean turned left at Kensington Road. The lights stayed green as far as the Royal Albert Hall, where he told Tiffany, "Utopia Avenue's going to fill that place, one o' these days."

"Reserve me the Royal Box. I'll gaze down at you adoringly."

You, Tiffany had said, not *all of you* or *the band,* and Dean's desire shifted up a gear. She conjured a little mirror out of thin air and touched up her lipstick. Dean went through the motions of cautioning himself as to why an affair would not be a smart move. She's a mother of two. Her husband would axe the band's now-confirmed role in *The Narrow Road to the Deep North* soundtrack. Levon, Elf, and Griff would be livid. If anyone found out.

Dean imagined unzipping her.

His pulse shifted up another gear.

"A penny for your thoughts," she said.

Dean wondered if all women were mind readers, or just some of them, or just the ones he slept with. "I keep my thoughts firmly under lock 'n' key, Tiffany Seabrook."

Tiffany did a Nazi villain voice. "Vell, Mr. Moss, ve have vays of mecking you talk zat you vill not so easily vithstand . . ."

SIDE ONE OF *Blonde on Blonde* clicks off. Tiffany unties Dean's blindfold and the cords binding his wrists. The breeze nudges the curtains of his room. London hums, drums, speeds up, brakes, and breathes. The cocaine has worn off. Dean's Swiss Army knife and a length of drinking straw are by the mirror. Tiffany could have stuck that knife in anywhere. He's no longer nervous about the clap, at least. Today is their third liaison since the Triumph Spitfire morning. He would be peeing battery acid by now if she had anything.

Tiffany lies down. "Sorry I got a bit bitey. When I met Tony, I was down to the last three for *Kiss of the Vampire.* Some American bimbo got the part . . ."

Dean touches the love-bite on his collarbone.

". . . then I fell pregnant with Martin, and that was that. On the bright side you've passed *your* audition with flying colors."

"Yeah?" Dean bites his half-eaten apple. "What's the part?"

"Funny." She takes his apple and bites the last big chunk. " 'Tiffany Moss' has a nicer ring to it than 'Tiffany Hershey.' "

She's just toying with you, Dean assures himself.

"I'll need a bigger engagement ring than Tony's when we go public. People notice these things."

Dean chews more slowly. *Just let the joke die away . . .*

"My lawyer says my chances of getting the Bayswater house go up if I establish Tony's adultery. I've kept notes, but it's best if you buy a place for us in the meantime. One needs a roof."

Dean looks at her to check she's joking.

"Chelsea's nice. Somewhere big enough for parties. A flat for a housekeeper and an au pair. The boys need rooms of their own. Crispin likes you. Martin'll stop hating you eventually . . ."

The apple sticks in his throat.

"Or sooner, if we give him a little brother."

The deeply unpleasant thought of a certain young woman named Mandy Craddock and her baby son arrives first; and is shoved aside the next instant by the equally unpleasant thought that Tiffany is *not* toying with him to get a rise, but is, in fact, stone cold serious. Dean sits up and backs away. "Look, Tiff . . . I-I-I . . . I don't think—"

"No, no, you're right. Chelsea's a frightful cliché. I'll settle for Knightsbridge. We'll have Harrods on the doorstep."

"Yeah but . . . I mean, we only just . . . but . . ."

Tiffany sits up, covering her breasts with a sweaty sheet. She's frowning, genuinely puzzled. "But what, darling?"

Dean stares at his adulterous lover. *How the bloody hell do I get out o' this?* Tiffany's face changes—into a big, naughty grin. Relief dissolves through his bloodstream like sugar. "You evil, *evil* bloody witch."

"It's a basic exercise at drama school."

"You *totally* bloody had me."

"Why thank you. I—" Her face changes to iffy disgust. "Just a minute." Tiffany snatches Kleenexes from the box, swivels away, and wipes herself. Turning back, she notices a yogurty smear on the back of her thumb. "Look at that." She peers at it. "Stuff of life."

TEN MORNINGS AGO, at their flat, Jasper was playing Dean a rough version of his new song when the phone rang. It was Levon, for Dean, sounding grim. "So here's the story. A girl called Amanda Craddock just visited Moonwhale with her mother, a family-law solicitor, and a three-month-old baby boy. They're claiming you're the baby's father."

First, Dean felt sick. Then, he tried to place the name. "Amanda Craddock." It wasn't familiar—but it wasn't unfamiliar.

"Dean? Are you hearing this?"

Dry mouth, tight throat. "Yeah."

"Is this girl lying or isn't she?"

"Dunno . . ." he croaked. "I . . . dunno."

" 'Dunno' isn't an option. We need a 'yes' or 'no.' Both are problematic, but one is much more expensively problematic than the other. Can you come to the office?"

"Right now? Is she still there?"

"No, she's gone. Yes, right now. Ted Silver's leaving for his golf weekend after lunch. We all need to talk."

Dean hung up. Jasper carried on strumming in the sunken lounge. *Amanda Craddock?* Three months plus nine equals June or July last year, around the time of Imogen's wedding, or the Gravesend gig. He had been with Jude. There had been extracurricular encounters. Dean had made it clear—or clear-ish—to the women involved that he wasn't in the market for a steady girlfriend. Casual sex with a celebrity stays very very casual. That's the unwritten contract. Unfortunately, Dean now realized, unwritten contracts have as much fine print as the written variety.

DEAN SET OFF for Denmark Street on foot, telling Jasper, an unreliable liar, he had an errand. As he walked through a warm and muggy Mayfair, he tried to put last summer's girls in order. There were two groupies he met at the party of a pal of Roger Daltrey's in Notting Hill. Was that May? There was the girl in the Land Rover round the back of the Young Farmers' gig at Loughborough. Was she a Craddock? Izzy Penhaligon in June. Or July. Dean had to admit, he had no idea. He hoped that he could sort this out before Nan Moss and Bill got to hear. In their world, if a guy gets a girl "into trouble" he marries her, plain and simple. Like Ray and Shirl. That's not Dean's world now, though. He would've paid for an abortion, if he'd known. They're legal now. Girls don't have to risk bleeding to death over a bucket in an old maid's back parlor somewhere. Dean trudged up Greek Street and entered the short tunnel under the Pillars of Hercules pub into Manette Street.

"Got the time, sir?" asked a girl. By Soho street-corner standards she was pretty. Dean paused. Her pimp emerged from the soot-encrusted shadows, mistaking Dean's hesitancy. "Lotta's fresh up from the country. Nice 'n' clean. Plump 'n' juicy."

Nauseous, Dean hurried into the seedy sunlight, past Foyles bookshop, wishing this was a film. Wishing he didn't have to face Bethany at Moonwhale, who would look at him over her typewriter and say, "Good morning, Dean"—almost as if nothing was the matter at all.

SIDE TWO OF *Blonde on Blonde* clicks off with a clunk. Tiffany's thigh is glued to his. He thinks, *If I had to get anyone pregnant, why couldn't it have been you? You five years ago minus husband 'n' kids, obviously, that is.* She says, "A penny for your thoughts."

That phrase was starting to grate. "Uh . . . Bob Dylan."

"Close friend of yours, is he?"

"Nah. Saw him at the Albert Hall a couple o' years ago."

"Tony had tickets for that concert, but Martin had chicken pox, so he took Barbara Windsor instead. I heard the show was stormy."

"Half the audience was expecting 'Blowing in the Wind.' They got *crash bang wallop!* instead. And were not happy."

"I never quite grasp Dylan. When he's singing how 'you fake just like a woman,' then—what was it?—loving like a woman, and aching like one, but then breaking like a little girl, is he criticizing *his* girl's fragility in particular? Or is he saying that *all* women are fragile? Or what? Why isn't he clearer?"

"It's open to interpretation, I s'pose. But I like that."

She traces a circle around his nipple. "I prefer your songs."

"Oh, I bet yer say that to all the boys."

"Your lyrics are stories. Or a journey. Elf's too."

"Jasper's?"

"Jasper's songs are a bit Dylan-esque, in a way . . ."

"Now I'll have to kill him out o' sheer jealousy."

"Don't. This flat's perfect for these liaisons."

"I liked the Hyde Park Embassy."

"One should vary the scenes of one's liaisons . . ." *Sounds like she's done this before,* thinks Dean. "The staff are discreet—if you tip them—but it's a gossipy town, and Tony's not a nobody."

"When's he due back from Los Angeles?"

"The end of the month. It keeps changing."

The phone *ring-rings* in the hallway.

It's Ted Silver, thinks Dean, *with Mandy Craddock news.*

The phone *ring-rings* in the hallway.

"Aren't you going to get it?" asks Tiffany.

The phone *ring-rings* in the hallway.

"Stuff it. I'm enjoying you too much."

The phone *ring-rings* in the hallway.

"Tony would be sprinting down the hall," says Tiffany. "He's Pavlov's dog when the phone goes."

The phone *ring-rings* in the hallway.

Dean guesses Pavlov's some arty Russian filmmaker. The phone stops ringing. Tiffany lets out an odd sigh. "It's been a while since I was valued more than a telephone call."

They hear the key in the door of the flat. Tiffany tenses. "It's only Jasper," says Dean. "My DO NOT DISTURB sign's up."

She's still nervy. "You said he'd be out all day."

"I guess his plans've changed. He won't come in."

"Nobody must know about us. I'm serious."

"Me too. I don't want anyone to know either. I'll go 'n' tell Jasper I've got a coy visitor. When you leave, he'll hide. He's the opposite of nosy. It's fine."

Dean pulls on his underpants and dressing gown . . .

IN THE KITCHEN Jasper is drinking a glass of milk.

"How was the exhibition?" asks Dean.

"Impressive, but Luisa had an interview with Mary Quant so she and Elf went off to that, and I came back early."

"Elf's seeing a lot of Luisa."

Jasper studies him. "You've had sex."

"Why'd yer ask?"

"Love-bites, underpants and dressing gown, and . . ." Jasper sniffs strongly ". . . the smell of overripe Brie."

Ugh. "Look, the young lady's shy, so if yer'd retreat to yer room when she leaves, I'd be obliged."

"Sure. Elf's coming over at six so your friend ought to be gone before then. I won't peep, but Elf will."

BETHANY AT MOONWHALE looked at Dean over her typewriter and said, "Good morning, Dean"—almost as if nothing was the matter at all.

"Morning, Bethany. So, um . . ."

"Ted's in with Levon now." *Tappety-tap-tap-tap.*

Dean knocked and opened Levon's sliding doors. His manager and the lawyer sat at the low tables, smoking.

"Speak of the devil." Ted looked amused.

"Have a seat." Levon looked a lot less amused.

Dean propped his Fender against the filing cabinet and sat down. He lit his fifth Marlboro of the morning.

"So," said Ted, "to ask one of humanity's oldest questions, are you the daddy-o?"

"I dunno. I don't remember an Amanda. I meet a lot o' girls. But I don't keep a desk diary o' their names or nothing."

Levon reached for his desk diary and took out a snapshot of a young woman holding a baby. She had dark hair, dark eyes, and an ambiguous smile. The baby looked like any baby. Dean would file its mother under "Wouldn't Say No."

"Well?" asks Levon. "Jog any memories loose?"

"Nothing specific."

"Miss Craddock *is* specific," says Levon. "July the twenty-ninth. The Alexandra Palace Love-in. You played a slot between Blossom Toes and Tomorrow. She says you met backstage during the Crazy World of Arthur Brown's set, that you went back to her flat, above a launderette, and that nine months later," Levon held up the photograph, "Arthur Dean Craddock was born."

Abruptly, Dean's big vague cloud of doubt dwindled to a little white dot, like the TV at shutdown—and disappeared. *Shit shit shit.* The launderette. "Mandy" not "Amanda." She'd asked, "So do I get to see you again?" Dean used his "Let's not spoil a beautiful night" line. Her mother was folding clothes downstairs. She looked at Dean and said nothing. He escaped onto the quiet Sunday road. "We slept together."

"Which is neither legal nor hereditary proof," said Ted Silver, "that young Arthur sprang from *your* loins. Unmarried mothers have been known to lie."

Dean looked at the baby with fresh hope and fresh guilt. Was there a Moss-ness—or Moffat-ness—about him? He wished he could show the photo to Nan Moss, and feared doing so. She'd be furious. "I heard there's a blood test yer can do . . ."

The lawyer waggled a hand. "The blood group test rules *out* paternity in thirty percent of cases. It's no smoking gun."

"So what are my choices?"

Ted Silver picked up a ginger biscuit. "You could claim that you never met Miss Craddock. Inadvisable. If it went to court, you'd have to perjure yourself." *Munch* on the ginger biscuit. "You could agree that you and Miss Craddock were *in concubitus* on the night, but refuse to acknowledge paternity of the child." *Munch munch.* "You could acknowledge the child as yours and talk turkey."

"What's the price tag on this turkey?"

"Figures are contingent upon negotiations, naturally."

"Naturally. But."

"But if I were representing the Craddocks, I'd demand a lump sum equal to what a tabloid newspaper would pay, plus index-linked monthly support payments until the child turns eighteen."

"Bloody hell. What year'll that be?"

"Nineteen eighty-six."

The date belonged to an impossibly distant future. "All in, then, we're talking . . ."

"North of fifty thousand pounds. Index-linked." The office tilted and whirled like a spinning teacup at a funfair. Dean shut his eyes to make it stop. "Fifty thousand quid for one shag? For a kid who may not even be mine? No way. She can fuck off."

"Provisionally, then," says Ted, "we're looking at option two. You admit that you and Miss Craddock shared physical intimacies, but you do not acknowledge paternity of the child."

Dean opened his eyes. The room was back to normal. "Yeah. Do that. And, why didn't she come after me till she saw I've got a few bob to my name? Smacks o' gold digging, does that."

Ted looked at Levon. "Thoughts? Concerns? Consequences?"

Levon lit a cigarette. "If we'd marketed the band as the Stones, people would just say, 'True to form.' If we'd sold you as a sort of British Peter, Paul and Mary, it would kill you. But Utopia Avenue? It could go either way. There may be an element in the press saying, 'We should have let him rot in an Italian jail after all.' Elf's female fans may wonder why she stays in a band with a love-cheat sperm-gun. On the other hand, Dean's more red-blooded followers will think, *Nice one, my son.* Nor are these reactions mutually exclusive. It'll add up to column inches, that's for sure."

"Agreed. Right now, we play for time. I'll tell the Craddocks' solicitor that Dean's in a state of shock. I'll ask for, say, a fortnight's grace for us to put together a proposal regarding the next step. I'll make it clear that if the Craddocks speak to the press, any deal will be off the table. I also propose we do this blood test now. If Miss Craddock *is* a gold digger, she may be spooked into backing off. Either way, the blood test will cast Dean in a responsible light if we go to court later."

Court. Newspapers. Scandal. Ugh. "They're piss-poor, right, the Craddocks? Do they have the money for legal action 'n' that?"

"Awash with money they certainly are not."

"So if suing me looks like it'll cost an arm 'n' a leg . . ."

"They *may* cut their losses." Ted Silver tapped his pipe. "Mind you, if thirty years of legal practice has taught me anything, it's that a plaintiff is a fickle beast."

SIDE THREE OF *Blonde on Blonde* clicks off. "When Martin came along, Tony and I did a deal." Tiffany taps her cigarette on the ashtray. "I'd take a hiatus from my career and be Tony's ideal stay-at-home mother. In return, after five years, he'd make a film and cast me as the lead. Quid pro quo. I *am* an actress. *Thistledown* was one of *the* British movies of 1961. People know me from *Carry On,* from *The Tempest* at the National, from *Battleship Hill.* I'd missed being Honey Ryder in *Dr. No* by a whisker. So it was agreed. I did the nappies, bottles, nanny-organizing, sleepless nights, while Tony made *Wigan Pier* and *Gethsemane.* My agent had inquiries, but Tony said I should keep my powder dry for the big Tiffany Seabrook comeback. Last year he *finally* started writing *Narrow Road.* By 'he' I mean 'we.' I wrote more of it than Max, Tony's co-writer. Piper—the rock star's dead sister—is a *peach* of a role and it was mine. Until a fortnight ago. The day you bought your car."

"What's my Spitfire got to do with it?"

"Nothing. But when I got home, Tony was waiting with the news"—Tiffany's jaw clenches—"that Warner Brothers love the script. They'll put in half a million dollars *if* Jane Fonda plays Piper."

"Jane Fonda? On a spiritual odyssey to the Isle of Skye?"

"They want to shoot in LA and call it *The Narrow Road to the Far West.* It'll be all tits, mojitos, and bimbos."

Dean hears Jasper run a bath. "That's bloody nuts."

"It's a betrayal! So I told Tony to tell the Yanks where to shove their half-million dollars. Guess what his answer was."

I doubt you liked the answer, whatever it was. "What?"

"That he hadn't paid for his house, my jewelry, 'my' Midsummer Balls and nannies by turning down half a million dollars. End of conversation. A fait accompli."

Fay what? Fay Who? "That's a knife in the back."

"He tried to fob me off with a new role Warner Brothers want to add—a demented lesbian psychopath. I told Tony to piss off. So he did. Off to LA. To put starlets through their paces."

So, thinks Dean, *I'm a revenge shag. Do I mind?*

"I didn't mean to tell you all this," says Tiffany. "A secret lover who moans about her husband can't be very—"

Can't say I do. Dean kisses her—and hears a key in the front door—and abruptly pulls back from the kiss, listening.

"What's up?" asks Tiffany.

"Jasper's in the bath. So who just came in?"

Dean hears voices. His body redistributes blood, instantly. He slips on his trousers and a T-shirt and grabs a wine-bottle candlestick that might, at a push, function as a club. He slips out into the hallway. Jasper's got the radio up loud in the bathroom, so he may not have heard. Up ahead Dean sees two intruders through the curtain of beads . . .

DEAN YELLS AS he bursts through the beads. One of the burglars yelps, jumps back, terrified, hits the coat stand, knocks it over, and trips backward. The older one is calm. About fifty, in a conservative suit and tie, he stares at Dean as if he owns the place. Dean brandishes the bottle. "Who the *fuck* are yer and what're yer doing in my flat?"

"I own the place," says the older man in a foreign accent. "I am Guus de Zoet. Jasper's father."

"Yer *what?*"

"Did you think he was made in a lab? This is my son Maarten." Maarten, who looks about thirty, picks himself up, scowling. "So we ask you the same. Who are you? What are you doing in *my* flat? Put the bottle down. You are embarrassing yourself."

Dean sees the family resemblance. "I'm Dean. Jasper's flatmate. Thought yer were burglars. Sorry 'bout that."

Jasper appears with a towel around his waist, dripping onto the floor. He exchanges a few Dutch phrases with his father and half-brother. The reunion looks joyless. Dean is referred to. Jasper tells them all, "Give me a minute, I'll be right out," and retreats to the bathroom.

Maarten de Zoet picks up the coat stand. "You play bass in Jasper's band, I think."

"Utopia Avenue isn't 'xactly Jasper's band. If yer'd just've rung the doorbell, I wouldn't've, uh, jumped to the wrong conclusion."

"I telephoned," says Guus de Zoet. "An hour ago. Nobody replied, so we assumed nobody was at home."

Oh, thinks Dean, *so that was you.*

"How long have you been my tenant, Dean?" asks Guus de Zoet.

Tenant? Rent? Awkward. "I'll let Jasper answer that."

"Surely you can remember when you moved in?"

"Have a seat. I'll make a pot o' tea."

"Very English," says Maarten.

. . .

TIFFANY WAS EAVESDROPPING in case she had to scream into Chetwynd Mews for help. She's worried about being trapped in the flat. The Hershey nanny is expecting her home by seven P.M., and it's now gone five. Dean returns to the kitchen, where the two visitors are smoking Chesterfields, Jasper is smoking a Marlboro, and conversation is in Dutch. Dean turns to go, but the kettle is starting to boil and none of the de Zoets is making a move. Dean prepares the tea. During what feels like a lull in the Dutch dialogue, Dean asks, "What brings yer to London, Mr. de Zoet?"

"We are here three or four times a year."

"And this is the first time yer drop in?"

"I come to London for business, not pleasure."

Dean's about to ask, "What about family?" but remembers the unvisited Harry Moffat, pushes away the thought of Mandy Craddock's son, and brings the teapot over.

"We are expanding," says Mr. de Zoet. "I may visit more."

"Great." Dean pours the tea. "Uh . . . milk?"

"Milk is acceptable," states Jasper's father.

"How 'bout you . . . uh, do I call yer Maarten or Mr. de Zoet too?"

"Our ages are close, so you may use my Christian name. Milk is acceptable for me also."

"Okey-dokey," says Dean. "Beans on toast? Bowl o' Shreddies?"

Missing the irony, Guus checks his wafer-thin watch. "We are dining with the Dutch ambassador soon, so we will resist the temptation. It is best we address the matter in hand and leave."

"Soon" and "leave" sound good. "Address away," says Dean.

"You must vacate this flat by the end of July."

Yer what? "But me 'n' Jasper live here." Dean looks at Jasper, who is not surprised. They must have told him in Dutch.

"Yes, and from the first day of August," says Guus de Zoet, "Maarten and his bride will live here."

Jasper asks his half-brother something in Dutch.

Maarten replies in English. "In April, in Ghent. Zoë's people are in banking. She's the daughter of a friend of Mother. *My* mother, I mean, of course."

This family is screwed up, thinks Dean, *even by Moffat-Moss standards.* Jasper says, "Congratulations."

Maarten answers with a few calm Dutch words.

"Hang on a mo." Dean is not calm. "Yer did *say* Jasper was yer son and not some random tenant? I didn't dream that bit?"

Guus de Zoet sips his tea. "Jasper has discussed his . . . origins?"

"There's a lot of hours to fill 'n' kill if yer in a band. Yer talk. So, yeah. I *do* know how yer got his mum up the duff in India. And how yer acted like he didn't exist till his granddad bloody well made yer."

Guus de Zoet puffs on his Chesterfield. "You paint me as the villain of this movie."

"How d'yer paint yerself, Mr. de Zoet? The victim?"

"Not entirely. I acknowledge Jasper in law. We, the de Zoets, allow him to use the family name."

"Yer want a sainthood for that, do yer?"

Guus de Zoet makes a face like a reasonable man in vexing circumstances. "Young men make mistakes. Don't you?"

A bloody ton, thinks Dean, *but bugger me if I admit it.*

The Dutchman blows smoke away. "I paid for Jasper's education. For his summers in Domburg. For a sanatorium. I presume you know?" He looks at Jasper, who nods. "For his conservatory in Amsterdam. And for this flat."

"Which yer now kicking him out of."

"The fact is," says Maarten, "Jasper *is* illegitimate. That is not his fault. But he cannot have the same claims on the de Zoet name as I. Sorry, but this is how the world works. He accepts that."

"There's only two real bastards here." Dean folds his arms and looks at Maarten and Guus de Zoet.

"I am pleased Jasper has an"—Jasper's father *tap-taps* on the ashtray—"advocate. But, Jasper, I was clear that your tenancy was likely to be temporary? Correct?"

Jasper inspects the calluses on his fingers. "Correct."

Oh, for fucksake, thinks Dean. *Why do I bother?*

"You were not entitled to sublet," adds Maarten.

"I didn't," replies Jasper. "Dean paid no rent."

"Ah," smirks Maarten, "no wonder he's so upset."

"And with all your success," adds Guus de Zoet, "you will not have to sleep on a bench in Kensington Gardens, I think."

Maarten stands up. "I will inspect the two bedrooms."

Dean stands up. "No, yer won't."

"You are forgetting who owns this flat."

Dean sizes Maarten up. He's a couple of inches taller, pudgier, better teeth, smooth skin. *And more afraid o' getting hurt.* "We'll leave by September the first. But till then our rooms're private, matey. So yer can fuck off."

De Zoet Senior stubs out his Chesterfield. "Perhaps Dean is hiding an embarrassing secret, Maarten. The inspection can wait." He converses in Dutch with Jasper and the language-shutter falls. Dean retreats to his room, where Tiffany's getting ready to leave . . .

THE UNWELCOME DE Zoets are gone, Jasper is in the bath, and Janis Joplin is on the turntable. Dean washes up the tea things, telling himself that any similarities between his recent conduct and the younger Guus de Zoet's are superficial. He never lied to Mandy Craddock. He didn't get her pregnant knowing he already had a family. He has no proof that he is her baby's father. Dean opens a beer and sinks onto the sofa. *So we need a new flat by September.* He could afford a place of his own now. *I'd miss Jasper,* Dean realizes. When Dean first met this unsmiling, public school, half-Dutch weirdo he was a free place to stay, a great guitarist, and that was that. Eighteen months later, he's a friend. *There's so much in that word.* Dean tunes his new acoustic Martin and feels around for the "Sad Eyed Lady of the Lowlands" chords. D . . . A . . . G . . . A? He fetches the double album from his room, where Tiffany's scent still lingers, and puts side four on the stereo in the lounge. *"With your mercury mouth in the missionary times"* is D, A, G, A7. *"And your eyes like smoke and your prayers like rhymes"* has the same pattern, but the third line is different, as third lines tend to be. G . . . D . . . E minor? Dean tries picking instead of strumming. *Better.* Better. *Try an F minor instead of the G.* No, F. One spoon of Dylan makes a gallon of meanings. *Why don't I try to write lyrics like this?* A song about how one brief phone call can change what you are. How a call from Tiffany Hershey—"Join me for a cocktail at the Hilton"—turned them into adulterous lovers. How stability is illusory. How certainty is ignorance. Dean gets a biro and starts writing. Time slips. Jasper's out of the bath. Time slips again. The doorbell rings. Jasper's getting it. *It's probably Elf.*

Jasper's saying, "It's for you."

IT TAKES DEAN a moment to recognize the scrawny, zombie-eyed couple at the door as Kenny Yearwood and his girlfriend, Floss. "Hey, Kenny. Floss. It's been ages." Dean's mind boomerangs to the day of the riot in Grosvenor Square, and back to now. He stops himself asking, "How are yer?" The answer's clear: *They're junkies.*

Kenny's tense. "Has Rod Dempsey called?"

"Not recently, no. Why?"

"Can we step inside?"

They want money. "Sure, but me 'n' Jasper're off out."

"We won't be staying." Floss glances around the mews.

Dean lets them step into the hallway. They both have rucksacks. "We want our thirty quid," declares Floss.

What thirty quid? "Yer what?"

"Kenny lent it you at the 2i's," says Floss. "Last year."

"*That?* That was a fiver. Kenny, I paid yer back at the Bag o' Nails. The night Geno Washington was playing. Remember?"

Kenny turns away his bloodshot eyes.

"Thirty, it was." Floss pushes back her hair, revealing the crook of her elbow, a lesion, and needle damage. "You can't plead poverty now, pop star."

Dean asks Kenny, "Mate, what's going on?"

Kenny looks barely alive. "Give us a minute, Floss."

Floss is no longer the head-in-the-clouds hippie girl Dean met. She's fractured and sharp-edged. "Don't let him fob you off. Give me the cigarettes."

"Yer smoked the last one on the tube, Floss."

Dean has a packet in his shirt pocket and offers her one. Floss takes five and goes outside. Kenny says, "She's nicer than that. Nothing fucks yer up as bad as shame. So I'm learning."

"Kenny, what's happened?"

Jasper is noodling on his Stratocaster in his room.

"Crash us a ciggie too, would yer?" asks Kenny.

"Take the pack. What Floss left, anyway."

Kenny's hand's trembling. Dean helps him light up. Kenny takes a grateful drag. "When did I see yer last?"

"March. Grosvenor Square. Day o' the big demo."

"Yeah, me 'n' Floss tried smack a bit after that. Ever done it?"

"I'm scared o' needles," admits Dean.

"Yer can cook it on a spoon and suck the fumes up a straw, but . . . whatever yer do, don't go near the stuff. Yer know how everyone tells yer, 'Don't touch drugs,' and yer do 'em, and yer think, *They were feeding me bullshit*? Well, smack's the one where it's not bullshit. First time, it was . . . a-fucking-*ma*-zing. Like coming. With angels. Can't describe it." Kenny rubs a sore on his nostril. "But yer *have* to get that feeling back. Not 'want to.' Have to. Only the second time, it's not as good. Third time's not as good as the second. Down it goes. Now . . . yer gums're bleedin', yer feel like shit, yer hate it, but . . . yer need it to feel normal. Lost my job. Flogged my guitar. Rod gave us a few bags o' weed to sell. To pay for the smack, like. As a favor. I kept it under the floorboards in our room."

"The commune in Hammersmith? Rivendell?"

"Nah, there was a bust-up." Kenny flinches. "Rod got us into a place he owns on Ladbroke Grove. A no-questions-asked sort o' bedsit. A friend o' Rod's minded the door, day 'n' night, so Floss felt safe. All our earnings from the weed, though, went on smack. But yer need more 'n' more o' the stuff. So, last week, Rod said he'd pay us a fiver plus an ounce o' Afghan White a week for 'storage.' Meaning, he stored a stash o' coke under the floorboards in our room. It was our job to mind it."

Why'd Rod Dempsey trust two junkies to mind a stash of drugs? Dean is afraid he can guess.

"The Afghan was the purest we'd had in ages. The high wasn't like the first time, but it was like the fifth or sixth. Better than it'd been for ages. Two days later"—Kenny sucks the life out of his cigarette—"the coke was gone. The floorboards'd been lifted. I told Rod. Straightaway. He's got a psycho side. He screamed at me. Asked if I thought he was stupid. But we never nicked it. I swear on my life. On Floss's life. On bloody everybody's life. We never."

Rod Dempsey nicked it, Dean thinks. "I believe yer."

"When Rod calmed down, he told me that me 'n' Floss owed him six hundred quid. I told him we didn't have six quid. Six bob. So Rod said me 'n' Floss could pay him back by . . ." Kenny's finding it hard to talk, ". . . going to parties."

"What kind o' parties?"

Kenny's breathing speeds up. "Yesterday night, we were taken to a . . . a place in Soho, behind the Courthouse. Quite classy. Me 'n' Floss was separated. I was given a bath, scrubbed down, shaved . . . They gave me a dab o' smack—and . . . there was three men . . ."

"What?"

"Don't make me spell it out. F'fucksake, Dean. Use yer imagination. Yeah? What yer thinking, that's what they did. In turns. Get the fucking picture?"

The words are "drugged" and "raped," realizes Dean.

Kenny wipes his eyes on his sleeve. He tokes on his cigarette, sharply. "Floss was in the car. After. She didn't speak. I didn't. The driver did. We'd earned back ten quid of our debt, he said. Five hundred and ninety more to go. He told us to forget the police. They're paid off. If we ran away, he said our families'd be liable. He showed Floss a photo of her sister and said, 'Lovely little thing, ain't she?' Back at Ladbroke Grove we had a sleeping tablet 'n' ice cream and this morning we got Methadone. Floss told me to get her out o' this or . . . she'd kill herself. I know she's not bluffing. 'Cause I'm the same."

"D'yer want to hide out here?"

"This'll be one o' the first places he'll look."

"Why didn't yer ask for help off the bat?"

"Floss didn't think yer'd believe me. Do yer?"

"I didn't know Rod did *this*—but . . . I've seen how he puts hooks into people. Plus, how could yer make this up? Why would yer?"

Kenny, in the half-gloom, grips Dean's wrist.

Dean takes everything he has from his wallet—over eleven pounds—and puts it into Kenny's hand. "The heroin. I'm no expert, I know from Harry Moffat that just saying 'Quit what's killing you' does nothing. But if yer don't get clean . . ."

Jasper's noodling turns into his "Nightwatchman" solo.

Kenny stuffs the money into his pocket. "I'll get us out to the middle o' nowhere. Somewhere there's no dealers. Isle o' Sheppey maybe. I dunno. Find a bit o' shelter, and . . . we'll try cold turkey again. Yer feel like yer bloody dying. But that house in Soho, it was worse than dying."

The telephone rings. Kenny stands up, pale and shaking.

"It's okay," says Dean. "It'll be Elf to say she's late."

Kenny crouches, like a frightened animal. "It's *him.*"

"Honest, Kenny. Apart from at a party last month, I've hardly seen him." Dean picks up the receiver. "Hello?"

"Dean, how the *hell* are yer? Rod Dempsey here."

The air is sucked out of Dean's lungs. "Rod?"

Kenny's backing off, shaking his head.

Rod Dempsey does a friendly little laugh. "Yer sound . . . funny. Case o' speak o' the devil, is it?"

If I needed proof, this is it.

Kenny's left the flat. The front door's half open to the pale dusk. *I can't help him, 'cept by lying well enough to fool a world champion.* "Yer must be a bloody mind reader, Rod. Swear to God, ten minutes ago—no, five—me 'n' Jasper were talking 'bout the best dope we ever smoked, and we thought o' that Helmand Brown. Yer brought it over last autumn, with Kenny 'n' Stew? Remember that?"

"An unforgettable night. I can get yer some more, if yer want. Different batch, but just as good."

"Perfect. Yeah. Uh. We're just finishing the new album, but soon after, maybe? I'll give yer a call."

"Will do. Speaking o' Kenny, have yer seen him? I'm trying to track him down."

"So'm I, actually." *Hide yer lie in a haystack of facts 'n' half-truths.*

"Not since Grosvenor Square. He was in a commune out Shepherd's Bush way. Have yer seen him? Is he okay?"

Rod Dempsey calculates. "I met him 'n' his lady friend last month. The Commune was giving him grief, so he asked me to keep my ear to the ground. A pal's renting a place in Camden, all mod cons, good price. It's *perfect* for him 'n' Floss. Problem is, I've lost his number. Could yer track him down for me? Urgent, like."

Rod Dempsey's hiding his lies in half-truths too. "I'd like to help. I'm trying to think who might know. But I'm drawing blanks."

"That's the thing 'bout London," says the drug dealer, pimp, and God knows what else. "There's no knowing who's coming round the next corner. Is there?"

THE ONLY SIGNS of Kenny and Floss are two cigarette stubs on the bottom step. Evening is pooling in Chetwynd Mews. Dean's mind is a noisy Top Five chart of problems and crises. He opens the garage doors to visit his Spitfire. He switches on the bulb and stares at her. *The new place has to have a lock-up garage,* he thinks, *or a beauty like you won't last fifteen minutes.* It's too late for a drive, but Dean climbs in and tries to find a moment's peace. He doesn't. He could be some kid's dad. *That's the last thing I want.* An affair with Tiffany Hershey's a gratifying thrill, but *How's that going to end?* Being turfed out by Jasper's father is a pain, but it won't end in homelessness. *Kenny 'n' Floss, though, that's another matter.* Nothing can ever undo what's already been done to them. Even if—*when, if, if, when*—they kick the heroin, Dean knows their peace will always be frayed, will always have shadows at the edges. *Floss is right to hate me. I've got a part in this.* Kenny came to London because of Dean, and Dean did nothing to help him. *Nothing.* A figure crosses the mouth of the garage, stops, and looks in. "Hello, Dean."

It just comes out: "Oh, yer've got to be bloody joking."

Harry Moffat takes a shallow breath. "Been a while."

He steps into the yellow light. Dean has a good view.

Harry Moffat is both the same and different.

His liver spots are splotchier. His eyes have sunk.

He's shaved. His hair's neat. He's made an effort.

Dean stays in his Triumph. "Ray tell yer my address, did he?"

Harry Moffat shakes his head. "There's only two de Zoets in the phone book and Mayfair's likelier than Pinner. Yer might want to go ex-directory."

Dean stopped scripting possible encounters years ago, so now he has no store of lines to fall back on. "What d'yer want?"

Harry Moffat has a new, sad, unsure half-smile. "Don't know if I know, Dean. I . . . Well, first off, yer album's brilliant."

Yer used to belt my mum, and Ray, and me.

" 'Specially 'Purple Flames.' Yer really put it across."

Dean wonders where his own anger and contempt have gone. *Time's a fire extinguisher,* he thinks.

Moths flutter around the garage bulb.

"Lovely motor," says Harry Moffat.

Dean says nothing.

"We was worried about yer while yer was banged up in Italy."

Who's the "we"? Moffats? Gravesenders?

"Feels like a long time ago," says Dean.

"Guess yer've been busy? Tourin', recordin', 'n' stuff?"

Following a path yer used to shit on, a dream yer once poured paraffin on and set alight. "Yep."

"Yer've done well for yerself."

Dean can't help it: "Must be all the encouragement yer gave me." Harry Moffat flinches. *No, I won't feel guilty.*

"There's lots o' things I wish I'd done," says Harry Moffat. "Lots o' things I wish I'd never." He indicates a stool in the mouth of the garage. "May I? I won't keep yer, but my legs ain't what they was."

Dean's gesture says, *It's all the same to me.*

He sits and takes off his cap. Dean sees he's stopped trying to hide his bald patch. "I'm in this group. For alcoholics. Thanks to them, I ain't had a drink since . . . the accident. Yer heard 'bout that?"

"The man who can't walk and the girl with one eye?"

Harry Moffat looks at his hands. "Yeah. There's this lady in our group, Christine, she's my sponsor. She says, 'Not even God can change the past.' It's true. Yer can't always fix stuff or put it right. But yer *can* say sorry. Maybe yer'll be told to bugger off, maybe they'll smack yer, but . . . yer can say it. So . . ." Harry Moffat takes a deep breath and scrunches his eyes shut. Dean was sure today had no surprises left in it, but the sight of tears on Harry Moffat's cheeks proves him wrong. "So. Sorry for hitting yer, and yer mum, and Ray. Sorry I let yer down. Sorry I . . . didn't see yer mum's cancer. Sorry I was all yer had. Sorry I went off the rails after yer mum died. As if I was ever *on* the bloody rails! Sorry I burned yer stuff. Yer guitar. Bonfire Night. Sorry 'bout that time you'n'Kenny'n'Stew were busking. *I* did all that." He opens his eyes and wipes his cheeks with his palms. "I'm not blaming the drink. It was there, God knows, but . . ." He shakes his head. "Lots o' men in the AA, they never hurt a fly. I hit my family. That's on me, that is. I'm sorry." Harry Moffat stands up and puts his cap on. He's about to say one last thing when Elf walks up.

"Evening."

"You're Elf. Yer in the band."

"Ye-es. I saw the garage was open and . . ."

"Harry Moffat."

Elf frowns, and unfrowns. "Oh, my God, you're . . ." She glances at Dean and stops herself saying, *Dean's dad.*

"Yep. *That* Harry Moffat. Yer got a lovely voice, pet."

"Thanks. Thank you." Elf is confused. "Wait till you hear Dean's vocals on the new LP, though. He's been taking harmony lessons and he's got this song called 'The Hook' and, I'm telling you, he's *airtight.*"

"Yeah? I'll look forward to hearing it. A lot."

The stockbroker neighbor with the dog walks by, lobbing in a "Lovely evening." Dean holds up a hand in greeting.

Elf says, "Isn't it just?" and the neighbor's gone. Elf asks Harry Moffat, "So . . . are you . . . coming up to the boys' flat? Or is this a garage party?"

Every word of what he just said, thinks Dean, *was real. But I can't just flick a switch. It's been too long now.* "He's leaving."

"Bless yer, Elf, but I'm heading back to Gravesend. British Rail waits for no man." He nods at Dean. "Look after each other, eh?"

With that he slips off, like a man in a story.

Elf turns to Dean. "Are you okay?"

Dean taps out a rhythm on the steering wheel. "No idea, Elf. None. Look, I'll, uh . . . be up in a few minutes."

THE THIRD PLANET

SIDE ONE

1. **CHELSEA HOTEL #939** (Holloway)
2. **WHO SHALL I SAY IS CALLING?** (De Zoet)
3. **WHAT'S INSIDE WHAT'S INSIDE** (Holloway)
4. **TIMEPIECE** (De Zoet)

CHELSEA HOTEL #939

"WAKE UP, ELF." *IT'S WHO? IT'S DEAN.*

She hauls herself out of the quicksand of sleep.

"Cop a load o' that," says Dean, inches to her left.

She opens her eyes to find she fell asleep on Dean's shoulder. Through the airplane window, far, far below, is a metropolis of grays and browns, needlepointed by lights, a tapestry sliding as the plane banks. Elf's brain plays the opening bars of Gershwin's *Rhapsody in Blue.* "Well, that's one of the most beautiful things I've ever seen," murmurs Elf through a mouth gummy with sleep. *It's Lilliput, Brobdingnag, and Laputa, all in one.* Manhattan floats on glassy dark, a raft laden with skyscrapers. Beveled skyscrapers; skyscrapers sharp enough to draw blood; skyscrapers stippled with windows, ledges, and braille-like dimples; burnished skyscrapers, lovingly polished. "There's the Statue of Liberty," says Dean. "See?"

"She looks bigger in her pictures," says Elf.

"Looks like a garden ornament from up here," says Griff.

Elf checks on Jasper, to her right. His woolly hat is pulled down to his nostrils. "You alive in there, Jasper? Nearly there."

Jasper unrolls his hat to reveal bloodshot eyes, fumbles in his bag, and extracts a pill bottle, which he drops. He swears in Dutch.

Elf reaches for the bottle. "It's okay."

"Did I lose any? Find them all. All of them."

"No—the lid's still on, look. Let me open it. How many?"

Jasper gulps air. "Two."

Elf reads the label—Queludrin—and tips a couple of pills onto Jasper's sweaty palm. They are big and pale blue.

Jasper swallows them and screws the lid onto the bottle.

"What are they for?" asks Elf. "Nerves?"

"Yes." *Meaning, "Leave me alone."*

"We'll be landing soon," says Elf.

Jasper pulls the hat over his eyes and Elf returns to the view. *New York* . . . a toponym, a symbol, a stage, a byword for Heaven and Hell—but only now, in Elf's mind, does it qualify as a real place. Frame by frame, her imaginary New York, assembled from *West Side Story,* Spider-Man comics, *On the Waterfront, Breakfast at Tiffany's, Valley of the Dolls,* and gangster movies, is dissolving into a solidity of girders, bricks, blocks, cladding, wiring, plumbing, paving, traffic lanes, the tops of buildings, shops, apartments, and eight million people . . . one of whom is Luisa Rey. Elf's heart thuds. It hurts. *But why hasn't she answered my calls? My telegrams? My telepathic commands?* For all of August, Luisa and Elf airmailed letters to each other every day and spoke for a ruinously expensive five minutes every week.

Eleven days ago, the cards and letters stopped. Until day five, Elf told herself there was a logical explanation: a postal strike, somewhere, or a family emergency at Luisa's end. On day six, she rang Luisa's apartment. The line was disconnected. On day seven she called the New York *Spyglass* office only to be told Luisa was "away until further notice." No further details were forthcoming, however craftily Elf probed. On day eight, the logical explanation began to look sickeningly obvious: Luisa didn't feel for Elf what Elf felt for Luisa, and this most startling love of Elf's life had ended as abruptly as it had begun.

Yet a part of Elf holds out hope that the logical explanation is not the correct one. *Surely, surely, Lu would have told me. She wouldn't have dumped me in this cruel limbo where I don't know if my heart is broken or not, and have no way to find out.*

Would she? What if I didn't know her as well as I thought I did? It wouldn't be the first time. Would it, Baby Wombat?

She's counting days. *Like I counted days with Bruce.* The cruelest twist is that she has to suffer alone. Not a living soul knows about her and Lu. *Not a living soul can know . . .*

AT THE HERSHEYS' Midsummer Ball, Elf and Luisa found a quiet back staircase with a window seat big enough for them to hide in. The curtain pulled across, and they were hidden from the garden below by a gingko tree in midsummer leaf. It could have been designed for assignations. They talked about music and politics; families and childhood; London, California, and New York; dreams and time. They shared a cigarette, using a glass ashtray placed between them. They talked about who they loved now, and why. Elf spoke about Mark, and all the birthday cakes she would never make for him. "Bake them anyway," said Luisa. "With candles. They do in Mexico." Footsteps descended, past their hiding place; Luisa made a comic-conspiratorial face; the footsteps carried on. Elf wanted to kiss her new friend, more urgently than she had ever wanted to kiss anyone. One voice in Elf's head warned her, *She's a girl. Stop it. This is not okay.* A stronger voice in Elf's head replied, *I know, and she's the most beautiful person I've ever met; and why should I stop?*

Luisa and Elf looked at one another.

"So this . . . is happening, isn't it?" said Luisa.

Elf's pulse was fast and hard. "Yes. You're so calm."

"I'm guessing I'd be your first," said Luisa. "If . . ."

Elf was ashamed and not. "That obvious, huh?"

"I can see your heartbeat. Look." Luisa touched a vein in Elf's left wrist and the left side of her body melted. Luisa spoke softly. "I know what you're feeling. Social conditioning is a radio. It's blaring, *'It's wrong! She's a girl!'*"

Elf nodded, gasped, and sighed all at once, messily.

"Turn off the radio. *Click.* Like that. Don't overanalyze. In fact, don't analyze. I did and there was no need. Don't fret. You're not about to step through a one-way looking glass. You won't grow horns. You're not swapping the tribe of the Respectable for the tribe of the Perverts. Nobody needs to know. I'm safe. It's only two people. Only us. Only"—*that smile again*—"love."

A whoosh, a rush, and they were kissing.

Elf pulled back, flushed and amazed.

Honey, tobacco, and Bordeaux wine.

"Love," said Luisa, "with a dash of lust."

Elf stroked Luisa's face. Like she would a man's. Luisa stroked hers. Elf's heart vibrated like a double bass. Desire, desire, desire, and desire.

"Don't forget to breathe," whispered Luisa.

Elf nearly giggled. She took a deep, deep breath.

A door opened up the stairs. Elf and Luisa sat back. Two friends, enjoying a quiet catch-up, away from the party. Light footsteps came down to the window seat, and a small hand pulled the curtain back. A miniature blond boy with baby blue eyes peered in. He wore a cowboy hat with a sheriff's star. "This is my den."

"Correct," said Luisa. "What's your name, Sheriff?"

"Crispin Hershey. What are you doing here?"

"Actually, we're not really here," said Elf.

Crispin frowned. "Oh yes you are."

"Oh no we're not," said Elf. "You're dreaming us. Right now. You're in bed, asleep. We're not real."

Crispin thought. "You look real."

"That's dreams for you," said Luisa. "When you're *in* one, like you are now, it feels very *very* real. Doesn't it?"

Crispin nodded.

"We'll prove you're dreaming," said Elf. "Go back to your bed, lie down, shut your eyes, then wake up. Then come back, and we won't be here. Why? Because we never were. Okay?"

Crispin thought. "Okay."

"Off you go then," said Luisa. "Back to your room. Chop chop. No time to waste."

The boy turned and ran back up the stairs. Elf and Luisa climbed out of the window seat and hurried downstairs. Before they re-entered the party, Luisa asked, "What now?"

Elf didn't analyze. "A taxi."

. . .

THE BAND QUEUE at immigration control in LaGuardia Airport for one hour and twenty minutes. Jasper recovers some of his composure, if not his color. Griff, Dean, and Levon run through, and expand upon, the band's repertoire of time-killing word games devised during sixteen months of driving around the United Kingdom in the Beast. Elf is ushered to the booth of an immigration officer. The official squints at Elf's passport photo, then at Elf, over his iron-framed glasses. He has sugar on his mustache. "Elizabeth—Frances—Holloway." His voice drags itself wearily to the end of his sentence. "Musician, it says here."

"That's correct."

"What kinda music you play?"

Don't mention rock 'n' roll, Levon advised, or psychedelia or politics. "Folk music, for the most part."

"Folk music. Like that Joan Baez."

"A little like Joan Baez, yes."

"A little like Joan Baez. You do antiwar songs?"

An instinct cautions Elf. "Not as such."

"My eldest son signed up for Vietnam."

Thin ice. "That must be tough."

"Wanna know the worst part?" The man removes his glasses. "Over *there,* it's a goddamn slaughterhouse. Over *here,* goddamn freaks are free to burn draft cards, rut like rabbits, riot, and sing about peace. Who buys them that freedom? Kids like my boy."

Of the twelve immigration booths, thinks Elf, *why did I have to get this one?* "My own repertoire would be more traditional than in the protest area."

"Yeah? Traditionally what?"

"Traditional folk. English, Scottish, Irish."

"I'm Irish. Sing me something Irish."

Elf assumes she misheard. "I beg your pardon?"

"Sing me something Irish. A folk song. Or is this"—he waggles her passport—"just so much bullcrap?"

"You mean . . . you want me to sing—right here?"

"Yeah. That's exactly what I mean."

There's no higher authority to appeal to. *Okay then, an impromptu gig.* Elf leans in, taps out a 4/4 rhythm on the desk, looks through the man's lenses into his pupils, and takes a breath:

On Raglan Road on an Autumn Day,
I saw her first and knew
That her dark hair would weave a snare
That I may one day rue.

I saw the danger, yet I walked
Along the enchanted way
And I said, "Let grief be a falling leaf
At the dawning of the day."

The immigration man's Adam's apple bobs. He guides his cigarette to his lips and inhales a lungful of smoke. "Pretty." He stamps Elf's passport and hands it back. "Yeah."

"I hope your son comes home soon."

"He worked at a fuel depot. Near the front. An artillery shell came outta nowhere. Whole frickin' place went up like the Fourth of July. Nothing left of my boy but his dog tag. Nineteen years old, he was. A bit of metal. That's all we've got."

Elf manages to say, "I'm so sorry."

The bereaved father stubs out his cigarette, peers back at the queue, and motions at the next supplicating foreigner. *"Next!"*

"GOOD GOLLY, MISS Molly." Max Mulholland, the pink-cheeked, feathery-haired, pomaded A&R man of Gargoyle Records, is waiting in Arrivals with a very large card on which WELCOMING THE NAKED GENIUS OF UTOPIA AVENUE is written. Luisa Rey, the only person Elf wants to see waiting in Arrivals, is nowhere. Max Mulholland embraces Levon and groans like a lover. "Lev, Lev, Lev, Lev, *Lev.* You're all skin and bone. Is rationing still a thing in England? What are you living on? Roots? Berries? Solid air?"

"Wings and prayers, Max. Thanks for coming out."

"*Psshaw!* It's not every day I get to welcome an old friend *and* a new signing. Griff, Jasper, Dean, Elf. The Avenue." He greets them handshake by handshake. "You, sirs and mademoiselle, are mag-*nif*icent. Oh, my dear sweet God, I've heard an early acetate of *Stuff of Life* and it—is—a . . ." he mouths, "masterpiece."

"We're glad yer think so," says Dean.

"Oh, but I *do.* And Jerry Nussbaum in *The Village Voice* agrees." With a flourish, he produces a newspaper open to the right page. " '*Question: Mix a shot of R&B with a glug of psychedelia, add a dash of folk and shake well, and what do you get? Answer: Utopia Avenue, whose debut LP* Paradise Is the Road to Paradise *made a big splash in the band's native England. With sophomore effort* Stuff of Life, *this idiosyncratic quartet look set to make waves on our shores. So who in hell are Utopia Avenue? Miss Elf Holloway, who wrote Wanda Virtue's Top Twenty hit "Any Way the Wind Blows" when she was sweet sixteen, lead guitarist Jasper de Zoet and bassist Dean Moss provide two or three songs per head, ably anchored by drummer-of-many-parts Griff Griffin.*' "

"Sounds as if my arms and legs unscrew," says Griff.

" '*Invention is unflagging across the album's nine tracks,*' " Max reads, " '*from outrageously catchy opener "The Hook" to the contagiously Dylanesque closer, "Look Who It Isn't." Having three distinct singer-songwriters affords a spectrum of musicality few bands can match. Moss's ode to liberty "Roll Away the Stone" broods and rises to a Hammond-swirling climax with hell-hounds on its tail. Holloway's "Prove It" is a tragicomic stomper about love and theft, while her instrumental "Even the Bluebells" captures a genie in a bottle of deep jazz-blues. Virtuosic guitarist de Zoet brings the evensong "Nightwatchman" to the party, and magnum opus "Sound Mind." Whether Utopia Avenue can recreate the studio wizardry onstage will be revealed at New York's Ghepardo club this week, but be in no doubt—*Stuff of Life *is one shit-hot record.*' " Max looks up. "Welcome to America."

"Who's Jerry Nussbaum?" asks Levon.

"The kind of critic who'd look at a Michelangelo and complain the marble's too pale and the dick's too small. Jasper, you look like you want to puke."

"I'm not the world's best flier."

"We have vomit bags in the cars." Max nods at the two drivers, who nod at porters. "Let's go."

. . .

THE TWO LIMOUSINES leave the futuristic airport up a ramp to a highway on pillars. Levon, Jasper, and Griff travel in the first car; Elf, Dean, and Max Mulholland follow in the second. Dean strokes the walnut trimmings. "Lincoln Continental." Highway lights dot a path across the urban dusk to the glittering city. Paul Simon's new song "America" plays itself in Elf's head. *I imagined I'd be making this journey with Lu.* Dean turns to Elf, looking tired but excited. "It's a long old way from Brighton Poly, eh?"

"A long, long, long, long way away."

Streetlamps slide overhead. Pylons stride across wastelands, like Martian invaders. American trucks would dwarf British lorries.

"This view still gives me goosebumps," says Max.

"Are yer from New York, Max?" asks Dean.

"No. I endured a childhood in Cedar Rapids, Iowa."

"It's an idyllic name," remarks Elf, "Cedar Rapids."

"Beware idyllic names in the New World."

"So where'd yer meet Levon?" asks Dean.

"On our first Monday at the now defunct Flake-Stern Agency. We arrived to be told that just the one job was available, and that on Friday each of us would be given five minutes to persuade Messrs. Flake and Stern why he should get the job and his rival the chop."

"How gladiatorial," says Elf.

" 'Shitty' was the word I used," says Max. "We had both given up jobs for the Flake-Stern offer—and had my rival been anyone but Levon Frankland, I'd have spent the week plotting and backstabbing to save my skin. But Lev spotted in me what I spotted in him. We devised a pact and hatched a plot. We borrowed files from Accounts and did some midnight sifting at my apartment. Cometh the hour of doom on Friday, we made a joint statement that the agency would be offering us *both* full-time positions. Otherwise, on Monday the agency's clients would learn about the discrepancy between earned monies received and monies paid out. On Tuesday the clients' lawyers would start calling. By close of business on Wednesday, Flake-Stern would likely cease to exist."

"Yer blackmailed yer prospective bosses?" asks Dean.

"We presented them with a joint offer."

"It only worked because neither you nor Levon stabbed the other in the back," remarks Elf.

"My point exactly," says Max. "If you don't skin Levon's rabbit, he won't skin yours; and an honest manager in show business is as rare as rocking-horse shit."

ELF CLIMBS OUT of the limo, stands on a real downtown New York sidewalk—*not "pavement"*—and stares up. A Victorian Gothic edifice of windows and balconies towers halfway to the moon. A vertical sign reads HOTEL over a smaller horizontal CHELSEA. "It's an institution," says Max. "Long-term lets, mostly. A town within a city. People raise families here, grow old here, die here. Not that Stanley the manager'll admit that anyone dies here. Losts of folks assume the neighborhood's named after the Chelsea, it's that iconic."

"The Stones keep a penthouse here," says Dean.

"It's one of the few places in New York that'll take musicians," says Max. "Nobody cares how you look and the walls are thick."

"What's the population?" asks Elf.

"I doubt there's been a census since the 1880s."

A man with blood clotted under his nose melts out of the shadows. "Hey, y'all, need any uppers, downers, out-of-towners?"

The two drivers block the dealer while Max ushers the band through the doors of the Chelsea. A giant porter greets him like an old friend and Max puts a banknote into his hand. "If you'd give a hand with the bags and accoutrements . . ."

"You got it, Mr. Mulholland."

The lobby contains thirty or forty people sitting on the low sofas, nursing drinks by the carved fireplace, arguing, smoking, seeing and being seen. Elf guesses they include professors, actors, hustlers, prostitutes, pimps, and activists of the type railed against by the immigration officer. None of them is Luisa Rey. *You're going to have to stop this.* Many have hair as long as Jasper's and a wardrobe at least as adventurous as Dean's. Artwork of mixed merit covers the walls. "Stanley accepts art in lieu of rent," Max tells Elf as they reach the desk.

"Stanley never learns." A man with a long face and a flop of brown hair straightens up with a retrieved pencil. "A dozen kids a week show up, clasping a portfolio and telling me, 'I'm the new Jasper Johns, this is worth three months' rent, I'll need a double bed and a TV.' Max Mulholland. How the hell are you?"

"Stanley, you're looking like a million dollars."

"I'm feeling like dimes and pocket lint. Utopia Avenue, I presume. Welcome to the Chelsea. I'm Stanley Bard. I tried to get you adjacent rooms. I managed adjacent floors. Dean, Griff, I have you both in eight twenty-two."

"I'll be needing my own room," states Dean.

"Aye, the needing is mutual," says Griff.

"Eight twenty-two's a suite with two bedrooms," says Stanley, "and I glean from *The Village Voice* you're a Dylan-fancier, Dean."

Dean is cautious. "Who isn't?"

"Bobby composed 'Sad Eyed Lady of the Lowlands' in eight twenty-two."

Dean's face changes. "Yer bloody codding me."

"He said it has a special vibe." Stanley Bard holds the key by its fob. "There *might* be separate rooms on the third, if you—"

"Eight twenty-two'll do nicely, cheers." Dean cradles the key in his hand like a believer holding a nail from the Holy Cross.

"Elf, you're nine thirty-nine. Levon, nine twelve. Jasper, I'm putting you in seven seventy-seven. A Chinaman assured me it's the luckiest room in any hotel."

Jasper takes the key, mumbling, "Thanks." Elf asks in a perfectly natural voice, "Are there any messages for me, Stanley?"

"I'll check." He goes into the back office. The others move to the lifts, except for Dean.

"Hoping to hear from Luisa?"

Elf answers brightly. "Just on the off chance. She's dead busy with work right now. A big story."

Stanley returns. "Nothing, Elf. Sorry."

"I wasn't expecting anything."

. . .

ROOM 939 IS stuffy and smells of roast chicken. It is furnished with items not worth stealing: chenille bedspread, a chipped ceramic lamp, a barometer whose needle erroneously claims STORMY, and a painting of an airship. Elf unpacks, imagining Mark Twain, Oscar Wilde, and a survivor of the *Titanic* unpacking before her in this very room. She puts her framed photograph of the three Holloway sisters and their mother, taken by a waiter last year on the day Imogen announced her pregnancy. *Mark's there too, kind of.* Elf washes her face, drinks a cup of New York tap water, fixes her hair, and reapplies her makeup at the cracked mirror above the dressing table. *I bet Jasper covers his mirror with the bedsheet.* If *Stuff of Life* does well and Utopia Avenue has to do more international tours, Jasper will need better medication than Queludrin.

Elf opens the door onto the balcony. A cool night. Nine stories down, cars, people, and shadows flit. London exists horizontally, mostly: New York is a vertical place, enabled by elevators.

America. So it's a real place after all.

The band are meeting for dinner downstairs. Elf changes into the black chiffon tunic top and frayed cream bell-bottoms she bought with Bea in Chelsea, five time zones and two days ago. What to do about Luisa's seraphinite pendant? *If I wear it, I'm a desperate dyke who can't face reality. If I don't wear it, I'm discarding her, and the dying hope that this is all some misunderstanding.* Elf wears the pendant.

WHEN THE ELEVATOR stops at the ninth floor, the busboy who operated the archaic cage on the way up is missing. A well-groomed man of about thirty is the only occupant. Elf tries to open the outer door, but the handle is stiff and awkward. "Allow me," he says. "It's quite the operation." He slides the inner door across, twists the handle of the outer door up, and swings it open. "Step aboard."

Elf steps in. "Thank you."

"Any time." The man knows he is tall, dark, and handsome. He has a wedding ring and his aftershave smells of tea and oranges. "Your final destination this evening, if I may ask?"

"Ground floor, please."

"Keep your thumb pressed on G."

It's an odd instruction, but Elf obeys.

The elevator doesn't move.

"Huh. Odd. Let me ask Eligius."

Nobody else is here. "Who?"

"Patron saint of elevators." He shuts his eyes and nods. "Got it. Eligius says you have to release your thumb . . ." Elf realizes he's now talking to her, "now." She obeys, and the elevator resumes its slow descent. "Good old Eligius," says the man.

Elf works out the trick: the lift won't move until the button is released. "Funny. Moderately. Not very."

His amused eyes have double-folded bags. "So are you a new inmate at the asylum, or just visiting?"

The elevator descends through the eighth floor.

"Visiting."

"Who is your fortunate host?"

Elf chooses an unobtainable male to deflect the man's charm offensive. "Jim Morrison."

"Why, madam, you are in luck. I *am* Jim Morrison."

Elf tries not to find this funny. "I've seen lollipop ladies in Blackpool who look more like Jim Morrison than you."

He gestures surrender. "You've wrestled the truth out of me. Friends call me Lenny. I hope you will, too."

Elf replies with an is-that-so face.

The elevator descends through the seventh floor.

Lenny doesn't press for her name. His shoes are polished to a high gloss. "Be warned, this is the slowest elevator in American hostelry. If you're in a hurry, walk. It's quicker."

"I'm in no mad rush."

"Good for you. The word 'faster' is becoming a synonym of 'better.' As if the goal of human evolution is to be a sentient bullet."

The elevator descends through the sixth floor.

He speaks like a writer, thinks Elf. She tries to think of a literary Lenny or Len. "Are you a resident here?"

"Periodically, but I'm an incurable itinerant. Toronto, here, Greece. Is yours what is called a 'Home Counties' accent?"

"Yes. Not bad. Richmond, west London."

"I was in London eight years ago on a kind of scholarship."

The elevator descends through the fifth floor.

"What kind of scholarship?"

"The literary kind. I wrote a novel by day and poetry by night."

"How very Bohemian. Good memories?"

The elevator descends through the fourth floor.

"My memories of Bohemia-on-the-Thames," says Lenny, "are of landladies diddling the gas meters; complaints about the loudness of my typewriter; not seeing the sun for months; and a wisdom-tooth extraction going horribly wrong. I wouldn't have survived without Soho. The saucy twinkle in Mother London's eye."

"It's twinkling as saucily as ever. I live there. Livonia Street."

"Then I envy you. In part."

The elevator descends through the third floor.

Elf recalls Bruce's friend Wotsit. "I've heard Greece is lovely."

"It's many things. Paradoxical. Governed by a far-right junta, yet out on the islands, it's live and let live."

"How did you end up there?"

"One day, at the fag end of an English winter, I went to the bank on Charing Cross Road. The teller had a perfect tan. I asked him where he'd been. He told me about Hydra and I thought, *I'm off.* A fortnight later, the ferry from Piraeus dropped me at the quay. Blue sky, blue sea, cypress trees, whitewashed buildings. Cafés where fifty cents get you a dinner of grilled fish, chilled retsina, olives, and tomatoes. No cars. Intermittent electricity. I rented a place for fourteen dollars a month. I own one now."

"Sounds like Paradise," says Elf, "in many ways."

"The snag with Paradise is, it's hard to earn a living there."

The elevator reaches the ground floor. Elf opens the door.

"I'm dining with friends at Union Square," says Lenny. "If you're heading that way, you're welcome to ride in my taxi."

"Thank you, no. I'm heading"—Elf points at the door to the El Quijote restaurant—"all the way there."

"I'm glad we shared this epic voyage, mysterious stranger."

"Elf Holloway."

Lenny repeats it approvingly, lifts his hat like an old-fashioned gentleman, and crosses the lobby—before reappearing at Elf's elbow. "Elf, forgive me if I'm overstepping a mark, but sometimes one gets a feeling about a person. My friend Janet is hosting a small gathering on the roof terrace later. Very informal. Just a few fellow misfits. Time and energy allowing, drop by. Or drop up. Companions in your coterie would also be welcome."

"Thank you, Lenny. I'll think about it."

SPANISH MUSIC, BRASSY and tasseled, crackles from the El Quijote's fuzzy speakers. The vocals are another reminder of Luisa. A vast mirror doubles the room's apparent size. Jasper sits with his back to it. Waiters glide over the chessboard floor carrying trays of food. Nothing Elf sees on the trays or other diners' tables is familiar. Their party of six is drinking a cocktail—also new to Elf—called an Old Fashioned. "I wasn't looking for trouble," Max Mulholland is saying. "I was looking for talent. My logic was, if half a million kids are flocking to Chicago for a week of music and protest, there'll be a hundred buskers on the fringes, and of that hundred, five might be shit hot. A buddy staying at the Conrad Hilton for the convention offered me his sofa to bunk on. Now, I was expecting a San Francisco–style flowers-in-gun-barrels affair. How wrong I was. Not a flower in sight. Last year's *ten* years ago. We've had Martin Luther King's murder. Riots all summer. Vietnam's going to shit. In the run-up to Chicago, the Yippies were dangling stories about spiking the water supply with LSD. Garbage, of course, but the press eat that shit, shit it out, and people believe it."

"What's a Yippie when it's at home?" asked Griff.

"Youth International Party," says Levon. "An umbrella group for anarchists, idealists, antiwar, pro-drugs groups. It's quite West Coast, Merry Prankster–ish in spirit—right, Max?"

"Right, but Chicago is more Mayor Richard Daley in spirit," says Max. "Rich as Croesus, corrupt as Nero. He issued a shoot-to-kill policy for arsonists during the summer riots. Cops shot. Cops killed." Max's levity ebbs away. "Long story short, the Yippies' liberal base finked out. Only the MC5 and Phil Ochs turned up for the concert in Lincoln Park. Instead of a sea of half a million, there was a pond of a few thousand. One in six of whom was a Fed in a floral shirt. My hopes of finding the next Bob Dylan evaporated and I headed back to the Hilton. On Michigan Avenue, I overtook a big antiwar demo. It was getting dark. At the hotel, the TV crew lights were up bright on a phalanx of National Guards on one side and long-haired kids waving Vietcong flags on the other. In Chicago! Two weeks later, describing it to you now, the danger's obvious: here's a match, here's the kerosene. At the time, I just figured, *Hey, I'm a guest at the hotel, it'll be fine, I'll just walk through the cops and go inside.*" Max sips his Old Fashioned. "It happened like a dam bursting. A roar boomed up and suddenly—urban warfare. Bedlam. Bricks. Screaming. The crowd surged. The cops surged back, armed with nightsticks. They'll crack bones like hard candy if wielded right. And wielded right they were. The *Tribune* called it 'a police riot,' but most riots are better behaved than Chicago. Anyone was fair game. Straights in suits. Women. Cameramen. Kids. A&R men. Anyone not in uniform. The cops went for faces, groins, kneecaps. They drove vehicles fitted with 'slammers' straight into the crowd. They tore their numbers off so they couldn't be identified. This one cop locked eyes with me. He was the predator, I was the prey. I don't know why he chose me, but he waded straight at me. His intent was to smash my skull. I *knew* I should've run. But it was . . . like one of those dreams where you're just not in charge. I just stood there, thinking, *This is how I die, now, today, on Michigan Avenue with my brains spilling out . . .*" Max lights a cigarette and gazes at the back of his hand. "A boot in the back of my knee saved me. I went down with my face pressed on the road. Someone fell on top of me. A tear-gas grenade bounced, inches away. A big red can with a steel nipple on top. I crawled off, through a screaming, stomping, shouting churn of bodies. I found a kid, lit by a TV light. Busted nose, half a lip torn off, teeth gone, blood from a gash where his eye should've been. I still see that kid's face. Like a Kodak print." Max draws a label in the air. *"Peace Activist, 1968."*

"I thought Grosvenor Square was bad," says Dean.

"Were you able to get him out?" asks Elf.

"I took a blast of tear gas to my face. It's like your eyeballs are melting. I staggered away, so . . . no, Elf, to my abiding shame I never learned what happened to that kid. I found the back of the hotel where a porter stood by the kitchen entrance. Six foot six, armed with a rolling pin, mean—as—*cuss.* I said, 'Let me in.' He said, 'One dollar.' I said, 'People are getting slaughtered.' He said, 'Two dollars.' I paid. And saved my skin."

"That's the free market for you," says Griff.

"I've never associated America with violence," says Elf.

"Violence is on every page of our history." Max mops up his gazpacho soup with a crust. "Brave settlers massacring Indians. Some days we'd cheat them with worthless treaties, but mostly it was massacres. Slavery. *Work for me for nothing till the day you die, or I'll kill you now.* The Civil War. We industrialized violence. We mass-produced it, years before Ford. Years before the trenches of Flanders. Gettysburg! Fifty thousand deaths in a single day. The Klan. Lynchings. The Frontier. Hiroshima. The Teamsters. War! We need war like the French need cheese. If there's no war, we'll concoct one. Korea. Vietnam. America's that junkie outside the hotel, only heroin's not the drug we're hooked on. No, sir."

"All empires rest on violence," says Jasper. "The colonized resist looting and pillage, so the colonizers have to suppress the natives. Or replace them. Or kill them. The USSR's at it now. The French, in North Africa. The Dutch in the Dutch East Indies, until recently. The Japanese in the last war. The Chinese in Tibet. The Third Reich all over Europe. The British, everywhere. The USA's hardly unique."

This is the most Jasper's said since they left London.

Elf's worried about him. *There's something wrong . . .*

Max dabs his lips with the linen napkin. "Here in the land of the free, you'll meet some of the gentlest, smartest, wisest people who ever lived. But when violence comes, it's merciless. Without warning. Out of the bluest sky. Quick as that." Max mimes a gun going off. "Enjoy the land of the free. But be careful."

. . .

DEAN AND GRIFF decide to join Elf at the rooftop gathering of Lenny's friend. Jasper bows out. Utopia Avenue's first show is tomorrow night, preceded by a day of media. Waiting for the elevator, a bearded man in an angel robe and wings approaches Griff: "I'll flagellate myself later if I don't ask you, where *did* you get those cheekbones?"

Griff reddens. "My cheekbones?"

"Your cheekbones are *deee*-vine."

"Uh . . . thanks. They came with the rest of me."

"Sweet God above. Your accent! A*dor*able. I'm Archangel Gabriel and you are?"

Elf helps out. "His friends call him Griff."

"I'll pray we'll be friends, Griff. Look, your elevator's here."

"Going our way, Gabriel?" asks Dean. "Griff'll be happy to make space for yer in the back."

"I'll fly up the shaft later, thank you."

Inside the elevator, Dean presses *R* for *Roof*. Jasper presses 7. The angel flutters her fingertips. "Don't be a stranger."

The elevator begins its grinding ascent. Dean peers at the drummer's cheekbones. "*Deee*-vine."

"Fook off," says Griff, amiably.

Elf asks Jasper, "Are you still feeling sick?"

Jasper doesn't realize he's being spoken to.

Dean clicks his fingers in front of Jasper's face.

"What?"

"Elf just asked if yer feeling any better."

Jasper frowns. "I have my doubts."

"Doubts?" asks Elf. "About what?"

"About what comes next," says Jasper.

Dean loses patience. "Don't be such a wet bloody blanket. We're playing New York. It's what we've always dreamed of."

Jasper presses 4. The elevator stops. He lets himself out and takes the stairs. Dean slams the doors and presses *R* again. "When he's in his tortured genius mood he's bloody impossible."

Jasper doesn't have "tortured genius moods," thinks Elf. She resolves to knock on his door later, after the party.

. . .

CAMELLIAS IN TUBS, topiary in planters, cosmos in pots are flourishing. Candles blink green-gold in jars and blue-gold in lanterns. A pyramid-shaped penthouse and a giant slabbed chimney enclose the rooftop garden on two sides, and railed walls complete the rectangle. Two or three dozen people sit around talking, smoking, and drinking. Dope flavors the air. A swashbuckling guitarist is sitting on a bench fingerpicking, superbly, with a trio of women at his feet. *Mum would call him a dreamboat,* thinks Elf. Then she thinks of Luisa. It hurts.

"Elf." Lenny appears, martini in hand. "I'm so very glad you're here, but I'm mortified that I didn't recognize you, earlier."

Dean recognizes him and blurts it out: "Leonard Cohen!"

The singer shrugs. "I've given up pretending otherwise."

Dean turns to Elf. "Why didn't yer warn us?"

"I . . ." Elf's blushing. "Lenny, sorry, I feel awful." She turns back to Dean. "He doesn't look like his picture on the LP."

"Which is *my* defense for not recognizing *you,*" says Lenny. "Griff, Dean, I know *Paradise.* My friend on Hydra plays it constantly."

"The number of times I've played 'Suzanne' in clubs," says Elf. "Lord, the royalties I must owe you . . ."

"For a bourbon on ice, and the chords to 'Mona Lisa,' I'll call off my lawyers. Do you know our hostess, Janis?"

A woman turns around. She wears a pink boa woven through her hair, the gown of a damsel in distress, and enough bracelets and chains to open a stall, and is one of America's most famous singers.

"Janis fookin' *Joplin*?" This time it's Griff who blurts.

"Utopia Avenue!" She has a ten-thousand-volt smile.

"You're *class* you are, Janis," says Griff. "Real class." He turns to Elf. "So yer didn't know this was her party?"

"I misheard Lenny," explains Elf. "I thought 'Janis' was 'Janet.' "

Janis Joplin puffs on her cigarette. "When Lenny told me he'd met a London Elf, I thought, *C'mon, how many Elves can there be?* So I phoned Stanley and, lo, the truth was revealed."

Elf blinks. *Janis Joplin knows my name.* "Did our airplane go down off Newfoundland? Is this Heaven?"

"Janis's parties are *much* more fun than Heaven," says Lenny.

"If fire could sing," Elf tells Janis, "it would sing like you."

Janis sighs. "I can't let compliments like that go, y'know, unanswered." Elf loves how her accent turns "can't" into "cay-ant." "I got a copy of *Stuff of Life.*" Janis twists a string of amber beads around her little finger. "I—*lost—my—shit.*"

Elf looks at Dean, who looks at Griff. "We're still learning American. Is losing shit a good thing or a bad thing?"

"A great thing," affirms Lenny. "We dug *Road to Paradise,* too. It helped me and Janis get through last winter."

Elf intercepts his glance at Janis. *They're together; or have been.* She points to the pyramid. "This is where you live, Janis?"

"It's from a fairy tale, isn't it? Not the cheapest pad in the Chelsea, but why work as hard as we do if you don't live a little?"

"The Pyramid has an illustrious guest book," says Lenny. "Arthur Miller and Marilyn Monroe rented it. Jean-Paul Sartre. Sarah Bernhardt. The one and only Janis Joplin . . ."

Janis looks around. "Where's Jasper?" she half whispers. "How do you say his surname?"

" 'Zoot,' " replies Elf. "Gone to bed. He and flying do *not* get on, and our four nights at the Ghepardo begin tomorrow."

"Some folks here'd like to meet him. Jackson, for one." She nods at the glossy-haired, fingerpicking dreamboat. "Come inside and try my peach punch. My daddy's recipe. And I do believe . . ." she squints at her watch, ". . . it's reefer o'clock."

THREE GUYS HAVE made passes at Elf. Each one makes her miss Luisa a little more. Janis Joplin finds her in a corner of the Pyramid and places an opaque cocktail in Elf's hand. "Try this. The Brutal Truth. That's its name. My cocktail man created it for me. Gin and nutmeg with a dash of damage." They clink their Brutal Truths and drink. "Holy God above," declares Elf.

"Was the runner-up name."

"That could propel missiles."

"Here's hoping, Lady Englisher. Tell me a thing. Have you worked out a method for this?"

The Brutal Truth anesthetizes Elf's esophagus. "A method?"

"How to do what we do, as a woman."

Close up, Elf sees crazed veins in the whites of Janis's eyes and scars on her face. "I don't have an answer. That's the brutal truth."

"Ain't it, though? If you're a guy, it's easy. Sing your songs, shake your tail feathers. After the show, go down to the bar and score chicks. But if you *are* a chick who's a singer, what're you supposed to do? *We're* the ones being scored. The bigger the star we are, the *more* that's true. We're like . . . we're like . . ."

"Princesses in the age of dynastic marriages."

Janis bites her lower lip and nods. "And our fame raises the value of locker-room bragging. Which the guys gain from. 'Oh, yeah, Janis Joplin? I know Janis. She gave me head on the unmade bed.' I hate it. But how do you fight it? Or change it? Or survive it?"

The Byrds sing "Wasn't Born to Follow" on a superb hi-fi.

"I'm not on your level yet," says Elf. "Have you any advice?"

"No advice. Only a fear and a name: Billie Holiday."

Elf takes a third sip of Brutal Truth. "Didn't Billie Holiday die a heroin addict with no functioning liver, under arrest on her deathbed, with only seventy cents in her bank account?"

Janis lights a cigarette. "That's the fear."

AN AMERICAN MOON is wedged between two skyscrapers, like a nickel fallen down a crack. Elf looks through the railing over the city. *The edge of a battlement on the eve of war.* Her core is buzzing from the Brutal Truth. Her extremities are buzzing from Janis's weed. She imagines Luisa appearing like the Virgin Mary in Janis's rooftop garden, and aches that it can't happen. Elf remembers feeling grief when Bruce dumped her for Vanessa the Model. Losing Luisa feels more like the loss of a body part. *What did I do wrong? It must have been me. It must have been.*

"Is that one"—Dean points—"the famous one?"

Elf has no idea what Dean means. Leonard Cohen replies. "The Empire State. The tallest building on the planet."

"Where's King Kong, swatting the biplanes?" asks Dean.

"He's had his hours cut," says Lenny. "Times is hard."

In the windows of nearer, lower buildings, a few lamps are still on. *Each square light,* thinks Elf, *is a life as big as mine.*

"Hear that?" asks Dean, cupping his ear.

"What are we listening to?" asks Elf.

"New York's soundtrack LP. *Shhhhhh . . .*"

Beneath the party chatter and Sam Cooke singing "Lost and Lookin' " lies a composite hum of engines, cars, trains, lifts, horns, sirens, dogs . . . everything. Doors, locks, drains, kitchens, robberies, lovers. "It's like an orchestra tuning up," says Elf, "except it's the main show. A cacophony symphony."

"She says things like that," says Dean to Lenny, "even when she's *not* on the baccy."

"Elf's a natural-born poet." He turns those I-see-your-soul brown eyes on her in the moonlight.

"You're a natural-born flirt, mister," thinks Elf, and realizes she just said it out loud. *Janis's weed. Hey-ho.*

"I've changed my plea to 'Guilty,' " concedes Lenny.

Elf imagines Lenny asking Dean about her boyfriends and Dean telling him, and Dean asking Lenny about Janis, and Lenny telling him. Women share intelligence in the Battle of the Sexes: *men, surely, do the same.* She misses Luisa more than ever. She is her refuge from all that. *Was. Is. Was. Is.*

"Why'd yer leave New York?" says Dean to Lenny, looking out at the city of their dreams. "Once yer were settled here?"

"I'm not one of life's settlers. I came here to write The—or just A—Great American Novel. I wince at the cliché. I fancied myself a big fish in a small pond, but I wasn't even a fish. I *was* susceptible to distraction. Greenwich Village. Beatnik readings. Folk sessions. I went on long walks, posing as a flâneur, but only the French can get away with that. I watched the boats on the East River. Once, I took the elevator up there." Leonard nods at the Empire State Building. "I looked over Manhattan and was seized by an absurd desire to take it. To *own* it. Do we write songs as a substitute for possession?"

"I write songs to discover what I want to say," says Elf.

"*I* write 'em 'cause I just bloody love it," says Dean.

"Maybe you're the purest artist here," remarks Lenny.

A stoned voice calls from the Pyramid. "Hey, Lenny! We need you to adjudicate."

Lenny calls back. "On what?"

"The difference between melancholy and depression."

Leonard Cohen looks apologetic: "Duty calls . . ."

"HE'D BE UP for it if you are," Dean tells Elf.

"You sound like a pimp. Or a go-between."

"Just worried my bandmate's not getting a lot."

Is that sweet? I don't know. "Janis tells me he has a kind-of wife and stepkid in Greece. Call me picky, but I'll pass."

Dean passes her the joint. "Nine months without any action . . . I'd be going bloody mental."

"Action"? Like a military exercise. Elf inhales, lets the smoke out, and warns herself that anything she says about Luisa can't be unsaid. Sam Cooke has moved on to "Mean Old World." "Men," says Elf, "*need* to get laid. For women it's less of a 'must' and more of a 'might be nice' or a 'possibly.' We can't win. If we don't play the game, we're frigid or we can't get a man. If we play the game too much, we're a slut, the village bike, damaged goods. Not to mention the joy of an unplanned pregnancy sitting in the corner of the room, watching you getting it on." Elf passes him the joint. "None of which is your fault. But you should know: patriarchy is a stitch-up."

"Yer an education." Dean flicks the dead joint into the void. "My paternity woes've shed a new light on casual hookups."

So he wants to talk. "Have you decided anything?"

"The test result'll be waiting when we fly back, but it ain't a straight yes or no. If I *ain't* the baby's father, there's a ten percent chance the blood groups'll say so for sure."

"That's hardly conclusive."

Dean says nothing for a while. "I s'pose we'll wait till the kid's old enough for family features to show up. Do I pay 'Miss Craddock' any money till then, though? That's the question. If I'm *not* the dad, and

I pay, I'm a bloody mug. But if I *am,* and I pay nothing, what's the difference between me 'n' Guus de Zoet?"

Shouts float up from the street thirteen floors below.

"If I had three wishes," says Elf, "I'd let you have one."

"When Levon first called me with the news, I'd've done anything to wish it away. Anything. But now, even if this kid isn't mine, he's someone's. Yer can't wish life away. Can yer?"

Elf thinks of Mark and Mark's tiny coffin.

"Oh, shit, sorry, Elf. My big mouth. I'm a bloody eejit."

Elf squeezes Dean's hand. "No. Life's precious. We forget it. All the time. We shouldn't wait until a funeral to remember."

Dean peels the label from his beer bottle. "Yeah."

"I LOVE YOU all," Janis Joplin stands on a pedestal in the garden, "but I've a session tomorrow, so I'm volunteering Jackson to play one of his for the road home, and he's volunteered me to sing it."

Jackson counts them in, then plays the same descending cascade, ending in a major seventh. The breeze ruffles his hair. Elf recognizes the opening of "These Days" from the *Chelsea Girl* LP, but where Nico sings it with icy Nordic sobriety, Janis scorches the song, varying the color from phrase to phrase. *It's a trick,* Elf thinks, *to keep your attention, and she's really good at it.* Jackson improvises a bridge before the final verse and Dean whispers in Elf's ear, "Handsome Pants is a player *and* a looker."

Elf whispers back, "Worried you've met your match?"

Janis serves up the last four lines a cappella. Jackson emulates a bell on his guitar, chiming ten times:

Please don't confront me with my failures
I had not forgotten them.

Two dozen people on a rooftop in New York applaud. Janis performs a wobbly curtsy. Jackson bows. Someone asks, "One more, Janis?" She laughs her bronco-bucking laugh—"For *free*? Get outta here! Maybe Lenny has something up his sleeve."

The Canadian permits himself to be cajoled to the front and receives Jackson's Gibson with a smile. "Friends. If you insist, here's a song I first learned at Camp Sunshine, aged fifteen. There, I acquired my trademark sunny disposition, and the rest is musical history." He tunes the guitar by ear. "Two Free French fighters-in-exile wrote it in London, and it's called 'The Partisan.' And a-one, two, three, four . . ."

Lenny's guitar skills are basic compared to Jackson's and his voice is both nasal and gravelly, but the song gives Elf goosebumps. Its narrator is a soldier who cannot, as ordered, surrender, as the enemy pour across the border. Instead he takes his gun and vanishes into the frontier to survive, somehow, until freedom comes. The lyrics are telegrammatic yet vivid, like instructions for a short play to be staged in the listener's imagination—*There were three of us this morning, I'm the only one this evening* . . . There is no wordplay. There are no tricks. The song barely rhymes. Elf thinks how hard "Prove It" tries to impress, and feels embarrassed. "The Partisan" just is. Leonard sings three verses in French, then the song ends in English in a graveyard with a resurrection, of sorts. Elf is gripped and moved. The bearded angel from the lobby earlier, whose arrival Elf didn't notice, murmurs in her ear, "It's as much a séance as a song." The applause is warm. Someone calls out, "A surefire smash from Lenny 'The Hit Factory' Cohen!" The Canadian smiles and shushes the applause. "I wish to nominate a new friend for the last song, but she only flew in today, so she mustn't feel pressured. However. Might Miss Elf Holloway bless us with her musical grace?"

Everyone looks at her. Dean looks hopeful.

It's easier to do it than not. "Okay, then, but—" Cheers smother Elf's disclaimer as she perches on the barstool and Lenny hands her Jackson's guitar. "If it all goes tits up, I'm blaming Janis's weed. Um . . ." *What to sing?* "I'll try something I wrote on the plane." *Back when I hoped Lu might be waiting at Arrivals.* She takes her notepad from her handbag and sits a candle-jar on the corner of the page. "It follows the tune of an old English folk song, 'The Devil and the

Pigman.' Could anyone lend me a plectrum?" Jackson hands her his. "Thanks." She counts herself in.

As far off as an icy glare
is from summer laughter—
as "Once upon a time" is from
"Happy ever after"—

As far off as the brutal truth
is from prose gone purple,
as far away as death from birth
unless life is a circle—

Pluto and the far-off Sun—
how far you are from me.
As far as "now" from "never" is,
philosophically—

Elf strums and hums a bridge but doesn't attempt a solo—Jackson's virtuosity is too fresh in her ears, and she hasn't written a song on the guitar since joining Utopia Avenue. "Insert a Jasper de Zoet solo here," she tells the roof garden, "on Spanish guitar, something frisky . . . with Dean on harmonica, *here,* maybe"—Elf gently howls how the solo might go—"like a homesick werewolf . . ." She glances at Dean who nods back *Yer got it.* Part two . . .

Yet love collapses distances—
love, and curiosity.
Love is a kind of telescope—
love is pure velocity.

Love ignores the rules of love—
those rules stamped on the heart.
Perhaps those rules had reasons, once.
Perhaps those reasons weren't so smart.

Love comes and goes, a feral cat—
unbound by human vow.
Humbly, then, I beg of love—
be here now.

Elf strums another vocal-less verse and inverts the melody, closing on a stumbled-upon chord she doesn't know the name of—an oddball F—that leaves a question hanging in the air. People applaud. *It works.* She looks at these new, brief acquaintances, these strangers, at Janis and Lenny, at Griff—*drunk*—and at Dean who's placed a hand on his heart to say, *I love it,* and at Luisa Rey, her hawkish eyes and faraway smile. *No no no—this is too much, too scripted.* Elf doesn't smile, yet; she can't. She's too astonished. It's too corny. *You don't just show up as I'm singing verses written specifically to conjure you.* Then Elf thinks, *This is New York—the moon is full—why am I even surprised?*

"THEY TOLD ME they'd kill me if I didn't leave the city," says Luisa. "My editor was warned by his NYPD guy that the threat was genuine."

"My sweet God, Lu." Elf wants to hug her close, and she could if Luisa was a boyfriend, but Janis Joplin's rooftop is too public.

"The cops told the *Spyglass* staff to hang up on anyone trying to find out where I was. That's why you got the brush-off. I'm only sorry my note didn't reach you. I assumed it would."

"Stuff that. You poor thing. It sounds . . . hideous."

"A story about protection rackets was never going to be popular. We just didn't think it would blow up so quickly."

"Where did you go?" asks Elf. "Your parents?"

"I didn't want to risk it. Dad's in Vietnam, Mom's alone. A friend has a log cabin in the mountains near Red Hook, upstate."

"And yer sure yer out o' danger now?" asks Dean.

"I got lucky. A Mafia feud came to a head. Six people were shot dead in New Jersey yesterday. Two of them were the . . . gentlemen who had threatened me and *Spyglass.* My editor's detective reckons we should be out of the woods. I live to write another day."

"It's a fookin' gangster movie," says Griff.

"Less fun, more squalid, a lot more real."

IN ROOM 939's tiny kitchenette, Elf makes hot chocolate for Luisa, fresh out of the shower. "My mind keeps replaying the last week and a half," says Elf. "While I was all 'Poor me' you were this far from a bullet."

"You didn't know." Luisa wraps her hair in a towel. "I didn't know you didn't know. I couldn't tell you. We've survived."

"Would asking you to stick to restaurant reviews work?"

"Would asking you to write bubblegum pop songs work?"

"Never get so numb to danger that you get blasé. Promise me."

"My dad warns me against *exactly* that danger." Luisa kisses her. "I promise." They step onto the balcony and sit in deck chairs with their hot chocolate, like two old people on holiday. Luisa lights them each a Camel. They watch each other, and take a drag simultaneously so the tips glow in unison—and laugh.

"Guess what I'm doing now," says Elf.

"What are you doing now?" asks Luisa.

"I'm sending a mind-telegram back in time to myself. To the night at Les Cousins when Levon and the boys invited me to a tryout. And in that mind-telegram, I'm telling myself, 'SAY YES.' "

"And?"

"And this: *Because if you say yes, then over the next twenty months, you'll record two LPs; go on* Top of the Pops; *play dozens and dozens of shows; earn some money; have a few ups and downs with your love life; go to New York; be flirted with by Leonard Cohen; share a sister-in-music confession with Janis Joplin; but best of all, you'll meet a smart, funny, brave, kind, future Pulitzer Prize–winning*"—she hushes Luisa's objections—"*and very sexy Mexican-Irish-American woman—yes, a woman. You'll make mad, passionate love with this woman—*"

"God, you sound *so* English."

"Shush —*You'll make mad passionate love in the Chelsea Hotel, and drink hot chocolate, and you won't ask yourself* 'Am I a lesbian now' *or* 'Am I bisexual?' *or* 'Was I repressed before?' *or* 'Am I now?' *or any of that. No. You'll feel true and right and . . . you'll run out of words for how good you feel. So for your own good . . . SAY YES.* Here ends my mind-telegram. STOP. Send."

"I love your telegram," says Luisa. "Though it's turned into a letter, really, hasn't it?"

Elf nods, smokes, sips her hot chocolate, and holds her lover's hand. Nine floors below, a yellow cab prowls West 23rd Street by the Chelsea Hotel, looking for a fare . . .

WHO SHALL I SAY IS CALLING?

JASPER WAS EIGHTEEN. QUELUDRIN WAS FAILING. KNOCK Knock was resurgent and eroding his mind. His resistance might last weeks. It wouldn't last months. Three mornings after Heinz Formaggio had embarked for his American future, Jasper decided that a quick release was better than being reduced to mental rubble. Jasper got dressed, washed his face, brushed his teeth, and went down to breakfast. The auctioneer from Delft narrated his dream in a quick-fire mumble. After breakfast, Jasper went to the dispensary, as usual. The ink of *J. de ZOET* on his pill-tray label was fading. Jasper took his two pale-blue Queludrins. Dr. Galavazi was away at a symposium.

Up in his room, Jasper put a note inside his guitar case: "For Formaggio, if he wants it." He put on his coat, retrieved a dusty rucksack from the top of his cupboard, went to the main entrance, and asked for a morning pass. The junior psychiatrist on duty was surprised by the shy agoraphobe's request. Jasper told a plausible lie about the benign influence of his friend Formaggio. The duty-doctor asked if he wanted a companion. "I want to conquer my demon myself," said Jasper. "I won't go far." Satisfied, the psychiatrist wrote out the pass, noted the time in his logbook, and signaled to the gatekeeper that the young patient had permission to leave . . .

OUTSIDE THE WALLS of Rijksdorp, Jasper found everything different and everything the same. The morning was muted. The sky was veiled. The woods smelt of autumn. Dead leaves drifted on the liquid wind. Pines shushed and soughed. Crows hatched plots. Faces surfaced from tree trunks. Jasper didn't meet their stares. The path twisted upward. The wood petered out. Dunes fell and rose. Surf pounded the shore, not far off. Grass whiplashed. Gulls cried. The sea looked dirty. A sign warned would-be swimmers: GEVAARLIJKE ONDERSTROOM. VERBODEN TE ZWEMMEN. The tide was in. Waves shunted shingle up the beach; the undertow sucked it back. Scheveningen cluttered the southern distance. Katwijk lay five miles to the northeast. Mud grays, sandy grays, pale grays. Slimy groins sloped into the surging water. Jasper filled his rucksack with big pebbles. This was less messy than razors, he told himself, more reliable than pills, less Gothic than a rope, with no witnesses to shock and scar. Jasper strapped on his rucksack. It felt as heavy as him. Jasper went over his instructions one last time: walk into the sea; keep walking; when the water is up to your chin, fall forward, with the weight pressing you down. Open wide. Everlasting Queludrin. Milly Wallace was buried at sea. The Only Sea. The Ceaseless Sea. The Last Sea.

Jasper asked, "Are you still sure?"

Jasper replied, "A person is a thing who leaves."

Jasper strode into the sea. It filled his shoes.

It wrapped around his knees, his thighs, his waist . . .

DON'T, SAID A voice. All noise ceased. No sea, no wind, no gulls. *You can't undo that ending.* A voice speaking Dutch with a foreign accent, inside Jasper's head, as if heard through headphones. *Get out of the water,* said the voice. It wasn't Knock Knock.

The sea swirled around Jasper. "Who are you?"

First, get out of the water.

Jasper deployed Formaggio's strategy of isolating known facts. One: this voice communicated in direct language. Two: it didn't want Jasper dead. Three . . .

Three, it said, *would you please get out of the water?*

Jasper waded back to shore and sat on a driftwood log.

Empty the stones from the bag, said the voice.

Jasper obeyed. "So who are you?"

A hesitation. *I don't know.*

"How is that possible?"

I don't know that either.

"So . . . what do you know?"

About myself?

"About yourself."

I'm a mind without a body of my own. I've existed for five decades in this form. I may be from Mongolia. I transfer between human hosts by touch. When Formaggio shook your hand, I transferred to you. My Dutch is poor, as you heard, so . . . The voice had switched to English. *Like I said, I don't know much.*

"If you don't know who you are, what are you?"

"Spirit," "ghost," "ancestor," "guardian angel," "noncorpum," "incorporeal." I'm not prescriptive.

"Why are you in my head?"

I found you in Formaggio's memory, and hoped Knock Knock might offer clues to my own origins. I've been sifting.

"So it's only chance you're here now?"

"If you believe in chance, yes."

A stranded jellyfish gleamed in the pale morning. "So you've spent the last day rummaging in my memory, uninvited?"

Do you ask a book for permission before you read it?

"I'd ask the book's owner."

From "Goodbye, cruel world" to "What about my privacy?" in only two minutes.

A trawler slid into a patch of silver light, a mile out.

Jasper asked, "What do I call you?"

If I pluck a name out of thin air, I fear I'll jinx my hopes of discovering who I really am. Mongolian feels like my mother tongue, so call me the Mongolian.

Far-off seagulls, tiny as close-up sand fleas, hovered behind the trawler. "Did you find the clues you were searching for?"

No. Knock Knock's another incorporeal, but we have little else in common. He wants you dead. I don't know why.

"Have you communicated?"

Certainly not. To wake him from his Queludrin stupor would be unwise. If— From nowhere, a giant black dog rocketed over the lip of the dune and Jasper fell off the log. The dog barked, barked, and barked—but without a soundtrack, as if on a silent film. Jasper felt his own lips, tongue, and vocal cords activated, saying, *"Zail! Zail!"* The dog's tail dipped; it crouched low; its head tilted. Jasper's hand back-slapped the air and the dog slunk off.

Jasper's heart pounded. "You can control your hosts?"

If I have no other choice.

"You have a way with dogs."

I told it to go away. In Mongolian.

"Why would a Dutch dog understand Mongolian?"

Don't underestimate dogs.

A mile out on the marbled sea, a yacht dived and rose.

"If you can take me over—like just now, with the dog—why didn't you force me out of the sea? Or stop me before I went in?"

I hoped you would stop yourself.

Jasper lies on the shingle. "I just . . . got tired."

I would have fished you out, if you hadn't listened to me. I'm in no hurry to discover what happens to me if my host dies. I'm glad of this conversation, however. I'm a solitary soul.

"Lonely? You have hosts to talk to."

It's dangerous. Most hosts would mistake me for insanity.

"I guess I'm inoculated. Or insane already."

You're not insane, Jasper, but you are host to a long-term lodger who does not wish you well. Knock Knock has damaged you already. Shall we walk as we talk? The young psychiatrist who let you out will be worrying, and you need dry clothes . . .

OVER THE FOLLOWING hours, Jasper's disembodied confessor helped him analyze his position in ways that Dr. Galavazi, who "knew" Knock Knock was a psychosis, could not. The Mongolian's perspective harvested a fresh crop of insights that, Formaggio-like, Jasper arranged in a list. *One:* Knock Knock must be unable to transfer between hosts, or he would have left Jasper at Ely. *Two:* Knock Knock's goal appeared to be Jasper's death. *Three:* Knock Knock's powers of coercion must be weaker than the Mongolian's, or he would have thrown Jasper off the SS *Arnhem* on the crossing from

Harwich. *Four:* Queludrin was choking Jasper's thyroid gland and eroding the cervical nerves in his spine. "So if Knock Knock doesn't get me," said Jasper, "the Queludrin will."

The Mongolian hesitated. *If you stay on this path, yes.*

"What other path is there?"

I could, so to speak, operate.

"You can cut out Knock Knock?"

No. He's too integrated. But if I cauterize the synapses surrounding Knock Knock in your brain, he would, effectively, be entombed. You should no longer need Queludrin. It's not a cure. Once you're off the medication, Knock Knock will awaken, detect his entrapment, and begin to graft new synapses. But this would take him a few years. A safer drug might come along, or a stronger ally. In the meantime, you could go out into the world. Live a little, as my American hosts might say.

Jasper found a dice in his pocket. White dots on a red plastic cube. He had no memory of it. "What are the risks?"

I'm inducing a localized stroke. It's not a riskless thing to do. Compared to spinal erosion, however, or a dead thyroid, or a hostile mind-visitor, or wading into the North Sea, the risks are manageable.

Dutch rain beat at Jasper's dark window. "When can you carry out this operation?"

JASPER WOKE TO blustery sunlight on the ceiling.

How do you feel? asked a Mongolian spirit.

"As if an object the size of an acorn, or bullet, is embedded in my brain. It doesn't hurt. But it's there. Like a benign tumor."

Benign on the outside, malign on the inside. That's the cauterized barrier I've cut around your guest. His cell, if you like.

"So I can stop taking Queludrin . . . from today?"

That's the point. Knock Knock can't get at you.

"Persuading Dr. Galavazi that I'm cured won't be easy."

I disagree. Your recovery is his medical triumph. Shake hands with him after breakfast. I'll transfer over and plant an idea or two. He's a good man.

"Why not announce yourself to him, like you did with me?"

I don't want him to lose his faith in psychiatry. The world has too many mystics and too few scientists.

"What should I tell him?"

The Mongolian thought. *Everything except the suicide attempt. Just say I came to you on your walk.*

"If I do, he'll definitely think I'm crazy."

Yet here you are, healthier and happier. I predict Dr. Galavazi will interpret your recovery and "the Mongolian" in psychiatric terms. Who knows? Good may come of it . . .

KNOCK-KNOCK ON THE door of Room 777 in the Chelsea Hotel. Jasper wakes. The sleeping pill dug him only a shallow grave. *Knock-knock. Maybe it's Elf or Griff or Dean.* Jasper doubts it. *Knock-knock.* Jasper gets up, goes to the door, and looks out through the spyhole.

Nobody.

He's back. It's official. My remission is over.

Knock-knock. Jasper opens the door. The yellow corridors stretch in both directions, punctuated by brown doors.

Nobody.

Jasper shuts the door, attaches the chain, and—

Knock-knock. Jasper senses him. The prey senses the predator. He goes to the bathroom to take another Queludrin. Twelve remain. Only six days' supply. *I'll have to get more, and soon.*

Knock-knock. Since the party at the Roundhouse for *Stuff of Life,* Jasper has heard these bleary nearby knockings.

Knock-knock. On the airplane, the knocking was loud and clear. Did Jasper's dread of flying somehow empower—

Knock-knock. Jasper's watch says 12:19 A.M. He took two Queludrins only six hours ago, when the airplane was circling over New York. At Rijksdorp, they lasted twelve hours, easily.

Knock-knock. Jasper tips two pale blue pills onto his palm and washes them down with half a glass of New York water. Pages of the *Times* are taped over the big mirror. AIR FRANCE FLIGHT 1611 CRASHES INTO SEA OFF NICE WITH LOSS OF 95 LIVES. Jasper cleans his teeth while the Queludrin penetrates his brain. After three or four minutes he puts his toothbrush in the glass, and—

A slow, mocking *knock . . . knock.*

What if it no longer works at all?

JASPER KNOCKS LOUD and hard on the door of Room 912 until Levon's bleary face appears over the safety chain.

"I have to call the Netherlands," says Jasper.

"What?" Levon blinks.

"I have to call the Netherlands."

"It'll be six in the morning there."

"I need to speak with my doctor."

"They have doctors in New York. I'll ask Max, in—"

"Do you want me to perform tomorrow or not?"

This works. Levon opens the door and gestures him inside. His pajamas are canary yellow. Jasper gives his manager a scrap of paper with Dr. Galavazi's number on it. Levon calls down to the switchboard, reads out the number, confirms the call, agrees, "Yes, I *know* it'll cost me," and hands Jasper the receiver. "Make it quick. Please. We aren't filling stadiums yet."

"I need privacy," states Jasper.

Levon's face goes doubly illegible. He puts a gown over his pajamas and leaves the room.

Jasper hears the Dutch ringtone from the earpiece.

Knock Knock *knock-knocks* over the *ring-rings* . . .

The doctor answers. "It's damned early, whoever you are."

Jasper speaks in Dutch. "Dr. Galavazi, I need your help."

A pause. "Good morning, Jasper. Where are you?"

"Levon's room in the Chelsea Hotel in New York."

"New York is a sucked orange, according to Emerson."

Jasper thinks about this. "Knock Knock's come back. Really, really back. Not just on his way."

A long pause. "Symptoms?"

"Knocking. Lots of knocking. It's not relentless yet, but I feel him. Smirking. Like a cat toying with a bird. And the Queludrin's losing its potency. Two pills last six or seven hours. I took another one as we landed, but Knock Knock's knocking again."

Knock-knock.

"Jasper? Are you still there?"

"He knocked. Just now. There's no Mongolian to save me this time. If Queludrin stops working, I'm defenseless."

"Then we need to find another drug that does."

"What if I ask a doctor, 'Give me a drug to stop these noises in my head?' and he locks me up in a padded cell? This is America. America's the world leader for locking people up."

A pause. "Getting agitated won't help."

"Then what will help, Dr. Galavazi?"

"Right now, sleep. Do you have any sleeping pills?"

"I took one, but Knock Knock woke me up."

"Take two. I'll contact my colleague, Dr. Yu Leon Marinus. The one I told you about when you visited. He's at Columbia University, so he shouldn't be far away from . . . It's the Chelsea Hotel, you say?"

"Yes. It's famous."

"I'll ask him to visit you. Urgently."

Jasper hears a *knock-knock, knock-knock, knock-knock* . . . Like sarcastic applause. "Thank you." He hangs up and leaves Levon's room. His manager tries to block his way. "What's going on?"

Jasper goes back to Room 777 to a mock death march of *Knock, knock, knock.* He takes two benzodiazepines, turns off the lamp, and sinks into a chemical limbo, where . . .

A CICADA NYMPH, bulbous and blind, is sucking sap from a tree root. It emerges from the soil into a raucous forest. In tiny increments the grub climbs a sapling growing in the shadow of a giant cedar. Under a twig the grub clings until, from a diaphanous carapace, a shiny black cicada hatches. The insect unfolds its gummy wings to dry them in the sun. Then . . . up, up, up it flies through crisscrossed, sun-streaked, dark-splotched air; over the roof of a cloister where pregnant women sweep the walkway; over the steep roofs of Zeeland; over Chetwynd Mews; over the Brooklyn Bridge, and down, down, through a gap in the sash window of Room 777 in the Chelsea Hotel where Jasper lies unconscious. A black aperture has opened between his eyebrows. The cicada lands on Jasper's forehead, tucks in its wings, and enters the hole.

Knock-knock. Jasper wakes up. Knock Knock is awake and present. He may as well be sitting on the chair in the corner, in person. *Perhaps he is.* Jasper's watch says 7:12 A.M. He goes to the bathroom and takes three Queludrins. *Only nine left.*

Dr. Galavazi always told Jasper that speaking to Knock Knock feeds and fortifies his psychosis, and urged him not to do so. Jasper decides that prohibition is now pointless. Back in the bedroom, he draws a Formaggio-style alphabet grid. "You know how this works. Will you speak to me?"

The noise of early traffic simmered seven floors below.

No knocks, but a voice: *If I choose to, de Zoet, I shall.*

Jasper gasps. The voice is as clear as the Mongolian's.

I hear your words, says Knock Knock. *I hear your thoughts.*

Jasper's mind spins. "This *is* Knock Knock?"

I am he whom you call by that name.

To Jasper's inner ear, the voice sounds patrician, cold and resolute. "Should I call you by another name?"

Would you care by what name a dog knows you?

Jasper works out that, in this metaphor, he is the dog and Knock Knock the master. He glances at the clock: 7:14 A.M. The Queludrin is having no effect. "Why do you want to destroy me?"

This body is my property. It is time you were gone.

"This body? This mind? They're mine. They're me."

My claim is older than yours.

"What claim? I don't understand."

A pause. *The dream of the cicada.*

More metaphors? "Am I the cicada? Are you? What are you going to do to me? Just tell me. Directly."

"Directly," then: the custom of my country allows even the lowliest thief a period of a few hours to prepare his spirit for death. Your period of grace begins now, and ends tonight.

"I don't want to die."

That is irrelevant. You die tonight.

"Is there no other way?"

None.

Jasper stares at his hands. The clock ticks.

This is your fate, de Zoet. No sword, bullet, exorcist, drug, stranger, or stratagem can change it. Accept this.

"If I kill myself first?"

Then I will inhabit another. There is no shortage of suitable bodies in this city. If you want anything of yourself to survive, however, surrender this body in good working order.

Knock Knock withdraws . . .

TRAFFIC SIMMERS SEVEN floors below Jasper's balcony. The air is cool and metallic. Autumn's here. The city rumbles, near and far. Early sunlight reflects off high east-facing windows. Jasper lists his options. *One.* Jump over the rail. *Deny Knock Knock my body.* Jasper waits for an intervention. None is forthcoming. *If this is my last day, why end it now? Two.* Act as if Knock Knock has not just served a death sentence and spend the day with Elf, Dean, and Griff in interviews with the press, answering questions about our first impressions of America and why Elf, a woman, is in Utopia Avenue.

Three. Go down to breakfast and tell Levon and the band that Knock Knock, a demon in his head, is going to kill him later. *Four.* Obey Knock Knock. Prepare for death. *How do you do that?* Jasper's not sure, but he finds himself cleaning his teeth, dressing in his stage gear, pocketing his wallet, putting his shoes on, walking down the echoey stairwell, out through the lobby, and onto 23rd Street, past unglamorous apartments, repair shops, garages, a bus depot, parking lots, and warehouses, where men in oil-stained overalls eyeball him as if he's an intruder who has no legitimate business there. Rats ferret through rubbish spilling from an upturned bin. Jasper walks under an elevated highway of angry cars. Beyond is a strip of wasteland. He watches the Hudson River slide past, toward its perpetual ending. *I am leaving the world.* Not in fifty years. *Tonight.* Whatever Knock Knock's plans for his future are, Jasper doubts very much they include Utopia Avenue. The band too, then, has only a few hours left, unless Elf and Dean carry on without him. *I'm half ghost already.* In a lean-to, a kid Jasper's age is injecting drugs into his lacerated forearm. He looks up at Jasper and slumps back, the tip of the needle still in his arm. Jasper walks on. He stops and reties an undone bootlace, marveling at the complexity of this everyday operation. Weeds corkscrew up from cracks in the path. Their flowers are sparks . . .

JASPER IS ENGULFED in a human river, dammed by a DON'T WALK sign; it changes to WALK and the river spills forward. Glass-fronted buildings reflect the sun, its own reflections and re-reflections.

In a gleaming perfume showroom, women stare at Jasper like sinister dolls. He tries a row of samples from wrist to elbow. Lavender, rose, geranium, sage. Bottled gardens. "Sir," says a serious guard. "We have a hair policy."

"What's a hair policy?" asked Jasper.

The guard's eyes narrow into slits. "Wise guy."

Jasper's confused. "Only accidentally."

"Scram, buddy. Go!"

Aggression, realizes Jasper. He leaves the showroom, passing a school bus, big and yellow and toylike, disgorging schoolchildren. "Quit *whining,* Snail!" scolds an older girl. Jasper thinks about his cousins in Lyme Regis—Eileen, Lesley, Norma, John, Robert—for the first time in a long, long time. Their faces are forgotten. One wave of the de Zoet magic wand and they vanished. They'll probably be married now, with children of their own. Maybe they saw Utopia Avenue on *Top of the Pops* without recognizing their small cousin from long ago. "Titch," they used to call him. "Shrimp." He wonders if they missed him, after the de Zoets' driver took him off to boarding school.

Hundreds, thousands of besuited men with briefcases surge along this sunless street. Few speak. None gives way. None makes eye contact. *They serve the god who made them.* Jasper has to dodge or get shoulder-barged. A busker is playing Big Bill Broonzy's "Key to the Highway." George Washington watches from his plinth, framed by Doric columns. Statues' faces are easier to read than people's—George Washington is not pleased to be there. Jasper sees a shop:

BOWLING GREEN PHARMACY. A rebel thought nudges Jasper inside to ask a pharmacist for an over-the-counter antipsychotic drug, and his skull is pummeled by KNOCK-*KNOCK* KNOCK-*KNOCK* KNOCK-*KNOCK* KNOCK-*KNOCK* KNOCK-*KNOCK* KNOCK-*KNOCK-KNOCK* KNOCK-*KNOCK* KNOCK-*KNOCK* KNOCK-*KNOCK* KNOCK-KNOCK-*KNOCK* KNOCK-*KNOCK* KNOCK-*KNOCK* KNOCK-*KNOCK* *KNOCK*-KNOCK *KNOCK*-KNOCK *KNOCK*-KNOCK *KNOCK*-KNOCK KNOCK-*KNOCK* KNOCK-*KNOCK* until his vision swims.

"No drugs," Jasper tells Knock Knock. "I understand."

Knock Knock does not reply, but stops pounding.

A pharmacist is staring. "Can I help you, son?"

"It's okay. I was talking to a voice in my head."

DOWN IN A subway station, booms and screeches echo all the way from the underworld to Jasper's eardrums. *An ogre's borborygmi.* An approaching train howls out of the tunnel and stops to disgorge and load up with more carcasses-in-waiting. The carriage contains all the racial variations Jasper knows of, with mixes he can only guess at. *Rivers of blood,* he thinks, *flow not in the street but through our species.* Passengers sway, snooze, and read. The genetic deck is reshuffled at every stop. *I wish I could live here.* He wonders if Knock Knock intends to erase his memories once he's moved in, or if he'll keep some, like the photograph albums of a man you murder. If Knock Knock hears, he offers no comment. Jasper gets off at the 86th Street stop. It looks close to Central Park on the map of the subway stops. A thin sheet of cloud is pulled tight across the sky. The sun shines through, like a torch. This neighborhood is home to old money and privilege, like Mayfair or the Prinsengracht. The park draws Jasper a few blocks along 86th Street and into its well-thumbed pages. Maples are pyrotechnic. Conkers spill from cat-jackets, like brains, under the spreading chestnut tree. Squirrels flit in and out of sight. A spiral path brings Jasper into a mossy omphalos. He sits on a bench and rests his aching feet. *We are porous.* "Old haunts fill me with melancholy." The elderly man has the beard of

God and the hat and pipe of a gentleman farmer. "Old haunts gladden my heart."

"It's a new haunt, for me," says Jasper.

"Time is the only difference."

"I don't have much of that left."

"To die is different from what anyone supposes." The old man touches Jasper's wrist. "Don't be afraid."

"Easy for you to say. You had a whole lifetime."

"As do we all. Not a moment more, nor a moment less."

Jasper wakes up. Nobody's there. He walks out of the spiral and onto a lawn where a military band is playing "The Ballad of the Green Berets." The Stars and Stripes flutters from a flagpole by an army tent. A banner reads, WANTED: AMERICAN HEROES—ENLIST TODAY! A couple of recruitment officers are surrounded by a dozen long-haired youths. "Heroes? You're burning children over there! Children! Wake the *fuck up* already! It's genocide!"

A recruitment officer shouts back: "You're a disgrace! Hiding behind that peace sign while REAL MEN do your fighting for you! Peace doesn't just happen! Peace has to be *fought for!*"

A crowd is gathering, but Jasper doesn't stay to watch. His death sentence has made most things that once mattered newly irrelevant. He leaves Central Park and finds a statue on a tall pillar on a traffic island. Christopher Columbus has lost his way and it's later than he thought. Jasper buys a bottle of something called Dr Pepper from a street vendor, but it doesn't taste of pepper. Jasper didn't bring his watch. He asks Knock Knock, "How much time do I have left?"

If Knock Knock hears, he does not answer.

Jasper enters a record shop. Cream's "Born Under a Bad Sign" is playing. He flicks through the racks of LPs, enjoying the updraft of air on his face with every sleeve flicked. He takes his leave of *Pet Sounds, Sgt. Pepper's, A Love Supreme;* of Etta James's *At Last!,* Aretha Franklin's *I Never Loved a Man the Way I Love You* and Love's *Forever Changes;* of *Otis Blue, The Psychedelic Sounds of the 13th Floor Elevators,* and *The Who Sell Out.* Jasper arrives at *Paradise Is the Road to Paradise* and *Stuff of Life.* The tarot card cover turned out well. Jasper wishes he could live long enough to hear Elf's and Dean's American songs. He'll miss his life. Except, of course, he won't. Only the living miss things.

"They're playing in town this week." The shopkeeper has a big belly, milky eyes, and stains on his polyester shirt. "The Ghepardo. Broadway at 53rd. That's the second album. *Stuff of Life.* The first one was good, but that's a step up."

"Is it selling well?"

"Sold five today. You sound English."

"My mother was. I went to school there."

"Yeah? Ever see the Beatles?"

"Only John. It was at a party."

"Woah. You *met* him? You're shitting me."

Is "shitting" lying? "We didn't really chat. It was under a table. He'd lost his mind and wanted it back."

The shopkeeper frowns. "Is that, like, British humor?"

"Not as far as I know."

"Born Under a Bad Sign" ends. "Try this," says the shopkeeper, and puts on "Look Who It Isn't." "Total motherfucker."

Jasper remembers Dean teaching him the riff at Fungus Hut, and Elf playing organ descents from Bach's *Toccata,* and Griff deciding, "This one needs the full Moon. Stand back . . ."

It hurts that he'll never see the band again.

They'll think I lost my nerve and vanished.

Jasper exits the shop. Evening submerges the streets and avenues. The traffic thickens and gets angrier. Jasper overtakes a Ferrari on foot. Horns honk. *Ya-honk, ya-hoooooonk, ya-hoooooooonk,* filling the geometry of Manhattan. Like most rage, it is perfectly futile. WASHINGTON SQUARE PARK, says a sign. Trees are turning. Somewhere a busker is playing Big Bill Broonzy's "Key to the Highway." *Profound aural schizophrenia.* Men are playing chess on benches, picnic chairs, and tables. The oldest of them is lean as a turkey neck, with cracked spectacles, a grimy tweed cap, and a sackcloth bag. His opponent knocks over his king and pays a cigarette. "I'll keep your bunk safe, Diz," he says, and goes.

Diz looks up at Jasper. "Want a game, Shotgun?"

"Is your name really 'Diz'?"

"That's what I go by. You in or not?"

"How does it work?"

"Easy." Diz's voice is a rasp. "I stake a dollar. You stake a dollar to play black, or a dollar-fifty for white. Winner takes the pot."

"I'll play as black."

Diz puts two fifty-cent coins into a chipped cup. Jasper puts in a dollar bill. His opponent opens with a variant on the Modern Benoni Attack. Jasper opts for the King's Indian Defense. A few spectators gather, and Jasper becomes aware of bets being placed on their game. At the tenth move, Diz sets up a pincer with his bishop. By sidestepping it, Jasper blunders into a two-way fork. He goes a knight down, and a slow war of attrition begins. Jasper manages to castle, but cannot avoid a queen exchange. Piece by traded piece, Jasper's chances of clawing back a knight or a bishop diminish. At the endgame, Jasper is a move away from promoting a pawn to queen, but Diz has it covered. "Check."

"The inevitable." Jasper knocks over his king. He sees the moon has risen. "That was a strong opening."

"They taught me good at my academy."

"You went to a chess academy?"

"Attica Prison Academy. Gimme a half-dollar, I'll teach you the Benoni."

"You already have." Under the table Jasper slips a five-dollar bill into his box of Dunhills, then gives it to the old man. "Tuition."

He pockets it. " 'Ppreciate that, Shotgun."

Signs around him tell Jasper this is Greenwich Village. He smells food but isn't hungry. He buys an iced tea at a café. Baseball is on the radio. A wall in Jasper's mind shudders under a powerful blow. It's a message. *Soon now . . .*

JASPER WANTS DARKNESS, privacy, and warmth for this death, but he doesn't want the others to find him dead in his room. The sight will upset Elf. *An empty church, or . . .* He enters a hospital of uncertain dimensions. The emergency room is a turbulent exhibition of human suffering, of fractures, breakages, a knife wound, a gunshot wound, burns. Some patients sit stoically and others don't. *Who can measure the pain of another?* Jasper passes a security guard unchallenged and climbs stairs, turns corners, and crosses corridors. The air smells of bleach, old masonry, and something earthy. *"Clear the way! Clear the way!"* A medical team rushes by with a trolley. Someone is sobbing in a stairwell, above or below, it's hard to be sure. Jasper reaches a door labeled PRIVATE WARD N9D. There is a window at head-height set into the door. It is curtained behind for privacy and reflects like a black mirror. Knock Knock examines Jasper with the eyes of time. *In here,* he says. Jasper opens the door a crack. By dim light the color of treacle, he sees a small ward containing two beds. One bed is occupied by a man. There is not much of him left but hollow folds and wrinkles wrapped in a hospital gown. *The Hollow Man.* The other bed is vacant. Quietly, Jasper shuts the door behind him, removes his shoes, and lies on the spare bed. If the Hollow Man notices his visitor, he gives no indication. Jasper's feet are throbbing after a day of walking. Sounds reach him, as if piped from a sinking ship. A band is playing on. A telephone is ringing. A woman answers: "Hello?" Pause. "Who shall I say is calling?" Six feet away, a rattle rattles in the Hollow Man's throat. *Split dried peas in a cardboard shaker.* Drool pools from a toothless mouth and falls in a filament from withered lips. It soaks into his pillow. The Hollow Man opens his eyes. He has none. Jasper wonders who he once was, and announces, "Goodbye." Jasper tells Knock Knock, "I'm ready."

The wall in his mind is shattered, and falls away.

Knock Knock bursts out, flooding his brain.

Jasper's sentience dims to near zero.

Presence reverts to Absence.

WHAT'S INSIDE WHAT'S INSIDE

NINE FLOORS BELOW, A YELLOW CAB PROWLS WEST 23RD Street by the Chelsea Hotel, looking for a fare. Elf considers how the metaphor of life as a journey underplays how the traveler herself is changed by the road, by misadventures, by what's inside. *By what's inside what's inside.* Luisa's arms encircle her waist and reach up to her seraphinite pendant. She smells of soap. She kisses Elf's neck. *No male stubble to pretend to not mind as it scrubs me raw. Bruce was a hedgehog. A plagiarizing hedgehog. It doesn't matter. If he hadn't left, I wouldn't have her. I wouldn't have this. Disaster is rebirth, seen from the front. Rebirth is disaster, seen from behind.* "You're that princess," says Luisa. "The one in the tower. Rapunzel."

"A New York Rapunzel's hair wouldn't reach the pavements."

"A New York Rapunzel would have a specially made wig." Luisa coils Elf's hair around her thumb and whispers in her ear, *"Rapunzel, Rapunzel, deja caer tu cabello."*

"I'm defenseless when you speak Spanish."

"Is that so? In that case . . ." Luisa whispers in Elf's ear. *"Voy a soplar y puff y volar su casa hacia abajo."*

Elf muffles a giggle. "What's that?"

"I'll huff and I'll puff and I'll blow your house down."

"You did that in London." Elf plants a kiss on Luisa's thumb. " 'O, wonder! How many goodly creatures are there here! How beauteous womankind is! O brave new world, That has such people in't!' "

"Which one's that?"

"*The Tempest.* Tweaked. My sister's playing Miranda and we went through her lines a few days ago."

The Chelsea Hotel's door-stepping drug-pusher's voice travels up to the ninth floor, very faintly. "Hey! Need any uppers, downers, out-of-towners?"

"You know how," says Elf, "when you go abroad, you learn more about where you're from than where you're visiting?"

"Definitely."

"You, us, this . . ."

" 'Mad, passionate affair.' "

"Thank you—this mad, passionate affair is 'abroad.' I look back at my old self, before I met you, and I understand her better than I did when I was her."

"And what have you gleaned, here where the Wild Dykes be?"

"Labels."

"Labels?"

"Labels. I stuck them on everything. 'Good.' 'Bad.' 'Right.' 'Wrong.' 'Square.' 'Hip.' 'Queer.' 'Normal.' 'Friend.' 'Enemy.' 'Success.' 'Failure.' They're easy to use. They save you the bother of thinking. Those labels stay stuck. They proliferate. They become a habit. Soon, they're covering everything, and everybody, up. You start thinking reality *is* the labels. Simple labels, written in permanent marker. The trouble is, reality's the opposite. Reality is nuanced, paradoxical, shifting. It's difficult. It's many things at once. That's why we're so crummy at it. People harp on about freedom. *All* the time. It's everywhere. There are riots and wars about what freedom is and who it's for. But the Queen of Freedoms is this: to be free of labels. Here endeth today's lesson. You're giving me a funny look."

Luisa strokes the pendant, once hers, now Elf's. "I was just mentally putting a label on you, that's all."

"What does it say?"

" 'Elf for President.' "

They hear a *knock-knock* on the outer door.

Luisa looks at Elf. "Expecting a visitor?"

"At this hour? God, no."

Knock-knock. Knock-knock.

"Some stray suitor from the party?" guesses Luisa. "Perhaps with the name LEONARD stitched onto his mittens?"

Knock-knock. Knock-knock. Knock-knock.

"Someone who knows I'm here," says Elf. "Levon?"

"Answer, then, but look through the eyehole first . . ."

THE FISH-EYE LENS shows Levon, in his pajamas and dressing gown. His frowning forehead is hugely magnified.

Elf whispers to her lover, "Levon."

Luisa whispers back: "Shall I hide?"

Elf hesitates. Griff and Dean knew Luisa was going to sleep in Elf's room; just not in Elf's bed. "Put a blanket and pillow on the sofa."

Luisa nods and goes back into the bedroom. Elf opens up. The corridor is margarine yellow.

"Sorry to come knocking at this hour."

"You wouldn't be if it wasn't urgent."

Levon looks around. "It's Jasper. He's acting weird."

"How can you tell?"

"He just came to my room and insisted that I have the switchboard put a call through to the Netherlands. I said 'What for?' He said it was medical. I pointed out how early it is in Europe. He threatened not to play at the Ghepardo if I didn't do as he said."

Elf's shocked. "Jasper said that?"

"Exactly. So I wanted to ask if he went with you to the party on the roof after all—and if he did any."

Elf shakes her head. "He went to his room and he never showed up. I meant to go and check up on him, but it got late, and I thought, *Let him sleep the flight off.* Did you place the call to Holland?"

"I had no choice. Jasper told me to wait outside. I did what any diligent manager would, but he spoke Dutch. The name 'Galavazi' cropped up a few times. Ring any bells?"

Elf shakes her head. "Sounds more Italian than Dutch."

"What about 'Quallydin' or 'Quellydrone'?"

"Queludrin?"

"Could've been."

"It's medication. Jasper took it on the flight. For nerves. A kind of sedative, I guess. How long did the call last?"

"Two or three minutes. After he hung up I asked him what the story was, but he ignored me. I sat in the dark for a few minutes, then decided to come see if you could shed a little light."

"I wish I could. We could go and knock on his door, but if Jasper doesn't want to discuss something, he won't. All I can suggest is to trust in a night's sleep."

Levon rubs his tired face. "Guess so. Sorry for dumping this on you at this hour. Breakfast at nine. Tomorrow's a busy day."

A CHELSEA MORNING, with sun through yellow curtains and a rainbow on the wall. The clock says 6:59. *A big day ahead.* The barometer's needle points to G in CHANGEABLE. Elf lies in bed and listens to the buzz of traffic on 23rd Street. *A kind of language.* Luisa, asleep, breathes in slow, deep rhythms. Her bare, slung hand rests on Elf's exposed midriff. Elf likes the contrast between their skin tones. It's erotic. Luisa smells of toast and thyme. Bruce smelt of cheddar and beer. Angus of salt-and-vinegar crisps. Luisa stirs, stretching like a young, superbly toned cat, yawns, and surrenders to sleep again. *To think that someone wanted her dead and she's just shrugged it off, like I might shrug off a shitty review.* Elf remembers the Jasper Question. It's too early to go and wake him up now. *He'll be asleep. He'll be all right. It's the flight. It's the success. It's happened so quickly. He's bound to need a period of adjustment. Wanting to speak to a doctor in Holland isn't so very weird. That's where his clinic was. Perhaps Levon cornered him into threatening not to play* . . . Elf thinks of other explanations for Jasper's ultimatum until sleep pulls her under by her ankles . . .

. . . AND SUDDENLY THEY'RE running late. Luisa dresses in jeans, a T-shirt, and jacket. She kisses Elf while Elf's putting on her makeup, promises to be at the Ghepardo later, and leaves for the *Spyglass* office after a ten-day absence. Ten minutes later, Elf finds Levon downstairs in the El Quijote restaurant reading *The New Yorker* and eating a glazed bread doughnut. Before Elf sits down, he asks, "Should we go and see if Jasper's up yet?"

"Let him sleep in a little. Beauty sleep . . ."

"After breakfast, then. Ever had one of these?" He holds up his bread. "It's a bagel. Have one . . ." Elf agrees, and in addition orders coffee and a grapefruit. American grapefruit are pink, not yellow. Dean and Griff arrive and order more things they've never heard of: grits, hash browns, avocados, and eggs over easy. At 9:40 A.M., Levon and Elf go to Reception to ask Stanley to call Jasper's room. He goes to the switchboard in the back. A minute later Stanley returns, shaking his head. "No reply."

Elf and Levon look at each other. "We've got a cab coming at a quarter after ten," Levon tells the manager. "Can I take a key and open up his room? I have to get him out of bed."

"I'll come," replies Stanley. "It's hotel policy." They go to the elevators. "It'll be with us in a jiffy."

A minute later, they are still waiting.

"Literally, any second now," says Stanley.

Two minutes later, Levon takes the stairs. Elf follows him. Stanley follows her. "People don't die in the Chelsea Hotel," insists the hotelier. "And anyway, Jasper's in the luckiest room in the building . . ."

777—SPECKLED GOLD-PAINT NUMBERS screwed onto walnut veneer. Elf knocks and telepathically orders Jasper to appear at the door, squinting at them through his messed-up red hair and a fog of jet lag and sleeping pills. Nobody replies.

Levon knocks harder. "Jasper?"

The only reply is a feeble echo: *Jasper?*

Elf swats away images of their guitarist in the bath with his veins opened up. She bangs on the door. "Jasper!"

A short man in a morning jacket with rouged cheeks approaches. His female companion towers over him in a ball gown. They say, "Good morning, Stanley." Her voice is bass: his, alto.

"Mr. and Mrs. Blancheflower," says Stanley. "We're well, I trust?"

"Quite well, thank you," says Mrs. Blancheflower.

"Any trouble?" Mr. Blancheflower nods at the door. "Has a guest checked out before checking out?"

Stanley smiles as if the question can't possibly be serious. "What a question, Mr. Blancheflower! This is the Chelsea."

The couple exchange a sad smile at the follies of the world, then continue their journey down the stairs. When the Blancheflowers are out of eyeshot, Stanley puts the key in the door. "I'll go in first," says Levon. Something makes Elf touch his arm and insist, "No." She's afraid. She goes in. "Jasper?"

No reply. The bathroom, off to the right, is empty—as is the bath. *Thank God.* Sheets of newspaper are taped over the mirror. *A bad sign.* "What's that about?" asks Stanley.

"He just hates reflections." Elf steels herself to enter the bedroom, but Jasper's dead body is not lying on the bed, or next to it, or anywhere. "Best pillowcases I ever bought, those," says Stanley. "From a Greek market over in Brooklyn."

Elf draws apart the curtains and slides open the balcony door. There's nobody on the balcony. All is well on the street below.

"What did I tell ya?" asks Stanley. "He's gone for a stroll, is all. It's a beautiful morning in New York City. He'll be back any minute."

"ALL ABOARD, ALL aboard, Locomotive 97.8 FM," says the DJ. "I am Bat Segundo bringing you *all* the best songs from Great to Late. It's coming up to five after three and *that* was 'Roll Away the Stone,' the new single by my old friends from across the pond, Utopia Avenue. Three-quarters of the band are here aboard the Bat Train to discuss their way-out new album, *Stuff of Life*—but, first, introductions are in order." Bat nods at Elf first.

"Hello, New York," Elf says, into her mic. "I'm Elf Holloway, I play keyboards and sing with the band, and"—*I'm so worried about our missing guitarist, I could puke*—"we know Bat from his disc jockey days in England, where he was the first DJ *on the planet* to play us. Enough about me. Over to Dean." Elf grimaces on the inside. *I sounded like an idiot.*

"Afternoon, all. I'm Dean Moss, I play bass, sing, and write. That last one was one o' mine, so I hope yer dug it. We think the sun shines out of *all* the Bat-holes. Griff?"

"I'm Griff the 'umble drummer. For those of you trying to picture me, imagine Paul Newman and Rock Hudson's love child."

"Missing," continues the Bat, "is the fourth Utopian, Jacob de— sorry, I mean, *Jasper* de Zoet—I just changed his name—Jasper, who plays guitar and *will* be back for tonight's show at the Ghepardo on 53rd Street, starting nine P.M., a few tickets still available so get—on—down."

I hope to hell he will be back, thinks Elf.

"So tell us, Elf, Dean, Griff," says Bat. "As citizens of one great city, what are your first impressions of *our* great city? In one word."

" 'Sandwiches,' " says Griff. "Back home, it's ham, egg, or cheese. Here, there's hundreds of breads, meats, cheeses, pickles, dressings. I didn't know where to start at the deli. I had to order by pointing at a customer's sandwich and saying, 'One of them.' "

"My word for New York is 'more,' " says Dean. "More buildings, more height, more noise, more beggars, more music, more neon, more races. More hustle, bustle, winners, losers. More more."

"More shrinks," offers Bat. "More rats. Elf?"

"I can't sum up the city in a single word," says Elf, "but if New York was a sentence, it would be 'Stay out of my hair, and I'll stay out of yours.' London would be, 'And who do you think you are?' "

"I could personify cities all day," says the DJ. "But let's talk music. Congratulations on busting the Top Thirty with 'Roll Away the Stone'—a song you wrote, Dean, in testing circumstances?"

"I did, Bat, yeah. Basically, the Italian police planted drugs on me and slung me into prison for a week. 'Roll Away the Stone' came out o' that. I was completely exonerated, I hasten to add."

"Corrupt cops?" Bat acts astonished. "Thank God we have none of *them* in New York City. And thank God that justice prevailed because *Stuff of Life,* the album you recorded after your release, is a *supernova.* Now, I loved your debut—*Paradise Is the Road to Paradise*— but *Stuff of Life* is up a gear. The writing's so assured. The sonic palette's wider. You got a harpsichord on 'Sound Mind.' String section on 'The Hook.' Sitar on 'Look Who It Isn't.' Lyrically, it's more adventurous. So I gotta ask: What in God's name have you been putting on your cornflakes?"

"Big Brother 'n' the Holding Company," says Griff.

"*Odessey and Oracle* by the Zombies," says Elf.

"The Band's *Music from Big Pink,"* says Dean. "Yer hear a record that good, yer think, *Shi–damn, we've got to up our game.*"

"Our friend Brian talks about 'The Scenius,' " says Elf. "The genius of the scene. Art's made by artists, but artists are enabled by a scene—*non*-artistic factors. Buyers, sellers, materials, patrons, technology, places to mingle and swap ideas. You see the fruits of scenius in Medici Florence. The Dutch Golden Age. New York in the twenties. Hollywood. Right now, the scenius of London, and Soho, is pretty perfect. We've the venues, studios with multitrack recorders, the radio stations, the music papers and magazines . . . even cafés where session players hang out. Even a few managers who won't rip you off." Through the studio glass, Levon blows Elf a kiss. "We made our album, sure. But it emerged from the scenius."

"Possibly *the* most erudite answer ever heard on Locomotive 97.8 FM," says Bat. "Yet *Stuff of Life*'s songs, you'll agree, come not from 'scenius' but from experiences you've lived through. Some are so personal, it hurts. In a good way."

Dean and Elf look at each other. Dean says, "True . . . it's been a bit of a roller-coaster year. In our personal lives, like. We've lived through stuff that, like, can't *not* get into the songs."

"Exposing your heart and fears isn't always pleasant or easy," says Elf. "But if a song isn't *felt*—if not even its writer ever *believed* it— it's phony. It's a steak sandwich made of paper and glue. It may look okay but it tastes wrong. I can't write fake songs. I know Dean and Jasper are the same."

"You've been quoted as saying 'Even the Bluebells' is an elegy for a young relative of yours who passed away, Elf?"

"My nephew died in May. The song's for him. For Mark. I . . . don't want to kill the vibes by sobbing on your live show, Bat, so . . ."

"My point is, *Stuff of Life* proves what a few of us have been saying since *Rubber Soul* and *Bringing It All Back Home:* the best pop music is art. And art is about whatever the artist wants it to be. Falling in love for the first time? Yes. But also grief. Fame. Madness. Betrayal. Theft. The whole caboodle."

"Even—can yer say 'sex' on the radio?" asks Dean.

Through the glass, Bat's producer is making a *NO* gesture.

"Sure," says the DJ, "as long as you *in no way* suggest sex might be pleasurable, because that would be pure filth. Elf, could we give 'Bluebells' a spin before we hear a message from our sponsors?"

"Fire away. It'll be a North American exclusive."

"Then to all you passengers aboard Locomotive FM"—Bat positions the stylus over the quiet groove on the LP and shucks an earphone over an ear—"Great till Late on 97.8 FM, this is 'Even the Bluebells,' by our special studio guests Utopia Avenue . . ."

ELF, DEAN, AND Griff slalom through the afternoon's interviews at the office of Gargoyle Records on Bleecker Street. After each round of questions, Elf hopes that Levon or Max will appear with the news that Jasper has shown up at the office or the Chelsea. This does not happen. Max is hunting for a session musician who knows *Paradise* and *Stuff of Life* and who might step in to save the Ghepardo show. This, so far, is too tall an order. Howie Stoker has called in a favor at the NYPD to put out a city-wide alert for a "tall white Caucasian with long red hair in a purple jacket." *Like looking for a needle in a needle factory,* thinks Elf. They return to the Chelsea Hotel at 6 P.M. to prepare for a show that may never happen. Dean is furious with the absent Jasper. Griff is silent. Elf's more worried than angry. She's also feeling guilty. She wishes she could rewind to last night when Levon told her about Jasper's behavior. *I should have checked on him then. I should have checked on him this morning . . .*

At 7 P.M. they depart for the Ghepardo. Levon brings Jasper's Stratocaster in case he appears at the club. Manhattan lights up, but Elf barely notices. She is certain Jasper would be here if he possibly could. Her rosiest explanations are now that Jasper's had a crack-up, or has been mugged; the bleakest ones end in a city morgue. Max still hasn't found anyone able to play Jasper's parts from *Stuff of Life,* but he has tracked down a session player who can make a decent fist of the *Paradise* songs. The plan is to wait until the very last minute, plead appendicitis, and perform Dean's and Elf's *Paradise* material plus a few covers. "It'll only be half as good as it should be," says Dean, "at bloody best."

The car turns onto Eighth Avenue and shunts along in stop-and-start traffic. Elf combs the crowd's countless selves for a tall, stooping figure. A man bangs on the car window, yelling, "I'm hungry! Hungry! Hungry! I'm hungry!"

The driver veers the Lincoln into the middle lane.

"He'd *better* be in hospital after this," says Dean.

"Don't wish that," says Elf. "However pissed off you are."

"Why bloody not? The selfish prick's—"

"I've been in hospitals, Deano," says Griff. "Elf's right."

A PINK NEON sign inscribes THE GHEPARDO on the glowing dusk over a street-level entrance under unlit anonymous offices. Max opens the car door. "No news." A poster says, TAKE A TRIP DOWN UTOPIA AVENUE, using the *Stuff of Life* font. Luisa is waiting in the lobby. Her smile vanishes when she sees the band's faces. "What?"

"Jasper's been missing all day," explains Elf.

"Don't assume the worst," says Luisa.

Brigit, the matriarch of the Ghepardo, is less fazed. "Hey, musicians may be walking asscracks or they may be God's mouthpiece on Earth, but punctual they ain't."

Elf looks at Levon. *Jasper is always punctual.*

Brigit shows the band onto the stage for the sound check. The Ghepardo is a big old once-grand ballroom. Nine glitterballs hang from a paneled ceiling in need of renovation. The shoulder-high stage is well equipped with speakers, lights, and a stage curtain. A capable sound technician helps Elf, Dean, and Griff find levels that suit them and the space. Dean plays the Stratocaster and guesses at the levels Jasper would ask for. Sound checks are usually fun. This one feels like a rehearsal for a funeral.

8:15 P.M. THE substitute session player is caught in uptown traffic and won't arrive for another half-hour. Even Brigit is concerned now. Max is glum. Levon maintains a calm façade, but Elf guesses he's screaming inside. Elf is resorting to prayer: not *Let him walk in now,* but *Let him be alive and well;* failing that, she'll take *Let him be alive.* She finds the words to "Prove It" have faded from memory. *How many hundreds of times have I sung those lines?* She studies her emergency crib sheet, with Luisa's help. Howie Stoker arrives with a honey-skinned girlfriend a third his age with green eyeshadow, arachnid eyelashes, and satin-white hair. He introduces her as Ivanka. Naturally, Howie is disturbed that the star guitarist in "his" first signing is nowhere to be found thirty minutes before their American debut. "Where *is* he?"

"Up my bloody arse," mutters Dean. "I hid him for a joke."

"Shouldn't bandmates look out for each other?" asks Howie.

Griff puffs a smoke-ring of indifference.

Howie's partly right, thinks Elf. *We're so used to Jasper's eccentricities, we stopped watching out for him.*

Levon comes back from the ballroom. "It's filling up."

IT'S 8:45 P.M. Neither Jasper nor his stand-in has arrived. Elf has a sense of déjà vu, and traces it to anxiety dreams where she has to perform at a pre-doomed show. *There's no waking from this one.* "Why don't the three of you just play a few of the new tunes?" suggests Howie.

"Why don't greyhounds have three fookin' legs?" asks Griff.

"Who exactly is impressed by your cussing?" asks Howie.

"Haven't got the fookiest idea, Howie."

Aretha Franklin's *Lady Soul* LP is playing on the Ghepardo's speakers. Elf wishes it was something less good. Howie lumbers over to meet Luisa. "I don't believe we've met."

"We haven't," Luisa confirms.

"Howie Stoker, mover and shaker. And you are?"

"A friend of Elf's."

Howie purses his lips and nods. "I connect with *señoritas.* An ex-wife was a past-life therapist. I was a matador in Cádiz in Viking times. We may be cousins. Sufficiently distant ones."

Luisa looks at Elf. They both look at Ivanka, ten steps away. *She can hear.* She gives no sign of caring. *Is she paid by the hour?* "We will not be connecting, Mr. Stoker. Not in any life."

"Is disaster!" Ivanka falls to her knees. "My eyelash . . . is lost! Everybody, look for!" She studies the dark carpet. "Is black!"

Levon enters: "Look who's arrived."

It's Jasper, walking in as if it's nine o'clock this morning, not ten minutes before the show. "I need a glass of water."

During the long and dramatic pause, Elf is tempted to go over and give him a hug; but something holds her back.

Dean finds his voice first. "Where the fucking hell were yer?"

"Walking. I need a glass of water."

Dean seizes a jug of ice water and empties it over Jasper.

Jasper stands there, soaked and dripping.

" '*Walking*'? We've been *shitting* ourselves 'bout yer *all day;* yer didn't tell us if yer was alive or *what;* just for sodding '*walking*'? Yer selfish bloody *pillock*!"

Jasper takes a glass of water from Elf and drinks it in one. "Another." Levon has magicked up a tea-towel and is dabbing Jasper's face dry. Elf gets him a second glass. "Are you all right, Jasper?"

"I am here to play. I want their energy."

"Are yer high?" asks Dean. "Yer high, aren't yer?"

"He said not," reports Levon. "His pupils are okay."

"The . . . instrument. The—"

"*That's* not high?" scoffs Dean.

"Let's focus on the show," Levon tells him, "and what help Jasper needs. You've made your displeasure clear."

"I bloody haven't. We had *promo,* de Zoet. Interviews. Work. Sound check. The set list. We're *professionals.* We're on in *ten minutes.* No. It's five now. 'I went for a walk' is not good enough."

Jasper is unmoved. "I gave him a day's grace. To make peace."

Him? Elf looks at Luisa. "Who, Jasper? Who's 'him'?"

Jasper stares at the dressing table mirrors. He walks over and brings his face up close. An ecstatic smile spreads across his face.

"Jasper?" asks Elf. "What are you doing? Jasper?"

Max and Brigit hurry in, having heard the news. "Glad you could join us, Jasper," says Max. "Can you play?"

"That question is off the bloody menu," says Dean.

"I wholeheartedly agree with Dean," says Howie Stoker.

"De Zoet will play." Jasper watches his reflection turn and tilt. *Anyone would think this was his first encounter with a mirror.* "What happened to you out there?" asks Elf.

"Later," Levon tells her, softly. "Later."

"Damn right," says Brigit. "We've got no warm-up act and you're on *now.* I'm Brigit. This is my club. Get your ass here earlier tomorrow or I'm cutting your fees in half."

Jasper walks past Brigit, takes his guitar out of its case, plugs it into a baby Vox in the corner, and begins to tune up.

Brigit shakes her head in disgust and leaves.

"All's well that ends well, it seems," says Howie Stoker.

All is not well, thinks Elf. "If you're having some kind of mental crisis, Jasper, you can—"

"Bloody well have it in England, a week Friday," says Dean.

Jasper plays a G. "I am here to play. I want their energy."

DEAN SPEAKS INTO the mic. "We've been waiting all our lives to"—a spike of feedback—"to say, *'Good evening, New York—we are Utopia Avenue!'*" The crowd clap at middling intensity. Griff plays a drumroll, Elf plays a line of "the Bronx is up and the Battery's down," and Jasper could be waiting for a bus. Dean and Elf exchange a worried glance. "With no further ado," says Dean, "here's our single, 'Roll Away the Stone.' *And* a-*one,* and a-*two,* and a-one two three—" Jasper comes in on the *four* and plays his guitar part as per the album. Griff and Dean are as tight as ever, Elf plays with as much verve as she can muster, but Jasper's a lifeless imitation of Jasper de Zoet. They get through the song, but Elf senses the audience is dubious about this alleged peer of Clapton and Hendrix. The same thing happens with "Mona Lisa Sings the Blues." Griff and Dean support Elf's performance as best they can, but Jasper's playing is sluggish and sclerotic. He's making no connection with the crowd. Many onlookers stand with folded arms. He's not looking at the band, either, so Elf, Griff, and Dean have to fit around his stinting guitar part. Next up is "Darkroom." He steps up to the mic. Someone calls, "Say a few words, Jasper." He says nothing, and merely counts the band in. *If that wasn't a deliberate Fuck You it definitely came over as one.* Jasper doesn't drop notes or forget lyrics, but he plays without the joy or musical acrobatics that make Utopia Avenue's shows a hot ticket. The applause for "Darkroom" is perfunctory. *He's behaving as if the Ghepardo is beneath him.* "The Hook" and "Prove It" follow. Both are, in Griff's phrase, three-legged greyhounds. *The reviews will range from mixed to submersion in a cesspit.* Elf senses the crowd's confusion: Why are three-quarters of Utopia Avenue playing their asses off, but the guitarist is only going through the motions? Dean's pissed off. Griff looks grim. Elf's sweating buckets. After a lackluster "Prove It" she glances into the wings and sees Luisa. She looks concerned. Jasper names the next song on the set list—"Sound Mind"—and pain distorts his face. He hunches up and shudders for a second or two. When he straightens up, he looks surprised, and Elf dares to hope the real Jasper is back and that pallid impostor is gone. Jasper looks out at the Ghepardo. Tinkerbells from the glitterballs dance across his face. "Thanks for coming out tonight, everyone."

Someone calls out, "More than *you've* fuckin' done, pal!"

Jasper turns to Dean: "Thanks." To Griff: "Nice work." To Elf: "Goodbye." Elf doesn't understand why he's saying this. *We're not at the halfway point yet.* Dean sends Elf a what's-going-on? look. Elf replies with a search-me look, but at least Jasper appears to be present again. He strums; asks the tech guy for more volume on his guitar; shuts his eyes . . . and slams into an amp-blowing, bent-string howl; and fires off a scale of triads, sliding from high E all the way down. *Was he playing some weird mind game with us all?* Jasper rewards his first cheer of the night with a new riff that isn't "Sound Mind" but gets the audience thunder-clapping in time. Griff punctuates the melody; Dean enters the fray with a three-note underlay. Elf launches slabs of Hammond chords. *This could be us jamming for fun at Pavel Z's on a Soho morning.* Jasper drives the improvisation over three laps of rocky blues before blasting it to pieces with a jangled, hammered, sustained B flat, the opening of "Sound Mind." Dean gets the message and plays the song's bass riff; Elf comes in on the next bar; and Griff chop-slaps on the next. Jasper leans in close to the mic to do the first verse in his psycho-whisper . . .

. . .

. . . JASPER SETS OFF firework after firework through "Sound Mind" 's nine verses. The Ghepardo is a beast transformed. At the third chorus the band drop away to let five hundred New Yorkers bellow out the final line. Jasper's eyes are half closed. He gallops into a rapid-fire outro. Elf summons a crescendo of bathybic, many-fingered runs; and Dean's hanging on for dear life, his faster-than-the-eye fingers skimming around his fretboard. Jasper takes measured steps toward the Marshall stack, flirting with frequencies until—a *yooooooooooooowl!* of feedback thrashes and tears the air; a glance at Griff reveals an eight-armed Oriental deity; and Elf is laughing, drunk on relief that Jasper's back, stoned on the dope of art. Jasper's cheeks are wet. *I didn't know he had tear glands.* The studio "Sound Mind" is long gone. Elf hammers along to Dean's riff with both hands, cross-hands, slam-hands. Jasper walks into the center of the stage and looks past Elf; his eyes track someone walking toward him, but Elf sees nobody. Jasper nods at the presence, and his eyeballs roll back in their sockets . . .

. . . AND HE SLUMPS like a discarded puppet. Elf stops playing. Dean stops. Griff stops and stands. The audience falls silent. Someone shouts, "What's going on?" Jasper's mouth's moving, forming a word Elf cannot read, and closing. *A fish drowning in air.* She recalls Dean's story about Little Richard's fake heart attack, but this isn't that. Jasper's nose is bleeding. Maybe he cracked it on the floor. Maybe it's more sinister. Levon and Brigit come skidding up. Levon shouts, "Lower that curtain!" Seconds later, the fire curtain drops down. Jasper spasms and snarls, like a dog in pain. Muscles are moving in his neck. Brigit shouts, "Get Dr. Grayling!" Elf remembers Brighton Polytechnic. Staff appear with a tarpaulin. They slip it under Jasper's body and, with Griff and Dean, carry him to the changing room. They lower him onto the red leatherette sofa. Jasper's only semiconscious, at best. Luisa checks for a pulse—*Of course she knows first aid: her dad's a war reporter*—while Dean dabs blood from Jasper's nose with a hanky. "Yer'll be fine, mate, don't worry, yer'll be okay." Luisa says his pulse is through the roof. A hefty, bison-faced man in flannel barrels in with Brigit. "This is Dr. Grayling, he's hip." He kneels by the sofa and peers into Jasper's face: "Can you hear me, Jasper?"

Jasper makes no response. His eyes flicker.

A scraping noise comes from Jasper's throat.

Dr. Grayling asks, "Anyone: Does he have a history of epilepsy?"

Elf forces a reply, "Not as far as we know."

"Diabetes?"

"No," says Dean.

"You know for certain?"

"I'm his flatmate."

"What drugs is he on? Do not lie."

"Only Queludrin," says Elf. "As far as we know."

The doctor looks skeptical: "The antipsychotic? Are you sure?"

"Yes. He took some yesterday."

"Any schizophrenic episodes of late?"

"I don't think so," says Elf.

"He was missing all day," says Dean. "We can't be sure what happened since this morning, or what he took."

"I'll give him a sedative to bring his pulse down." The doctor readies a hypodermic needle. "Brigit, you'd better call an ambu—"

The doctor's mouth stops moving, as do his arms, hands, fingers, and eyelids. He is a 3D photograph of himself . . . except for a vein. Elf sees it throb. Dean, also, is motionless, except for his chest rising and falling. Elf turns her head to Luisa—who is motionless, biting her fingernail. "Lu? Can you—"

TIMEPIECE

THE WALL IN JASPER'S MIND IS SHATTERED, AND FALLS AWAY. Knock Knock bursts out, flooding his brain.

Jasper's sentience dims to near zero.

Presence reverts to Absence.

Jasper's body is now Knock Knock's. He can no more command it than the viewer of *Lawrence of Arabia* can command Peter O'Toole, up on the screen. No vocabulary exists for this non-death. Jasper must resort to metaphor. *I used to drive this car where, when, and how I wished; now I'm a passenger in the back, tied and gagged.* Or, *I was once a lighthouse: now I'm a memory of a lighthouse in a mind unraveling.* Through the eyes that were his, he sees the interior of Private Ward N9D. Through the ears that were his, he hears textured silence. The Hollow Man has stopped breathing.

Yet, thinks Jasper, *I'm thinking this, so a piece of me must still exist.* He senses Knock Knock's emotions: the joy of liberation; a curiosity about this tall, strong young body he can now call his. Knock Knock flexes his fingers, stands, inhales deeply. He puts on Jasper's shoes, leaves the ward, and retraces Jasper's steps from the emergency room back through the hospital.

Can you hear me? asks Jasper.

If I wish to, replies Knock Knock.

Am I dead? asks Jasper.

You are an ember, replies Knock Knock.

Will I live like this? asks Jasper.

Do embers live long?

Where are we going?

There is no "we."

Where are you going?

To the place of ceremony, of song, of worship.

Church? asks Jasper.

The venue, replies Knock Knock.

The Ghepardo? Why are you—

A connection is cut, and Jasper receives blurrier, dreamier pictures and the sounds of Knock Knock exiting the hospital and hailing a cab. "The Ghepardo on Broadway and 53rd," says Knock Knock, in Jasper's ex-voice. New York slides by in fits and starts. Cars, lights, shops, buses, storefronts, other passengers in other taxis. Jasper watches it all from inside Knock Knock. He is a passenger within a passenger. *Knock Knock knows what I know, but I don't know what Knock Knock knows.* Jasper's lost his former fluency of thought. Deduction takes effort. *Does this asymmetry of knowledge mean Dr. Galavazi was right or wrong? Am I insane, or is this real?* Jasper doesn't know. Jasper doesn't know how to know.

LEVON IS OUTSIDE the Ghepardo. A poster says, TAKE A TRIP DOWN UTOPIA AVENUE. The cab stops and Knock Knock gets out, bringing what's left of Jasper with him. "Hey!" shouts the driver. "HEY! Mister! Two sixty!" Levon's already there, handing him three dollars. "Keep the change, keep the change. Thanks. Bye." The taxi roars off. Levon grips Knock Knock's shoulders, believing them to be Jasper's. Jasper wants to explain, to apologize, to beg for help, but his tongue, lips, and vocal cords won't work for him. Levon's frowning. *Worry,* Jasper guesses, *relief, and anger.* "Can you play?" asks Levon. "Have you taken anything?"

Knock Knock speaks: "I am here to play."

Jasper hears his own voice convey another's words.

"Good," says Levon. "You've cut it fine, but that's great."

Around them, people are entering the venue.

Someone says, "That's him, that's Jasper de Zoet."

But it's not! It's not me! It's my body, hijacked!

Levon steers Knock Knock down an alley, through a stage door, and down a corridor, where Levon tells a stagehand, "Tell Max and Brigit the Prodigal Son is home." They enter a changing room with dressing tables and two big red sofas in the center. Elf is sitting on one, with her friend Luisa. *Good,* thinks Jasper. *I'm glad you found her, or she found you.* Howie Stoker is here, dressed like Dracula, with a girlfriend—*or his daughter?*—whose eyelashes curl and interlace like Venus flytraps. Elf stands up in her lucky suede jacket from *Top of the Pops* and says his name. Griff's in his loose shirt with his chest hair showing. Dean's shouting at him. Knock Knock asks for water. Dean flings a jugful into Knock Knock's face. Knock Knock enjoys the sensation. Dean is still shouting. A fleck of spittle lands on Knock Knock's cheek. *You're not shouting at who you thinking you're shouting at,* Jasper wants to tell him—but will never be able to tell anyone anything ever again. Elf's calmer. There are mirrors. *This gets complicated.* Through Jasper's ex-eyeballs, Jasper sees his ex-body, steered by Knock Knock, approach the mirror. Knock Knock is smiling with Jasper's face. *So that's what my smile looks like.* It is strange beyond strange. Knock Knock turns away and tunes Jasper's Stratocaster, drawing on Jasper's knowledge. Luisa touches his ex-forehead. "No fever," says the woman. Max Mulholland arrives, pink and sweaty, followed by a bustling woman who Jasper guesses is the venue owner. Speech multiplies. What's left of Jasper can't keep words in the right order as easily as his old self could. *It's like a roomful of radios.* His ex-fingers pluck a G. "I am here to play," says Knock Knock. "I want their energy."

"ROLL AWAY THE Stone"; "Mona Lisa"; "Darkroom." The Ghepardo show is bizarre and painful. Bizarre, because Jasper's ex-body is playing songs Jasper knows inside out as he passively observes. Painful, because performance is not only technique: performance is technique and soul, and Knock Knock minus Jasper is merely competent. Utopia Avenue should be playing far better on their American debut. Elf, Dean, and Griff must think Jasper's letting them down. Five or six hundred New Yorkers will believe the same—that Jasper de Zoet couldn't be bothered. It hurts him that Utopia Avenue die in a whimper of disappointment. *Ironic that, as I'm fading away, I'm feeling emotions more clearly than I did when I had a body.* The band play "The Hook." It's as lackluster a version as the others. Jasper wonders at Knock Knock's motive for bringing his new body here, to play this show. *Not from a sense of duty.* He feels Knock Knock's thrill at the noise and attention. Knock Knock was somebody before Jasper knew him; perhaps that somebody was a performer as well, or somebody who commanded, or was worshipped. *Well?* Jasper asks his jailer. *Will you tell me who you were?* There is no reply. The band play "Prove It." The magical feedback loop between the band and the audience is not happening, and it is Jasper's fault. *Except it's really your fault, Knock Knock . . . Look, the ember's almost out . . . if you'll grant me a dying wish, let me spend the last of myself on "Sound Mind." They'll worship you.* Knock Knock heard him. He's thinking it over. Jasper senses it. His reply arrives with a surge of voltage. Jasper shudders at the shock of possessing his own nervous system once again. Private Ward N9D can only be eighty or ninety minutes ago, but the sensation is giddying and raw. Tinkerbells from the glitterballs dance across Jasper's vision. "Thanks for coming out tonight, everyone."

Someone calls out, "More than *you've* fuckin' done, pal!"

Last words nobody knows will be last words. Jasper turns to Dean: "Thanks." To Griff: "Nice work." To Elf: "Goodbye." Jasper strums; asks the tech guy for more volume on his guitar; shuts his eyes . . . and slams into an amp-blowing, bent-string howl; and fires off a scale of triads, sliding from high E all the way down. Jasper rewards his first cheer of the night with a new riff that isn't "Sound Mind"; nobody will ever know it's a rip-off of Cream's "Born Under a Bad Sign." It gets the audience thunder-clapping in time. Griff, Dean, and Elf join in on drums, bass, and Hammond. Jasper steers the jam through three cycles before wrapping it up in a wah-wah'd B flat, the opening of "Sound Mind." Dean comes in with the bass riff; Elf comes in on the next bar; and Griff chop-slaps on the next. Jasper leans in for his psycho-whisper . . .

Tomorrow I heard a knock at a door—
a door that won't be there before—

couldn't tell if it was criminal,
didn't know it was subliminal, so . . .

Griff gongs the gong. Ghepardo patrons smile. Dean moves in to the mic for his vocal turn as Nobody:

I opened up and Nobody spoke,
"Son, you've become a serious joke;
Old Father Sanity left you behind—
sad truth is, you're not of sound mind."

The band have never played a better "Sound Mind." The crowd belt out the third chorus, and Jasper's eyes are mysteriously wet. *I'm glad it happened once before I went.* Jasper's running out of fuel, of road, of himself. He gallops into a rapid-fire outro. Elf spins out a whirlwind on her Hammond. Griff summons an earthquake from a mile down. Dean's fingers zig-zag faster than the eye. Jasper moves toward the speaker, inch by inch, until it finds Hendrix's Goldilocks spot—and *yooooooooooowl!* A banshee's orgasm. Beyond Elf, Jasper sees Knock Knock pass by Luisa Rey and approach him. This must be a dying illusion. *Knock Knock's in my head.* The phantom turns to the audience to bask in its roaring heat, then he looks at Jasper the way a moneylender looks at a debtor.

He touches the spot between Jasper's eyebrows.

The pain is over before he knew it arrived.

Jasper's body slumps like a discarded puppet.

He sees it on the stage from a few feet above.

So it's true, you really do float upward.

"Sound Mind" has clattered off the tracks.

The Ghepardo trickles away, like sand.

Levon's distant voice: *"Lower that curtain!"*

An irresistible velocity takes him away . . .

TO A SAND dune, steep and high, ending in a ridge, up ahead. The wind and the sand are the only sounds. Behind him, the blankness is blanker the deeper you look. Pale lights stream past Jasper at knee-height or waist-height, toward the ridge. *A multitude.* The wind pushes Jasper up the slope as, surely, it propels the pale lights, like tumbleweed. He tries to catch one, but it passes through his palm. *Souls?* Jasper examines his hand. *Only my memory of my hand.* Perhaps every pale light sees itself as a person. The high ridge is close now, and closer with every step. The sky—*if it is sky*—is darkening to dusk. Soon—*if it is "soon"*—Jasper stands on the crest of the high ridge and looks into the dusk. The Dusk. Dunes slope down to a sea of void. It appears to be four or five miles away, but Jasper doubts that distances work the same way here. The pale lights follow the contours of the dunes, at varying speeds and heights, down to the sea. The soul of Jasper de Zoet steps off the high ridge . . .

Somebody issues an order: *"Turn back."*

The soul of Jasper de Zoet stops at the brink.

The seaward wind pushes at the soul, harder.

The soul resists. A tug-of-war breaks out . . .

JASPER IS SLUNG into his body on the sofa backstage at the Ghepardo. He tries to move. He can't. Not a limb, not a finger. Eyeballs and eyelids, yes. *Otherwise, I'm paralyzed.* The eight people visible to Jasper are motionless. *Not just standing still: motionless.* Dean is a life-size model of Dean, holding a blood-dappled handkerchief close to Jasper's face. *My nose is bleeding.* Griff is standing behind Dean. Luisa, holding Jasper's wrist, is as still as a photograph. Howie's girlfriend is discharging a sneeze. Howie Stoker's fingernail is inside his nostril. Levon and Max appear to be in conversation with a shaggy-haired stranger holding a syringe—*a doctor?* Jasper thinks of Joseph Wright's *Experiment on a Bird in the Air Pump. I can still remember and still access facts.* Noise seeps in from the Ghepardo's ballroom. *Time has stopped in here, but not out there.* Jasper recalls collapsing onstage at the end of "Sound Mind."

He remembers the dunes. The Dusk. *I died.*

Why am I back here? Something brought me.

Where is Knock Knock? Still here in my mind.

What causes paralysis in eight people?

. . .

A MAN AND a woman enter the room. A copper-skinned, middle-aged woman in a khaki tunic, trousers, desert boots, and beads of many colors; and a slim Asian man in a bespoke suit, with silvering hair and gold-rimmed glasses. Neither looks perturbed by the human waxworks.

"The nick of time, I'd say," remarks the woman. She prizes the syringe from the doctor's fingers. "God knows what's in this."

The Asian man approaches the sofa and squats on his heels. "Did you see the high ridge? The Dusk, the souls . . ."

Jasper is still as voiceless as before.

The man touches Jasper's throat.

"Who are you?"

"Dr. Yu Leon Marinus. 'Marinus' is fine. Ignaz Galavazi sent me. I was out of the city, but Esther here"—he glances at his companion—"tracked you after our friend Walt reported seeing you in the park."

The man's speech is precise. His accent is difficult to locate. Jasper's mind scrambles to gain traction. He gestures at the others. "Did you freeze my friends like that? Will they be okay?"

"It's called 'psychosedation.'" Esther Little speaks with a buzzing Australian twang. "They'll be fine. Unlike you"—she frowns at a spot on Jasper's brow—"unless you undergo surgery. Soon."

A young woman enters with a wheelchair. "Xi Lo's suasioning like a flamethrower out there. If you don't want reports of a mass delusion in *The New York Times* tomorrow, we have to go."

"Pardon the bluntness, Jasper," says Marinus, "but your choices are clear and stark. Stay and die when 'Knock Knock' gets free of his temporary straitjacket or come with us and, if you're lucky, live."

A CONTINUUM OF Jasper's recent past flies by, viewed from an impossible train, hurtling through sharp images and blurry tunnels. Here's the band boarding the airplane at Heathrow Airport to fly to New York; here's Dean confronting Guus de Zoet and Maarten; here's the band at Fungus Hut, discussing vocals for "Absent Friend." Most scenes Jasper forgot ever forgetting. Here's the jumble and smell of Berwick Street market near Elf's flat; here's a cherry-red Triumph sports car overtaking the Beast on a downhill stretch lined with orchards; here's Jasper's audition for Archie Kinnock's Blues Cadillac, two Christmases ago. Memories glimpsed from this backward-flying Memory Train are imbued with smell, taste, touch, sound, and moods: here is the dining room at Rijksdorp sanatorium, infused with the aroma of soup and herring. Jasper himself appears in none of them. *A camera can't photograph itself . . . except in mirrors, which I avoid.* Upon reaching Rijksdorp, the memories decelerate; day and night pulse light and dark like a slowing strobe light. Here's Jasper's room, up at the top of the house. An owl hoots. Blustery sunlight shivers on the ceiling. *Benign on the outside, malign on the inside.* The Mongolian is describing his containment of Knock Knock. *It's a void I've cut around your guest. His padded cell, if you like.* Slow blur. The early morning regresses into darkness and nothing . . . until it's the night before, when the Mongolian explained how he could isolate Knock Knock and buy Jasper a few years' peace. Now it's the day before the night. Now it's the episode at the shore, where the Mongolian announced himself to Jasper, waist high in the North Sea with a rucksack full of pebbles . . . Then the Memory Train picks up speed again and travels back through Jasper's months as a psychiatric patient; his guitar classes, lots of Dr. Galavazi . . .

. . . AND IT DAWNS on Jasper that if he isn't controlling this train, someone else must be, and that someone else must be here.

Jasper mind-speaks, *Who are you?*

Only Marinus, replies a familiar voice, here in Jasper's mind. *I didn't want to startle you.*

I don't remember leaving the Ghepardo.

Esther put you under psychosedation, the doctor mind-answers. *There was, and is, no time to waste.*

Where are we? Why am I seeing these memories?

Marinus's pause may contain a sigh. *Imagine trying to explain satellite technology to a mule-driver in fifth-century Italy. You—your body—are at 119A, our redoubt in Manhattan. You're in a secure upstairs room, on a futon, in an induced coma. You're safe. For now.*

The news alarms Jasper. *Will I be all right?*

That depends on what we find. We're currently inside your brain, in your mnemo-parallax. It connects your cerebellum with your hippocampus and functions as a lifelong memory archive.

Did you just say, checks Jasper, *you are inside my brain?*

Incorporeally, yes. My body is on a futon three feet from yours. Esther can transverse standing. I have to lie down.

This is a lot to take in, mind-replies Jasper.

Try, mule-driver. Try. Meanwhile, look at the pictures.

The mnemo-parallax shows autumn at Rijksdorp giving way to summer. Fallen leaves fly up to twigs, attach themselves, and blush from brown to red to orange to green.

Everything's happening backward.

You're re-experiencing your memories in reverse. We're rewinding.

Why is everything sharper than my usual memories?

Marinus extends the analogy. *The mnemo-parallax is a master tape. Full, 4D, multisensory, stereo-surround Technicolor. Regular memories are courtroom sketches, elaborated and eroded at every viewing.*

Summer at Rijksdorp turns to spring. A fox darts backward through the dappled shadows.

You could get lost in here forever and never come out, thinks Jasper. Speech and thought appear to be equal. *Where's Knock Knock?*

In a jury-rigged brig that won't hold for long. He is furious and dangerous.

Can you make a secure cell for him? mind-asks Jasper.

Alas, the Mongolian's procedure was a one-time-only solution. There's not enough spare mass in the brain to do it twice.

How long do I have before Knock Knock's free again?

Hours, replies Marinus. *Hence the urgency.*

In the mnemo-parallax, puddles launch droplets of rain up to twigs and clouds. Tulips shrink into their bulbs.

Jasper asks, *What are we looking for?*

We're sifting the proximate circadian cycles for data on Knock Knock. I've read Dr. Galavazi's reports on "Patient JZ," but that information passed through filters. Your mnemo-parallax is the primary source. When did you first see his face?

My last day at Ely. Seven years earlier. Knock Knock was in the mirror in the wardrobe in my room.

Then let's take a look. The Memory Train picks up speed. Jasper glimpses patients at Rijksdorp unrolling a snowman out of existence. He asks, *How did you "psycho-sedate" everyone back at the Ghepardo? How are you doing all this?*

A branch of applied metaphysics called psychosoterica.

Jasper considers the word. *It sounds like quack science.*

Our fifth-century mule-driver would not know the words "orbital velocity." Does his ignorance mean that aeronautics is quack science?

No, admits Jasper. *Psychosoterica. What is it?*

The devil's box of tricks, to some. To others, it's an arsenal. To us, it's an evolving discipline.

You keep saying "us." Jasper sees his first year at Rijksdorp passing by at a backward canter. *Who are "us"?*

We are Horology, replies Marinus.

Jasper's heard of the word. *Clockmaking?*

In recent decades, yes. Words evolve. In the past a horologist studied time itself. Look, here's you arriving at Rijksdorp . . .

Jasper sees a six-years-younger Dr. Galavazi. Rijksdorp recedes through its gates, viewed at night from Grootvader Wim's Jaguar. Formaggio is in the car, too. The car appears to drive backward to Hook of Holland port in thirty seconds, as night gives way to evening. *I feel like Scrooge in* A Christmas Carol, says Jasper.

I'm not as jolly as the Ghost of Christmas Past, believe me.

The SS *Arnhem* crosses the North Sea toward the morning. A stomachful of vomit flies up from the waves into Formaggio's mouth, and Formaggio rushes backward to the lounge.

The day before this, says Jasper. *The morning before.*

Fast as flight, the ferry arrives at Harwich, a car travels across Norfolk to Ely, night swallows the day, and sixteen-year-old Jasper is back in the bedroom he shares with Formaggio. The *knock-knock-knock-knock-knocking* speeds into a rapid-fire buzz. *Go slow here,* Jasper tells Marinus. *It happened any second . . .*

. . .

NOW. TIME SLOWS to its usual speed, albeit in reverse gear. Here is the moment when Jasper's sixteen-year-old self opens the wardrobe in his and Formaggio's room at Swaffham House. An Oriental cleric with a shaven head stares out of the mirror. The Memory Train stops. Jasper would prefer to look away, but his incorporeal self has no neck muscles or eyelids to shut, so he must scrutinize Knock Knock's scrutiny. *Hatred? Jealousy? Vengefulness?*

Marinus releases a long phrase in a foreign language.

I don't know that language, says Jasper.

He swore, says a dry Australian growl, *in Hindi.*

Jasper would look around for the owner of the voice, but can't.

G'day, kiddo, says the voice. *I'm Esther Little. The other spook.*

Jasper remembers the Aboriginal-looking woman in the changing room at the club. *Is anyone else in here?*

Just us two little mice, says Esther. *Speak, Marinus.*

I've forgotten thousands of faces during my meta-life, says Marinus. *But this one I can't. Nor shall I. Ever.*

Jasper's confused. *You know Knock Knock?*

Our paths crossed years ago. Dramatically.

When? asks Jasper. *Where? How?*

Back in the early 1790s, says Marinus.

Jasper assumes he misheard. *Back in the when?*

Right first time, says Esther. *The 1790s.*

A joke? A metaphor? There's no face for Jasper to try to read, so he asks directly. *Dr. Marinus, how old are you?*

Later. For now, I want more of your backstory.

THE JOURNEY THROUGH Jasper's life accelerates toward the beginning. Nights blink shut, days open up, clouds streak across the sky. Seasons turn, anticlockwise. Summer terms at Bishop's Ely. Easters. Lent terms. Christmases, spent at Swaffham House with boarders whose families lived overseas. Michaelmas terms. Augusts and Julys in Zeeland. Another summer term. The vantage point loses altitude as Jasper's growth is reversed. A balsa-wood glider off the summer dunes at Domburg. A cricket victory. Singing "To Be a Pilgrim" in the school choir. Swimming in the Great Ouse. Conkers, marbles, jacks, and Stuck-in-the-Mud. Soon Jasper is six, and the black car sent by the de Zoets to transport him to a gentleman's life reverses up to his aunt's boarding house in the seaside town of Lyme Regis. Jasper shrinks into his fifth, fourth, and third years, surrounded by giants whose moods are as unaccountable as the weather. Here are Jasper's invalid uncle, scoldings, hide-and-seek, a go-kart, a sparkler writing on the dark, a sunny day, a scary dog as big as a cow, a pram, with a view of a granite seawall curving into a dull jade sea. Seagulls attack a dropped bag of chips. Children—Jasper's cousins—scream. The procession of images pauses on the face of a careworn woman. *That's my aunt Nelly,* says Jasper. *My mother's sister.*

You're twelve months old here, says Marinus. *Now things get indistinct . . .* The images melt into each other. A dog-eaten golliwog. Baked beans squelched between fingers. Rain at a window. A bottle of baby formula. Aunt Nelly's sleepless face crying softly, *"Milly, why did you have to do this to us?"* Howling. Incontinence. Contentment. All lines are smudged lines, and perspective has stopped working. *Babies can't focus their eyes for eight weeks,* explains Marinus. *For Temporals this is the end of the line. Ordinarily. If my hypothesis holds water, however . . .*

The motion continues, turgid and dragging——

——until a jolt occurs, a slip, an imperfect join in the tracks. If Jasper had a body, he would have steadied himself.

The sensation of motion continues, but now it arcs away from the horizontal and toward the vertical. *As if I'm falling down a well,* thinks Jasper. Through windows in the walls of the well he glimpses fireworks and Milly Wallace. Diamond Head, the famous hill at Cape Town. A glimpse of a captain's cabin. The images are clearer than those of Jasper's infancy, but not as sharp as those from his own boyhood. Like pictures of pictures, or recordings of recordings. *But these aren't my memories,* remarks Jasper.

These are fragments of your father's life, says Marinus.

Here is Guus's wife in a wedding veil. Leiden University in, Jasper guesses, the 1930s. Flying a kite. Learning to skim stones . . .

Another jolt occurs. *What is that sensation?* asks Jasper.

A generational join, says Marinus. *We've reached your grandfather, before he fathered your father.* European bodies lie under an African sky. *This looks like the Boer War, I remember it well . . . a bloody, stupid mess.*

Here's a church full of people in old-fashioned clothes. *I know this church,* says Jasper. *It's Domburg, in Zeeland.*

You know it sixty years later, points out Marinus.

He only migrates to boys, I see, observes Esther.

Who is not a product of their times? says Marinus.

Visionaries, replies Esther, *for starters.*

Jasper glimpses Dutch-style canal-side houses under a tropical sky. Horse-drawn carriages. A plantation. Java. A shipwreck. A crocodile attacking a water buffalo. A lamplit Melanesian woman under a mosquito net. A blur of lamplit sex. A volcano. A duel—and incorporeal shock, at a bullet wound. *It feels so real, Marinus.*

Much as early films did, to early cinemagoers.

Jasper asks, *Do memories flow down a bloodline?*

Ordinarily, no, says Esther. *A mnemo-parallax dies with the brain it resides in. But Horology doesn't deal with the ordinary.*

Then how can it be, asks Jasper, *that we are watching memories from before I existed?*

We are no longer inside your *mnemo-parallax,* says Marinus. *These are memories of your ancestors' experiences: but they were archived by a "de Zoet family guest," who passes from father to son, to son, to you. This is the guest's mnemo-parallax, made of his hosts' memories, stitched together.*

Like a giant meta-scarf, says Esther, *made of single scarves.*

A guest the Mongolian? asks Jasper.

With differences, Marinus tells him. *The de Zoet guest didn't, or couldn't, migrate from his hosts. Nor was he ever fully conscious until your lifetime.*

The smell of mothballs. Open chests of white crystals. *Camphor,* says Marinus. *A valuable cargo from Japan in the nineteenth century. We're getting close.* A sloping city of brownish roofs, with green rice terraces higher up. Fishing junks, moored along a wharf. A sailing ship from the Napoleonic era enters a bay, approaching—

backward—a small fan-shaped island, connected to the mainland by a short bridge. A Dutch flag flies on a tall pole. *Peking? Siam? Hong Kong?*

Nagasaki, says Marinus. *A Dutch East Indies Company trading post called Dejima.* The sound of a funeral bell. Incense. A grave inscribed with the name LUCAS MARINUS.

That's your name, says Jasper.

So it is, replies Marinus, in a strange tone. The sound of a harpsichord. A big bear of a man in an early operating theater.

You were fond of the pies, observes Esther Little. *Look at the belly on you.*

I was stuck on Dejima for ten years. Marinus sounds defensive. *The British plundered Dutch shipping. Pies were one of my few pleasures. I died there. Thanks, Britannia. Watch closely, Jasper, you're going to meet someone . . .*

The mnemo-parallax reveals a Westerner's face, a man in his late twenties, freckled and red-haired. He dabs beads of sweat from his brow. *That's Jacob de Zoet,* says Marinus. *Your great-great-great-grandfather.* The scene would be normal enough, except for a small black hole between Jacob's eyebrows. Jacob is writing in a ledger with a quill. Numbers vanish as the quill scratches the paper. The hole in Jacob's head dwindles to nothing. There are inchoate shouts from outside.

That was it, says Esther. *That was the moment.*

I don't understand, says Jasper. *What moment?*

The moment Knock Knock entered your ancestor, explains Marinus, *and began his journey, all the way to you . . .*

THE VIEWPOINT WHEELS in reverse over Nagasaki. Smoke billows into a cooking fire. Gulls spiral backward alongside the "eye." The trajectory passes through a paper screen on a balcony and stops, abruptly, in a room. The image is frozen still. This memory is not blurry but needle-sharp. The woven rush mats smell fresh. Sliding screens are decorated with chrysanthemums. A Go table lies overturned, with a bowl of white pieces spilling across the floor. Four corpses lie slumped. The youngest is a monk. One is an elderly official, with wispy eyebrows. A third appears to be a high-ranking Samurai. The last body is Knock Knock in death. A red gourd has toppled over on its side and four soot-black drinking cups are scattered nearby. *What is this place?* asks Jasper.

The Room of the Last Chrysanthemum, says Marinus. *A room I never expected to see again.*

Poison, I presume, says Esther. *Something quick and nasty.*

That's what the rumors said, confirms Marinus. *Let's begin with our antagonist. Knock Knock was the abbot of an esoteric Shinto order. His real name was, and is, Enomoto. It's the year 1800, if memory serves. His order operated a kind of harem at its mother monastery at Mount Shiranui, two days away up in the remote Kirishima Mountains. The harem's purpose wasn't the usual one, however. It was a type of livestock farm, to ensure a supply of babies.*

Jasper asks, *Why did a religious order want babies?*

To distill their souls into a liquid they called tamashi-abura—Oil of Souls. By imbibing it, the monks postponed death. Inevitably.

Jasper looks at dead Abbot Enomoto. His lips are black. *Enomoto believed he was a necromancer?*

Marinus hesitates. *Oil of Souls, to use an anachronism, did what it said on the label. Those who drank it did not age.*

If I told any of this to Dr. Galavazi, Jasper thinks—

He would call it a schizophrenic episode, Marinus agrees, *in a trice. He's a good psychiatrist, but his frames of reference are limited.*

But elixirs of immortality aren't real, says Jasper.

Two or three in a thousand are, says Esther. *Horology exists for those two or three.*

The psychosedation at the Ghepardo, says Marinus. *The mnemoparallax. This. Esther and me. Are you imagining all this?*

I don't think so, says Jasper. *But how can I be sure?*

God give me strength, huffs Esther.

Follow Formaggio's advice, then, says Marinus. *File us under Theory X. Not reality, not delusion, but a phenomenon awaiting proof.*

Jasper doesn't know how to respond. Theory X is the only way forward. He returns to the four dead bodies. *Who killed them?*

The chain of events would fill a hefty novel, replies Marinus. *Governor*

Shiroyama—the samurai in this frieze—learned about Enomoto's infanticidal regime. He devised a plot to decapitate the order by poisoning its powerful abbot. Enomoto was wisely paranoid about poison, so the plot required both the governor and his secretary to consume the toxin, too. As you see, the plot worked. Enomoto's young novice accompanied his master to the wrong tea party.

Jasper looks at the crime scene. It's sad and real. *If the plot worked, how did Knock Knock—Enomoto—survive?*

Occult knowledge of the Shaded Way, replies Esther Little. *His soul resisted the Sea Wind for long enough to find a host—your ancestor Jacob de Zoet, down in the warehouse. But why him, Marinus? Of all the potential hosts in Nagasaki, what links the abbot of an obscure order to a foreign clerk a quarter-mile away?*

There was a woman, says Marinus.

Aha, says Esther.

One Orito Aibagawa. The first female scholar of Dutch Studies in Japan. I taught her midwifery and medicine at my surgery on Dejima. Jacob fell for Miss Aibagawa, as white knights do in these tales, but Enomoto abducted her to Mount Shiranui, two days away. The abbot wanted the best midwife in Japan to care for the women in his breeding farm.

Why is this link strong enough, asks Esther, *to draw Enomoto's soul halfway across the city at the moment of death?*

Marinus selects his words. *Jacob de Zoet, an interpreter named Ogawa, and I each played a part in bringing Enomoto's crimes to the attention of Governor Shiroyama. From Abbot Enomoto's point of view*—they look at the dead cleric—*we were accomplices in his murder.*

Esther weighs this up. *A karmic thread, then. Enomoto's soul followed it like a beeline. Or a song-line, my people might say.*

Jasper feels left behind. *So my ancestor in the warehouse wrongs this "real" necromancer in the year 1800. Upon dying, Enomoto's soul "flies" into Jacob de Zoet's head and burrows inside. There he stays, dormant, like a larva. This larva gets passed down from father to son, to son, to Grootvader Wim, to my father, to me. All the while, he's "acquiring" his hosts' memories and stitching an ever-longer memory-scarf. Then in the 1960s—sixteen decades later—Enomoto is finally replenished enough to "wake up," shatter my mind, and take over my body.*

That's about the size of it, kiddo, says Esther.

Is there a cure? asks Jasper.

We can't just evict Enomoto, says Esther, *like we're a pair of bailiffs, if that's what you're hoping.*

That's exactly what I'm hoping, admits Jasper.

If we use force and Enomoto resists, explains Marinus, *the brain damage will kill you. Neurologically* and *psychosoterically, he's too deeply anchored.*

What can we do, then? asks Jasper.

A deal, says Esther. *Though even if he agrees to the procedure, the psychosurgery will be very,* very *delicate.*

We need to speak with him, says Marinus.

Wait. Jasper's alarmed. *How will I know if the "psychosurgery" is successful?*

If it works, says Marinus, *you'll wake up here, in 119A.*

If it doesn't work? asks Jasper.

The next thing you see will be the High Ridge and the Dusk, says Esther, *but this time we won't be able to bring you back.*

I don't have much choice, do I? asks Jasper.

The Room of the Last Chrysanthemum fades.

THE CEILING IS plain. The room is spacious. He's on a futon. *Not the slope to the High Ridge.* The floor is wooden. Jasper explores the inside of his skull and finds Knock Knock—or Enomoto—gone. Not partitioned off, like after the Mongolian's operation, but gone, like an extracted wisdom tooth or a paid-off debt. *Gone.* Pale curtains filter daylight. Jasper sits up. He's wearing yesterday's underwear. His clothes are folded and hung on a Queen Anne chair. The room is sparsely, curiously furnished: a wall scroll of a monkey trying to touch its own moonlit reflection, an art nouveau bookcase, a carpet of symbols, an antique harpsichord, and a writing bureau on which sit a fountain pen, an ink pot, and nothing else. Silence.

Jasper stands up and draws the curtains. The window is about five stories up. Manhattan roofs rise, fall, and slant. Not far off, the beveled edges of the Chrysler Building rise into low clouds. It's raining, gently. The bookshelves house books in alphabets varied and unknown to Jasper: *The Perpetuum* by Jamini Marinus Choudary (ed.); *Een beknopte geschiedenis van de Onderstroom in de Lage Landen* by H. Damsma and N. Miedema; *The Great Unveiling* by L. Cantillon; *On Lacunae* by Xi Lo; and, propped up face outward, *Récit d'un témoin de visu de la Bataille de Paris, de la Commune et du bain de sang subséquent, par le citoyen François Arkady, fier Communard converti à l'Horlogerie* by M. Berri. Sheet music of a Scarlatti sonata is on the harpsichord. Jasper lifts the lid. It's old. Jasper's sight-reading isn't as good as Elf's, so he plays the opening bars of "A Raft and a River." The timbre of the notes is spindly and vitreous. There's a small en-suite bathroom he uses. He dresses, but can't see his shoes, so he shuffles to the door in his socks. It slides open into a paneled elevator. Jasper steps inside. The door slides shut. Five unmarked buttons sit in a row; a sixth is marked "*." Jasper presses the asterisk. He waits for the elevator to move, but there are no clunking gears, no slow grinding, like its counterpart at the Chelsea Hotel. Nothing happens.

JASPER SLIDES THE elevator door open and finds an elegant ballroom with a high ceiling and chandeliers. At the end of the long table sits Yu Leon Marinus. "You might want to step out of there," says the doctor. "The elevator has a mind of its own."

Jasper enters the ballroom. Three large windows are semi-opaque. A vast mirror doubles the space and light. Jasper averts his gaze, then averts it back. *One less phobia.* Pictures from many eras adorn the walls, including Agnolo Bronzino's *Venus, Cupid, Folly and Time.* Jasper thought the painting was in London's National Gallery. "Knock Knock's gone," he tells Marinus. "So I guess last night was real."

"He is gone. It was real." Marinus indicates a seat near his and lifts a silver dome of the type used to keep food warm. There are poached eggs, mushrooms, brown toast, grapefruit juice, and a pot of tea.

"That's what I like to eat at home."

"Fancy that. Tuck in, if you're hungry."

Jasper finds that he is, sits down—and realizes they've been speaking Dutch. "A psychiatrist, a Horologist, *and* a linguist."

"My Dutch is rusty, so"—Marinus reverts to English—"I'll spare you further earache. I was reborn in Haarlem six lifetimes ago, but Dutch evolves so rapidly. Really, I should go and live there for a few months to brush up. Perhaps Galavazi can organize a residency."

Jasper grinds black pepper onto his egg. "You really do come back? Lifetime after lifetime after lifetime?"

"Same soul, old mind, new body. Now, let's not insult the chef by letting our breakfast cool. *Bon appétit.*"

Under Marinus's dome is a bowl of rice and miso soup. They eat in silence for a minute. Normals feel awkward in the absence of conversation, but Marinus is no Normal. Jasper notices Marinus's newspaper is the Russian edition of *Pravda.* "Were you Russian in a previous life?"

"Twice." Marinus dabs his mouth. "Any newspaper named 'Truth' is bound to be stuffed with lies. Yet lies may illuminate."

Jasper's yolk bleeds yellow-orange. "So Knock Knock agreed to leave without a fight, and the psychosurgery was successful."

Marinus tips a small dish of pickles onto his rice. "We made a proposal. Esther is persuasive."

Jasper pours some tea into a Wedgwood cup. "A proposal?"

"If he granted you your lifetime," Marinus lifts his bowl and chopsticks, "we would grant him one in return."

"How? He doesn't have a body."

"I found him a spare."

Jasper is flummoxed.

"Last June, a teenage male in a city on the eastern seaboard took a drug overdose. His soul left his body that night, but his body saved itself by entering a coma. The police couldn't identify him and nobody came looking for him. In August John Doe's coma was downgraded to a persistent vegetative state. American hospitals are businesses, and care is costly. Life support was to be withdrawn on Friday. Approximately . . ." Marinus pulls out a timepiece on a chain, ". . . ninety minutes ago, John Doe regained consciousness. His team are calling it a miracle. The word 'miracle' is a disservice to Esther's psychosurgery, but no matter. John Doe's body is Enomoto's new, and last, host body. Barring accidents, he should live to eighty."

"A soul transplant."

Marinus sips his miso soup. "You could say so."

Tulips in a vase are wine-red and snow-streaked.

"What if Enomoto starts brewing Oil of Souls again?"

"Then he becomes an enemy of Horology." Marinus munches a pickle. "It's a risk. The ethics of what we do are gray, I admit. But if ethics aren't gray they aren't really ethics."

Jasper eats a mushroom. "So horology is a kind of . . . psychosoteric FBI. What a job."

There may be a smile under Marinus's frown.

Jasper has cleared his plate. He runs his thumb over his guitarist's calluses. "What do I do now?"

"What do you want to do?"

Jasper considers. "Write a song. Before this fades."

"Then go back to the Chelsea Hotel and write a song. Everyone's at it there, I'm told. Go forth. Multiply. Your body looks good for five or six more decades."

Levon and the band . . . "The others! They'll think . . . I've been kidnapped. Or . . . What about last night at the Ghepardo?"

Marinus dabs his mouth with his napkin. "Xi Lo redacted a few minutes from the mnemo-parallaxi of all the witnesses."

"I have no idea what that sentence means."

"Their memories of what happened backstage have been wiped and replaced by a cover story. You collapsed on stage. An ambulance took you to the private clinic of a colleague of your Dutch doctor for tests and observation. It's not far from the truth. I telephoned Mr. Frankland earlier with the good news that I've identified the cause of your collapse: an endocrinal imbalance, treatable with a course of anticoagulants." He takes a pillbox from inside his jacket and slides it to Jasper. "A stage prop. They're only sugar, but they're big and impressive."

Jasper takes the box. *I'll never need Queludrin again.* "Can I play tonight's gig at the Ghepardo?"

"You'd better, after all this trouble." A young woman has arrived. She has oil-black hair, a heather-colored dress, and a silent way of moving. "Your color's back, de Zoet." She's familiar.

"You brought in the wheelchair for me last night."

"I'm Unalaq. I'm driving you to your hotel."

Time to go. Marinus is walking him to the elevator.

"I had more questions I was hoping to ask."

"I'm not surprised," says the serial reincarnatee, "but further answers would be superfluous."

Jasper steps inside the paneled elevator. "Thank you."

Marinus studies him over his glasses. "I see your ancestor Jacob in you. A middling billiards player, but a good man."

UNALAQ SAYS VERY little as she drives Jasper across a drizzly Manhattan. *Horologists don't talk much.* Carlo Gesualdo's haunted madrigals fill the silence. The anonymous black car crosses Central Park, where Jasper got lost only a night and half a day ago. The streets beyond the park become scrubbier, and soon they pull up at the Chelsea Hotel. Unalaq peers up at the brick cliff face of windows, balconies, and masonry. "The opening party lasted a whole week."

"I won't remember any of this, will I?"

Unalaq doesn't say yes and doesn't say no.

"I understand. If the government knew about Horology, they'd put you all in a lab and you'd never see sunlight again."

"I'd like to see them try," says Unalaq.

"Or if the public knew about predators like Enomoto . . . or that death is postponeable . . . What wouldn't change? What wouldn't the powerful do for a supply of Oil of Souls?"

A garbage truck growls by. Glass smashes in its innards.

"Your life is waiting, Jasper."

"Could I just ask if Horology—"

Jasper is on the pavement looking at Unalaq's Arctic eyes.

"Horology?" she asks. "Isn't that repairing old clocks? I don't know much about it, I'm afraid. Bye, then."

Jasper watches the car vanish around the corner.

"Buddy," says a drug dealer at Jasper's shoulder. "Whadd'ya need? If I ain't got it, I'll get it. Tell me. Whadd'ya *really* need?"

ELF, DEAN, GRIFF, and Levon sit around a Spanish breakfast.

"Eh up," says Griff. "Here comes Trouble."

"Of all the ways to dodge an encore," says Elf.

"Got a decent review, considering." Dean holds up the *New York Star.* " 'Pparently yer collapsed 'cause of . . ." he searches for the line, ". . . 'incandescent creative genius.' Who knew?"

Levon stands up and clasps Jasper's shoulder. "I woke up and thought, *Shit, I don't even have the name of the clinic!* Then the phone went, and it was Dr. . . . Marino telling me all was well. I nearly died of relief."

"Indestructible, is our Jasper," says Dean. "He's prob'ly immortal but hasn't told anyone."

"What *is* 'an endocrinal imbalance' exactly?" asks Elf.

"Elf," says Dean. "Let the poor guy catch his breath. Jasper, mate. Sit down. Have a splash o' coffee. How d'yer feel?"

From now on, Jasper decides, *I am a student of feelings.* "I feel . . ." He looks at his friends. "As if my life is beginning."

utopia avenue
THE THIRD PLANET
SIDE TWO
1. I'M A STRANGER HERE MYSELF (Moss)
2. EIGHT OF CUPS (Moss)
3. THE NARROW ROAD TO THE FAR WEST (Moss)

I'M A STRANGER HERE MYSELF

WHY BLOODY NOT? DEAN LOOPS THE STRAP OF HIS BROWNIE around his neck, climbs onto the balcony railing, grabs the arching trunk of the tree, and starts to shimmy up it, koala-like. The bark is scaly and warm against his skin. Below, Laurel Canyon falls away. Shallow-angled roofs, flat roofs, plants from Tarzan films, and swimming pools in backyards. *Not "back gardens" in America.* Dean reaches a Y in the trunk and perches there. The ground's a long way down. *Broken limbs if not a broken neck.* He looks through the Brownie's viewfinder, doubtful that the camera could capture a tenth of the majesty of the view. Los Angeles, gridded by streets, flat as a puddle, a mile off. The Pacific Ocean is a navy stripe, tinseled. *I'm the first known Moss or Moffat to see it.* The Californian sky is the one real true-blue sky. British blue skies are just a cheap knockoff. *Same goes for flowers.* Flowers here spill, explode, and riot. Scarlet trumpets, frothy lilacs, blushing stars, twisted spires. *What a place, what a day, what a time . . .* Cars rumble. Insects wind and unwind. Birds call strange notes. Dean takes a photo, just to show Ray and Shanks when he gets back. Landward is Joni Mitchell's veranda, almost level with the Y that Dean is perched on. She's trying out versions of a first line: *"I slept last night in a fine hotel . . ."* Then, *"I spent last night in a good hotel."* Then, *"I love to stay in a fab hotel . . ."* The melody's beautiful. *I'm going to ask Elf for piano lessons . . .*

THE LONGER DEAN'S away from London, the less he wants to go back. *Reverse homesickness.* In England's favor, "Roll Away the Stone" is now at number twelve on the UK charts. Utopia Avenue, if it was a football team, has spent its life knocking about in the lower reaches of Division Three. Almost overnight, they've been promoted to the top half of Division One. People are starting to recognize Dean, and ask for his autograph. Including bouncers at nightclubs. He has a cherry red Triumph Spitfire in a lockup behind Levon's flat in Bayswater. *Not to mention regular nookie with Tiffany Seabrook, foxier than all my old girlfriends rolled into one.* On the other hand, England also means the Craddocks, a baby boy who might be Dean's son, and the Craddocks' lawyer, who is proving to be no pushover. England means Rod Dempsey, who is acting more like a Kray Twin by the day. England is 80 percent income tax, miserable weather, strikes, only one flavor of ice cream—white. *Plus, if Great Britain likes the band, America bloody loves us.* After their rocky opening night at the Ghepardo, the band played three strong shows to growing houses. Jimi Hendrix hung out backstage on the Friday. Ginger Baker wants Dean on his next LP. A black model made a move on him several nights ago at the Chelsea. *How could a gentleman refuse?*

"Dean?" Elf's on the balcony in her yellow hippie-chick shift, looking around. Her hair's bundled up in a towel. She can't see him. He's tempted to hide, but: "Me Tarzan," he calls down, "you Jane."

"Jesus! Is that safe?"

"Relax. I've read a million Spider-Man comics."

"You have a phone call."

Here? "Well, yer can tell whoever that I'm up a palm tree in Laurel Canyon, and I'm never coming down. Unless it's Jimi, Ginger, or Janis. I'll come down for them."

"What about Rod?"

"Rod Stewart? Seriously?"

"No, you dolt. Rod Dempsey. Your pal."

The forty-foot drop below lurches into four hundred. Dean grips tight. "Uh . . ." *If I avoid him, he'll guess it's 'cause I helped Kenny 'n' Floss skip town.* "Tell him I'm on my way . . ."

. . .

"ALL HAIL THE King of America!"

"Yer voice is dead clear." Dean tries to sound casual. "Who knew the phone lines stretched this far?"

"Age o' the satellite, matey. Tour going well? The *NME* said yer went down a storm in New York."

Dean feels like a defendant having his guard lowered by a few easy openers. "Jasper collapsed onstage the first night, but he's fine now. This'll be costin' yer an arm 'n' a leg. What can I do for yer?"

"First off, my estate agent says yer 'n' Jasper can move into the Covent Garden flat. No deposit needed for a pal o' yours truly."

"T'riffic, Rod. Thanks a lot."

"Happy to help. Item two's a bit less t'riffic, I'm afraid."

He knows about Kenny 'n' Floss. "Yeah?"

"Delicate one, this, so I'll jump straight in. Two days ago I heard a nasty rumor 'bout a set o' shall-we-say 'artistic' pictures of the missus of a famous filmmaker doing the dirty with a young British bass player on the top floor o' the Hyde Park Embassy."

How? How? Down the wooden hallway, Elf and Jasper are harmonizing on Jasper's "Who was that in Central Park? Who was laughing in the dark?" line.

Rod asks, "Yer still with me?"

"Yer seen 'em? The pics? With yer own eyes?"

"I took the liberty, yeah. 'Cause we're mates. I needed to check if the rumor was bollocks or kosher. 'Fraid to say, it's kosher."

Dean forces himself to ask: "What can yer see?"

"Handcuffs. Faces. Coke. Not only the faces. They've got yer."

Beads in the doorway clack in the draft. "Who took 'em?"

"Prob'ly an insider at the Hilton recognized yer and tipped off a specialist. Looks like a hole was drilled through the adjoining wall. They're top quality. All very James Bond."

"Who'd bother? I'm not John bloody Profumo. Tiffany's no spy."

"Yer've both a public reputation and money to pay to protect it."

"I'm not rich compared to"—*drug dealers and pimps*—"stockbrokers or estate agents."

"The *News o' the Screws*'d pay upward o' three grand for pics o' you 'n' Mrs. Hershey. Stings like this're commoner'n yer'd think."

Dean imagines the scandal and Anthony Hershey's reaction. The film deal would be off. Tiffany's career would be over. *She'll be "the adulterous mother of two" for the rest of her days.*

"Yer've gone all quiet on me," says Rod.

"It's a bloody nightmare, is why."

"Cheer up, yer got a few options. Well, three."

"Revolver, noose, or sleeping pills?"

"Stick, carrot, or 'scarrot.' The stick is, yer tell the bright spark who took the photos that if the pics surface yer'll have him put in a wheelchair. People get persuadable when it comes to kneecaps."

"I can't blame them. So do I."

"Trouble is, what if they call yer bluff? Yer've either got to back off or carry out the threat. Conspiracy to commit GBH'll earn yer two to four years."

"If that's the stick, what's the carrot?"

"Cough up the bread for the negs."

"What stops the bastards coming back for more?"

" 'Xactly. That's the problem with carrots. My friendly advice is, respond with a 'scarrot.' Stick *and* carrot. Yer say, 'Congrats, yer got me fair 'n' square. I like a quiet life, so here's a contract. Sign it, and a thousand quid'll appear in yer account three days from now. Send the negs and another grand'll appear three days later. But if yer ever darken my door again, it's war. If one o' them pictures appears, anywhere, by fuck you will regret it. Deal? Good. Sign on the dotted line and no funny business.' Or language o' that ilk. Then yer can also get 'em for blackmail, if they Judas yer."

The beads clack as if somebody has just passed through. "I don't think I could say all o' that," says Dean. "Not convincingly."

"It ain't yer specialty. But give me the nod and I'll administer the scarrot. Since I've already had dealings."

Dean thinks of the money. "Two bloody grand."

"When knobbing married actresses, change yer hotel. Yer can afford it, mate. What yer can't afford is for this to get out. Yer lady friend, she'd be well 'n' truly pokered. The divorce. The disgrace."

He's right. "Do it, Rod. Please. The scarrot."

A car pulls up in the driveway outside. *Levon 'n' Griff.*

"Leave it with me," says Rod. "But, Dean, first—give me yer word yer won't breathe a thing to yer manager or yer lady friend. If it all goes tits up, the fewer the people yer've told, the better. Yeah?"

"Agreed. I promise. And thanks."

"It's Gravesend boys versus the world. We'll get through this. I'll call again soon to let yer know how it went." *Click.*

Purrr. . . . . Dean hangs up.

"The *LA Times* loves you." Levon enters the house, carrying a box of groceries. "You're the hottest ticket in town."

"Look at this." Griff holds up a real pineapple. "Just like off the front of a can. Cost less than a can. What a fookin' country!"

"Good news," says Dean. "Rod Dempsey just called from London. Me 'n' Jasper can move into that flat in Covent Garden."

Levon can't quite hide how pleased he is. "It was a pleasure to have you and Jasper camping in my flat for a week, but . . ."

"Yer can have too much of a good thing, right?"

IN A ZAP of Californian daylight, Anthony Hershey enters the wood-lined control room at Gold Star Studios. Dean's glad of the low lighting. He feels as if the word GUILT is written across his face. He presses the talkback switch and tells Elf, Jasper, and Griff, "Tony's arrived, guys."

The Californian Anthony Hershey is brasher than his London version, and sports a new goatee and a Hawaiian-print shirt. Dean looks for signs of cuckolded venom, but finds none. "Tiff says hi, Dean," Hershey tells him. "We spoke last night."

"Bless her. Say hi back. How is she?"

"Oh, you know Tiff. Busy busy busy. Handling the boys, running the house, staying on top of the paperwork . . ."

He doesn't know. "Brilliant lady is your missus. She had that Triumph salesman eating out of her hand."

"I'm a lucky man. I know it."

Elf, Griff, and Jasper file in from the studio. "Howdy, all," says Hershey. "Congratulations on the *LA Times* piece this morning. Sounds like a heck of a show. I'll be there tonight if I can."

"I'll put your name on the comp list," says Levon. "Doug Weston says after last night the tickets are hot enough to give third-degree burns. The band were damn tight at the Ghepardo, but folks will be talking about Utopia Avenue's run at the Troubadour in 1968 for the rest of the century. Mark my words."

"It's true," says Jasper, innocently. "We are playing well."

Anthony Hershey flips aside the awkward moment. "You're working like Trojans, that's for sure. I saw your itinerary. San Francisco after here. Press conference later today. What's the TV slot? *Smothers Brothers?*"

"Randy Thorn Goes Pop!" Levon checks his watch. "Forgive me for turning all managerial, Tony, but time's a little tight."

"To business, then. Band. Levon's told me that between conquering the United States, you've found time to think about our *Narrow Road* project."

"Dean's taken the lead on this one," says Elf.

"Then speak to me, Dean."

"I'm not the world's biggest reader, but that screenplay yer sent, I picked it up, and uh . . . yeah. It really got under my skin."

"Good," says Hershey. "I'm very proud of it."

So was Tiffany, thinks Dean. "Strikes me, the whole film's 'bout freedom. Pilgrim's this star, but he's still a slave. It's 'Keep making records,' 'Keep feeding the machine,' 'Keep touring.' That bit where his manager says, 'You want to know what freedom is? It's over there!' and points to the tramp in the doorway. Pilgrim's only jolted out o' the Great Showbiz Machine when he's told he's got just three months to live. So off he goes 'n' finds the Commune o' the Free, but once he's inside, it's a psychedelic concentration camp. Being square's a hanging offense. Literally. The Guru's just another king, or a god, or Chairman Mao. And when Pilgrim's forced to sing his old hits, he's just as much a slave as he ever was, right?"

"We're in talks with Rock Hudson to play the Guru," says the director. "But carry on. Freedom."

"Freedom runs through this story like letters through seaside rock," says Dean. "What freedom isn't: not a jingle, not a slogan, not an anthem, not a lifestyle, not a drug, not a status symbol. Not even power. But when Pilgrim 'n' Piper're on the road, the story looks at what freedom *is*. It's inner. It's limited. It's fragile. It's a journey. It's easily robbed. It's not selfish. It's not commandable. Only the not-free can see it. Freedom's a struggle. It's *in* the struggle. Like *Paradise Is the Road to Paradise,* maybe freedom's the road to freedom." Dean feels self-conscious and lights a cigarette. Elf and Levon are watching him in a new way. Griff ought to crack a joke, but he doesn't. Anthony Hershey's looking serious. "So, yeah, in my four-four rhythm sort o' way, I'm doing a song that captures all o' this. Or trying to. Elf's got a cracking piano figure we're weaving in, and Mr. Stratocaster there is working his usual magic. And that's where we're up to. Sorry if I've read yer script wrong, Tony."

"Far from it." Hershey lights a Chesterfield. *Same brand as Guus de Zoet.* "Everything you said is bang on the nail. I'm delighted you've connected with the script so perceptively."

Sorry I'm nibbling Tiff on the side, thinks Dean, *but if yer weren't knobbing starlets, she wouldn't've come on to me . . .*

"Griff's just added percussion," says Levon, "and we're in the process of getting it down to a three-and-a-half-minute radio edit."

"May I hear it as a work-in-progress?" asks Hershey.

"Dean, I think, should do the honors," says Levon.

"My vocal's rough as old guts"—Dean presses rewind on the console—"and the *scooby-dooby-doobies* are placeholders, but . . ." Tape goes from reel to reel. "Welcome to 'The Narrow Road to the Far West,' take eleven."

Stop.

Play.

NEEDLES OF SWEAT ooze through Dean's pores, coated with makeup. *It's like an extra plastic skin—how do women stand this?* A brunette blows him a pouty kiss from the front row as he lip-syncs the dying notes of "Roll Away the Stone." The production on *Randy Thorn Goes Pop!* is far slicker than on *Top of the Pops* and the audience livelier than their British counterparts. They whoop at Randy Thorn, a Brylcreemed, sequined singer whose clutch of singles fizzled out during the British Invasion in the wake of the Beatles. "A seeen*sation*al song, by a seeen*sation*al band: 'Roll Away the Stone' by Utopian Avenue. Now let's meet the leader of the pack." He holds the mic in front of Dean. "And you are?"

Dean gets a blast of Randy Thorn's egg-and-whisky breath. "Dean Moss. But I'm not the leader."

Randy's smile is undimmed. "You *are* the lead singer?"

"On 'Roll Away the Stone,' yeah, but the three of us"—he indicates Jasper and Elf—"all sing lead on songs we've written."

"Democracy in action, folks. Now, something tells me"—Randy switches to a Texan drawl—*"y'all ain't from these parts, boy."*

A sign is held up: LAUGHTER. The audience laughs.

"Right. We're from Great Britain."

"And how are you finding Great America so far?"

"Pretty cool. As a boy, America was the Land of Elvis 'n' Little Richard 'n' Roy Orbison. I'd dream about playing here. Now—"

"Seeensational. Randy Thorn makes another dream come true." He winks at the camera and strolls over to Griff. "Let's meet this, uh . . . and you are?"

"Griff."

"What's that?"

"Griff."

"Like the 'Billy Goat Gruff'?"

Up goes the LAUGHTER board: out comes the laughter.

"Griff," says Griff. "With an *i*."

"And where's that adorable accent from, Gruff?"

"Yorkshire."

" 'Yorkshire'? What country's that?"

"It's up on the English border with Norway. Visit us when you're over. We do love a pillocky prat in Yorkshire."

Randy turns to the camera. "Who knew, Mom 'n' Pop? The things you learn on *Randy Thorn Goes Pop!* Now let's quit Gruff while the going's good and pay a call to . . ." he steps down from the riser, "the fair *lady* of Utopia." He walks toward Elf, then veers to Jasper, acts confused, gurns at the camera, looks back at Jasper, and covers his mouth in fake mortification.

Up goes the LAUGHTER board: out comes the laughter.

"Just my little gag—hope you're not offended."

"I'm not good at getting offended."

"That's a red flag to a bull, my friend. What's your name?"

"My first name or my full name?"

Randy Thorn gurns at the camera. "Your first name's enough."

"It's Jasper."

"You know, I thought Jasper was a boy's name?"

Up goes the LAUGHTER board; out comes the laughter.

That's not bloody funny, thinks Dean.

"Couldn't resist it, folks," says Randy Thorn, "Could *not* resist."

"I'm surprised you think my hair's effeminate, Mr. Thorn," says Jasper. "Many American men have long hair. Have you considered that your culture's moving on, but you aren't?"

Randy Thorn's grin strains its seams. "Folks, Jasper the joker! Last but not least is the rose among the thorns, or is she . . ." the presenter crosses the stage to Elf, ". . . the she-wolf among the sheep? Let's find out! What's your name, sweet cheeks?"

"Elf Holloway."

"Elf? 'Elf'? As in 'Pixie'?"

"It's a nickname, from when I was little."

"And are you hiding pointy ears under those golden locks?"

"It's a nickname, from when I was little."

"Do you work on Santa's Naughty 'n' Nice lists? I'm both, by the way. Very naughty *and* very nice." Up goes the LAUGHTER board. The studio laughter, at last, is dimming. "What's it like being Little Orphan Annie in a band of big bad boys, like Jasper, Gruff, and Derek? Boys *will* be boys, right?"

Elf looks around at the producer offstage who has the decency to look embarrassed: "They're gentlemen."

"Wh*oooooo*psie! Folks, I think we've touched a raw nerve!"

"Oy, Randy!" says Dean. "We've written a special song for yer."

Randy Thorn walks over and into the trap. "A special song?"

"Yeah. It's called"—Dean takes the mic and looks into the live camera, enunciating each word like a newsreader: " 'Randy Thorn's Career Lies a-Mouldering in Its Grave.' Want to hear it?"

The silence in the studio is silent.

Dean drops the mic at Randy's feet, pats his cheek, drops the fake bass, and makes a throat-slashing gesture at the others. Utopia Avenue walk off the set. Low-level chaos is boiling over. A hand grips Dean's collar from behind and squeezes, constricting his windpipe. "Shitty limey cocksucker!" Randy Thorn drags Dean back a few paces. "This is MY SHOW! NOBODY walks off MY SHOW!" He hurls Dean to the studio floor, his eyes bulging. He kicks Dean's ribs. Dean rolls back, trying to get up, but another kick lands in his jaw. He tastes blood. Then he glimpses Elf, swinging the fake bass smack into Randy Thorn's face. She must have wielded it with force to make it shatter the way it does. Bits of instrument fly off. A few rain on Dean.

Randy Thorn's face has gone from blood-lustful to dazed. Griff and Levon are helping Dean up when a voice shouts out, "KILL THE CAMERAS! NOW! ALEX! *KILL THE CAMERAS!*"

Kill the cameras? They were still rolling? This show's live—so people at home saw that? Through a haze of pain, implications swarm into Dean's brain.

THE BAND TROOP onto a low stage and sit at a table in a conference room at the Wilshire Hotel. Cameras click like a locust attack. The big clock says 7:07 P.M. Dean's face is still throbbing. Elf pours him a glass of ice water and mutters, "Keep an ice cube on where it hurts." Dean nods. A TV camera is recording the proceedings. Thirty or forty reporters and photographers are seated in rows. Max sits with Griff and Jasper on one side and Elf and Dean on the other. He taps the microphone. "Folks, can everyone hear me?"

A few nods and "Yep"s and a "Loud and clear."

"I'm Max Mulholland, head of Gargoyle Records. Apologies for keeping you past happy hour. Send your complaints to Randy

Thorn, who went *pop* live this afternoon." Genuine laughter from the press pack. "It's great to see so many of you. Clearly the old maxim 'Nothing travels faster than light except gossip in Hollywood' is still as true as it's ever been . . ."

Dean looks out through the glass wall of the conference room over a lush lawn to a row of palm trees. His jaw hurts.

"Griff, Jasper, Elf, and Dean are here to answer any questions," Max is saying. "Time's short, so with no further ado, fire away."

"Los Angeles Times," says a man with the air and five o'clock shadow of a Raymond Chandler detective. "A question for Mr. Moss regarding his future best man Randy . . ."

"Please don't make me smile." Dean touches his jaw. "It's tender."

"Apologies. Randy Thorn issued this statement an hour ago: 'That faggoty English sonofabitch set out to provoke me, just to get attention for his shitty music. Deport that drug fiend now.' Any responses?"

Dean sips his water. "It's one o' my better reviews." Laughter. "Is Randy saying that *I* knew—in advance—that he'd be grabbing my neck, decking me, and kicking my face? How? How could I know that?" Dean shrugs. "I'll let yer draw yer own conclusions."

"Will you file assault charges?" asks the journalist.

Max swoops in: "We'll be consulting our lawyers."

"Nah," says Dean. "I'm not suing anyone. Randy was drunk before the show. His career's over. Anyway, it was worth it, just to see Elf do a Pete Townshend on his head."

There's a cheer; Elf buries her embarrassed grin in her hands and shakes her head.

"Was that the love and peace we hear so much about from the counterculture?" asks a reporter in a banana-yellow jacket.

Elf uncovers her face. "Love and peace aren't pushovers."

"*Billboard* magazine." The reporter puts Dean in mind of the jack of spades. "Hi. I'd like to ask each of you to name one U.S. artist who inspires you, and why."

"Cass Elliot," says Elf. "For proving that female singers don't have to look like a *Playboy* bunny."

"Elvis," says Dean, "for *Jailhouse Rock.* He showed me what I wanted to do with my life."

"A drummer died," says Griff, "and at the Pearly Gates he heard drumming so incredible, it *had* to be Buddy Rich. So he said to Saint Peter, 'I didn't know Buddy Rich had died.' Saint Peter said, 'No no, that's God. He *thinks* he's Buddy Rich.' That's my answer."

"Emily Dickinson," says Jasper. The reporter looks surprised. An approving murmur breaks out. Dean wonders, *Who?*

"I'm from *Ramparts.*" A reporter stands up. He's the only black reporter in the room. "What are your views on the ongoing carnage in Vietnam?"

Huffs, clucks, and phews break out. Max says, "Look, I'm not sure if that's really relevant, so—"

" 'Roll Away the Stone' references an antiwar demo in London, or were you *not* actually there in Grosvenor Square, Dean?"

"Dean," Max leans behind Elf, "you don't have to—"

"No, I'll answer. Took balls to ask that. Yeah, I *was* there," he tells the *Ramparts* man. "Mate, I'm British. Vietnam's not my war. But if Vietnam was winnable, then after all these months gone, all that money spent, all them bombs dropped, all them lives lost, America would've won it already. Wouldn't yer?"

"Herald Examiner." A man raises a pen. "What do you say to those who maintain that by defending Vietnam, the USA is defending *all* liberal democracies from a domino effect of Communist takeovers?"

" '*Defending* Vietnam' did you say?" Elf asks. "Have you not seen the pictures? Does Vietnam look 'defended' to you?"

"Sacrifices happen in war, Miss Holloway," says *Herald Examiner.* "It's a nastier job than singing about rafts and rivers."

"The immigration man who stamped my passport in New York had a son in Vietnam," says Elf. "That son was blown up. Do you have sons, sir? Have they been drafted?"

Herald Examiner shifts his body. "This is your press conference, Miss Holloway. I'm not sure if—"

"I'll translate," says the *Ramparts* reporter. "He's telling you, 'Yes, I *do* have sons: no, they will *not* be going to Vietnam.' "

"They have legitimate medical exemptions!"

"How much did those bone spurs set you back, Gary?" asks *Ramparts.* "Five hundred bucks? A thousand?"

"Questions for Utopia Avenue over here," announces Max. "Political kickboxing outside, gentlemen, please."

"*San Diego Evening Tribune.*" The speaker is a woman. "A simpler question than Gary's: Can songs change the world?"

Too much like hard work for me, thinks Dean, looking at Elf, who looks at Griff, who says, "Hey, I just drum along."

"Songs do not change the world," declares Jasper. "People do. People pass laws, riot, hear God, and act accordingly. People invent, kill, make babies, start wars." Jasper lights a Marlboro. "Which raises a question. 'Who or what influences the minds of the people who change the world?' My answer is 'Ideas and feelings.' Which begs a question. '*Where do ideas and feelings originate?*' My answer is, 'Others. One's heart and mind. The press. The arts. Stories. Last, but not least, songs.' Songs. Songs, like dandelion seeds, billowing across space and time. Who knows where they'll land? Or what they'll bring?" Jasper leans into the mic and, without a wisp of self-consciousness, sings a miscellany of single lines from nine or ten songs. Dean recognizes "It's Alright, Ma (I'm Only Bleeding)," "Strange Fruit," and "The Trail of the Lonesome Pine." Others, Dean can't identify, but the hardboiled press pack look on. Nobody laughs, nobody scoffs. Cameras click. "Where will these song-seeds land? It's the Parable of the Sower. Often, usually, they land on barren soil and don't take root. But sometimes, they land in a mind that *is* ready. *Is* fertile. What happens then? Feelings and ideas happen. Joy, solace, sympathy. Assurance. Cathartic sorrow. The idea that life could be, should be, better than this. An invitation to slip into somebody else's skin for a little while. If a song plants an idea or a feeling in a mind, it has already changed the world."

Bloody hell, thinks Dean. *I live with this guy.*

"Why's everyone gone quiet?" Slightly alarmed, Jasper asks the band. "Was that weird? Did I go too far?"

MAX USHERS THE band out and along a corridor carpeted in blood-and-coffee-colored zigzags. "The photographer's set up in the big room at the end. I'll quickly call Doug Weston to say we'll be a little late." Dean walks on ahead, following the twists and turns of the corridor, and finds himself alone. *They'll be along in a minute.* He passes through swing doors into a makeshift photo studio. A slim woman stands with her back to him, taking a light meter reading as a flash bounces off a reflector. She turns and looks at Dean. Skinny, blond, thickish lips . . . *Have we slept together?* She takes a picture with the camera around her neck. "Mecca? Bloody hell!"

Click. Scrit-scrit. "How's things, Dean?"

"But . . ."

"I am your photographer."

"But . . ." *Get a grip.* "So you live here in LA?"

"Now, yes. I've been traveling around since London. But I started working for an agency here exactly two weeks ago."

"Your accent's gone all . . . German-American."

"Language is a virus, like Burroughs says."

Burroughs? A new boyfriend? "Does Jasper know?"

The doors open. Elf's mouth gapes like a cartoon character: *"Mecca!"* She sails over for a long hug. Mecca looks over Elf's shoulder at Jasper and her face says, *Hello,* and Dean feels envy and an unpleasant recollection of the morning's call about photographs and blackmail. Mecca finishes the hug. "Hello, Griff. Hello, Levon."

Levon does not look surprised. *The Dark Arts,* thinks Dean. Griff looks delighted. "Small world, eh?"

"It is. Hello, Mr. de Zoet."

The ex-lovers stare at each other for a few seconds.

"You look a little bit older," says Jasper. "Around the eyes."

"Oh, dear God, Jasper," groans Elf. "I despair of you . . .' "

Mecca's laughing. "Your Troubadour show last night was *very* great. I thought the first album was out of this world, but *Stuff of Life* blows my mind."

"Hang on," says Elf. "You were at the Troubadour?"

"I bought a ticket when I hear you play there."

"Why didn't yer bloody *tell* us?" asks Dean.

"I did not want to be the girl who says, 'Hey, I used to date the guitar god, so give me special treatment.' Also . . ."

"Oh, Jasper's single," says Dean. "Since you left, none o' the babysitters've lasted more than a week or two."

"Are you free this evening?" asks Jasper. "Come to the show."

"There's a party at Cass Elliot's house after," says Levon.

Mecca sighs and looks uncertain. "Unfortunately, Friday night is my Black Forest Gateau and Lederhosen Club Night. So sad . . ."

Jasper needs a few seconds. "Irony." Then he's not so sure. "Or a lie? No. A joke. Dean? Was it a joke?"

Max Mulholland sails in. "Doug Weston says every last ticket sold within a quarter-hour of Elf whacking Randy Thorn on his head. There's a line outside already. We'd best hurry . . ."

THE QUEUE IS still there an hour later. The band, Levon, and Mecca watch from across Santa Monica Boulevard. Under a roof of dark glare, warm lights illuminate the club's frontage and a sign in a Gothic font: DOUG WESTON'S TROUBADOUR. Lower down, in block letters: UTOPIA AVENUE. Mecca's holding Jasper's hand, Dean notices. *Looks like they're picking up where they left off . . . No "Who have you slept with?" No fuss. No love child. No paternity lawsuit.* A gunmetal gray Ford Zodiac cruises by. Next, an eye-blue Corvette Sting Ray. Then a ruby-red Pontiac GTO.

"Night four," says Griff. "Anybody getting used to it yet?"

"Not me," says Elf. "Not yet."

"I was shitting myself the first night," says Dean. "But now I'm like, *Ah, we knocked it for six before, we will again.*"

"Tuesday to Thursday," says Levon, "you were building buzz. Tonight's the payoff. A good run at the Troubadour unlocks Los Angeles. Los Angeles unlocks California. And California's the key to America. Not New York. Here. Things are falling into place."

Dean smells car fumes and his own aftershave. "Bet it's raining in England now. Here we are in short sleeves. They'll never know. Our families, I mean. We can describe it, but unless they've been here, unless they've lived it . . ."

"I've had that thought too," says Elf. "It's melancholic."

"Turn around, everyone," instructs Mecca.

They obey—*Click 'n' FLASH! Scrit-scrit . . .*

"Yer don't tend to ask, do yer?" remarks Dean.

"No, she does not," says Jasper.

"Either you ask politely," replies Mecca, "or you get good photographs." *Click 'n' FLASH! Scrit-scrit . . .*

"Let's go tell Doug we're here," says Levon.

DOUG WESTON'S UPSTAIRS office vibrates in time to the support act's bass. 101 Damn Nations, a local band, are good enough to "warm the seat" but not so good as to threaten Utopia Avenue. Doug Weston, a giant in green velvet with anarchic blond hair, is the most affable club owner Dean has ever met, and when the rest of the band go downstairs, he stays to chat a while longer. Doug discusses the Randy Thorn episode and takes out a Sucrets throat-lozenge tin. "It was *the* most compelling live TV since . . . well, I'd propose Lee Harvey Oswald's assassination, but that would be tasteless. People were phoning in on KDAY-FM, KCRW. They've been playing 'Roll Away the Stone.' You're the conversation in LA today. If Levon wasn't so Canadian, I'd be thinking, *Shit, did he set the whole thing up?*"

"That's Randy Thorn's theory, I'm told," says Dean. " 'Cept in *his* version, *I* set the whole thing up."

"Randy Thorn's days of being taken seriously by anyone except his mother and his dog are over." Doug clears space on his desk, pushing aside bills, papers, letters, acetates, ashtrays, shotglasses, a Pirelli calendar, and a framed photograph of Doug and Jimi Hendrix. Doug opens the small tin and takes out a loaded spatula's worth of cocaine, deposits it on the cover of *Newsweek,* and makes a white line running between Hubert Humphrey and Richard Nixon. He hands Dean a rolled-up dollar bill and tells him, "Rocket fuel."

Dean snorts the cocaine up his nostril and flips his head back. It burns, freezes, and exhilarates. *Ten espressos at once.* "Liftoff."

"Ain't that just the *smoothest* shit?"

"The stuff at home just butchers my nose."

"Keith Richards preaches two cardinal rules: know your dealer and buy the best. If you don't, your shit'll be cut with cornstarch, baby milk, or worse."

Dean glows. "What's worse than cornstarch?"

"Rat poison's worse than cornstarch."

"Why would a dealer poison his customers?"

"Profit. Indifference. Homicidal urges." Doug tips out a second heaped spatula onto *Newsweek.* "I've twice your body mass," he explains. He snorts—*"Aaahhhhhh . . ."*—and smiles like an ugly horse attaining Nirvana.

I wrote a few songs, thinks Dean, *they got recorded, and look at me now. I've bloody won, Gravesend. See? I won . . .*

Doug Weston locks his cocaine stash away. "Let's get you back now. Mustn't let Levon think I'm leading you down the starry path of rock 'n' roll depravity . . ."

THE BAND, LEVON, and Mecca wait on the stairs leading down to the stage. The Troubadour is packed, twice over. The smoke is thick. Dean's coming down from his cocaine bump but still feeling semi-indestructible. "Here at the Troubadour," says Doug Weston onstage, "we've always taken pride in introducing the hottest talent from England to our City of the Fallen Angels. Utopia Avenue is playing their last night of an un-for-*gettable* stay here. Randy Thorn sure as hell ain't going to forget anytime soon, anyhow." Laughter and cheers surge up the stairs. Dean squeezes Elf's hand and Elf squeezes his back. "But I know the band'll be playing again at the Troubadour very soon because—"

"You made 'em sign a blood oath to come back and do shows for the next twenty years?" calls a heckler.

Doug presses his hand to his wounded heart. "Because they have a cosmic future. So with no further ado . . ." he turns to face the band at the top of the stairs, ". . . Utopia Avenue!"

The applause has grown from a low boil on Tuesday to a roar spiked with catcalls tonight. Dean and Doug pat shoulders as they pass and Doug speaks in his ear: "Slay 'em." The band take their positions. Dean looks into the dim, brick-walled venue, full of glinting eyes, and thinks, *They're here to see yer 'cause yer the best thing on in LA tonight.* He gets a nod back from Elf, Griff, and Jasper, comes in close to his mic, and fills his lungs:

I-i-i-i-f life has shot yer full of holes—

His voice detonates—it is scorched and tortured, like Eric Burdon's on "House of the Rising Sun" . . .

a-a-a-a-nd hung yer out to dry . . .

A figure on the side catches his eye; Dean's pretty sure it's David Crosby, late of the Byrds—that hat, that cape—*breathe* . . . Dean reaches for the next line . . . which is . . . which was . . . Gone.

What's the next bloody line?

How can I have forgotten?

I've sung it five hundred times!

Then what is it? There's just a noisy druggy glow in his brain where the words should be. *Why why why did I do the fucking cocaine?* Now Dean's panicking, all hope of finding the lyrics is gone, *and they're going to realize I'm an amateur and an impostor and I shouldn't bloody be here,* and Dean feels the eyes on him *finding me out, finding me out, finding me—*

and slung you in a pauper's grave

Elf's voice arrives, like a sonic angel, as if the long pause was deliberate. Dean turns to her. *I love yer,* he thinks. *Not like a boyfriend: I love yer deeper than that.* She nods to say, "You're welcome," and sings the next line:

down where the dead men lie —

On "lie," Dean and Griff come in. Four bars later, Elf joins in and Jasper *keranggg*s his guitar into urgent life.

If life has shot yer full of holes
and hung yer out to dry —
and slung yer in a pauper's grave
down where the dead men lie —

He fluffs the riff a little—if his fingers were a sports car, the brakes would need seeing to—but at least he remembers the words. *Swear to God, I'll never do cocaine before a show again, ever, ever.* Here come Jasper and Elf to join in the chorus:

I'll roll away the stone, my friend,
I'll roll away the stone —
put my shoulder to the rock
and roll away that stone.

Verse two: the Ferlinghetti Verse. Dean plays his Fender safely and solidly, a fraction of a beat behind Griff, like a drunk sober enough to know he's drunk and needs to let someone else lead:

If Ferlinghetti frames yer
and throws away the key —
if you were there in Grosvenor Square
where Anarchy killed Tyranny —

Dean realizes his mistake immediately: it's "Tyranny killed Anarchy." *Anarchy killed Tyranny means the good guys won. Maybe no one will notice,* he tells himself, *or maybe everyone noticed.* Jasper adds fills to the chorus's second and fourth lines:

We'll roll away the stone, my friend,
we'll roll away the stone —
we'll get you on yer feet again
and roll away that stone.

Jasper keeps his first solo close to the album's. They have ninety minutes to fill and, as Eric Clapton told them, always keep your best fireworks for the second half.

The eunuchs in the harem
will twist the words yer meant,

but they can't make yer hate yerself
without yer give consent.

Elf plays the Hammond part with her left hand and adds piano with her right:

So ro-oooll away that stone, my friend,
Ro-oooll away that stone —
grip it, heave it, kick its arse and
roll that goddamn stone.

Last is the verse Elf suggested. Dean thinks it's the best, but finds that cocaine has boosted not his confidence but his self-doubt, and he's afraid the verse will sound glib. Dean lets his Fender hang and grips the mic like a man throttling a chicken that refuses to die:

If death touches one yer love,
if grief grips yer in its fist,
honor those who left too soon —

Dean looks over at Elf, knowing who she's thinking about. On one side is her nephew, an infant everybody wanted but who didn't survive past the bluebell season. On the other side is Amanda Craddock's boy. Dean, at least, would rather the boy didn't exist; but there he is, in a poky flat in North London, thriving and growing and being. *Life has a sick sense of humor.* The band waits for four beats . . .

exist, exist, exist.

Until recently, Griff tapped the four beats on the rim of his drum, but they've been so musically tight over the last month that he stopped. Dean is so anxious not to jump the gun—and jittery with the coke—that he jumps the gun half a beat earlier. *I keep misfiring 'n' slipping gears.* The others stumble to catch up:

Let's roll away the stone, my friends,
let's roll away the stone —
persistence is resistance, so
roll away that stone.

The applause is solid, but not ecstatic. Dean is furious with himself. He wants to rush offstage. *I want to hide for the rest of the century.*

"Stay," says Jasper, into his ear. "You'll be fine."

Yer mystery, de Zoet, thinks Dean. "Sorry." Jasper clasps Dean's shoulder. *He's never, ever touched me before . . .*

Elf has picked up the slack. "It's great to be here, and not in a cell in the county jail facing a charge of aggravated assault with a plywood guitar." More laughter. "This next is a voodoo curse about art, love, and theft. It's called 'Prove It.' " She checks everyone's ready. Still floored by Jasper's empathy, Dean nods.

"A-*one* and a-*two* and a one-two-*three*—"

DEAN STEPS INTO the illuminated garden of Cass Elliot's house. The pool is twice the size of Anthony Hershey's. Lanterns glow in the trees. Revelers laugh. Lovers enter wigwams and lie in hammocks smoking weed. *This is the party I've been looking for all my life,* thinks Dean. The band's temporary neighbor Joni Mitchell's vodka-on-ice voice escapes through a window. The song is "Cactus Tree." Her voice pulses, dives, aches, swivels, regrets, consoles, avows. Dean peers in through the insect screen. Joni's hair and skin are golden under a marigold lamp. She sings with her half-closed eyes watching her fingers. Her tuning never stays still. This song is DADF#AD with the capo on the fourth fret. *I should mess around with tunings more . . . It changes the voice o' yer guitar.* Mama Cass looks on with a face like that of a woman in prayer. Graham Nash sits cross-legged, gazing up at his candlelit girlfriend. California has worked its King Midas magic on him, too. Everybody here is 15 percent better-looking than they are elsewhere. A white moth lands on Dean's watch. Joni finishes the final verse on a strummed discordant *ka-dannngggg.*

Dean heads for the lookout deck at the end of the garden. Peacocks wander aimlessly underneath the orange tree. A pockmarked half-moon hangs above the wooded mountain. *Moonlight is sunlight, bounced.* The moon is eclipsed by a black cowboy hat. "Congratulations, Dean." The cowboy is soft-spoken and intense. "Tonight was quite something."

" 'Ppreciate yer saying so. It had its ups 'n' downs."

"Your downs are higher than most artists' ups. If I'm any judge of these matters, you're destined for greatness."

"Nobody knows what's waiting round the next bend."

"Prophecy is a fancy name for an intelligent guess. Joint?" A silver box of reefers is produced from thin air.

"Why not?"

The cowboy lights one for Dean and slips a second into his jacket pocket. "What one thing do all bands have in common?"

"What one thing *do* all bands have in common?"

"One fine day, they cease to exist."

"Yeah, but yer can say that 'bout anything."

"Jasper and Elf are gifted, yes. But you're the best songwriter. You also have the looks and charisma to be a solo star. I don't deal in flattery, Dean. I deal in facts. 'Roll Away the Stone' should be a worldwide Top Five hit. With the right marketing, it would be."

"What did yer say yer name was?"

"My name's Jeb Malone. I work for Mr. Allen Klein."

Dean knows the name. "The Stones' new manager?"

"None other. Mr. Klein admires your songs, your voice, your spirit, and your potential. Here's his direct line." Jeb Malone slips a card into Dean's shirt pocket. "If your situation changes vis-à-vis the band, Mr. Klein will be happy to discuss your options."

Take that card out, Dean tells himself, *and rip it up.*

Dean looks around to check nobody saw. "I'm already in a band. I already have a deal. I already have a manager."

"And Levon is a very nice guy. Very Canadian. But business is a jungle, and you need carnivores, not nice guys. Mr. Klein could close you a deal for two solo records worth a quarter of a million dollars. Not 'in theory.' No ifs, no buts. Now."

The party sound recedes, leaving only the number, which Dean can't quite believe. "Did you just say . . ."

"One quarter of a million dollars. A life-altering sum. Think about it. Mr. Klein will be expecting your call. Enjoy the party." Jeb Malone vanishes in a puff of joint smoke.

Dean heads for the lookout deck at the end of the garden. *A quarter of a million dollars.* On a nearby roof, cats screech songs of feline lust. "Dean Moss," says a woman, who might have slid off an Egyptian vase. Kohled eyes, linen shift, stern black hair. "I'm Callista, and I have an unusual passion. Maybe you've heard of me."

"Or maybe I haven't." Dean drinks from his bottle of beer.

"I take plaster casts of the penises of rock stars."

Most of Dean's beer exits via his nostrils.

"I've done Jimi Hendrix," Callista recounts, "Noel Redding, Eric Burdon, but his broke in two. The cast, I mean. Not the penis."

She's serious. "Why?"

"If the penis droops in mid-session, a crack can appear."

"No, I mean why d'yer do plaster casts o' knobs?"

"A girl needs a hobby. It'll only take an hour, and my friend comes along to plate you, so don't worry about stage fright."

"Try Griff. A drummer'll do a lot for free plating."

"There's only one man in Utopia Avenue I *really* want . . ."

"Good luck with yer collection, Callista."

"Booo-*rrr*ing." Plaster-caster Callista exits the scene.

Dean continues his journey over to the lookout deck.

"Quite a show you guys put on," says a face with a horseshoe mustache. He looks like a Mexican bandit who gets shot first in a Spaghetti Western. " 'Look Who It Isn't' kinda oiled my gun."

"Jesus bloody Christ. Yer Frank bloody Zappa."

"On my better days I am," says Frank Zappa.

Dean shakes his hand. "Janis Joplin put me on to *We're Only In It for the Money*. It's indescribable. It's—"

"I'll take 'indescribable.' Like Charles Mingus says, writing about music is like dancing about architecture."

A woman nestles into Frank Zappa's side. She's holding a glass of milk. "Hi, I'm Gail. The dreaded wife. We dig your band."

Mr. Zappa smiles at Mrs. Zappa with pride and affection.

"Nice to meet yer." He tokes on his reefer. "Care for a puff?"

"We're abstainers," says Frank. "The world is majestic enough."

Frank Zappa doesn't do drugs? "That's cool. So, Frank, how'd yer get MGM to release the least commercial LP ever made?"

"My guile and MGM's ignorance. If you think my stuff's uncommercial, try Stravinsky. Try Halim El-Dabh. Or try braining Randy Thorn with a guitar on live TV. Pure performance art."

"That was just . . . an unplanned accident," says Dean.

"Accidents are often art's best bits," remarks Frank.

"It'll buy you an authenticity that money can't," says Gail. "Utopia Avenue are now the Anti-Monkees."

A diver belly flops into the pool. Onlookers go, *"Woooooo!"*

"So what do you think of the place?" asks Frank.

"Laurel Canyon? It's like the Garden of Eden."

"The Garden of Eden's no Paradise," says Frank.

"I thought it was the original Paradise," says Dean.

"It's the original horror show. God creates Eden and puts a naked man and a naked woman in charge. 'All this is yours,' His Omniscience says, 'but whatever you do, DON'T eat this apple dangling HERE on the Tree of Knowledge, or BAD SHIT will go down.' Why not go the whole hog and hang an EAT ME sign on it? Adam and Eve deserve medals for holding out so long. God has to crack them with the old phallic talking-snake trick. So they eat the knowledge—as God intended all along—and get punished with menstruation, work, and corduroy pants. The carnivores turn on the herbivores and the soil of Eden is soaked in blood. See? The original horror show."

Dean frowns. "What're yer saying, Frank? That Laurel Canyon's a bloodbath waiting to happen?"

"I'm saying," replies Frank, "that if you ever think, *I've found Paradise,* you are not in possession of the facts. Don't be dazzled by peacocks either. They're vain, ornery sons-of-bitches who shit like it's going out of style."

DEAN STANDS ON the lookout deck at the end of the garden, smoking Jeb Malone's second joint, imagining himself on the prow of a ship. Insects trill by the million. Stars run rampant by the billion. *If, just if, in the future, or a next-door universe where Utopia Avenue is over, and I'm a free agent, and I call Allen Klein and if,* if, *I got that quarter-million . . . which one o' them houses'd I fancy?* He settles on a big house three properties over. It's all arches and terra-cotta with giant ferns. A couple are enjoying a late hot tub under the half-moon and stars. Dean imagines he's watching himself and Tiffany. Tiffany's kids don't exist in this universe. There's a garage for Dean's Triumph Spitfire, which he'd have shipped over, naturally, and space for Nan Moss and Bill, and Ray and his family to come and stay . . . *And what about Harry Moffat? I don't know. I still don't know. Some things are so much easier not to think about—and America is an endless, world-class distraction, if nothing else.* Elf joins him at the rail. "Which house are you planning to splurge your ill-gotten gains on, then?"

"That one." He points. "With the hot tub."

"All mod cons. Outstanding views. Nice choice."

"Hell of a party. Met any eligible bachelors?"

"Oh, not especially. Met any eligible ladies of the canyon?"

"A woman just offered to make a plaster cast of my knob."

Elf checks that he's serious—and shrieks with laughter. Dean's happy that she's happy. When she's able to speak, Elf asks, "What did you say?"

"Thanks but no thanks."

"Why? You could've gone into mass production. Whole warehouses stuffed to the gills with 'The Dean Machine.' Batteries not included."

Dean snorts out a laugh. "Hey, I just met Frank Zappa. He gave me a short sermon about why Laurel Canyon isn't Paradise."

"Clever old Frank," says Elf. "I was thinking how it's the Land of the Lotus Eaters."

She can't mean the car. "Go on, then, Prof. Holloway. Lotus Eaters?"

"It's from *The Odyssey.* Odysseus spies land and rows ashore with some of his men. He sends three off to forage. They meet a tribe of hippies called the Lotus Eaters who greet them with love and peace and say, 'Hey, guys, try this lotus stuff, you'll love it.' Love it they do.

They forget about getting home. They forget who they are. All they want is more lotus. Odysseus drags them back to the boat and orders the others to row like hell. The three 'wept bitter tears as the oars smote the gray sea.' "

"Who wouldn't? Saying goodbye to all that free dope."

"Odysseus gave them their lives back. Lotus Eaters don't create anything. Or love. Or live. They're kind of the living dead."

"Who's dead here? Cass isn't. Joni 'n' Graham aren't. Zappa isn't. They write, record, go on tour. Have careers."

"Sure. But reality creeps in wherever you live, however pretty the flowers are, however blue the sky, however great the parties. The only people who actually live in dreams are people in comas."

The sound of wind chimes floats up the hill.

"Nice try, but I still don't want to go back," says Dean.

"That's what you said in Amsterdam, I recall."

"Yeah, but I was high in Amsterdam."

"And that's a Dunhill you're smoking, is it?"

Night blooms scent the breeze.

"Thanks," says Elf. "For earlier. At the TV studio."

"Yer thanking me? For getting us barred from networks?"

"Thorn was a creep. You stood up for me. Women are usually told to get a sense of humor or to take it as a compliment."

"Thanks for braining him with a guitar," says Dean. "Thanks for saving my arse in 'Roll Away the Stone.' "

"Any time. Though don't do cocaine before a show again."

Dean winces. "Bloody idiot. I didn't even do it for a reason. At least Doug's a proper addict. I just thought, *Yeah, why not?*"

"Don't beat yourself up about it. All four of us are handling new stuff. Everything's happening so quickly."

They hear owls.

"Seen Jasper or Mecca recently?" asks Dean.

"They slipped off. We'll see them back at the house. Or, possibly, hear them."

"Slander. I can vouch that Jasper is no shrieker."

Elf makes an *ugh* face. "What about Griff?"

"Griff *is* a shrieker. I needed earplugs at the Chelsea."

Elf's *ugh* becomes a *glurggheugh.* "All I was asking is, has he hooked up with—"

"Yeah, I know. I saw him go into one o' the Wigwams of Love and he was *not* alone, but to say any more would be indiscreet." Dean tokes on his reefer. "Smash a guitar on my head if I'm a Mr. Stoner crossing a line, Elf, but . . . you and Luisa."

Elf doesn't reply for a while. "Ye-es?"

Can't backtrack now. "She's got a heart o' gold, she's sharp as a whip, and if I've read the clues right . . . good on yer."

Elf takes Dean's reefer from his fingers. "What clues?"

"Well . . . partly the way Levon was protective of yer both in New York. Mostly, it's the way yer light up when she walks in. Plus . . . yer ain't denied it yet."

Elf takes a long drag on the reefer. "I won't deny it. I assert it." She gives Dean a defiant smile. "But this is personal, Dean. Not just to me but to Luisa, too. So . . . I'm trusting you."

"I like it when yer trust me. Brings out the best in me."

"Have Jasper and Griff said anything?"

"No. Who knows what Jasper knows? I doubt he'll bat an eyelid. Not after ten years at an all-boys boarding school. Same with Griff. He's got no problem with Levon. Touring jazzers are a broad-minded tribe, I've found. I 'xpect he'll just be, 'Fine, so Elf was into Bruce, now it's Luisa, right, got it . . . Where d'yer want that drum-fill again?' So is Luisa yer first . . ." Dean can't quite say it yet.

" 'Girlfriend' could be the word you're after."

Dean smiles a little. "I reckon it is."

Elf smiles a little. "She is, yes. It's . . . wonderful. Love, though, eh? They sure as Billy-O don't give you a map."

The wind stirs the trillion leaves and needles of Laurel Canyon. The night is all blues, indigos, and blacks, except for the pale yellows around the lamps and streetlights. Dean thinks of an ocean shelf, dropping away. "I wish I could give yer directions," he says a little later, "but I'm a stranger here myself."

EIGHT OF CUPS

DEAN BALANCES ON THE FOOTBOARD OF THE DOUBLE BED, stretches his arms out, and falls, *flumph*ing onto a snowy eiderdown. He inhales the smell of soap powder . . . and thinks of a launderette in North London. He turns onto his back. A space-age light fitting, a huge TV housed in its own cabinet, with doors, an abstract print in its aluminum frame. It's everything his old bedsit at Mrs. Nevitt's wasn't. The British upper classes, Dean thinks, favor ugly furniture from olden times, Rolls-Royces, grouse-shooting, inbreeding and an accent like the Queen's. Wealthy Americans appear to be content with just *being* rich, and feel less need to rub the noses of the poor in their money. Dean checks Allen Klein's card is still safe in his wallet. *A visa, a ticket, an insurance policy.* He hasn't told the others about Jeb Malone's overture at Cass's party. It's a hard subject to broach. *Sorry 'n' all that, but a music mogul thinks I'm the real star and he's offering a quarter of a million dollars.* The thought of the money still makes his heart quiver. *I could pay the blackmailers in London as easy as buying a packet o' cigarettes.* He still hasn't heard back from Rod Dempsey. *Which could be good news, or bad, or neither . . .*

Dean goes to the window. New York was vertical; Los Angeles was a spillage; San Francisco dips, rises, levels out, dips, rises, and falls sharply to the bay. Crazy gradients are the price of keeping to the grid pattern. The big telephone emits one long loud *rrrrrringgggggg,* not the jumpy *rrring-ringgg . . . rrring-ringgg* like at home. His heart pumping, Dean picks up the receiver. "Hello?"

A woman speaks: "Hello, Mr. Moss, hotel switchboard here. We have a call from London for you. A Mr. Ted Silver."

"Uh, yeah. Put him through, please."

"Hold the line one moment, sir."

Click; scratch; clunk. "Dean, my boy, can you hear me?"

"Loud and clear, Mr. Silver."

"Splendid, splendid. How's America treating you?"

Who gives a shit? "Are the results of the paternity test through?"

"They are indeed. The verdict is 'Inconclusive.' Your blood group is O. So is Miss Craddock's and so is her son's. According to the laws that govern these things, you might be the daddy, as might any other man with the blood group O. Which, I am told, constitutes eighty-five percent of the British population, give or take. So there you have it."

Fat lot o' bloody use that was. "What now?"

"For now, dear boy, enjoy the States, make hay while the sun shines, and we'll discuss your next move back in Blighty . . ."

At £15 an hour. "Okay, Mr. Silver."

"Chin up, my boy. This, too, shall pass."

"Not if I'm that baby's father, it won't."

"The fact may not, but the anguish it provokes in your breast shall. I guarantee it. Is today the big festival?"

"Yeah. Just flew in from Los Angeles, and a car's coming to pick us up in a bit. Then we're recording tomorrow, ditto Tuesday, back on Wednesday."

"Until Thursday or Friday, then. Good luck and bon voyage." Ted Silver hangs up and the line goes *prrrrrrrr* . . .

Dean hangs up. *So I am a dad, I'm not a dad, and I'm a possible dad, all at once.* He'd like to tell Elf the non-news, but she'll be unpacking and may need some girl time. He unpacks. He takes his Martin from its case, tunes it to DADF#D with the capo on the fourth fret, and strums a tune he's been working on. This time the music's arrived first, but what Elf said the other day about uncharted waters being where you grow has lodged in his head. What rhymes with "waters"? Daughters . . . *Maybe* . . . Mortars . . . *Definitely not* . . . There's a knock at his door.

It's Levon. "We're pushed for time, so order yourself a bite of lunch on room service."

"Room service? Seriously?"

"Welcome to the big time. Gargoyle's dime."

"Right yer are." Dean shuts the door and picks up the phone. Room service. He's seen this in films. You say what you want on the phone, and the food arrives on a trolley under a silver dome. There's a button marked ROOM SERVICE. He presses it.

A man answers: "Room service."

"Uh, hi, I'd like a bite o' lunch if that's okay."

"What's that now, sir? A *what* for lunch?"

"A *bite* o' lunch. Some lunch. Please."

"Oh, a 'bite' of lunch. What did you have in mind?"

"Um . . . what is there?"

"There's a menu right by the telephone, sir."

"Oh. Yeah." He opens the menu but it's in a foreign language, or most of it is. *Croque monsieur; John Dory; avocado; boeuf bourguignon; lasagna; tiramisu; crème brûlée* . . . Dean can't even pronounce most of these, let alone guess what they are. "A sandwich?"

"We have the club sandwich, sir."

"Thank God. One o' them, please."

"And would you like that on poppy seed, sourdough, walnut . . ."

"In bread, please. Just normal white bread."

"You got it, sir. And vinaigrette or Thousand Island dressing?"

Dressing? "Mate, are yer taking the piss?"

A pause. "Perhaps just a little ketchup on the side, sir?"

"Now yer talking. Cheers."

"It'll be with you in thirty minutes, sir."

Dean puts down the receiver. Stress ebbs away.

The telephone emits one long loud *rrrrrringggggg.*

Oh God, something else about the sandwich. "Hello?"

"Mr. Moss, this is the hotel switchboard again. We have a second call from London for you: a Mr. Rod Dempsey."

Dean's whole body tightens. "I'll take it."

"Hold the line one moment, sir."

Click; scratch; clunk. "God of Rock, how are yer?"

"Hi, Rod. That kind o' depends on yer news."

"The news is, the ballistic missile o' scandal 'n' shit that *was* about to destroy yer life has been knocked out o' the sky."

Thank fuck for that. "So I'm in the clear?"

"Yep. The Other Party dug their heels in for three and a half grand, but yer won't be short of a few bob now yer've a hit single, I know. I wrote a check for the first two thousand, so yer can reimburse me once yer back."

Enough to buy a house on Peacock Road. "Right. Thanks. And they'll send the negs once yer check clears?"

"They'll send the what?"

"The negatives. O' the photos. So they can't use 'em."

"Ah, well, what we said was, we'll meet in No Man's Land, they'll show me the negs, and burn 'em in front of me."

Something's fishy. "Oh. Is that—"

"Diplomacy's a delicate art, Dean. Both sides need to be happy with the outcome, or there *is* no outcome."

"So . . . I'll come along to No Man's Land and see the job done."

"No can do, I'm afraid. The Other Party don't want yer meeting 'em. They're very clear. No face to face."

Something's wrong. "Rod, how'm I s'posed to know that the negs've been destroyed? Or . . ." Dean feels a free-falling sensation, and arrives at the truth, a few seconds later.

This is all Rod Dempsey's scam. The photographs don't exist. Ditto "The Other Party." Dean and Tiffany may have been seen at the Hyde Park Embassy, but that's all. *He's reeled me in like a trout.* Dean grasps at reasons why this can't be true. *How could he know 'bout the blindfolds 'n' cuffs?*

Dean recalls the night they went out to the Bag o' Nails. Four guys, out on the lash, in a nightclub. *I blurted it out myself.* Just the sort of tidbit an extortionist would file away.

But why now?

Why d'yer think? Rod knows Dean helped Kenny and Floss get out of his clutches and out of London.

Rod's voice turns gentle. "Or what, Dean?"

"In my shoes, wouldn't yer want to see these pictures with yer own eyes before forking out three 'n' a half grand?"

A pause. An exhalation. "Only if I thought yer'd fucked me over, Deano. So tell me. Is that what yer thinking? Or have I misunderstood?" Rod's intimidating . . .

Which proves it. Why would a practiced blackmailer insist on negotiating with hard-knock ex-con Rod Dempsey and not helpless Dean Moss, the object of the blackmail? *He must've been laughing his tits off.* "Yer must've been laughing yer tits off."

Rod Dempsey's voice turns icy. "I've saved yer arse, Rock God. You *and* yer married actress. Is this the thanks I get?"

What if yer wrong? "It ain't adding up, Rod."

"Here's what ain't adding up: two grand. *You—owe—me.*"

"Cancel the check."

"I paid in cash, genius. Checks leave a trail."

"Ah, but yer just told me yer paid with a check."

"Who gives a *shit* how I paid? Yer owe me two grand!"

He's lying. "What happened to 'Gravesend boys against the world'? What did I do to yer?"

Nine time zones and five thousand miles away, Rod Dempsey lights a cigarette. "Yer know what yer did. Yer think fame makes yer untouchable? Yer think Mrs. Shag-a-bag's Bayswater address keeps her safe? Wrong. Dead wrong. Yer shoved yer fat beak into my business. Yer'll pay for that, Moss. Yer'll *pay.*"

The line goes *prrrrrrrr* . . .

THE DRIVER SENT by the festival is a man-mountain by the name of Bugbear. He's maybe Dean's age but moves lumberingly and limps. He helps the band into the VW Camper and hunches behind the wheel, like a boy too big for his go-kart. "Climb aboard, y'all. It's a squeeze. Can't adjust the frickin' seats." Dean sits up front, with Elf, Levon, and Griff behind, Jasper and Mecca and her camera in the back. The Camper coasts down a steep street, growls up a steeper one, and waits at a crossroads. *Intersection.* The others are enjoying the streetscapes, but Rod Dempsey's threat and a not-yet-digested club sandwich sit ill in him. Dean knows he should call Tiffany and warn her, but he's afraid she'll fly off into a pointless panic. Dempsey's bluffing about targeting her. Surely? She's Tiffany Hershey née Seabrook. Not some exploitable nobody like Kenny and Floss.

Elf asks Bugbear if he's from San Francisco.

"Uh-huh. Nebraska, originally."

"What brought yer to California?" asks Dean.

"A twelve-hour army transport from Hawaii."

Dean asks, "Vietnam?"

Bugbear gazes forward. "Uh-huh."

"I've heard it's bad out there."

Bugbear puts in a stick of gum. "In the morning, my platoon had forty-two men. By evening, there were six left. Of those six, three made it back to base. So, yeah. It's bad out there."

Griff, Elf, Dean, and Levon exchange looks, not sure what to say. *Jesus bloody Christ,* thinks Dean. *And I think I've got problems.* A streetcar full of tourists rumbles by. Mecca leans from the window and takes photographs. The lights turn green, and the van shunts off, slipping onto a faster road and now the Bay Bridge. The first eastbound section is roofed by the westbound section and walled by flickering girders. Dean sees ships and boats on the blue-green-gray water far below. Towns fringe the distant shoreline. Mountains crumple up behind them. *Places I'll never go.* The double-decked span of the bridge ends in an eight-lane tunnel drilled through Yerba Buena Island, halfway across . . .

Rod Dempsey can't know I helped Kenny and Floss get out of London, Dean thinks, *unless he's got hold of them again, and forced them to tell him . . . in which case, God help them. I could get Ted Silver to force the law to get involved, but it'll get very messy very quickly . . . and Dempsey'll blow the lid off me 'n' Tiffany . . .* "What a bloody mess."

"Say something, our Deano?" asks Griff.

"Nah. Just . . . working on lyrics."

Griff lights a cigarette. "As you were."

At the very least, Dean is going to have to tell Levon and Jasper that the Covent Garden flat has fallen through and offer a version of why. *I'll have to call Tiffany, too. Even if Dempsey was bluffing, she should be taking sensible precautions.* It is not a conversation Dean is looking forward to. He asks for a drag of Griff's cigarette. He wishes it was a joint, but after the Troubadour, he's promised himself to abstain from drugs before a show. The van emerges from the tunnel onto the eastern section of the bridge, where all eight west- and eastbound lanes are open to the sky. The cables are as thick as trees. The suspension towers could be parts of a galactic cruiser.

The entirety is steel, mighty, permanent, real . . .

. . . *and was once just a dream in somebody's head.*

THE CAMPER TURNS off the freeway at a sign for Knowland Park. Further down the slip road, a sign reads, GOLDEN STATE INTERNATIONAL POP FESTIVAL.

"Are we the 'international' bit?" asks Griff.

"Us," replies Levon, "plus Procol Harum, the Animals, and Deep Purple, who played here yesterday."

"Who's Deep Purple?" asks Elf.

"A Birmingham band," says Griff. "They've been supporting Cream on tour here. They're getting quite a name in the States."

The Camper enters the showground proper. Ranks and files of cars are parked to one side, with tents and camper vans on the other. There are dozens of stalls offering food, drinks, and hippie trinkets. A grandstand and a Ferris wheel are visible above a tall wall. Crowds enter through turnstiles.

"More organized than I'd expected," says Elf.

"It's big," says Griff, "but not big big *big* big."

"Twenty thousand punters paying three bucks a head," says Levon, "is much, much tastier than a half-million paying nothing. The word 'free' in 'free concert' means 'bankrupt.' Walls and turnstiles. That's the future of festivals, right there."

A guard recognizes Bugbear and waves the van into a fenced-off compound of neatly parked trailers. Two men are lugging a huge Marshall speaker out of a truck. José Feliciano's soulful croon and Latin guitar figures fill the middle distance. Bugbear takes them to a trailer with a handwritten UTOPIA AVE sign taped to the door. "I'll be taking y'all back later, so break a leg." He walks off without a backward glance.

"A man o' few words," remarks Dean.

"Maybe he left his words in Vietnam," says Jasper.

"I'll slip away and take some pictures," says Mecca. She kisses Jasper and exits the compound. "See you all later."

"Could you take a few of the band when they're on?" asks Levon. "I'll find something in the budget if we use any."

"Sure." She tells Jasper, "Break your legs," and goes.

"I love how she says that," says Jasper.

INSIDE THE TRAILER is a kitchenette with jugs of water, overflowing ashtrays, bottles of beer, Pepsi, and bowls of grapes and bananas. Marijuana smoke hangs in the air. When everyone is settled with a beer, Levon springs a surprise. "Band meeting. Max has put together a possible package of four days' worth of dates, here in the States."

Thank God, thinks Dean. *I can put off London.*

"It's intense. Portland on Thursday, Seattle on Friday, Vancouver on Saturday, then Chicago on Sunday to a show at the Aragon Ballroom—also known as the Aragon 'Brawl-room'—to be broadcast across the Midwest and Canada. You can say no. But this could shunt *Stuff of Life* up ten places. Possibly into the Top Ten."

"I vote yes," says Elf.

"I vote yes," says Jasper.

"I vote 'Shit, yes,' " says Griff.

"This will give us an extra day to record," says Dean. "Could you say we'll do it if the record company pay our studio fees?"

"We'll make a manager of you yet," says Levon.

"Being skint's my superpower," replies Dean.

"Studio fees are in the deal. If we're agreed, I'll tell Max—"

There's a *knock-knock* at the door. A sunburned man with sweat-patches and a clipboard peers in. "Utopia Avenue? Bill Quarry. I'm the operator of this smooth-running festival machine."

"Welcome to your trailer, Bill. Levon Frankland."

Bill shakes everyone's hand. "José finishes in twenty minutes, then Johnny Winter is on from five till six, then it's you guys. Why don't I show you backstage, so you can get the lay of the land?"

Dean is mugged by a huge yawn. "I'll catch forty winks."

"Forty 'winks'?" checks Griff.

"I despair of you two," says Elf.

"Don't worry, boss," Dean tells Levon. "I won't do anything you wouldn't. Or take anything."

"The thought never entered my mind," lies Levon.

DEAN SINKS INTO the sofa bed. Something smooth sticks against his cheek. He sits up again and peels off a tarot card. It shows a figure walking away, up a mountain across a channel of water. The figure carries a staff, like a pilgrim, and wears a red cape. The pilgrim's hair is shoulder length and brownish, like Dean's, though his face is turned away. The yellow moon watches him from a twilit sky. Three cups sit on a bottom row of five cups in the foreground, and the words "VIII of CUPS" are written along the top.

The breeze rustles the net curtain. A woman laughs like Dean's mother used to. The pilgrim won't be coming back this way again. A nearby crowd of thousands roars its applause as José Feliciano finishes his fluid version of "Light My Fire." Dean puts the tarot card into his wallet, next to Allen Klein's business card. He lies back down and shuts his eyes. *There's Rod Dempsey to worry about; there's Mandy Craddock and my possible son; there's what to do about Harry Moffat. I'm sure there are more I've forgotten . . .* Problems tangle up like clothes in a tumble dryer.

No. Enough. Dean leaves the launderette and follows a path, up a mountain, under a yellow moon both crescent and full, with a staff in his hand. He's left his worries behind him, on the other side of the river. He won't be going back . . .

. . . AND ARRIVES AT the Captain Marlow pub in Gravesend. Dave the publican says, "Thank God you're here. Upstairs is on fire and the firemen are on strike." So it's up to Dean, Harry Moffat, and Clive from the Scotch of St. James to work their way up, floor by floor, fighting the fire with buckets of water and sand that are brought by half-strangers. The flames are purple, noisy, and drenched in feedback. At the top of the pub is an attic room. Inside, a scrawny boy with black corkscrew hair is munching grapes . . .

DEAN IS IN a trailer in California where a scrawny boy with black corkscrew hair is munching grapes. He's wearing sandals, shorts, and a baggy Captain America T-shirt, and looks about ten. His skin-tone is from everywhere. Dean is unimpressed with Bill Quarry's security arrangements. "What rabbit hole did *you* pop out of?"

"Sacramento," says the boy.

Dean has no idea where, what, or who Sacramento might be. *Try again.* "What're yer doing in my trailer?"

The boy flips a top off a bottle of Dr Pepper with a bottle opener. "My parents wandered off. Again."

Dean sits up. "Who're yer parents?"

"My mom's name is Dee-Dee. My honorary dad's Ben."

"Don't yer think yer should go back to them?"

"I've been looking. Ever since the man with the sore throat sang about the bad mood rising. No luck yet."

"So . . . yer lost?"

The boy sips his Dr Pepper. "My parents are lost."

All I wanted was a bit o' shut-eye. Dean goes to the door of the trailer. A few muscled roadies are milling around. They don't look likely to help a lost boy. In lieu of a more purposeful action, Dean asks him, "What's yer name?"

"What's yours?"

Dean's surprised into answering, "Dean."

"I'm . . ." the boy says something like "Bolly Var."

"Oliver?"

"*Bo-li-var.* Bolívar. After Simón Bolívar, the revolutionary from the early 1800s. Bolivia's named after him."

"Right. Bolívar. Look, I've got to go and perform soon, so why don't yer take those grapes, and . . ." Dean realizes he can't tell a ten-year-old to go and hunt for two people in a crowd of thousands. He wishes Levon or Elf was here. He sees the security man at the gate to the VIP compound under his big sun-umbrella. "We'll go ask that sort o' policeman over there. He'll know what to do."

Bolívar looks amused. "Whatever you say, Dean."

They leave the trailer and walk over. Security Man wears a hunter's hat, reflective sunglasses, and a combat jacket. " 'Scuse me," says Dean, "but this kid just appeared in my trailer."

"So?"

"So, he's separated from his parents."

"That big blue flag." Security Man points toward a pavilion across a field of campers. "That there's the lost kid tent."

"But I'm Dean Moss. I'm in Utopia Avenue."

"So in Utopia lost kids are someone else's problem, are they?"

"No, but I'm a musician. Lost kids aren't my responsibility."

"Ain't mine neither, pal. I can't abandon my post."

"So whose responsibility is it to walk this kid to that tent?"

"That's a procedural matter. Ask Bonnie or Bunny."

Dean sees his incredulous face reflected in Security Man's sunglasses. "Where are Bonnie or Bunny?"

He gestures at Heaven and Earth. "Could be anywhere."

Oh f' fucksake. Dean crouches. "Look, Bolívar. See that blue flag over there?" He points. "That's the lost kid tent."

"Let's get going, then, Dean."

"Great idea," says Security Guy.

Smarmy git, thinks Dean. "We can't encourage a boy to go wandering off with strangers."

"But you ain't a stranger," says Security Guy. "You're Dean Moss. You're in Utopia Avenue."

Dean has been outplayed. *If I don't spend ten minutes walking him over, I'll spend seventy years wondering what happened to him.* "Okay, Bolívar. Let's go."

"IF I RIDE on your shoulders," says Bolívar, a few paces into their journey, "Dee-Dee or Ben might spot me." Dean hoists him up. Bolívar presses his hands on Dean's skull like a faith healer. *He shouldn't trust strangers this much,* thinks Dean. Yet now Dean has been chosen, he is determined not to let the boy down. Guitar chords from inside the showground crisscross their own echoes. Women are sunbathing on blankets. Teens sit around smoking. Couples canoodle. Families eat in the shade of tents. Girls are having their faces painted. A woman breastfeeds her baby like it's no big deal. *Yer don't see that in Hyde Park.* Clowns are patrolling on stilts. Teenagers are strumming on guitars. *I know that tune . . .* They're working out the chords to "Roll Away the Stone." They're arguing over whether it's a D or a D minor. *I'll let them work it out,* thinks Dean. *I had to.*

Bolívar asks, "How old are you?"

"Twenty-four. How old are you?"

"Eight hundred and eight."

"Huh. I guess yer use face cream."

"Are you from London, Dean?"

"Yeah, I am. How d'yer know?"

"You speak like the chimney sweep in *Mary Poppins.*"

"Where I'm from, you sound funny too."

A scrimmage of wild children rushes by, shrieking.

"Are you a dad?" asks Bolívar.

"Wow, look at that balloon-bender."

"Do you have any kids?"

Sharp as a tack. "The jury's still out on that one."

"Why don't you know if you have any kids or not?"

"Grown-up reasons."

Bolívar shifts his weight. "Did you have sex with a lady who had a baby, but you don't know if her baby grew from the seed you put in her womb or not?"

Bloody—hell. Dean twists his head to look at Bolívar.

The boy looks victorious.

"How d'yer know that? How *could* yer know?"

"Educated guess."

"God, yer grow up quick in America." Dean carries on toward the blue flag. A biplane hauls a banner reading, THIRSTY? GRAB A COKE! across the nearly cloudless sky.

"Why don't you want to be a dad?" asks Bolívar.

"Why d'yer ask so many 'why?' questions?"

"Why did you stop asking 'why?' questions?"

" 'Cause I grew up. 'Cause it's bloody annoying."

"You'd have to put a quarter in the Profanity Jar if you were in our family," says the boy. "Mom started it because she doesn't want me growing up in a sewer. So why don't you want to be a dad?"

"What makes yer think I don't?"

"You change the subject when I bring it up."

Dean stops to let a watermelon vendor push his cart by. "I s'pose . . . I'm afraid of being a dad I wouldn't want *as* a dad."

Bolívar pats his head as if to say, *There, there.*

A FRECKLED MAN in a San Francisco Giants shirt and a floppy hat is hovering in the mouth of the lost kid tent, puffing nervously on a cigarette. When he sees Bolívar his face transforms from bottled panic to sheer relief. *It was worth bringing the kid over just to see that,* thinks Dean. "*Jesus Christ,* Bolly," says the freckled man, "you gave us a fright."

"Profanity Jar," says Bolívar. "Two quarters. One for the 'Jesus' and one for the 'Christ.' I won't forget."

The man makes a God-give-me-strength face and tells Dean, "Thanks. I'm Benjamin Olins—just 'Ben' is fine. I'm his stepdad."

" 'Honorary dad,' " insists the boy.

"Honorary dad." Ben lifts Bolívar off Dean's shoulders. "Mom is having a cow. Where were you?"

"Looking for you. I found him"—the boy points at Dean—"in a trailer. His name's Dean, he's from London, and he isn't sure if he's a dad or not. Speak to him, Ben. Old guy to old guy."

Ben listens to this, frowns, and looks at Dean properly. "Dean Moss? From Utopia Avenue? Holy *crap.* It *is* you."

"One more quarter," says Bolívar. "You're up to three now."

"But Utopia Avenue's why we're here today, and—"

"No ifs, no buts: three quarters. And Mom's here for Johnny Winter, not Dean. Sorry, Dean. There's a lady over there giving candy to lost kids. I'll be right back. Don't wander off."

"Yer said it was yer mum 'n' Ben who got lost," points out Dean.

"She's not going to hand out lollipops to a grown-up, is she? Think it through, Dean." Bolívar goes over.

"Not yer average kid," Dean tells Ben.

"Jeez Louise—you have no i*de*a."

"Eight hundred and eight years old, he said he was."

"He's been keeping that up since he was five. Acute meningitis. Nearly died, poor kid, and he came out of his coma kinda . . . different than before. Sometimes Dee-Dee—Bolly's mom—thinks we should get him looked at, but . . . he's a happy enough kid, so I'm not sure what we'd be trying to fix. But, Dean, I *really* dig your music. I run a record store over in Sacramento. If I've hand-sold one copy of *Stuff of Life,* I've hand-sold fifty. Your first album sells too, of course, but *Stuff of Life* is . . ." Ben mimes an airplane gaining altitude.

"Cheers. Guess I owe yer a royalty check."

"Just make a third album. Please."

"I'll see what we can do. Yer boy's struck gold." The lollipop lady is holding the jar for Bolívar.

"Oh, he could charm the birds and fishes," says Ben. "Do you have kids, or . . . I didn't get what Bolly was saying just now."

The smell of toasted chestnuts wafts by. *No, I can't tell a total stranger about my legal woes when I haven't even told my own family.* "He asked if I had kids and I was just saying I don't feel ready to be a father. That's all."

" 'Ready'? Forget it. I'm winging it, every single day." Ben offers Dean a Marlboro; Dean accepts. "To Dad or Not To Dad? That is the question. It *is* heavy shit. I won't say, 'Do it,' if you don't want to." He puffs the smoke away. "But if you're on the fence and want a nudge, I'll nudge you. You won't miss what you think you'll miss. You'll have more headaches but you'll have more joy. Joy and headaches. The A side and the flip side." Bolly returns with a fistful of candy. "Look at you, you hunter-gatherer."

Bolly spots someone behind Dean. He waves. "Mom! Mom! It's okay—I found Ben. He's here."

Dee-Dee, a heavily pregnant woman with beaded, braided hair, lets out a long, earthy groan of relief and smothers her son in an enormous hug. *"Damn it,* Bolly, *please* don't go wandering off like that . . ."

The boy wriggles free. "One quarter! One whole dollar for the Profanity Jar. I got us a lollipop each, plus one for the baby. Dean, this is Mom. She's in her third trimester. Mom, Dean helped me find you. What do you say to him?"

"Bolly, it's *you* who went off—"

Bolly holds up an admonitory finger.

Dee-Dee takes a deep breath. "Thank you."

THE CROWD OF seven or eight thousand is the biggest by far the band have played. Dean feels stage fright bubbling under. The sky is the sky from the Eight of Cups, on the cusp of evening. "Please welcome," booms Bill Quarry at the central mic, "all the way from England, the one, the only UTOPIA AVENUE!" Levon slaps Dean on the back; Dee-Dee, Ben, and Bolívar slap his shoulder, and he's following Elf onto the stage. *Can't turn back now.* The crowd blast out a roar that Dean wasn't expecting: he feels it on his face. Elf turns and grins. The band take their positions. Jasper and Dean plug in while Elf speaks into her mic. "Thanks, California. We weren't sure if anyone here knows us, but I guess—" The roar and whistles intensify, and a chant spreads out from a spot Dean can't locate: to the tune of "John Brown's Body Lies a-Mouldering in the Grave," the crowd sings: "Randy Thorn's career lies a-mouldering in the grave, Randy Thorn's career lies a-mouldering in the grave . . ." Jasper picks out the melody on his guitar; the notes are burnished and golden. For the "Glory, Glory Hallelujah" chorus, Elf vamps on the organ, and Dean conducts like Herbert von Karajan. His stage fright has evaporated.

"We love you too," says Elf. "So, our first song was written by Dean in a dungeon." A roar of approval. She nods at Dean.

Dean deploys a trick Mama Cass told him for opening a song with an unaccompanied vocal: run through the line once, in your mind's ear, at the pitch you want, then replay it, but join in:

I-i-i-i-f life has shot yer full of ho-o-ooooles —
a-a-a-a-nd hung yer out to-ooo-oo-o dry . . .

Mick Jagger told Dean the hardest part of his job was singing "Satisfaction" for the five hundredth time as if he'd only written it an hour before, but there's no danger of "Roll Away the Stone" sounding tired this evening. The size of the crowd heightens Dean's senses. His voice booms out over the PA and off into the universe like the voice of God . . .

a-a-aaa-and slung you in a pau-au-auper's grave
down where the dead men li-i-i-iiiii-i-i-ie —

Griff clicks his sticks to launch the first chorus. The song grows bigger to fill the bowl of the showground. Dean's stagecraft is more theatrical than usual and Jasper's playing is fiercer. During Elf's roller-coasting Hammond solo, Dean looks at people in the crowd nodding in time and swaying as they drink beers and toke on roll-ups. Where the crush is less, near-naked revelers perform the shamanistic dance beloved of film crews at mad hippie festivals.

The song ends in applause that goes on much longer than Dean would expect for act number eleven on day two. "Prove It" gets a similar reception. Combed-out clouds glow incandescent as the sun sinks. As Jasper hits the first chord of "Darkroom," the stage lights come on. Jasper's posh English voice carries an exoticness in the oncoming American twilight that it lacks when they perform the song at home. The rapid punch of "The Hook" grounds the set. They extend the bridge and swaths of audience clap in time. Dean sings with a harnessed ferocity. Everything he tries works. Griff takes a drum solo and gets into a call-and-response sequence with Elf. Somehow it's funny. Jasper takes a solo that burns up slowly, like a meteor, and smashes to bits at the end of the song. The applause is long and loud. *Cocaine's a pale imitation o' this,* thinks Dean. He mops his face with a damp towel. *I hope someone somewhere's making a quality bootleg o' this 'cause tonight we're bloody brilliant.* He glances at Levon in the wings, and sees Jerry Garcia of the Grateful Dead clapping with four fingers against his palm. Dean nods back. Bolívar and his parents are sitting up on some scaffolding.

Elf plays a few lines of the *Moonlight Sonata* for fun before seguing into "A Raft and a River." After the riff-sticky madness of "The Hook," her song is a cool glass of water. Faces stare at her, hypnotized. Griff pitter-patters and shushes on his cymbals and hi-hat. Dean and Jasper join in on Elf's new three-part-harmony chorus, inspired by hearing Graham Nash, Stephen Stills, and David Crosby singing in Mama Cass's kitchen. It's risky—there's nowhere to hide if harmony turns bad—but they've been practicing and the applause is vigorous. Bill Quarry calls from the side, tapping his watch and megaphoning through his hands, "One more big one!" It's Jasper's pick. Dean's expecting "Sound Mind," but Jasper calls, "Let's do 'Who Shall I Say Is Calling?' " He wrote the entire song on the flight from New York. His onstage seizure appears to have had the benign side effect of curing Jasper's fear of flying. It's a brave choice. They've only played the piece through a few times in the studio, but it does feel like one of those gigs when the songs half play themselves. Elf nods at Dean, who nods at Jasper, who addresses the crowd. "Our last song's our newest. It's one day old and it's called 'Who Shall I Say Is Calling?' " He looks at Dean, nods, "And one, and two, and three, and—"

Dean's there with the blues riff. A, G, F, back to A.

Elf's Hammond gate-crashes the party, finds its feet, and dances a drunken jig. Griff joins in with a round of backbeats, the snare, and distant thunder on the bass drum. Jasper's guitar picks out a hovering Grateful Dead–style intro before he sings into the mic:

You loved him in the tropics,
they labeled you "Immoral";
you gave me life and kissed my head,
then sank among the coral.

You loved her in the tropics,
when Europe was aflame.
I'm your indiscretion,
I have your name.

Dean wonders if the words make any sense at all to people who don't know it's about Jasper's father. "Nightwatchman" and "Darkroom" feel personal but, actually, aren't. The first two verses of this new one are raw. In lieu of a chorus, Elf plays a half-jazz-half-blues piano solo of cascading runs before the next verse:

A priest from long ago,
hid in the family tree.
Generations passed until
the priest demanded liberty.

A stranger from Mongolia,
turned me back from suicide.
He walled the priest up in my mind,
and gave me five more years to hide.

When Dean asked Jasper who the priest and the Mongolian were, he just replied, "A long story. The short version is, they were voices in my head." Jasper now plays a solo. The level's wrong on his wah-wah pedal and it buzzes, half drowning the guitar. It sounds like an icebreaker smashing through ice. *Actually it sounds bloody great,* thinks Dean. Jasper must agree: he waves away the sound guy and extends the solo by another round. *Even the mishaps are on our side tonight.* Jasper steps up to his mic:

One dark day, the walled-up priest
erupted from the past —
I tripped into Hell in the Chelsea Hotel.
I wasn't the first, I won't be the last.

A psycho-surgeon for the damned,
A shelter in the gale —
If not for Marinus of Tire,
I'd not be here to tell the tale.

These two verses have been modified since Dean last heard them: "Marinus of Tire"? Is "Tire" a place? Or just a tire? The song's like "Desolation Row," Dean decides. *I can't say I understand it, but I know 'xactly what it means.* He notices Mecca crouching between the spotlights, taking an upward shot of Jasper. Jasper sees her too, and gives her a look. Since his collapse at the Ghepardo, Jasper's been present and calm and different. *If I believed in curses, I'd say a curse was lifted.* Jasper's third cosmic solo spirals over the showground, like a thing with wings. Dean joins Jasper at his mic and Elf leans into hers for the final three repeats of—verse? Chorus? Bridge? Who cares?

Who shall I say is calling?
Who shall I say is calling?
A ghost now asks a ghost-to-be,
"Who shall I say is calling?"

The ending is a minute-long *Wait for it* of whirling dervish keyboards, bass runs, yowling feedback, and drum cascades before the band comes to a sudden, perfect stop.

The crowd doesn't react. *What's wrong?*

Dean looks at Elf. *Did we fuck it up?*

The showground ignites with the noise of eight thousand people yelling, cheering, whistling, and clapping as loud as they possibly can.

All that it cost us to get here was worth it.

Griff, Elf, and Jasper line up by his side.

Venus is a glint in the eye of the sky.

Utopia Avenue take a bow.

THE NARROW ROAD TO THE FAR WEST

On Monday, the band went to record in Studio C at Turk Street Studios, a short walk from their hotel. They laid down solid demos of Elf's "Chelsea Hotel #939," a bluesy waltz about their New York digs, and "What's Inside What's Inside," a love song with zithers, an Appalachian dulcimer, and a flute solo played by a friend of Max's from the San Francisco Symphony Orchestra. They finished at ten P.M., ate at a Chinese restaurant, and crawled into bed. Yesterday, the band recorded a diamond-bright version of "Who Shall I Say Is Calling?" during the course of the morning, then an eight-minute composition of Jasper's called "Timepiece" featuring amplified clockwork, wind chimes, Elf on harpsichord, a backward twelve-string guitar solo, an ethereal vocal stack, and recordings Mecca made on Monday of a funeral bell, the sea, and a railway terminus. Today, their last full day in San Francisco, has been spent on two new songs of Dean's: a riff-heavy number, "I'm a Stranger Here Myself," and a spacier, mystical song, "Eight of Cups." Dean, Elf, and Jasper are offering and accepting suggestions for each other's songs more than they ever did at their Fungus Hut sessions. Griff listens closely to each new song as its writer introduces it, and by the third or fourth run-through is laying down a rhythm track.

Levon comes from an afternoon of meetings and the band stop to play him the latest take of "Eight of Cups." He leans back, listens intently, and pronounces, "Glorious. *Paradise* was a few months behind the trend. *Stuff of Life* is kind of marching in lockstep with the trend. This new stuff is going to be the trend. When Max hears it, he'll wet his pants."

"Is that a good thing or a bad thing?" asks Jasper.

"Good," says Dean. "What about Günther?"

"Günther's not a pants-wetter, but he will tap along with one finger. During the racier passages, maybe two."

"Bloody hell. Yer reckon?"

The light flashes on the telephone. Levon picks up. "Hello?" Pause. "Oh, yeah, sure. Put him through." Levon cups the mouthpiece and tells the others, "It's Anthony Hershey."

Of course it is. He's found out 'bout me 'n' Tiff. Dean's not as scared as he should be. *What's there to be scared of?*

"Tony," begins Levon. "How the hell *are* you? Did—" A pause. Levon frowns at Dean. "Uh . . . Okay. Is it anything I can help with?" A pause. "Then let me see if he's still around." Levon cups the mouthpiece and whispers, "He wants to speak to you, but he sounds homicidal."

Let's get it over with. Dean presses the speakerphone button so everyone can hear. "Tony. How's the weather down in Los Angeles?"

Anthony Hershey's outraged upper-class voice blasts through the tinny speaker. "How *dare* you? How RUDDY DARE you?"

"How dare I what, 'xactly, Tony?"

"Oh, you *know*! You've VIOLATED my marriage."

"Howdy, Mr. Pot—have you met Mr. Kettle?" Elf's jaw has dropped. Griff is frowning. Levon is already making calculations. Jasper lights a cigarette and passes it to Dean. "It's an eight-hour drive up from LA, if yer fancy pistols at dawn. Or I could meet yer halfway."

"You'd not be worth the bullet, you pig-ignorant, yobbish, flash-in-the-pan, coke-snorting, wife-snatching . . . oik."

Griff has shut his eyes and is shaking his head.

"Nobody's perfect, Tony, but at least I didn't snatch my wife's career off her and give it to Jane Fonda. I mean, if *you* were Tiff, would *you* think, *Oh, well, I'll just have to put up 'n' shut up 'n' scrub Tony's shirts 'n' undies?* Or would yer think, *Sod this for a lark, what's good for the gander's good for the goose?*"

"My wife is the mother of my children!"

"See, that's yer problem, Tony." Dean mimics Hershey's accent. 'My wife is the mother of my children.' Yer not a feudal lord, matey. Tiff's not yer possession. She's a human being. If yer care so much, go back to *The Narrow Road to the Deep North* starring Tiffany Seabrook. She's a great actor. So what if she's not a Hollywood name? Make it anyway. It'll be a better film. Yer'll rescue yer marriage."

Anthony Hershey makes outraged popping, hissing noises, then: "I'm not taking marital advice from *you*!"

"Yer bloody need it from someone. Acting is Tiff's art. You took it from her. Give it back. She still likes yer, deep down. Even if yer do drop her like a dishrag the moment the phone goes."

The timbre of Hershey's anger goes from hot to icy. "You'll do film work in London or LA over my dead body."

"Oh, Tony, don't tempt Death like that. Look, before one of us hangs up on the other, I'm curious: Were these glad tidings brought to yer by one Rod Dempsey? East End gangster-y kind o' voice?"

The director does not say, "Who?"; he hesitates, then says, "If you touch my wife again, I'll *crush you like a cockroach*. If I see you again, I'll give you the thrashing of your ruddy life. Am I clear?"

"Does that mean Utopia Avenue isn't going to be doing the soundtrack for—"

The phone line from Los Angeles goes dead.

If that's Rod Dempsey's revenge, Dean thinks, *I can take it.* "Sorry," he tells the band. "There goes our shot at Hollywood glory."

"And I thought *I* was a dark horse," says Elf.

"On the bright side," says Jasper, "we don't have to worry about hacking ninety seconds off 'Narrow Road' any more."

"I can't say I don't wish you'd keep it in your trousers," says Levon, "but Warners' lawyers were a pain in the hole."

"Tiffany Seabrook?" Griff winces with admiration. "Back o' the fookin' net, Deano." His stomach growls. "Is Jerry Garcia still expecting us for a bite to eat?"

710 ASHBURY STREET is a tall, bay-and-gable, wood-fronted, black-and-white house on a hefty slope. Steep steps climb from the pave-

ment to an arched porch on the second floor. Up on the porch sits a man in a rocking chair. A baseball bat leans against a pillar. To Dean's eyes, he looks Red Indian. "My sisters and I had a doll's house like this," says Elf. "The front opened up like a book."

Jasper faces the afternoon sun. "Everything's a few degrees more real after a day in the studio."

A small tour bus painted in psychedelic swirls pulls up. "This, folks," declares the guide, "is the home of Jerry Garcia, Phil Lesh, Bob Weir, and Ron 'Pigpen' McKernan—better known to the world as rock phenomenon the Grateful Dead."

"No mention of the fookin' drummers," says Griff. "Typical."

Tourists jostle to take a photograph. The possible Indian on the porch blesses the coach with a finger.

"If this house could talk," says the tour guide, "Ashbury Street would blush. Who dares to imagine what scenes of rock 'n' roll abandon are going down behind those windows right now?"

The bus pulls off. "Fingers crossed," says Dean. They begin the ascent, gripping the handrail. A stumble could cost a broken neck. Up on the porch, the possible Indian has a moon-gray cat on his lap. "Hello," says Dean. "We're Utopia Avenue."

"You're expected." The possible Indian leans back to call through the half-open door. "Jerry, your guests are here."

The cat rubs against Elf's legs. Elf picks the animal up. "Aren't *you* adorable?" Its leaf-green eyes stay on Dean.

"Utopians!" Jerry Garcia, beaming, bearded, flannel-shirted, and barefoot, appears. "I thought I heard friendly voices climbing up the stairway to Heaven. So, you found us okay."

"We told our taxi, 'Follow that tourist bus,'" says Griff.

Jerry Garcia's smile turns to a grimace. "First they revile us, then they turn us into an attraction. Come in. Marty and Paul from Jefferson Airplane have dropped by. They're cool. Obviously."

TIBETAN MANDALAS, AN American Stars and Stripes, and scrolls decorate the wall. Somewhere in 710, John Coltrane's saxophone is playing. Dope smoke, incense, and the aroma of Chinese food mingle in the air. A few people drift in and out of the kitchen, including a girl wearing nothing but a sheet. Nobody seems too sure who lives here and who is visiting. Dean dunks a spring roll in the sweet chili sauce. "God, I bloody love these."

"Too bad you're not staying longer," says Pigpen, who, Dean can't help thinking, looks like his name. "I'd take you to Chinatown. One dollar, you eat like an emperor."

Dean thinks of Allen Klein's offer to meet and discuss a quarter of a million. "Next time."

At a corner of the table, Jerry Garcia and Jasper are swapping scales over a pair of guitars. "This one's called the Mixolydian," the Deadhead tells the Utopian, "and it uses a flattened seventh . . ." He plays it through. Marty Balin—short, round, and mushroom-colored—is flirting with Elf.

Good luck with that, thinks Dean, as the eerily golden Paul Kantner asks him, "So did you ever run into Jimi in his London period?"

"Only in passing," says Dean. "We never hung out."

"Jimi played at the Fillmore the week after Monterey," says Paul. "Started below us on the bill, but after a couple of days, he was headlining. What—a—*cat.*"

Marty slurps noodles. "You and me, we play with hands and fingers, right? We taught ourselves, sitting down in rooms. Jimi's a street guitarist. Plays with his whole body. Calves, waist, hips."

"Balls, ass, and cock," adds Pigpen. "He's the first black cat who white women, y' know, frothed for. I've never seen anything like it. They kinda . . . *dripped* lust."

"*Some* white women," Elf corrects Pigpen.

"Sure, I hear ya. But lots. Guys too, that's the thing. The first black leather pants I ever saw were Jimi's."

"That scarf round the knee and scarf round the head thing he does?" adds Paul. "It spread through San Francisco faster than the clap during the Summer of Love."

"My Summer of Love was spent driving a van up and down the M1 with this lot." Griff indicates the band. "Right time, wrong place."

"Sixty-*six* was the year." Marty slurps egg-drop soup. "The summer before the Summer of Love. You agree, Jerry?"

"Yup." Jerry Garcia looks up from his fretboard. "The Summer of Granted Wishes. If you were a band, you had an audience. Bill Graham opened the Fillmore and put on four or five bands a night. You didn't even need to be that good. A whole new scene sprang up, unlike anything in America. Or on Earth. Or in history."

"This is *the* Bill Graham?" asks Dean. "The same Bill Graham who manages Jefferson Airplane?"

Marty makes a face and looks at Paul, who munches a rice cracker. "Uh-huh, though Bill's only technically our manager."

"You'll hear many views about Bill," says Jerry. "Detractors say he's only fed the psychedelic cow to milk it. But he works like crazy, he never denies wanting to get rich, he holds benefits for HALO—lawyers for busted kids—and for the Diggers, a radical community group who feed hungry people."

"Most revolutionary of all," says Pigpen, "he actually pays bands what he promises to pay. There's none of this 'We didn't make as much on the door as we hoped, so here's a beer and a ball of dope, now piss off' bullshit. Not ever. Not with Bill."

"Levon's having breakfast with him tomorrow," says Dean.

"He'll want you for the Fillmore," states Pigpen. "Word's getting round about your set at Knowland Park. That was some show."

Griff twists his fork into his chow mein. "How did Knowland Park festival compare to the Human Be-in?"

"Chalk and cheese," says Golden Paul. "Knowland Park was to make its organizers money, while pretending not to. The Be-in made nobody jack-shit, but it *will* make the history books."

"It was *waaay* bigger," says Marty. "Thirty thousand of us at the Polo Fields in Golden Gate Park. Haight-Ashbury hippies preaching peace and love. Berkeley radicals preaching revolution. Comedians, poets, gurus. Big Brother with Janis, the Dead, Quicksilver, us. Tibetan chanters to greet the sun."

"And no violence," says Pigpen. "No muggings. Owsley Stanley handing out LSD like there's no tomorrow."

"Free LSD?" asks Dean. "What 'bout the cops?"

"Acid wasn't illegal yet," says Paul. "City Hall hated it, but how could they withhold permission that nobody had asked for?"

"The mayor of Chicago found a way," said Elf.

"San Francisco's not Chicago," says Pigpen.

"And just for a while," says Jerry, "maybe a few months, enough of us believed that a new way of living might be possible. Starting right here. The Diggers gave out free meals. There's still a free clinic on Haight Street."

"What changed?" asks Elf.

"Exposure," says Pigpen. "Word got out. The media pumped the whole thing up. 'Middle America! Your kids too could fall into Satan's trap of free love, free dope, and free music!' Which made damn sure those kids showed up, all wearing flowers in their hair."

"By the hundreds of thousands," says Jerry. "Heading right here. Where, it turned out, Diggers didn't dig up meals, not literally. They needed hard cash from the likes of Bill Graham. Demand was infinite. Supply was not."

"Drug dealers saw pay dirt," says Paul. "Turf wars kicked off. A kid got stabbed to death thirty feet from this house. Then the first acid burnouts showed up. Owsley gave *everyone* the same dose. Beefy jocks and skinny chicks. People just ain't built the same."

Dean thinks of the sorry state of Syd Barrett.

"Anti-commercialism got commercialized," says Jerry.

"We saw all the head shops from the taxi," says Jasper.

"Exactly," says Marty. "It's T-shirts, I Ching sets, pentagrams. Racks of crap. It's all gotten less 'Turn on, tune in, drop out' and more 'Roll up, cash in, sell out.' "

"Here's the difference between then and now." Paul dabs sauce off his substantial chin. "A friend of mine was flying back to New Mexico in June of last year. He's a classic hippie who doesn't wear shoes. At San Francisco Airport, the clerk said the airline wouldn't let him on board barefoot. So my friend looked around, saw a fellow freak arriving *in* San Francisco, and asked, 'Hey, man, could I borrow your sandals? I'll miss my flight if I don't find some shoes right now.' This total stranger said, 'Sure,' handed them over, and my friend flew home with no further trouble. Now, that exchange could only have happened in a narrow window of a few months between sixty-six and sixty-seven. Sixty-five would've been too early.

The stranger would've said, 'Are you *nuts*? Buy your own frickin' sandals.' Now, in 1968, it's too late. The stranger would say, 'Sure you can have them—five bucks, plus sales tax.' "

Jerry Garcia fires off a closing blues riff.

"Is anything left of that time?" asks Elf.

The San Franciscans look at each other.

"I'd say not a lot," says Paul Kantner.

"Only a few hollow slogans," says Pigpen.

Jerry strums his guitar. "Every third or fourth generation is a generation of radicals, of revolutionaries. We, my friends, are the bottle-smashers. We release the genies. We run riot, get shot, get infiltrated, get bought off. We die, go bust, sell out to the man. Sure as eggs is eggs. But the genies we let loose *stay* loose. In the ears of the young the genies whisper what was unsayable. 'Hey, kids—there's nothing wrong with being gay.' Or 'What if war isn't a patriotism test, but really fucking dumb?' Or 'Why do so few own so goddamn much?' In the short run, not a lot seems to change. Those kids are nowhere near the levers of power. Not yet. But in the long run? Those whispers are the blueprints of the future."

"WHO'S IN THE mood for acid?" asks Jerry.

"Me and Paul have an early flight over to Denver," says Marty Balin. "Bill's got us on a treadmill."

"LSD and I do not get along," says Elf. "I'll bow out."

"Same story here, Elf." Pigpen pours himself a tumbler of Southern Comfort. "My last trip—freakin' nightmare."

"I'll regret turning down an acid trip with Jerry Garcia," says Griff, "for a date with two kickboxers, but the flesh is weak."

"Jasper?" asks Jerry. "You can't tell me 'Sound Mind' and 'Darkroom' came from smoking Marlboros."

"If my mind was one of the three little pigs' houses," replies Jasper, "it would not be the house made of bricks."

"Man," Pigpen turns to Elf. "Does this dude *ever* give a straight answer to a straight question?"

Elf pats Jasper's hand. "His answers are either alarmingly straight or cryptic crossword clues."

"Schizophrenia is an old friend of mine," says Jasper. "It was trippy enough for a lifetime. My girlfriend's going to a cabal of West Coast photographers, so I'll join her."

Jerry looks at Dean. "You're my only hope, Mr. Moss."

Tonight's the night. "I'm in, Mr. Garcia."

"Ever tripped before?"

"I have not," admits Dean. "Not properly."

"Then, as a virgin, I'll give you a light dose."

Elf, Jasper, and Griff stand up to go. "Look after our Dean," Elf tells Jerry. "Good bassists are hard to find."

"If we venture out, I'll summon up a guardian angel. Dean can crash on our sofa, so he won't have to get back to your hotel."

"See yer all at the studio in the morning," says Dean.

"Session starts nine sharp," says Griff. "There or square."

Jasper tells him, "Bring us back a souvenir."

"ACID IS A box of mystery chocolates." Dean and his host sit on the floor of Jerry's room, on cushions at a low table made of a slab of tree trunk. "Ten lines of coke from the same batch'll give you the same bump. Ten reefers of the same weed will give you the same buzz. Ten trips with LSD of the same potency is ten *different* trips. A lot depends on where your head's at, so only do this if you've got your shit together. This trip has no ejector seat."

Mandy Craddock? Her son? Rod Dempsey? My father? "My shit is as together as it can be, right now, right here."

"Then behind you is a big red book. Jules Verne."

Dean turns: "*Journey to the Center of the Earth*?"

"Put it on the table." Dean does as asked. Jerry turns to the rear cover and lifts a hidden flap in the thick board. Under the flap is a tiny brown envelope, one inch by three. Using tweezers, Jerry extracts a square of yellow paper the size of a postage stamp. "This is rice paper, impregnated with a dose of liquid acid. Lick your thumb." Jerry puts the yellow paper on the damp patch, and follows suit. "Here we go."

They put the papers onto their tongues.

Dean's dissolves in seconds.

"The magic carpet will arrive shortly. Pick out a record." Jerry returns his stash and replaces Jules Verne while Dean pulls out the Band's *Music from Big Pink* and puts on side two. Jerry and Dean bongo along until "Chest Fever" ignites with a fiery burst of organ.

"Bloody incredible playing, this," says Dean.

"It's a Lowrey. Garth's the Band's secret weapon. Sweetest guy you ever met, too. How're you feeling now?"

"Like I need a dump."

"That's your body saying, 'Something celestial's on its way, I'll attend to the earthier stuff now.' Bathroom's thataway." Dean goes and Dean goes. He washes his hands. The water feels silky. Gravity is lessening. Back in Jerry's room, Jerry asks, "Is it kicking in?"

"I feel atoms of air bouncing in my lungs, like popcorn."

"Let's go out for a walk in the park."

THE POSSIBLE INDIAN'S name turns out to be Chayton. "One-half Navajo," he tells Dean, as they descend to the street, "one-quarter Sioux, one-quarter who the hell knows?" He follows a step or two behind Dean and Jerry. Jerry talks about the neighborhood. Chayton walks with a panther's gait, emanating a force field that the hustlers, beggars, and sightseers of Haight Street detect and do not test. Jerry's wearing a vast-brimmed hat and mirror sunglasses, and nobody bothers him. His cigarette smells of sage. The sky is a no-man's-land between afternoon and evening. Clouds are few, high, and puffy, like dragon smoke. Three jet trails make a triangle.

The high windows of a bowling alley are propped open.

Dean hears the trundle of balls and the clatter of pins.

A girl walks by, leaving a trail of herself in her slipstream. Dean is entranced by the impossible sight. A tramp, too, leaves a dozen selves in his wake. Haight Street is filled with visual slipstreams.

Dean swivels his arm and a fan of forearms opens up.

"You ghosting?" Jerry is at the front of Comet Jerry.

"Guess I am," replies Dean. *Ghosting.* They cross Stanyan Street and pass under the wrought-iron gate of Golden Gate Park, where the colors are doubling, trebling, quadrupling in intensity. Green shrubs glow green, the blue sky sings blue, and a band of pink cloud oscillates through all the pinks there are and some there aren't. "Does acid cure you of color blindness?" asks Dean.

"No," says Jerry, "but it makes you wonder if you've actually been living not in the real world but only a description of it."

"Can I have that line? I want to put it in a song."

"If you remember it, my friend, it is all yours."

Fiery maples snap, crackle, and pop scarlets and golds into the air. Up they swirl. "Bloody bloody bloody hell . . ."

The three sit on a bench. The long grass around them is wriggling. *Really?* Dean takes a closer look, and it stops. *No, it's just grass.* But when Dean looks away, it reverts to its wriggling ways, only to stop again when Dean focuses his attention. *Like a schoolboy waiting till the teacher's back's turned.* "So when we look at a thing," says Dean, "we change what it is."

"Which is exactly why we never see things as they are," says Jerry. "Only as we are." A big dog tows a girl on roller skates.

Where Dean and Jerry walk, Chayton follows. They stop to watch tennis players. The soundtrack is slipping out of sync. The whack of the racquet hitting the ball happens only after impact. As the rally progresses, the players grow bigger. Dean turns to tell Jerry, but Jerry's head, too, has swollen to twice its normal size, though it deflates again when he exhales. The tennis players' skin turns first albino-milky, then see-through, like cellophane. Their veins, arteries, muscles, and fascia are on full display. A greyhound darts by. Dean sees its bones, its heart, its lungs, its cartilage. A gull, by a bin, is a living, meaty fossil of a gull.

At a burger van, a picture of a cheeseburger is, in fact, not a picture at all, but a real cheeseburger. It drips globules of hot fat. Melting cheese stretches down to the pavement. Ketchup shines like blood at the scene of a fresh accident. The bun is a real, soft, puffy bread bun that breathes in and out and in and out. "Your big mistake," the bun tells Dean, "is to assume your brain generates a bubble of consciousness you call 'Me.' "

"Why is that a mistake?" Dean asks the talking bun.

"The truth is that you're not your own private 'I.' You are to consciousness what the flame of a match is to the Milky Way. Your brain only *taps into* consciousness. You aren't a broadcaster. You're a transceiver."

"Bloody hell," says Dean. "So when we die . . ."

"When a match dies does light cease to exist?"

The burger man in a burger van is shooing at Dean with his fry-slice: "Never Never Land's *thataway,* kid."

Dean looks all the way down the Narrow Road to the Far West and sees Bolívar, the boy he took to the lost kid tent at the festival, in the eye of the setting sun. "Hey, Bolívar . . . are yer real?"

Bolívar's voice travels down the light-rays. "Are *you*?"

Where Dean and Jerry walk, Chayton follows.

In the shadows of a bandstand, Dean pees diamonds. They vanish into the earth. *Nobody will ever know.* He hears a brass band approaching. The last diamond gone forever, he joins Jerry on the bandstand. "Can yer hear the brass band?"

The pink sun is reflected in Jerry's glasses. "I hear the engines of the Earth. It's a choral roar. What's the band playing?"

"I'll tell yer when I work it out. Here they come . . ." Under the spreading chestnut tree, a hundred skeletons march in ragged uniforms that hang off their herky-jerky frames. Their instruments are made of human bones. The melody is the forgotten soundtrack of Creation. *If we can only get that down on record,* thinks Dean, *we'll alter reality . . . It's up to you, Moss . . . Remember . . .*

Parakeets and herons hang in the dusk, stringlessly.

Dean lifts his thumb and a heron's wing moves.

Dean puffs a puff of air, and a cloud is pushed along.

Separateness is an illusion, Dean realizes. *What we do to another, we do to ourselves.* "How obvious." *A ghost now asks a ghost-to-be, "Who shall I say is calling?"*

A small boy brings up the rear in his dressing gown and slippers. It's Crispin, Tiffany's younger son, pointing his index finger at Dean. *You're shagging my mum.*

"These things happen," Dean calls back. "Yer'll understand, one day."

A second finger joins Crispin's first. They form a gun. He shoots Dean. *Bang bang, you're dead.*

Where Dean and Jerry walk, Chayton follows.

"This is the Polo Fields," Jerry tells him, "the sacred turf, where Ginsberg led the chanting for the sun moon and stars until the end of time"

Dean wonders if he's gone deaf; or if Jerry's voice is gone; or if God the Father has slid the volume fader of the cosmos down. Before any answer emerges, Dean's groin is gouged open by an axe-blade of hot pain. His knees fold apart and collapse. He drops backward onto the grassy bank. The agony is beyond anything Dean has ever felt. He cannot scream; or wonder where his jeans or underpants went; or guess how he could have been so utterly wrong about his gender all his life; or worry about the risks of exposing himself in a public park in San Francisco.

Dean wonders, *Am I dying?*

"No," replies Chayton. "The opposite. Look."

Between his legs, Dean sees the gluey bulge of a fontanelle. *I'm giving birth.* Dean's mother is with him, smiling like she does in the photograph on Nan Moss's piano: "Push, Dean . . . Push, love . . . One more push!" With the rip of a root uprooted, Dean's baby slithers out in a gush of fluids. Dean lies back, gasping and whimpering.

His mother says, "It's a boy," and hands him his baby.

Dean's baby is a tiny, bloodied, vulnerable Dean.

Dean is his own baby, peering up at Harry Moffat.

Eyes shining with love and wonder, Harry Moffat cradles Dean in the crook of his arm. "Welcome to the loony bin, son."

DEAN WAKES ON a sofa. He smells cold Chinese food, dope, and a kitchen bin that needs emptying. Here are books; a long-necked snakeskin banjo that must be something else; a giant candle from a cathedral; a stereo; a stratum of records. Through an arch, he sees the Grateful Dead's kitchen at 710 Ashbury. A Playboy bunny clock says it's 7:41 A.M. A perky American DJ is talking about the weather before the opening bars of "Look Who It Isn't," off *Stuff of Life,* come on. *I love this city,* thinks Dean. *One day, I'm moving here to live.* He feels good. Sane. Stable. *Bit sticky . . . I could do with a bath.* He sits up. His body parts are where they should be, and what they were: yesterday's birth canal was only on loan. The shutters of a large bay window slice bright morning light. *I'm Dean Moss, I passed the acid test, and I gave birth to myself. If there's not a song in that, I'll eat my Fender.* His eyes settle on a battered book entitled *The Way of Tarot* by Dwight Silverwind. He opens it. Each card has its own page. Dean looks up the Eight of Cups. *"The Eight of Cups,"* writes Dwight Silverwind, *"is a card of change. The pilgrim is turning away from the viewer—the Now—and embarking on a journey across a narrow channel into arid mountains. Belonging to the Minor Arcana, the Eight of Cups symbolizes a turning away from old patterns and behaviors to commence a search for deeper meaning. Note the orderliness of the eight cups 'left behind': our pilgrim is moving on, without fuss and drama. Some authorities associate the Eight of Cups with desertion or abandonment, but to my mind the traveler's decision is an act of self-emancipation."* Dean closes the book.

Nobody else is up. He puts on his shoes and socks, uses the bathroom, and does not pee diamonds. He drinks a mug of water, takes an apple from a crystal bowl, writes a note on a phone memo saying, *Jerry, I leave you not quite the same as you found me. Cheers, Dean—PS I borrowed an apple,* and slips it under Jerry's door. The air on the elevated porch is crisp and cool. The trees across Ashbury Street break Dean's heart. He can't say why. Chayton is on his rocking chair, reading *The New Yorker.* "Another beautiful morning," says the confirmed Indian. "It may rain later."

"Thanks for minding me yesterday."

Chayton makes an it's-nothing face.

"Where's that cat o' yours?"

"That cat is no man's cat. She comes, she goes."

Dean goes down a few steps, then turns. "Can yer walk to Turk and Hyde from here?"

Chayton illustrates his directions with his vertical palm. "Go down Haight Street, all the way to Market. Carry on straight. Hyde is six blocks on your left. Turk's four blocks up. Forty minutes."

" 'Ppreciate it."

"Be seeing you soon."

THE SUNNY SIDE of Haight Street is too bright, so Dean crosses to the shady side where his eyeballs work better. The neighborhood puts him in mind of the morning after an epic unauthorized house party. *Slip off before the bills fall due.* Few humans are about. Overturned bins spill their trashy guts into the gutter. Crows and mangy dogs bicker over the spoils. He bites the borrowed apple. It's golden and zesty, like an apple from a myth. Dean passes what looks like a bingo hall, but is in fact a church. He wonders if it's the church in the Mamas and the Papas' "California Dreamin'," and remembers that he can now phone Cass Elliot and just ask her.

Three or four blocks later, the hippie vibe gives way to humdrum frontages. A hilly park rears up where birds Dean can't name sing in trees he can't name. He prefers the world in its shabbier clothes, he decides. *My trip was a revelation,* he thinks, *but yer can't live in a revelation.* He knows Griff and Elf are going to quiz him about his acid trip; and knows he won't be able to convey a thousandth of it in words. *It's like trying to perform a symphony with a skiffle group.* Dean remembers the skeleton band. A few sketchy fragments of the Music of Creation are near, he's sure . . . tantalizingly near . . .

But it wouldn't sound like it did. A teenage couple are asleep under a ragged blanket on a park bench under a tree that mutters to itself. *Twins in a womb.* Dean thinks of Kenny and Floss and hopes the couple are here as the epilogue of a magical night, and not because they have nowhere else to go. He hears a tram—*called a "streetcar"*—up ahead, and thinks of a milk-float making its way up Peacock Street in Gravesend. Ray'll be home now, after a nine-hour shift at the engineering plant. Dean arrives at an intersection. A sign says MARKET STREET. A café is opening, right by the streetcar stop. It's cool and shady and Dean thinks, *Why not?*

He goes in, sits by the open window, and orders a coffee from a waitress in her forties whose name badge says, I'M GLORIA! *America loves exclamation marks.* He tries to summon up the names and faces of the waitresses he worked with at the Etna Café. He's forgotten them. One worried about him, that January night he had nowhere to sleep. She wanted to let him sleep on her floor, but was afraid of her landlady. *The night Utopia Avenue began.*

Dean takes Allen Klein's business card out of his wallet. He holds one corner in the flame of his lighter and incinerates it in the ashtray. It burns purplishly. He's not sure what his logic is, but it feels right. *We're a band.* When the card is gone, Dean feels as if a heavy weight has been removed. Out on Market Street, two vans stop for a red light. The side of the front van is emblazoned with the slogan *THE* BEST TV RENTALS IN TOWN. The second reads, L&H MOVERS—ACROSS THE PLANET! A few seconds later, another van stops in the nearest lane, half-eclipsing the two behind. Its side panel reads THIRD STREET DRY CLEANERS, the four words stacked one above the next. The alignment and position of the vans is such that, at Dean's eye level, a phrase is spelled out: *THE*—THIRD—PLANET. Dean takes out his notebook from his jacket and writes it down. "The Third Planet." By the time he's finished, the vans have departed. Behind the bar, steam is being blasted through his ground coffee beans . . .

. . . AND HERE is his coffee, served in a big blue bowl, like poets and philosophers drink it in Paris, Dean imagines. He takes a sip. The temperature's just right. He slurps up a third of the cup and holds it in his mouth, letting the coffee work its magic. Dean swallows, and all his tangled thinking about his possible son comes unknotted. *I'll assume Arthur's my son. I'll pay his mother maintenance. Every month, no pissing about. Enough so they don't have to scrimp 'n' save. We won't get married, 'cause her 'n' me both deserve to find someone we love, but we'll aim at friendly relations. In a couple o' years, when Arthur's a walking, talking boy and not a blobby baby, I'll invite Amanda 'n' him to Gravesend to meet Nan Moss and the aunts. They'll know if he's my son or not. Even I'll know by then, I reckon. If it's a yes, I'll shunt my life around so Arthur knows I'm his dad. I'll teach him how to fish on the pier up past the old fort. If it's a no, I'll offer to be Arthur's godfather, and I'll still teach him how to fish.* Dean opens his eyes.

"That should work," he murmurs to himself.

"How's your coffee?" asks Gloria the waitress.

Dean knows he's supposed to just say, "Fine," but he decides to be Jasper for a moment. "Let's see. Temperature: warm, not scalding. Taste . . ." Dean sips. "Good blend, nicely toasted, smooth, not bitter. It's bloody perfect. The danger is that all future coffees sort o' pale in comparison. But who knows? Maybe it'll usher in the dawn of a new Coffee Age. Only time will tell. And that, Gloria, if I may use yer name, I'm Dean by the way, *that* is how my coffee is. Thank yer for asking."

"Wow. My gosh. Glad to hear it. I'll tell Pedro. He made it. So, um . . . that'll be thirty cents, then, when you're ready."

"Rightio." *She thinks yer too stoned to pay.* He puts a dollar on the table. "Keep the change. You 'n' Pedro."

Her anxiety vanishes. "Are you sure?"

"It's yours. And Pedro's."

"Thank you." The dollar vanishes into her apron.

"It's a big day. I . . ." *say it,* ". . . am going to be a dad."

"Congratulations, Dean! When's the baby due?"

"Three months ago."

Gloria's confused. "So, he's already born?"

"Yeah. Bit of a long story. His name's Arthur. It's new territory for me, but . . ." Dean thinks of the pilgrim on the Eight of Cups. "Life's a journey, don't yer think?"

The waitress looks out at Market Street, thinks of other times, and looks back. "It should be. The best of luck with Arthur. You helped make him, but he'll make a man of you."

DEAN PASSES NOT-YET-OPEN shops, boarded-up shops, low offices, a building site, a plot of wasteland, a depot. *Nothing to write home about.* Every twenty or thirty paces a tree is losing its leaves to the warm wind. Traffic stampedes between the intersections of Market Street. Motorbikes swerve between the bigger beasts. A truck is pulled up outside a butcher's. Carcasses hang on racks. Dean inhales the breath of the abattoir. A force that is not him runs through him, like the current in the streetcars' overhead cable. *What if ley lines aren't total bollocks?* The buildings grow as downtown approaches. Dean finds Hyde Street and remembers Chayton's instructions. *Now I know where I am.* Where Hyde crosses Turk Street, that's the studio. Dean checks his watch. The band will be at the studio in thirty minutes or so. *I'll be there in fifteen.* Carry on up to Sutter Street, and there's the hotel. He'll have time for a shower. *I'd better: I'm hot 'n' sweaty 'n' stinking.* He passes the Opera House, a big heavy building you might find in Haymarket or Kensington Gardens, with columns and Georgian windows. Hyde Street slopes uphill. It's not a posh district. Dean passes a pawn shop with steel mesh over the windows. A down-at-heel laundromat. *Not launderette.* TENDERLOIN GIRLIE SHOW. A parking lot where a rusty sedan has no wheels. Brambles twist out of cracks. A bundled figure is slumped in a doorway. A biro-on-cardboard sign says, I BEEN DOING THIS SHIT FOR 20 YEARS. Poverty in California looks as miserable as poverty anywhere. He puts fifty cents into the man's hand. Grimy fingers close. He has red eyes and he says, "That all you got?" At the corner of Eddy Street, a shop is open: Eddy Turk's General & Liquor.

Dean sees a cold cabinet with bottles of milk.

It's been a long walk. *A nice cold glass o' milk . . .*

THE SHOP SMELLS of overripe fruit and brown paper. The Sikh shopkeeper has black glasses, a navy turban, and a white shirt. He's reading *Valley of the Dolls* and eating grapes. Bottles of spirits line the shelves behind his till. He sizes Dean up. "Fine day."

"Let's hope so. Just came in for a bottle o' milk."

He nods at the cabinet. "Help yourself."

Dean gets a half-pint and holds the cold glass against his face. He brings it to the counter. "Twenty Marlboro, too." There's a rack of postcards. Dean picks one out of the Golden Gate Bridge.

"Sixty cents." He sounds as American as John Wayne. "For sixty-two cents, I'll throw in an airmail stamp."

"Cheers." Dean digs out the coins. "Could I rent yer pen?"

The Sikh deposits the coins and hands Dean a pen. "On the house. You're welcome to use the table at the back."

" 'Ppreciate that." Dean finds a stool under an old school desk with a liftable lid and inkwell. He sits, looks at the message side of the postcard, and wonders where to start. *Maybe I ought to ask Elf.* Dean drinks half his milk. It's refreshing. *What matters is the fact I'm writing.* Dean takes up the pen:

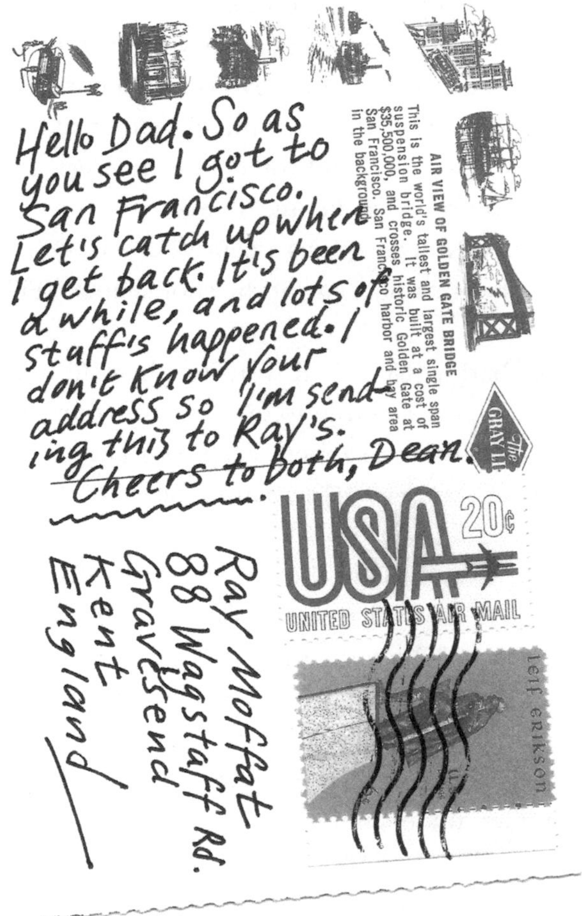

Hello Dad. So as you see I got to San Francisco. Let's catch up when I get back. It's been a while, and lots of stuff's happened. I don't know your address so I'm sending this to Ray's.
Cheers to both, Dean.
AIR VIEW OF GOLDEN GATE BRIDGE
This is the world's tallest and largest single span suspension bridge. It was built at a cost of $35,500,000, and crosses historic Golden Gate at San Francisco. San Francisco harbor and bay area in the background
USA 20¢
UNITED STATES AIR MAIL
leif erikson
Ray Moffat
88 Wagstaff Rd.
Gravesend
Kent
England

Yeah, that'll do. He writes Ray's address, and stands up as one, two, three men stream into the shop, wearing balaclavas. *Like bank robbers in a film,* thinks Dean, just as they pull guns out. Real guns—the first Dean has ever seen. One yells, "Hands in the air, Ali Baba!"

Glowering with contempt, the shopkeeper obeys.

The robbers haven't noticed Dean but he decides he'd better follow suit. All three robbers turn their guns on him and Dean cringes. "Don't shoot! It's okay! Don't shoot!"

Chief Robber demands, "What's he doing here?"

"Just a customer," says Dean. "I'll leave if, uh—"

"Stay *right there*!" Chief Robber turns to a shorter partner in crime. "The joint was s'posed to be *EMPTY.*"

Short Robber's freckles are visible through his eyeholes. "I was watching the store for five minutes. No one came in. That's why I gave you the all-clear." He sounds young, fifteen or sixteen.

Chief Robber snaps back, "Did you check the *aisles*?"

A pause. "This is my first stakeout. It's a—"

"You *shitferbrains*! Now we got us a *witness*!"

The tallest robber thrusts a bag at the shopkeeper. "Fill it."

"With what?"

Chief Robber barks, "No! He'll stuff it with small notes an' shit an' say, 'That's all I got.' Get him to open the till, then *you* fill it."

Tall Robber tells the shopkeeper, "Step back and open the till."

The shopkeeper pauses. "How can I open the till after I've stepped back?"

Short Robber shouts, "Play the SMART-ASS with us, I'll shoot your *FAG ASS* OFF." His voice squeaks on the *ass. He sounds about fourteen,* thinks Dean. "Open the till *first. Then* step back." The shopkeeper sighs and does as he's told. Tall Robber transfers its contents into the cloth bag. It doesn't take long.

"Now take out the cash drawer," says Chief Robber. "The real money'll be hidden under there."

Tall Robber rattles at the drawer. "It won't budge."

Chief Robber waves his gun at the shopkeeper. "Do it."

"The cash drawer doesn't come out of that till."

Short Robber shouts, or tries to: "TAKE IT OUT!" There's a coked-up jaggedness to him, Dean notices, with concern.

The shopkeeper looks over his glasses. "It's a till from the forties, son. The drawer isn't removable. There's nothing more."

Chief Robber snatches the bag from Tall Robber and peers in. "There's only twenty-five bucks? You're shitting us."

"I sell liquor and groceries. Not diamonds. It's nine A.M. on a Thursday morning. How much were you expecting?"

Tall Robber levels his gun. "Open the office safe."

"What office? There's a stockroom the size of a closet and a broke-ass john. Why would I keep money on the premises in *this* neighborhood? Too many robberies. That's why I put the sign up on the way in, 'No Money Kept on Premises.' "

"He's lying," growls Chief Robber. "You're lying."

Short Robber has gone to the door. "Wait up." He reads, with difficulty: 'No Money Kept on . . . Promises.' He ain't lying, Dex."

"No fucking *names*!" shouts Chief Robber.

Now Tall Robber turns on Dex the Chief Robber. "*You* staked this job out. *You* said we'd clear two hundred bucks each, *easy*."

"Each? Six hundred dollars?" The shopkeeper is flabbergasted. "On a graveyard shift? Do you know the first thing about retail?"

"Shut *up*," snarls Chief Robber, "and give me your wallet."

"I never bring my wallet to work. Too many muggings."

"Bull*shit*—what if you need to buy something?"

"I mark my purchases in the stock book. Search my pockets."

What a bunch o' bloody amateurs, thinks Dean.

Chief Robber turns to Dean. "What're *you* looking at?"

"Um . . . an armed robbery?"

"Shorty, get his wallet."

Short Robber waggles his gun: "Wallet."

Dean has about ten dollars, but coked-up idiots and guns are a bad combination so he places his half-drunk bottle of milk on a pile of Pinkerton's pretzel boxes. He reaches into his inside jacket pocket for his wallet, just as a car screeches to a halt outside the shop. Startled, Short Robber turns and biffs the tower of boxes, knocking off the milk bottle. As Dean tries to catch it, a demonic force flings him back . . .

DISJOINTED SENTENCES REACH Dean, as if from radios swinging by on long ropes. "You *dumbass* motherfucker!"

I'm shot . . . I'm actually bloody shot . . .

"He was reaching for a gun, Dex."

"I told him to give me his wallet!"

"Who keeps his wallet in a jacket?"

I can't die . . . I can't die . . . Not now . . .

"He does! Look! He's holding it!"

"But he moved, Dex, and . . . and . . ."

Not like this . . . this is too, too stupid . . .

"Don't use my name, you dumbass motherfucker!"

I WON'T DIE . . . I WON'T . . . I'M STAYING . . .

"You can't, Dean, I'm sorry." Chayton is here.

How can yer be here? Yer at Jerry's house . . .

"Don't be afraid. I'll walk you up to the ridge."

But I've still got songs I need to record.

"You'll have to leave them here."

Elf, Jasper, Griff, Ray . . . can't I just tell them . . .

"You know how this works, Dean."

The voices in Eddy Turk's General & Liquor dwindle as the velocity increases. The Sikh shopkeeper is barely audible: "I'm calling an ambulance for my customer. Shoot me if you want. Then you'll be looking at Death Row. Or just run and take your chances."

I don't need an ambulance, Dean thinks.

"People not yet born will play your songs," says Chayton.

Will Arthur play my songs?

"I reckon so. It's time now."

Dean is falling upward.

No last words . . .

LAST WORDS

"ALL BANDS BREAK UP," LEVON FRANKLAND WRITES IN HIS memoir, *"but nearly all bands get back together again. All it takes is time and a hole in the pension pot."* When Jasper, Griff, and I disbanded Utopia Avenue in 1968, we well and truly meant it. Our friend and bandmate Dean Moss had been shot and killed in a grocery-store robbery in San Francisco, and we didn't have the heart to carry on. The very next day calamity compounded our grief when a fire broke out at Turk Street Studios and robbed us of Dean's last work. A Utopia Avenue album without Dean's musicianship, vocals, and songwriting would, we felt, have violated the Trade Descriptions Act. And so, for half a century, Utopia Avenue persisted as one of those exceptions that proved the validity of Frankland's Law. So how has it come about that now, fifty-one years after our last show, I am writing these sleeve notes (as they used to be called) for a new Utopia Avenue LP featuring Dean Moss on bass, vocals, harmonica, and a twenty-three-minute trilogy of original Moss songs? An explanation is in order.

WE FLEW TO New York in September 1968 for our first and only string of American performances. Dean's anthem "Roll Away the Stone" was a minor hit of the summer on both sides of the Atlantic, and our second LP, *Stuff of Life,* was knocking on the door of the Top Twenty of the Billboard 100. Our American label arranged a short tour in the hopes of kicking that door open. After four nights at the Ghepardo club in New York and a sheep-dip of media interviews, we flew to Los Angeles for a short residency at the fabled Troubadour club and an appearance on the not-so-fabled *Randy Thorn Goes Pop!* TV show. Two days later we played the Golden State International Pop Festival in bucolic Knowland Park, on the back of which gigs in Portland, Seattle, Vancouver, and Chicago were hastily arranged. For four British kids born in the forties and raised on the forbidden fruits of American music, the trip was less the stuff of life and more the stuff of dreams.

Transformative dreams, at that. The politics of 1968 were febrile and visionary. The future felt shapeable. This conviction wouldn't reoccur until the revolutions of 1989, the Arab Spring and, arguably, the #MeToo and climate activism of the current era. Utopia Avenue were not a political band with a capital *P*, but the summer of riots following Martin Luther King Jr.'s assassination, the mounting body count in Vietnam, and the "police riot" at the Democratic Convention in Chicago, beamed to every TV set in the nation, filled both public and private discourse. The antiwar movement was spilling out of its radical and hippie enclaves. In that highly charged atmosphere, indifference was rare. I remember Jerry Garcia telling us, "In 1966, whatever you wished for came true." In 1968, whatever you *didn't* wish for also came true.

Against this volatile backdrop, the four kids we were encountered whole new ways of thinking and being. My long walk out of the closet took a major step forward during our stay at the Chelsea Hotel. Jasper was exorcizing some old demons of his own, and the lyrics Dean wrote in his last few weeks spoke of a seismic self-recalibration. Musically, all of us took a quantum leap. America presented us with an all-you-can-eat musical buffet. We met peers, masters, heroes, and villains. I recall conversations with Leonard Cohen about poetry; with Janis Joplin and Mama Cass Elliot about vocal technique and coloratura; with Frank Zappa about satire and fame; with a still-teenage Jackson Browne about finger-picking; with Janis Joplin about thriving as a woman in a business run by, and for, men; with Jerry Garcia about polyrhythm; and with the not-yet-signed Crosby, Stills & Nash about harmony. No young songwriter could emerge unchanged from such a milieu. What young songwriter would *want* to?

Between shows, Jasper, Dean, and I worked on new material at our hotels and on planes, and at Gold Star Studios in Los Angeles and Turk Street Studios in San Francisco. We egged each other on. I'd think, *Well, if Jasper's got tubular bells on "Timepiece," then I'll damn well get a sitar for "What's Inside What's Inside."* I remember Dean, during the session we recorded "I'm a Stranger Here Myself," telling me, "Okay, Holloway—I'll meet your dulcimer and raise you a harpsichord—and *in five/four time.* Match that!" Of course, the results could have been disastrous, but during our American sessions an *esprit de corps* spurred us all on to work in unison to make our mad ideas succeed. Griff's role cannot be overstated. He followed where the music led and kept the rhythms purring once he got there. A band *is* a band because it is greater than the sum of its parts. Otherwise, why bother? By the morning of October 12, 1968, Jasper and I had laid down the bones of two new songs each, while a song Dean had written for a soundtrack expanded, like fractals, into a three-part unfinished masterpiece.

ONCE UPON A time in the sixties, masters were stored on magnetic reel-to-reels. If these were lost or damaged, the music stored on them was irretrievably gone. Less than forty-eight hours after Dean's death, while we were still in San Francisco awaiting the coroner's report, Turk Street Studios burned to the ground and Levon had to tell us that the tapes from our sessions had melted in the fire. There was no hard-drive backup, no memory sticks, no Cloud. We felt that Dean had been taken from us a second time. We felt Utopia Avenue was well and truly cursed.

We flew back to London with an urn containing Dean's ashes a few days later. The plan was to scatter them from a pier a few miles downstream from Gravesend, where Dean's father had taught him to fish, in a low-key ceremony with just a few friends and family. As Dean used to say, however, "There are no secrets in Gravesend," and over a thousand people turned up—including, thankfully, some off-duty coppers who kept the crowds away from the elderly wooden jetty. As Dean's brother, father, and grandmother emptied the urn onto the water, Jasper played "Roll Away the Stone" on an amplified acoustic guitar. A thousand voices joined in. As the final note died, Jasper threw the guitar into the river. The Thames carried it and Dean's ashes out to sea.

IS THE SOUL a real thing? I wondered then as I wonder now. Are the unscientific majority right? Does some essence of Dean persist somehow, somewhere? Or is the notion of the soul a placebo, a comfort blanket, a blindfold we use to spare ourselves the full awfulness of the cold, hard truth that when we die we *stop*? Is Dean, in fact, as gone, as utterly gone, as a gusty autumn morning on the Thames estuary fifty-one years ago? All I know is, I don't know—and so the answer is, "Maybe." I'll take that "Maybe," however. I prefer it to "Definitely not." There's solace in "Maybe."

LEVON LEFT MOONWHALE and returned to Toronto to head up Atlantic's new Canadian office. Griff returned to the jazz circuit before moving to LA in 1972, where he established himself as a go-to session and tour drummer. I released my first solo album, *Driftway to Astercote,* in 1970. Jasper, to the dismay of his fans, retired from music and vanished into the wild blue yonder. For a few years my only contact with him was through enigmatic postcards sent from places not known for postcards. Our next face-to-face encounter was in 1976 at a Greek restaurant in New York, where he was completing a doctorate in psychology. Thereafter, Dr. de Zoet would appear at my door once a year, stay for a day or two, swap stories, listen to my works-in-progress and leave. He still played the guitar for pleasure and his virtuosity was undimmed, but he resisted all attempts to lure him back into the studio. He used to shrug and say, "I've already done that. Why do it again?"

THE MUSIC OF Utopia Avenue outlasted the band, in a curious, up-and-down way. Dean's death brought him even more fame than his false imprisonment, and both *Paradise* and *Stuff of Life* went gold and sold solidly for three or four years. The pages of the calendar flickered by, and glam, prog rock, disco, and punk each took turns to consign all that had gone before to the bargain bins of history—including that curious psychedelic-folk-rock moment that Utopia Avenue embodied for a few months in 1967 and 1968. Moonwhale Music was bought by EMI, which filleted its small-but-perfectly-formed catalogue, and the little office at the top of the stairs in Denmark Street became a photo library. By the mid-seventies, it was increasingly rare to find Utopia Avenue nestled between James Taylor and the Who in record racks. Another new decade arrived, and to teenagers brought up on New Order, Duran Duran, and the Eurythmics, Utopia Avenue's songs sounded like musical antiques from an earlier age.

If you hang on long enough, however, antiques can accrue a value they never had when new. The early nineties brought an unexpected revival of interest in the band. The Beastie Boys sampled "The Hook" on their seminal LP *Paul's Boutique*. Mark Hollis of Talk Talk cited *Stuff of Life* as a formative influence. Original vinyl copies of our singles and LPs were changing hands for serious sums of money—a market kept buoyant by legal issues that postponed the two albums' CD release. Damon MacNish's grunge version of "Smithereens" became a Top Five hit in 1994. The biggest hit of my solo career, "Be My Religion," followed in 1996, thanks to its use in a Volkswagen advert. (What can I say? I needed the money.)

Utopia Avenue reappeared in the record shops, piled high in the nineties megastores. Nieces and nephews told me that we were being played in the artier college dorms. Teenagers appeared at my shows in growing numbers, asking for songs I hadn't played since decimalization. (Google it.) I remember turning down a request for "Prove It" at Cambridge Folk Festival on the grounds that I doubted I still knew the words. A kid with tattoos and a mullet yelled back, "Don't worry, Elf, we'll sing 'em for you!" They didn't let me down. Then, in the early days of the Internet, my nephew typed "Utopia Avenue" into my new computer—and page after page scrolled up about the band. Views, opinions, trivia, chatrooms, fan clubs, reviews, set lists of gigs we'd played, new images I'd never seen. Some of the photos moved me to tears, especially those of Dean.

In 2001, Levon—by this time an Oscar-nominated film producer—presented me with a high-quality bootleg of our Knowland Park show that he had obtained through, as he put it, "serendipity and the Dark Arts." If I do say so myself, we sounded shit hot. The eight-song set included an in-progress version of Jasper's track "Who Shall I Say Is Calling?," lost in the Turk Street fire. Digger and I digitally remastered the entire album at Fungus Hut, and Ilex Records issued it. To everyone's astonishment, our little vanity project—snappily titled *Utopia Avenue Live at Knowland Park, 1968*—charted at thirty-nine on the first week and hovered in the Top Thirty for three months. When YouTube got up and running, snippets of interviews and TV shows the band had done began to pop up. (I still play our exchange with Henk Teuling on Dutch TV on gloomy days. Comedy gold.) In 2004, the year I turned sixty, Glastonbury invited me to play a set. My sister took me aside and told me, "Sorry, sis, but it's time to stop deluding yourself and face the facts: you're just not properly *obscure* anymore . . ."

I will not deny this was all very gratifying, but while Utopia Avenue's music was re-oxygenated, the band itself remained moribund. What was true in 1968 was true in the twenty-first century: without Dean, there could be no band. Promoters approached Jasper, Griff, and me regularly to see if we had changed our minds. Even Dean's son, Arthur Craddock-Moss, a film and TV composer, had offers to take the "New Utopia Avenue" on the road. Our answer was always the same: "We'll only do it if Dean says yes."

FAST-FORWARD TO AUGUST 2018. I was getting ready for bed when I heard a knock on my door. It was Jasper in a long black coat, like a man in a Bob Dylan song, clutching a battered guitar case. The following dialogue is a reconstruction, but reasonably accurate:

JASPER: I've got them.
ME: Nice to see you too, Jasper.

JASPER: Nice to see you, but I've got them.

ME: Got what?

JASPER: (*Holding up a MacBook like an exorcist brandishing a Bible*) Our songs. On here.

ME: Our albums? I've got them too. So?

JASPER: No, Elf, our *lost* songs. The California sessions. On hard drive. I've heard them. It's us. Here.

ME: (*Croak.*)

MY WIFE: Evening, Jasper, come in—Elf, would you ever shut the door before every moth in the county joins the party?

Jasper came in, and explained that a suitcase of twelve reel-to-reels from our sessions in LA and San Francisco had surfaced at a car-boot sale in Honolulu earlier in the year. How had they escaped the fire at Turk Street? Nobody knew. Was the tapes' preservation due to accident, theft, misfiling, or divine intervention? Anybody's guess. How and when had the suitcase arrived in Hawaii? Another mystery.

One thing was known. A young man named Adam Murphy had acquired the tapes at a car-boot sale while honeymooning in Oahu. Adam, who blogs as "Heritage Audiophile," possessed two items crucial to this story. One: a 1966 Grundig reel-to-reel player capable of playing the 1965 BASF and TDK tape. Two: the nous to position top-of-the-range Neumann microphones by the speakers on the very first playback, to capture the sounds onto a digital file in case the fifty-year-old tapes disintegrated. At least half did exactly that. Let the record show that without Adam Murphy's foresight you would not be reading these lines.

Once all the music was preserved, Heritage Audiophile set about identifying the artists. Soon after, Jasper received a call from a stranger with some rather special news . . .

BACK IN MY kitchen, Jasper Bluetoothed his Mac to my speakers and clicked Play and there we were: Dean, Jasper, Griff, and me, aged twenty-three or -four, playing, singing, laying down tracks. "Temporal vertigo" doesn't come close. Here was my New York love song,

"Chelsea Hotel #939"; Jasper's bluesy psychodrama, "Timepiece"; and chunks of Dean's musical trilogy, "The Narrow Road." It's not every day you hear your younger self play with a long-dead, long-missed bandmate, and I was reduced to emotional jelly.

Afterward, Jasper, my wife, and I sat around our table. Outside, owls hooted and foxes barked. Eventually, I was able to speak again. I asked, "Incredible, but what do we do with it?"

"We make our third album," said Jasper.

We spent that weekend in my garden studio poring through the full nine hours. The material could be subdivided into "Mostly finished," "Needs fleshing out," and "Sketchy." Sound quality was variable. The LA tapes had more hiss than the Turk Street sessions. Luckily, Dean hadn't really got to work on "Narrow Road" until San Francisco, so his irreplaceable vocals were sufficiently bright. The tracks sequenced themselves. Jasper's and my two songs, conceived in and/or inspired by New York and the Chelsea Hotel, belonged on what vinyl lovers still think of as "side one." Dean's "Narrow Road" trilogy, which started life as a possible soundtrack for an Anthony Hershey film that never saw the light of day, was an uninterruptible sequence. Its only logical home was "side two." "I'm a Stranger Here Myself" and "Eight of Cups" belonged between the "mostly finished" and "needs fleshing out" categories, while the third song—"The Narrow Road to the Far West"—was a hypnotic but skeletal eight-minute bass track. We had planned to work on it the morning Dean was shot. As Jasper and I debated what to do with "The Narrow Road," we hit a dilemma: Was our job to make the album we would have made over the winter of 1968/9, had Dean lived? Or should we, instead, use the tapes as raw material for an album that Jasper and I wished to make now, in 2019? Were we purist restorers or postmodern creators?

Through trial and error, a guiding principle evolved. Jasper and I licensed ourselves to do whatever we wanted to do with the material, as long as we did not deploy post-1968 musical technology. Yes, then, to the mandolin on "Who Shall I Say Is Calling?" and to Old Elf's harmonies with Young Elf on "What's Inside What's Inside." But no to sampling, auto-tune and rap (as if), and loops. I cheated only by programming my Fairlight to reproduce the sound of my old Hammond organ. Griff joined us for a few days to overlay percussion or replace his original drum tracks where the sound was unsatisfactory. Arthur—old enough now to be his father's father—filled in bass runs on Dean's old Fender and laid down some blood-harmonies on "Eight of Cups." Levon joined us to fill a Levon-shaped hole in proceedings, and the photographer Mecca Rohmer, who shot our very first publicity snaps in March 1967, documented the brief resurrection of Utopia Avenue for posterity.

Why *The Third Planet*? The project's working title was *The California Sessions,* but when Arthur visited, he brought the notebook found in Dean's pocket on the morning of his death. The final words, on a page of their own, read "The Third Planet." We can only guess what caught Dean's eye about this phrase, but they struck us all as an apt title for Utopia Avenue's third and final LP.

Dean, the last words are yours.

Elf,
Kilcrannóg, 2020

Acknowledgments

Thank you to my family.

Thank you to Sam Amidon, Tom Barbash, Avideh Bashirrad, Nick Barley, Sally Beamish, Manuel Berri, Ray Blackwell of De Barras Bar & Folk Club in Clonakilty, Jess Bonet, Chris Brand, Craig Burgess, Kate Brunt, Evan Camfield, Gina Centrello, Louise Court, Harm Damsma, Louise Dennys, Walter Donohue, Benjamin Dreyer, Lorraine Dufficey, Barbara Fillon, Helen Flood, Jonny Geller, Evelyn Glennie, Ted Goossen, Roy Harper, Paul Harris, Viola Hayden, Stephen Housden, Kazuo Ishiguro and family, Hellen Jo ("criminal/subliminal"), John Kelly, Trish Kerr and team at Kerr's Bookshop in Clonakilty, Martin Kingston, Hari Kunzru, Tonya Ley, Dixie Linder, Nick Marston, Katie McGowan, Mrs. McIntosh, Niek Miedema, Callum Mollison, Carrie Neill, Lawrence Norfolk and family, Alasdair Oliver, Hazel Orme, Marie Pantojan, Lidewijde Paris, Bridget Piekarz, Stan Rijven, Susan Spratt, Simon Sullivan, The Unthanks, Amanda Waters, Andy Ward, Charles Williams, John Wilson.

Thank you to the Pit.

Numerous details were extracted from many sources, but particularly helpful were Joe Boyd's *White Bicycles* (Serpent's Tail, 2007) and Simon Napier-Bell's *You Don't Have to Say You Love Me* (Ebury Press, 2005) for the Lennon encounter.

Finally, thanks to my editor Carole Welch for superhuman patience in the face of multiple busted deadlines.

. . .

Lyrics quoted briefly in the novel are from the following songs:

"Art for Art's Sake" written by Eric Stewart and Graham Gouldman; "House of the Rising Sun" by Alan Price; "A Day in the Life" by John Lennon and Paul McCartney; "Life's Greatest Fool" by Gene Clark; "It Ain't Necessarily So" by Dorothy Heyward, Du Bose Heyward, George Gershwin and Ira Gershwin; "Just Like a Woman" and "Sad Eyed Lady of the Lowlands" by Bob Dylan; "Chelsea Hotel #2" and "Who by Fire" by Leonard Cohen; "I've Changed My Plea to Guilty" by Steven Morrissey and Mark Edward Cascian Nevin; "Chelsea Morning" by Joni Mitchell; "These Days" by Jackson Browne; "The Partisan" by Hy Zaret and Anna Marly; "Guinevere" by David Crosby; and "Mercy Street" by Peter Gabriel.

"For Free" by Joni Mitchell is overheard as a work in progress, so does not quite match the recorded version.

"Have You Got It Yet?" is an unfinished, unreleased Syd Barrett song/practical joke from 1967.

Music enthusiasts will spot the lyrical anachronisms but agree, I trust, that music is timeless.

About the Author

David Mitchell is the author of the novels *Ghostwritten, Number9Dream, Cloud Atlas, Black Swan Green, The Thousand Autumns of Jacob de Zoet, The Bone Clocks,* and *Slade House.* He has been shortlisted twice for the Booker Prize and has won the John Llewellyn Rhys, Geoffrey Faber Memorial, and South Bank Show literature prizes, as well as the World Fantasy Award. In 2018, he received the Sunday Times Award for Literary Excellence, given in recognition of a writer's entire body of work.

In addition, David Mitchell together with KA Yoshida has translated from the Japanese two books by Naoki Higashida: *The Reason I Jump: The Inner Voice of a Thirteen-Year-Old Boy with Autism* and *Fall Down 7 Times Get Up 8: A Young Man's Voice from the Silence of Autism.*

Born in 1969, Mitchell grew up in Worcestershire and, after graduating from university, spent several years teaching English in Japan. He now lives in Ireland with his wife and their two children.

davidmitchellbooks.com
Facebook.com/davidmitchellbooks
Twitter: @david_mitchell

About the Type

This book was set in Baskerville, a typeface designed by John Baskerville (1706–75), an amateur printer and typefounder, and cut for him by John Handy in 1750. The type became popular again when the Lanston Monotype Corporation of London revived the classic roman face in 1923. The Mergenthaler Linotype Company in England and the United States cut a version of Baskerville in 1931, making it one of the most widely used typefaces today.